A CENTURY OF NOIR

Thirty-two Classic Crime Stories

Thirty-two
Classic
Crime
Stories

A CENTURY OF NOIR

Edited by
MICKEY SPILLANE
and
MAX ALLAN COLLINS

NEW AMERICAN LIBRARY

NEW AMERICAN LIBRARY
Published by New American Library, a division of
Penguin Putnam Inc., 375 Hudson Street, New York, New York 10014, U.S.A.
Penguin Books Ltd, 80 Strand, London WC2R 0RL, England
Penguin Books Australia Ltd, Ringwood, Victoria, Australia
Penguin Books Canada Ltd, 10 Alcorn Avenue, Toronto, Ontario, Canada M4V 3B2
Penguin Books (N.Z.) Ltd, 182–190 Wairau Road, Auckland 10, New Zealand

Penguin Books Ltd, Registered Offices: Harmondsworth, Middlesex, England

First published by New American Library, a division of Penguin Putnam Inc.

First Printing, April 2002
10 9 8 7 6 5 4 3 2 1

Page 519 constitutes an extension of this copyright page.

LIBRARY OF CONGRESS CATALOGING-IN-PUBLICATION DATA:

A century of noir : thirty-two classic crime stories / edited by Mickey Spillane and Max Allan Collins.
p. cm.
ISBN 0-451-20596-0 (alk. paper)
1. Detective and mystery stories, American. I. Spillane, Mickey, 1918– II. Collins, Max Allan.

PS648.D4 C435 2002
813'.087208—dc21

2001058708

Printed in the United States of America

CONTENTS

INTRODUCTION

First of all, you have to understand that Mickey Spillane hates the term *noir*. He will groan and he will moan and he will downright bitch at me when he sees that this title prevailed for our collection of what used to be called hard-boiled—or sometimes "tough guy"—crime and detective fiction.

It is characteristic of Mickey to "hate" the term, as opposed to simply dislike it or even detest it. Though Mickey is one of the nicest, easiest-going of stand-up guys, he even now can tap into hate . . . which was part of what made his character Mike Hammer perhaps the definitive tough P.I. of the twentieth century. To dislike the term—well, that would be too soft, even sissy. To detest it—well, that would be worse, because that would be pretentious.

For years Mickey made fun of me for using the term *genre,* which he considered pompous and would willfully mispronounce ("john-er"), long after he knew exactly how to pronounce it. He hates pretensions (not dislikes, not despises) and his insistence on being called a writer and not an author is well-known. To Mickey an author is a guy who writes one book—a college professor, or a retired general or ex-president. Writers are blue-collar men and women who pound the keys to make a living and, along the way, entertain the hell out of a hell of a lot of readers.

Who's going to argue the point with him? Not me.

Besides, Mickey was one of those readers, once. Like me, he is a fan who grew up to be a published writer. Just as I once consumed his Mike Hammer novels like a famished kid gobbling jelly beans, he sat under the covers of his bed—reading by flashlight—the violent, racy, pulp-magazine adventures of Race Williams by Carroll John Daly, the forgotten writer who is considered the inventor of the modern tough P.I.

In a friendship I have cherished, Mickey and I have talked writing and writers many times over the years. Mickey prefers *Red Harvest* to *The Maltese Falcon* (not surprising, if you're familiar with both Hammett's novel and Mickey's work), and thinks Chandler never wrote a better book than *Farewell, My Lovely* (I agree). He thought his idol Carroll John Daly was a lousy (a key Spillane word) novelist, but a great short story writer; and he himself prefers the novella form to any other, and is dismayed that the market for such short fiction is not what it once was.

Mickey remains a controversial figure, but few would deny him his position as the most famous living mystery writer. Christie is gone; so are Hammett and Chandler. Erle Stanley Gardner, Dorothy L. Sayers, and Rex Stout have gone the way of the cousins who wrote the Ellery Queen books. But as the twentieth century wound down, Mickey Spillane was still with us—even writing the very occasional Mike Hammer novel—and that seemed the perfect moment to put together this book.

I don't remember whether the idea was mine or Martin H. Greenberg's. Marty had worked with Mickey and me on a trio of anthologies for NAL a few years ago, attempting to bring back the glory days of such pulps as *Black Mask* and *Manhunt*; briefly, we succeeded. At some point, Marty and I got around to the notion of seeking Mickey's input on a definitive anthology of noir fiction in the twentieth century . . . even if Mickey did hate the term *noir*.

About that term: We are referring to film noir, the French film critics' post–World War II description of black-and-white crime and mystery movies, often B-movies like *Detour* (1945), *Gun Crazy* (1949), and a certain Spillane adaptation (often called the last great film of the original *noir* cycle), *Kiss Me Deadly* (1955). Movie term or not, its roots are literary, deriving from Serie Noire, French publisher Gallimard's still-running series of translations of American crime novels, many of them by writers in this book (Mickey and myself included). Fittingly, one of our writers, Chester Himes, was an expatriate whose American crime novels—the wonderful Coffin Ed Johnson and Grave Digger Jones yarns—were expressly written for Serie Noire and weren't published in the United States until later, at first as cheap paperback originals . . . the market opened up by Mickey Spillane's paperback success.

In recent years, the term *noir* has extended itself—in circular fashion—to crime fiction, as well as film. It's a more commercial term than "hard-boiled," and that's something Mickey can understand, since he claims to have no fans or readers, merely customers.

A while back I used the word "definitive," and as thrilled as I am with the contents of this book, I would not be so bold as to make that claim for it. Several key writers—Dashiell Hammett, Raymond Chandler, and Cornell Woolrich, among others—were out of our reach; fortunately, the first two remain widely in print, and you can seek them out for your further noir enjoyment. The permissions to reprint a number of others we wanted very much to represent could not be cleared in time to be included here—the lack of stories by Horace McCoy and Roy Huggins were two particular disappointments for me.

The selections herein represent writers that are not necessarily favorites of Mickey Spillane, or for that matter of mine. Mickey has never been a James M. Cain fan, for instance—"I don't like stories written by guys in jail cells," he says—and Cain's inclusion here was at my insistence, since he is one of my handful of top favorites. Mickey's favorite short story writer is Fredric Brown, but it was yours truly who picked the example, as the tale included here is one I've cited frequently as a great short story. A number of the selections were suggestions by Marty Greenberg and his staff, and John Helfers made numerous good suggestions, and handled the clearances. Thank you, John.

The co-editors are also represented by stories here. Mickey didn't want to have a story included, but I insisted (and picked it); and I was embarrassed about having one of my Nate Heller stories included, but Mickey insisted . . . but left the selection up to me. And I left it up to Marty. (The introductions to our stories were written by John.)

The rest we leave up to you: the enjoyment of this collection of tales, many of which are hard-boiled enough to chip a tooth on. You will find in the pages ahead some of the best writers of—and finest examples of—noir stories of the twentieth century . . . just don't tell my co-editor I used that term, okay?

Max Allan Collins
February 2001

CHESTER HIMES

Chester Himes (1909–1984) was nearly fifty when he began writing detective stories and novels. But what a fifty years it was. He had served seven years in the Ohio State Penitentiary, where he had discovered *Black Mask* magazine. "When I could see the end of my time inside, I bought myself a typewriter and taught myself touch typing. I'd been reading stories by Dashiell Hammett in *Black Mask* and I thought I could do them just as well. When my stories finally appeared, the other convicts thought the same thing. There was nothing to it. All you had to do was tell it like it is."

And tell it he did. His stories about Grave Digger Jones and Coffin Ed Johnson were not throwaway violent pulp stories, but angry tales about growing up in a bleak city with an even bleaker future. As the timeline in the novels progresses, the characters grow more disillusioned and cynical about their jobs, their own people, and the world they live in. A longtime staple in France, his first crime novel, *A Rage in Harlem*, which was written at the request of Marcel Duhamel, editor of the famous Serie Noire line of Gallimard, was awarded the Grand Prix de Littérature Policière in 1958.

The Meanest Cop in the World

How he got there, and how long he had been there, Jack didn't know: but there he was, sitting on the steps of the Administration building. He had some books under his arm and a little red cap perched on the back of his head, and he knew that he would not have suffered these ignominies had he not been a freshman.

A couple of girls hove into view from the direction of the Chemistry Building and attracted Jack's attention. They were pretty girls and Jack uncurled his long, slim frame and bowed to them with his cap in his hand and his dark hair glinting in the sunshine. There was a touch of hesitancy in his actions, a hint of shyness in the corners of his infectious grin, that counteracted the offense of his boldness.

The girl on the inside, a brunette with a tinge of gold in the bronze of her skin and nice curves beneath her simple little dress, nodded to Jack and smiled a dimpled, wide-mouthed smile. She found something strangely appealing about Jack's incongruous mixture of shyness and boldness. And then she looked into Jack's eyes and knew with the subtle intuition of a woman's heart that Jack was only lonely.

Jack's heart did a little flip-flop and his eyes sparkled with delight as his mind registered the warmness of her smile. For a moment he seemed enraptured, and all by a mere smile from a common co-ed. That seemed very peculiar, for a young man as handsome as Jack should have known and been admired by many pretty girls.

The girl felt well repaid for her nod and little smile: and little wonder, for the heart of any girl would have been warmed by the patent delight in Jack's brown eyes.

The next day at the same time Jack met the girl again as she came out of the Chemistry Building. It was a little after noon and he screwed up his courage and asked her to lunch with him. She accepted, as he should have known that she would, but he hadn't—he was that dumb in the ways of modern maids. He took her to one of those cosy, intimate little cafés which seniors and part-time instructors usually avoid.

She smiled across the table at him and told him that her name was Violet: and she ate a dollar and sixty cents' worth of tit-bits. And Jack then understood why underpaid instructors and economic seniors avoided such nice little cafés. He couldn't eat a thing himself after he had looked into her eyes and felt the glow of her smile: and he felt emptier still when the waiter presented him the bill.

But he smiled and paid it like more money was the least of his worries. He and Violet left the café and sauntered down the lazy, tree-shaded college lane, and the first thing they knew, they were holding hands in the darkened mezzanine of the University Circle Theatre. The picture was Southern romance, and the warm intimate darkness of the interior seemed to draw them together. They stole a precious, fleeting kiss in the darkness that marked the end of the feature picture, and a subtle understanding was created between them.

When they left the theatre the gentle gray of twilight had descended upon the land leaving a faint touch of rose in the Western sky. Jack knew that he had lost his job in the bookstore where he worked as a clerk in the afternoons, but he didn't care. He was drunk, they were both drunk, with youth and understanding and the mellow wine of first love. They walked the streets 'til late that night: and he whispered in her ear those things that lovers have whispered since time immemorial: and they looked at the moon and dreamed: and she stored way in that deep fastness of her woman's heart his stammered love words—so meaningless, so worthless to the rest of the world—but to her, they were priceless.

Jack awoke the next morning to a world of realities, and things such as money and jobs once more attained their right importance. He realized that he was very poor and that a job was vital to the continuance of his education; and what was more important than that, the continuation of his relationship with Violet. But jobs were very scarce that year, even such jobs as clerking in bookstores.

But he continued to take Violet to lunch, even though he owed two weeks' room rent and hadn't been able to find any kind of employment. Violet loved him, he loved her: and what else under the sun mattered to them except their love? But he was to learn that food mattered, for he had spent his scant savings treating and entertaining Violet, and now only the Lord knew where his next meal was coming from.

And then, to top it off, Violet invited him to a formal dance given by the pledges of her sorority. Jack didn't have any money, and he didn't have a tuxedo, and he didn't see how he could possibly make it—until his eyes lighted upon his portable typewriter, his one outstanding asset.

So he took his typewriter to a pawnshop and returned with a rented tuxedo, rented dance pumps, rented silk topper and cane—all slightly the worse for wear—and ninety cents in his pocket which he had wrangled from Abie, the pawnbroker, by virtually out-talking him. He bought a pint of gin and a package of mints with the ninety cents and swaggered down to the sorority house like a millionaire playboy on an afternoon stroll.

He and Violet had a swell time that night—he ceased to think of his predicament: and what did she have to think of, other than him, when she was in his arms? They had such a grand and noisy time of it that the other Kappa girls, or Omega girls, or whatever girls they were, began to take notice of the handsome freshman that Violet had in tow.

It was late when Jack got back to his room in a somewhat dilapidated rooming house over back of the stadium: and Jack was pretty drunk and not nearly so quiet about it as he should have been, knowing that he owed two weeks' room rent. The landlady, a devout church sister of Amazonian proportions, awoke from pleasant dreams of the coming of Gabriel the third time that Jack yelled: "Who-o-o-p-e-ee!" She promptly stalked out into the hall with her faded pink kimono drawn closely about her ample body and asked Jack for his room right then, that very minute.

If Jack showed a slight reluctance at granting her rather abrupt request, you can't much blame him, for he didn't have a place in the whole wide world to go. But still, you can't blame the landlady much either for tossing Jack out on the posterior end of his anatomy, for Jack's yelling was annoying, to say the least, and doubly so in light of the fact that he owed two weeks' back rent.

Jack got up from his semi-reclining position in the street and dusted his rented tuxedo with the palms of his hands, then he stumbled drunkenly down the street, his silk topper slanted on the back of his head, the collar of his rented tuxedo pulled up about his neck, and a maudlin grin upon his face. He didn't have a place in the world to go, and that's exactly where he went.

It was six weeks later, a few minutes before the beginning of the season's last football game, that Jack showed up again. He was all togged out in a well-fitting worsted with a camel's-hair topcoat tossed across his shoulders, and he felt like the million dollars he looked, even if he did have only a dollar and ten cents to his name after he had bought a nine dollar and ninety cents box-seat ticket.

When he got to his seat he found that there were strangers all about him and even the game wasn't very interesting for the first three quarters. The ball was mostly in the air, one put after another—both teams were cautious, using a few power plays of simple variety and putting on the third down if they had more than three yards to go.

Jack drowsed a little, and then suddenly he sat up straight, as the halfback of the opposing team got loose on an off-tackle play and was romping through the open field like a leaf in the wind. Jack stood up, one hand extended: his voice stuck in his throat as he tried to yell. But the safety man got the runner just a scant two yards before it was too late, and Jack sighed with relief and relaxed into his seat. But the ball was on his home team's two yard line and it was first down, two yards to go—for a touchdown and victory.

There was a tense moment of play, a power drive straight through center against a stonewall defense. A foot was gained and a player was hurt. The referee blew time out, the doctor scampered across the field with his bag to administer first aid. Finally the player got to his feet and limped to the sidelines with his arms about the shoulders of two of his teammates.

Down at the end of the stadium in the bleachers the whole section was cheering the hurt player at the tops of their voices, but the spectators about Jack were glum and silent. Jack looked about him with cool eyes and he noticed that the people in his section were downtown business people who had paid their ten bucks to see a winning team and not a hurt tackle. That made Jack angry. He jumped to his feet and yelled:

"Cheer, you lousy slobs, cheer! This ain't no horse race, this is college football!" And then he gave an Indian war whoop to show them just how it was done.

People turned and stared at him. A girl down in front of him turned about and looked into his eyes. They both gave a start, then he cried:

"Violet!"

"Jack!" she answered, and the tone of her voice made him think that she had missed him almost as much as he had missed her, and that was a whole lot. "Where have you been all these years?" she asked, and there was reproach in her voice.

He wanted to tell her all about it, as a man does when he is in love but she stopped him with a gesture. It was not because she didn't want to hear him, but she didn't want to be rude to the man who was escorting her.

So she said: "Come around to the house and tell me about it this evening." She spoke like she would be breathless in anticipation until they met that night—at least that was the way she sounded to him.

Jack went around to the Kappa house or the Omega house, or whatever house it was, that evening about eight o'clock. A girl met him in the foyer and took his hat and coat, and when he mentioned Violet, she said "Oh yes," and took him into a dimly lit reception room.

There were several girls and a couple of young men grouped in a circle on the carpeted floor. Violet got up from the davenport where she had been sitting and took him by the arm.

She said, "The matron is away and we were planning to play some stud poker on the floor. Come on, it's great fun."

But Jack hesitated. He was slightly embarrassed, for he only had a dollar and ten cents to his name and he didn't want to win, but he couldn't afford to lose for that dollar and ten cents was his meal ticket. One of the girls went out for a deck of cards and Jack took advantage of the delay to edge Violet over to a settee in a corner where there wasn't much light.

He tried to kiss her but she told him to wait until some of the gang cleared. And then suddenly, before either one of them was really aware of it, she was in his arms and their lips were sealed together. He had been away six weeks and six weeks is a long time when you are young and in love. Jack realized then that he loved her a lot more than he had any business loving anyone with his capital amounting to only a dollar and ten cents.

A girl came into the room then and called Jack's name, jarring him out of the ethereal loveland of Violet's arms back to the cold concreteness of reality. The girl told Jack that there was someone at the door to see him and Jack got up reluctantly and went out into the foyer.

A huge policeman with a hard bronze face and slitted eyes awaited Jack. The policeman wore a high blue helmet pulled down over his forehead and the brass buttons of his leather-belted overcoat gleamed like lobster eyes in the softened light of the foyer. The policeman held a three foot nightstick in his right hand and a dull black service revolver in his left. The round muzzle of the gun was pointing at Jack's stomach, and Jack felt goosefleshy about the nape of his neck.

The policeman commanded Jack to stick up his hands. Jack stretched his arms ceilingward. Then the policeman asked Jack if he knew how to pray. Jack nodded, wondering what it was all about, and getting kind of angry at the policeman's bulldozing methods.

The policeman told Jack to get on his knees and pray. Jack frowned, beginning to get a little frightened. He dropped to his knees, still holding his hands above his head. The policeman pushed the revolver straight into Jack's face—and Jack sat up in his bed yelling bloody murder.

The guy across the darkened cell turned over in his bunk and said "Aw, pipe down, mugg, and let a guy sleep, will ya?"

And then suddenly Jack realized that he wasn't a freshman in a nice old college, and he wasn't in love with a pretty girl called Violet, that he didn't even know such a girl, that he was just convict number 10012 in a dark, chilly cell, and he had eaten too many beans at supper. But for hours afterward he lay there silently cursing the huge policeman who had made him realize this.

CARROLL JOHN DALY

Race Williams pretty much started it all. You take your Hammetts, Chandlers, Cains, MacDonalds (John D. and Ross Macdonald)—and you're still talking Carroll John Daly (1889–1958), the creator of Race Williams. Because no matter how you gussy up, trick up, Seriously Literaur-ize the private eye novel, the source will always be the inimitable, reckless antics of Race Williams, who never met a man he didn't want to kill.

Frequently published in pulp magazines such as *Black Mask* and *Dime Detective*, Daly broke away from the genteel sleuthing of his predecessors, bringing the dirty streets and double-dealing criminals onto the magazine pages. His short story "The False Burton Combs" is acknowledged to be the first hard-boiled detective story. In more than fifteen novels published from the 1920s to the 1950s, his detectives lived by their own moral code, punishing the guilty and protecting the innocent.

Just Another Stiff

Chapter One

A Corpse on Me

The door of my private office crashed back, and the man hurled himself in. Jerry, my assistant, was following him, grabbing at his right arm. Then followed the prettiest bit of gun-work you'd want to look at.

Both the man's hands moved at once; both of them held guns. The left one was trained on me. The right one crashed with a thud against bone, and I saw the blood on Jerry's forehead start to trickle down before he sank to the floor and lay quietly there. My visitor's foot moved too, and the door was kicked closed.

Some entrance!

I was caught with my coat off—and that's no figure of speech. It was warm. My shoulder holster was sporting a gun, but it was over on the bookcase. A bad set-up for a guy who fancies himself with heavy hardware and should be ready day and night? I don't know. I had a gun fastened beneath my desk that was handy enough. Well, nearly enough.

But I was getting a good look at this smart duck. He was high class on the outside—that is if expensive scenery makes for high class. Spats, a ninety-buck suit, a twelve-dollar hat. Things had happened to his face. Someone must have taken a sledge hammer and knocked his nose flat into the middle of it.

My hands went up and he spoke. "You don't have to play any Hold-Up-Your-Hands game with me, Race Williams. If you have any wish to use a gun, why go ahead and use it. How's that?"

I nodded and said that was fine. I wondered what he'd do if I slipped one hand under the desk, let my gun drop into it. Then I wondered what I'd do. I'd have to raise my hand to shoot; he only had to press a finger on a trigger—either trigger. So I waited—and lived on.

"So you're Williams. The wise dick, Race Williams—smartest gunman in the racket. You didn't think a guy could come from across the pond and put the finger on you—lay you right on the spot."

"Across the Atlantic?" I tried.

He shook his head. "The Orient. Don't know my face, eh?"

"Well—" I looked at that thick-lipped, flattened puss of his and said: "Maybe I knew it before you had it renovated."

He didn't get that last crack, and maybe it was just as well. He didn't look like a guy who'd take a joke, and I was in a pretty position to take a face full of forty-fives.

There was my own forty-four sprung nicely beneath my desk. Just an outward thrust, an upward jerk, and the pressure of a finger. I've done it before and gotten away with it, and I'd have done it then. But this guy could do things with guns and the best I could hope for was a double death. Besides he looked like a man who wanted to talk. And if he wanted to talk, I wanted to listen; he wouldn't be the first lad who'd talked himself to death.

"Brother," he said, "you've got a chance to live if you do exactly what I tell you. Don't go around with the wrong people. You understand that?"

"Sure"—I looked straight into his eyes—"sure, I understand that. What's the show?"

"The show is dope. Millions of dollars' worth of narcotics coming into the country through Morse and Lee, Fifth Avenue jewelers. Coming in easily until you killed Frank Morse, saved Conklyn Lee's life after he had discovered the racket Frank Morse was running. Then you even wised up the real owner of the firm—the girl, Mary Morse—and for the time being put the easy money out of business."

"Anything else I did you didn't like?"

"Yes," he said. "The killing of Gentle Jim Corrigan, the man who started to take Frank Morse's place—that's why I came."

"You were a long time coming." I stopped and looked toward Jerry. "How about putting the boy on the couch." And when he only grinned, "He may come to and bother you."

He laughed—a very assured laugh. "He won't come to for a bit, and if he does, he won't bother me." For a fraction of a second his head jerked toward Jerry, his eyes rolled. And I took the chance. My right arm shot slightly forward, my fingers touched metal, and a forty-four dropped into my hand.

Did he see me? I knew that he didn't, for his guns never changed—nor did either of his fingers tighten. He went on talking.

"Certainly, we were a long time coming. A long time figuring out the set-up, and making new plans. You see, we figured that after the first shooting you would be out of the case, because Mary Morse didn't have any money—and wouldn't have until she was twenty-one. So she couldn't hire you. But somehow you fell for her blue eyes, and took a hand in things. And now—"

He went for his inner jacket pocket. He simply crossed his left arm, tucked the gun under his right armpit—never took his right-hand gun off me—and pulled out a long folded piece of paper. He tossed it on the desk before me. I had to move my gun into my left hand as I leaned forward to reach it. I didn't dare come up shooting then, for he was leaning far over the desk.

"Look that over," he said.

He waited while I read it. It was hot stuff—a written statement of everything that had taken place in the dope-smuggling game. My protection of Mary Morse; her own knowledge of what was going on; the fact that her stepfather, Conklyn Lee, also knew; and that I, too, had kept such information from the government. It was all there right up to the shooting of Frank Morse. It looked like a confession that awaited only my signature.

Where did he get his information? Mary Morse wouldn't talk and ruin the Morse business to say nothing of being accused of helping her uncle. Conklyn Lee wouldn't tell for the same reason. Then it must be—

"Where did you get this information?" I asked Flat-Face.

From his indifference, I knew I was never supposed to live to repeat his answer. He said simply, and without hesitation: "The little lady known as the Flame supplied the information. But take a sheet of paper, copy that document there in your own handwriting. That will assure us that in the future, you'll stay out of this case—stay away from Mary Morse."

It wasn't the time to laugh, so I didn't. Up to date, the Morse case had not only paid me nothing, but had actually been a loss. I had thought it was over. Oh, she had buzzed me a few times on the phone, tried to see me, and then—like that—a dead silence. Which suited me, I guess.

I looked at Flat-Face's gun, thought, "Now is the time for it," pulled up my right hand and started to reach for the pen. The left with the gun in it was ready to follow, when he leaned far forward and killed that motion. "Get paper! What's the matter with your left hand? Are you a cripple?"

I dropped my gun onto my knees, and brought up my left hand. And I was right. If black had showed against the white of my hand I would have been dead, for his eyes were glued on that left.

For a moment I was glad I hadn't chanced death—I mean chanced his death, for mine would have been sure. Then I wasn't so glad. I was beginning to copy the paper. Hell, I know it's the proper thing for a real hero to throw out his chest, tell the guy that the sweet child, Mary Morse, came first and die like a man. But the hard thing to do is live like a man—if you're in a position like I was. I wanted to see a turn of his head, a second's lowering of that gun—and I wouldn't bore him with any more conversation. But I guess the main reason I was exercising my penmanship was because I was simply writing, *Now is the time for all good men to come to the aid of the party.*

After watching my moving fingers a while, he said: "You're making good time, Williams. Turn the paper around so I can see what you wrote."

I breathed easier. This was the break. He'd have to look down at that paper, and when he did—Simple? Sure. It's just playing a waiting game, having a bit of patience. I swung the paper around, slid my left hand back to the edge of the desk.

"There you are. Just what you—"

His eyes never lowered. They stayed right on my hands. He said simply: "Put both your hands in the air—both of them."

I did, and he looked down at the paper—just a quick glance. Then his right hand moved with incredible speed. I felt more than saw that the gun turned in his hand as he gun-whipped me. Sure—he just tore a thin line down the side of my face, dug backwards, and gouged out a hunk of flesh almost beneath my ear. Mad? Of course I was. This lad's technique was perfect.

His voice never raised as he said simply: "Take another sheet of paper and try again." And when both my hands were once more on that desk, and a fresh sheet ready, "Listen, Williams, the cops know I'm in town. They're looking for me. You write it and sign it and I'll pass down the back stairs and be safely hidden away. They can't possibly suspect I'm here at your office. Don't write it—and I'll blast your head off or maybe simply cut your throat."

He parked a gun then; his left hand shot beneath his jacket and out again. Silver streaked in the light—and there was a long-bladed knife sticking in my desk.

He said: "That might as well have been in your chest—or in your throat!" And his crooked mouth twisting, "Though I like cutting throats from behind—it isn't such a mess. I mean for the cutter."

Now, as I wrote, he leaned forward and picked up the knife. He was trying to see, but no matter how he bent, the writing was still upside down. So he pulled a fast one.

"Keep on writing word for word, Williams. A mistake, and I'll let the whole thing go. To be perfectly honest with you, I didn't like the looks of a couple of men outside your office building. They looked copper, and they smelled copper." He was moving around the desk as he spoke.

"Look here"—I kept my right hand on the desk, but let my left slide naturally off it and onto my knees as I turned and faced him—"how do I know that you won't kill me after it's written?"

"You don't know—only that I tell you and that my gun would make too much noise."

The knife! I thought of the knife then, and I knew what he intended to do, just as if he had told me himself. Once the final word was written, once my signature was there, it would be a single stretch of his arm behind my back, a sharp twist of his wrist and he'd cut my throat.

Then what? Why, they'd have that girl, Mary Morse, under their thumbs, have her money, the cellar of her great store to keep their dope in. The famous house of Morse and Lee that was beyond suspicion would become a huge central receiving and distributing point for the narcotic trade. And I signed that paper—with all the threats, intimidation, blackmail and extortion that were contained therein.

The killer—with the knife in his left hand the gun in his right—was coming around the end of the desk. He was going to pass almost in full view of me. Would he see the gun? Would he see it before his body was directly in the line of my fire? Of course he would. I wouldn't dare move the hand that held it; I wouldn't dare move the arm or the shoulder that controlled that hand. Suddenly he moved forward, was directly before my gun—and he saw it.

Sure he saw the gun! He couldn't help see it. It was spewing orange-blue flame as soon as enough of his body was visible. It wasn't a nice shot; it wasn't a clean shot. But then it wasn't meant to be. It spun him as if he were a top. His own gun exploded, tore into the bookcase behind me. For a moment he swung back toward me and his gun was stretched out in his hand. And that was all of that. I squeezed lead once more and made a hole where his flat nose had been.

He was further away this time, but he was dead—dead right there on his feet. I saw it in his eyes, saw the light go out of them as if you'd switched off an electric bulb, just before he collapsed there between the desk and the window.

A voice said: "Nice work, boss. You don't often let me in on the kill." It was Jerry, half up on one knee.

"*He* let you in on it and—" I paused, picked up the original paper and the copy I was making and started to tear them up. A door slammed. Heavy feet beat across the outer office and once again my private door burst open. I slipped my gun into my pocket as a face appeared in the doorway—the hard, weather-beaten face of my worst enemy on the police force. Yep, you guessed his name. It was Iron Man Nelson. All the things I had pulled on him and taken my laugh at, at the time, didn't seem quite so funny to me now with those papers clutched in my left hand.

Inspector Nelson saw Jerry who was getting slowly to his feet; saw the deep cut in his forehead, the blood beginning to dry on Jerry's face, and for the first time in his life Nelson was solicitous. Evidently he thought I had been knocking Jerry around and he was going to make the most of it. Apparently Iron Man Nelson hadn't heard those shots. He'd come in for some other reason. Of course, he wasn't in a position to see the body of Flat-Face.

"What did this man, Williams, do to you, son?" Iron Man had an arm around Jerry, and the "son" sounded as though a couple of other words were missing. "He smacked you with a gun, eh? Well that's a pastime of Williams'."

"Mr. Williams was showing me a new gun-twist," Jerry lied easily, though I knew his head was near busting as he bathed it at the water-cooler. Before Nelson could blow up he added: "Then I tried it on him and—"

I dropped the papers into the ashtray, lit a butt, and tossed the match in after them.

Nelson's eyes were wide as he looked at my face, the thin line of red down it, the dig behind the ear, for I turned my head so he could see it. Then he saw the sudden blaze in the tray, said: "What the hell! Want to burn up the place?" He stepped forward and reached for that ashtray, but I was before him and had awkwardly knocked it from the desk.

Jerry dropped to his knees, was picking up the white sheets, grinding in the partly burnt edges—and I had a real break. Sergeant O'Rourke stamped into the room, stood there in the doorway with a couple of city dicks behind him as Jerry walked by him with the papers. Good old Jerry! Walking out with a bit of writing that would have given Nelson the happiest moment of his life, and O'Rourke—well, friend or no friend, I'd have been in plenty of trouble. But the cops were ready for an argument between themselves. Nelson always was. O'Rourke gave him the chance this time.

"Now look here, Nelson"—O'Rourke worked close to the commissioner and didn't have to take guff from any cop, not even an inspector—"I tipped you to this lay, and you go in the back way alone."

"What lay?" I cut in as Nelson said something about O'Rourke being too friendly with a "private dick" and making those two words stink to high heaven.

O'Rourke began to explain then. "Why—Spats Willis. Wanted here ten or twelve years ago for murder, went to the Orient—Singapore last time we heard of him—and mixed up in some dope-smuggling. We think he's Raftner's man—Nick Raftner."

"Who's Raftner?" I wanted to know.

"Who knows?" said Nelson. "No one has ever seen him. However, he's real. Sits pretty in the Malay States and has a big idea about filling America with dope."

"Yeah?" I said. "But why would he come here? I mean this other bloke—Spats Willis."

"We don't know, Race." And when I just stared at him, "It's not a hunch or anything like that. We had a call Willis would be found here at your office, and to come up right after one o'clock. No suspicion of you—nothing like that, Race."

"No? That's just O'Rourke's opinion," Nelson sneered. "We got a good description of Willis. He was seen entering this building, and it's fairly well established that he came to this floor. He's got a face that isn't hard to place."

I shrugged. "Who told you he was here?"

"We don't know. You didn't anyway!" Nelson blasted. "What's that got to do with it? We got to search the place—maybe take you down for a little questioning."

I looked at O'Rourke. He looked back very soberly, said: "He's wanted for at least one murder we can lay on him. It's serious business, Race, if you let him come and go."

"What would you do with him?"

Though I spoke to O'Rourke I got the answer where I hoped I'd get it—from Nelson. "We'd fry him. Or better still lay a couple of slugs in his head."

"Oh, you want him dead." I tried putting on a child-like wonder which I knew always infuriated Nelson.

"Of course, we want him dead. If Raftner's money's behind him it'll take a couple of years to get a conviction—if we get one even then. Now, Race, what do you know about—"

He stopped, followed the direction of my jerking thumb—first with his eyes, then with his head, and finally with his moving feet. His bellow of surprise as he spotted the body was pleasant to my ears. Then O'Rourke was on his knees beside him and I saw them swing the dead head around.

"It's Spats Willis all right. I remember him years back," Nelson said and I liked the awe in his voice. "And what a mess!"

"That's right—a mess," I told him. "Get him out of here. He's all yours."

Nelson came to his feet, turned on me viciously. He accused me of everything right up to the murder of a poor unfortunate traveler named Willis, who had returned to his native shores after these many years. Maybe those weren't his exact words, but they're close enough. And they made me mad; damned good and mad. I let him have it.

"By God!" I said. "You pound in here hollering for Willis's death. And me—am I paid to sit around and wait until someone you happen to approve of knocks over your wanted man? Then you give me abuse, accuse me of about everything in the calendar." And going to the cooler and taking a drink, "Look at my rug! That's the thanks I get for spilling a public enemy's guts all over it. He's yours. Take him out of here. I'll complain to the commissioner that you got word I was to be shot to death and waited until you thought the job was done."

Nelson started toward me as I turned to leave the room, but O'Rourke reached me first. "All right. All right. How did it happen, Race?"

"How did it happen!" I flared back. "Why, he just talked himself to death." And I banged on into the outer office.

Mad? Well, not now. I went to the rear of the room and laughed for a good five minutes.

O'Rourke came out and stood looking at me. He shook his head. "I can't understand you, Race. I've been twenty-five years in this business—and I have never yet been able to see anything funny in death."

"Funny!" I told him. "Of course, it's funny. Damn it, O'Rourke! If you couldn't get an occasional laugh in this business, you'd go nuts. But I've got to go out and eat. Haven't had lunch yet."

I swung back into my private office, hopped over the late lamented Mr. Spats Willis, swung both my shoulder holsters into place and put on my jacket.

"Don't scowl like that, Nelson." I winked at the sour-pussed inspector. "They don't come much deader than that one. I'll expect the city to pay for the rug at the cleaner's. There, there—not a word of thanks. That corpse is on me."

Chapter Two

Table for Three

I hit my favorite restaurant, ready for a thick steak, and I saw the girl; the woman, if you like—for the Flame could be either one—a sort of flesh-and-blood Doctor Jekyll and Miss Hyde, if you get what I mean. There were times when she was young and lovely, the sparkle of youth in her eyes—and times, too, when she was hard, cold, cruel, a woman of the night. Beautiful—sure, but in a sinister way.

I couldn't tell which was she now, as I walked down the room. She was tapping a cigarette on the table, looking toward the door, and suddenly she saw me. Her eyes brightened, her head moved slightly, and I went toward her. What a coincidence finding the Flame occupying my special booth in my special restaurant? Well, if you're young and in love you might look on it like that. But the Flame has no coincidence in her life—and I have none in mine. I knew she was waiting for me.

She didn't show surprise and neither did I as she started to move over to make room for me beside her. My surprise came when I saw that the seat across from her was occupied. Long, slender, neatly manicured fingers lay upon the whiteness of the table cloth. Sleek black hair, soft oily skin—I don't have to tell you. It was Armin Loring—One Man Armin—the most dangerous man in the city of New York.

The Flame moved further into the booth. Armin just looked at me, smiled pleasantly enough when I sat down beside her.

I didn't let the Flame talk first. I said: "I suppose you wish me to sit down—right?"

"Right. Would you believe me, Race, if I said I'm surprised to see you—but delighted?"

"Maybe you are surprised to see me—alive, but I rather doubt the delighted part."

"And you may well doubt that, Williams." Armin Loring showed more of his even white teeth, watched the Flame open her purse. He took the five hundred-dollar bills she stretched across to him. "Will we tell Williams about the bet, honey?" And when the Flame stiffened, "It's too good to keep. You see, Race, Florence bet me those five centuries that I'd never see you alive again." And twisting up his lips as he pocketed the money, "Even money, too, Race. You must be slipping."

Graceful shoulders went up and down. The Flame turned, blew a smoke ring at me, said: "You always did let me down, Race. Seriously, Armin, you're not really jealous because Race was once madly in love with me?" She looked at me steadily. "Sometimes I think he still is."

"That's the way it goes." Armin beckoned a waiter and I ordered. And then, "They say that once a man loves the Flame he always loves her."

I said: "And they say also that to love the Flame is to die."

"Yet," said Armin, "you and I are both alive. There, Williams, you can be the first to congratulate me. Florence and I have given up the racket, discovered that underneath it all we are both very conventional people. We are going to be married—and sail away on our honeymoon."

"Not to Singapore by any chance?" I asked.

Armin Loring jerked erect. I had hit him a wallop all right. He showed it and knew that he showed it. "What do you mean by that?" he demanded.

"Well"—I stuck my tongue in my cheek—"I had a visitor from Singapore today. He said you sent him."

Armin Loring looked straight at me. He seemed puzzled. I knew he spoke the truth when he said: "I never sent anyone." He looked at the Flame; back to me.

"Race"—he spoke very slowly, very distinctly, and without any dramatics—"you have never really crossed me yet." He scowled. "Except for that one time when you took Miss Morse from the Royal Hotel. Forget me—forget Singapore. I haven't got an enemy in the world—a dangerous enemy—that is a live one. Don't make me think I have." He leaned forward now and I believe he meant every word he said. "You've walked up and down the Avenue for years, Race. Lads fear you because they fear death. They recognize you as one of their own kind. A man who has no interest in courts of justice, no interest in stupidly gathering evidence that won't stand up. You're a killer, just like—"

"Just like you're a killer," I finished for him.

"No." He was deadly serious. "Speed with a gun like speed in everything else is only relative. You don't know it, don't believe it, but I can draw and shoot in less than one second."

"Yeah?" I said. "Right now?"

"Right now—one second. What do you say to that?"

I said: "Armin, you'd be exactly one-half second too late."

And Armin did it. I had heard about his speed and was interested to see it operate. Now I did. He just swept the handkerchief from his outside jacket pocket and I saw plainly the nose of the tiny gun beneath it.

"By God!" Armin said, and I didn't like his eyes. "I've a good mind to do it here." And his eyes shifting up and down the room, "I will, too—unless you give me your word that you will never mention my name and Singapore. Poor sap, you never even raised a hand to save yourself."

I said easily: "Be your age, Armin. You don't think I go around letting guys pull guns on me—at least not twice in one day. Put that handkerchief away or comes it a sudden pain in your stomach."

His eyes narrowed. His thin lips tightened. I saw the Flame half rise in the booth.

I said: "There's a gun covering you under the table, Armin." And when doubt came into his eyes I added lightly: "A nice conventional guy like you wouldn't want a lot of strangers to know what you had for lunch."

"I don't believe you." Those were Armin Loring's words, but he did believe me just the same. And he was right. Why, a gun fell into my hand almost the moment I sat down.

I shrugged my shoulders and told him what was on my chest. "We sat like this once before, Armin. Remember? I do. Only that time both our guns were under the table. But have it your own way. Press the trigger of that toy gun—" I leaned forward suddenly, spat the words at him. "Park that gun, Armin; park it damn quick or I'll blow hell out of your insides!"

Armin's eyes brightened to twin beads of fire. For a moment I thought he was going to do his stuff and my finger tightened on the trigger. I could feel the hammer of my forty-four slipping back.

Armin smiled suddenly and said his well known line. "No fooling, Race?"

"No fooling, Armin," I answered.

Three things happened. His handkerchief twirled back into his pocket.

My gun slipped back into its holster. The waiter brought my steak. And—I'm not sure—but I think the Flame opened the bag that lay on her lap and slipped something stubby and black into it. Was I ungentlemanly enough to think it was a gun? Yeah, I guess I was. But the steak was good and I was hungry.

There were several minutes of silence then—that is conversational silence. I like my steak and I don't care who hears it.

After a while the Flame said: "You run along if you want, Armin. I'd like to talk to Race—of our old love." And damn it, she put a hand across the table and patted the back of his.

He took a dumb look and pulled his hand away—but he liked it. He said: "All right, kitten. Just a word with Race first." And to me, "Now about this Mary Morse case and the unfortunate fact that unscrupulous people have been using her jewelry firm for dishonest acts." He grinned at his own cleverness in the wording. "You haven't made a nickel on the deal. I have been offered a big fee—a very big fee to keep you out of this case. Because of your old friendship with Florence, my future wife, and my dislike for trouble just before our honeymoon, I'll give you half of this fee to stay out of your own accord."

"The laugh's on you, Armin," I told him. "I am out of it."

"Certain?"

"As certain as a man can be." I shrugged. "I have no intention of seeing Mary Morse."

"That's a promise—your word?"

"That's nothing to you," I told him flat. "It simply means that I don't want to see her—don't want to go to her if she sends for me. But I would go in a minute if I felt like it. Threat from you—or no threat from you."

The Flame clapped her hands. "Waving the old flag, eh Race? You have to understand him, Armin. He's free, white and twenty-one, and he just won't be threatened."

"Threatened, hell!" Armin drew a small case from his pocket, flipped it open, tossed a cigarette into his mouth and popped a match to the end of it. "This, Race, is a plain statement of the facts. You never bluff; I never bluff. If you're seen with Mary Morse again—so much as talk to her in a hotel or restaurant—you'll be shot to death at once."

"By you?" was all I asked.

"By me the second time."

"You expect to kill me twice, eh?"

"I expect to kill you if the first attempt fails, though I can hardly see failure." He was tossing his napkin on the table now. "This man I have in mind would shoot you even in a crowded restaurant."

"Restaurant, eh?" I rubbed my chin as he pulled that "restaurant" line the second time, watched him start to slide out of the booth. I looked at the check for the meal beside his plate, said quickly: "It's you who are going to marry the girl, Armin. I'm damned if I'll pay the check."

It was strange to see the sudden color come into Armin's face, but he fished out a five-spot and tossed it on the table. I turned over the check, took a squint and nodded, said: "The Flame must be trying to reduce. On your way. Nothing else I should know, is there?"

Armin didn't like my light banter. His teeth showed when he leaned over and spoke to me, but there was nothing of a smile on his face—just the baring of his teeth which was anything but pleasant. "I'm going to pay you a great compliment, Race," he said. "I'm going to steal your line. If you so much as see or speak to Mary Morse again and live—then I'll shoot you to death the first time we meet."

I shook my head, smiled and filled in the missing words for him. He had left my favorite line out. "Any place, any time—at Forty-Second Street and Broadway during the lunch hour. That's what you mean, isn't it, Armin?"

"That," said Armin, "is exactly what I mean." Without another word he turned and left the table. I watched him walk slowly down the length of the room toward the door. Then I turned to the Flame.

For a long moment I looked steadily into those brown eyes. They looked steadily back, didn't even blink slightly. I tried: "Too bad about the bet you lost, Florence. So you sent Spats Willis to kill me."

"To kill the man I used to love—do love?" She leaned forward.

"You bet Armin he'd never see me alive again. And Willis was fast with a gun."

"So"—arched eyebrows went up—"you admit that others can be fast with a gun. Willis—What happened to him?"

"In this hot weather they'll bury him quickly."

Red ran in and out of her face; her right hand tapped the table. If that was emotion, it was all she showed. She said simply: "It's part of the price men must pay who want to make money—a lot of money."

"And women, too," I told her.

"Mary Morse, for instance." She pretended to miss my crack. And then, "How do you know I sent him—to kill you?" And after a pause, "Maybe I sent him for you to kill."

"But why—why?" I'd had that thought, too. But I was never sure that it was an honest thought or a wish—something I wanted to believe, yet really didn't.

"I saved your life once, and you believed that I did it because I was more anxious for someone else to die. Perhaps I sent Willis to you that you might kill him."

"Yeah." I looked at her. "You've lined up with a dope outfit so you can set guys up for me to shoot down. Let me tell you something. This Willis boy very nearly got your intentions mixed and gave me the dose. After this when you set a lad up for me, give me a ring he's coming. Hell, Florence, you wouldn't expect a child to believe that!"

"I'm not expecting you to believe anything; certainly not as much as a child. A child has a clean honest mind." And suddenly sticking out a hand and gripping mine tightly; gripping it while her fingers against my skin went colder and colder, "Let's chuck it all, Race. Let's go away together—"

I jerked my hand away, put hard eyes on her—then lowered them slightly. Damn it, the woman was a marvel of—well, maybe deceit. I could have sworn her eyes were wet and warm. But I said: "I thought you were going to marry Armin Loring."

She shrugged. "You told me once that I would make a charming widow."

I let that slide and spoke what was on my mind. "They wish to keep me away from Mary Morse. Why? She doesn't want me, doesn't need me now."

"She needs you more than she ever needed you. Armin would like an excuse to kill you. Someone watches over Mary day and night. Someone who came from the Orient. Someone who could shoot you to death right in a public place and wield enough influence—what with your reputation for shooting—to escape punishment. If you want to live don't go near Mary Morse."

I didn't get it, but I drew in my knees and let the Flame slide from the booth. Certainly, I admitted, she was a gorgeous woman, but if I were Armin, I'd have her searched upon her wedding night.

She turned her lithe, feline body there at the end of the booth and said: "There are a million tiny cells in every human brain, Race. Try using just one of them. Remember, the police arrived in time. They might have been late."

That they had been late was my only thought as she swung down the room.

A minute later I picked up my check and saw the small envelope under it. I drew out the oblong bit of cardboard about as big as a visiting-card. It was from the Flame, of course. But it wasn't. It read simply—

> Race—Race, don't come to the Green Room. Don't come to my table. It means your death. Don't come no matter what I say—how I plead. It's a trap to kill you—I won't mean it.
>
> Mary Morse

CHAPTER THREE

Champagne Supper

I stalled around a bit before going back to my office. When I got there the body was gone. O'Rourke wanted to hear my story again. Nelson wanted to hear it again. The D. A. wanted to hear it and so did the commissioner of police. Also a dozen or more reporters wanted to hear it.

By that time I didn't want to hear it and had boiled it down to a few words. I simply said: "His name, the cops say, was Willis. Why he tried to kill me I don't know. He fired and missed. I fired and didn't miss." After all, there wasn't a hell of a lot more to it.

One reporter said: "You killed him." And when he saw the expressions on the faces of boys who had been around and knew my record, added hastily, "Of course."

I shrugged my shoulders. "If I didn't kill him, you've got a great story. 'Cops Bury Man Alive'."

You just can't go around the city shooting people to death, nor are you even allowed to pull off promiscuous killings in your own office. But it was routine to me. I knew all the answers, and if I didn't, I had a damn good lawyer who did. Spats Willis was wanted for murder. It was easier to find reasons for killing him than it was to find reasons for not killing him. Everybody was pleased—even Nelson.

After I went downtown and traded dirty words with the D.A., O'Rourke got me alone in his room and talked straight out. We liked each other O'Rourke and me.

"Race," he said, "there's a new angle to this case. You see, we got word that Spats Willis was coming to America, also that Raftner was coming. Now, Spats was known, but no one has ever seen Raftner. Raftner is also supposed to be here in New York. He's the biggest narcotic agent in the world. Yet, if he walked into police headquarters this minute no one could arrest him. You know—that knowledge-without-the-evidence stuff. Wanted in England, Germany, France, Italy—"

"I know." I nodded. "But what of that? He's in New York now."

"Yeah, that's right." O'Rourke eyed me shrewdly. "We were tipped off he was coming by the G-men. They could have dragged in Spats Willis any time they wanted to; they've been following him ever since he landed. Lost him last week—and we wanted him for murder here. But the G-men have been following someone else longer than they have been following Willis."

"Who—Raftner?"

"No. Take another guess."

"I'm not good at riddles."

"You," said O'Rourke. "You, Race."

"Hell! I should have known it. There's been a dozen or more lads playing lamb to my little Mary." And suddenly, "How long? What did they find?"

O'Rourke grinned. "You seem excited, Race. They drew a blank on you, passed you up over a week ago. Gave you a clean bill of health."

I breathed easier, said: "What put me into their heads? They didn't suspect I was in the racket?"

"I don't know what they suspected; or how they picked up your trail. But they knew drugs had entered the country and that a big man handled it. Gentle Jim Corrigan was wanted, but they weren't sure he headed the dope-ring. They only had to read the newspapers to know that you shot Corrigan to death smack in front of Nelson and myself. So they figured some place along the line you had a client in the racket—and they sat down on your tail."

"Well"—I looked straight at O'Rourke—"I haven't got a client, in or out of the racket."

"Have you met the Flame lately?"

"Haven't seen her in three or four months." My attitude was one of total indifference.

"You mean since lunchtime today." O'Rourke tossed his bomb as casually.

"My God!" I cried out. "You—spying on me like that. How did you find that out?"

O'Rourke chided me lightly. "Now, now. You've been seeing too many movies with dumb cops in them, Race. You shot a man to death and walked out for your lunch. The police were interested in whom you met. You won't argue with me, Race, when I say that the Flame is the most beautiful and the most dangerous woman in New York. And today she was with the most dangerous man in New York—Armin Loring. That's a combination a single man can't beat. No, not even a single man like you. Women are dangerous to men in the racket. Armin never had a woman before—and such a woman."

"The Flame is not—" I started, but O'Rourke cut in.

"I know. I know." A long pause and then, "He'd think nothing of having you killed. And Armin can think fast."

"Fast with his brain as well as with his gun," I thought half aloud.

"Correct," O'Rourke agreed. "Just fast with a gun won't keep a man from being shot in the back of the head." And with a smile, "Your being alive sort of disproves that theory, eh Race?"

"Yeah," was the best I could do.

O'Rourke laid a hand on my shoulder. "You have something that none of them have, boy. You've got instinct. You feel danger before you see it. That's what keeps you alive."

"What about these federal men. Are they going to question me?"

"No. In fact, they've decided to drop you as useless to them."

"Even though I killed Willis?"

"Even though you killed Willis. They didn't make me promise not to tell you about them, but I think a demand for such a promise was coming when we were interrupted. Now, Race, those are my cards. I want yours."

"Mine? I have none. You don't think Armin is in the dope racket? As for the Flame—" I stopped there. Sure, she was in it.

O'Rourke went on and his voice was low. "I never pushed you, Race. I won't push you now. You worked with the G-men once—they owe you something now. It would be a great feather in my hat if we beat them to the pinch." And after a moment, "I'd stretch a point for your client, too."

"O'Rourke!" I looked indignant. "You don't think I'd help anyone who—"

"Never mind what I think. Will you play ball with me when the big moment comes? I don't want our city to be flooded openly with dope. I'd like to think that I was the guy—even through you—who helped prevent that." And suddenly, "Did you know that Armin has been to Singapore?"

"No, but I know he intends to go."

"And for some reason or other he intends to have you killed. That's a fact, Race. It's common gossip in the underworld. Do you know why?"

I grinned broadly, thought of Mary Morse and grinned more. "Is it about a woman?" I asked innocently.

"A woman?" O'Rourke seemed surprised so I switched that.

"Well—I don't know just who Mr. Armin Loring will get to alibi him in my death."

O'Rourke said rather sadly: "The lad who knocks you over won't even need a lawyer. Any self-defence plea will save the man who kills you. With your record any judge, any jury will feel that if you didn't try to kill the man first it was simply an oversight on your part."

I took a bow. "I won't worry about the lad who does me in." And in sudden thought, "Now, O'Rourke, you think Armin is going to kill me. Armin, perhaps, thinks the same thing. Just how would you feel if I—well, prevented Armin from killing me?"

"What do you mean?"

"I mean that if he wasn't alive, why he couldn't kill anyone."

"You mean that you'd murder him?"

My shoulders went up and down. "Why make a nasty word out of it?"

"I'm telling you now that he can shoot circles around you."

"That'll be fine." I grinned. "If I'm standing in the middle of that circle while he's doing his act, then good-bye, Mr. Armin Loring. Suppose"—I leaned forward—"suppose seriously, O'Rourke, because I have a great respect for Armin and his gun, that it was kill or be killed. Just one bullet from one gun—whichever lad fired first. How would you like it if Armin took the dose?"

"Personally," said O'Rourke, "I'd like it fine."

"All right." I turned toward the door. "I'll see what I can do for you—personally."

"Personally—" He started suddenly, stopped, then blurted it out. "You said it was a woman. Good God, it's not the Flame!"

"Good God—it's not." I had the door half open and O'Rourke had his mouth half open. I knew what he was going to say; what he always said. His personal opinion had nothing to do with that of the department, so I didn't give him a chance to say it. I just closed the door and took it on the run down the hall. If anything happened to Armin now, I'd tell O'Rourke I thought he wanted it that way. And truth is truth—I think he did.

* * *

I went whistling out of the building and grabbed the subway uptown. Oh, I know taxis are the thing for private investigators. You can't very well say to subway motormen: "Follow that man." But then I had no man to follow—and more to the point, no client to pay for the taxi.

When I reached my own apartment I dropped into an easy chair, picked up the evening papers. I liked the streamers on a couple of the papers. *Wanted Murderer Shot To Death* and *Hoodlum Killed As He Threatens Death*. But one sheet did its stuff and wouldn't hurt my business any. Yep, the blazing banner I liked best read—*Race Williams Does It Again*.

On the second page I took a laugh. The photograph was good; the wording under it better. There was a picture of Iron Man Nelson leaning over the body of Spats Willis in my office. And the caption read—*Inspector Nelson First to Find the Dead Body*. Get it? Of course, you do—and so would Nelson. He had been making it a habit lately of finding bodies—after I laid those bodies out for him.

The phone rang. It was Mary Morse and she was crying. There was terror in her voice. She had hard work in getting her words out over the phone, and I had a sight harder work understanding them. Then she cleared up.

"Race," she said finally, very slowly and distinctly, "I need you more than I have ever needed you. I am at the Green Room of the Hotel York Terrace. There is a man with me called Raftner. He is controlling my every move, because—well, you know why."

I didn't get the idea, but I said simply: "Sure, Mary. I'll come around and have a talk with you."

"But this man—he'll kill you if you come!"

"Nonsense." I put it lightly. "I'll stick you for the supper check."

"But this Raftner—he's here with me."

"Then we'll stick him for the check," I chuckled.

Her voice lowered. Someone muttered beside her. Mary Morse pulled an aside in a hoarse whisper. "I won't. I won't. He's coming." A pause and then, "Close the door of the booth. Wait on the outside, and I will—Oh, I will!"

I didn't cut in on the little comedy—or tragedy—that took place in that booth. I just listened. I heard a single step, a soft swish which sounded like the telephone-booth door closing, then Mary Morse's voice.

"They are making me do this. Raftner is making me. They want me to plead with you to come. They want to find out if you would come. Race, Race! I've caused you enough danger. Don't come—don't come. This Raftner is different; has influence. He's—he's bad."

"He's kidding you, Mary. I'll just trot over to the York Terrace and see how bad he really is."

"No—no!" Her voice wasn't low now. "Don't come! He'll kill you right here at—"

There was a slight thud, a stifled scream, the click of the receiver—and I dropped my own phone back in its cradle.

I whistled softly as I adjusted my shoulder holsters, slipped into my jacket, picked up my hat. Armin Loring had warned me not to see Mary Morse again. The Flame had told me not to see her again. Mary Morse herself had told me not to come—both on that card and over the phone. And a lad called Raftner—so bad that he admitted it himself—threatened my death if I visited the Green Room of the Hotel York Terrace.

There was only one answer to that.

The York Terrace is a rather classy, high-priced hotel, and the Green Room some parsnips in the night life of a great city. Yet, I didn't get into evening clothes. I can wear the boiled shirt as well as the next fellow and talk so I won't be taken for a waiter. But a shoulder holster isn't so good with a tux, unless you sport a small gun. Me—I don't like twenty-twos. When I put a hole in a guy I don't embarrass half a dozen doctors who try to find it. My motto is: There isn't much sense in shooting the same guy over and over.

The exclusive Hotel York Terrace was having something put over on it. I spotted him as soon as I entered the lobby. He was all decked out in fish-and-soup and leaning against a pillar—a bad boy of the night. He had the size to look down at you, and the twisted kisser to scare people to death. Now he grabbed my arm and started to work on me as soon as I reached the pillar.

"Listen, Williams," he said, and despite my six feet, I had to raise my head slightly to look at him, "I'm working for Armin—Armin Loring. You're not to go in that Green Room. You're to beat it from the hotel now before I—"

I stopped him there. I knew why he repeated Armin's name. It was like whistling in the dark. His heart wasn't in his threat. I said simply: "Take your hand off me, Sam, before I shoot your arm away at the shoulder." And when he dropped his hand as if he were gripping a hot iron, "Now—tell me what you'll do. And if I don't like it—you'll be surprised."

His face got a bit white. "Well—" He hedged trying to get us a little back from the entrance to the Green Room which made me turn my head and see Mr. Armin Loring sitting at a table by the door with the Flame. His face was sideways to us. "Well," Sam tried again, "I was just to say it wouldn't be healthy for you." And as I carelessly crossed my right hand to my left armpit, "God, Mr. Williams! It was just a message I had to give and—and—"

I watched him back away then, fade to the left and out of sight of the crowd in the Green Room. He didn't speak again. When he got far enough away he turned sideways and did a little ballet dance toward the main entrance. And he was right. I don't take talk from guys like him; never did; never will.

I spun on my heel and entered the Green Room. Armin turned his head and saw me just as I saw Mary Morse—frightened, white-faced little Mary Morse who had gone through so much with her head up—and the gent beside her. Big shoulders, big neck, big head—and so help me God!—nose-glasses with a wide black ribbon running down from them and half twisted about the huge cigar that decorated his thick-lipped puss. They were far down in a corner of that room.

"Hello, Armin." I leaned on Armin's table and smiled at him; smiled just as the lights dimmed, a spotlight flashed, and a dame started to sing. "Is Raftner still tough? Is he the guy with the crape on his glasses?"

Armin said very slowly: "That is Raftner—and he'll shoot you to death right at the table. So don't go near Mary Morse."

I smiled cheerfully over at the Flame. She wasn't the young girl now. She was the hard, calculating woman of the night. It was in her eyes, her face, her tight lips—in the very movement she made pulling the high-priced fur piece over her bare right shoulder.

I said to Armin above the singer who had hit her stride and was raising hell all over the room: "And if Raftner isn't as bad as you think, then you'll—"

He almost snarled as he cut in. "Any time and place."

"Fine." I patted Armin—the dangerous Armin—on the back. "Get ready for the fireworks."

"You fool!" Armin clutched at my arm, looked at me as if he were figuring out if I were drunk or not. "Don't try anything here. I tell you this man will kill you."

"You asked for it, brother," I told him and then almost viciously as I jerked my arm free, "If Raftner's half the man you think he is, we'll give the Green Room a floor-show that will be entirely different."

I moved around the edge of the dance-floor, cut across it on the fringe of the light, nearly lost an eardrum as the singing girl, feeling that she was not annoying enough people, began to circle around.

I went straight down the lane of light toward those wide, staring terror-stricken eyes of Mary Morse. I saw Raftner, too. He was half turned now. One arm—his left—hung over the side of his chair. His right hand was holding a glass of champagne. The silver ice-bucket was plainly visible beside him.

I got a good look at his face. He wasn't any gunman—that is a gunman as we picture one. He was smiling at me and his bulging, fish-like eyes had a film over them; a film that seemed to magnify instead of dim them through the lenses of his glasses.

He never changed his position as I reached the table—just smiled and said very low: "You're Race Williams, of course. I have seen your picture. I have come to this country for the purpose of looking at you—just once."

"That's fine," I said, and since his voice was not unpleasant, I tried to keep mine the same, though I daresay I didn't make much of a go of it. "You're Mr. Raftner. Well, I've got some bad news for you. Your very charming companion is coming along with me."

"That is not the truth," he said very solemnly. "She will not go. She will remain here with me. It is her preference—her privilege—and her comfort." And very slowly, "She is used to every luxury of life. Prison cells are cold and damp."

"Hell!" I didn't like this backing and filling. "I thought you were dynamite. Armin gave me the idea that this was the table of death."

"You could, of course, make Armin's words come true." Those great shoulders hunched. His left hand still hung over the chair; his right still held the almost full glass of champagne.

"Come on, Mary," I said. "Your fat friend has proved a bust. You and I are going places."

Mary started to her feet. Raftner spoke, "The dear child has a cold on her chest Mr. Williams. She will be escorted home carefully so that the night air will not hurt her. Then she will place her feet in a hot bath." He paused a long moment, turned his head and looked directly at the girl. "Sit down, child," he said, and his voice was like fingernails drawn along a wall. "I knew a young girl once who found the hot bath so severe that she never walked again." He made a queer noise in his throat. "Both her feet were amputated."

So that was it. Here was a guy who was supposed to be good with a gun making cracks with certainly more than a hint of torture. Mary Morse put one hand to her throat; the other stretched limply toward me as she fell rather than slipped back in the chair.

"Go, Race," she said. "Go—I'll—I'll stay with him. I've got to. I've got to."

"Nonsense," I told her and as my voice rose a little I took a quick look-see around. Tables on either side of us were vacant; people beyond were looking from the semi-darkness beneath the balcony into the light, and watching the singer. I went on: "Don't mind this big bust, Mary. You heard what was going to happen to me if I came here. Now what? A lot of wind. Why, this big stiff couldn't—"

The big stiff did. He just moved his right hand back and tossed it up again. The "insult direct" or something like that in the book of etiquette, I guess. For his cigar puffed, smoke blew straight into my face the moment the champagne splashed all over my map.

Mad? Of course I was mad. So would you be. I just can't shoot lads to death unless there is some reason for it. Though you and I may think a face full of champagne is sufficient reason—twelve beer-drinking men on a jury might not.

Anyway, I didn't like it. His eyes were watching my right hand. Hard eyes and cold; no fish now, but steel through his glasses. And his right hand was ready to cross as soon as mine. Oh, I won't believe any man is quicker than I am, and—

I don't go in for light humor often, but I did now. I stretched out my right hand, pulled the cigar out of his wide, surprised mouth, then shoved it back into his face again. That I turned it around and shoved in the wrong end of the cigar—that is, the wrong end from his point of view—is what caused the trouble. But if he wanted to play—why, so did I.

If you have ever pushed the lighted end of a cigar in your own mouth during a fast evening, you'll know the sensation of surprise. But you'll probably have to guess how it feels when someone else does it—then screws it in like a cork in a bottle.

No, I don't know how dangerous Mr. Raftner was, but I do know what he did. He spit bits of cigar, ashes, and fire, and jumped up and down like a maniac. Sure, he stopped the show. He had half a dozen waiters around, poured glasses and glasses of water into his mouth, and just made a mess of himself as the waiters tried to stop him. He tried to talk, but didn't make much of a go of it.

To the first waiter I said: "He's drunk."

The head-waiter was disturbed—greatly disturbed. He said sort of awed: "He's the Baron from Antwerp, is he not? It is most regrettable, Miss Morse—this head of a great jewelry firm." And when I put a bug in his ear, "But certainly, *monsieur*. Miss Morse need not be further embarrassed. The door there— through the kitchen. No, no—no one knows him by name, and few saw—and none, I believe, recognized Miss Morse."

I wasn't mad any more when a captain led the girl and me to the little door and into the kitchen. Of course, Mary was well known in the best places. For some time now she had been the actual head of Morse and Lee. Poor kid—trying to stimulate the jewelry trade by appearing in fashionable places.

I was careful as we left that dining-room. No fear that Mr. Raftner, alias, the Baron, would stick a bullet in my back. Like Mount Vesuvius, he was having another eruption. It was Armin I was watching. I saw him come to his feet and start across the dining-room toward the vanishing figure of Raftner who was being pushed more than just escorted between red curtains in one corner of the room. Then Armin hesitated, hurried back to the Flame who was quickly leaving the room.

Yes, I was chuckling. But we can't have our little joke without paying for it. That's life, I suppose. The captain who saw us to the side entrance and sent for a taxi was very polite. He said quite close to my ear: "*Monsieur le Baron* was rather too clever with the champagne. But you, *monsieur*, with the revolving cigar were superb."

So just as I was about to help Mary Morse into the taxi I parted with a tenspot. Another donation to a cause that had paid no dividends. But I shook my head. After all, where could I have gone and had so much fun for ten bucks. Mr. Raftner had taken it, and wasn't likely to go around and tell people what had happened. I frowned. Nothing to worry me, maybe. But what of Mary Morse?

That had been my mental question. Now as I turned and started to climb into the taxi it became a physical one. Mary Morse was not in the taxi. Mary Morse was gone. She was nowhere on that side street. By the time I reached the corner Mary Morse was not on the main thoroughfare either.

Chapter Four

On the Kill

I climbed into the taxi and gave the address of my apartment. Then I did a little thinking. My main thought was that Raftner was flooding the city with narcotics and the place he would use to distribute the drugs from would be Mary Morse's jewelry shop—one of the most respected establishments in the city. The last place to suspect, it had never even come under observation when her dear Uncle Frank Morse had hidden drugs in the basement. He'd kept the stuff in vases that sold for prices that would amaze you—did me, not having an eye for Ming's Dynasty or any other guy's dynasty for that matter. Now Raftner was threatening Mary Morse with exposure of her dead uncle's activities, the fact that she'd kept her knowledge of them from the police. Also threatening to expose the bit of killing I'd pulled off in her interest.

One thing they did wish to make sure of—and that was that I was out of the picture, and out of it quickly. If I were willing to fade myself they'd let it go at that. If I weren't, they wanted to find it out right away and knock me over.

Anyway, I couldn't get the truth out of Mary Morse—at least at once—since I didn't know where she was. Then who could talk? And I had it. Her stepfather, Conklyn Lee. He had managed that firm since Mary's grandfather's death.

I'm not a sentimental fool. Anyone who knows me knows that. Oh, if it comes to a show-down, I'll die for a cause, but I'd much rather kill the cause and live for another one. And I'm not a guy who got his knowledge of drugs and the vicious part they play in the life and death of a great city by reading articles in the magazines. I have seen the real thing. Criminals turned into mad dogs by dope, murders and tortures, decent women leaving their husbands and children and walking the streets because of it. Young lives ruined, old lives taken by a jump from a window.

Of course I couldn't let lugs like Armin or Raftner tell me where to get off but when I reached Conklyn Lee's old brown-stone front, I like to think there was something else beside that urging me—something of the crusader if you want to go DeMille on me. Lee let me in himself and I followed him down the hall to the library. He may have been hot stuff in the jewelry business and made quite a front, but then I guess he didn't go walking about the great floor of the shop with his nightshirt flapping out from under his bathrobe.

He had more things to do before he could get settled than a bride getting ready for her wedding. He had to get his glasses, mix himself a whisky and soda without hardly enough whisky to kill the taste of the soda. He kept walking around offering me cigarettes and lighting one himself every time I shook my head, until he had two in the ashtray and one in his hand—all lit. And all the time he kept saying: "Mary—where is Mary? No cigarette, Mr. Williams, no whisky? Some tea then?"

"I never eat or drink or smoke in a place I'm not sure of," I told him flat. "I lost some good friends that way." And when his face grew blank, I explained simply, "Poison."

"Good gracious," he said, and if the words themselves seemed trite, old-fashioned and childish, he put enough expression into them to make them sound almost profane.

I didn't waste time; I gave him straight talk. I said bluntly, and as if I knew every word of it to be gospel: "The shop is being used again to store and ship narcotics."

"The idea"—he puffed and blew a bit—"is impossible."

"Have you met the Baron from Antwerp?" I chucked at him.

"Baron Von Stutz? Yes."

"And Armin Loring?"

"Armin Loring? No."

"Maybe not under that name." I shook my head. "Now, Mr. Lee, we're getting too deep into this thing to go on with it. I may have trouble explaining my knowledge of the former use of your store for narcotics, and those men I shot up in Mount Vernon. And it may ruin the Morse firm, may give you and Mary a jolt up the River. I've got to hear talk from you—real words—or I'm going to blow the works. You're opening up a passage that will make the almost uncontrollable crime situation in the country get out of hand entirely."

He got up, paced the room, said: "I don't know. I hope not. I—God, Williams! I've thought of it day and night and have been tempted to go right to the government officials. It's Mary—just Mary. But there are times when I thought it would be best for her if I should talk to you. After all you have done it would seem so unfair—such ingratitude—to let you pay the penalty for your loyalty and help. Yes, I think I will go straight to the police with the whole truth."

So we reversed positions. It was he who threatened to go to the cops, and now I who talked him out of it. I told him all that had happened tonight. Of Mary's fear, of my attempt to help her, of the threats against my life. I watched his face while I talked. Then I watched his face while he talked, and I'm used to reading faces. His was an honest one; so honest it stood out. I'd have bet my last dollar on that—but what the hell! I've bet my last dollar on a lot of things and lost. But he gave me the story.

"Mary has taken an active part in the business lately. Even built it up considerably. After Gentle Jim Corrigan's death we felt that we had nothing more to fear. Mary tried to see you then—thank you. The past seemed so definitely the past. Then it became the present—a deadly horrible present."

He paused and I helped by saying: "Let's have it."

"Mary began to be worried. Began to spend much of her time in the basement below the store. Then she introduced me to Baron Von Stutz who was interested in vases. Then out of a clear sky she told me that the Baron would take charge for a while of the buying and selling of vases to private collectors. He would come and go by the rear entrance to the basement itself. No one but men he selected would handle the shipments of vases. There was such a fear in her eyes, such a plea, such a—I—" His hands spread far apart. "So she asked for the key to the heavy steel door that led to the basement, and the next morning"—with great emphasis on the single word, *next*—"I gave it to her, and for the first time in the history of the shop the basement on that side was shut off from the shop itself."

"Why do you say—*next* morning?" I asked him.

He coughed, looked me straight in the eyes and finally said: "We had but the one key which I kept in a drawer in the safe. I had a duplicate made."

"You were suspicious, then?" The old boy had his good points.

"Suspicious!" His voice raised slightly. "I was alarmed, frightened, distraught."

I liked that last word so I threw it back at him. "When you visited the basement later with that key were you still distraught?"

He didn't smile, simply nodded. "This Baron knew nothing of vases. Even in the semi-darkness and without handling them I knew that a great many pieces he'd brought in were made here in America by the thousands to be sold at cheap auction-rooms. I spoke to Mary, and she told me the truth. It was blackmail. This dark man who was often with the Baron and called himself Mr. Armitage had discovered the secret of her uncle's—Frank Morse's—death. They were using our basement for the cutting and resetting of smuggled or stolen gems. It was the price we must pay for their silence."

"Did you believe her?"

"Of course." Conklyn Lee seemed surprised, and if he were an actor he was a damned good one. "You think it's drugs. No, Mr. Williams. I thought of that, too, but after what you told Mary the first time—she'd—yes, she'd sacrifice everything—name, business before she'd agree to that."

I shrugged my shoulders as I came to my feet. "Go on believing what you like, Mr. Lee. But it's drugs just the same."

We talked after that. And I believed in Conklyn Lee, just as Mary Morse believed in him. I believed in Mary Morse, too. Believed even now that she did not suspect the real truth. Illegal diamonds, unlike dope, could not corrupt the youth of a country. Sure, she would believe what they told her. Who wouldn't believe it? And I gulped. I didn't like the answer to that thought. The Flame wouldn't believe it. Not be fooled a minute. And the Flame was in it. Criminal mind, eh? She must have developed a criminal stomach, too.

Before I left I made arrangements to meet Conklyn Lee at the shop the following night.

The Flame was nervous; Armin Loring was nervous; Raftner was nervous, for he had sent Spats Willis to kill me. Willis, of course, was both nervous and dead. But I recognized the signs. It affects all big crooks the same. They get fidgety, suspicious, ready to act quickly; kill quickly just before the big pay-off.

The pay-off was soon, then. The drugs must be in that basement ready to be shipped. The cheap vases gave that away. That's how the dope came there and that would be how the dope left.

What would the government, the police, give for a bit of information like that? They'd give us freedom. They'd have to. It would be a great story that Mary Morse suspected something wrong, hired me and I uncovered the greatest drug-ring that ever got ready to encircle a city— a country even. The other story about Uncle Frank Morse—my killing him— why, we'd just forget that and begin with the coming of Baron Von Stutz, alias Raftner, and Armin Loring. So I was humming as I left the house.

I wasn't humming when the taxi drew up before my apartment door. My pleasant thoughts busted like a child's balloon. We could forget it all right. But what good would that do us while Raftner and Armin Loring still remembered it and could talk about it?

As I stepped from the taxi my thought was to make them forget it. Which was impossible unless—unless—And my right hand mechanically slid under my left armpit as I swung around. Yep, I thought, imagination is a great thing, as I actually caressed my gun—and I was right. For that little bit of imagination saved my life, saved it right then and there in the fraction of a split second.

Sure, for I swung my face almost against the barrel of a Tommy gun. I saw the steel drum which hid steady fingers, saw a face behind that tommy gun. I don't know if the man spoke, if the man threatened. I don't think so. Just narrowing eyes, a droop to the lower lip, the sudden assurance of death, and I flipped back my hand and shot that face straight out of my life—and his too, for that matter.

The City of New York may seem insufficiently policed. You can walk the streets at night and not see a cop; you'd think you didn't have any protection. But try shooting a man to death and see how quickly the boys turn up and want to know why. Yep, they were on their way before I skipped over the corpse and stepped into my apartment house.

I bumped into Frosty, the night-man. His eyes popped; he dropped the paper he had been reading on the floor, mouthed the words: “Lord, Mr. Williams, sah! I just read it in the paper and—and you ain’t gone an’ done it again?”

“That’s right, Frosty. I gone an’ done it again.” I handed him a five-spot. “Tell the cops I’m upstairs and pay the taxi-man if he squawks.” Without losing my stride I entered the automatic lift and started up. One thing was certain. The boys in the dope racket meant business.

I reached my apartment in time to get O’Rourke out of bed and tell him to hop over—there might be trouble with the police. O’Rourke was half asleep, but he came to quick enough when he realized a dead guy was lying out front.

“What the hell!” I cut in on his sermon. “I’m a citizen and I want some police protection. I want it pretty damn quick, too, or these cops will drag me downtown and keep me from shooting a guy who—”

“Another one?”

“Yeah—another one.” I stopped. The bell of my apartment was ringing, and someone was trying to kick the door in at the same time. “Wait, O’Rourke. Don’t go back to sleep.” I put the phone down on the table leaving the connection open and went to the door, flung it wide. A sergeant was there and a couple of harness cops behind him.

The sergeant was fat, officious and had been used to scaring pickpockets and milk-bottle thieves half to death by glaring at them. I knew him and he knew me.

“Hello, Halorhan.” I pushed him in the stomach. “The commissioner has let the ropes down, and you’re filling up the waist-line, eh?”

“Now look here, Williams.” Sergeant Halorhan came into the room as if he expected guys to pull guns on him from behind every chair. “You can’t be doing this, you know—not so steadily on the public streets. I’ve got to—”

“You’ve got to talk to O’Rourke.” I managed to roll him across to the phone, even lifted it and put it in his hand. The talk was one-sided. It went like this—

“That’s right, O’Rourke. . . . No, I guess Williams admits the killing. . . . There was a Tommy gun in this hood’s hand. . . . Recognize him! Why, he hasn’t got any face.”

There was more, but I wasn’t listening. I invited in the cops who stood in the doorway. Jerry was around by now and I had him get them a drink and saw Halorhan looking at the glasses and hurrying his talk with O’Rourke. At last he hung up the phone and when I didn’t say anything, asked point-blank for a “snort.” He was a “one-drink man” when on duty, but he made that drink go a long ways. It knocked hell out of a bottle.

Now he rubbed the back of his hand across his mouth, smacked his lips and said partly sarcastic, partly humorous: "I wonder, Mr. Race Williams, if it would be asking too much to ask just how it happened. Sergeant O'Rourke seems to think that you're too busy killing people to talk about it."

"No trouble at all." I was affable. "I stepped out of a cab. This lad put a Tommy gun against my head, and I shot him."

"Then?" said Halorhan falling into the trap.

"Why then he died," I told him.

The cops laughed, stopped at once as Halorhan moved toward the door. Then they were gone.

The phone rang and it was Mary Morse. She talked before I could get started. "Race—you're alive then! You're all right? Armin Loring swore he'd kill you if I so much as talked to you. That's why I ran away from you tonight. I thought they'd know, understand. I telephoned Armin that I'd never see you again if he spared you and—"

"Spared me! That grease ball! Listen here, Mary—" And I damn near choked over the words. I thought I'd shown her enough to let her know I didn't need any nursemaid. "Wherever did you get such an idea? You saw how I handled Raftner."

"I was told, Race—yes, told by your friend—to warn you to keep out of this affair, never to see me again or you'd be killed by Armin who can"—yes, her very words were—"who can shoot circles all around you. Don't you see, Race—don't you understand! It was your own assistant who told me."

"My assistant—Jerry?" I fairly gasped, before the truth struck me.

"No, that woman. The one who helped you and me when we were prisoners. The woman with the queer name—the Flame."

The Flame. Sure, I saw what she meant then. The Flame had told her she was my assistant and I had never told Mary any different. At the time I'd kept silent, perhaps to protect the Flame. Later there was no need. Now—I just gasped, let the thing go, and asked her: "Where are you—home?"

"No, I've been walking the streets. I don't know what to do. I've got to see Armin or he'll kill you."

Dumb? For a bright girl she was certainly dumb. Poor kid. No, she wasn't dumb—except in one thing. How anyone above the age of seven who had seen me in action could think for a moment that Armin Loring would take away my appetite, I don't know. But I told her simply: "Let me run things for a day or two. Go to some hotel, register under another name and—"

"But I can't. I telephoned Armin. I must go over and see him in half an hour. He said I must. I saw your assistant with him in the Green Room tonight. Does that mean—"

I cut her off. "What's Armin's telephone number?" And when she hesitated, "I want to ring him up and tell him I won't bother with you any more"—I gulped—"then he won't want to kill me."

She gave me his telephone number at once. So her dumbness served me some purpose that time. But when I started to talk to her like a Dutch uncle she hung up on me.

Mad? I was fit to be tied. Why should I wait around for Armin to have first shot at me? Wait to let Armin set the time and the place—murder by his watch? Just wait until he was ready—then try my luck against his. No, I had had enough of that. Two could play his game.

I snapped up the phone and buzzed Armin's number. It was early in the morning, yet he answered the phone almost at once. His voice was low and expectant—expectant of another voice maybe, a girl's voice—but he got exactly what was on my mind.

"Williams calling, Armin," I told him. "You've broken that one-man record. There was an attempt on my life a few minutes ago. Friend of yours—nice boy."

"Yes?" There was interest in Armin's voice, anxiety too, I thought. "What happened?"

"He's dead," I said. "Spread all over the sidewalk, and I'll have to talk to the district attorney early in the morning."

"I'm sorry you have to get up early, Race, but I'm sure the D.A. will be pleased."

"I won't have to get up early," I told him. "At least, I don't think I will. I'll already be up."

"Insomnia—conscience?" He laughed. "I don't quite understand."

"Listen, Armin—about that promise of yours—or was it a threat? You know—any place, any time. Does it still go?"

His laugh was light. "It got under your skin, eh Race? Well, when I talk like that and something like that machine-gun business comes off, it is unnerving. Yes, it still goes—maybe quicker than you think."

"That's right." I was very serious now. "Maybe quicker—much quicker—than even you think. I'm giving you a chance to withdraw that threat, Armin. I know you don't bluff, and it does bother me."

"Any time, any place—the five-o'clock rush hour on Forty-Second Street. Do I make myself clear enough?"

"O.K." I got down to the point. "I'll be leaving here in five minutes and I'm coming directly to your apartment. If you're to make good on that threat, you've got to make good on it within the next twenty minutes."

"What do you mean by that?" I think he was a bit startled.

"I mean," I said, "some people have an idea that you're faster with a gun than I am. In twenty minutes one of us will find out—but only one of us."

"Hell," he said. "You can't try that, not tonight."

"Listen, Armin. When you open your door, open it shooting or you're never going to shoot again. I'm on the kill."

"No fooling, Race?" And something had gone out of his voice.

"No fooling, Armin," I said and hung up the phone. And I wasn't fooling when I put on my hat and walked out the door. I know it doesn't sound nice; doesn't look nice in black and white. But it was the truth. Armin Loring had to make good within the next twenty minutes or I'd shoot him to death.

Chapter Five

The Flame

I won't say it was exactly pleasant walking up the stairs to Armin's top-floor apartment, but I didn't think he'd had time enough to call in any friends, and I didn't think he'd show the yellow streak anyway—at least not to those friends.

Nothing happened as I reached the fifth floor, went down the corridor, and stood there in the dim hall-light right smack before his door. Then I lifted both my guns from their holsters, shoved one against the bell-button and trained the other on the door.

But the door didn't open. Didn't open, though I heard feet—a sort of soft pressure as if a body leaned against that door, maybe with an ear cocked to listen. I tapped lightly with my gun, moved the gun close to the lock, half tightened my finger on the trigger, then looked up and down the hall.

I shrugged and shook my head. That wouldn't do at all. This was no secret mission on my part but still—I looked toward the flight of stairs that led to the roof, jerked back my gun and sped up them. No tricks there, no lock to shoot. I simply slipped the hook off the door and walked out onto the flat roof. I didn't need the light in the window below to tell me which fire-escape led to Armin's apartment.

I don't like to loiter and pussy-foot around. In less than two minutes after I left that apartment door, I was crouching on the fire-escape by the window. And what's more the window was open a bit. A look-see under the shade did me no good. There was a window-seat, and beyond that heavy curtains. Well, I was there on business. I pushed the window quietly up, slipped onto that window-seat and parting the drapes, peered through just as the doorbell to the apartment rang. There was another visitor, then. Perhaps half a dozen of them. Armin wasn't taking chances.

I sat down on the window-seat behind those curtains, made sure that they were long enough to hide my feet, held a gun in each hand and waited; waited as I looked between those curtains at the man who stood in the center of that room. He stood there with a gun hanging in his hand, fear in his eyes, uncertainty in his manner, as he turned from the ringing bell to the curtains behind which I sat.

It was my boy friend, Sam, of the Hotel York Terrace—the big mutton who had started out to be a tough guy and turned into a ballet-dancer. The bell rang once more. Sam stiffened and listened as he backed toward me. I took a silent laugh. He was backing to that window to escape me at the door! So Armin had run out on me.

But I was listening just as Sam was listening. His hand was on the curtain when the key turned in the lock and the door to the apartment opened and closed. Feet came down the hall—light, tapping feet—the feet of a woman. Mary Morse, of course.

And I was wrong. So wrong I damn near fell off the window-seat. Sam shot his gun into his shoulder holster and sighed with relief. It was the Flame, and if she had ever been the laughing happy young girl, you wouldn't know it now. Her face was hard, set; her brown eyes, twin balls of ice. She squeezed her green handbag close in her two slender, ungloved hands and popped right out with, "Where's Armin?"

"He's out. Got a message from this Williams guy and beat it along." Sam shook his head. "This cheap dick was coming down to have it out with Armin. Armin hated to leave, but couldn't afford a shoot-up here with things ready to move."

The Flame nodded, said: "Is it tonight?" And shaking her head, "It's too early in the morning for that. Is the stuff to move tomorrow night, Sam?"

I could see the man's eyes narrow. "Don't you know? You're going to marry Armin and you don't—"

The Flame raised her head, sniffed at the air, said: "Where's the woman. Did he leave her here?"

"Why, there ain't no woman here, Florence."

"Miss Drummond," she snapped back at him. "Armin's got an eye on that Morse girl for more than just the money in it. She's been writing him letters."

"Naw." Sam let his broad thick lips part. "And what of it, Florence. You're a knock-out when you're mad. Armin was always One Man Armin—not One Woman Armin." He put a hand around her shoulders, drew her to him. "Let him run out with the dame if he wants. I'll be around to make it up to you." And suddenly grabbing her to him with both his arms, "Hell—the Flame—that's the name for you."

Did I step out to protect the frail little body of the Flame from this giant. I did not. And I didn't need to. Her arms moved like twin pistons, the hands on the ends of those arms flashing white. Just the crack, and the marks of fingers upon the man's face. A curse as sharp pointed toes pounded against his legs.

He dropped her, stepped back, muttered: "And I seen you going through Armin's desk looking for letters from some moll and never peeped. He'd strangle you for that. You want to play rough, well I'll play rough. You can't talk—can't tell Armin afterwards—or I'll talk. There, don't run. It won't do you any good."

The Flame wasn't running. She didn't even step back, didn't give an inch—just stood there clutching her green bag. This time as his hand shot out, her right hand came up and down. I saw the tiny gun, saw it turn in her hand, saw its sight rip down his face and the blood come. He raised his hand to his face, staggered slightly.

The Flame watched him—calm. Her voice was even, steady, when she spoke. "Don't be a fool, Sam," she said. "I could have emptied the twenty-twos in this rod down your throat. There, that's better. I'm giving orders here. Where's that dame?"

The man eyed her, lifted his hands twice, let them fall to his sides again, said finally: "I'm sorry. It won't happen again. I swear it."

"There's nothing to apologize for," she said bluntly. "You keep your mouth closed and so will I." Her smile was not pleasant. "And it can happen again any time you want to be a fool. I always take care of myself." As if dismissing the subject, she stretched up a hand, grabbed at the lapel of his coat. "Was Williams here?"

"He was at the door and left." Sam was willing to forgive and forget, too. There was a nasty dig in his face. "I begged Armin to let me meet Williams. I'd have killed him right there in the doorway as soon as—"

The Flame laughed. "Race Williams would have shot your head right off your shoulders before you had time to tell him what a real dangerous man you are, Sam. About this dame, Mary Morse. Did she go with Armin or—"

The Flame stopped; both listened. Someone was at the door. There was the click of metal against metal as if that someone were having trouble placing a key in a lock.

"That's the girl—the Morse girl." The Flame just breathed the words. "Keep your face closed, Sam, or I'll tell Armin the trouble you have with your hands. I'll get her to go with me—say Williams sent me."

"You—you'd kill her?" He shrugged. "Well, it would save Armin the trouble."

"He was going to kill her tonight?"

"Maybe. She knows too much. Armin's afraid she'll blow to Williams. He—"

The door had opened and closed again. This time the feet were anything but steady. Mary Morse wobbled slightly as she stood in the doorway. Then she was speaking.

"Armin sent for me—and I came. I can't go through with it. I—I—" Her blue eyes grew even wider; the fear went out of them as they turned from Sam to the Flame. "You—you—Race's assistant. Oh, God, I wish I had your courage now!" She ran to the Flame, clung to her sobbing. I saw the Flame look up over her shoulder, wink at Sam.

I was tempted to step out then, but I didn't. Here was a chance to get an earful. It didn't seem like Armin was coming back.

The Flame was saying: "Armin had to leave, my dear. I'm going to take you along with me."

"You—Yes, I can go any place with you. But I must see Mr.

Williams—Race Williams. I must tell him everything. I know the truth. It mustn't happen—mustn't—"

"I understand," the Flame said quietly as she patted the girl's head. "There, don't cry. Race Williams will make things come out all right for you; he always has. Don't shake like that—let me hold you."

If I wasn't on to the show I would have believed it myself. Just an older woman who had seen a lot of life comforting a younger one who hadn't. Yes, I'd have trusted the Flame, and I didn't blame Mary Morse for trusting her. Besides, there was that first time when Mary had taken the Flame for my assistant and I had let her believe it. I should have told her the truth. And suddenly she did know the truth.

It was the ballet-dancer, good old tactful Sam, who made his ugliest face when he spoke. "Why feed the kid baloney, sister. I think Armin may want her to live for a few days until he's sure."

Mary Morse screamed as she jumped back from the Flame. "That man—what is he doing here?" And there was recognition in her eyes followed by terror. "He's going to kill me—kill me before I can right my wrong."

She was running for the hall when Sam grabbed her and swung her back. She was screaming, too, but her words were clear until Sam clapped a hand over her mouth. "It's narcotics—drugs—not diamonds! I know it now!"

The man's left hand went over her face, tore her head back against his chest. His right hand shot awkwardly behind him, jerked a blackjack from a hip pocket. He was staggering under her weight, straightening, trying to regain his balance, his back almost against the curtain. Then his hand went up, the blackjack started down, and I parted the curtains slightly and struck—viciously, brutally. My gun bounced hard against his head—damn good and hard.

Ballet-dancer or not, Sam didn't trip the light fantastic this time. He just dropped his arm from around Mary Morse's throat and hit the floor.

As for me, I merely stepped over his body in time to strike with my gun again and knock the twenty-two from the Flame's hand. I wasn't any too gentle. Involuntarily her right hand went to her mouth, sucking suddenly at those fingers.

"I'm sorry, Florence, if I hurt your fingers." My apology was meant to be the height of sarcasm. "But it was that or shoot you to death."

She was a remarkable woman, all right. If she were surprised she gave no sign. Certainly, she was not struck with any terror. She said simply and as if she meant it: "It's too bad I didn't lift the gun. I'd like to know if you'd have—" And looking at the curtains behind me, "Well, throw out the body. I suppose Armin's lying dead there."

"No such luck." I shook my head as I helped Mary Morse to her feet. "You were playing the game pretty low on the kid here. Was it money or jealousy?" And as her brown eyes flashed, "It was money, then. You wouldn't recognize jealousy. You wouldn't recognize any other woman's chance against you."

"That's right." She looked from me to Mary Morse, sobbing on my arm, and back to me. "Not even with you, Race. Your trouble is that you're too sensational. Let her go, Race."

But I wasn't going to let Mary Morse go this time. I started after her as she ran toward the hall door. Then I stopped, swung quickly around and said to the Flame: "Don't touch it!"

She shrugged her shoulders and straightened from the gun.

"O.K., Race," she cut in when I would have spoken. "I know your line. 'There is no sex in crime,' you were going to say. Then gallantly spare my life by shooting three fingers off my right hand." And biting her lips, "I am very proud of my hands. I wouldn't want to live without the fingers that make them so clever."

"I wonder," I said, "why you want to live at all." This as the door slammed and I picked up the Flame's gun. No, I didn't follow Mary Morse. I might have caught her, probably would, but the Flame still had the little green bag in her hand and I didn't know what all was in it. I might very easily catch a bullet in the back.

"I live simply for you, dear." Her smile was rather unpleasant. "Is Sam dead?"

"I'm not a doctor," I told her gruffly. "If his head is as thick as the thoughts that come out of it, he won't have much more than a dent."

She shook her head at me, smiled. "They couldn't arrest you for killing Sam. It would just be one of those mercy killings."

Not a bad crack at all, but I didn't feel in a light humor. Damn it! I had loved the Flame, had— And she was putting those eyes on me now, with a brightness, yes, a sparkle of youth in them. And—And I snapped out of it.

I said when I reached the door: "Has Armin Loring got much money, Florence?"

"Enough. Why?"

"Because if you want to inherit as the widow you'd better marry him at once. He hasn't much longer to live."

I started to turn, but didn't. I felt almost as if she were laughing at me as I backed through that doorway to the hall. Well, after all, I'd rather have her laughing at me than be dead. Did I mean that the Flame might kill me? Truth is truth—that is exactly what I meant.

CHAPTER SIX

An Earful of Murder

Jerry and I hopped out of the taxi and hustled into the Morse and Lee jewelry-shop the following night. Though the weather was warm we were both sporting topcoats—Jerry's, a somber blue, mine a light, noticeable brown. What's more, we had our coat collars turned up. If anyone watched us enter or not, I don't know. I didn't see anyone; didn't expect anyone, but I like to do things as if the whole town were watching.

Conklyn Lee was nervous as a mother hen when we stepped into his private office and fumbled with the key at least a full minute before he got that door locked. He finally said: "Why is that young man with you, Mr. Williams? And why are you wearing coats this time of year."

"We forgot to look at the calendar." I gave him a dig in the ribs. "You have your assistant manager in the other room there?" I jerked a thumb toward the door to the right. "About my size you said on the phone."

"Yes—but I don't understand."

"Fine, fine. If you don't understand, then others won't. No word from Mary?"

"No, not a word. You think they're keeping her prisoner until they finish their work below? But if they kill you, then—"

"Never mind about my life. I've taken care of it for years. And I intend to live to dance on the graves of Armin Loring, Baron Stutz, et al. You'd better think about her life and your own and do everything I asked you to do."

He had a first-class chill right away. Maybe I didn't hear his bones rattle, but I heard the change in his pocket.

Jerry remained behind and I got a slant at the assistant manager, standing in the room beyond when we passed through it. He was about my height and build, but not weight. He'd have to do something about that stomach of his first. And his face—well, I'm not so hot-looking I can complain. But his walk, as he opened the far door for us, bothered me. And the way he moved his hands looked as if he might break into Mendelssohn's *Spring Song* any moment. A couple of minutes later Conklyn Lee and I stood before the steel door in the back of the shop.

"I don't think anyone is down there now," he jittered. "But I don't know—I couldn't know. They come and go by the entrance on the alley."

"Open her up," I told him. "They wouldn't be around this early, and if they are—that suits me, too."

He got the key working and we went down to the basement. There was no one there—we covered it thoroughly. It wasn't such a big room—that is, as cellars go.

Just a little way from the foot of the stairs and beneath a green-shaded lamp was a stretch of carpet, a flat desk, and two comfortable chairs. There were no windows in the room, but tiny ventilators up near the ceiling.

Conklyn Lee lost his nervousness as he began to show me rare vases—far back in the dimness. He lifted them, held them as if they were a king's first born and looked childishly hurt when I told him flat they didn't look any better than five-buck ones to me. I was interested in those cheap ones he'd been telling me about. The ones Raftner, alias the Baron, had brought in.

We found them at once—and Conklyn Lee gasped. They were all close to the wide steel door which led to the alley. They were small and packed six to a partly opened crate.

"These are the ones?" I asked him. "Crated just like this? Why"—I went down the line and counted the crates, one upon the other—"there are enough here to flood the whole country with dope." I stretched a hand between the slats, had difficulty feeling inside of one, turned the crate over and slipped in my flashlight. Every vase was empty.

"There's nothing in them," Lee told me. "I have looked into every one. But if you're thinking of drugs—well, those vases are just a cheap pottery. The drug could be placed right in the mold. Do you want to break one and see?"

"No. The stuff might be in only one vase in ten. Besides, they'd notice a broken one, and I don't want to rouse suspicion."

"But if the drug is there why not—"

I cut in on him: "But I don't know it's there. They may bring the stuff with them later—tonight even—place it in the vases then take them away in a truck. A crate sent here and there—all open and above-board; just drop half a dozen vases at second-hand shops throughout the city. Nice distribution. I'll wait and see."

"Wait—and see. What do you mean?"

I didn't answer that one then. I was looking at two immense vases. Boy, they were big! Over six feet tall each one of them. If some of those small ones were worth dough why these must have been worth a cool fortune. They were both off the rug—just in the shadows away from that single overhead light. Still you could see animals and dragons dancing all over them. They were class. I told Lee so.

Conklyn Lee laughed. "Monstrosities," he said. "Valueless—sickening."

"How come you have them then?" They looked hot stuff to me.

"We give exhibitions above occasionally. A salesman on the road picked these up when the Chicago World's Fair closed. Had some fool idea that they would look nice on either side of the entrance to our little display of rare pieces."

He seemed disgusted at the thought and maybe a little disappointed that I didn't give him a chance to tell me about how they fired that salesman. I was pulling a chair over, looking at the short wide neck, trying to see things in the blackness of one of the vases.

"A man could get in there—hide in there," I said.

"Can and did." Lee smiled. "A burglar hid in one all night at the Fair, robbed the place, climbed back into the vase and the next morning mixed with the crowd and was never caught."

"A man about my size?" I was examining that opening.

"About—" Conklyn Lee nodded. "Maybe not so broad of shoulder. Good God, Mr. Williams! You weren't thinking of hiding in there. Why—these are desperate men. One of them could look down from the top and shoot you to death."

"If that one didn't lose his head."

Conklyn Lee pondered a moment. "They are very level-headed men," he said seriously.

I didn't explain how the guy who looked in would lose his head. I just took Conklyn Lee by the arm, led him to the stairs. I had seen the telephone that stood on the desk. He sat beside me on those steel steps as if his last ounce of dignity had left him.

"Mr. Lee," I said, "how far would you go for Mary?"

He said without hesitation: "I would give my life—everything for that child."

"O.K.," I told him. "There's a phone on that desk. Go to your home. Stay awake. Mary Morse is missing. They won't harm her until after the stuff is safe away from here—if it's here—or if they intend to bring it here and carry it away in those vases. You have let things go too far and so have I. I'd have the feds in here now if it weren't for the danger to Mary. I'm going to blow the works tonight—come what may. But I'm going to find out where Mary is first."

"But they won't tell you where she is. And they will kill her later."

"Mr. Lee," I said very seriously, and meant it, "if they don't tell me they won't be alive to kill her later. Now—go home. I have your number. If I don't telephone you before twelve, call this number." I handed him a card. "Ask for Sergeant O'Rourke. Tell him to come here. Then skip yourself and tell it all to a good lawyer. You'll need one."

"But what of you?"

"Oh, I'll have missed out."

"You'll be dead."

"That's right. But get O'Rourke here, tell him about the vases. No matter what happens to me that dope must not get into the city." And after a pause, "You're not worth it. The firm is not worth it—Mary is not worth it. No, and by God, I'm not worth it!"

I dropped his hand quickly when I found I was holding it like a leading-man in a cheap road-show. Sure, that's right. I was even beginning to feel sorry for myself, and the sacrifice I was making for my fellow citizens.

I snapped out of that, said: "Jerry, my boy upstairs, will walk out to your car with your assistant manager, who will wear my brown coat, and my slouch hat. He'll turn the collar of my coat up high. If anyone is watching they'll think I've left."

Conklyn Lee proceeded me up the steps to the closed door. "Mr. Williams," he said and his voice was husky. "I have read enough about you, seen enough of you to understand that this is—well, part of your business, part of your life—maybe routine with you. But it is the most fearful night of my whole life. Is there anything else I can do?"

I smiled at him. "Brother," I said. "I have a feeling it is going to be the most fearful of my life, too." And just before he closed the door, "Yeah, there is one thing you can do. Make your assistant manager keep his hands in my overcoat pocket when he leaves the store." I was thinking of the airy-fairy way he used those hands. If I was to die—well, there might be people outside who would take that lad for me, and I didn't want to be remembered doing any Spring Dance.

After Conklyn Lee left I took a look-see over that cellar again. The boys had to come in that sliding door which led to the alley. It would be simple to stick each one up and wait for the next. I looked at those huge vases, too. They'd be swell places to dump a stray body or two if a lad felt like tossing a few corpses around.

I felt I had lots of time. No one would show up until late; until the side-street would be deserted. I went over to those crates of vases and examined them again. The Morse and Lee name was painted in great black letters on wide slats. Respectability that—keen thinking. And the vases weren't completely boxed. All the world could see what was being carried. And I saw it—or thought I did.

I took out my flash and examined the boards of a crate; then another and another. By God, the stuff must be in them! I'm not an expert carpenter; I didn't need to be. One or two boards on every crate had been hammered up far enough to remove the vases, then nailed down again. Did that mean the stuff was in them, hidden away in a secret place in those vases? Little movable parts in the bottom, perhaps, put there for that very purpose.

Should I bust hell out of them? Stand at the door afterwards and knock everyone for a loop that came in? Should I call O'Rourke and—But Mary Morse came first. But hell, she didn't come first—not before an entire city!

I went to the desk, looked at the telephone on it. The telephone! And I thought back to a mistake I had made in my younger days. Forgetting a telephone, caving in a guy's head who was supposed to use that phone to tell others the coast was clear. So it might be tonight.

My eyes raised and rested on one of those huge vases. A place to hide—a damn good place to hide. Plenty of room for a crouching man inside, and one of those vases had held "a man about my size!" Would they look inside the vase? Would the first man who came look inside it? Well, he couldn't see anything unless he stuck a light in. And if he stuck a light in, he'd never see anything again. I'd shoot his head right off his shoulders and damn near through the ceiling.

The vase was the place, obviously. I couldn't see once I was in there, but I could hear, wait, pop out with a couple of guns and do my stuff if the boys wanted it that way. No more fooling around, then. Into the vase I'd have to go.

Trouble? Of course there was trouble. First, I had to turn out the light. Second, I had to use my flash in the deep blackness. Third, I had to put the flash in my pocket while I scrambled up. And I made it—at least I was lying on my stomach on top of it. Getting inside was another thing. One leg at a time didn't seem to work, but I finally managed to get on my feet, straddling with one foot on either side of the thick circular rim around the top of the neck.

Why so fancy? Well, I wanted another chance to look inside that vase, with the flash directed straight in. I felt for my flash; the vase wobbled. I regained my balance, breathed a sigh of relief, then stuck my feet together and dropped right into that vase. It was dark and my judgment wasn't so good. My shoulders caught for a moment in the neck, slipped through and I landed bent up like a jackknife inside that vase.

Why did I pull that quick drop? Well, a bolt had clicked; a heavy iron bar was removed from the alley door. I'd heard it distinctly, as even now I heard the door beginning to slide back. But I was safe inside.

The door opened and closed. Groping feet crossed the stone floor, the feet of a lone man. Then the feet left the stone and settled on the rug. A light flashed and after a moment or two the feet moved again upon stone, passed close to the vase, hesitated. I looked up and raised my gun. My position was certainly good. If he looked in I'd simply have to decide whether he saw me or not. And on my decision would rest his life. What could be fairer than that?

After a bit the dial on the phone clicked several times. A husky voice said: "O.K., boss. All quiet here. I think you're wise to move the stuff early. . . . What . . . ? Yeah, I'd like to see Williams come here, too. He bounced a gun off my head last night."

So it was Sam. Poor dumb Sam. And the Flame had wondered if he were dead. His very next words made me feel that perhaps after all Sam wasn't so dumb.

"What?" he said. "The Flame's turned Armin's head? I don't know about that. But I tell you she's a wildcat, Raftner. See you in an hour then."

An hour. That was not so good. That vase was built funny, maybe thicker than I thought. Anyway I couldn't stand up and I couldn't sit down; I had to crouch like a guy playing squat-tag. I could turn, but I had to be careful of noise; had to be careful that neither one of the two guns I clutched in my hands pounded against the sides of the vase and rang out like chimes. How did I know they would ring out like chimes? I didn't. I didn't know what that vase was made of. But I did feel that the burglar who'd robbed the World's Fair was entitled to all he got if he spent most of the night in that crouched position.

There was little sound after the phone was hung up. Just the pounding of Sam's heels on the desk where he sat and waited. And I just crouched and waited.

An hour passed and there was a knock, followed by Sam's feet beating across the hard stone, then the opening door.

This time more than one pair of feet crossed the floor. Each sound, each word came to me hollowly.

Armin Loring's voice snapped: "We don't need Sam here, Raftner. The trucks will be along any minute now—we'll want to get rolling."

The door closed and I guess Sam left.

Raftner said: "Sure, sure, Armin." And his voice changing to a harsh note, "Sit down. Yes—that thing in your back is a gun."

"God, are you mad!" Armin said and his breath whistled in his throat. It was a regular radio play for me from then on with sound effects and all. I saw nothing; heard everything. And I heard plenty.

Raftner was speaking and his voice was soft, pleasant. "I heard about you, Armin—One Man Armin. Yes, one man—running a great racket; building up for this great racket until you became head of it. I thought Frank Morse was at the top. When he died I thought Gentle Jim Corrigan was head of it, and when he died—I knew the real head. The last man to be suspected because you built up the one-man idea, the working-alone idea. You've been head of it all along—and neither Frank Morse nor Corrigan even suspected it."

"Well," said Armin, "why the gun in my back? What the hell! You knew you had a boss—now you know who he is. I had to come out in the open sometime—at least to you."

"Well," said Raftner, "it goes like this. Frank Morse got onto the Flame. She was shoving herself in, getting into his papers. He didn't kill her; he wrote me he wasn't going to kill her. He felt pretty cocky in having that brilliant criminal mind working for him. And he died—she planned his death."

"Hell, you're crazy," said Armin.

"There was Jim Corrigan," Raftner went on. "She played him along. He got wise, wrote me exactly how Morse died, then died himself. And *his* death was planned by the Flame. She was there in the house with Corrigan when Williams killed him. Williams didn't expose her then. He didn't expose her because she'd set Corrigan up for Williams to kill."

"Williams didn't expose her because they were once—well, to know the Flame is—"

"To love the Flame is to die," Raftner snapped in. "That went for all the others. It's going for you tonight, too."

"You mean—you're going to kill me?"

"I'm not going to have the Flame set me up for death."

"You're out of your head, man," Armin said. "It was just a coincidence."

"All right"—Raftner didn't argue—"have it your way. I'm not going to die by coincidence. But you—"

I could hear Armin's quick breath, felt that Raftner must have shoved his gun tighter against him. Armin's voice was hoarse when he spoke. "What—what do you want me to do?"

"I want you to pick up that phone, tell the Flame to come here—now."

"Then what?"

"I'm going to prevent any more coincidences. I'm going to kill her."

Armin laughed. "And you think I'd bring her here for that?"

"I think—just that?"

Armin spoke out like a man. I always thought he had it in him, but I had always thought also, and always believed and so stated, that all murderers were yellow inside; would do any rotten act, right up to tossing a knife into their best friend's back, if it would save their own skin. Now Armin made me out a liar.

"Raftner," he said, "I have always played the game without a woman. That's where I got the name, One Man Armin. Now—this is something new in my life. I'm taking on a wife not a woman. If you were to cut me to ribbons I wouldn't lift that phone from its cradle."

Raftner said very seriously: "I'm not going to cut you to ribbons. I'm simply going to shoot you to death."

"Go ahead and shoot then." Armin raised his voice. "I love that girl and—and—What are you going to do?"

"Count five and shoot."

"Why the Flame means more to me than life."

"One—"

"Death would mean nothing and—"

"Two."

"You can't bluff me by—"

"Three."

"I tell you I'd die a hundred times before—" And Armin's voice had raised to an almost hysterical shriek.

"Four," said Raftner.

A sudden cry from Armin. A dead silence. Then a clicking noise. After a few minutes I heard the voice of Armin say: "This is Armin, gorgeous. I'm at the den. Come over at once. . . . Wrong? No, everything is fine. . . . Right away then. Good. . . . Sure, I have good news for you."

"That," said Raftner, "is more like it."

"That," I said to myself, "is more like what I expected also." No, there was nothing yellow about Armin but his soul.

Chapter Seven

Up Popped the Devil

They talked low after that—very low—Armin trying to convince Raftner, Raftner on his guard. Then I heard them cross the room, heard muffled conversation, and Armin curse and exclaim: "The vases—the one I marked with X. Look—the ones that had the stuff in them!"

"Yeah, I see. No tricks now, Armin. They still have the X on them."

"Yes, but they are not the same vases, not the same design or color even. Look there! Remember? And the crate. By God, it's been opened and nailed up again!"

Loud talk then. Plenty of cursing, the pound of something heavy, and smashing crockery. More pounding, more smashing crockery—and Armin cried out: "Millions—and it's gone! Someone has taken it away."

"Who? Who—Williams!" Raftner shouted and then, "Don't go near that door! Only you could have—"

"Me!" The door was opening, Armin was calling low now: "Sam, come here." Feet then, and the closing door and Armin's, "You were wrong about the Flame, Raftner. She was not building me up; she's building up herself or—or—By God, she's working for—"

Mumbled words; quick questions. The voice of Sam, stupid, slow, unexcited. I damned near popped out of the vase, but didn't.

Sam was saying: "The Flame gave me money when I found her going through your desk. I thought it was love-letters, Armin. She always seemed jealous about you. I thought nothing of her looking through your things and—"

"The book," said Raftner. "The list of where the stuff was to go. What have you told her, Armin?"

"The book is in my pocket. I told her nothing—very little. Yes, she knew it was dope; didn't know I was head of the organization. She wanted me to make money. She had a key to the door here. I—I—Take that gun off me, Raftner. She made a fool of me. I'll attend to her when she gets here."

Yep, it was just like a good radio program. I could feel Raftner looking at Armin, reading the truth in that cold, cruel face of his.

It was after they chased Sam outside again that Raftner said: "All right, Armin. But I'll make her tell where she put the stuff."

"No," said Armin very slowly, "I'll make her tell. I'll cut tiny pieces from every last inch of her beautiful body—"

"You'll kill her too soon—before she can talk."

"No," said Armin, "I won't kill her too soon. I won't even kill her after she talks. I'll promise her death just as she promised me life on that trip abroad." And after a long pause, "But I'll make it a most horrible death. Yes, I'll make her tell."

That was my cue. Just to pop up with a couple of guns before the Flame even entered the place. I was happy, too, for the first time since I had met the Flame months back and believed she was in this, the rottenest of all rackets. Then I had another thought. Perhaps they were wrong and the Flame was working just for herself.

I'm of a suspicious nature and so I didn't pop up. Perhaps I would hear more when the Flame came. Maybe she'd talk. Maybe they'd talk. Maybe I'd hear where the drugs were hidden. But I was listening to other pleasant conversation.

"About this Mary Morse"—it was Raftner's voice—"she's apt to gum up the works any time. She's safe?"

Armin laughed. It was like static. "Another cute bag of tricks. I missed her going into my apartment because of Williams last night. But I caught her coming out. Yes, she was ready to holler the business from the housetops. She's tied up on the thirty-seventh floor of the Hampton Hotel." He paused for a moment. Then, "It would be just like her to jump from the window, toss herself to the street below."

"God!" said Raftner. "You haven't done that."

"Not yet. I was afraid the police might find some way of identifying her body. That'd mean an investigation and cops and government men here in the shop. Williams will have to die first. The fool nearly forced me into shooting it out with him at my apartment. It's the first time I ever ran from any man, but I couldn't chance the investigation at this time. With Williams dead—and he will be dead—there is no one to know the truth. Conklyn Lee hardly counts. He doesn't know your real identity and he doesn't know mine. I might even keep the girl alive." And talking rapidly and excitedly as if he had just had the thought, "With Williams dead—we might let Mary Morse live. She gets money—plenty of it. If Conklyn Lee knew I had her and would kill her unless she—"

"No, no," Raftner said quietly. "There's more than a million in this for us. You said you had laid the foundation for the next distribution from a house in Brooklyn. The home of a respected lawyer with a big name—slated to be senator—who killed a man twenty years ago. No, Armin. This place will be too hot after tonight. I think your idea of Mary Morse jumping from the window must stand."

I heard Armin's feet move, heard his hand come down upon the desk. I imagined his eyes narrowing and his lips tightening. "O.K.," he said. "The Flame must talk. You've got the men outside. There's no danger from anyone but Williams—"

"Yes." I didn't need to see Raftner's face; the hate was in his words. He spat as if he still tasted that cigar. "There are two men with machine guns in the alley. I had hoped to be well away in the truck before Williams could act and now—"

A sudden silence. I heard the opening door, Sam's voice, then the closing door again and a single pair of feet across that hard floor. Quick steps, woman's steps; steps that stopped before they reached the rug. Then a voice said: "What's up, Armin? You and Raftner look white as ghosts. Anything wrong?" The voice was the voice of the Flame.

Feet went toward her, I guess. Armin spoke softly. "Why nothing, beautiful. What could be wrong with us?" Then, "To love the Flame is to die. To rat out on Armin Loring is—" A half scream, a muffled curse, a dull thud and a falling body.

Raftner spoke. "You fool, Armin! What did you hit her for? She must talk, must—"

"I couldn't help it—the two-timing little tart. Besides—her purse. Look at that gun. She'd use it, too."

I damned near popped out then, but I didn't. I waited and guessed what was going on outside. Moving feet, low voices; something knocked against the side of the desk, I think. Raftner was saying something about making the Flame trap me much as Armin had trapped her.

It was hard waiting till she came to five minutes later—maybe ten. Anyway it seemed a long time before they were hammering questions at her and she was answering defiantly.

Finally she said: "That's right, boys. I got the filthy stuff you wanted to flood the city with. You'll never find it now. Armin, you're a fool. One Man Armin—taken in by a woman. Now you'd torture the woman. Well—see how that woman takes it."

"You worked with Williams, didn't you?" Raftner shot the words through his teeth. "Race Williams—that was it, wasn't it? By God, you were the woman to fool Armin—to fool men! But Williams was clever."

The Flame laughed. It wasn't a nice laugh. "Clever? Williams is dumb. He couldn't have fooled you two for a minute. He wouldn't have let me try. No, I wasn't working with him. I was working for him—but without his knowing it. It was I who made you clever men threaten him. Mary Morse couldn't have brought him back by pleading with him. I couldn't have brought him into it again by pleading with him. He's built backward. You forced him back by threats he wouldn't take, and they were at my suggestion. Mary Morse told him not to come, fearing for his life—and I put that fear into her head. You attempted to kill him—I put the attempt into your heads. And it was an attempt that nearly succeeded when Armin kept me, so that I failed to warn him. Yes, Race is a stupid, gun-toting fool. Yet he's worth a dozen of either of you because he wins out through his lack of fear—his very conceit."

Maybe I turned slightly red in that tight-fitting vase, but Raftner said: "And just why did you do this—risk your life for Race Williams?"

"Because he saw no good in me. Because he saw only bad. Because he never believed in me. Because I wanted him to believe me—and want me. Not because I'm the Flame who can make any man love her—including the great One Man Armin. No, I wanted Race to like the girl he once thought me to be. I know I'm going to die."

There was passion in Armin's voice, a passion that he could not control. He said: "But you don't know how you're going to die."

"I didn't fail." There was a proud ring in the Flame's voice. "The drugs are gone, hidden far away where you'll never find them. I don't care what you do—no, not even if you cut me to ribbons."

"What a coincidence," said Armin Loring. "My dear, that is exactly what we are going to do. Cut you to ribbons."

"Unless," said Raftner, "you tell us where the drugs are."

"And," added Armin, "trap Race Williams for us."

"Trap him!" she said. "The only man I ever loved! Why—"

She didn't scream exactly. It was more a quick breath, a sucking sort of breath.

And the show was over. The curtain was to ring down on the final act. I felt good way down inside me. The thing was so simple, too. These men were busy with the girl. Feared, desperate killers both of them. Yet, I had nothing to do but pop out of that vase like a jack-in-the-box, throw a couple of guns over the rim and give them both the dose if they preferred it that way.

Dramatic? Sure it was dramatic. I knew that when the Flame winced again—yes, an audible wince if you understand what I mean. So I took my cue. I gripped both my guns firmly, straightened my body as best I could, braced my feet and started my body upward.

My head went up into the neck of that vase, but my shoulders didn't. They stuck; stuck there in that neck just as my head came out over the top. And I knew the truth—the horrible truth. I had gotten into the vase through the very force of my falling body. Now—I could not get out!

Chapter Eight

Blast-Out

The Flame cried out and I made another desperate effort, felt the vase rock slightly, nearly got my shoulders wedged so that I could go neither up nor down. What if my head stuck out with my arms pinned down at my sides? What if the vase should turn over and—and—I couldn't save the Flame then. Good God! I could kill them afterward, of course—sometime, someplace. I shuddered. Kill them after the Flame was dead; after I had crouched there helpless while they tortured her to death!

Minutes must have passed since my brain went dead. Things must have changed outside. The Flame was saying: "Telephone Race?" Her laugh was high pitched, but determined just the same. "Trap him to his death—to watch you torture him so I will tell you where the rotten stuff is. No, no, no! I want him to live—live to kill you! I left a note to be delivered to him if I was murdered. I wanted him to know the truth about me then. He'll kill you—both of you. Good, old stupid Race. He'd like it that way. He'd—What are you going to do with that knife! My mouth!"

Armin said very slowly: "You wish to laugh at us, Florence. I wish to make your mouth wider so that you may better enjoy that laugh. So we, too, can enjoy that laugh. Like this—"

God! I couldn't see. I didn't know what was happening. There was a struggle. I heard that and—

A hole in the vase would mean a chance to see; a second, a chance to shoot. I placed my guns against the side of that vase, one above the other. Two holes—or would there be any holes? What was the damned vase made of? It might be steel; it might be copper. The lead might strike, ricochet and—and—No, I couldn't live to get them then. I couldn't live to get them anyway, once I fired that gun. No chance at all. A single bullet-hole—two holes. With the best of luck—the greatest of luck, I might hit one man. But the shots would be heard and the other man—No, I didn't dare shoot.

"All right, Raftner." Armin's voice was high now, gloating as he said: "Hold her so. The left side first. That pretty mouth slit close to the left ear before we crop that ear. Hold her steady—steady. That's it."

Both my fingers closed. My body stiffened, tightened. The roar was terrific!

God! What had happened? I was choked with smoke and burned powder. The entire room had collapsed around me, not on me, for I was there; there in the center of the room, crouched low, blinking in the light; blinking straight up into the surprised eyes of Raftner. Raftner who had turned from the Flame; turned from the back of the chair in which he held her while Armin—

I knew then. The vase was gone, smashed into a thousand pieces. And Raftner hurled his huge body toward me—over me. He was crashing down upon me, both arms out, both hands grasping for my throat.

Then I heard Armin Loring's voice. "On top of him, Raftner! Pin him to the floor. I've got—"

That's all I heard then. I fired twice—just an upward flip of both guns and a split second between the shots. Did he fall dead on me pinning me to the floor? Not him—not a guy with forty-fours pounding into his chest. He picked himself up like an acrobat in the circus. Yes picked himself up and went out on his back. I never saw or heard a man hit the floor harder with his head.

My head still rang with those first two shots and the smashing vase. I staggered to my feet and shouted the words above the din in my head. "I'm on the kill, Armin!" I bellowed out like a madman. "On the kill!"

Whether it was the busting vase, the crashing body of Raftner or my shouting voice, I don't know. But Armin lost his head. He gave me a chance to rise and face him as he rushed to the Flame, raised his knife and yelled: "Drop the guns, Race, or she takes the—"

I lowered one gun and shot at the only part of his body I could see as he crouched there before the Flame, huddled in the chair. It was his leg—just below the knee. Did I hit it? Hell—you know me. I don't shoot at things I don't hit.

Armin regained his head then. I saw him step back and I saw that famous draw of his—that double draw—just both hands across his chest. You couldn't tell if they went under his coat or not, but they were both holding guns, both blazing as mine were blazing.

I had a sort of numb feeling as if I were going to drop. Then a sudden stab of pain in my cheek—sharp, quick pain that cleared that numb feeling.

There was blood on Armin's face—on mine, too, I guess. Warm—I felt it. But the blood was in Armin's eyes. He fired again before I did. I'll give him credit for that. But he either fired too soon or the blood blocked his vision. But he saw enough. Saw death and threw himself toward the Flame there in the chair for protection. I pushed out both my arms, twisted my guns in and fired twice.

Maybe Armin intended to kill the Flame then. Maybe he thought more of killing the Flame than of killing me; maybe it wasn't protection he sought after all—only vengeance. But I had fired directly—and surely—and calmly. Armin Loring was hurled backward. He half sank, straightened, crashed against the desk behind him. Then we hit it off together. Just crashing lead. If a Tommy gun had opened up in that cellar, the staccato notes of spitting steel couldn't have been closer together.

Wildly, blindly we fired? Well, maybe Armin did. I didn't. My lead spun him from the desk, turned him completely around. I took a slug in the right side just above the hip bone.

And I did it. Two shots into his stomach, another one into his chest. He was spinning like a top now, firing as he spun, and I got him—just as clean as I ever got any man.

Eyes that were bright and hateful dimmed, faded, and went blank. A small hole started to widen in his forehead, turn from black to blue, then a dull sort of red with tiny bubbles in it.

He didn't pound to the floor—not Armin. He sank very slowly to his knees, stayed there a moment, then twisted grotesquely and rolled over on his back. I wasn't any too steady myself now as I stood above him. I was nodding my head, saying over and over: "No fooling, Armin. No fooling."

The Flame! She had been in the chair. Now she was close to me, under my arm, holding me there. Had they done it? Had Armin done it? Had he ripped that knife across her face and—and—

"Florence," I said. "Your mouth—your mouth."

"Yes, Race, yes," was all she said as she pulled down my head and put her mouth hard against mine.

* * *

I had never really known if I loved the Flame. I didn't know then. But I stretched out my arms, pulled her to me, felt the guns still tight in my hands and—Suddenly I turned and faced the door that was opening. The machine-gunners—the men Raftner had there! I had saved the Flame. We were alive. I wanted to live and now—

The door slid wider. Figures were there in the gloom. I felt the Flame grab at my arms, but I was aiming straight at those figures as the trigger fingers of both my hands closed tightly.

Click, click. No more. Both my guns were empty, and—and Sergeant O'Rourke was pounding flat-footed toward me. There was Nelson, too. A couple of harness bulls and some plainclothesmen. And sneaking along on the side I saw the trembling figure of Conklyn Lee.

I guess Lee was talking to me. Anyway he was saying: "Mary was gone—no word from her. You were here—no word from you. I—I telephoned Sergeant O'Rourke and here I am. I—I had to."

I said to Conklyn Lee: "What did you tell him—tell the sergeant—these others?" I saw things going after all.

"He didn't tell us anything, Race," O'Rourke said. "He met us before the shop. There were guys with tommy guns outside. But they dropped them and ran when they saw us. Flannigan and his men will get them on the block behind. Suppose you tell us."

"Suppose I tell you, Sergeant—and you, too, Inspector." The Flame was as serene now as if nothing had happened. "You never believed in me, Sergeant, but Race did; kept it from you, but believed in me. These men here—one, Raftner, whom you've wanted for a long time—were blackmailing Mary Morse for something her Uncle Frank Morse, who disappeared, had done. They made use of her store. She came straight to Race. We advised her to pretend to submit to the blackmail, once Race suspected it was the narcotic crowd. You nearly spoiled it a couple of times, Sergeant—the government men, too. You see, I had to pose as a friend of Armin Loring."

Now you've got to admit that was a good story. I couldn't have told a better one myself—maybe not so good a one.

I added my bit by saying that Mary Morse was safe. I didn't say where; she might speak out of turn. I wanted to see her first—regardless of the lead in me.

"And the narcotics?" It was Nelson who shot that one in as he nearly stumbled over Armin's outstretched legs.

"In the vases over there—the real ones in the back," the Flame said almost indifferently. "Race and I moved them away from the other vases to be sure nothing would go wrong if Race were killed. Race is hurt, Inspector. He'll have to have treatment. No hospital—I'll take care of him." And looking at me, "And what's more, Race, you've got an assistant who'll see that you collect this time from the Mary Morse fund or there'll be a surrogate shot around here." And when I started to ask her what of Mary Morse she whispered, "I'll set her free when I have you home in bed and a good surgeon digging into you."

O'Rourke, with the help of Conklyn Lee, had found the drugs. Nelson was looking at the body of Armin Loring—bending closer. He straightened finally and paid me a compliment. Oh, maybe he didn't mean to, but it was in his voice more than his words.

"You, Race—" he said. "You shot it out man to man with—with Armin Loring. Why he was the most feared man in the city. No one—"

I cut in waving my hand deprecatingly as the Flame took my arm, supporting my slightly sagging body. But I got my final crack in before she sat me in a chair. I said: "It was really nothing, Nelson. Armin Loring. Nothing to me, Inspector—just another stiff."

NORBERT DAVIS

Norbert Davis (1909–1949) was one of a handful of thirties and forties pulp writers who wound up making a good living writing for the slicks. All the more mysterious, then, was his death by suicide when all seemed to be going well in his life.

A number of pulp crime writers tried to blend the screwball comedies, then fashionable at the movies, with the soft-boiled crime story. Craig Rice and Norbert Davis had the greatest success with this fusion, both with the public and with the critics.

Davis had an affection for oddballs. He created Doan and Carstairs, the former who is a rather snooty and uppity Great Dane, and the latter a perpetually hungover private eye not exactly in league with Sam Spade as far as trench-coated competence goes.

As John D. MacDonald once noted, what gets lost in all the hilarity and high jinks of the Davis stories is what a damned fine writer the man was.

Something for the Sweeper

Jones limped slowly along, his rubbers making an irregular squeak-squish sound on the wet cement of the sidewalk. He was not a large man and, walking as he was now, humped forward in an unconscious effort to favor his feet, he looked small and insignificant. He wore an old trench-coat with grease stains running jaggedly down the front. The sun was bright on the slick-black wetness of the asphalt paving, and he had his hat-brim pulled low over his tired eyes.

The houses on this street were gaunt, ugly and brown, and as alike as the teeth in a saw. They all had a wide flight of worn stairs leading up to the front door with another flight beside it leading down into the basement. They had all been built by one man, those houses, and he evidently was a person who believed in getting a good, plain plan and then sticking to it.

Jones was watching house numbers out of the corners of his eyes. He was coming pretty close now, and he began to walk even slower. His mouth twisted up at one side every time he came down on his right foot.

Ahead of him he could see a man's head and shoulders. The man was halfway down one of the basement flights of stairs. His head and shoulders moved back and forth in a sort of a jigging rhythm. Approaching, Jones saw that he was sweeping up the stairs of the basement. He swept in careful, calculating little dabs, as precisely as if he were painting a picture with his broom.

"Hi," said Jones, stopping and standing on his left foot.

The man made another dab with his broom, inspected the result, and then looked up at Jones. He was an old man, small and shrunken and wiry, with white, smooth hair that was combed straight back from his softly plastic face. He nodded silently at Jones, solemn and wordless.

"Hendrick Boone live here?" Jones asked.

The old man sniffed and rubbed his nose. "Who?"

"Hendrick Boone."

The old man considered for a moment. "Live where?"

"Here," said Jones.

"Yes," said the old man.

Jones stared at him sourly. "Thanks a lot," he said at last.

"Oh, that's all right," the old man said, and smiled.

Jones went up the stairs, grunting painfully, and, when he got to the top, leaned over and pinched the toe of his right rubber and muttered to himself under his breath. He straightened up and looked at the closed double doors ahead of him. There was a narrow frosted-glass panel in each one, and the pair of stiff-legged storks, with toothpick beaks depicted on them, leered disdainfully at him with opposite eyes. Jones looked around for a doorbell, finally located a little iron lever that protruded out of a slit in one of the doors. He pulled it down and then up again, and a bell made a dismal *blink-blink-blink* sound inside.

Jones waited, standing on his left foot, and the door opened slowly, squeaking a little. Jones touched his hat and said: "Hello. Is Mr. Hendrick Boone here, and if so, can I talk to him for a minute?"

"He's not here. He's really not here."

"Oh," said Jones.

She was a very small woman with gray hair that was puffed up in a wide knot on the top of her head. She wore thick, rimless glasses and behind them her eyes were a distorted blue, wide and a little frightened and anxious to please. She wore a long skirt that rustled and a white waist with lace stiff on the front. She had a timid, wavering smile.

"Where is he?" Jones asked.

"He's in the hospital."

"Hospital?" Jones repeated.

"Yes. He fell downstairs. Are you the man from the installment company?"

"No," said Jones. "I'm a detective, believe it or not. I know I don't look like one. I can't help that. I didn't pick this face, and, to tell the truth, I don't think so much of it myself."

"Oh, but he didn't do it! Really he didn't, officer! He couldn't have, you see. He's been in the hospital, and his condition is very serious, really it is, and he couldn't have done it."

"Done what?" said Jones.

She moved her hands a little, helplessly. "Well—well, whatever you think he did. Was it—windows again?"

"Windows?" Jones asked.

"I mean, did you think he broke some windows, like he usually does?"

"He makes a habit of breaking windows?"

She nodded. "Oh, yes. But only plate glass ones."

"Particular, huh? What does he break windows for?"

Her sallow face flushed slightly. "He sees his image. You know, his reflection. And he thinks he is following himself again. He thinks he is spying on himself. And so he breaks the windows."

"Well, maybe it's a good idea," said Jones. "Is he ever troubled with pink elephants?"

"Yes, he is. He often sees them walking on the ceiling when he wakes up in the morning."

"What does he do for them?"

"Oh, he always saves a half pint, and as soon as he drinks that they go away."

"I should think they would," said Jones. "I'm still talking about Hendrick Boone, by the way? Are you?"

"Yes. My husband."

"Oh," said Jones. "You're Mrs. Boone. Could I come in and sit down and speak to you for a moment? I've got some news for you, and besides my feet hurt."

"Oh, yes. Surely. Excuse me, please. I was a little flustered when you said 'detective'—"

The hall was dark and small and narrow with a carpeted staircase running up steeply just to the right of the front door. The wallpaper was a stained brownish-black. There was a hole worn in the carpet at the foot of the stairs.

"Right in here," Mrs. Boone said anxiously.

It was the parlor that stretched across the narrow front of the house. The furniture was stiff and awkward, mellowed with age, and there was a clumsy cut-glass chandelier that had been originally designed to burn gas.

Jones sat down on a sofa that creaked mournfully under him and looked down at his feet, wincing involuntarily.

"Now," said Mrs. Boone. She was sitting primly upright, looking very small against the high carved back of the chair, with her hands folded on her lap and smiling a little, timidly. "Now—you wished to speak to me?"

Jones nodded, still thinking about his feet. "Yes. Your husband was born in Awkright, Idaho, wasn't he?"

She nodded brightly. "Yes."

"Had one brother—by the name of Semus Boone?"

"Yes."

"Not any more," said Jones. "Semus Boone died a couple of months ago."

"Oh," said Mrs. Boone. She was silent for a moment. "We hadn't seen him for over twenty years. He didn't like Hendrick. He invited us to a Christmas party, and Hendrick took a drop too much and broke the plate glass window in Semus' living room. Semus was very angry."

"He must have gotten over it," said Jones. "He left your husband all his money."

"Oh!" said Mrs. Boone. She smiled vaguely. "Was it enough to pay his funeral expenses?"

Jones nodded. "Yes. And a little bit to spare. About a million and a half."

Mrs. Boone's hands gripped tight. Her eyes glazed behind the thick glasses, and her lips moved soundlessly. After a while she drew a deep breath. "You're not—joking?"

"No," said Jones.

"You're—you're sure there's no mistake?"

"No," said Jones. "I don't make mistakes—not when there's a million and a half in the pot. I've been hunting your husband for two months."

"A million and a half!" said Mrs. Boone dreamily.

"Yes," said Jones. "Your husband can't touch the principal, though. It's in trust. That's where I come in. I'm an investigator for the Suburban Mortgage and Trust Company. The company's the trustee—handles the principal. Your husband gets the income—he and his heirs and assigns and what not—for twenty years. Then the principal sum goes to certain charities. The income amounts to over a thousand a week."

"Oh!" said Mrs. Boone. "Oh!" Her eyes began to gleam behind the glasses, and she swallowed. "Sarah!" she called, and there was a gasping catch in her voice. "Sarah! Sarah!"

There was the flip-flop of slippers in the hall, and a girl came and stopped in the doorway. She had a wide red mouth and cigarette drooping in the corner of it that slid a smooth blue stream of smoke up past her cheek and the faded blondness of her hair. She was big and heavy-boned, but had a lazy, cat-like gracefulness. Her eyes were a deep-sea blue, set far apart. They were narrowed sullenly now, and she looked Jones up and down.

"Well," she said. "And now what?"

She wore a blue kimono with the sleeves rolled back and was wiping her hands on a towel. Her forearms were white and smoothly muscled. There were birthmarks on both of them.

"Sarah," said Mrs. Boone. "This gentleman here just came to tell us that your Uncle Semus died."

"Too bad," said Sarah. "What'd he do—bite himself on the tongue and die of hydrophobia?"

"No," said Jones. "As a matter of fact he had a heart attack."

"Somebody must have cheated him out of a nickel," said Sarah. "That would do it, all right."

"Don't speak ill of the dead," Mrs. Boone said in a gently reproving voice. "He left your father a lot of money."

"How much?"

"The income from a million and a half," Jones told her.

Sarah's wide set eyes blinked once and then narrowed slowly. "Oh yeah? What's the gag, mister?"

"No gag," Jones said. "I don't have anything to do with it. The trust company that handles the principal hired me to find you, and here you are. I'm through."

"A million and a half," said Sarah slowly. "About how much would that be a month?"

"Around five thousand."

Sarah's breath made a little hissing sound between her white teeth. "Five thousand a month! The old man will drink himself to death in a week."

"Won't make any difference to you if he does," Jones said. "The income will go to your mother in that case."

"Oh," said Sarah thoughtfully. "It would, hey? That's something that needs a little thinking about."

Jones got up. "I'll run down and see Mr. Boone before I leave town."

Mrs. Boone blinked at him, worried. "He's in the City Hospital. But, I don't know. He's really pretty seriously ill. I don't know whether they'll let you in his room."

"I just want to look at him," Jones said. "I'll have to put it in my report. You say he fell?"

"Yes," said Mrs. Boone. "He came home late, and he was—"

"Fried," said Sarah. "Drunk as a skunk. He crawled up the front steps and started walking around in circles looking for the front door and fell down again. He cracked his noggin on the sidewalk. He'll get over it, though, I'm afraid."

"Sarah," said Mrs. Boone. "Sarah, now. He's your father."

"That's your fault," said Sarah. "Not mine."

"Well, I'll be going," Jones said.

"Mr. Morganwaite," Mrs. Boone said brightly, getting up with a sudden swish of her long skirt. "I must tell him! He'll be so pleased! I won't have to worry—" She hurried out of the room.

"Morganwaite?" Jones said inquiringly, looking at Sarah.

"He's an old stooge we keep around to clean up the joint now and then," Sarah told him. "He takes care of the old man when he gets potted. You probably saw him when you came in. He was sweepin' the basement stairs."

"Oh, yes," Jones said. "Well, so long."

"So long," Sarah said. "Lots of thanks, mister, for coming around and doing a Santa Claus for us."

Jones smiled. "I got paid for it." He went down the dark hall and out the doors past the two storks that were still leering at him and the world in general.

The city hospital was a great square pile of brick, masonry and steel that covered a complete city block. Three hours after he had visited the Boones, Jones rode up and down on seven elevators and limped through a mile and a half of silent cork-floored corridors and finally located the section he wanted. He went in through a glass door in a glass partition that blocked off the short end of a hall. There was a middle-aged woman sitting behind a flat desk in a little cubby-hole off the corridor.

"Yes?" she said. Her voice had a low, practiced hush, and her face looked as stiff and white and starched as her uniform and cap.

"Hendrick Boone?" Jones inquired wearily.

She nodded. "Mr. Boone is in Room Eighteen Hundred."

"Hah!" said Jones triumphantly, and shifted his weight from one foot to the other. "Can I see him?"

"No. Mr. Boone is allowed to receive no visitors except the members of his immediate family. His condition is very serious."

"I'm not a visitor," said Jones. "I just want to look at him. Don't worry—it's not curiosity. It's my job. I was hired to find him."

"He's here."

"Look," said Jones. "How do you think that would sound in my report? I can't say I think he's here, or he's supposed to be here, or somebody by his name is here, or you told me he's here. I got to *know* he's here. I've got to see him. They're not paying me for guessing."

The nurse regarded him silently.

"Just a peek," said Jones. "Just open his door and give me a squint. I've got his picture and description. I won't say a word to him."

The nurse picked up a precisely sharpened pencil, opened a leather-bound notebook. "Your name, please?"

"Jones," said Jones.

"Your first name?"

"Just Jones."

The nurse looked up at him, and her lips tightened a little.

"All right," said Jones quickly. "Don't get mad. You asked for it, and that's really my name—just plain Jones. J. P. Jones. See, my mother had a lot of kids, and she always thought she ought to give them something fancy in the way of first names on account of there being lots of Joneses around. She named 'em Horatius and Alvimina and Evangeline and things like that. But she began to run out of names pretty soon, and she had an awful time with Number Twelve. She said: 'If there's any more, I'm not going to all this trouble. The next one is going to be just plain Jones.' So here I am."

The nurse wrote in her book. "Address?"

"Suburban Mortgage and Trust—New York City."

She closed the notebook, laid the pencil carefully beside it. "This way, please." She went along the hall to the last door on the right and, standing in front of it, turned to look at Jones. "You are not to speak to him. You understand?"

"Right," said Jones.

The door swished a little, opening slowly. The room was a small one, and the high iron bed was in the corner beside the big window. The man in the bed made a bulging mound of the covers. He was lying on his back, and there was a white bandage like an adhesive and gauze skullcap on his head. There was something the matter with his face.

The nurse made a gasping sound, and her starched stiffness seemed to crack. She ran across to the bed, and Jones trailed right behind her. She fumbled under the covers, found the man's limply slack wrist. It was a thick wrist, big-boned, and the hand was big and square and powerful.

The nurse's voice was breathlessly small. "No—pulse. He strangled himself—"

"He didn't have to do it, himself," Jones said. "He had some help." He pointed to the red blotches, slowly turning dark now, on the thick throat.

"Pulmotor," the nurse said, and started for the door.

Jones caught her arm, spun her around. "No. A pulmotor won't do him any good. Look at the color of those marks on his throat. Who came to see him this afternoon?"

The nurse jerked against his grip. "His daughter. She left a half hour ago. Said—he was asleep."

"He was, all right," said Jones. "You sure it was his daughter? Sarah? You've seen her before?"

"Yes—yes. Let go!"

"You sure it was Sarah?" Jones repeated. "You positively saw her?"

"Yes! She was veiled, but her arms—the birthmarks—"

"Oh, yeah," said Jones. "Anybody else come?"

"No!" She twisted free, ran out the door.

Jones looked closely at the face of the man on the bed. It was Hendrick

Boone. Jones went out of the room. There was no one in sight in the corridor, and he went out through the glass partition and walked along the hall until he found a stairway and went down it.

In five minutes, he came out in the main entrance hall of the hospital and entered one of the public telephone booths beside the reception desk. He consulted the directory, finally deposited a nickel and dialed a number. He could hear the telephone at the other end ring and ring. It rang for a long time while Jones squinted at the black hard-rubber mouthpiece in front of him and muttered to himself inaudibly. Finally, the line clicked.

"Hello," a voice said casually.

"Is Sarah Boone there?" Jones asked.

"Who?"

"Sarah Boone."

"Where?"

Jones drew a deep breath. "Oh, it's you again, is it? Listen, Morganwaite, this is Jones, the detective that was there this morning. I want to know if Sarah Boone is there and by there I mean where you are. Now, quit playing around and answer me."

"No," said Morganwaite.

Jones choked and then recovered himself. "Are you saying no, you won't answer me, or no, she isn't there?"

"No, she isn't here."

"Is Mrs. Boone there?"

"No. She left as soon as she got Sarah's message."

"Message?" Jones said. "Sarah sent her a message?"

"Yes."

"How do you know?"

"Mrs. Boone told me."

"When?"

"When she got it."

"That's what I want to know!" Jones said explosively. "When did she get it?"

Morganwaite was silent while he evidently considered the matter at some length. "About a half hour ago."

"What did the message say?" Jones asked.

"I don't know. Mrs. Boone didn't say. She just left."

"What kind of a message was it? Telephone—telegraph?"

"No."

"Well, what kind?"

"A written message—in an envelope."

"Who brought it? Come on now, shake yourself and think hard."

"It was a boy," said Morganwaite pensively. "A boy in a gray uniform on a red bicycle. A small boy with freckles."

"Thanks," said Jones. He hung up, took out his handkerchief and wiped his forehead. Then he got up and walked quickly out of the hospital.

There was a taxi-stand across the street. Only one taxi was there now, and its driver was sitting disconsolately on the running-board cleaning his fingernails with a jackknife. He stood up when Jones approached and said, "Taxi?" in a not very hopeful voice.

"Is there a messenger service around town that specializes in red bikes and gray uniforms?" Jones asked him.

"Sure. Bullet Service."

"Have they got a branch office near here?"

"Sure, on Court Street. Three blocks down and one to your right."

"Show me," said Jones. He opened the door of the taxi, climbed in, and plumped himself down on the seat with a sigh of relief.

It was a small, neat office with a big plate glass window that ran clear across the front and had an enormous bullet painted on it with red lines trailing behind to show it was traveling at tremendous speed. There were several people waiting when Jones limped up to the high counter and leaned on it with his elbow, looking as mysterious and hard-boiled as possible in view of the fact that his feet were hurting him more and more all the time.

A clerk with a polished haircut and a vacantly cordial smile stepped up to the other side of the counter. "Yes."

"I'm a detective," Jones sneered at him. "Don't act funny. Just be natural. Treat me like anybody else."

The clerk gulped. "Police! What—"

"Shut up," said Jones. "I said act natural. I want some information about a party who sent a message by one of your boys to Mrs. Hendrick Boone at Forty-five–fifteen Raleigh Street. Was it sent from this branch?"

The clerk nodded once, then again, and finally said, "Yes," in a frightened stage whisper.

"When?"

"About—about an hour ago."

"Did a woman send it?"

"Yes," the clerk said. He swallowed and then said: "Her name was Sarah Boone."

"So?" said Jones sharply. "And how do you know that?"

"Well, we have a rule about messages. A few months ago someone started sending poison-pen letters—anonymous—through our messenger service. Brought us a lot of bad publicity. Now, we require anyone sending a sealed message to sign it in our presence. This lady did."

"What'd she look like?" Jones asked.

The clerk stared. "Well, she was a woman—I mean, sort of young, I think. She was veiled. I didn't notice. She had a lot of birthmarks on her arms."

"Yeah," said Jones absently. He squinted thoughtfully at the clerk for a moment, then suddenly pulled one of the blank pads of paper on the counter toward him, picked up a pencil, and wrote rapidly *You're a liar*.

"I'm not!" the clerk denied, instantly indignant. "You—"

Jones slapped the pad down. "I thought so! You're a shark at reading handwriting upside down, aren't you? That's the why of your signature rule, to give you boys a chance to spot a poison-pen letter before it goes out. Now, what did Sarah Boone's message say? Don't stall me."

The clerk shifted uneasily. "Well, I can't repeat it, word for word. I didn't pay enough attention. I saw right away it wasn't anything like what we've been looking for. It was headed 'Dear Mother,' and it said something about a lot of serious trouble and for the mother to meet her right away at Ten-eleven Twelfth Avenue."

"Where?" Jones asked.

"Ten-eleven Twelfth Avenue. I remembered that on account of the sequence of figures—ten, eleven, twelve. I was thinking that ought to be a lucky address—"

"Maybe not so lucky," said Jones. "Keep this under your hat—if you have a hat. Thanks."

Half the pickets were gone out of the fence, and it swayed backward wearily toward the wet brown square of earth that had once been a lawn. The house was gaunt and weather-beaten and ugly, and it had boards nailed haphazardly across the windows on the lower floor. It looked long deserted. A sign beside the gate said *For Sale or Lease* and gave the name of a realty company.

Jones looked from the sign to the house and back again, squinting thoughtfully. He turned his head slowly. There were no other houses within a half block.

Jones said, "Huh," to himself. He dropped his right hand into the pocket of the trench-coat. He was carrying a pair of flat brass knuckles in the pocket, and he slid his fingers through the metal loops and closed his fist. He unfastened the middle button of the coat with his left hand and touched the butt of the .38 Police Positive he carried in his waistband. Then he nudged the sagging gate open with his knee and strolled aimlessly up the narrow walk.

There were some children playing in the street a block away, and their excited cries carried high and shrill in the stillness. Jones' feet made hollow thumps on the steps, on the damp-warped boards of the porch. The front door was open about an inch. Jones took his right hand out of his coat pocket and rapped with the brass knuckles. The echoes came back from empty rooms, hollow and thin and ghostly. Jones put his right hand behind him and waited. Nothing happened.

Jones closed the fingers of his left hand more firmly around the grip of the Police Positive and then suddenly kicked the door open and stepped to one side. The door swung in a dark, silent arc and banged against the wall. After about thirty seconds, Jones looked cautiously around the edge of the doorway and saw Mrs. Boone and Sarah.

Mrs. Boone was lying in front of the door. She wore a long, old-fashioned coat with a thin fur collar and an old-fashioned hat that sat high on her gray hair. The hat was tipped sidewise now at a grotesquely jaunty angle. She was lying on her back, and she had one arm thrown across her face.

Sarah was crumpled in a heap under one of the boarded windows, and the failing sunlight made a barred pattern across her broad face. A little trickle of blood on her cheek glistened brightly. One smooth white arm was flung limply wide. Jones could see the birthmark on it. The lax fingers just touched a stubby automatic lying there beside her.

Jones came inside the room, taking one cautious step, then another. He knelt beside Mrs. Boone. She was breathing faintly. There was a swollen, blue-black welt on her cheek. Jones leaned over Sarah and touched the smooth white arm. Then he suddenly spun around and ran out of the room. He ran down the walk, through the gate, on down the street. He ran two blocks to a corner drugstore, dodged into a telephone booth, dropped a nickel in the instrument, and dialed the operator.

"Ambulance," he said breathlessly.

Dusk was a soft-gray smoothness closing down slowly over the row of houses that were just alike when Jones stopped on the sidewalk in front of the Boones' and looked up the steep front stairs at Morganwaite. Morganwaite was sitting on the top step, leaning forward weakly, as if he had collapsed there. His broom was lying beside him, and he had the evening paper spread across his knees.

"Hello," Jones said, and climbed the steps slowly and sat down beside him.

Morganwaite's hand was trembling a little, and he touched the paper on his knees with his forefinger gingerly. "This paper—I picked it up. The newsboy—delivered it just like any other night. It says that Sarah killed her father and tried to kill her mother and then—had an attack of remorse and killed herself."

"It's mostly right," said Jones. "Only Sarah didn't kill herself. She isn't dead."

"Not dead," Morganwaite repeated dully.

"No. They thought she was, at first. I did, too. I never saw anybody that looked deader. But the bullet was a small-caliber one. It didn't penetrate her brain. Gave her a multiple skull-fracture. It's a toss-up whether she'll pull through or not. The doc thinks she's got a good chance. Funny thing—she's in the same room her father was in at the hospital. That's the wing where they put the head injuries, and it was the only room vacant. She doesn't know it, of course. She's unconscious."

"Mrs. Boone," Morganwaite said. "There—there was no mistake about her? She's—all right?"

Jones nodded. "Just a concussion and shock. She's not even in the hospital. She's staying at a private nursing-home."

"Sarah," said Morganwaite. "I can't believe it. I can't think she'd do that."

"People do," said Jones. He stretched his feet out on the stairs, grunting painfully. "Chilblains—I get 'em every spring. They're killing me. Ever have 'em?"

"No," said Morganwaite.

Jones sighed. "You're lucky. Can you look after things around the place here for a couple days? Mrs. Boone will be O.K. by then."

"Yes," said Morganwaite.

Jones got up. "Well—I've got to go. So long."

Morganwaite didn't answer. He sat staring straight ahead with eyes that were wide and unseeing.

There were two big stone pillars on either side of the broad walk that led up to the entrance of the City Hospital. Jones was leaning against one of them, a thin indistinguishable shadow in the darkness, with his hat pulled low over his eyes. He was peering around the edge of the pillar, up toward the entrance of the hospital. After a moment, he stepped from behind the pillar, walked quickly up to the steps, pushed the plate glass door open.

A thick-set man with square, heavy shoulders was standing just inside the door. He wore a blue overcoat and a black felt hat, and he had a thin white scar on his face that ran from the corner of his left eye straight down across his cheek to the line of his jaw.

"Jones?" he asked softly.

"Yes," said Jones in a surprised voice.

The scarred man stepped forward and picked up Jones by the front of the trenchcoat. He swung Jones around and slammed him against the wall.

"Careful," said Jones. "Don't step on my feet, or I'll kill you."

He said it in such a murderously calm voice that the scarred man let go of him. Jones straightened the front of his coat with a jerk and a shrug of his shoulders. "You don't have to tell me," he said. "I know you're a cop."

"Yeah," said the scarred man. "Maybe you didn't think there were any cops in this town. Maybe you think you've been playing a little game of hide-and-seek with yourself. What's the big idea of trying to make us look like monkeys?"

"I can't help what you look like. You wanted to see me, you said."

"All right. You've been in this case from the first. In fact, you started the ball rolling. You found Hendrick Boone. Did you stick around? No, you ducked out before we got here. You found the other two. Now, just what do you think you're doing?"

"Trying to find a murderer."

The scarred man stared at him. "Are you so dumb you haven't figured it out yet? Sarah Boone did for her father and tried to do for her mother so she'd get the money her uncle left."

"Did she?" said Jones.

"Why, sure. What—" The scarred man's hard eyes narrowed. "Oh, so you've got something else up your sleeve, have you? All right, then. Who is the murderer?"

"The person I was following. You can come along and take the credit for the arrest, if you don't bother me with a lot of dumb questions."

The feet of Jones and the scarred man were soft and noiseless on the cork flooring. They walked side by side, tensely, and ahead of them was the bright, clean glitter of the glass partition that blocked off the short corridor where Hendrick Boone's room had been.

Through it they could see the nurse sitting behind her desk and looking up into Mrs. Hendrick Boone's thick glasses and shaking her head in a blank, surprised way. Jones nodded at the scarred man and then reached down and turned the knob on the glass door very softly.

"No," said Jones. "Sarah isn't here. That was just a gag to see if I couldn't get you out from under cover. You really killed Sarah. She's in the morgue. Your feet are too big, Mrs. Boone."

Mrs. Boone's skirt rustled silkily. Mrs. Boone's white-kid gloves made a blurred streak rising above the collar of her old coat, flipping down again. The knife was a flat, hissing glitter coming at Jones.

The scarred man ducked with an inarticulate cry. Jones dove under the knife and it smashed through the glass partition and rattled on the corridor floor beyond. Jones' shoulder hit against bony knees. There was a strangled cry, and Mrs. Boone's coat ballooned clumsily, falling.

Jones got up, drawing in a long breath. "You were a big help," he said to the scarred man. "Thanks." He looked at the white-faced nurse. "Sorry, Miss. I didn't figure on any knife-throwing."

The scarred man pointed. "She—Mrs. Boone—she killed her husband and daughter?"

"No," said Jones. "Of course not. Morganwaite killed them. What do you think I just tackled him for?"

"Him?" the scarred man said blankly.

Jones leaned down and picked up Mrs. Boone's glasses and loosened the collar of Mrs. Boone's coat and pulled it down. Morganwaite's face looked white and peaceful and kindly.

"Morganwaite killed Sarah and Hendrick Boone," Jones said. "He did it so he could marry Mrs. Boone and live in comfort on her money. He had been planning it even before I turned up. Mrs. Boone had a little property. The news I brought about the trust fund just gave him added incentive. I don't think there's any doubt that he would have married Mrs. Boone had his plan gone through. She was a timid, trusting soul, beaten down by years of living with her drunken husband. She wouldn't be hard for anyone as clever as Morganwaite."

"Well, how?" said the scarred man.

"Easy for him," said Jones. "He's quite a female impersonator. Must have been an old-time actor. He looks like one. First, he got rid of Sarah. On some pretext, he got her to go to that old house on Twelfth Street. He'd picked out the spot a long time ago. He shot her when he got her there—in the temple, close enough so it would look like suicide. Then he dressed himself in Sarah's clothes, painted some birthmarks on his arms, came down here and finished Hendrick Boone. Then, still pretending to be Sarah and laying a nice plain trail, he sent a note to Mrs. Boone and signed Sarah's name to it, asking Mrs. Boone to meet Sarah at the house on Twelfth."

"Huh!" said the scarred man. "You mean the old lady didn't even know her kid's writing?"

Jones held up the thick glasses. "Morganwaite thought of that, too. He stole Mrs. Boone's glasses. Look at 'em. They're an inch thick. Mrs. Boone couldn't read anything without 'em. Some neighbor read the note to her, or else the messenger did. Of course, she didn't question the writing. She went right down to the house on Twelfth. Morganwaite was waiting there for her. He hit her on the head as she came in, before she saw him, and left her there. The set-up was supposed to look as if Sarah had planned to kill her father and mother, but that, when she got to the point of actually doing for her mother, she had an attack of remorse and killed herself, instead.

"I was pretty sure of the set-up, but I didn't have any proof. So I went around and told Morganwaite Sarah wasn't dead—that she was here. Well, that upset his whole apple cart. Sarah knew he shot her, and, if she told, why there he'd be in the soup. So he came down to finish the job. This time he dressed up in Mrs. Boone's clothes to keep from being identified. He knew Mrs. Boone wouldn't be suspected, actually, because she was in a rest-home and would have an airtight alibi."

Jones looked around. "If you've got any more questions, we'll have to go somewhere where I can sit down. My feet are killing me."

LEIGH BRACKETT

Leigh Brackett (1915–1978) finished her extraordinary career by writing the screenplay for *The Empire Strikes Back*. Yes, that *Empire Strikes Back*. She wrote a number of other screenplays as well, most notably for *The Big Sleep* and *Rio Bravo*.

Despite her Hollywood reputation, her fine stories and novels have been somewhat overlooked. She worked in two genres essentially, science fiction and hard-boiled crime, although the Western Writers of America awarded her the Spur award for fiction in 1964. But she was magnificent in noir and science fiction. Look up such novels as *No Good from a Corpse* and *The Tiger Among Us* if you want to see a first-rate writer at the top of her talent.

I Feel Bad Killing You

1

Dead End Town

LOS ANGELES, APR. 21.—The death of Henry Channing, 24, policeman attached to the Surfside Division and brother of the once-prominent detective Paul Channing, central figure in the Padway gang-torture case, has been termed a suicide following investigation by local authorities. Young Channing's battered body was found in the surf under Sunset Pier in the beach community three days ago. It was first thought that Channing might have fallen or been thrown from the end of the pier, where his cap was found, but there is no evidence of violence and a high guard rail precludes the accident theory. Sunset Pier was part of his regular beat.

Police Captain Max Gandara made the following statement: "We have reliable testimony that Channing had been nervous and despondent following a beating by *pachucos* two months ago." He then cited the case of the brother, Paul Channing, who quit the force and vanished into obscurity following his mistreatment at the hands of the once-powerful Padway gang in 1934. "They were both good cops," Gandara said, "but they lost their nerve."

Paul Channing stood for a moment at the corner. The crossing-light, half a block along the highway, showed him only as a gaunt shadow among shadows. He looked down the short street in somber hesitation. Small tired houses crouched patiently under the wind. Somewhere a rusted screen door slammed with the protesting futility of a dying bird beating its wing. At the end of the deserted pavement was the grey pallor of sand and, beyond it, the sea.

He stood listening to the boom and hiss of the waves, thinking of them rushing black and foam-streaked through the pilings of Sunset Pier, the long weeds streaming out and the barnacles pink and fluted and razor sharp behind it. He hoped that Hank had struck his head at once against a timber.

He lifted his head, his body shaken briefly by a tremor. *This is it*, he thought. *This is the deadline*.

He began to walk, neither slowly nor fast, scraping sand under his feet. The rhythm of the scraping was uneven, a slight dragging, off-beat. He went to the last house on the right, mounted three sagging steps to a wooden porch, and rapped with his knuckles on a door blistered and greasy with the salt sweat of the sea. There was a light behind drawn blinds, and a sound of voices. The voices stopped, sliced cleanly by the knocking.

Someone walked heavily through the silence. The door opened, spilling yellow light around the shadow of a thick-set, powerful man in shirtsleeves. He let his breath out in what was not quite a laugh and relaxed against the jamb.

"So you did turn up," he said. He was well into middle age, hard-eyed, obstinate. His name was Max Gandara, Police Captain, Surfside Division, L.A.P.D. He studied the man on the porch with slow, deliberate insolence.

The man on the porch seemed not to mind. He seemed not to be in any hurry. His dark eyes looked, unmoved, at the big man, at him and through him. His face was a mask of thin sinewy flesh, laid close over ruthless bone, expressionless. And yet, in spite of his face and his lean erect body, there was a shadow on him. He was like a man who has drawn away, beyond the edge of life.

"Did you think I wouldn't come?" he asked.

Gandara shrugged. "They're all here. Come on in and get it over with."

Channing nodded and stepped inside. He removed his hat. His dark hair was shot with grey. He turned to lay the hat on a table and the movement brought into focus a scar that ran up from his shirt collar on the right side of his neck, back of the ear. Then he followed Gandara into the living room.

There were three people there, and the silence. Three people watching the door. A red-haired, green-eyed girl with a smouldering, angry glow deep inside her. A red-haired, green-eyed boy with a sullen, guarded face. And a man, a neat, lean, swarthy man with aggressive features that seemed always to be on the edge of laughter and eyes that kept all their emotion on the surface.

"Folks," said Gandara, "this is Paul Channing." He indicated them, in order. "Marge Krist, Rudy Krist, Jack Flavin."

Hate crawled into the green eyes of Rudy Krist, brilliant and poisonous, fixed on Channing.

Out in the kitchen a woman screamed. The swing door burst open. A chubby pink man came through in a tottering rush, followed by a large, bleached blonde with an ice pick. Her dress was torn slightly at the shoulder and her mouth was smeared. Her incongruously black eyes were owlish and mad.

Gandara yelled. The sound of his voice got through to the blonde. She slowed down and said sulkily, to no one in particular, "He better keep his fat paws off or I'll fix him." She went back to the kitchen.

The chubby pink man staggered to a halt, swayed, caught hold of Channing's arm and looked up at him, smiling foolishly. The smile faded, leaving his mouth open like a baby's. His eyes, magnified behind rimless lenses, widened and fixed.

"Chan," he said. "My God. Chan."

He sat down on the floor and began to cry, the tears running quietly down his cheeks.

"Hello, Budge." Channing stooped and touched his shoulder.

"Take it easy." Gandara pulled Channing's arms. "Let the little lush alone. Him and—that." He made a jerky gesture at the girl, flung himself heavily into a chair and glowered at Channing. "All right, we're all curious—tell us why we're here."

Channing sat down. He seemed in no hurry to begin. A thin film of sweat made the tight pattern of muscles very plain under his skin.

"We're here to talk about a lot of things," he said. "Who murdered Henry?" No one seemed particularly moved except Budge Hanna, who stopped crying and stared at Channing. Rudy Krist made a small derisive noise in his throat. Gandara laughed.

"That ain't such a bombshell, Chan. I guess we all had an idea of what you was driving at, from the letters you wrote us. What we want to know is what makes you think you got a right to holler murder."

Channing drew a thick envelope from his inside pocket, laying it on his knee to conceal the fact that his hands trembled. He said, not looking at anybody, "I haven't seen my brother for several years, but we've been in fairly close touch through letters. I've kept most of his. Hank was good at writing letters, good at saying things. He's had a lot to say since he was transferred to Surfside—and not one word of it points to suicide."

Max Gandara's face had grown rocky. "Oh, he had a lot to say, did he?"

Channing nodded. Marge Krist was leaning forward, watching him intently. Jack Flavin's terrier face was interested, but unreadable. He had been smoking nervously when Channing entered. The nervousness seemed to be habitual, part of his wiry personality. Now he lighted another cigarette, his hands moving with a swiftness that seemed jerky but was not. The match flared and spat. Paul Channing started involuntarily. The flame seemed to have a terrible fascination for him. He dropped his gaze. Beads of sweat came out along his hairline. Once again, harshly, Gandara laughed.

"Go on," he said. "Go on."

"Hank told me about that brush with the *pachucos*. They didn't hurt him much. They sure as hell didn't break him."

"Flavin, here, says different. Rudy says different. Marge says different."

"That's why I wanted to talk to them—and you, Max. Hank mentioned you all in his letters." He was talking to the whole room now. "Max I knew from the old days. You, Miss Krist, I know because Hank went with you—not seriously, I guess, but you liked each other. He liked your brother, too."

The kid stared at him, his eyes blank and bright. Channing said, "Hank talked a lot about you, Rudy. He said you were a smart kid, a good kid but headed for trouble. He said some ways you were so smart you were downright stupid."

Rudy and Marge both started to speak, but Channing was going on. "I guess he was right, Rudy. You've got it on you already—a sort of greyness that comes from prison walls, or the shadow of them. You've got that look on your face, like a closed door."

Rudy got halfway to his feet, looking nasty. Flavin said quietly, "Shut up." Rudy sat down again. Flavin seemed relaxed. His brown eyes held only a hard glitter from the light. "Hank seems to have been a great talker. What did he say about me?"

"He said you smell of stripes."

Flavin laid his cigarette carefully in a tray. He got up, very light and easy. He went over to Channing and took a handful of his shirt, drawing him up slightly, and said with gentle kindness, "I don't think I like that remark."

Marge Krist cried, "Stop it! Jack, don't you dare start trouble."

"Maybe you didn't understand what he meant, Marge." Flavin still did not sound angry. "He's accusing me of having a record, a prison record. He didn't pick a very nice way of saying it."

"Take it easy, Jack," Gandara said. "Don't you get what he's doing?

He's trying to wangle himself a little publicity and stir up a little trouble, so that maybe the public will think maybe Hank didn't do the Dutch after all." He pointed at Budge Hanna. "Even the press is here." He rose and took hold of Flavin's shoulder. "He's just making a noise with his mouth, because a long time ago people used to listen when he did it and he hasn't forgotten how good that felt."

Flavin shrugged and returned to his chair. Gandara lighted a cigarette, holding the match deliberately close to Channing's sweaty face. "Listen, Chan. Jack Flavin is a good citizen of Surfside. He owns a store, legitimate, and Rudy works for him, legitimate. I don't like people coming into my town and making cracks about the citizens. If they step out of line, I'll take care of them. If they don't, I'll see they're let alone."

He sat down again, comfortably. "All right, Chan. Let's get this all out of your system. What did little brother have to say about me?"

Channing's dark eyes flickered with what might have been malice. "What everybody's always said about you, Max. That you were too goddam dumb even to be crooked."

Gandara turned purple. He moved and Jack Flavin laughed. "No fair, Max. You wouldn't let me."

Budge Hanna giggled with startling shrillness. The blonde had come in and sat down beside him. Her eyes were half closed but she seemed somehow less drunk than she had been. Gandara settled back. He said ominously, "Go on."

"All right. Hank said that Surfside was a dirty town, dirty from the gutters up. He said any man with the brains of a sick flea would know that most of the liquor places were run illegally, and most of the hotels, too, and that two-thirds of the police force was paid to have bad eyesight. He said it wasn't any use trying to do a good job as a decent cop. He said every report he turned in was thrown away for lack of evidence, and he was sick of it."

Marge Krist said, "Then maybe that's what he was worried about."

"He wasn't afraid," said Channing. "All his letters were angry, and an angry man doesn't commit suicide."

Budge Hanna said shrilly, "Look out."

Max Gandara was on his feet. He was standing over Channing. His lips had a white line around them.

"Listen," he said. "I been pretty patient with you. Now I'll tell you something. Your brother committed suicide. All these three people testified at the inquest. You can read the transcript. They all said Hank was worried; he wasn't happy about things. There was no sign of violence on Hank, or the pier."

"How could there be?" said Channing. "Hard asphalt paving doesn't show much. And Hank's body wouldn't show much, either."

"Shut up. I'm telling you. There's no evidence of murder, no reason to think it's murder. Hank was like you, Channing. He couldn't take punishment. He got chicken walking a dark beat down here, and he jumped, and that's all."

Channing said slowly, "Only two kinds of people come to Surfside—the ones that are starting at the bottom, going up, and the ones that are finished, coming down. It's either a beginning or an end, and I guess we all know where we stand on that scale."

He got up, tossing the packet of letters into Budge Hanna's lap. "Those are photostats. The originals are already with police headquarters in L.A. I don't think you have to worry much, Max. There's nothing definite in them. Just a green young harness cop griping at the system, making a few personal remarks. He hasn't even accused you of being dishonest, Max. Only dumb—and the powers-that-be already know that. That's why you're here in Surfside, waiting for the age of retirement."

Gandara struck him in the mouth. Channing took three steps backward, caught himself, swayed, and was steady again. Blood ran from the corner of his mouth down his chin. Marge Krist was on her feet, her eyes blazing, but something about Channing kept her from speaking. He seemed not to care about the blood, about Gandara, or about anything but what he was saying.

"You used to be a good reporter, Budge, before you drank yourself onto the scrapheap. I thought maybe you'd like to be in at the beginning on this story. Because there's going to be a story, if it's only the story of my death.

"I knew Hank. There was no yellow in him. Whether there's yellow in me or not, doesn't matter. Hank didn't jump off that pier. Somebody threw him off, and I'm going to find out who, and why. I used to be a pretty good dick once. I've got a reason now for remembering all I learned."

Max Gandara said, "Oh, God," in a disgusted voice. "Take that somewhere else, Chan. It smells." He pushed him roughly toward the door, and Rudy Krist laughed.

"Yellow," he said. "Yellower than four Japs. Both of 'em, all talk and no guts. Get him out, Max. He stinks up the room."

Flavin said, "Shut up, Rudy." He grinned at Marge. "You're getting your sister sore."

"You bet I'm sore!" she flared. "I think Mr. Channing is right. I knew Hank pretty well, and I think you ought to be ashamed to push him around like this."

Flavin said, "Who? Hank or Mr. Channing?"

Marge snapped, "Oh, go to hell." She turned and went out. Gandara shoved Channing into the hall after her. "You know where the door is, Chan. Stay away from me, and if I was you I'd stay away from Surfside." He turned around, reached down and got a handful of Budge Hanna's coat collar and slung him out bodily. "You, too, rumdum. *And* you." He made a grab for the blonde, but she was already out. He followed the four of them down the hall and closed the door hard behind them.

* * *

Paul Channing said, "Miss Krist—and you too, Budge." The wind felt ice cold on his skin. His shirt stuck to his back. It turned clammy and he began to shiver. "I want to talk to you."

The blonde said, "Is this private?"

"I don't think so. Maybe you can help." Channing walked slowly toward the beach front and the boardwalk. "Miss Krist, if you didn't think Hank committed suicide, why did you testify as you did at the inquest?"

"Because I didn't know." She sounded rather angry, with him and possibly herself. "They asked me how he acted, and I had to say he'd been worried and depressed, because he had been. I told them I didn't think he was the type for suicide, but they didn't care."

"Did Hank ever hint that he knew something—anything that might have been dangerous to him?" Channing's eyes were alert, watchful in the darkness.

"No. Hank pounded a beat. He wasn't a detective."

"He was pretty friendly with your brother, wasn't he?"

"I thought for a while it might bring Rudy back to his senses. He took a liking to Hank, they weren't so far apart in years, and Hank was doing him good. Now, of course—"

"What's wrong with Rudy? What's he doing?"

"That's just it, I don't know. He's 4-F in the draft, and that hurts him, and he's always been restless, never could hold a job. Then he met Jack Flavin, and since then he's been working steady, but he—he's changed. I can't put my finger on it, I don't know of anything wrong he's done, but he's hardened and drawn into himself, as though he had secrets and didn't trust anybody. You saw how he acted. He's turned mean. I've done my best to bring him up right."

Channing said, "Kids go that way sometimes. Know anything about him, Budge?"

The reporter said, "Nuh-uh. He's never been picked up for anything, and as far as anybody knows even Flavin is straight. He owns a haberdashery and pays his taxes."

"Well," said Channing, "I guess that's all for now."

"No." Marge Krist stopped and faced him. He could see her eyes in the pale reflection of the water, dark and intense. The wind blew her hair, pressed her light coat against the long lifting planes of her body. "I want to warn you. Maybe you're a brilliant, nervy man and you know what you're doing, and if you do it's all right. But if you really are what you acted like in there, you'd better go home and forget about it. Surfside is a bad town. You can't insult people and get away with it." She paused. "For Hank's sake, I hope you know what you're doing. I'm in the phone book if you want me. Good night."

"Good night." Channing watched her go. She had a lovely way of moving. Absently, he began to wipe the blood off his face. His lip had begun to swell.

Budge Hanna said, "Chan."

"Yeah."

"I want to say thanks, and I'm with you. I'll give you the biggest break I can in the paper."

"We used to work pretty well together, before I got mine and you found yours, in a bottle."

"Yeah. And now I'm in Surfside with the rest of the scrap. If this turns out a big enough story, I might—oh, well." He paused, rubbing a pudgy cheek with his forefinger.

Channing said, "Go ahead, Budge. Say it."

"All right. Every crook in the Western states knows that the Padway mob took you to the wall. They know what was done to you, with fire. They know you broke. The minute they find out you're back, even unofficially, you know what'll happen. You sent up a lot of guys in your time. You sent a lot of 'em down, too—down to the morgue. You were a tough dick, Chan, and a square one, and you know how they love you."

"I guess I know all that, Budge."

"Chan—" he looked up, squinting earnestly through the gloom, his spectacles shining—"how is it? I mean, can you—"

Channing put a hand on his shoulder, pushing him around slightly. "You watch your step, kid, and try to stay sober. I don't know what I may be getting into. If you want out—"

"Hell, no. Just—well, good luck, Chan."

"Thanks."

The blonde said, "Ain't you going to ask me something?"

"Sure," said Channing. "What do you know?"

"I know who killed your brother."

2

Badge of Carnage

The blood swelled and thickened in Channing's veins. It made a hard pain over his eyes and pressed against the stiff scar tissue on his neck. No one spoke. No one moved.

The wind blew sand in riffles across the empty beach. The waves rushed and broke their backs in thunder and slipped out again, sighing. Up ahead Sunset Pier thrust its black bulk against the night. Beyond it was the huge amusement pier. Here and there a single light was burning, swaying with the wind, and the reaching skeletons of the roller coaster and the giant slide were desolate in the pre-season quiet. Vacant lots and a single unlighted house were as deserted as the moon.

Paul Channing looked at the woman with eyes as dark and lonely as the night. "We're not playing a game," he said. "This is murder."

The blonde's teeth glittered white between moist lips.

Budge Hanna whispered, "She's crazy. She couldn't know."

"Oh, couldn't I!" The blonde's whisper was throatily venomous. "Young Channing was thrown off the pier about midnight, wasn't he? Okay. Well, you stood me up on a date that evening, remember, Budgie dear? And my room is on the same floor as yours, remember? And I can hear every pair of hoofs clumping up and down those damn stairs right outside, remember?"

"Listen," Budge said, "I told you I got stewed and—"

"And got in a fight. I know. Sure, you told me. But how can you prove it? I heard your fairy footsteps. They didn't sound very stewed to me. So I looked out, and you were hitting it for your room like your pants were on fire. Your shirt was torn, and so was your coat, and you didn't look so good other ways. I could hear you heaving clear out in the hall. And it was just nineteen minutes after twelve."

Budge Hanna's voice had risen to a squeak. "Damn you, Millie, I— Chan, she's crazy! She's just trying—"

"Sure," said Millie. She thrust her face close to his. "I been shoved around enough. I been called enough funny names. I been stood up enough times. I loaned you enough money I'll never get back. And I ain't so dumb I don't know you got dirt on your hands from somewhere. Me, I'm quitting you right now and—"

"Shut up. Shut up!"

"And I got a few things to say that'll interest some people!" Millie was screeching now. "You killed that Channing kid, or you know who did!"

Budge Hanna slapped her hard across the mouth.

Millie reeled back. Then she screamed like a cat. Her hands flashed up, curved and wicked, long red nails gleaming. She went for Budge Hanna.

Channing stepped between them. He was instantly involved in a whirlwind of angry flailing hands. While he was trying to quiet them the men came up behind him.

There were four of them. They had come quietly from the shadows beside the vacant house. They worked quickly, with deadly efficiency. Channing got his hand inside his coat, and after that he didn't know anything for a long time.

Things came back to Channing in disconnected pieces. His head hurt. He was in something that moved. He was hot. He was covered with something, lying flat on his back, and he could hardly breathe. There was another person jammed against him. There were somebody's feet on his chest, and somebody else's feet on his thighs. Presently he found that his mouth was covered with adhesive, that his eyes were taped shut, and that his hands and feet were bound, probably also with tape. The moving thing was an automobile, taking its time.

The stale, stifling air under the blanket covering him was heavy with the scent of powder and cheap perfume. He guessed that the woman was Millie. From time to time she stirred and whimpered.

A man's voice said, "Here is okay."

The car stopped. Doors were opened. The blanket was pulled away. Cold salt air rushed over Channing, mixed with the heavy sulphurous reek of sewage. He knew they were somewhere on the road above Hyperion, where there was nothing but miles of empty dunes.

Hands grabbed him, hauled him bodily out of the car. Somebody said, "Got the Thompson ready?"

"Yeah." The speaker laughed gleefully, like a child with a bass voice. "Just like old times, ain't it? Good ole Dolly. She ain't had a chansta sing in a long time. Come on, honey. Loosen up the pipes."

A rattling staccato burst out, and was silent.

"For cripesake, Joe! That stuff ain't so plentiful. Doncha know there's a war on? We gotta conserve. C'mon, help me with this guy." He kicked Channing. "On your feet, you."

He was hauled erect and leaned against a post. Joe said, "What about the dame?"

The other man laughed. "Her turn comes later. Much later."

A fourth voice, one that had not spoken before, said, "Okay, boys. Get away from him now." It was a slow, inflectionless and yet strangely forceful voice, with a hint of a lisp. The lisp was not in the least effeminate or funny. It had the effect of a knife blade whetted on oilstone. The man who owned it put his hands on Channing's shoulders.

"You know me," he said.

Channing nodded. The uncovered parts of his face were greasy with sweat. It had soaked loose the corners of the adhesive. The man said, "You knew I'd catch up with you some day."

The man struck him, deliberately and with force, twice across the face with his open palms.

"I'm sorry you lost your guts, Channing. This makes me feel like I'm shooting a kitten. Why didn't you do the Dutch years ago, like your brother?"

Channing brought his bound fists up, slammed them into the man's face, striking at the sound of his voice. The man grunted and fell, making a heavy soft thump in the sand. Somebody yelled, "Hey!" and the man with the quiet lisping voice said, "Shut up. Let him alone."

Channing heard him scramble up and the voice came near again. "Do that again."

Channing did.

The man avoided his blow this time. He laughed softly. "So you still have insides, Chan. That makes it better. Much better."

Joe said, "Look, somebody may come along—"

"Shut up." The man brought something from his pocket, held his hand close to Channing's ear, and shook it. "You know what that is?"

Channing stiffened. He nodded.

There was a light thin rattling sound, and then a scratching of emery and the quick spitting of a match-head rubbed to flame.

The man said softly, "How are your guts now?"

The little sharp tongue of heat touched Channing's chin. He drew his head back. His mouth worked under the adhesive. Cords stood out in his throat. The flame followed. Channing began to shake. His knees gave. He braced them, braced his body against the post. Sweat ran down his face and the scar on his neck turned dark and livid.

The man laughed. He threw the match down and stepped away. He said, "Okay, Joe."

Somebody said, sharply, "There's a car coming. Two cars."

The man swore. "Bunch of sailors up from Long Beach. Okay, we'll get out of here. Back in the car, Joe. Can't use the chopper, they'd hear it." Joe cursed unhappily. Feet scruffed hurriedly in the sand. Leather squeaked, the small familiar sound of metal clearing a shoulder clip. The safety snicked open.

The man said, "So long, Channing."

Channing was already falling sideways when the shot came. There was a second one close behind it. Channing dropped into the ditch and lay perfectly still, hidden from the road. The car roared off. Presently the two other cars shot by, loaded with sailors. They were singing and shouting and not worrying about what somebody might have left at the side of the road.

Sometime later Channing began to move, at first in uncoordinated jerks and then with reasonable steadiness. He was conscious that he had been hit in two places. The right side of his head was stiff and numb clear down to his neck. Somebody had shoved a red-hot spike through the flesh over his heart-ribs and forgotten to take it out. He could feel blood oozing, sticky with sand.

He rolled over slowly and started to peel the adhesive from his face, fumbling awkwardly with his bound hands. When that was done he used his teeth on his wrist bonds. It took a long time. After that the ankles were easy.

It was no use trying to see how much damage had been done. He decided it couldn't be as bad as it felt. He smiled, a crooked and humorless grimace, and swore and laughed shortly. He wadded the clean handkerchief from his hip pocket into the gash under his arm and tightened the holster strap to hold it there. The display handkerchief in his breast pocket went around his head. He found that after he got started he could walk quite well. His gun had not been removed. Channing laughed again, quietly. He did not touch nor in any way notice the burn on his chin.

It took him nearly three hours to get back to Surfside, crouching in the ditch twice to let cars go by.

He passed Gandara's street, and the one beyond where Marge and Rudy Krist lived. He came to the ocean front and the dark loom of the pier and the vacant house from behind which the men had come. He found Budge Hanna doubled up under a clump of Monterey cypress. The cold spring wind blew sand into Hanna's wide-open eyes, but he didn't seem to mind it. He had bled from the nose and ears—not much.

Channing went through Hanna's pockets, examining things swiftly by the light of a tiny pocket flash shielded in his hand. There was just the usual clutter of articles. Channing took the key ring. Then, tucked into the watch pocket, he found a receipt from Flavin's Men's Shop for three pairs of socks. The date was April 22. Channing frowned. April 21 was the day on which Hank Channing's death had been declared a suicide. April 21 was a Saturday.

Channing rose slowly and walked on down the front to Surfside Avenue. It was hours past midnight. The bars were closed. The only lights on the street were those of the police station and the lobby of the Surfside Hotel, which was locked and deserted. Channing let himself in with Budge Hanna's key and walked up dirty marble steps to the second floor and found Budge Hanna's number. He leaned against the jamb, his knees sagging, managed to force the key around and get inside. He switched on the lights, locked the door again, and braced his back against it. The first thing he saw was a bottle on the bedside table.

He drank straight from the neck. It was scotch, good scotch. In a few minutes he felt much better. He stared at the label, turning the bottle around in his hands, frowning at it. Then, very quietly, he began to search the room.

He found nothing until, in the bottom drawer of the dresser, he discovered a brand new shirt wrapped in cheap green paper. The receipt was from Flavin's Men's Shop. Channing looked at the date. It was for the day which had just begun, Monday.

Channing studied the shirt, poking his fingers into the folds. Between the tail and the cardboard he found an envelope. It was unaddressed, unsealed, and contained six one hundred dollar bills.

Channing's mouth twisted. He replaced the money and the shirt and sat down on the bed. He scowled at the wall, not seeing it, and drank some more of Budge Hanna's scotch. He thought Budge wouldn't mind. It would take more even than good scotch to warm him now.

A picture on the wall impressed itself gradually upon Channing's mind.

He looked at it more closely. It was a professional photograph of a beautiful woman in a white evening gown. She had a magnificent figure and a strong, provocative, heart-shaped face. Her gown and hairdress were of the late twenties. The picture was autographed in faded ink, "Lots of Luck, Skinny, from your pal Dorothy Balf."

"Skinny" had been crossed out and "Budge" written above.

Channing took the frame down and slid the picture out. It had been wiped off, but both frame and picture showed the ravages of time, dust and stains and faded places, as though they had hung a long time with only each other for company. On the back of the picture was stamped:

SKINNY CRAIL'S
Surfside at Culver
"Between the Devil and the Deep"

Memories came back to Channing. Skinny Crail, that bad-luck boy of Hollywood, plunging his last dime on a night club that flurried into success and then faded gradually to a pathetically mediocre doom, a white elephant rotting hugely in the empty flats between Culver City and the beach. Dorothy Balf had been the leading feminine star of that day, and Budge Hanna's idol. Channing glanced again at the scrawled "Budge." He sighed and replaced the picture carefully. Then he turned out the lights and sat a long while in the dark, thinking.

Presently he sighed again and ran his hand over his face, wincing. He rose and went out, locking the door carefully behind him. He moved slowly, his limp accentuated by weakness and a slight unsteadiness from the scotch. His expression was that of a man who hopes for nothing and is therefore immune to blows.

There was a phone booth in the lobby. Channing called Max Gandara. He talked for a long time. When he came out his face was chalk-colored and damp, utterly without expression. He left the hotel and walked slowly down the beach.

The shapeless, colorless little house was dark and silent, with two empty lots to seaward and a cheap brick apartment house on its right. No lights showed anywhere. Channing set his finger on the rusted bell.

He could hear it buzzing somewhere inside. After a long time lights went on behind heavy crash draperies, drawn close. Channing turned suddenly sick. Sweat came out on his wrists and his ears rang. Through the ringing he heard Marge Krist's clear voice asking who was there.

He told her. "I'm hurt," he said. "Let me in."

The door opened. Channing walked through it. He seemed to be walking through dark water that swirled around him, very cold, very heavy. He decided not to fight it.

When he opened his eyes again he was stretched out on a studio couch. Apparently he had been out only a moment or two. Marge and Rudy Krist were arguing fiercely.

"I tell you he's got to have a doctor!"

"All right, tell him to go get one. You don't want to get in trouble."

"Trouble? Why would I get in trouble?"

"They guy's been shot. That means cops. They'll be trampling all over, asking you why he should have come here. How do you know what the little rat's been doing? If he's square, why didn't he go to the cops himself? Maybe it's a frame, or maybe he shot himself."

"Maybe," said Marge slowly, "you're afraid to be questioned."

Rudy swore. He looked almost as white and hollow as Channing felt. Channing laughed. It was not a pleasant sound.

He said, "Sure he's scared. Start an investigation now and that messes up everything for tonight."

Marge and Rudy both started at the sound of his voice. Rudy's face went hard and blank as a pine slab. He walked over toward the couch.

"What does that crack mean?"

"It means you better call Flavin quick and tell him to get his new shirt out of Budge Hanna's room. Budge Hanna won't be needing it now, and the cops are going to be very interested in the accessories."

Rudy's lips had a curious stiffness. "What's wrong with Hanna?"

"Nothing much. Only one of Dave's boys hit him a little too hard. He's dead."

"Dead?" Rudy shaped the word carefully and studied it as though he had never heard it before. Then he said, "Who's Dave? What are you talking about?"

Channing studied him. "Flavin's still keeping you in the nursery, is he?"

"That kind of talk don't go with me, Channing."

"That's tough, because it'll go with the cops. You'll sound kind of silly, won't you, bleating how you didn't know what was going on because papa never told you."

Rudy moved toward Channing. Marge yelled and caught him. Channing grinned and drew his gun. His head was propped fairly high on pillows, so he could see what he was doing without making any disastrous attempt to sit up.

"Fine hood you are, Rudy. Didn't even frisk me. Listen, punk. Budge Hanna's dead, murdered. His Millie is dead, too, by now. I'm supposed to be dead, in a ditch above Hyperion, but Dave Padway always was a lousy shot. Where do you think you come in on this?"

Rudy's skin had a sickly greenish tinge, but his jaw was hard. "You're a liar, Channing. I never heard of Dave Padway. I don't know anything about Budge Hanna or that dame. I don't know anything about you. Now get the hell out."

"You make a good Charlie McCarthy, Rudy. Maybe Flavin will hold you on his knee in the death-chair at San Quentin."

Marge stopped Rudy again. She said quietly, "What happened, Mr. Channing?"

Channing told her, keeping his eyes on Rudy. "Flavin's heading a racket," he said finally. "His store is just a front, useful for background and a way to make pay-offs and pass on information. He doesn't keep the store open on Sunday, does he, Rudy?"

Rudy didn't answer. Marge said, "No."

"Okay. Budge Hanna worked for Flavin. I'll make a guess. I'll say Flavin is engineering liquor robberies, hijacking, and so forth. Budge Hanna was a well-known lush. He could go into any bar and make a deal for bootleg whiskey, and nobody would suspect him. Trouble with Budge was, he couldn't handle his women. Millie got sore, and suspicious and began to yell out loud. I guess Dave Padway's boys overheard her. Dave never did trust women and drunks."

Channing stared narrow-eyed at Rudy. His blood-caked face was twisted into a cruel grin. "Dave never liked punks, either. There's going to be trouble between Dave and your pal Flavin, and I don't see where you're going to come in, except maybe on a morgue slab, like the others. Like Hank."

"Oh, cripes," said Ruby, "we're back to Hank again."

"Yeah. Always back to Hank. You know what happened, Rudy. You kind of liked Hank. You're a smart kid, Rudy. You've probably got a better brain than Flavin, and if you're going to be a successful crook these days you need brains. So Flavin pushed Hank off the pier and called it suicide, so you'd think he was yellow."

Rudy laughed. "That's good. That's very good. Marge was out with Jack Flavin that night." His green eyes were dangerous.

Marge nodded, dropping her gaze. "I was."

Channing shrugged. "So what? He hired it done. Just like he hired this tonight. Only Dave Padway isn't a boy you can hire for long. He used to be big time, and ten years in clink won't slow him up too much. You better call Flavin, Rudy. They're liable to find Budge Hanna any time and start searching his room." He laughed. "Flavin wasn't so smart to pay off on Saturday, too late for the banks."

Marge said, "Why haven't you called the police?"

"With what I have to tell them I'd only scare off the birds. Let 'em find out for themselves."

She looked at him with level, calculating eyes. "Then you're planning to do it all by yourself?"

"I've got the whip hand right now. Only you two know I'm alive. But I know about Budge Hanna's shirt, and the cops will too, pretty soon. Somebody's got to get busy, and the minute he does I'll know for sure who's who in this little tinpot crime combine."

Marge rose. "That's ridiculous. You're in no condition to handle anyone. And even if you were—" She left that hanging and crossed to the telephone.

Channing said, "Even if I were, I'm still yellow, is that it? Sure. Stand still, Rudy. I'm not too yellow or too weak to shoot your ankle off." His face was grey, gaunt, infinitely tired. He touched the burn on his chin. His cheek muscles tightened.

He lay still and listened to Marge Krist talking to Max Gandara.

When she was through she went out into the kitchen. Rudy sat down, glowering sullenly at Channing. He began to tremble, a shallow nervous vibration. Channing laughed.

"How do you like crime now, kiddie? Fun, isn't it?"

Rudy gave him a lurid and prophetic direction.

Marge came back with hot water and a clean cloth. She wiped Channing's face, not touching the handkerchief. The wound had stopped bleeding, but the gash in his side was still oozing. The pad had slipped. Marge took his coat off, waiting while he changed hands with the gun, and then his shoulder clip and shirt. When she saw his body she let the shirt drop and put her hand to her mouth. Channing, sitting up now on the couch, glanced from her to Rudy's slack pale face, and said quietly,

"You see why I don't like fire."

Marge was working gently on his side when the bell rang. "That's the police," she said, and went to the front door. Channing held Rudy with the gun. He heard nothing behind him, but quite suddenly there was a cold object pressing the back of his neck and a voice said quietly,

"Drop it, bud."

It was Joe's voice. He had come in through the kitchen. Channing dropped his gun. The men coming in the front door were not policemen. They were Dave Padway and Jack Flavin.

Flavin closed the door and locked it. Channing nodded, smiling faintly. Dave Padway nodded back. He was a tall, shambling man with white eyes and a long face, like a pinto horse.

"I see I'm still a bum shot," he said.

"Ten years in the can doesn't help your eye, Dave." Channing seemed relaxed and unemotional. "Well, now we're all here we can talk. We can talk about murder."

Marge and Ruby were both staring at Padway. Flavin grinned. "My new business partner, Dave Padway. Dave, meet Marge Krist and Rudy."

Padway glanced at them briefly. His pale eyes were empty of expression. He said, in his soft way, "It's Channing that interests me right now. How much has he told, and who has he told it to?"

Channing laughed, with insolent mockery.

"Fine time to worry about that," Flavin grunted. "Who was it messed up the kill in the first place?"

Padway's eyelids drooped. "Everyone makes mistakes, Jack," he said mildly. Flavin struck a match. The flame trembled slightly.

Rudy said, "Jack. Listen, Jack, this guy says Budge Hanna and his girl were killed. Did you—"

"No. That was Dave's idea."

Padway said, "Any objections to it?"

"Hanna was a good man. He was my contact with all the bars."

"He was a bum. Him and that floozie between them were laying the whole thing in Channing's lap. I heard 'em."

"Okay, okay! I'm just sorry, that's all."

Rudy said, "Jack, honest to God, I don't want to be messed up in killing. I don't mind slugging a watchman, that's okay, and if you had to shoot it out with the cops, well, that's okay too, I guess. But murder, Jack!" He glanced at Channing's scarred body. "Murder, and things like that—" He shook.

Padway muttered, "My God, he's still in diapers."

"Take it easy, kid," Flavin said. "You're in big time now. It's worth getting sick at your stomach a couple times." He looked at Channing, grinning his hard white grin. "You were right when you said Surfside was either an end or a beginning. Dave and I both needed a place to begin again. Start small and grow, like any other business."

Channing nodded. He looked at Rudy. "Hank told you it would be like this, didn't he? You believe him now?"

Rudy repeated his suggestion. His skin was greenish. He sat down and lighted a cigarette. Marge leaned against the wall, watching with bright, narrow-lidded eyes. She was pale. She had said nothing.

Channing said, "Flavin, you were out with Marge the night Hank was killed."

"So what?"

"Did you leave her at all?"

"A couple of times. Not long enough to get out on the pier to kill your brother."

Marge said quietly, "He's right, Mr. Channing."

Channing said, "Where did you go?"

"Ship Cafe, a bunch of bars, dancing. So what?" Flavin gestured impatiently.

Channing said, "How about you, Dave? Did you kill Hank to pay for your brother, and then wait for me to come?"

"If I had," Padway said, "I'd have told you. I'd have made sure you'd come." He stepped closer, looking down. "You don't seem very surprised to see us."

"I'm not surprised at anything anymore."

"Yeah." Padway's gun came smoothly into his hand. "At this range I ought to be able to hit you, Chan." Marge Krist caught her breath sharply. Padway said, "No, not here, unless he makes me. Go ahead, Joe."

Joe got busy with the adhesive tape again. This time he did a better job. They wrapped his trussed body in a blanket. Joe picked up the feet. Flavin motioned Rudy to take hold. Rudy hesitated. Padway flicked the muzzle of his gun. Rudy picked up Channing's shoulders. They turned out the lights and carried Channing out to a waiting car. Marge and Rudy Krist walked ahead of Padway, who had forgotten to put away his gun.

3

"I Feel Bad Killin' You . . ."

The room was enormous in the flashlight beams. There were still recognizable signs of its former occupation—dust-blackened, tawdry bunting dangling ragged from the ceiling, a floor worn by the scraping of many feet, a few forgotten tables and chairs, the curling fly-specked photographs of bygone celebrities autographed to "Dear Skinny," an empty, dusty band platform.

One of Padway's men lighted a coal-oil lamp. The boarded windows were carefully reinforced with tarpaper. In one end of the ballroom were stacks of liquor cases built into a huge square mountain. Doors opened into other rooms, black and disused. The place was utterly silent, odorous with the dust and rot of years.

Padway said, "Put him over there." He indicated a camp cot beside a table and a group of chairs. The men carrying Channing dropped him there. The rest straggled in and sat down, lighting cigarettes. Padway said, "Joe, take the Thompson and go upstairs. Yell if anybody looks this way."

Jack Flavin swore briefly. "I told you we weren't tailed, Dave. Cripes, we've driven all over this goddam town to make sure. Can't you relax?"

"Sure, when I'm ready to. You may have hair on your chest, Jack, but it's no bulletproof vest." He went over to the cot and pulled the blanket off Channing. Channing looked up at him, his eyes sunk deep under hooded lids. He was naked to the waist. Padway inspected the two gashes.

"I didn't miss you by much, Chan," he said slowly.

"Enough."

"Yeah." Padway pulled a cigarette slowly out of the pack. "Who did you talk to, Chan, besides Marge Krist? What did you say?"

Channing bared his teeth. It might have been meant for a smile. It was undoubtedly malicious.

Padway put the cigarette in his mouth and got a match out. It was a large kitchen match with a blue head. "You got me puzzled, Chan. You sure have. And it worries me. I can smell copper, but I can't see any. I don't like that, Channing."

"That's tough," Channing said.

"Yeah. It may be." Padway struck the match.

Rudy Krist rose abruptly and went off into the shadows. No one else moved. Marge Krist was hunched up on a blanket near Flavin. Her eyes were brilliant green under her tumbled red hair.

Dave Padway held the match low over Channing's eyes. There was no draft, no tremor in his hand. The flame was a perfect triangle, gold and blue. Padway said somberly, "I don't trust you, Chan. You were a good cop. You were good enough to take me once, and you were good enough to take my brother, and he was a better man than me. I don't trust this setup, Chan. I don't trust you."

Flavin said impatiently, "Why didn't you for godsake kill him the first time? You're to blame for this mess, Dave. If you hadn't loused it up—okay, okay! The guy's crazy afraid of fire. Look at him now. Put it to him, Dave. He'll talk."

"Will he?" said Padway. "Will he?" He lowered the match. Channing screamed. Padway lighted his cigarette and blew out the match. "Will you talk, Chan?"

Channing said hoarsely, "Offer me the right coin, Dave. Give me the man who killed my brother, and I'll tell you where you stand."

Padway stared at him with blank light eyes, and then he began to laugh, quietly, with a terrible humor.

"Tie him down, Mack," he said, "and bring the matches over here."

The room was quiet, except for Channing's breathing. Rudy Krist sat apart from the others, smoking steadily, his hands never still. The three gunsels bent with scowling concentration over a game of blackjack. Marge Krist had not moved since she sat down. Perhaps twenty minutes had passed. Channing's corded body was spotted with small vicious marks.

Dave Padway dropped the empty matchbox. He sighed and leaned over, slapping Channing lightly on the cheek. Channing opened his eyes.

"You going to talk, Chan?"

Channing's head moved, not much, from right to left.

Jack Flavin swore. "Dave, the guy's crazy afraid of fire. If he'd had anything to tell he'd have told it." His shirt was open, the space around his feet littered with cigarette ends. His harsh terrier face had no laughter in it now. He watched Padway obliquely, his lids hooded.

"Maybe," said Padway. "Maybe not. We got a big deal on tonight, Jack. It's our first step toward the top. Channing read your receipt, remember. He knows about that. He knows a lot of people out here. Maybe he has a deal on, and maybe it isn't with the cops. Maybe it isn't supposed to break until tonight. Maybe it'll break us when it does."

Channing laughed, a dry husky mockery.

Flavin got up, scraping his chair angrily. "Listen, Dave, you getting chicken or something? Looks to me like you've got a fixation on this bird."

"Look to me, Jack, like nobody ever taught you manners."

The room became perfectly still. The men at the table put their cards down slowly, like men playing cards in a dream. Marge Krist rose silently and moved towards the cot.

Channing whispered, "Take it easy, boys. There's no percentage in a shroud." He watched them, his eyes holding a deep, cruel glint. It was something new, something born within the last quarter of an hour. It changed, subtly, his whole face, the lines of it, the shape of it. "You've got a business here, a going concern. Or maybe you haven't. Maybe you're bait for the meat wagon. I talked, boys, oh yes, I talked. Give me Hank's killer, and I'll tell you who."

Flavin said, "Can't you forget that? The guy jumped."

Channing shook his head.

Padway said softly, "Suppose you're right, Chan. Suppose you get the killer. What good does that do you?"

"I'm not a cop anymore. I don't care how much booze you run. All I want is the guy that killed Hank."

Jack Flavin laughed. It was not a nice sound.

"Dave knows I keep a promise. Besides, you can always shoot me in the back."

Flavin said, "This is crazy. You haven't really hurt the guy, Dave. Put it to him. He'll talk."

"His heart would quit first." Padway smiled almost fondly at Channing. "He's got his guts back in. That's good to know, huh, Chan?"

"Yeah."

"But bad, too. For both of us."

"Go ahead and kill me, Dave, if you think it would help any."

Flavin said, with elaborate patience, "Dave, the man is crazy. Maybe he wants publicity. Maybe he's trying to chisel himself back on the force. Maybe he's a masochist. But he's nuts. I don't believe he talked to anybody. Either make him talk, or shoot him. Or I will."

"Will you, now?" Padway asked.

Channing said, "What are you so scared of, Flavin?"

Flavin snarled and swung his hand. Padway caught it, pulling Flavin around. He said, "Seems to me whoever killed Hank has made us all a lot of trouble. He's maybe busted us wide open. I'd kind of like to know who did it, and why. We were working together then, Jack, remember? And nobody told me about any cop named Channing."

Flavin shook him off. "The kid committed suicide. And don't try manhandling me, Dave. It was my racket, remember. I let you in."

"Why," said Padway mildly, "that's so, ain't it?" He hit Flavin in the mouth so quickly that his fist made a blur in the air. Flavin fell, clawing automatically at his armpit. Padway's men rose from the table and covered him. Flavin dropped his hand. He lay still, his eyes slitted and deadly.

Marge Krist slid down silently beside Channing's cot. She might have been fainting, leaning forward against it, her hands out of sight. She was not fainting. Channing felt her working at his wrists.

Flavin said, "Rudy. Come here."

Rudy Krist came into the circle of lamplight. He looked like a small boy dreaming a nightmare and knowing he can't wake up.

Flavin said, "All right, Dave. You're boss. Go ahead and give Channing his killer." He looked at Rudy, and everybody else looked, too, except the men covering Flavin.

Rudy Krist's eyes widened, until white showed all around the green. He stopped, staring at the hard, impassive faces turned toward him.

Flavin said contemptuously, "He turned you soft, Rudy. You spilled over and then you didn't have the nerve to go through with it. You knew what would happen to you. So you shoved Hank off the pier to save your own hide."

Rudy made a stifled, catlike noise. He leaped suddenly down onto Flavin. Padway motioned to his boys to hold it. Channing cried out desperately, "Don't do anything. Wait! Dave, drag him off."

Rudy had Flavin by the throat. He was frothing slightly. Flavin writhed, jerking his heels against the floor. Suddenly there was a sharp slamming noise from underneath Rudy's body. Rudy bent his back, as though he were trying to double over backwards. He let go of Flavin. He relaxed, his head falling sleepily against Flavin's shoulder.

Channing rolled off the cot, scrambling toward Flavin.

Flavin fired again, twice, so rapidly the shots sounded like one. One of Padway's boys knelt down and bowed forward over his knees like a praying Jap. Another of Padway's men fell. The second shot clipped Padway, tearing the shoulder pad of his suit.

Channing grabbed Flavin's wrist from behind.

"Okay," said Padway grimly. "Hold it, everybody."

Before he got the words out a small sharp crack came from behind the cot. Flavin relaxed. He lay looking up into Channing's face with an expression of great surprise, as though the third eye just opened in his forehead gave him a completely new perspective.

Marge Krist stood green-eyed and deadly with a little pearl-handled revolver smoking in her hand.

Padway turned toward her slowly. Channing's mouth twitched dourly. He hardly glanced at the girl, but rolled the boy's body over carefully.

Channing said, "Did you kill Hank?"

Rudy whispered, "Honest to God, no."

"Did Flavin kill him?"

"I don't know . . ." Tears came in Rudy's eyes. "Hank," he whispered, "I wish. . . ." The tears kept running out of his eyes for several seconds after he was dead.

By that time the police had come into the room, from the dark disused doorways, from behind the stacked liquor. Max Gandara said,

"Everybody hold still."

Dave Padway put his hands up slowly, his eyes at first wide with surprise and then narrow and ice-hard. His gunboy did the same, first dropping his rod with a heavy clatter on the bare floor.

Padway said, "They've been here all the time."

Channing sat up stiffly. "I hope they were. I didn't know whether Max would play with me or not."

"You dirty double-crossing louse."

"I feel bad, crossing up an ape like you, Dave. You treated me so square, up there by Hyperion." Channing raised his voice. "Max, look out for the boy with the chopper."

Gandara said, "I had three men up there. They took him when he went up, real quiet."

Marge Krist had come like a sleepwalker around the cot. She was close to Padway. Quite suddenly she fainted. Padway caught her, so that she shielded his body, and his gun snapped into his hand.

Max Gandara said, "Don't shoot. Don't anybody shoot."

"That's sensible," said Padway softly.

Channing's hand, on the floor, slid over the gun Flavin wasn't using anymore. Then, very quickly, he threw himself forward into the table with the lamp on it.

A bullet slammed into the wood, through it, and past his ear, and then Channing fired twice, deliberately, through the flames.

Channing rose and walked past the fire. He moved stiffly, limping, but there was a difference in him. Padway was down on one knee, eyes shut and teeth clenched against the pain of a shattered wrist. Marge Krist was still standing. She was staring with stricken eyes at the hole in her white forearm and the pattern of brilliant red threads spreading from it.

Max Gandara caught Channing. "You crazy—"

Channing hit him, hard and square. His face didn't change expression. "I owe you that one, Max. And before you start preaching the sanctity of womanhood, you better pry out a couple of those slugs that just missed me. You'll find they came from Miss Krist's pretty little popgun—the same one that killed her boy friend, Jack Flavin." He went over and tilted Marge Krist's face to his, quite gently. "You came out of your faint in a hurry, didn't you, sweetheart?"

She brought up her good hand and tried to claw his eye out.

Channing laughed. He pushed her into the arms of a policeman. "It'll all come out in the wash. Meantime, there are the bullets from Marge's gun. The fact that she had a gun at all proves she was in on the gang. They'd have searched her, if all that pious stuff about poor Rudy's evil ways had been on the level. She was a little surprised about Padway and sore because Flavin had kept it from her. But she knew which was the better man, all right. She was going along with Padway, and she shot Flavin to keep his mouth shut about Hank, and to make sure he didn't get Padway by accident. Flavin was a gutty little guy, and he came close to doing just that. Marge untied me because she hoped I'd get shot in the confusion, or start trouble on my own account. If you hadn't come in, Max, she'd probably have shot me herself. She didn't want any more fussing about Hank Channing, and with me and Flavin dead she was in the clear."

Gandara said with ugly stubbornness, "Sounded to me like Flavin made a pretty good case against Rudy."

"Sure, sure. He was down on the ground with half his teeth out and three guys holding guns on him."

Marge Krist was sitting now on the cot, while somebody worked over her with a first aid kit. Channing stood in front of her.

"You've done a good night's work, Marge. You killed Rudy just as much as you did Flavin, or Hank. Rudy had decent stuff in him. You forced him into the game, but Hank was turning him soft. You killed Hank."

Channing moved closer to her. She looked up at him, her green eyes meeting his dark ones, both of them passionate and cruel.

"You're a smart girl, Marge. You and your mealy-mouthed hypocrisy. I know now what you meant when you accused Rudy of being afraid to be questioned. Flavin couldn't kill Hank by himself. He wasn't big enough, and Hank wasn't that dumb. He didn't trust Flavin. But you, Marge, sure, he trusted you. He'd stand on a dark pier at midnight and talk to you, and never notice who was sneaking up behind with a blackjack." He bent over her. "A smart girl, Marge, and a pretty one. I don't think I'll want to stand outside the window while you die."

"I wish I'd killed you, too," she whispered. "By God, I wish I'd killed you too!"

Channing nodded. He went over and sat down wearily. He looked exhausted and weak, but his eyes were alive.

"Somebody give me a cigarette," he said. He struck the match himself. The smoke tasted good.

It was his first smoke in ten years.

FREDRIC BROWN

Fredric Brown (1906–1972) was a puckish little man who remained puckish even after a night's drinking. No easy task, especially when all those around you are throwing punches or sleeping it off in a corner booth.

Something of this is found in most of his work, too. There's an irony in his fiction, a sense that he's just offstage, telling you how dangerous but amusing life is. But Brown knew that just because it might be amusing, that made life no less dangerous.

His very best work—*The Fabulous Clipjoint, The Far Cry, The Screaming Mimi, Knock Three-One-Two*—are about as good as it gets in crime fiction. In fact, they get richer and more haunting with the passing years. He was a master technician with the heart of a forlorn but wry poet. And no one wrote the surprise-ending short story better . . . not even O. Henry.

Don't Look Behind You

Just sit back and relax, now. Try to enjoy this; it's going to be the last story you ever read, or nearly the last. After you finish it you can sit there and stall awhile, you can find excuses to hang around your house, or your room, or your office, wherever you're reading this; but sooner or later you're going to have to get up and go out. That's where I'm waiting for you: outside. Or maybe closer than that. Maybe in this room.

You think that's a joke of course. You think this is just a story in a book, and that I don't really mean you. Keep right on thinking so. But be fair; admit that I'm giving you fair warning.

Harley bet me I couldn't do it. He bet me a diamond he's told me about, a diamond as big as his head. So you see why I've got to kill you. And why I've got to tell you how and why and all about it first. That's part of the bet. It's just the kind of idea Harley would have.

I'll tell you about Harley first. He's tall and handsome, and suave and cosmopolitan. He looks something like Ronald Colman, only he's taller. He dresses like a million dollars, but it wouldn't matter if he didn't; I mean that he'd look distinguished in overalls. There's a sort of magic about Harley, a mocking magic in the way he looks at you; it makes you think of palaces and far-off countries and bright music.

It was in Springfield, Ohio, that he met Justin Dean. Justin was a funny-looking little runt who was just a printer. He worked for the Atlas Printing & Engraving Company. He was a very ordinary little guy, just about as different as possible from Harley; you couldn't pick two men more different. He was only thirty-five, but he was mostly bald already, and he had to wear thick glasses because he'd worn out his eyes doing fine printing and engraving. He was a good printer and engraver; I'll say that for him.

I never asked Harley how he happened to come to Springfield, but the day he got there, after he'd checked in at the Castle Hotel, he stopped in at Atlas to have some calling cards made. It happened that Justin Dean was alone in the shop at the time, and he took Harley's order for the cards; Harley wanted engraved ones, the best. Harley always wants the best of everything.

Harley probably didn't even notice Justin; there was no reason why he should have. But Justin noticed Harley all right, and in him he saw everything that he himself would like to be, and never would be, because most of the things Harley has, you have to be born with.

And Justin made the plates for the cards himself and printed them himself, and he did a wonderful job—something he thought would be worthy of a man like Harley Prentice. That was the name engraved on the card, just that and nothing else, as all really important people have their cards engraved.

He did fine-line work on it, freehand cursive style, and used all the skill he had. It wasn't wasted, because the next day when Harley called to get the cards he held one and stared at it for a while, and then he looked at Justin, seeing him for the first time. He asked, "Who did this?"

And little Justin told him proudly who had done it, and Harley smiled at him and told him it was the work of an artist, and he asked Justin to have dinner with him that evening after work, in the Blue Room of the Castle Hotel.

That's how Harley and Justin got together, but Harley was careful. He waited until he'd known Justin awhile before he asked him whether or not he could make plates for five- and ten-dollar bills. Harley had the contacts; he could market the bills in quantity with men who specialized in passing them, and—most important—he knew where he could get paper with the silk threads in it, paper that wasn't quite the genuine thing, but was close enough to pass inspection by anyone but an expert.

So Justin quit his job at Atlas and he and Harley went to New York, and they set up a little printing shop as a blind, on Amsterdam Avenue south of Sherman Square, and they worked at the bills. Justin worked hard, harder than he had ever worked in his life, because besides working on the plates for the bills, he helped meet expenses by handling what legitimate printing work came into the shop.

He worked day and night for almost a year, making plate after plate, and each one was a little better than the last, and finally he had plates that Harley said were good enough. That night they had dinner at the Waldorf-Astoria to celebrate and after dinner they went the rounds of the best nightclubs, and it cost Harley a small fortune, but that didn't matter because they were going to get rich.

They drank champagne, and it was the first time Justin ever drank champagne and he got disgustingly drunk and must have made quite a fool of himself. Harley told him about it afterward, but Harley wasn't mad at him. He took him back to his room at the hotel and put him to bed, and Justin was pretty sick for a couple of days. But that didn't matter, either, because they were going to get rich.

Then Justin started printing bills from the plates, and they got rich. After that, Justin didn't have to work so hard, either, because he turned down most jobs that came into the print shop, told them he was behind schedule and couldn't handle any more. He took just a little work, to keep up a front. And behind the front, he made five- and ten-dollar bills, and he and Harley got rich.

He got to know other people whom Harley knew. He met Bull Mallon, who handled the distribution end. Bull Mallon was built like a bull, that was why they called him that. He had a face that never smiled or changed expression at all except when he was holding burning matches to the soles of Justin's bare feet. But that wasn't then; that was later, when he wanted Justin to tell him where the plates were.

And he got to know Captain John Willys of the police department, who was a friend of Harley's, to whom Harley gave quite a bit of the money they made, but that didn't matter either, because there was plenty left and they all got rich. He met a friend of Harley's who was a big star of the stage, and one who owned a big New York newspaper. He got to know other people equally important, but in less respectable ways.

Harley, Justin knew, had a hand in lots of other enterprises besides the little mint on Amsterdam Avenue. Some of these ventures took him out of town, usually over weekends. And the weekend that Harley was murdered Justin never found out what really happened, except that Harley went away and didn't come back. Oh, he knew that he was murdered, all right, because the police found his body—with three bullet holes in his chest—in the most expensive suite of the best hotel in Albany. Even for a place to be found dead in Harley Prentice had chosen the best.

All Justin ever knew about it was that a long-distance call came to him at the hotel where he was staying, the night that Harley was murdered—it must have been a matter of minutes, in fact, before the time the newspapers said Harley was killed.

It was Harley's voice on the phone, and his voice was debonair and unexcited as ever. But he said, "Justin? Get to the shop and get rid of the plates, the paper, everything. Right away. I'll explain when I see you." He waited only until Justin said, "Sure, Harley," and then he said, "Attaboy" and hung up.

Justin hurried around to the printing shop and got the plates and the paper and a few thousand dollars' worth of counterfeit bills that were on hand. He made the paper and bills into one bundle and the copper plates into another, smaller one, and he left the shop with no evidence that it had ever been a mint in miniature.

He was very careful and very clever in disposing of both bundles. He got rid of the big one first by checking in at a big hotel, not one he or Harley ever stayed at, under a false name, just to have a chance to put the big bundle in the incinerator there. It was paper and it would burn. And he made sure there was a fire in the incinerator before he dropped it down the chute.

The plates were different. They wouldn't burn, he knew, so he took a trip to Staten Island and back on the ferry and, somewhere out in the middle of the bay, he dropped the bundle over the side into the water.

Then, having done what Harley had told him to do, and having done it well and thoroughly, he went back to the hotel—his own hotel, not the one where he had dumped the paper and the bills—and went to sleep.

In the morning he read in the newspapers that Harley had been killed, and he was stunned. It didn't seem possible. He couldn't believe it; it was a joke someone was playing on him. Harley would come back to him, he knew. And he was right; Harley did, but that was later, in the swamp.

But anyway, Justin had to know, so he took the very next train for Albany. He must have been on the train when the police went to his hotel, and at the hotel they must have learned he'd asked at the desk about trains for Albany, because they were waiting for him when he got off the train there.

They took him to a station and they kept him there a long, long time, days and days, asking him questions. They found out, after a while, that he couldn't have killed Harley because he'd been in New York City at the time Harley was killed in Albany but they knew, also, that he and Harley had been operating the little mint, and they thought that might be a lead to who killed Harley, and they were interested in the counterfeiting, too, maybe even more than in the murder. They asked Justin Dean questions, over and over and over, and he couldn't answer them, so he didn't. They kept him awake for days at a time, asking him questions over and over. Most of all they wanted to know where the plates were. He wished he could tell them that the plates were safe where nobody could ever get them again, but he couldn't tell them that without admitting that he and Harley had been counterfeiting, so he couldn't tell them.

They located the Amsterdam shop, but they didn't find any evidence there, and they really had no evidence to hold Justin on at all, but he didn't know that, and it never occurred to him to get a lawyer.

He kept wanting to see Harley, and they wouldn't let him; then, when they learned he really didn't believe Harley could be dead, they made him look at a dead man they said was Harley, and he guessed it was, although Harley looked different dead. He didn't look magnificent, dead. And Justin believed, then, but still didn't believe. And after that he just went silent and wouldn't say a word, even when they kept him awake for days and days with a bright light in his eyes, and kept slapping him to keep him awake. They didn't use clubs or rubber hoses, but they slapped him a million times and wouldn't let him sleep. And after a while he lost track of things and couldn't have answered their questions even if he'd wanted to.

For a while after that, he was in a bed in a white room, and all he remembers about that are nightmares he had, and calling for Harley and an awful confusion as to whether Harley was dead or not, and then things came back to him gradually and he knew he didn't want to stay in the white room; he wanted to get out so he could hunt for Harley. And if Harley was dead, he wanted to kill whoever had killed Harley, because Harley would have done the same for him.

So he began pretending, and acting, very cleverly, the way the doctors and nurses seemed to want him to act, and after a while they gave him his clothes and let him go.

He was becoming cleverer now. He thought, "What would Harley tell me to do?" And he knew they'd try to follow him because they'd think he might lead them to the plates, which they didn't know were at the bottom of the bay, and he gave them the slip before he left Albany, and he went first to Boston, and from there by boat to New York, instead of going direct.

He went first to the print shop, and went in the back way after watching the alley for a long time to be sure the place wasn't guarded. It was a mess; they must have searched it very thoroughly for the plates.

Harley wasn't there, of course. Justin left and from a phone booth in a drugstore, he telephoned their hotel and asked for Harley and was told Harley no longer lived there; and to be clever and not let them guess who he was, he asked for Justin Dean, and they said Justin Dean didn't live there anymore either.

Then he moved to a different drugstore and from there he decided to call up some friends of Harley's, and he phoned Bull Mallon first and because Bull was a friend, he told him who he was and asked if he knew where Harley was.

Bull Mallon didn't pay any attention to that; he sounded excited, a little, and he asked, "Did the cops get the plates, Dean?" and Justin said they didn't, that he wouldn't tell them, and he asked again about Harley.

Bull asked, "Are you nuts, or kidding?" And Justin just asked him again, and Bull's voice changed and he said, "Where are you?" and Justin told him. Bull said, "Harley's here. He's staying under cover, but it's all right if you know, Dean. You wait right there at the drugstore, and we'll come and get you."

They came and got Justin, Bull Mallon and two other men in a car, and they told him Harley was hiding out way deep in New Jersey and that they were going to drive there now. So he went along and sat in the back seat between two men he didn't know, while Bull Mallon drove.

It was late afternoon then, when they picked him up, and Bull drove all evening and most of the night and he drove fast, so he must have gone farther than New Jersey, at least into Virginia or maybe farther, into the Carolinas.

The sky was getting faintly gray with first dawn when they stopped at a rustic cabin that looked like it had been used as a hunting lodge. It was miles from anywhere, there wasn't even a road leading to it, just a trail that was level enough for the car to be able to make it.

They took Justin into the cabin and tied him to a chair, and they told him Harley wasn't there, but Harley had told them that Justin would tell them where the plates were, and he couldn't leave until he did tell.

Justin didn't believe them; he knew then that they'd tricked him about Harley, but it didn't matter, as far as the plates were concerned. It didn't matter if he told them what he'd done with the plates, because they couldn't get them again, and they wouldn't tell the police. So he told them, quite willingly.

But they didn't believe him. They said he'd hidden the plates and was lying. They tortured him to make him tell. They beat him, and they cut him with knives, and they held burning matches and lighted cigars to the soles of his feet, and they pushed needles under his fingernails. Then they'd rest and ask him questions and if he could talk, he'd tell them the truth, and after a while they'd start to torture him again.

It went on for days and weeks—Justin doesn't know how long, but it was a long time. Once they went away for several days and left him tied up with nothing to eat or drink. They came back and started in all over again. And all the time he hoped Harley would come to help him, but Harley didn't come, not then.

After a while what was happening in the cabin ended, or anyway he didn't know any more about it. They must have thought he was dead; maybe they were right, or anyway not far from wrong.

The next thing he knows was the swamp. He was lying in shallow water at the edge of deeper water. His face was out of the water; it woke him when he turned a little and his face went under. They must have thought him dead and thrown him into the water, but he had floated into the shallow part before he had drowned, and a last flicker of consciousness had turned him over on his back with his face out.

I don't remember much about Justin in the swamp; it was a long time, but I just remember flashes of it. I couldn't move at first; I just lay there in the shallow water with my face out. It got dark and it got cold, I remember, and finally my arms would move a little and I got farther out of the water, lying in the mud with only my feet in the water. I slept or was unconscious again and when I woke up it was getting gray dawn, and that was when Harley came. I think I'd been calling him, and he must have heard.

He stood there, dressed as immaculately and perfectly as ever, right in the swamp, and he was laughing at me for being so weak and lying there like a log, half in the dirty water and half in the mud, and I got up and nothing hurt anymore.

We shook hands and he said, "Come on, Justin, let's get you out of here," and I was so glad he'd come that I cried a little. He laughed at me for that and said I should lean on him and he'd help me walk, but I wouldn't do that, because I was coated with mud and filth of the swamp and he was so clean and perfect in a white linen suit, like an ad in a magazine. And all the way out of that swamp, all the days and nights we spent there, he never even got mud on his trouser cuffs, nor his hair mussed.

I told him just to lead the way, and he did, walking just ahead of me, sometimes turning around, laughing and talking to me and cheering me up. Sometimes I'd fall but I wouldn't let him come back and help me. But he'd wait patiently until I could get up. Sometimes I'd crawl instead when I couldn't stand up anymore. Sometimes I'd have to swim streams that he'd leap lightly across.

And it was day and night and day and night, and sometimes I'd sleep, and things would crawl across me. And some of them I caught and ate, or maybe I dreamed that. I remember other things, in that swamp, like an organ that played a lot of the time, and sometimes angels in the air and devils in the water, but those were delirium, I guess.

Harley would say, "A little farther, Justin; we'll make it. And we'll get back at them, at all of them."

And we made it. We came to dry fields, cultivated fields with waist-high corn, but there weren't ears on the corn for me to eat. And then there was a stream, a clear stream that wasn't stinking water like the swamp, and Harley told me to wash myself and my clothes and I did, although I wanted to hurry on to where I could get food.

I still looked pretty bad; my clothes were clean of mud and filth but they were mere rags and wet, because I couldn't wait for them to dry, and I had a ragged beard and I was barefoot.

But we went on and came to a little farm building, just a two-room shack, and there was a smell of fresh bread just out of an oven, and I ran the last few yards to knock on the door. A woman, an ugly woman, opened the door and when she saw me she slammed it again before I could say a word.

Strength came to me from somewhere, maybe from Harley, although I can't remember him being there just then. There was a pile of kindling logs beside the door. I picked one of them up as though it were no heavier than a broomstick, and I broke down the door and killed the woman. She screamed a lot, but I killed her. Then I ate the hot fresh bread.

I watched from the window as I ate, and saw a man running across the field toward the house. I found a knife, and I killed him as he came in at the door. It was much better, killing with the knife; I liked it that way.

I ate more bread, and kept watching from all the windows, but no one else came. Then my stomach hurt from the hot bread I'd eaten and I had to lie down, doubled up, and when the hurting quit, I slept.

Harley woke me up, and it was dark. He said, "Let's get going; you should be far away from here before it's daylight."

I knew he was right, but I didn't hurry away. I was becoming, as you see, very clever now. I knew there were things to do first. I found matches and a lamp, and lighted the lamp. Then I hunted through the shack for everything I could use. I found clothes of the man, and they fitted me not too badly except that I had to turn up the cuffs of the trousers and the shirt. His shoes were big, but that was good because my feet were so swollen.

I found a razor and shaved; it took a long time because my hand wasn't steady, but I was very careful and didn't cut myself much.

I had to hunt hardest for their money, but I found it finally. It was sixty dollars.

And I took the knife, after I had sharpened it. It isn't fancy; just a bone-handled carving knife, but it's good steel. I'll show it to you, pretty soon now. It's had a lot of use.

Then we left and it was Harley who told me to stay away from the roads, and find railroad tracks. That was easy because we heard a train whistle far off in the night and knew which direction the tracks lay. From then on, with Harley helping, it's been easy.

You won't need the details from here. I mean, about the brakeman, and about the tramp we found asleep in the empty reefer, and about the near thing I had with the police in Richmond. I learned from that; I learned I mustn't talk to Harley when anybody else was around to hear. He hides himself from them; he's got a trick and they don't know he's there, and they think I'm funny in the head if I talk to him. But in Richmond I bought better clothes and got a haircut and a man I killed in an alley had forty dollars on him, so I had money again. I've done a lot of traveling since then. If you stop to think you'll know where I am right now.

I'm looking for Bull Mallon and the two men who helped him. Their names are Harry and Carl. I'm going to kill them when I find them. Harley keeps telling me that those fellows are big time and that I'm not ready for them yet. But I can be looking while I'm getting ready so I keep moving around. Sometimes I stay in one place long enough to hold a job as a printer for a while. I've learned a lot of things. I can hold a job and people don't think I'm too strange; they don't get scared when I look at them like they sometimes did a few months ago. And I've learned not to talk to Harley except in our own room and then only very quietly so people in the next room won't think I'm talking to myself.

And I've kept in practice with the knife. I've killed lots of people with it, mostly on the streets at night. Sometimes because they look like they might have money on them, but mostly just for practice and because I've come to like doing it. I'm really good with the knife by now. You'll hardly feel it.

But Harley tells me that kind of killing is easy and that it's something else to kill a person who's on guard, as Bull and Harry and Carl will be.

And that's the conversation that led to the bet I mentioned. I told Harley that I'd bet him that, right now, I could warn a man I was going to use the knife on him and even tell him why and approximately when, and that I could still kill him. And he bet me that I couldn't and he's going to lose that bet.

He's going to lose it because I'm warning you right now and you're not going to believe me. I'm betting that you're going to believe that this is just another story in a book. That you won't believe that this is the *only* copy of this book that contains this story and that this story is true. Even when I tell you how it was done, I don't think you'll really believe me.

You see I'm putting it over on Harley, winning the bet, by putting it over on you. He never thought, and you won't realize, how easy it is for a good printer, who's been a counterfeiter too, to counterfeit one story in a book. Nothing like as hard as counterfeiting a five-dollar bill.

I had to pick a book of short stories and I picked this one because I happened to notice that the last story in the book was titled "Don't Look Behind You" and that was going to be a good title for this. You'll see what I mean in a few minutes.

I'm lucky that the printing shop I'm working for now does book work and had a typeface that matches the rest of this book. I had a little trouble matching the paper exactly, but I finally did and I've got it ready while I'm writing this. I'm writing this directly on a Linotype, late at night in the shop where I'm working days. I even have the boss's permission, told him I was going to set up and print a story that a friend of mine had written, as a surprise for him, and that I'd melt the type metal back as soon as I'd printed one good copy.

When I finished writing this I'll make up the type in pages to match the rest of the book and I'll print it on the matching paper I have ready. I'll cut the new pages to fit and bind them in; you won't be able to tell the difference, even if a faint suspicion may cause you to look at it. Don't forget I made five- and ten-dollar bills you couldn't have told from the original, and this is kindergarten stuff compared to that job. And I've done enough bookbinding that I'll be able to take the last story out of the book and bind this one in instead of it and you won't be able to tell the difference no matter how closely you look. I'm going to do a perfect job of it if it takes me all night.

And tomorrow I'll go to some bookstore, or maybe a newsstand or even a drugstore that sells books and has other copies of this book, ordinary copies, and I'll plant this one there. I'll find myself a good place to watch from, and I'll be watching when you buy it.

The rest I can't tell you yet because it depends a lot on circumstances, whether you went right home with the book or what you did. I won't know till I follow you and keep watch till you read it—and I see that you're reading the last story in the book.

If you're home while you're reading this, maybe I'm in the house with you right now. Maybe I'm in this very room, hidden, waiting for you to finish the story. Maybe I'm watching through a window. Or maybe I'm sitting near you on the streetcar or train, if you're reading it there. Maybe I'm on the fire escape outside your hotel room. But wherever you're reading it, I'm near you, watching and waiting for you to finish. You can count on that.

You're pretty near the end now. You'll be finished in seconds and you'll close the book, still not believing. Or, if you haven't read the stories in order, maybe you'll turn back to start another story. If you do, you'll never finish it.

But don't look around; you'll be happier if you don't know, if you don't see the knife coming. When I kill people from behind they don't seem to mind so much.

Go on, just a few seconds or minutes, thinking this is just another story. Don't look behind you. Don't believe this—*until you feel the knife.*

WILLIAM P. MCGIVERN

Never bet on whose work will survive beyond the grave.

Few writers in the fifties were as fashionable as William P. McGivern (1922–1982). Anthony Boucher compared him favorably to Graham Greene. At least two of his books, including *The Big Heat* and *Odds Against Tomorrow*, were filmed and appear regularly on movie cable channels today. *Odds* may just be the single best suspense novel of its decade. It is as lacerating today as it was upon first publication.

So what happened? Only one McGivern novel is in print. He is rarely mentioned in discussion of fifties crime fiction. He's gone.

One hopes this won't always be the case. His work deserves to be brought back, and with real fanfare, for new generations to read and appreciate.

Death Comes Gift-Wrapped

Sergeant Burt Moran was a tall man with hard flat features and eyes that were cold and dull, like those of a snake. He was that comparatively rare thing among cops, a man equally hated by crooks and by his fellow officers. Operators on both sides of the law forgot their differences and came to agreement on one point at least: that Moran was a heel by any or all standards.

Moran was a bully who shook down petty crooks for a few bucks whenever he got the chance. But he left the big boys alone. He lacked the imagination to serve them and, consequently, he never got in on the important payoff. There would have been some dignity in being a big grafter, but Moran grubbed for his few extra dollars the hard way, the cheap way, the way that earned him nothing else but contempt.

There was a streak of savage brutality in him that caused the underworld to mingle their contempt with a certain fear. Moran had killed six men in the line of duty, three of whom were unarmed at the time, and another who had died after Moran had worked him over with a sap for fourteen hours. The story of the men he'd killed wasn't told because a corpse is an unsatisfactory witness. Moran knew this. He knew all about killing.

Now, at two o'clock in the morning, in the cheap room of a cheap hotel, Moran was going to learn about murder. He had to commit a murder because of something new in his life, something that he had always sneered at in the lives of other men.

Moran was in love. And he had learned that love, like anything else, costs money.

He stood just inside the doorway of the room and watched the scrawny, thin-faced man who was staring at him from the bed. The man was Dinny Nelson, a small-time bookie who, Moran knew, carried all his assets in a hip wallet.

Dinny brushed a hand over his sleep-dulled features and said, "What's the pitch, Moran? You got no right busting in here."

Moran drew his gun and leveled it at Dinny. He knew what would happen with crystal clarity, not only to Dinny and the portions of his body hit by the heavy slugs, but after that, to Dinny's corpse, to the police department and to himself, Moran. It was an old story to him. He had killed six men in the line of duty and he knew the way everything worked. No one would doubt his story.

Dinny saw his fate in Moran's face. He began to beg in a cracked voice. "No, no, you can't," he said. "There's no reason to kill me—I ain't done nothing. Don't."

Moran fired three shots and they were very loud in the small, thin-walled room. Dinny's body jack-knifed with the impact of the slugs, rolled from the bed to the floor. He didn't live long. Moran watched expressionlessly as Dinny's limbs twisted spasmodically, then became rigid and still. Underneath Dinny's body the roses in the faded pattern of the rug bloomed again, bright and scarlet.

There was two thousand, three hundred and thirty dollars in Dinny's wallet. Moran left thirty. The money made a comfortable bulge against his leg as he sauntered to the phone . . .

While the coroner did his work and two lab technicians went over the room, Moran told his story to Lieutenant Bill Pickerton, his immediate superior at Homicide.

"Tonight I seen him taking bets in the lobby," Moran said. "This was eleven. I started across to him but he seen me and ducked into the bar and then out to the street. So I drifted away. Around two I came back, came right up here to his room. I told him to get dressed but the fool went for me. I had to shoot him."

Lieutenant Pickerton rubbed his long jaw. "This stinks worse than your usual stuff, Moran. You could have handled him with your fists. He doesn't have a gun."

Moran shrugged. "Why should I risk getting beat over the head with a chair or something?"

Pickerton looked at him with active dislike. "Okay, turn in a written report tomorrow morning. The old man won't like this, you know."

"To hell with the old man," Moran said. "He wants us to bring 'em in with a butterfly net, I suppose."

"All right," Pickerton said. He paid no more attention to Moran, but studied the body and the room with alert, careful eyes.

Downstairs, Moran hailed a cab and gave the driver the address of the Diamond Club. He stared out the window at the dark streets of the Loop, his impassive face hiding the mirth inside him.

When Moran had realized that a night club singer couldn't be impressed by a cop's salary, he had looked around in his dull, unimaginative fashion for a way to get some money. Nothing had occurred to him for quite a while. Then the idea came, the idea that a cop could literally get away with murder.

After he got that much, the rest was easy. He had picked Dinny because he wasn't big-time, but big enough as far as money went. Now it was all over and he had the money. There would be a routine investigation of course, but there was no one to come forward with Dinny's version of what had happened. Therefore, the department would have to accept Moran's story. They might raise hell with him, threaten him some, but that didn't matter.

Moran's hand touched the unfamiliar bulge of money in his pocket and a rare smile touched the corner of his mouth. It didn't matter at all.

He paid off the driver in front of the Diamond Club on Randolph Street and walked past the headwaiter with a familiar smile. The headwaiter smiled cordially, for Moran's visits to the club had been frequent over the past two months, dating from the time Cherry Angela had joined the show.

Moran found a corner table and watched the girl singing at the mike. This was Cherry Angela. The blue spot molded her silver evening dress to her slim, pliant body, revealing all the curving outlines. She wore her platinum hair loose, falling in soft waves to her shoulders, and her eyes and features were mocking as she sang an old, old story about a man and a woman.

Moran forgot everything watching the girl. And there was an expression of sullen hunger on his face.

She came to his table after the number and sat down with lithe grace. "Hi, copper," she said, and her voice was amused. "Like my song?"

"I liked it," Moran said.

Her lean face was mocking. "I should do a black-flip from sheer happiness, I suppose. Would a beer strain your budget?"

"Go ahead," Moran said, flushing. "I've spent plenty on you, baby."

"You tired of it?" she said lightly.

Moran put his hands under the table so she wouldn't see their trembling. She was in his blood like nothing else had ever been in his life. But he got nothing from her but mockery, or sarcasm that shriveled him up inside.

He knew that she let him hang around for laughs, enjoying the spectacle of a forty-year-old flatfoot behaving like an adolescent before her charms. For just a second then he wanted to tell her what he had done tonight, and about the money in his pocket. He wanted to see her expression change, wanted to see respect for him in her eyes.

But he resisted that impulse. Fools bragged. And got caught. Moran wasn't getting caught.

Some day he'd have her where he wanted. Helpless, crawling. That was what he wanted. It was a strange kind of love that had driven Moran to murder.

He took her home that night but she left him at the doorway of her apartment. Sometimes, if he'd spent a lot of money, she let him come up for a nightcap, but tonight she was tired.

Leaving her, Moran walked the five miles to his own apartment, hoping to tire himself out so that he could sleep without tormenting himself with visions of what she might be doing, or who she might be with.

But once in bed, he knew the walk hadn't helped. He was wide awake and strangely nervous. After half an hour of tossing he sat up and snapped on the bed lamp. It was five-thirty in the morning, and he had a report to make on the murder in about four hours. He needed sleep, he needed to be rested when he told his story, and thinking about that made sleep impossible.

He picked the evening paper from the floor, glanced over the news. There was a murder on page one, not his, but somebody else's. He thought about his murder then and realized with a slight shock of fear that it had been on his mind all the time. It was the thing keeping him from sleep. Not Cherry Angela.

He frowned and stared out the window at the gray dawn. What was his trouble? This killing tonight was just like the others. And they hadn't bothered him. There must be a difference somewhere, he decided. It came to him after a while. The others had been killings. This one was murder. And the difference was that murder made you think.

Moran lay back in the bed, but he didn't go to sleep. He kept thinking.

At ten after eleven Moran had finished his report. He read it over twice, frowning with concentration, then took it down to Lieutenant Bill Pickerton's office.

There was someone with Pickerton, a young man with mild eyes and neatly combed hair. He was sitting beside Pickerton's desk, and the two men were talking baseball.

Pickerton nodded to Moran, said, "This is Don Linton from the commissioner's office, Moran."

Moran shook hands with Linton and put his report before Pickerton. Pickerton handed it to Linton. Linton said, "Excuse me," put on rimless glasses and bent his head to the report.

Moran lit a cigarette and dropped the match in Pickerton's ashtray. He guessed that Linton was here to look into the Dinny Nelson killing. His eyes were hot from his sleepless night and he was irritable.

"Is that all you want?" he asked Pickerton.

Linton answered. He said, "No. I've got a few questions. Have a chair, Sergeant."

Pickerton remained silent.

Moran sat down, trying to control the heavy pounding of his heart. They had nothing on him. It was his word, the word of a cop, and it was the only word they'd get.

"Okay, this seems clear," Linton said. He put his glasses away, studied Moran directly. "I'm from the commissioner's office, Moran. The commissioner wants me to ascertain that the shooting of Dinny Nelson was justified. Let's start with this. You're a homicide sergeant, assigned to roving duty in the Loop. Why did you make it your business to go to Nelson's room to arrest him on a gambling charge?"

Moran was ready for that one. He explained that he'd seen Dinny taking bets in the hotel lobby, that it seemed a pretty flagrant violation, so he'd decided to pick him up, even though it wasn't his beat.

Moran's voice was steady as he talked. All of this was true. He *had* seen Dinny taking a bet, had tried to pick him up, and Dinny had given him the slip. On that ground Moran felt confident.

"Okay," Linton said casually. "Now according to our information Dinny Nelson usually carried a sizeable amount of cash with him. But there was just thirty dollars on his body after you shot him. Got any ideas about that, Sergeant?"

"No," Moran said.

There was silence. Pickerton and Linton exchanged a glance. Then Linton put his fingertips together precisely and looked at Moran. "Did you leave the hotel room at any time after the shooting? I mean did you step out and leave the body alone?"

"No," Moran said. He wondered what Linton was getting at.

"You see, there was a bellhop on the floor at the time. He had brought some aspirin up to a woman. He has a record for theft and it occurred to us that if you left the room for any length of time, he might have slipped in, stolen the money and left before you returned."

"I didn't leave the room," Moran said. He felt scared. They might be telling the truth, but he doubted it. They were setting a trap, leaving an opening for him to dive into. A man guilty and scared would grab any out. Moran wet his lips and kept quiet. Crooks who got caught got scared. They started lying, blundered, and hung themselves talking. That wouldn't happen to him. They had his story.

Linton asked him then why he hadn't subdued Dinny with his fists. That was better. That was the sort of stuff he expected. Half an hour later Linton said he had enough, and Moran walked to the door. He was sweating. He was glad to get out. Linton might look like a law student, but his mind was sharp, strong like a trap.

As he reached the door, Linton said, "By the way, you know Cherry Angela, don't you?"

Moran's hand froze on the knob. He turned and his body was stiff and tense. "Yeah," he said. His voice wasn't steady.

Linton looked pleasantly interested, that was all. "I've heard her sing," he said. "And I heard you were a friend of hers." He said nothing else, volunteered no other information, but continued to watch Moran with a polite expression.

Moran stood uncertainly for a moment, then nodded quickly to the two men and went to the elevators. Waiting for a car, he wondered how Linton knew he was a friend of Cherry's. They must already have done some checking into his activities. Moran lit a cigarette and wasn't surprised to notice that his fingers were trembling . . .

That day was hell. He couldn't sleep, and food tasted like sawdust. Also, he kept thinking, turning everything over in his mind a thousand times. That made him tense and jumpy.

That night Moran went to the Diamond Club for Cherry's early show. When he walked through the archway he saw her sitting at a corner table with a man. There was a champagne bottle beside them in an ice bucket and they were talking very seriously. Moran felt a bitter anger and unconsciously his hands balled into fists.

He started toward their table, moving deliberately. This is the time for a show-down, he thought. I'll chase that punk out of here and have it out with her.

Then he recognized the young man with her, and the shock of that recognition sent a cold tremor through his body.

It was Linton, the investigator from the commissioner's office.

Moran's face felt hot and stiff. He turned clumsily, hoping they hadn't seen him, and went back across the room, forcing himself to walk casually.

But splintered thoughts were flicking into his mind with frightening intensity. What was Linton doing here? What was Cherry telling him? More important, what was Linton asking her?

Ignoring the headwaiter's puzzled smile, Moran hurried out of the club. He walked a block quickly before his heart stopped hammering and he was able to think. He knew he had behaved foolishly. He should have gone to her table, said hello and sat down. Any change in his normal routine would look suspicious now.

Lighting a cigarette, he realized that he must see Cherry tonight, find out what Linton had been after. He retraced his steps until he came to a doorway about fifty feet from the entrance of the Diamond Club. There he stopped and prepared to wait. For he had to be sure that Linton was gone before going in to see Cherry.

It was a long wait.

The last show ended, noisy customers streamed out, but still Linton had not appeared. Moran's throat was dry from too many cigarettes, and his eyes burned from lack of sleep. But he waited, a deep shadow in the doorway.

Then Linton appeared and Moran cursed bitterly under his breath. For Cherry was with him, bundled up in furs and chattering so that her voice carried along the street to him.

The doorman went out in the street to hail them a cab. There were plenty of cabs out and that was a break. Linton and Cherry climbed into one, and Moran hurried down the block from the club and caught the next cruiser. He told the driver to follow Linton's cab and it led them to Cherry's apartment.

Moran ordered his driver to stop half a block away. He watched while Cherry and Linton got out and went into her building. But their cab waited and in a few seconds Linton appeared again and drove away.

Moran let out a relieved sigh. He paid off his cab and walked slowly along the darkened street until he came abreast of Cherry's entrance. For a second he hesitated, wetting his lower lip uncertainly. It was stupid for him to barge in on Cherry now. It would look as if he were afraid, guilty.

But he felt he had to know what Linton had wanted. That was the only way he could release the tight, aching feeling in his stomach. He made up his mind and turned into her entrance.

She opened the door in answer to his knock, her eyes widening with surprise. "Well, it's a small world," she said. "I just left one of your buddies."

"I know," Moran said, and stepped inside. She had changed into a green robe and as she turned he saw the flash of her legs, slim, smooth and bare. But they didn't distract him now.

"What did he want?" he said watching her closely.

"The copper?" She shrugged and went to a table for a cigarette. "What does any copper want? Information."

He walked to her side and suddenly all the twisted feeling he had for her crystalized to hatred. She was so cool, so bored and indifferent, while he was ready to crack in pieces from the pressure inside him.

Raising his thick hand he struck the cigarette from her mouth with brutal force. She staggered, face whitening with shock and anger. But he caught her shoulders and jerked her close to him.

"Now," he said, in a low hard voice. "You talk, baby. What did that guy want?"

"You're hurting me," she said, breathing angrily. "He wanted to know about you. Now let me go."

"What did you tell him?" he asked hoarsely.

She turned from him and sat down on the couch. "I didn't tell him anything," she said, rubbing her bruised shoulders. "Now you can get the hell out of here. No guy pushes me around, Moran."

"Forget that," Moran said. "I didn't mean to get rough. But I'm in a jam, baby. I had to shoot a guy last night and the old women in the commissioner's office are on my tail. They're trying to frame me, and that's why that guy Linton was snooping around you."

Cherry's lean face was interested. She said, "Did you kill the guy, Moran?"

"I shot him. He went for me and I shot him, that's all."

"Oh," she said. She smiled. "You wouldn't do anything original, I guess. Nothing that might put an extra buck in your pocket."

"I get along on my pay," Moran said.

"And your friends have to, too," she said. "That's why you haven't got any, I suppose."

"I didn't get anything out of shooting the guy," Moran said. That was smart. Not talking, not bragging. Guys talked to dames, then the dames talked. That wasn't for Moran.

Cherry grinned ruefully and leaned back against the fat pillows on the couch. There was one light in the room, a lamp on an end table that caught lights in her loose blonde hair and accentuated the soft curves of her body. Yawning, she put her legs onto the couch. The green robe parted revealing her slim calves in the soft light. She didn't seem to notice.

She was smiling, but there was a hard light in her eyes. "Tell me, Moran," she said, "how does it feel to kill a man?"

Moran swallowed heavily. He couldn't wrench his eyes from her long bare legs, or stop the sudden drumming in his temples.

When he spoke, his voice was dry. "It's like anything else you do, like smoking a cigarette or buying a paper, that's all."

She sighed. "You're such a clod, Moran. You're like a big heap of dough that's turning sour."

He came closer to her. "I could be different with you," he said. "You drive me crazy, baby."

She laughed with real amusement. "In the Casanova role you're a riot."

"Damn you," he said hoarsely.

She laughed again and sat up, putting her feet on the floor. "Let's break this up," she said. "You're a jerk and always will be, Moran. I might have liked you a little if you were smart, or if you had a spare buck to spend on a girl, but as you stand you're hopeless. So beat it, will you? And stop hanging around the club."

"Now wait," Moran said. His anger broke, melted away. "You don't mean that. I'll go, but let me see you again."

Her voice was hard. "No. You're all through. Beat it."

Moran stood beside her, reached for her hand. "What would you think if I was smart, if I did have a little dough?"

"I don't want to play twenty questions," she said coldly.

"This is no gag," he said. When he saw interest in her face, he slid on the couch beside her and began speaking rapidly, the words spilling out in a rush. "I got a little dough," he said. "I got it from Dinny Nelson last night. He was the guy I shot. I blew him out like a candle, then took his bundle. It's all yours, baby, for anything you want. But we got to play it quiet until I get a clean bill from the commissioner's office. You see that, don't you?"

"Are you on the stuff?" she said. "Is this story coming out of a pipe?"

"No, no it's on the level," he said. "I did it for you, baby. I shot hell out of him and got the dough. And I'm in the clear."

"Let's see the dough," she said skeptically.

He took the roll from his pocket. He had kept it on him because there was no safer place. Now he spread it in her lap and watched her face. She fingered the money gently and gradually a little smile pulled at her lips. "I might change my ideas about you," she said at last.

"Sure you will," Moran said eagerly. "I'm okay, baby. You'll see."

"I kind of want to find out," she said, grinning at him. "Want to excuse baby a minute?"

He watched her as she walked to the bedroom door. Something tightened in him as he saw the way her shoulders tapered gracefully to her slender waist, and the way her hips moved under the silken robe. She turned at the doorway and winked at him, and he saw the gleam of her long legs before she disappeared.

It was worth it, Moran thought exultantly. He felt happy for the first time since the murder. This was going to make it all right, and the tight ache inside him melted away and he knew it was gone for good.

He lit a cigarette and leaned back against the cushions, closing his eyes. Linton could go to hell, and so could Pickerton. They had nothing on him, now or ever.

He opened his eyes when he heard the click of the doorknob. Straightening up, he crushed out a cigarette and got to his feet, a grin on his face.

The bedroom swung open and Moran's heart lurched sickeningly.

Lieutenant Pickerton walked into the room, a gun in his hand. The gun was pointed at Moran's stomach.

"You're all through," he said.

Moran stood still, the grin pasted on his face, his mind frozen in the paralysis of panic. He tried to speak but no words came out, and the noise he made was like the grunt of an animal.

There was the sound of a key in the front door and then Linton came in, gun in hand.

He glanced at Pickerton. "You get it all?"

"The works," Pickerton nodded.

Linton came to Moran's side, deftly slipped the gun from his shoulder holster. "You're under arrest for the murder of Dinny Nelson," he said formally. "Anything you say may be used against you. As you know," he added dryly.

"Yeah, I know," Moran said numbly. Linton's words, the old familiar words, released him from paralysis.

Cherry appeared in the bedroom doorway, stepped around Pickerton and entered the room. She picked up a cigarette and smiled. Her fingers moved to the mark on her cheek where he had struck her.

Then she looked at Moran. "They wanted me to get you to talk," she said. "I wasn't going to, because I'm no informer. I might have warned you that Pickerton was hiding in the bedroom, but after you hit me, I had to pay you back."

"That was just one of the stupid things you did," Pickerton said. He shook his head disgustedly. "What made you think you were smart enough to get away with murder? Your speed is the little stuff, Moran."

Moran wet his lips. "What did I do wrong?" he asked. He didn't know what was happening to him but he felt weak and drained.

Pickerton glanced at Linton. "You tell him," he said.

"We had nothing on you," Linton said, "except your bad record, and the fact that Dinny's money had been taken. But you acted from the start in a suspicious manner. During our first talk you were nervous, sweating. Later you came to the Diamond Club, but when you saw me with Cherry, you turned and got out. We saw you, of course.

"Pickerton came here to Cherry's apartment because we knew you'd come here. A smart man wouldn't have. I took Cherry home, drove off. You immediately barged into the building and I came back and followed you up here."

He glanced at Cherry, then back at Moran. "You were too nervous to be subtle with her, or to go easy. You pushed her around and that did what we hadn't been able to do, convinced her to help us. She played you like a sucker. You spilled everything to her, which is the thing only a fool would have done. Fortunately for us, Moran, you're a fool." His face became curious. "A cop should have known better. Didn't you stop to think at all?"

"I was thinking about the murder," Moran said slowly. "It was on my mind. That left no room for any thinking about the smart thing to do."

Pickerton took his arm and started him toward the door.

Linton walked over and shook hands with Cherry. "Thanks for the help," he said. He hesitated, then smiled. "I'd like to see you some time when I'm off duty."

Cherry pulled the robe tight around her slim waist. "Any old time—just any old time."

Linton grinned. "I'll call you."

He took Moran's other arm and the three men went out the door.

Moran walked like a dead man.

JOHN D. MACDONALD

John D. MacDonald (1916–1986) was one of the most successful writers ever to come out of the pulp magazines. He took what he learned there, combined it with the interest he had in the literary novels of his time, and created a form of crime fiction that owed as much to John O'Hara and Irwin Shaw as to Dashiell Hammett and Raymond Chandler.

As good as his peer group of pulpsters was, you find, even in MacDonald's earliest work, a desire to work outside the confines of formula. He did this largely through backstory. He told you in some depth about his people, good people and bad people alike, how they'd grown up, what they liked and disliked, and what they wanted out of life at this particular point in their lives. This is why he found such a wide audience for his books. Because men and women alike could relate to them, find commonalities lacking in too much crime fiction of the day.

Travis McGee made him famous and rich, yes. But there are a lot of MacDonald readers who prefer his other, earlier work. His was one of the largest talents in the crime genre. And nobody seems likely to fill his particular shoes for some time to come.

Murder for Money

Long ago he had given up trying to estimate what he would find in any house merely by looking at the outside of it. The interior of each house had a special flavor. It was not so much the result of the degree of tidiness, or lack of it, but rather the result of the emotional climate that had permeated the house. Anger, bitterness, despair—all left their subtle stains on even the most immaculate fabrics.

Darrigan parked the rented car by the curb and, for a long moment, looked at the house, at the iron fence, at the cypress shade. He sensed dignity, restraint, quietness. Yet he knew that the interior could destroy these impressions. He was in the habit of telling himself that his record of successful investigations was the result of the application of unemotional logic—yet his logic was often the result of sensing, somehow, the final answer and then retracing the careful steps to arrive once more at that same answer.

After a time, as the September sun of west-coast Florida began to turn the rented sedan into an oven, Darrigan pushed open the door, patted his pocket to be sure his notebook was in place, and walked toward the front door of the white house. There were two cars in the driveway, both of them with local licenses, both of them Cadillacs. It was perceptibly cooler under the trees that lined the walk.

Beyond the screen door the hallway was dim. A heavy woman came in answer to his second ring, staring at him with frank curiosity.

"I'd like to speak to Mrs. Davisson, please. Here's my card."

The woman opened the screen just enough for the card to be passed through, saying, with Midwest nasality, "Well, she's resting right now. . . . Oh, you're from the insurance?"

"Yes, I flew down from Hartford."

"Please come in and wait and I'll see if she's awake, Mr. Darrigan. I'm just a neighbor. I'm Mrs. Hoke. The poor dear has been so terribly upset."

"Yes, of course," Darrigan murmured, stepping into the hall. Mrs. Hoke walked heavily away. Darrigan could hear the mumble of other voices, a faint, slightly incongruous laugh. From the hall he could see into a living room, two steps lower than the hall itself. It was furnished in cool colors, with Florida furniture of cane and pale fabrics.

Mrs. Hoke came back and said reassuringly, "She was awake, Mr. Darrigan. She said you should wait in the study and she'll be out in a few minutes. The door is right back here. This is such a dreadful thing, not knowing what has happened to him. It's hard on her, the poor dear thing."

The study was not done in Florida fashion. Darrigan guessed that the furniture had been shipped down from the North. A walnut desk, a bit ornate, leather couch and chairs, two walls of books.

Mrs. Hoke stood in the doorway. "Now don't you upset her, you hear?" she said with elephantine coyness.

"I'll try not to."

Mrs. Hoke went away. This was Davisson's room, obviously. His books. A great number of technical works on the textile industry. Popularized texts for the layman in other fields. Astronomy, philosophy, physics. Quite a few biographies. Very little fiction. A man, then, with a serious turn of mind, dedicated to self-improvement, perhaps a bit humorless. And certainly very tidy.

Darrigan turned quickly as he heard the step in the hallway. She was a tall young woman, light on her feet. Her sunback dress was emerald green. Late twenties, he judged, or possibly very early thirties. Brown hair, sun-bleached on top. Quite a bit of tan. A fresh face, wide across the cheekbones, heavy-lipped, slightly Bergman in impact. The mouth faintly touched with strain.

"Mr. Darrigan?" He liked the voice. Low, controlled, poised.

"How do you do, Mrs. Davisson. Sorry to bother you like this."

"That's all right. I wasn't able to sleep. Won't you sit down, please?"

"If you don't mind, I'll sit at the desk, Mrs. Davisson. I'll have to make some notes."

She sat on the leather couch. He offered her a cigarette. "No, thank you, I've been smoking so much I have a sore throat. Mr. Darrigan, isn't this a bit . . . previous for the insurance company to send someone down here? I mean, as far as we know, he isn't—"

"We wouldn't do this in the case of a normal policyholder, Mrs. Davisson, but your husband carries policies with us totaling over nine hundred thousand dollars."

"Really! I knew Temple had quite a bit, but I didn't know it was that much!"

He showed her his best smile and said, "It makes it awkward for me, Mrs. Davisson, for them to send me out like some sort of bird of prey. You have presented no claim to the company, and you are perfectly within your rights to tell me to be on my merry way."

She answered his smile. "I wouldn't want to do that, Mr. Darrigan. But I don't quite understand why you're here."

"You could call me a sort of investigator. My actual title is Chief Adjuster for Guardsman Life and Casualty. I sincerely hope that we'll find a reasonable explanation for your husband's disappearance. He disappeared Thursday, didn't he?"

"He didn't come home Thursday night. I reported it to the police early Friday morning. And this is—"

"Tuesday."

He opened his notebook, took his time looking over the pages. It was a device, to give him a chance to gauge the degree of tension. She sat quite still, her hands resting in her lap, unmoving.

He leaned back. "It may sound presumptuous, Mrs. Davisson, but I intend to see if I can find out what happened to your husband. I've had reasonable success in such cases in the past. I'll cooperate with the local police officials, of course. I hope you won't mind answering questions that may duplicate what the police have already asked you."

"I won't mind. The important thing is . . . to find out. This not knowing is. . . ." Her voice caught a bit. She looked down at her hands.

"According to our records, Mrs. Davisson, his first wife, Anna Thorn Davisson, was principal beneficiary under his policies until her death in

1978. The death of the beneficiary was reported, but it was not necessary to change the policies at that time as the two children of his first marriage were secondary beneficiaries, sharing equally in the proceeds in case of death. In 1979, probably at the time of his marriage to you, we received instructions to make you the primary beneficiary under all policies, with the secondary beneficiaries, Temple C. Davisson, Junior, and Alicia Jean Davisson, unchanged. I have your name here as Dinah Pell Davisson. That is correct?"

"Yes, it is."

"Could you tell me about your husband? What sort of man is he?"

She gave him a small smile. "What should I say? He is a very kind man. Perhaps slightly autocratic, but kind. He owned a small knitting mill in Utica, New York. He sold it, I believe, in 1972. It was incorporated and he owned the controlling stock interest, and there was some sort of merger with a larger firm, where he received payment in the stock in the larger firm in return for his interest. He sold out because his wife had to live in a warmer climate. She had a serious kidney condition. They came down here to Clearwater and bought this house. Temple was too active to retire. He studied real estate conditions here for a full year and then began to invest money in all sorts of property. He has done very well."

"How did you meet him, Mrs. Davisson?"

"My husband was a sergeant in the Air Force. He was stationed at Drew Field. I followed him here. When he was sent overseas I had no special place to go, and we agreed I should wait for him here. The Davissons advertised for a companion for Mrs. Davisson. I applied and held the job from early 1974 until she died in 1978."

"And your husband?"

"He was killed in a crash landing. When I received the wire, the Davissons were very kind and understanding. At that time my position in the household was more like a daughter receiving an allowance. My own parents died long ago. I have a married sister in Melbourne, Australia. We've never been close."

"What did you do between the time Mrs. Davisson died and you married Temple Davisson?"

"I left here, of course. Mrs. Davisson had money of her own. She left me five thousand dollars and left the rest to Temple, Junior, and Alicia. Mr. Davisson found me a job in a real estate office in Clearwater. I rented a small apartment. One night Mr. Davisson came to see me at the apartment. He was quite shy. It took him a long time to get to the reason he had come. He told me that he tried to keep the house going, but the people he had hired were undependable. He also said that he was lonely. He asked me to marry him. I told him that I had affection for him, as for a father. He told me that he did not love me that way either, that Anna had been the only woman in his life. Well, Jack had been the only man in my life, and life was pretty empty. The Davissons had filled a place in my life. I missed this house. But he is sixty-one, and that makes almost exactly thirty years' difference in ages. It seemed a bit grotesque. He told me to think it over and give him my answer when I was ready. It occurred to me that his children would resent me, and it also occurred to me that I cared very little what people thought. Four days later I told him I would marry him."

Darrigan realized that he was treading on most dangerous ground. "Has it been a good marriage?"

"Is that a question you're supposed to ask?"

"It sounds impertinent. I know that. But in a disappearance of this sort I must consider suicide. Unhappiness can come from ill health, money difficulties, or emotional difficulties. I should try to rule them out."

"I'll take one of those cigarettes now, Mr. Darrigan," she said. "I can use it."

He lit it for her, went back to the desk chair. She frowned, exhaled a cloud of smoke.

"It has not been a completely happy marriage, Mr. Darrigan."

"Can you explain that?"

"I'd rather not." He pursed his lips, let the silence grow. At last she said, "I suppose I can consider an insurance man to be as ethical as a doctor or a lawyer?"

"Of course."

"For several months it was a marriage in name only. I was content to have it go on being that way. But he is a vigorous man, and after a while I became aware that his attitude had changed and he had begun to . . . want me." She flushed.

"But you had no feeling for him in that way," he said, helping her.

"None. And we'd made no actual agreement, in so many words. But living here with him, I had no ethical basis for refusing him. After that, our marriage became different. He sensed, of course, that I was merely submitting. He began to . . . court me, I suppose you'd call it. Flowers and little things like that. He took off weight and began to dress much more youthfully. He tried to make himself younger, in his speech and in his habits. It was sort of pathetic, the way he tried."

"Would you relate that to . . . his disappearance?"

For a moment her face was twisted in the agony of self reproach. "I don't know."

"I appreciate your frankness. I'll respect it, Mrs. Davisson. How did he act Thursday?"

"The same as always. We had a late breakfast. He had just sold some lots in the Lido section at Sarasota, and he was thinking of putting the money into a Gulf-front tract at Redington Beach. He asked me to go down there with him, but I had an eleven o'clock appointment with the hairdresser. His car was in the garage, so he took my convertible. He said he'd have lunch down that way and be back in the late afternoon. We were going to have some people in for cocktails. Well, the cocktail guests came and Temple didn't show up. I didn't worry. I thought he was delayed. We all went out to dinner and I left a note telling him that he could catch up with us at the Belmonte, on Clearwater Beach.

"After dinner the Deens brought me home. They live down on the next street. I began to get really worried at ten o'clock. I thought of heart attacks and all sorts of things like that. Of accidents and so on. I phoned Morton Plant Hospital and asked if they knew anything. I phoned the police here at Redington and at St. Petersburg. I fell asleep in a chair at about four o'clock and woke up at seven. That was when I officially reported him missing.

"They found my car parked outside a hotel apartment on Redington Beach, called Aqua Azul. They checked and found out he'd gone into the Aqua Azul cocktail lounge at eight thirty, alone. He had one dry martini and phoned here, but of course I had left by that time and the house was empty. He had another drink and then left. But apparently he didn't get in the car and drive away. That's what I don't understand. And I keep thinking that the Aqua Azul is right on the Gulf."

"Have his children come down?"

"Temple, Junior, wired that he is coming. He's a lieutenant colonel of ordnance stationed at the Pentagon."

"How old is he?"

"Thirty-six, and Alicia is thirty-three. Temple, Junior, is married, but Alicia isn't. She's with a Boston advertising agency, and when I tried to phone her I found out she's on vacation, taking a motor trip in Canada. She may not even know about it."

"When is the son arriving?"

"Late today, the wire said."

"Were they at the wedding?"

"No. But I know them, of course. I met them before Mrs. Davisson died, many times. And only once since my marriage. There was quite a scene then. They think I'm some sort of dirty little opportunist. When they were down while Mrs. Davisson was alive, they had me firmly established in the servant category. I suppose they were right, but one never thinks of oneself as a servant. I'm afraid Colonel Davisson is going to be difficult."

"Do you think your husband might have had business worries?"

"None. He told me a few months ago, quite proudly, that when he liquidated the knitting-company stock he received five hundred thousand dollars. In 1973 he started to buy land in this area. He said that the land he now owns could be sold off for an estimated million and a half dollars."

"Did he maintain an office?"

"This is his office. Mr. Darrigan, you used the past tense then. I find it disturbing."

"I'm sorry. It wasn't intentional." Yet it had been. He had wanted to see how easily she would slip into the past tense, showing that in her mind she considered him dead.

"Do you know the terms of his current will?"

"He discussed it with me a year ago. It sets up trust funds, one for me and one for each of the children. He insisted that it be set up so that we share equally. And yet, if I get all that insurance, it isn't going to seem very equal, is it? I'm sorry for snapping at you about using the past tense, Mr. Darrigan. I think he's dead."

"Why?"

"I know that amnesia is a very rare thing, genuine amnesia. And Temple had a very sound, stable mind. As I said before, he is kind. He wouldn't go away and leave me to this kind of worry."

"The newspaper picture was poor. Do you have a better one?"

"Quite a good one taken in July. Don't get up. I can get it. It's right in this desk drawer."

She sat lithely on her heels and opened the bottom desk drawer. Her perfume had a pleasant tang. Where her hair was parted he could see the ivory cleanness of her scalp. An attractive woman, with a quality of personal warmth held in reserve. Darrigan decided that the sergeant had been a most fortunate man. And he wondered if Davisson was perceptive enough to measure the true extent of his failure. He remembered an old story of a man held captive at the bottom of a dark, smooth-sided well. Whenever the light was turned on, for a brief interval, he could see that the circular wall was of glass, with exotic fruits banked behind it.

"This one," she said, taking out a 35-millimeter color transparency mounted in paperboard. She slipped it into a green plastic viewer and handed it to him. "You better take it over to the window. Natural light is best."

Darrigan held the viewer up to his eye. A heavy bald man, tanned like a Tahitian, stood smiling into the camera. He stood on a beach in the sunlight, and he wore bathing trunks with a pattern of blue fish on a white background. There was a doggedness about his heavy jaw, a glint of shrewdness in his eyes. His position was faintly strained and Darrigan judged he was holding his belly in, arching his wide chest for the camera. He looked to be no fool.

"May I take this along?" Darrigan asked, turning to her.

"Not for keeps." The childish expression was touching.

"Not for keeps," he said, smiling, meaning his smile for the first time. "Thank you for your courtesy, Mrs. Davisson. I'll be in touch with you. If you want me for any reason, I'm registered at a place called Bon Villa on the beach. The owner will take a message for me."

Darrigan left police headquarters in Clearwater at three o'clock. They had been as cool as he had expected at first, but after he had clearly stated his intentions they had relaxed and informed him of progress to date. They were cooperating with the Pinellas County officials and with the police at Redington.

Temple Davisson had kept his appointment with the man who owned the plot of Gulf-front property that had interested him. The potential vendor was named Myron Drynfells, and Davisson had picked him up at eleven fifteen at the motel he owned at Madeira Beach. Drynfells reported that they had inspected the property but were unable to arrive at a figure acceptable to both of them. Davisson had driven him back to the Coral Tour Haven, depositing him there shortly after twelve thirty. Davisson had intimated that he was going farther down the line to take a look at some property near St. Petersburg Beach.

There was one unconfirmed report of a man answering Davisson's description seen walking along the shoulder of the highway up near the Bath Club accompanied by a dark-haired girl, some time shortly before nine o'clock on Thursday night.

The police had no objection to Darrigan's talking with Dynfells or making his own attempt to find the elusive dark-haired girl. They were reluctant to voice any theory that would account for the disappearance.

Following a map of the area, Darrigan had little difficulty in finding his way out South Fort Harrison Avenue to the turnoff to the Belleaire causeway. He drove through the village of Indian Rocks and down a straight road that paralleled the beach. The Aqua Azul was not hard to find. It was an ugly four-story building tinted pale chartreuse with corner balconies overlooking the Gulf. From the parking area one walked along a crushed-shell path to tile steps leading down into a pseudo-Mexican courtyard where shrubbery screened off the highway. The lobby door, of plate glass with a chrome push bar, opened off the other side of the patio. The fountain in the center of the patio was rimmed with small floodlights with blue-glass lenses. Darrigan guessed that the fountain would be fairly garish once the lights were turned on.

Beyond the glass door the lobby was frigidly air-conditioned. A brass sign on the blond desk announced that summer rates were in effect. The lobby walls were rough tan plaster. At the head of a short wide staircase was a mural of lumpy, coffee-colored, semi-naked women grinding corn and holding infants.

A black man was slowly sweeping the tile floor of the lobby. A girl behind the desk was carrying on a monosyllabic phone conversation. The place had a quietness, a hint of informality, that suggested it would be more pleasant now than during the height of the winter tourist season.

The bar lounge opened off the lobby. The west wall was entirely glass, facing the beach glare. A curtain had been drawn across the glass. It was sufficiently opaque to cut the glare, subdue the light in the room. Sand gritted underfoot as Darrigan walked to the bar. Three lean women in bathing suits sat at one table, complete with beach bags, tall drinks, and that special porcelainized facial expression of the middle forties trying, with monied success, to look like middle thirties.

Two heavy men in white suits hunched over a corner table, florid faces eight inches apart, muttering at each other. A young couple sat at the bar.

They had a honeymoon flavor about them. Darrigan sat down at the end of the bar, around the corner, and decided on a rum collins. The bartender was brisk, young, dark, and he mixed a good drink.

When he brought the change, Darrigan said, "Say, have they found that guy who wandered away and left his car here the other night?"

"I don't think so, sir," the bartender said with no show of interest.

"Were you on duty the night he came in?"

"Yes, sir."

"Regular customer?"

The bartender didn't answer.

Darrigan quickly leafed through half a dozen possible approaches. He selected one that seemed suited to the bartender's look of quick intelligence and smiled ingratiatingly. "They ought to make all cops take a sort of internship behind a bar. That's where you learn what makes people tick."

The slight wariness faded. "That's no joke."

"Teddy!" one of the three lean women called. "Another round, please."

"Coming right up, Mrs. Jerrold," Teddy said.

Darrigan waited with monumental patience. He had planted a seed, and he wanted to see if it would take root. He stared down at his drink, watching Teddy out of the corner of his eye. After the drinks had been taken to the three women, Teddy drifted slowly back toward Darrigan. Darrigan waited for Teddy to say the first word.

"I think that Davisson will show up."

Darrigan shrugged. "That's hard to say." It put the burden of proof on Teddy.

Teddy became confidential. "Like you said, sir, you see a lot when you're behind a bar. You learn to size them up. Now, you take that Davisson. I don't think he ever came in here before. I didn't make any connection until they showed me the picture. Then I remembered him. In the off season, you get time to size people up. He came in alone. I'd say he'd had a couple already. Husky old guy. Looked like money. Looked smart, too. That kind, they like service. He came in about eight thirty. A local guy. I could tell. I don't know how. You can always tell them from the tourists. One martini, he wants. Very dry. He gets it very dry. He asks me where he can phone. I told him about the phone in the lobby. He finished half his cocktail, then phoned. When he came back he looked satisfied about the phone call. A little more relaxed. You know what I mean. He sat right on that stool there, and one of the regulars, a Mrs. Kathy Marrick, is sitting alone at that table over there. That Davisson, he turns on the stool and starts giving Mrs. Marrick the eye. Not that you can blame him. She is something to look at. He orders another martini. I figure out the pitch then. That Davisson, he went and called his wife and then he was settling down to an evening of wolfing around. Some of those older guys, they give us more trouble than the college kids. And he had that look, you know what I mean.

"Well, from where he was sitting he couldn't even see first base, not with Mrs. Marrick, and I saw him figure that out for himself. He finished his second drink in a hurry, and away he went. I sort of decided he was going to look around and see where the hunting was a little better."

"And that makes you think he'll turn up?"

"Sure. I think the old guy just lost himself a big weekend, and he'll come crawling out of the woodwork with some crazy amnesia story or something."

"Then how do you figure the car being left here?"

"I think he found somebody with a car of her own. They saw him walking up the line not long after he left here, and he was with a girl, wasn't he? That makes sense to me."

"Where would he have gone to find that other girl?"

"I think he came out of here, and it was just beginning to get dark, and he looked from the parking lot and saw the lights of the Tide Table up the road, and it was just as easy to walk as drive."

Darrigan nodded. "That would make sense. Is it a nice place, that Tide Table?"

"A big bar and bathhouses and a dance floor and carhops to serve greasy hamburgers. It doesn't do this section of the beach much good."

"Was Davisson dressed right for that kind of a place?"

"I don't know. He had on a white mesh shirt with short sleeves and tan slacks, I think. Maybe he had a coat in his car. He didn't wear it in here. The rules here say men have to wear coats in the bar and dining room after November first."

"That Mrs. Marrick wouldn't have met him outside, would she?"

"Not her. No, sir. She rents one of our cabañas here."

"Did she notice him?"

"I'd say she did. You can't fool Kathy Marrick."

Darrigan knew that Teddy could add nothing more. So Darrigan switched the conversation to other things. He made himself talk dully and at length so that when Teddy saw his chance, he eased away with almost obvious relief. Darrigan had learned to make himself boring, merely by relating complicated incidents which had no particular point. It served its purpose. He knew that Teddy was left with a mild contempt for Darrigan's intellectual resources. Later, should anyone suggest to Teddy that Darrigan was a uniquely shrewd investigator, Teddy would hoot with laughter, completely forgetting that Darrigan, with a minimum of words, had extracted every bit of information Teddy had possessed.

Darrigan went out to the desk and asked if he might see Mrs. Marrick. The girl went to the small switchboard and plugged one of the house phones into Mrs. Marrick's cabaña. After the phone rang five times a sleepy, soft-fibered voice answered.

He stated his name and his wish to speak with her. She agreed, sleepily. Following the desk girl's instructions, Darrigan walked out the beach door of the lobby and down a shell walk to the last cabaña to the south. A woman in a two-piece white terry-cloth sun suit lay on an uptilted Barwa chair in the hot sun. Her hair was wheat and silver, sun-parched. Her figure was rich, and her tan was coppery. She had the hollowed cheeks of a Dietrich and a wide, flat mouth.

She opened lazy sea-green eyes when he spoke her name. She looked at him for a long moment and then said, "Mr. Darrigan, you cast an unpleasantly black shadow on the sand. Are you one of the new ones with my husband's law firm? If so, the answer is still no, in spite of the fact that you're quite pretty."

"I never heard of you until ten minutes ago, Mrs. Marrick."

"That's refreshing, dear. Be a good boy and go in and build us some drinks. You'll find whatever you want, and I need a fresh gin and tonic. This glass will do for me. And bring out a pack of cigarettes from the carton on the bedroom dressing table."

She shut her eyes. Darrigan shrugged and went into the cabaña. It was clean but cluttered. He made himself a rum collins, took the two drinks out, handed her her drink and a pack of cigarettes. She shifted her weight forward and the chair tilted down.

"Now talk, dear," she said.

"Last Friday night at about eight thirty you were alone in the bar and a bald-headed man with a deep tan sat at the bar. He was interested in you."

"Mmm. The missing Mr. Davisson, eh? Let me see now. You can't be a local policeman. They all either look like fullbacks from the University of Florida or skippers of unsuccessful charter boats. Your complexion and clothes are definitely northern. That might make you FBI, but I don't think so somehow. Insurance, Mr. Darrigan?"

He sat on a canvas chair and looked at her with new respect. "Insurance, Mrs. Marrick."

"He's dead, I think."

"His wife thinks so too. Why do you?"

"I was alone. I'm a vain creature, and the older I get the more flattered I am by all little attentions. Your Mr. Davisson was a bit pathetic, my dear. He had a lost look. A . . . hollowness. Do you understand?"

"Not quite."

"A man of that age will either be totally uninterested in casual females or he will have an enormous amount of assurance about him. Mr. Davisson had neither. He looked at me like a little boy staring into the candy shop. I was almost tempted to help the poor dear, but he looked dreadfully dull. I said to myself, Kathy there is a man who suddenly has decided to be a bit of a rake and does not know just how to go about it."

"Does that make him dead?"

"No, of course. It was something else. Looking into his eyes was like looking into the eyes of a photograph of someone who has recently died. It is a look of death. It cannot be described. It made me feel quite upset."

"How would I write that up in a report?"

"You wouldn't, my dear. You would go out and find out how he died. He was looking for adventure last Friday night. And I believe he found it."

"With a girl with dark hair?"

"Perhaps."

"It isn't much of a starting place, is it?" Darrigan said ruefully.

She finished her drink and tilted her chair back. "I understand that the wife is young."

"Comparatively speaking. Are you French?"

"I was once. You're quick, aren't you? I'm told there's no accent."

"No accent. A turn of phrase here and there. What if the wife is young?"

"Call it my French turn of mind. A lover of the wife could help your Mr. Davisson find . . . his adventure."

"The wife was with a group all evening."

"A very sensible precaution."

He stood up. "Thank you for talking to me."

"You see, you're not as quick as I thought, Mr. Darrigan. I wanted you to keep questioning me in a clever way, and then I should tell you that Mr. Davisson kept watching the door during his two drinks, as though he were expecting that someone had followed him. He was watching, not with worry, but with . . . annoyance."

Darrigan smiled. "I thought you had something else to tell. And it seemed the quickest way to get it out of you, to pretend to go."

She stared at him and then laughed. It was a good laugh, fullthroated, rich. "We could be friends, my dear," she said, when she got her breath.

"So far I haven't filled in enough of his day. I know what he did up until very early afternoon. Then there is a gap. He comes into the Aqua Azul bar at eight-thirty. He has had a few drinks. I like the theory of someone following him, meeting him outside. That would account for his leaving his car at the lot."

"What will you do now?"

"See if I can fill in the blanks in his day."

"The blank before he arrived here, and the more important one afterward?"

"Yes."

"I'm well known up and down the Gulf beaches, Mr. Darrigan. Being with me would be protective coloration."

"And besides, you're bored."

"Utterly."

He smiled at her. "Then you'd better get dressed, don't you think?"

He waited outside while she changed. He knew that she would be useful for her knowledge of the area. Yet not sufficiently useful to warrant taking her along had she not been a mature, witty, perceptive woman.

She came out wearing sandals and a severely cut sand-colored linen sun dress, carrying a white purse. The end tendrils of the astonishing hair were damp-curled where they had protruded from her shower cap.

"Darrigan and Marrick," she said. "Investigations to order. This might be fun."

"And it might be dull."

"But we shan't be dull, Mr. Darrigan, shall we. What are you called?"

"Gil, usually."

"Ah, Gil, if this were a properly conceived plot, I would be the one who lured your Mr. Davisson to his death. Now I accompany the investigator to allay suspicion."

"No such luck, Kathy."

"No such luck." They walked along the shell path to the main building of the Aqua Azul. She led the way around the building toward a Cadillac convertible the shade of raspberry sherbet.

"More protective coloration?" Darrigan asked.

She smiled and handed him the keys from her purse. After he shut her door he went around and got behind the wheel. The sun was far enough gone to warrant having the top down. She took a dark bandanna from the glove compartment and tied it around her hair.

"Now how do you go about this, Gil?" she asked.

"I head south and show a picture of Davisson in every bar until we find the one he was in. He could have called his wife earlier. I think he was the sort to remember that a cocktail party was scheduled for that evening. Something kept him from phoning his wife."

"Maybe he didn't want to phone her until it was too late."

"I'll grant that. First I want to talk to a man named Drynfells. For this you better stay in the car."

The Coral Tour Haven was a pink hotel with pink iron flamingos stuck into the lawn and a profusion of whitewashed boulders marking the drive. Drynfells was a sour-looking man with a withered face, garish clothes, and a cheap Cuban cigar.

Darrigan had to follow Drynfells about as they talked. Drynfells ambled around, picking up scraps of cellophane, twigs, burned matches from his yard. He confirmed all that the Clearwater police had told Darrigan.

"You couldn't decide on a price, Mr. Drynfells?"

"I want one hundred and forty-five thousand for that piece. He offered one thirty-six, then one thirty-eight, and finally one forty. He said that was his top offer. I came down two thousand and told him that one forty-three was as low as I'd go."

"Did you quarrel?"

Drynfells gave him a sidelong glance. "We shouted a little. He was a shouter. Lot of men try to bull their way into a deal. He couldn't bulldoze me. No, sir."

They had walked around a corner of the motel. A pretty girl sat on a rubberized mattress at the side of a new wading pool. The ground was raw around the pool, freshly seeded, protected by stakes and string.

"What did you say your name was?" Drynfells asked.

"Darrigan."

"This here is my wife, Mr. Darrigan. Beth, this man is an insurance fellow asking about that Davisson."

Mrs. Drynfells was striking. She had a heavy strain of some Latin blood. Her dark eyes were liquid, expressive.

"He is the wan who is wanting to buy our beach, eh?"

"Yeah. That bald-headed man that the police were asking about," Drynfells said.

Mrs. Drynfells seemed to lose all interest in the situation. She lay back and shut her eyes. She wore a lemon-yellow swimsuit.

Drynfells wandered away and swooped on a scrap of paper, balling it up in his hand with the other debris he had collected. "You have a nice place here," Darrigan said.

"Just got it open in time for last season. Did pretty good. We got a private beach over there across the highway. Reasonable rates, too."

"I guess things are pretty dead in the off season."

"Right now we only got one unit taken. Those folks came in yesterday. But it ought to pick up again soon."

"How big is that piece of land you want one hundred and forty-five thousand for?"

"It's one hundred and twenty feet of Gulf-front lot, six hundred feet deep, but it isn't for sale any more."

"Why not?"

"Changed my mind about it, Mr. Darrigan. Decided to hold onto it, maybe develop it a little. Nice property."

Darrigan went out to the car. They drove south, stopping at the obvious places. There were unable to pick up the trail of Mr. Davisson. Darrigan bought Kathy Marrick dinner. He drove her back to the Aqua Azul. They took a short walk on the beach and he thanked her, promised to keep in touch with her, and drove the rented sedan back to Clearwater Beach.

It was after eleven and the porch of the Bon Villa was dark. He parked, and as he headed toward his room a familiar voice spoke hesitantly from one of the dark chairs.

"Mr. Darrigan?"

"Oh! Hello, Mrs. Davisson. You startled me. I didn't see you there. Do you want to come in?"

"No, please. Sit down and tell me what you've learned."

He pulled one of the aluminum chairs over close to hers and sat down. A faint sea breeze rattled the palm fronds. Her face was a pale oval, barely visible.

"I didn't learn much, Mrs. Davisson. Not much at all."

"Forgive me for coming here like this. Colonel Davisson arrived. It was as unpleasant as I'd expected. I had to get out of the house."

"It makes a difficult emotional problem for both of you—when the children of the first marriage are older than the second wife."

"I don't really blame him too much, I suppose. It looks bad."

"What did he accuse you of?"

"Driving his father into some crazy act. Maybe I did."

"Don't think that way."

"I keep thinking that if we never find out what happened to Temple, his children will always blame me. I don't especially want to be friends with them, but I do want their . . . respect, I guess you'd say."

"Mrs. Davisson, do you have any male friends your own age?"

"How do you mean that?" she asked hotly.

"Is there any man you've been friendly enough with to cause talk?"

"N-no, I—"

"Who were you thinking of when you hesitated?"

"Brad Sharvis. He's a bit over thirty, and quite nice. It was his real estate agency that Temple sent me to for a job. He has worked with Temple the last few years. He's a bachelor. He has dinner with us quite often. We both like him."

"Could there be talk?"

"There could be, but it would be without basis, Mr. Darrigan," she said coldly.

"I don't care how angry you get at me, Mrs. Davisson, so long as you tell me the truth."

After a long silence she said, "I'm sorry. I believe that you want to help."

"I do."

She stood up. "I feel better now. I think I'll go home."

"Can I take you home?"

"I have my car, thanks."

He watched her go down the walk. Under the streetlight he saw her walking with a good long stride. He saw the headlights, saw her swing around the island in the center of Mandalay and head back for the causeway to Clearwater.

Darrigan went in, showered, and went to bed. He lay in the dark room and smoked a slow cigarette. Somewhere, hidden in the personality or in the habits of one Temple Davisson, was the reason for his death. Darrigan found that he was thinking in terms of death. He smiled in the darkness as he thought of Kathy Marrick. A most pleasant companion. So far in the investigation he had met four women. Of the four only Mrs. Hoke was unattractive.

He snubbed out the cigarette and composed himself for sleep. A case, like a score of other cases. He would leave his brief mark on the participants and go out of their lives. For a moment he felt the ache of self-imposed loneliness. The ache had been there since the day Doris had left him, long ago. He wondered sourly, on the verge of sleep, if it had made him a better investigator.

* * *

Brad Sharvis was a florid, freckled, overweight young man with carrot hair, blue eyes, and a salesman's unthinking affability. The small real estate office was clean and bright. A girl was typing a lease agreement for an elderly couple.

Brad took Darrigan back into his small private office. A window air conditioner hummed, chilling the moist September air.

"What sort of man was he, Mr. Sharvis?"

"Was he? Or is he? Shrewd, Mr. Darrigan. Shrewd and honest. And something else. Tough-minded isn't the expression I want."

"Ruthless?"

"That's it exactly. He started moving in on property down here soon after he arrived. You wouldn't know the place if you saw it back then. The last ten years down here would take your breath away."

"He knew what to buy, eh?"

"It took him a year to decide on policy. He had a very simple operating idea. He decided, after his year of looking around, that there was going to be a tremendous pressure for waterfront land. At that time small building lots on Clearwater Beach, on the Gulf front, were going for as little as seventy-five hundred dollars. I remember that the first thing he did was pick up eight lots at that figure. He sold them in 1980 for fifty thousand apiece."

"Where did the ruthlessness come in, Mr. Sharvis?"

"You better call me Brad. That last name makes me feel too dignified."

"Okay, I'm Gil."

"I'll tell you, Gil. Suppose he got his eye on a piece he wanted. He'd go after it. Phone calls, letters, personal visits. He'd hound a man who had no idea of selling until, in some cases, I think they sold out just to get Temple Davisson off their back. And he'd fight for an hour to get forty dollars off the price of a twenty-thousand-dollar piece."

"Did he handle his deals through you?"

"No. He turned himself into a licensed agent and used this office for his deals. He pays toward the office expenses here, and I've been in with him on a few deals."

"Is he stingy?"

"Not a bit. Pretty free with his money, but a tight man in a deal. You know, he's told me a hundred times that everybody likes the look of nice fat batches of bills. He said that there's nothing exactly like counting out fifteen thousand dollars in bills onto a man's desk when the man wants to get seventeen thousand."

Darrigan felt a shiver of excitement run up his back. It was always that way when he found a bit of key information.

"Where did he bank?"

"Bank of Clearwater."

"Do you think he took money with him when he went after the Drynfells plot?"

Sharvis frowned. "I hardly think he'd take that much out there, but I'll wager he took a sizable payment against it."

"Twenty-five thousand?"

"Possibly. Probably more like fifty."

"I could check that at the bank, I suppose."

"I doubt it. He has a safe in his office at his house. A pretty good one, I think. He kept his cash there. He'd replenish the supply in Tampa, picking up a certified check from the Bank of Clearwater whenever he needed more than they could comfortably give him."

"He was anxious to get the Drynfells land?"

"A very nice piece. And with a tentative purchaser all lined up for it. Temple would have unloaded it for one hundred and seventy thousand. He wanted to work fast so that there'd be no chance of his customer getting together with Drynfells. It only went on the market Wednesday, a week ago today."

"Drynfells held it a long time?"

"Several years. He paid fifty thousand for it."

"Would it violate any confidence to tell me who Davisson planned to sell it to?"

"I can't give you the name because I don't know it myself. It's some man who sold a chain of movie houses in Kansas and wants to build a motel down here, that's all I know."

Darrigan walked out into the morning sunlight. The death of Temple Davisson was beginning to emerge from the mists. Sometime after he had left the Coral Tour Haven and before he appeared at the Aqua Azul, he had entangled himself with someone who wanted that cash. Wanted it badly. They had not taken their first opportunity. So they had sought a second choice, had made the most of it.

He parked in the center of town, had a cup of coffee. At such times he felt far away from his immediate environment. Life moved brightly around him and left him in a dark place where he sat and thought. Thought at such a time was not the application of logic but an endless stirring at the edge of the mind, a restless groping for the fleeting impression.

Davisson had been a man whose self-esteem had taken an inadvertent blow at the hands of his young wife. To mend his self-esteem, he had been casting a speculative eye at the random female. And he had been spending the day trying to engineer a deal that would mean a most pleasant profit.

Darrigan and Kathy Marrick had been unable to find the place where Davisson had taken a few drinks before stopping at the Aqua Azul. Darrigan paid for his coffee and went out to the car, spread the road map on the wheel, and studied it. Granted that Davisson was on his way home when he stopped at the Aqua Azul, it limited the area where he could have been. Had he been more than three miles south of the Aqua Azul, he would not logically have headed home on the road that would take him through Indian Rocks and along Belleaire Beach. He would have cut over to Route 19. With a pencil Darrigan made a circle. Temple Davisson had taken his drinks somewhere in that area.

He frowned. He detested legwork, that dullest stepsister of investigation. Sharing it with Mrs. Marrick made it a bit more pleasant, at least. It took him forty-five minutes to drive out to the Aqua Azul. Her raspberry convertible was under shelter in the long carport. He parked in the sun and went in, found her in the lobby chattering with the girl at the desk.

She smiled at him. "It can't be Nero Wolfe. Not enough waistline."

"Buy you a drink?"

"Clever boy. The bar isn't open yet. Come down to the cabaña and make your own and listen to the record of a busy morning."

They went into the cypress-paneled living room of the beach cabaña. She made the drinks.

"We failed to find out where he'd been by looking for him, my dear. So this morning I was up bright and early and went on a hunt for somebody who might have seen the car. A nice baby-blue convertible. They're a dime a dozen around here, but it seemed sensible. Tan men with bald heads are a dime a dozen too. But the combination of tan bald head and baby-blue convertible is not so usual."

"Any time you'd like a job, Kathy."

"Flatterer! Now prepare yourself for the letdown. All I found out was something we already knew. That the baby-blue job was parked at that hideous Coral Tour Haven early in the afternoon."

Darrigan sipped his drink. "Parked there?"

"That's what the man said. He has a painful little store that sells things made out of shells, and sells shells to people who want to make things out of shells. Say that three times fast."

"Why did you stop there?"

"Just to see if anybody could remember the car and man if they had seen them. He's across the street from that Coral Tour thing."

"I think I'd like to talk to him."

"Let's go, then. He's a foolish little sweetheart with a tic."

The man was small and nervous, and at unexpected intervals his entire face would twitch uncontrollably. "Like I told the lady, mister, I saw the car parked over to Drynfells's. You don't see many cars there. Myron doesn't do so good this time of year."

"And you saw the bald-headed man?"

"Sure. He went in with Drynfells, and then he came out after a while."

"After how long?"

"How would I know? Was I timing him? Maybe twenty minutes."

Darrigan showed him the picture. "This man?"

The little man squinted through the viewer. "Sure."

"You got a good look at him?"

"Just the first time."

"You mean when he went in?"

"No, I mean the first time he was there. The second time it was getting pretty late in the day, and the sun was gone."

"Did he stay long the second time?"

"I don't know. I closed up when he was still there."

"Thanks a lot."

The little man twitched and beamed. "A pleasure, certainly."

They went back out to Darrigan's car. When they got in Kathy said, "I feel a bit stupid, Gil."

"Don't think I suspected that. It came out by accident. One of those things. It happens sometimes. And I should have done some better guessing. I found out this morning that when Temple Davisson wanted a piece of property he didn't give up easily. He went back and tried again."

"And Mr. Drynfells didn't mention it."

"A matter which I find very interesting. I'm dropping you back at the Aqua Azul and then I'm going to tackle Drynfells."

"Who found the little man who sells shells? You are not leaving me out."

"It may turn out to be unpleasant, Kathy."

"So be it. I want to see how much of that tough look of yours is a pose, Mr. Darrigan."

"Let me handle it."

"I shall be a mouse, entirely."

He waited for two cars to go by and made a wide U-turn, then turned right into Drynfells's drive. The couple was out in back. Mrs. Drynfells was basking on her rubberized mattress, her eyes closed. She did not appear to have moved since the previous day. Myron Drynfells was over near the hedge having a bitter argument with a man who obviously belonged with the battered pickup parked in front.

Drynfells was saying, "I just got damn good and tired of waiting for you to come around and finish the job."

The man, a husky youngster in work clothes, flushed with anger, said, "Okay, okay. Just pay me off, then, if that's the way you feel. Fourteen hours' labor plus the bags and the pipe."

Drynfells turned and saw Darrigan and Kathy. "Hello," he said absently. "Be right back." He walked into the back door of the end unit with the husky young man.

Mrs. Drynfells opened her eyes. She looked speculatively at Kathy. "Allo," she said. Darrigan introduced the two women. He had done enough work on jewelry theft to know that the emerald in Mrs. Drynfells's ring was genuine. About three carats, he judged. A beauty.

Drynfells came out across the lawn, scowling. He wore chartreuse slacks and a dark blue seersucker sport shirt with a chartreuse flower pattern.

"Want anything done right," he said, "you got to do it yourself. What's on your mind, Mr. Darrigan?"

"Just checking, Mr. Drynfells. I got the impression from the police that Mr. Davisson merely dropped you off here after you'd looked at the land. I didn't know he'd come in with you."

"He's a persistent guy. I couldn't shake him off, could I, honey?"

"Talking, talking," Mrs. Drynfells said, with sunstruck sleepiness. "Too moch."

"He came in and yakked at me, and then when he left he told me he could find better lots south of here. I told him to go right ahead."

"How long did he stay?"

Drynfells shrugged. "Fifteen minutes, maybe."

"Did he wave big bills at you?"

"Sure. Kid stuff. I had my price and he wouldn't meet it. Waving money in my face wasn't going to change my mind. No, sir."

"And that's the last you saw of him?" Darrigan asked casually.

"That's right."

"Then why was his car parked out in front of here at dusk on Friday?"

"In front of here?" Drynfells said, his eyes opening wide.

"In front of here."

"I don't know what you're talking about, mister. I wasn't even here, then. I was in Clearwater on a business matter."

Mrs. Drynfells sat up and put her hand over her mouth. "Ai, I forget! He did come back. Still talking, talking, I send him away, that talking wan."

Drynfells stomped over to her and glared down at her. "Why did you forget that? Damn it, that might make us look bad."

"I do not theenk."

Drynfells turned to Darrigan with a shrug. "Rattleheaded, that's what she is. Forget her head if it wasn't fastened on."

"I am sorree!"

"I think you better phone the police and tell them, Mr. Drynfells, just in case."

"Think I should?"

"The man is still missing."

Drynfells sighed. "Okay, I better do that."

The Aqua Azul bar was open. Kathy and Darrigan took a corner table, ordered pre-lunch cocktails. "You've gone off somewhere, Gil."

He smiled at her. "I am sorree!"

"What's bothering you?"

"I don't exactly know. Not yet. Excuse me. I want to make a call."

He left her and phoned Hartford from the lobby. He got his assistant on the line. "Robby, I don't know what source to use for this, but find me the names of any men who have sold chains of movie houses in Kansas during the past year."

Robby whistled softly. "Let me see. There ought to be a trade publication that would have that dope. Phone you?"

"I'll call back at five."

"How does it look?"

"It begins to have the smell of murder."

"By the beneficiary, we hope?"

"Nope. No such luck."

"So we'll get a statistic for the actuarial boys. Luck, Gil. I'll rush that dope."

"Thanks, Robby. 'Bye."

He had sandwiches in the bar with Kathy and then gave her her instructions for the afternoon. "Any kind of gossip, rumor, anything at all you can pick up on the Drynfellses. Financial condition. Emotional condition. Do they throw pots? Where did he find the cutie?"

"Cute, like a derringer."

"I think I know what you mean."

"Of course you do, Gil. No woman is going to fool you long, or twice."

"That's what I keep telling myself."

"I hope, wherever your lady fair might be, that she realizes by now what she missed."

"You get too close for comfort sometimes, Kathy."

"Just love to see people wince. All right. This afternoon I shall be the Jack Anderson of Madeira Beach and vicinity. When do I report?"

"When I meet you for cocktails. Sixish?"

On the way back to Clearwater Beach he looked in on Dinah Davisson. There were dark shadows under her eyes. Temple Davisson's daughter had been reached. She was flying south. Mrs. Hoke had brought over a cake. Darrigan told her he had a hunch he'd have some real information by midnight. After he left he wondered why he had put himself out on a limb.

At four-thirty he grew impatient and phoned Robby. A James C. Brock had sold a nine-unit chain in central Kansas in July.

Darrigan thanked him. It seemed like a hopeless task to try to locate Brock in the limited time before he would have to leave for Redington Beach. He phoned Dinah Davisson and told her to see what she could do about finding James Brock. He told her to try all the places he might stop, starting at the most expensive and working her way down the list.

He told her that once she had located Mr. Brock she should sit tight and wait for a phone call from him.

Kathy was waiting at her cabaña. "Do I report right now, sir?"

"Right now, Operative Seventy-three."

"Classification one: financial. Pooie. That Coral Tour thing ran way over estimates. It staggers under a mortgage. And he got a loan on his beach property to help out. The dollie is no help in the financial department. She's of the gimme breed. A Cuban. Miami. Possibly nightclub training. Drynfells's first wife died several centuries ago. The local pitch is that he put that plot of land on the market to get the dough to cover some postdated checks that are floating around waiting to fall on him."

"Nice work, Kathy."

"I'm not through yet. Classification two: Emotional. Pooie again. His little item has him twisted around her pinkie. She throws pots. She raises merry hell. She has tantrums. He does the house-keeping chores. She has a glittering eye for a pair of shoulders, broad shoulders. Myron is very jealous of his lady."

"Any more?"

"Local opinion is that if he sells his land and lasts until the winter season is upon him, he may come out all right, provided he doesn't have to buy his little lady a brace of Mercedeses and minks to keep in good favor. He's not liked too well around here. Not a sociable sort, I'd judge. And naturally the wife doesn't mix too well with the standard-issue wives hereabouts."

"You did very well, Kathy."

"Now what do we do?"

"I buy you drinks. I buy you dinner. Reward for services rendered."

"Then what?"

"Then we ponder."

"We can ponder while we're working over the taste buds, can't we?"

"If you'd like to ponder."

They went up to the bar. Martinis came. Kathy said, "I ponder out loud. Davisson's offer was too low. But he waved his money about. They brooded over that money all day. He came back and waved it about some more. Mrs. Drynfells's acquisitive instincts were aroused. She followed him, met him outside of here, clunked him on the head, pitched him in the Gulf, and went home and hid the money under the bed."

"Nice, but I don't like it."

"Okay. You ponder."

"Like this. Drynfells lied from the beginning. He sold the land to Temple Davisson. They went back. Drynfells took the bundle of cash, possibly a check for the balance. Those twenty minutes inside was when some sort of document was being executed. Davisson mentions where he's going. In the afternoon Drynfells gets a better offer for the land. He stalls the buyer. He gets hold of Davisson and asks him to come back. Davisson does so. Drynfells wants to cancel the sale. Maybe he offers Davisson a bonus to tear up the document and take his money and check back. Davisson laughs at him. Drynfells asks for just a little bit of time. Davisson says he'll give him a little time. He'll be at the Aqua Azul for twenty minutes. From here he phones his wife. Can't get her. Makes eyes at you. Leaves. Drynfells, steered by his wife's instincts, has dropped her off and gone up the road a bit. She waits by Temple Davisson's car. He comes out. He is susceptible, as Mrs. Drynfells has guessed, to a little night walk with a very pretty young lady. She walks him up the road to where Drynfells is waiting. They bash him, tumble him into the Drynfells car, remove document of sale, dispose of body. That leaves them with the wad of cash, plus the money from the sale to the new customer Drynfells stalled. The weak point was the possibility of Davisson's car being seen at their place. That little scene we witnessed this morning had the flavor of being very well rehearsed."

Kathy snapped her fingers, eyes glowing. "It fits! Every little bit of it fits. They couldn't do it there, when he came back, because that would have left them with the car. He had to be seen someplace else. Here."

"There's one fat flaw, Kathy."

"How could there be?"

Just how do we go about proving it?"

She thought that over. Her face fell. "I see what you mean."

"I don't think that the dark-haired girl he was seen with could be identified as Mrs. Drynfells. Without evidence that the sale was consummated, we lack motive—except, of course, for the possible motive of murder for the money he carried."

Kathy sat with her chin propped on the backs of her fingers, studying him. "I wouldn't care to have you on my trail, Mr. Darrigan."

"How so?"

"You're very impressive, in your quiet little way, hiding behind that mask."

"A mask, yet."

"Of course. And behind it you sit, equipped with extra senses, catching the scent of murder, putting yourself neatly in the murderer's shoes, with all your reasoning based on emotions, not logic."

"I'm very logical. I plod. And I now plod out to the phone and see if logic has borne any fruit."

He went to the lobby and phoned Dinah Davisson.

"I found him, Mr. Darrigan. He's staying at the Kingfisher with his wife."

"Did you talk to him?"

"No. Just to the desk clerk."

"Thanks. You'll hear from me later, Mrs. Davisson."

He phoned the Kingfisher and had Mr. Brock called from the dining room to the phone. "Mr. Brock, my name is Darrigan. Mr. Temple Davisson told me you were interested in a plot of Gulf-front land."

"Has he been found?"

"No, he hasn't. I'm wondering if you're still in the market."

"Sorry, I'm not. I think I'm going to get the piece I want."

"At Redington Beach?"

Brock had a deep voice. "How did you know that?"

"Just a guess, Mr. Brock. Would you mind telling me who you're buying it from?"

"A Mr. Drynfells. He isn't an agent. It's his land."

"He contacted you last Friday, I suppose. In the afternoon?"

"You must have a crystal ball, Mr. Darrigan. Yes, he did. And he came in to see me late Friday night. We inspected the land Sunday. I suppose you even know what I'll be paying for it."

"Probably around one seventy-five."

"That's too close for comfort, Mr. Darrigan."

"Sorry to take you away from your dinner for no good reason. Thanks for being so frank with me."

"Quite all right."

Gilbert Darrigan walked slowly back into the bar. Kathy studied him. "Now you're even more impressive, Gil. Your eyes have gone cold."

"I feel cold. Right down into my bones. I feel this way when I've guessed a bit too accurately." She listened, eyes narrowed, as he told her the conversation.

"Mr. Drynfells had a busy Friday," she said.

"Now we have the matter of proof."

"How do you go about that? Psychological warfare, perhaps?"

"Not with that pair. They're careful. They're too selfish to have very much imagination. I believe we should consider the problem of the body."

She sipped her drink, stared over his head at the far wall. "The dramatic place, of course, would be under the concrete of that new pool, with the dark greedy wife sunbathing beside it, sleepy-eyed and callous."

He reached across the table and put his fingers hard around her wrist. "You are almost beyond price, Kathy. That is exactly where it is."

She looked faintly ill. "No," she said weakly. "I was only—"

"You thought you were inventing. But your subconscious mind knew, as mine did."

It was not too difficult to arrange. The call had to come from Clearwater. They drove there in Kathy's car, and Darrigan, lowering his voice, said to Drynfells over the phone, "I've got my lawyer here and I'd like you to come in right now, Mr. Drynfells. Bring your wife with you. We'll make it business and pleasure both."

"I don't know as I—"

"I have to make some definite arrangement, Mr. Drynfells. If I can't complete the deal with you, I'll have to pick up a different plot."

"But you took an option. Mr. Brock!"

"I can forfeit that, Mr. Drynfells. How soon can I expect you?"

After a long pause Drynfells said, "We'll leave here in twenty minutes."

On the way back out to Madeira Beach, Darrigan drove as fast as he dared. Kathy refused to be dropped off at the Aqua Azul. The Coral Tour Haven was dark, the "No Vacancy" sign lighted.

They walked out to the dark back yard, Kathy carrying the flash, Darrigan carrying the borrowed pickaxe. He found the valve to empty the shallow pool, turned it. He stood by Kathy. She giggled nervously as the water level dropped.

"We'd better not be wrong," she said.

"We're not wrong," Darrigan murmured. The water took an infuriating time to drain out of the pool. He rolled up his pants legs, pulled off shoes and socks, stepped down in when there was a matter of inches left. The cement had set firmly. It took several minutes to break through to the soil underneath. Then, using the pick point as a lever, he broke a piece free. He got his hands on it and turned it over. The flashlight wavered. Only the soil underneath was visible. Again he inserted a curved side of the pick, leaned his weight against it, lifted it up slowly. The flashlight beam focused on the side of a muddy white shoe, a gray sock encasing a heavy ankle. The light went out and Kathy Marrick made a moaning sound, deep in her throat.

Darrigan lowered the broken slab back into position, quite gently. He climbed out of the pool.

"Are you all right?" he asked.

"I . . . think so."

He rolled down his pants legs, pulled socks on over wet feet, shoved his feet into the shoes, laced them neatly and tightly.

"How perfectly dreadful," Kathy said in a low tone.

"It always is. Natural death is enough to give us a sort of superstitious fear. But violent death always seems obscene. An assault against the dignity of every one of us. Now we do some phoning."

They waited, afterwards, in the dark car parked across the road. When the Drynfellses returned home, two heavy men advanced on their car from either side, guns drawn, flashlights steady. There was no fuss. No struggle. Just the sound of heavy voices in the night, and a woman's spiritless weeping.

At the Aqua Azul, Kathy put her hand in his. "I won't see you again," she said. It was statement, not question.

"I don't believe so, Kathy."

"Take care of yourself." The words had a special intonation. She made her real meaning clear: Gil, don't let too many of these things happen to you. Don't go too far away from life and from warmth. Don't go to that far place where you are conscious only of evil and the effects of evil.

"I'll try to," he said.

As he drove away from her, drove down the dark road that paralleled the beaches, he thought of her as another chance lost, as another milepost on a lonely road that ended at some unguessable destination. There was a shifting sourness in his mind, an unease that was familiar. He drove with his eyes steady, his face fashioned into its mask of tough unconcern. Each time, you bled a little. And each time the hard flutter of excitement ended in this sourness. Murder for money. It was seldom anything else. It was seldom particularly clever. It was invariably brutal.

Dinah Davisson's house was brightly lighted. The other houses on the street were dark. He had asked that he be permitted to inform her.

She was in the long pastel living room, a man and a woman with her.

She had been crying, but she was undefeated. She carried her head high. Something hardened and tautened within him when he saw the red stripes on her cheek, stripes that only fingers could have made, in anger.

"Mr. Darrigan, this is Miss Davisson and Colonel Davisson."

They were tall people. Temple had his father's hard jaw, shrewd eye. The woman was so much like him that it was almost ludicrous. Both of them were very cool, very formal, slightly patronizing.

"You are from Guardsman Life?" Colonel Davisson asked. "Bit unusual for you to be here, isn't it?"

"Not entirely. I'd like to speak to you alone, Mrs. Davisson."

Anything you wish to say to her can be said in front of us," Alicia Davisson said acidly.

"I'd prefer to speak to her alone," Gil said, quite softly.

"It doesn't matter, Mr. Darrigan," the young widow said.

"The police have found your husband's body," he said bluntly, knowing that bluntness was more merciful than trying to cushion the blow with mealy half-truths.

Dinah closed her lovely eyes, kept them closed for long seconds. Her hand tightened on the arm of the chair and then relaxed. "How—"

"I knew a stupid marriage of this sort would end in some kind of disaster," Alicia said.

The cruelty of that statement took Darrigan's breath for a moment. Shock gave way to anger. The colonel walked to the dark windows, looked out into the night, hands locked behind him, head bowed.

Alicia rapped a cigarette briskly on her thumbnail, lighted it.

"Marriage had nothing to do with it," Darrigan said. "He was murdered for the sake of profit. He was murdered by a thoroughly unpleasant little man with a greedy wife."

"And our young friend here profits nicely," Alicia said.

Dinah stared at her. "How on earth can you say a thing like that when you've just found out? You're his daughter. It doesn't seem—"

"Kindly spare us the violin music," Alicia said.

"I don't want any of the insurance money," Dinah said. "I don't want any part of it. You two can have it. All of it."

The colonel wheeled slowly and stared at her. He wet his lips. "Do you mean that?"

Dinah lifted her chin. "I mean it."

The colonel said ingratiatingly, "You'll have the trust fund, of course, as it states in the will. That certainly will be enough to take care of you."

"I don't know as I want that, either."

"We can discuss that later," the colonel said soothingly. "This is a great shock to all of us. Darrigan, can you draw up some sort of document she can sign where she relinquishes her claim as principal beneficiary?" When he spoke to Darrigan, his voice had a Pentagon crispness.

Darrigan had seen this too many times before. Money had changed the faces of the children. A croupier would recognize that glitter in the eyes, that moistness of mouth. Darrigan looked at Dinah. Her face was proud, unchanged.

"I could, I suppose. But I won't," Darrigan said.

"Don't be impudent. If you can't, a lawyer can."

Darrigan spoke very slowly, very distinctly. "Possibly you don't understand, Colonel. The relationship between insurance company and policyholder is one of trust. A policyholder does not name his principal beneficiary through whim. We have accepted his money over a period of years. We intend to see that his wishes are carried out. The policy options state that his widow will have an excellent income during her lifetime. She does not receive a lump sum, except for a single payment of ten thousand. What she does with the income is her own business, once it is received. She can give it to you, if she wishes."

"I couldn't accept that sort of . . . charity," the colonel said stiffly. "You heard her state her wishes, man! She wants to give up all claims against the policies."

Darrigan allowed himself a smile. "She's only trying to dissociate herself from you two scavengers. She has a certain amount of pride. She is mourning her husband. Maybe you can't understand that."

"Throw him out, Tem," Alicia whispered.

The colonel had turned white. "I shall do exactly that," he said.

Dinah stood up slowly, her face white. "Leave my house," she said.

The colonel turned toward her. "What do—"

"Yes, the two of you. You and your sister. Leave my house at once."

The tension lasted for long seconds. Dinah's eyes didn't waver. Alicia shattered the moment by standing up and saying, in tones of infinite disgust, "Come on, Tem. The only thing to do with that little bitch is start dragging her through the courts."

They left silently, wrapped in dignity like stained cloaks.

Dinah came to Darrigan. She put her face against his chest, her brow hard against the angle of his jaw. The sobs were tiny spasms, tearing her, contorting her.

He cupped the back of her head in his hand, feeling a sense of wonder at the silk texture of her hair, at the tender outline of fragile bone underneath. Something more than forgotten welled up within him, stinging his eyes, husking his voice as he said, "They aren't worth . . . this."

"He . . . was worth . . . more than . . . this," she gasped.

The torment was gone as suddenly as it had come. She stepped back, rubbing at streaming eyes with the backs of her hands, the way a child does.

"I'm sorry," she said. She tried to smile. "You're not a wailing wall."

"Part of my official duties, sometimes."

"Can they turn this into . . . nastiness?"

"They have no basis. He was of sound mind when he made the

provisions. They're getting enough. More than enough. Some people can never have enough."

"I'd like to sign it over."

"Your husband had good reasons for setting it up the way he did."

"Perhaps."

"Do you have anyone to help you?" he asked impulsively. He knew at once he had put too much of what he felt in his voice. He tried to cover by saying, "There'll be a lot of arrangements. I mean, it could be considered part of my job."

He detected the faintly startled look in her eyes. Awareness made them awkward. "Thank you very much, Mr. Darrigan. I think Brad will help."

"Can you get that woman over to stay with you tonight?"

"I'll be all right."

He left her and went back to the beach to his room. In the morning he would make whatever official statements were considered necessary. He lay in the darkness and thought of Dinah, of the way she was a promise of warmth, of integrity.

And, being what he was, he began to look for subterfuge in her attitude, for some evidence that her reactions had been part of a clever act. He ended by despising himself for having gone so far that he could instinctively trust no one.

In the morning he phoned the home office. He talked with Palmer, a vice-president. He said, "Mr. Palmer, I'm sending through the necessary reports approving payment of the claim."

"It's a bloody big one," Palmer said disconsolately.

"I know that, sir," Darrigan said. "No way out of it."

"Well, I suppose you'll be checking in then by, say, the day after tomorrow?"

"That should be about right."

Darrigan spent the rest of the day going through motions. He signed the lengthy statement for the police. The Drynfellses were claiming that in the scuffle for the paper, Davisson had fallen and hit his head on a bumper guard. In panic they had hidden the body. It was dubious as to whether premeditation could be proved.

He dictated his report for the company files to a public stenographer, sent it off airmail. He turned the car in, packed his bag. He sat on the edge of his bed for a long time, smoking cigarettes, looking at the far wall.

The thought of heading north gave him a monstrous sense of loss. He argued with himself. Fool, she's just a young, well-heeled widow. All that sort of thing was canceled out when Doris left you. What difference does it make that she should remind you of what you had once thought Doris was?

He looked into the future and saw a long string of hotel rooms, one after the other, like a child's blocks aligned on a dark carpet.

If she doesn't laugh in your face, and if your daydream should turn out to be true, they'll nudge each other and talk about how Gil Darrigan fell into a soft spot.

She'll laugh in your face.

He phoned at quarter of five and caught Palmer. "I'd like to stay down here and do what I can for the beneficiary, Mr. Palmer. A couple of weeks, maybe."

"Isn't that a bit unusual?"

"I have a vacation overdue, if you'd rather I didn't do it on company time."

"Better make it vacation, then."

"Anything you say. Will you put it through for me?"

"Certainly, Gil."

At dusk she came down the hall, looked through the screen at him. She was wearing black.

He felt like a kid trying to make his first date. "I thought I could stay around a few days and . . . help out. I don't want you to think I—"

She swung the door open. "Somehow I knew you wouldn't leave," she said.

He stepped into the house, with a strange feeling of trumpets and banners. She hadn't laughed. And he knew in that moment that during the years ahead, the good years ahead of them, she would always know what was in his heart, even before he would know it. And one day, perhaps within the year, she would turn all that warmth suddenly toward him, and it would be like coming in out of a cold and rainy night.

JAMES M. CAIN

Not many writers of crime fiction can claim to have been a seminal influence on the great French writer Albert Camus. Yet throughout his career Camus praised the novels of James M. Cain (1892–1977) and, indeed, structured two of his novels along Cainian lines.

Cain, when all the arguments and arguers have been silenced, may just be the great crime fiction writer of all time. Chandler wrote B-movie fantasies; Hammett, a better writer, wrote well of his mean streets but buried his passion beneath a stoic style. Objective prose narrows the field of vision. Cain gave us criminals as they frequently are—confused, trapped, self-pitying, not terribly bright people who more often than not stumble into crime rather than seek it out. He did so in a style that was almost diarylike in its intimacy and yet was far richer in implication than anything done by Chandler or Hammett. The last chapter of *Double Indemnity* is beyond the talent of virtually all crime fiction writers. Camus himself might not have been capable of writing it.

In addition to straight crime, he gave us *Mildred Pierce,* in which he did something very few writers of any kind can ever do—made the life of a fundamentally decent and mostly unremarkable woman profoundly interesting and valuable.

Cigarette Girl

I'd never so much as laid eyes on her before going in this place, the Here's How, a nightclub on Route 1, a few miles north of Washington, on business that was 99 percent silly, but that I had to keep to myself. It was around eight at night, with hardly anyone there, and I'd just taken a table, ordered a drink, and started to unwrap a cigar when a whiff of perfume hit me, and she swept by with cigarettes. As to what she looked like, I had only a rear view, but the taffeta skirt, crepe blouse, and silver earrings were quiet, and the chassis was choice, call it fancy, a little smaller than medium. So far, a cigarette girl, nothing to rate any cheers, but not bad either, for a guy unattached who'd like an excuse to linger.

But then she made a pitch, or what I took for a pitch. Her middle-aged customer was trying to tell her some joke, and taking so long about it the proprietor got in the act. He was a big, blond, blocky guy, with kind of a decent face, but he went and whispered to her as though to hustle her up, for some reason apparently, I couldn't quite figure it out. She didn't much seem to like it, until her eye caught mine. She gave a little pout, a little shrug, a little wink, and then just stood there, smiling.

Now I know this pitch and it's nice, because of course I smiled back, and with that I was on the hook. A smile is nature's freeway: it has lanes, and you can go any speed you like, except you can't go back. Not that I wanted to, as I suddenly changed my mind about the cigar I had in my hand, stuck it back in my pocket, and wigwagged for cigarettes. She nodded, and when she came over said: "You stop laughing at me."

"Who's laughing? Looking."

"Oh, of course. That's different."

I picked out a pack, put down my buck, and got the surprise of my life: She gave me change. As she started to leave, I said: "You forgot something, maybe?"

"That's not necessary."

"For all this I get, I should pay."

"All what, sir, for instance?"

"I told you: the beauty that fills my eye."

"The best things in life are free."

"On that basis, fair lady, some of them, here, are tops. Would you care to sit down?"

"Can't."

"Why not?"

"Not allowed. We got rules."

With that she went out toward the rear somewhere, and I noticed the proprietor again, just a short distance away, and realized he'd been edging in. I called him over and said: "What's the big idea? I was talking to her."

"Mister, she's paid to work."

"Yeah, she mentioned about rules, but now they got other things too. Four Freedoms, all kinds of stuff. Didn't anyone ever tell you?"

"I heard of it, yes."

"You're Mr. Here's How?"

"Jack Conner, to my friends."

I took a V from my wallet, folded it, creased it, pushed it toward him. I said: "Jack, little note of introduction I generally carry around. I'd like you to ease these rules. She's cute, and I crave to buy her a drink."

He didn't see any money, and stood for a minute thinking. Then:

"Mister, you're off on the wrong foot. In the first place, she's not a cigarette girl. Tonight, yes, when the other girl is off. But not regular, no. In the second place, she's not any chiselly-wink that orders rye, drinks tea, takes the four bits you slip her, the four I charge for the drink—and is open to propositions. She's class. She's used to class—out west, with people that have it, and that brought her east when they came. In the third place she's a friend, and before I eased any rules I'd have to know more about you, a whole lot more, than this note tells me."

"My name's Cameron."

"Pleased to meet you and all that, but as to who you are, Mr. Cameron, and what you are, I still don't know—"

"I'm a musician."

"Yeah? What instrument?"

"Any of them. Guitar, mainly."

Which brings me to what I was doing there. I do play the guitar, play it all day long, for the help I get from it, as it gives me certain chords, the big ones that people go for, and heads me off from some others, the fancy ones on the piano, that other musicians go for. I'm an arranger, based in Baltimore, and had driven down on a little tune detecting. The guy who takes most of my work, Art Lomak, the band leader, writes a few tunes himself, and had gone clean off his rocker about one he said had been stolen, or thefted as they call it. It was one he'd been playing a little, to try it and work out bugs, with lyric and title to come, soon as the idea hit him. And then he rang me, with screams. It had already gone on the air, as twenty people had told him, from this same little honky-tonk, as part of a ten o'clock spot on the Washington FM pickup. He begged me to be here tonight, when the trio started their broadcast, pick up such dope as I could, and tomorrow give him the lowdown.

That much was right on the beam, stuff that goes on every day, a routine I knew by heart. But his tune had angles, all of them slightly peculiar. One was, it had already been written, though it was never a hit and was almost forgotten, in the days when states were hot, under the title "Nevada." Another was, it had been written even before that, by a gent named Giuseppe Verdi, as part of the *Sicilian Vespers*, under the title "O Tu Palermo." Still another was, Art was really burned and seemed to have no idea where the thing had come from. They just can't get it, those big schmalzburgers like him, that what leaks out of their head might, just once, have leaked in. But the twist, the reason I had to come and couldn't just play it for laughs, was: Art could have been right. Maybe the lift *was* from him, not from the original opera, or from the first theft, "Nevada." It's a natural for a three quarters beat, and that's how Art had been playing it. So if that's how they were doing it here, instead of with "Nevada's" four fourths, which followed the Verdi signature, there might still be plenty of work for the lawyers Art had put on it, with screams, same like to me.

Silly, almost.

Spooky.

But maybe, just possibly, moola.

So Jack, this boss character, by now had smelled something fishy and suddenly took a powder, to the stand where the fiddles were parked, as of course the boys weren't there yet, and came back with a Spanish guitar. I took it, thanked him, and tuned. To kind of work it around in the direction of Art's little problem, and at the same time make like there was nothing at all to conceal, I said I'd come on account of his band, to catch it during the broadcast, as I'd heard it was pretty good. He didn't react, which left me nowhere, but I thought it well to get going.

I played him "Night and Day," no Segovia job, but plenty good, for free. On "day and night," where it really opens up, I knew things to do, and talk suddenly stopped among the scattering of people that were in there. When I finished there was some little clapping, but still he didn't react, and I gave thought to mayhem. But then a buzzer sounded, and he took another powder, out toward the rear this time, where she had disappeared. I began a little beguine, but he was back. He bowed, picked up his V, bowed again, said: "Mr. Cameron, the guitar did it. She heard you, and you're in."

"Will you set me up for two?"

"Hold on, there's a catch."

He said until midnight, when one of his men would take over, she was checking his orders. "That means she handles the money, and if she's not there, I could just as well close down. You're invited back with her, but she can't come out with you."

"Oh. Fine."

"Sir, you asked for it."

It wasn't quite the way I'd have picked to do it, but the main thing was the girl, and I followed him through the OUT door, the one his waiters were using, still with my Spanish guitar. But then, all of a sudden, I loved it and felt even nearer to her.

This was the works of the joint, with a little office at one side, service bar on the other, range rear and center, the crew in white all around, getting the late stuff ready. But high on a stool, off by herself, on a little railed-in platform where waiters would have to pass, she was waving at me, treating it all as a joke. She called down: "Isn't this a balcony scene for you? You have to play me some music!"

I whapped into it quick, and when I told her it was *Romeo and Juliet*, she said it was just what she'd wanted. By then Jack had a stool he put next to hers, so I could sit beside her, back of her little desk. He introduced us, and it turned out her name was Stark. I climbed up and there we were, out in the middle of the air and yet in a way private, as the crew played it funny, to the extent they played it at all but mostly were too busy even to look. I put the guitar on the desk and kept on with the music. By the time I'd done some *Showboat* she was calling me Bill and to me she was Lydia. I remarked on her eyes, which were green and showed up bright against her creamy skin and ashy blond hair. She remarked on mine, which are light, watery blue, and I wished I was something besides tall, thin, and red-haired. But it was kind of cute when she gave a little pinch and nipped one of my freckles, on my hand back of the thumb.

Then Jack was back, with Champagne iced in a bucket, which I hadn't ordered. When I remembered my drink, the one I *had* ordered, he said scotch was no good, and this would be on him. I thanked him, but after he'd opened and poured, and I'd leaned the guitar in a corner and raised my glass to her, I said: "What's made him so friendly?"

"Oh, Jack's always friendly."

"Not to me. Oh, no."

"He may have thought I had it coming. Some little thing to cheer me. My last night in the place."

"You going away?"

"M'm-h'm."

"When?"

"Tonight."

"That why you're off at twelve?"

"Jack tell you that?"

"He told me quite a lot."

"Plane leaves at one. Bag's gone already. It's at the airport, all checked and ready to be weighed."

She clinked her glass to mine, took a little sip, and drew a deep, trembly breath. As for me, I felt downright sick, just why I couldn't say, as it had to all be strictly allegro, with nobody taking it serious. It stuck in my throat a little when I said: "Well—happy landings. Is it permitted to ask which way the plane is taking you?"

"Home."

"And where's that?"

"It's—not important."

"The West, I know that much?"

"What else did Jack tell you?"

I took it, improvised, and made up a little stuff, about her high-toned friends, her being a society brat, spoiled as all get-out, and the heavy dough she was used to—a light rib, as I thought. But it hadn't gone very far when I saw it was missing bad. When I cut it off, she took it. She said: "Some of that's true, in a way. I was—fortunate, we'll call it. But—you still have no idea have you, Bill, what I really am?"

"I've been playing by ear."

"I wonder if you want to know?"

"If you don't want to, I'd rather you didn't say."

None of it was turning out quite as I wanted, and I guess maybe I showed it. She studied me a little and asked: "The silver I wear, that didn't tell you anything? Or my giving you change for your dollar? It didn't mean anything to you that a girl would run a straight game?"

"She's not human."

"It means she's a gambler."

And then: "Bill, does that shock you?"

"No, not at all."

"I'm not ashamed of it. Out home, it's legal. You know where that is now?"

"Oh! *Oh!*"

"Why oh? And *oh*?"

"Nothing. It's—Nevada, isn't it?"

"Something wrong with Nevada?"

"No! I just woke up, that's all."

I guess that's what I said, but whatever it was, she could hardly miss the upbeat in my voice. Because, of course, that wrapped it all up pretty, not only the tune, which the band would naturally play for her, but her too, and who she was. Society dame, to tell the truth, hadn't pleased me much, and maybe that was one reason my rib was slightly off key. But gambler I could go for, a little cold, a little dangerous, a little brave. When she was sure I had really bought it, we were close again, and after a nip on the freckle her fingers slid over my hand. She said play her "Smoke"—the smoke she had in her eyes. But I didn't, and we just sat there some little time.

And then, a little bit at a time, she began to spill it: "Bill, it was just plain cockeyed. I worked in a club, the Paddock, in Reno, a regular institution. Tony Rocco—Rock—owned it, and was the squarest bookie ever—why he was a senator, a civic, and everything. And I worked for him, running his wires, practically being his manager, with a beautiful salary, a bonus at Christmas, and everything. And then wham, it struck. This federal thing. This ten percent tax on gross. And we were out of business. It just didn't make sense. Everything else was exempted. Wheels and boards and slots, whatever you could think of, but us. Us and the numbers racket, in Harlem and Florida and Washington."

"Take it easy."

"That's right, Bill. Thanks."

"Have some wine."

". . . Rock, of course, was fixed. He had property, and for the building, where the Paddock was, he got two hundred fifty thousand—or so I heard. But then came the tip on Maryland."

That crossed me up, and instead of switching her off, I asked her what she meant. She said: "That Maryland would legalize wheels."

"What do you smoke in Nevada?"

"Oh, I didn't believe it. And Rock didn't. But Mrs. Rock went nuts about it. Oh well, she had a reason."

"Dark, handsome reason?"

"I don't want to talk about it, but that reason took the Rocks for a ride, for every cent they got for the place, and tried to take me too, for other things besides money. When they went off to Italy, they thought they had it fixed; he was to keep me at my salary, in case Maryland *would* legalize, and if not, to send me home, with severance pay, as it's called. And instead of that—"

"I'm listening."

"I've said too much."

"What's this guy to you?"

"Nothing! I never even saw him until the three of us stepped off the plane—with our hopes. In a way it seemed reasonable. Maryland has tracks, and they help with the taxes. Why not wheels?"

"And *who* is this guy?"

"I'd be ashamed to say, but I'll say this much: I won't be a kept floozy. I don't care who he thinks he is, or—"

She bit her lip, started to cry, and really shut up then. To switch off, I asked why she was working for Jack, and she said: "Why not? You can't go home in a barrel. But he's been swell to me."

Saying people were swell seemed to be what she liked, and she calmed down, letting her hand stay when I pressed it in both of mine. Then we were really close, and I meditated if we were close enough that I'd be warranted in laying it on the line, she should let that plane fly away and not go to Nevada at all. But while I was working on that, business was picking up, with waiters stopping by to let her look at their trays, and I hadn't much chance to say it, whatever I wanted to say. Then, through the IN door, a waiter came through with a tray that had a wine bottle on it. A guy followed him in, a little noisy guy, who said the bottle was full and grabbed it off the tray. He had hardly gone out again when Jack was in the door, watching him as he staggered back to the table. The waiter swore the bottle was empty, but all Jack did was nod.

Then Jack came over to her, took another little peep through the window in the OUT door, which was just under her balcony, and said: "Lydia, what did you make of him?"

"Why—he's drunk, that's all."

"You notice him, Mr. Cameron?"

"No—except it crossed my mind he wasn't as tight as the act he was putting on."

"Just what crossed *my* mind! How could he get that drunk on a split of Napa red? What did he want back here?"

By now the waiter had gone out on the floor and come back, saying the guy wanted his check. But as he started to shuffle it out of the bunch he had tucked in his vest, Jack stopped him and said: "He don't get any check—not till I give the word. Tell Joe I said stand by and see he don't get out. *Move!*"

The waiter had looked kind of blank but hustled out as told, and then Jack looked at her. He said: "Lady, I'll be back. I'm taking a look around."

He went, and she drew another of her long, trembly breaths. I cut my eye around, but no one had noticed a thing, and yet it seemed kind of funny they'd all be slicing bread, wiping glass, or fixing cocktail setups, with Jack mumbling it low out of the side of his mouth. I had a creepy feeling of things going on, and my mind took it a little, fitting it together, what she had said about the bag checked at the airport, the guy trying to make her, and most of all the way Jack had acted the second she showed with her cigarettes, shooing her off the floor, getting her out of sight. She kept staring through the window, at the drunk where he sat with his bottle, and seemed to ease when a captain I took to be Joe planted himself pretty solid in a spot that would block off a run-out.

Then Jack was back, marching around, snapping his fingers, giving orders for the night. But as he passed the back door, I noticed his hand touched the lock, as though putting the catch on. He started back to the floor but stopped as he passed her desk, and shot it quick in a whisper: "He's out there, Lydia, parked in back. This drunk, like I thought, is a finger he sent in to spot you, but he won't be getting out till you're gone. You're leaving for the airport right now."

"Will you call me a cab, Jack?"

"Cab? I'm taking you."

He stepped near me and whispered: "Mr. Cameron, I'm sorry, this little lady has to leave for—"

"I know about that."

"She's in danger—"

"I've also caught on to that."

"From a no-good imitation goon that's been trying to get to her here, which is why I'm shipping her out. I hate to break this up, but if you'll ride with us, Mr. Cameron—"

"I'll follow you down."

"That's right, you have your car. It's Friendship Airport, just down the road."

He told her to get ready while he was having his car brought up and the boy who would take her place on the desk was changing his clothes. Step on it, he said, but wait until he came back. He went out on the floor and marched past the drunk without even turning his head. But she sat watching me. She said: "You're not coming, are you?"

"Friendship's a little cold."

"But not mine, Bill, no."

She got off her stool, stood near me and touched my hair. She said: "Ships that pass in the night pass so close, so close." And then: "I'm ashamed, Bill, I'd have to go for this reason. I wonder, for the first time, if gambling's really much good." She pulled the chain of the light, so we were half in the dark. Then she kissed me. She said: "God bless and keep you, Bill."

"And you, Lydia."

I felt her tears on my cheek, and then she pulled away and stepped to the little office, where she began putting a coat on and tying a scarf on her head. She looked so pretty it came to me I still hadn't given her the one little bouquet I'd been saving for the last. I picked up the guitar and started "Nevada."

She wheeled, but what stared at me were eyes as hard as glass. I was so startled I stopped, but she kept right on staring. Outside a car door slammed, and she listened at the window beside her. Then at last she looked away, to peep through the venetian blind. Jack popped in, wearing his coat and hat, and motioned her to hurry. But he caught something and said, low yet so I could hear him: "Lydia! What's the matter?"

She stalked over to me, with him following along, pointed her finger, and then didn't say it but spat it: "He's the finger—that's what's the matter, that's all. He played "Nevada," as though we hadn't had enough trouble with it already. And Vanny heard it. He hopped out of his car and he's under the window right now."

"Then OK, let's go."

I was a little too burned to make with the explanations and took my time, parking the guitar, sliding off, and climbing down, to give them a chance to blow. But she still had something to say, and to me, not to him. She pushed her face up to mine, and mocking how I had spoken, yipped: "Oh! . . . *Oh!* OH!" Then she went, with Jack. Then I went, clumping after.

Then it broke wide open.

The drunk, who was supposed to sit there, conveniently boxed in while she went slipping out, turned out more of a hog-calling type, and instead of playing his part jumped up and yelled: "Vanny! *Vanny!* Here she comes! She's leaving! VANNY!"

He kept it up while women screamed all over, then pulled a gun from his pocket and let go at the ceiling, so it sounded like the field artillery, as shots always do when fired inside a room. Jack jumped for him and hit the deck as his feet shot from under him on the slippery wood of the dance floor. Joe swung, missed, swung again, and landed, so Mr. Drunk went down. But when Joe scrambled for the gun, there came this voice through the smoke: "Hold it! As you were—and leave that gun alone."

Then hulking in came this short-necked, thick-shouldered thing, in homburg hat, double-breasted coat, and white muffler, one hand in his pocket, the other giving an imitation of a movie gangster. He said keep still and nobody would get hurt, but "I won't stand for tricks." He helped Jack up, asked how he'd been. Jack said: "Young man, let me tell you something—"

"How you been, I asked."

"Fine, Mr. Rocco."

"Any telling, Jack—I'll do it."

Then to her: "Lydia, how've *you* been?"

"That doesn't concern you."

The she burst out about what he had done to his mother, the gyp he'd handed his father, and his propositions to her, and I got it at last who this idiot was. He listened, but right in the middle of it he waved his hand toward me and asked: "Who's this guy?"

"Vanny, I think you know."

"Guy, are you the boyfriend?"

"If so I don't tell you."

I sounded tough, but my belly didn't feel that way. They had it some more, and he connected me with the tune and seemed to enjoy it a lot that it had told him where to find her, on the broadcast and here now tonight. But he kept creeping closer to where we were all lined up with the drunk stretched on the floor, the gun under his hand, and I suddenly felt the prickle that Vanny was really nuts and in a minute meant to kill her. It also crossed my mind that a guy who plays the guitar has a left hand made of steel, from squeezing down on the strings, and is a dead sure judge of distance to the last eighth of an inch. I prayed I could forget it, told myself I owed her nothing at all, that she'd turned on me cold with no good reason. I concentrated, to dismiss the thought entirely.

No soap.

I grabbed for my chord and got it.

I choked down on his hand, the one he held in his pocket, while hell broke loose in the place with women screaming, men running, and fists trying to help. I had the gun hand all right, but when I reached for the other he twisted, butted, and bit, and for that long I thought he'd get loose and that I was a gone pigeon. The gun barked, and a piledriver hit my leg. I went down. Another gun spoke and he went down beside me. Then there was Jack, the drunk's gun in his hand, stepping in close and firing again to make sure.

I blacked out.

I came to, and then she was there, a knife in her hand, ripping the cloth away from the outside of my leg, grabbing napkins, stanching blood, while somewhere ten miles off I could hear Jack's voice as he yelled into a phone. On the floor right beside me was something under a tablecloth.

That went on for some time, with Joe calming things down and some people sliding out. The band came in, and I heard a boy ask for his guitar. Somebody brought it to him. And then, at last, came the screech of sirens, and she whispered some thanks to God.

Then, while the cops were catching up, with me, with Jack, and what was under the cloth, we both went kind of haywire, me laughing, she crying, and both in each other's arms. I said: "Lydia, Lydia, you're not taking that plane. They legalize things in Maryland, one thing specially, except that instead of wheels they generally use a ring."

Still holding my leg with one hand she pulled me close with the other, kissed me and kept on kissing me, and couldn't speak at all. All legalized now, is what I started to tell about—with Jack as best man, naturally.

ROSS MACDONALD

The mystery field had long needed a Proust, and it got it in Kenneth Millar (1915–1983), who wrote under the pseudonym Ross Macdonald. Here was a writer who believed that most truths about the present could be found in the past, and he revealed that idea with incredible grace and style in his novels.

His private eye Lew Archer was an antique dealer of sorts, though instead of objects, he dealt in souls. Macdonald's version of southern California of the fifties and sixties is comparable to what Nathanael West and Horace McCoy achieved in the thirties. Archer was a refined man in a vulgar time, and yet one sensed that for all his surface calm, he was just as deeply troubled as the people he pursued. *The Way Some People Die, The Ivory Grin,* and *The Far Side of the Dollar* are particularly good novels. *The Chill* is most likely his masterpiece.

Tom Nolan's biography *Ross Macdonald* is heartily recommended if you want to know more about this intriguing author.

Guilt-Edged Blonde

(Lew Archer)

A man was waiting for me at the gate at the edge of the runway. He didn't look like the man I expected to meet. He wore a stained tan windbreaker, baggy slacks, a hat as squashed and dubious as his face. He must have been forty years old, to judge by the gray in his hair and the lines around his eyes. His eyes were dark and evasive, moving here and there as if to avoid getting hurt. He had been hurt often and badly, I guessed.

"You Archer?"

I said I was. I offered him my hand. He didn't know what to do with it. He regarded it suspiciously, as if I was planning to try a Judo hold on him. He kept his hands in the pockets of his windbreaker.

"I'm Harry Nemo." His voice was a grudging whine. It cost him an effort to give his name away. "My brother told me to come and pick you up. You ready to go?"

"As soon as I get my luggage."

I collected my overnight bag at the counter in the empty waiting room. The bag was very heavy for its size. It contained, besides a toothbrush and spare linen, two guns and the ammunition for them. A .38 special for sudden work, and a .32 automatic as a spare.

Harry Nemo took me outside to his car. It was a new seven-passenger custom job, as long and black as death. The windshield and side windows were very thick, and they had the yellowish tinge of bullet-proof glass.

"Are you expecting to be shot at?"

"Not me." His smile was dismal. "This is Nick's car."

"Why didn't Nick come himself?"

He looked around the deserted field. The plane I had arrived on was a flashing speck in the sky above the red sun. The only human being in sight was the operator in the control tower. But Nemo leaned towards me in the seat, and spoke in a whisper:

"Nick's a scared pigeon. He's scared to leave the house. Ever since this morning."

"What happened this morning?"

"Didn't he tell you? You talked to him on the phone."

"He didn't say very much. He told me he wanted to hire a bodyguard for six days, until his boat sails. He didn't tell me why."

"They're gunning for him, that's why. He went to the beach this morning. He has a private beach along the back of his ranch, and he went down there by himself for his morning dip. Somebody took a shot at him from the top of the bluff. Five or six shots. He was in the water, see, with no gun handy. He told me the slugs were splashing around him like hailstones. He ducked and swam under water out to sea. Lucky for him he's a good swimmer, or he wouldn't of got away. It's no wonder he's scared. It means they caught up with him, see."

"Who are 'they,' or is that a family secret?"

Nemo turned from the wheel to peer into my face. His breath was sour, his look incredulous. "Christ, don't you know who Nick is? Didn't he tell you?"

"He's a lemon-grower, isn't he?"

"He is now."

"What did he used to be?"

The bitter beaten face closed on itself. “I oughtn’t to be flapping at the mouth. He can tell you himself if he wants to.”

Two hundred horses yanked us away from the curb. I rode with my heavy leather bag on my knees. Nemo drove as if driving was the one thing in life he enjoyed, rapt in silent communion with the engine. It whisked us along the highway, then down a gradual incline between geometrically planted lemon groves. The sunset sea glimmered red at the foot of the slope.

Before we reached it, we turned off the blacktop into a private lane which ran like a straight hair-parting between the dark green trees. Straight for half a mile or more to a low house in a clearing.

The house was flat-roofed, made of concrete and fieldstone, with an attached garage. All of its windows were blinded with heavy draperies. It was surrounded with well-kept shrubbery and lawn, the lawn with a ten-foot wire fence surmounted by barbed wire.

Nemo stopped in front of the closed and padlocked gate, and honked the horn. There was no response. He honked the horn again.

About halfway between the house and the gate, a crawling thing came out of the shrubbery. It was a man, moving very slowly on hands and knees. His head hung down almost to the ground. One side of his head was bright red, as if he had fallen in paint. He left a jagged red trail in the gravel of the driveway.

Harry Nemo said, “Nick!” He scrambled out of the car. “What happened, Nick?”

The crawling man lifted his heavy head and looked at us. Cumbrously, he rose to his feet. He came forward with his legs spraddled and loose, like a huge infant learning to walk. He breathed loudly and horribly, looking at us with a dreadful hopefulness. Then he died on his feet, still walking. I saw the change in his face before it struck the gravel.

Harry Nemo went over the fence like a weary monkey, snagging his slacks on the barbed wire. He knelt beside his brother and turned him over and palmed his chest. He stood up shaking his head.

I had my bag unzipped and my hand on the revolver. I went to the gate. “Open up, Harry.”

Harry was saying, “They got him,” over and over. He crossed himself several times. “The dirty bastards.”

“Open up,” I said.

He found a key ring in the dead man’s pocket and opened the padlocked gate. Our dragging footsteps crunched the gravel. I looked down at the specks of gravel in Nicky Nemo’s eyes, the bullet hole in the temple.

“Who got him, Harry?”

“I dunno. Fats Jordan, or Artie Castola, or Faronese. It must have been one of them.”

“The Purple Gang.”

“You called it. Nicky was their treasurer back in the thirties. He was the one that didn't get into the papers. He handled the payoff, see. When the heat went on and the gang got busted up, he had some money in a safe deposit box. He was the only one that got away."

"How much money?"

"Nicky never told me. All I know, he come out here before the war and bought a thousand acres of lemon land. It took them fifteen years to catch up with him. He always knew they were gonna, though. He knew it."

"Artie Castola got off the Rock last spring."

"You're telling me. That's when Nicky bought himself the bullet-proof car and put up the fence."

"Are they gunning for you?"

He looked around at the darkening groves and the sky. The sky was streaked with running red, as if the sun had died a violent death.

"I dunno," he answered nervously. "They got no reason to. I'm as clean as soap. I never been in the rackets. Not since I was young, anyway. The wife made me go straight, see?"

I said: "We better get into the house and call the police."

The front door was standing a few inches ajar. I could see at the edge that it was sheathed with quarter-inch steel plate. Harry put my thoughts into words.

"Why in hell would he go outside? He was safe as houses as long as he stayed inside."

"Did he live alone?"

"More or less alone."

"What does that mean?"

He pretended not to hear me, but I got some kind of an answer. Looking through the doorless arch into the living room, I saw a leopardskin coat folded across the back of the chesterfield. There were redtipped cigarette butts mingled with chair butts in the ash trays.

"Nicky was married?"

"Not exactly."

"You know the woman?"

"Naw." But he was lying.

Somewhere behind the thick walls of the house, there was a creak of springs, a crashing bump, the broken roar of a cold engine, grinding of tires in gravel. I got to the door in time to see a cerise convertible hurtling down the driveway. The top was down, and a yellow-haired girl was small and intent at the wheel. She swerved around Nick's body and got through the gate somehow, with her tires screaming. I aimed at the right rear tire, and missed. Harry came up behind me. He pushed my gun-arm down before I could fire again. The convertible disappeared in the direction of the highway.

"Let her go," he said.

"Who is she?"

He thought about it, his slow brain clicking almost audibly. "I dunno.

Some pig that Nicky picked up some place. Her name is Flossie or Florrie or something. She didn't shoot him, if that's what you're worried about."

"You know her pretty well, do you?"

"The hell I do. I don't mess with Nicky's dames." He tried to work up a rage to go with the strong words, but he didn't have the makings. The best he could produce was petulance: "Listen, mister, why should you hang around? The guy that hired you is dead."

"I haven't been paid, for one thing."

"I'll fix that."

He trotted across the lawn to the body and came back with an alligator billfold. It was thick with money.

"How much?"

"A hundred will do it."

He handed me a hundred-dollar bill. "Now how about you amscray, bud, before the law gets here?"

"I need transportation."

"Take Nicky's car. He won't be using it. You can park it at the airport and leave the key with the agent."

"I can, eh?"

"Sure, I'm telling you you can."

"Aren't you getting a little free with your brother's property?"

"It's my property now, bud." A bright thought struck him, disorganizing his face. "Incidentally, how would you like to get off my land?"

"I'm staying, Harry. I like this place. I always say it's people that make a place."

The gun was still in my hand. He looked down at it.

"Get on the telephone, Harry. Call the police."

"Who do you think you are, ordering me around? I took my last order from anybody, see?" He glanced over his shoulder at the dark and shapeless object on the gravel, and spat venomously.

"I'm a citizen, working for Nicky. Not for you."

He changed his tune very suddenly. "How much to go to work for me?"

"Depends on the line of work."

He manipulated the alligator wallet. "Here's another hundred. If you got to hang around, keep the lip buttoned down about the dame, eh? Is it a deal?"

I didn't answer, but I took the money. I put it in a separate pocket by itself. Harry telephoned the county sheriff.

He emptied the ash trays before the sheriff's men arrived, and stuffed the leopardskin coat into the woodbox. I sat and watched him.

We spent the next two hours with loud-mouthed deputies. They were angry with the dead man for having the kind of past that attracted bullets. They were angry with Harry for being his brother. They were secretly angry with themselves for being inexperienced and incompetent. They didn't even uncover the leopardskin coat.

Harry Nemo left for the courthouse first. I waited for him to leave, and followed him home, on foot.

Where a leaning palm tree reared its ragged head above the pavements, there was a court lined with jerry-built frame cottages. Harry turned up the walk between them and entered the first cottage. Light flashed on his face from inside. I heard a woman's voice say something to him. Then light and sound were cut off by the closing door.

An old gabled house with boarded-up windows stood opposite the court. I crossed the street and settled down in the shadows of its veranda to watch Harry Nemo's cottage. Three cigarettes later, a tall woman in a dark hat and a light coat came out of the cottage and walked briskly to the corner and out of sight. Two cigarettes after that, she reappeared at the corner on my side of the street, still walking briskly. I noticed that she had a large straw handbag under her arm. Her face long and stony under the streetlight.

Leaving the street, she marched up the broken sidewalk to the veranda where I was leaning against the shadowed wall. The stairs groaned under her decisive footsteps. I put my hand on the gun in my pocket, and waited. With the rigid assurance of a WAC corporal marching at the head of her platoon, she crossed the veranda to me, a thin high-shouldered silhouette against the light from the corner. Her hand was in her straw bag, and the end of the bag was pointed at my stomach. Her shadowed face was a gleam of eyes, a glint of teeth.

"I wouldn't try it if I were you," she said. "I have a gun here, and the safety is off, and I know how to shoot it, mister."

"Congratulations."

"I'm not joking." Her deep contralto rose a notch. "Rapid fire used to be my specialty. So you better take your hands out of your pockets."

I showed her my hands, empty. Moving very quickly, she relieved my pocket of the weight of my gun, and frisked me for other weapons.

"Who are you, mister?" she said as she stepped back. "You can't be Arturo Castola, you're not old enough."

"Are you a policewoman?"

"I'll ask the questions. What are you doing here?"

"Waiting for a friend."

"You're a liar. You've been watching my house for an hour and a half. I tabbed you through the window."

"So you went and bought yourself a gun?"

"I did. You followed Harry home. I'm Mrs. Nemo, and I want to know why."

"Harry's the friend I'm waiting for."

"You're a double liar. Harry's afraid of you. You're no friend of his."

"That depends on Harry. I'm a detective."

She snorted. "Very likely. Where's your buzzer?"

"I'm a private detective," I said. "I have identification in my wallet."

"Show me. And don't try any tricks."

I produced my photostat. She held it up to the light from the street, and handed it back to me. "So you're a detective. You better do something about your tailing technique. It's obvious."

"I didn't know I was dealing with a cop."

"I was a cop," she said. "Not any more."

"Then give me back my .38. It cost me seventy dollars."

"First tell me, what's your interest in my husband? Who hired you?"

"Nick, your brother-in-law. He called me in Los Angeles today, said he needed a bodyguard for a week. Didn't Harry tell you?"

She didn't answer.

"By the time I got to Nick, he didn't need a bodyguard, or anything. But I thought I'd stick around and see what I could find out about his death. He was a client, after all."

"You should pick your clients more carefully."

"What about picking brothers-in-law?"

She took her head stiffly. The hair that escaped from under her hat was almost white. "I'm not responsible for Nick or anything about him. Harry is my responsibility. I met him in line of duty and I straightened him out, understand? I tore him loose from Detroit and the rackets, and I brought him out here. I couldn't cut him off from his brother entirely. But he hasn't been in trouble since I married him. Not once."

"Until now."

"Harry isn't in trouble now."

"Not yet. Not officially."

"What do you mean?"

"Give me my gun, and put yours down. I can't talk into iron."

She hesitated, a grim and anxious woman under pressure. I wondered what quirk of fate or psychology had married her to a hood, and decided it must have been love. Only love would send a woman across a dark street to face down an unknown gunman. Mrs. Nemo was horse-faced and aging and not pretty, but she had courage.

She handed me my gun. Its butt was soothing to the palm of my hand. I dropped in into my pocket. A gang of Negro boys at loose ends went by in the street, hooting and whistling purposelessly.

She leaned towards me, almost as tall as I was. Her voice was a low sibilance forced between her teeth:

"Harry had nothing to do with his brother's death. You're crazy if you think so."

"What makes you so sure, Mrs. Nemo?"

"Harry couldn't, that's all. I know Harry, I can read him like a book. Even if he had the guts, which he hasn't, he wouldn't dare to think of killing Nick. Nick was his older brother, understand, the successful one in the family." Her voice rasped contemptuously. "In spite of everything I could do or say, Harry worshipped Nick right up to the end."

"Those brotherly feelings sometimes cut two ways. And Harry had a lot to gain."

"Not a cent. Nothing."

"He's Nick's heir, isn't he?"

"Not as long as he stays married to me. I wouldn't let him touch a cent of Nick Nemo's filthy money. Is that clear?"

"It's clear to me. But is it clear to Harry?"

"I made it clear to him, many times. Anyway, this is ridiculous. Harry wouldn't lay a finger on that precious brother of his."

"Maybe he didn't do it himself. He could have had it done for him. I know he's covering for somebody."

"Who?"

"A blonde girl left the house after we arrived. She got away in a cherry-colored convertible. Harry recognized her."

"A cherry-colored convertible?"

"Yes. Does that mean something to you?"

"No. Nothing in particular. She must have been one of Nick's girls. He always had girls."

"Why would Harry cover for her?"

"What do you mean, cover for her?"

"She left a leopardskin coat behind. Harry hid it, and paid me not to tell the police."

"Harry did that?"

"Unless I'm having delusions."

"Maybe you are at that. If you think that Harry paid that girl to shoot Nick, or had anything—"

"I know. Don't say it. I'm crazy."

Mrs. Nemo laid a thin hand on my arm. "Anyway, lay off Harry. Please. I have a hard enough time handling him as it is. He's worse than my first husband. The first one was a drunk, believe it or not." She glanced at the lighted cottage across the street, and I saw one half of her bitter smile. "I wonder what makes a woman go for the lame ducks the way I did."

"I wouldn't know, Mrs. Nemo. Okay, I lay off Harry."

But I had no intention of laying off Harry. When she went back to her cottage, I walked around three-quarters of the block and took up a new position in the doorway of a dry-cleaning establishment. This time I didn't smoke. I didn't even move, except to look at my watch from time to time.

Around eleven o'clock, the lights went out behind the blinds in the Nemo cottage. Shortly before midnight the front door opened and Harry slipped out. He looked up and down the street and began to walk. He passed within six feet of my dark doorway, hustling along in a kind of furtive shuffle.

Working very cautiously, at a distance, I tailed him downtown. He disappeared into the lighted cavern of an all night garage. He came out of the garage a few minutes later, driving a prewar Chevrolet.

My money also talked to the attendant. I drew a prewar Buick which would still do seventy-five. I proved that it would, as soon as I hit the highway. I reached the entrance to Nick Nemo's private lane in time to see Harry's lights approaching the dark ranch house.

I cut my lights and parked at the roadside a hundred yards below the entrance to the lane, and facing it. The Chevrolet reappeared in a few minutes. Harry was still alone in the front seat. I followed it blind as far as the highway before I risked my lights. Then down the highway to the edge of town.

In the middle of the motel and drive-in district he turned off onto a side road and in under a neon sign which spelled out TRAILER COURT across the darkness. The trailers stood along the bank of a dry creek. The Chevrolet stopped in front of one of them, which had a light in the window. Harry got out with a spotted bundle under his arm. He knocked on the door of the trailer.

I U-turned at the next corner and put in more waiting time. The Chevrolet rolled out under the neon sign and turned towards the highway. I let it go.

Leaving my car, I walked along the creek bank to the lighted trailer. The windows were curtained. The cerise convertible was parked on its far side. I tapped on the aluminum door.

"Harry?" a girl's voice said. "Is that you, Harry?"

I muttered something indistinguishable. The door opened, and the yellow-haired girl looked out. She was very young, but her round blue eyes were heavy and sick with hangover, or remorse. She had on a nylon slip, nothing else.

"What is this?"

She tried to shut the door. I held it open.

"Get away from here. Leave me alone. I'll scream."

"All right. Scream."

She opened her mouth. No sound came out. She closed her mouth again. It was small, fleshy and defiant. "Who are you? Law?"

"Close enough. I'm coming in."

"Come in then, damn you. I got nothing to hide."

"I can see that."

I brushed in past her. There were dead Martinis on her breath. The little room was a jumble of feminine clothes, silk and cashmere and tweed and gossamer nylon, some of them flung on the floor, others hung up to dry. The leopardskin coat lay on the bunk bed, staring with innumerable bold eyes. She picked it up and covered her shoulders with it. Unconsciously, her nervous hands began to pick the wood-chips out of the fur. I said:

"Harry did you a favor, didn't he?"

"Maybe he did."

"Have you been doing any favors for Harry?"

"Such as?"

"Such as knocking off his brother."

"You're way off the beam, mister. I was very fond of Uncle Nick."

"Why run out on the killing then?"

"I panicked," she said. "It would happen to any girl. I was asleep when he got it, see, passed out if you want the truth. I heard the gun go off. It woke me up, but it took me quite a while to bring myself to and sober up enough to put my clothes on. By the time I made it to the bedroom window, Harry was back, with some guy." She peered into my face. "Were you the guy?"

I nodded.

"I thought so. I thought you were the law at the time. I saw Nick lying there in the driveway, all bloody, and I put two and two together and got trouble. Bad trouble for me, unless I got out. So I got out. It wasn't nice to do, after what Nick meant to me, but it was the only sensible thing. I got my career to think of."

"What career is that?"

"Modeling. Acting. Uncle Nick was gonna send me to school."

"Unless you talk, you'll finish your education at Corona. Who shot Nick?"

A thin edge of terror entered her voice. "I don't know, I tell you. I was passed out in the bedroom. I didn't see nothing."

"Why did Harry bring you your coat?"

"He didn't want me to get involved. He's my father, after all."

"Harry Nemo is your father?"

"Yes."

"You'll have to do better than that. What's your name?"

"Jeannine. Jeannine Larue."

"Why isn't your name Nemo if Harry is your father? Why do you call him Harry?"

"He's my stepfather, I mean."

"Sure," I said. "And Nick was really your uncle, and you were having a family reunion with him."

"He wasn't any blood relation to me. I always called him uncle, though."

"If Harry's your father, why don't you live with him?"

"I used to. Honest. This is the truth I'm telling you. I had to get out on account of the old lady. The old lady hates my guts. She's a real creep, a square. She can't stand for a girl to have any fun. Just because my old man was a rummy—"

"What's your idea of fun, Jeannine?"

She shook her feathercut hair at me. It exhaled a heavy perfume which was worth its weight in blood. She bared one pearly shoulder and smiled an artificial hustler's smile. "What's yours? Maybe we can get together."

"You mean the way you got together with Nick?"

"You're prettier than him."

"I'm also smarter, I hope. Is Harry really your stepfather?"

"Ask him if you don't believe me. Ask him. He lives in a place on Tule Street—I don't remember the number."

"I know where he lives."

But Harry wasn't at home. I knocked on the door of the frame cottage and got no answer. I turned the knob and found that the door was unlocked. There was a light behind it. The other cottages in the court were dark. It was long past midnight, and the street was deserted. I went into the cottage, preceded by my gun.

A ceiling bulb glared down on sparse and threadbare furniture, a time-eaten rug. Besides the living room, the house contained a cubbyhole of a bedroom and a closet kitchenette. Everything in the poverty-stricken place was pathetically clean. There were moral mottoes on the walls, and one picture. It was a photograph of a tow-headed girl in a teen-age party dress. Jeannine, before she learned that a pretty face and a sleek body could buy her the things she wanted. The things she thought she wanted.

For some reason, I felt sick. I went outside. Somewhere out of sight, an old car-engine muttered. Its muttering grew on the night. Harry Nemo's rented Chevrolet turned the corner under the streetlight. Its front wheels were weaving. One of the wheels climbed the curb in front of the cottage. The Chevrolet came to a halt at a drunken angle.

I crossed the sidewalk and opened the car door. Harry was at the wheel, clinging to it desperately as if he needed it to hold him up. His chest was bloody. His mouth was bright with blood. He spoke through it thickly:

"She got me."

"Who got you, Harry? Jeannine?"

"No. Not her. She was the reason for it, though. We had it coming."

Those were his final words. I caught his body as it fell sideways out of the seat. I laid it out on the sidewalk and left it for the cop on the beat to find.

I drove across town to the trailer court. Jeannine's trailer still had light in it, filtered through the curtains over the windows. I pushed the door open.

The girl was packing a suitcase on the bunk bed. She looked at me over her shoulder, and froze. Her blond head was cocked like a frightened bird's, hypnotized by my gun.

"Where are you off to, kid?"

"Out of this town. I'm getting out."

"You have some talking to do first."

She straightened up. "I told you all I know. You didn't believe me. What's the matter, didn't you get to see Harry?"

"I saw him. Harry's dead. Your whole family is dying like flies." She half-turned and sat down limply on the disordered bed. "Dead? You think I did it?"

"I think you know who did. Harry said before he died that you were the reason for it all."

"Me the reason for it?" Her eyes widened in false naivete, but there was thought behind them, quick and desperate thought. "You mean that Harry got killed on account of me?"

"Harry and Nick both. It was a woman who shot them."

"God," she said. The desperate thought behind her eyes crystallized into knowledge. Which I shared.

The aching silence was broken by a big diesel rolling by on the highway. She said above its roar:

"That crazy old bat. So *she* killed Nick."

"You're talking about your mother. Mrs. Nemo."

"Yeah."

"Did you see her shoot him?"

"No. I was blotto like I told you. But I saw her out there this week, keeping an eye on the house. She's always watched me like a hawk."

"Is that why you were getting out of town? Because you knew she killed Nick?"

"Maybe it was. I don't know. I wouldn't let myself think about it."

Her blue gaze shifted from my face to something behind me. I turned. Mrs. Nemo was in the doorway. She was hugging the straw bag to her thin chest.

Her right hand dove into the bag. I shot her in the right arm. She leaned against the doorframe and held her dangling arm with her left hand. Her face was granite in whose crevices her eyes were like live things caught.

The gun she dropped was a cheap .32 revolver, its nickel plating worn and corroded. I spun the cylinder. One shot had been fired from it.

"This accounts for Harry," I said. "You didn't shoot Nick with this gun, not at that distance."

"No." She was looking down at her dripping hand. "I used my old police gun on Nick Nemo. After I killed him, I threw the gun into the sea. I didn't know I'd have further use for a gun. I bought that little suicide gun tonight."

"To use on Harry?"

"To use on you. I thought you were on to me. I didn't know until you told me that Harry knew about Nick and Jeannine."

"Jeannine is your daughter by your first husband?"

"My only daughter." She said to the girl: "I did it for you, Jeannine. I've seen too much—the awful things that can happen."

The girl didn't answer. I said:

"I can understand why you shot Nick. But why did Harry have to die?"

"Nick paid him," she said. "Nick paid him for Jeannine. I found Harry in a bar an hour ago, and he admitted it. I hope I killed him."

"You killed him, Mrs. Nemo. What brought you here? Was Jeannine the third on your list?"

"No. No. She's my own girl. I came to tell her what I did for her. I wanted her to know."

She looked at the girl on the bed. Her eyes were terrible with pain and love. The girl said in a stunned voice:

"Mother. You're hurt. I'm sorry."

"Let's go, Mrs. Nemo," I said.

GIL BREWER

Gil Brewer (1922–1983) came out of World War II determined to become a writer. He held all the usual menial jobs.

He seemed, by nature, to have been the prototypical working-class stiff—hard-drinking, hard-loving, hard-dreaming. Right time right place, too. He wrote the kind of tough-tender hard-boiled novels and stories that the men and women of his generation preferred. The Golden Age of crime fiction was waning. People wanted a more believable kind of story, one that had at least a passing emotional connection to their own lives. They were never in danger of becoming a Duke and solving mysteries before a cozy Victorian fire. But they could see themselves trapped in a painful romance with somebody who was dragging them into trouble.

He's largely forgotten now. But at his very best—*A Killer Is Loose, The Red Scarf*—he was very much his own man. There is a Woolrichian darkness and desperation in his best work. It stays with you a long, long time.

The Gesture

Nolan placed both hands on the railing of the veranda, and unconsciously squeezed the wood until the muscles in his arms corded and ached. He looked down, across the immaculately trimmed green lawn, past the palms and the Australian pines, to the beach, gleaming whitely under the late morning sun.

The Gulf was crisply green today, and calm, broken only by the happy frolicking of the man and woman—laughing, swimming. His wife, Helen, and Latimer, the photographer from the magazine in New York, down to do a picture story of the island.

Nolan turned his gaze away, lifted his hands and stared at his palms. His hands were trembling and his thin cotton shirt was soaked with perspiration.

He couldn't stand it. He left the veranda, and walked swiftly into the sprawling living room of his home. He paced back and forth for a moment, his feet whispering on the grass rug. Then he stood quietly in the center of the room, trying to think. For two weeks it had been going on. At first he'd thought he would last. Now he knew it no longer mattered, about lasting.

He would have to do something. He strode rapidly across the room into his study, opened the top drawer of his desk, and looked down at the .45 automatic. He slammed the drawer shut, whirled and went back into the living room.

Why had he ever allowed the man entrance to the island?

Oh, he knew why, well enough. Because Helen had wanted it. And now he couldn't order Latimer away. It would be as good as telling Helen the reason. She knew how much he loved her; why did she act this way? Why did she torture him? She *must* realize, after all these years, that he couldn't stand another man even looking at her beauty.

Why did she think they lived here—severed from all mainland life?

He stiffened, making an effort to wipe away the frown on his face. He reached for his handkerchief, and swabbed at the perspiration on his arms and forehead. They were coming, laughing and talking, up across the lawn.

Quickly, he selected a magazine from the rack and settled into a wicker chair with his back to the front entrance. He flipped the periodical open and was engrossed in a month-old mystery story when they stomped loudly across the veranda.

Every step was a kind of unbearable thunder to Nolan. He was reaching such a pitch of helpless irritability that he nearly screamed.

"Darling!" Helen called. "Where are you—oh, there!"

She stepped toward him, her bare feet softly thumping the grass rug. He half-glanced up at her. She was coffee-brown, her eyes excited and happier than he'd seen them in a long time. She wore one of the violent-hued red, yellow and green cloth swimming suits that she'd designed for herself.

He abruptly realized how meager the suit was and his neck burned. He had contrived to have her make the suit with the least expenditure of material. It was his pleasure to look at her.

But not now—not with Latimer here!

"What *have* you been doing?" she asked.

He started to reply, looking across at Latimer standing at the entranceway, but she rippled on. "You really should have come swimming with us, dear. It was wonderful this morning." She reached out and tousled his hair. "You haven't been near the water in days."

Nolan cleared his throat. "Well," he said. "Well, Mister Latimer. About caught up? About ready with your story?"

He wanted to shout: *When are you leaving!* He could not. He sat there, staring at Latimer. The sunny days here on the island had done the man good. He was bronzed and healthy and young and abrim with a vitality that had not been present when he'd first come over from the mainland.

"A few more days, I guess," Latimer said. "I wish you'd call me Jack. And I sure wish you two would pose for a few pictures. It's nice enough, the way you've been about letting me photograph the island, your home, but—" Latimer left the protest unspoken, smiling halfheartedly.

Nolan glanced at his wife. She reached down and touched his arm, her fingers trembling. "After lunch Jack and I are going to take a walk, clear around the island," she said. "You know, we haven't done that in a terribly long while. Why don't you come along?"

"Sorry," Nolan said quickly. "I've some things I've got to attend to."

"Sure wish you'd come," Latimer said.

Nolan said nothing.

"Well," Latimer said. "I've got to write a letter. Guess I'll do it while you're fixing lunch, Helen."

"Right," Helen said. "I'd better get busy." She turned, and hurried off toward the kitchen, humming softly.

"By the way," Latimer said to Nolan. "Anything you'd like done in town? I'll be taking the boat across this evening, so I can mail some stuff off."

"Thank you," Nolan said. "There's nothing."

"Well," Latimer said. He sighed and started across the room toward the hallway leading to his bedroom. It had been a storage room, but Nolan had fixed it up with a bed and a table for Latimer's typewriter when Helen insisted the photographer stay on the island. Latimer paused by the hallway. "Sure you won't come with us this afternoon?"

Nolan didn't bother to answer. He couldn't answer. If he had tried, he knew he might have shouted, even cursed—maybe actually gone at the man with his bare hands.

He would not use his bare hands. He wouldn't soil them. He would use the gun. He listened as Latimer left the room, and sat there breathing stiffly, his fingers clenched into the magazine's crumpled pages.

Yes, that's what he would do. Latimer's saying he was going to remain on the island longer still clinched it. Nolan knew why Latimer had said that. He wasn't fooling anybody. Taking advantage of hospitality for his own sneaking reasons. Didn't Helen see what kind of a man Latimer was? Was she blind? Or did she want it this way?

The very thought of such a thing sent Nolan out of the chair, stalking back and forth across the room. He could hear Latimer's typewriter ticking away from the far side of the house.

Their paradise. Their home. Their love. Torn and twisted and broken by this insensitive person. He heard Helen call them to lunch then, and, moving toward the table in the dining room, he felt slightly relieved. He knew that while they were gone this afternoon, he would get everything ready.

With Latimer's unconscious aid, Nolan knew exactly how he was going to do it. He sat at the table, picking at his food, listening to them talk and laugh. He tried vainly to concentrate away from the sounds of their voices.

"This salad's terrific," Latimer said. "Helen, you're wonderful! You two've got it made, out here!"

Helen lowered her gaze to her plate. Nolan stared directly at Latimer and Latimer reddened and looked away. Nolan grinned inside. He had caught the man. But the victory was empty. The long afternoon, thinking about her out there with Latimer would be painful.

They finished lunch in silence. Almost before Nolan realized it, the house was again empty. He could hear them laughing still, their voices growing faint as they moved down along the beach.

Helen had even insisted on taking several bottles of cold beer wrapped in insulated bags to keep cool, and carried in the old musette.

Nolan could not stand still. He paced back and forth across the extent of the house, thinking about tonight. If he didn't do it tonight, it might be too late. He did not want Helen too attached to Latimer and he felt sure it had gone very far already.

He knew Latimer intended to stay on and stay on—until he could take Helen away with him. But tonight would end it. He would go along with Latimer to the mainland. Only Latimer would never reach the mainland. The boat would swamp.

Nolan knew how to swamp a boat. He knew Latimer wasn't much of a swimmer, and anyhow, a man couldn't swim with a .45 slug in his heart. But Nolan could swim well. He would kill Latimer, take him out into the Gulf, weight him and sink him. Then he'd bring the boat in and swamp it and swim ashore. He would report it, and rent a boat and come home. He knew they were in for a bit of heavy weather tonight. It would be just perfect.

And Helen and he would be happy again. The way they had always been.

He looked back, thinking over the good times. The time before they'd come to the island, when he'd been hard-working at the glass-cutting business he'd inherited from his father. Then more and more he'd become conscious of Helen's beauty and the effect she had on men. And loving her as wildly as he did, he could no longer bear the endless suspense; the knowledge that sooner or later, she would leave him. So he sold the business, retired. His little lie. So far as she knew, he simply wanted island life—quite, unhurried, alone with her. It was true. But not a complete truth.

All this time they had been happy. Until now. Somebody'd got wind of the beauty of the island and Latimer had shown up, to do his story. Under conditions imposed by Nolan—no pictures of either himself or Helen. He had allowed one fuzzy negative of them standing against a blossoming hibiscus near the house, at twilight—that was all.

Wandering through the house, trying not to think of what they were doing now, he found himself in Latimer's room. The unmade bed, the photographic equipment, the typewriter set up on the table.

Beside the machine was a typewritten letter.

Nolan turned away. But something drew him over to the table. Pure curiosity in this man Latimer. He stood there, staring down at the obviously unfinished letter. An addressed envelope lay beside it. There was a half-completed sentence on the sheet in the typewriter, numbered *Page Two*.

The letter was addressed to the editor of the magazine where Latimer worked.

Nolan began reading, at first leisurely, then feverishly.

> "Dear Bart:
>
> Really have this thing wrapped up, but I'm staying on a while longer, just to settle a few things in my own mind and maybe I'll come up with a bunch of pix and a yarn that'll knock your head off . . . sure beautiful scenery on the island . . . house is a regular bamboo and cypress mansion . . . unhealthy, Bart, really sick . . . he watches her like a hawk. He's ripped with jealousy and it would be laughable, except that they're both so very old. He must be in his eighties, but she's a bit harder to read. I did a lousy thing. I confronted her with it. You would have, too. She's so obviously just enduring everything for his sake. Humoring him. My God, think of it! All these years he's kept her out here, away from everybody, imprisoned. It's pure hell. She as much as admitted it. I'm staying on, just to see if I can't work it somehow. Get her back to civilization, if only for a vacation, Bart. She deserves it. You should hear her ask how things are out there—it would break your damned heart . . ."

There was more and Nolan read all of it through twice. For a moment longer, he stood there, seeing everything clearly for the first time in nearly a half century.

Then he walked through the house to his study, opened the desk drawer, took out the .45 automatic. He sat down in his chair by the desk, put the muzzle of the gun into his mouth and pulled the trigger.

DAVID GOODIS

David Goodis (1917–1967) wrote what was probably the darkest, most existential fiction of all the post–World War II noir writers. His first four novels were published to great critical and public acclaim, with one of them, *Dark Passage*, filmed with Humphrey Bogart and Lauren Bacall. His next books, published in paperback, were darker than any that had gone before, tales of men and women trying to fight against the inexorable suffering fate had in store for them.

Every one of his books follows this pattern, men and women clinging to any desperate shred of hope, yet knowing deep down inside that nothing will save them. Alcoholism, poverty, crime, failure, hopelessness form an urban whirlpool that sucks down anyone who gets caught in it. His short fiction followed this same pattern, but condensed, so that the pain and suffering fairly leap off the page.

The Plunge

Seven out of ten are slobs; he was thinking. There was no malice or disdain in the thought. It was more a mixture of pity and regret. And that made it somewhat sickening, for he was referring specifically to the other men who wore badges, his fellow-policemen. More specifically still, he was thinking of the nine plainclothesmen attached to the Vice Squad. Only yesterday they'd been caught with their palms out, hauled in before the Commissioner, and called all sorts of names before they were suspended.

But, of course, the suspensions were temporary. They'd soon be back on the job, their palms extended again, accepting the shakedown money with the languid smile that seemed to say, *It's all a part of the game.*

He'd never believed in that cynical axiom, had never let it touch him during his seventeen years on the city payroll. From rookie to Police Sergeant and on up to Detective Lieutenant he'd stayed away from the bribe, rakeoff and conniving and doing favors for certain individuals who required official protection to remain in business.

Of course, at times he'd made mistakes, but they were always clean mistakes. He'd been trying too hard or he was weary from nights without sleep. It was honest blundering and it put no shadows on his record. In City Hall he was listed Grade-A and they had him slated for promotion.

His name was Roy Childers and he was thirty-eight years old. He stood five-feet-ten and weighed a rock-hard one-ninety. It was really rock-hard because he was a firm believer in physical culture and wholesome living. He kept away from too much starches and sweets, smoked only after meals, had a beer now and then, but nothing more than that, and the only woman he ever slept with was his wife.

They'd been married eleven years and they had four children. In a few months Louise would be having the fifth. Maybe five was too many, considering his salary and the price of food these days. But, of course, they'd get along. They'd always managed to get along. He had a fine wife and a nicely arranged way of living and there was never anything serious to worry about.

That is, aside from his job. On the job he worried plenty. It was purely technical worriment because he took the job very seriously and when things didn't go the way he expected, he'd lose sleep and it would hurt his digestion. When he'd been with the Vice Squad, it hadn't happened so frequently. But a year ago he'd become fed up with the Vice Squad, with all the shenanigans and departmental throatcutting and, of course, the never-ending shakedown activity he saw all around him.

He'd requested a transfer to Homicide, and within a few months his dark brown hair showed grey streaks, pouches began to form under his eyes, the unsolved cases put creases at the corners of his mouth. But mostly it was the fact that Homicide also had its slobs and manipulators, its badge-wearing bandits who'd go in for any kind of deal if the price was right.

On more than one occasion he'd been close to grabbing a wanted man when someone tipped off someone who tipped off someone else, with the fugitive sliding away or building an alibi that caused the District Attorney to shrug and say, "What's the use? We've got no case."

So that now, after eleven months of working with Homicide, there was a lot of grey in Childers' hair, and his mouth was set tighter, showing the strain of work that demanded too much effort and paid too little dividends.

He was sitting at his desk in Homicide, which was on the ninth floor of City Hall. His desk was near the window and the view it gave him from that angle was the slum area extending from Twelfth and Patton Avenue to the river. Along the riverfront the warehouses looked very big in contrast to the two-story rat-traps and fire-traps where people lived or tried to live or didn't care whether they lived or not.

But he wasn't focusing on the slum-dwellings that breeded filth and degeneracy and violence. His eyes sought out the warehouses, and narrowed in concentration as they came to rest on the curved-roof structure labeled "No. 4" where not so very long ago there'd been a $15,000 payroll robbery, with one night-watchman killed and another permanently blinded from a pistol-whipping.

He'd been assigned to the case three weeks ago, after coming to the Captain and saying it looked like a Dice Nolan job. For one thing, he'd said, Dice Nolan was a specialist at payroll robbery, going in for warehouses along the riverfront and using a boat for the getaway. Nolan had used that method several times before they'd caught up with him some ten years ago.

They gave him ten-to-twenty, and according to the record he'd been let out on parole this year—in the middle of March. Now it was the middle of April and that just about gave him time enough to get a mob together and plan a campaign and make a grab for loot.

Another angle was the pistol-whipping. Dice Nolan had a reputation for that sort of thing, always going for the eyes for some weird reason planted deep in his criminal brain. Childers had said to the Captain, "What makes me sure it's Nolan, I've checked with the parole officers and they tell me he hasn't reported in for the past ten days. He's on a strict probation and he's supposed to show them his face every three days."

The Captain had frowned. "You figure he's still in town?"

"I'm betting on it," Childers had said. "I know the way he operates. He wouldn't be satisfied with a fifteen-grand haul. He'll stick around for a while and then go for another warehouse. He knows every inch of that neighborhood."

"How come you're wise to him?"

"It goes back a good many years," Childers had said. "We were raised on the same street."

The Captain was quiet for some moments. And then, without looking at Childers, he's said, "All right, go out and find him."

So he'd gone out to look for Nolan and the search took him along Patton Avenue going toward the river, past the rows of tenements where now they were strangers who'd been his childhood playmates, past the gutters where he'd sailed the matchbox-boats, unmindful of the slime and filth because it was the only world he'd known in that far-off time of carefree days.

Days of not knowing what poisonous roots were in the squalor of the neighborhood. Until the time when ignorance was ended and he saw them going bad, one by one, Georgie Mancuso and Hal Berkowski and Freddie Antonucci and Bill Weiss and Dice Nolan.

He'd pulled away from it with a teeth-clenched frenzy, like someone struggling out of a messy pit. He'd promised himself that he'd never breathe that rotten air again, never come near that dismal area where the roaches thrived and a switchblade nestled in almost every pocket. He'd gone away from it, telling himself the exit was permanent, feeling clean. And that was the important thing, to be clean, always to be clean.

He'd been acutely conscious of his own cleanliness as he'd questioned the men in the taprooms and poolrooms along Patton. They looked at him with hostile eyes but were careful to keep the hostility from their voices when they told him, "I don't know" and "I don't know" and "I don't know."

And some of them went so far as to state they were unacquainted with anyone named Dice Nolan. They'd never even heard of such a person. Of course he knew their lying and evasive answers were founded more on their fear of Nolan than on their instinctive dislike of the Police Department.

It told him his theory was correct. Nolan had engineered the payroll heist, and certainly Nolan was still in town.

But that was as far as he'd got with it. There were no further leads, and nothing that could come to a lead. Night after night he'd come home with a tired face to hear his wife saying, "Anything new?" And he'd try to give her a smile as he shook his head.

But it was getting more and more difficult to smile. He knew if he didn't come in with something soon, the Captain would take him off the case. He hated the thought of being taken off the case, he was so very sure about his man, so acutely sure the man was hiding somewhere near. Very near—.

The ringing phone sliced into his thoughts. He lifted it from the hook and said hello and the switchboard girl downstairs said to hold on for just a moment. Then a man's voice said, "This Childers?"

Instantly he had a feeling it was something. He could almost smell it. He said, "Yes," and waited, and heard the man saying, "I'm gonna make it fast before you trace the call. Is that all right with you?"

He didn't say anything. For a moment he felt awfully weary, thinking: It's just some crank who wants to call me some dirty names—.

But then the man was saying, "It's gonna be good if you wanna use it. I got some personal reasons for not liking Dice Nolan. Thing is, I can get you to his girl friend."

Childers reached automatically for a pencil and a pad. The man gave him a name and an address, and the pencil moved very rapidly. Then the call hung up, and Childers leaped from the desk, ran out of the office and down the hall to the elevator.

It was a seventeen-story apartment house on the edge of Lakeside Park. He went up to the ninth floor and down the corridor to room 907. It was early afternoon and he doubted she'd be there. But his finger was positive and persistent on the doorbell-button.

The door opened and he saw a woman in her middle-twenties, and his first thought was, a bum steer. This can't be Dice Nolan's girl.

He was certain she couldn't be connected with Nolan because there was nothing in her make-up that indicated moll or floosie or hard-mouthed slut. She wore very little paint and her hair-do was on the quiet side. There was no jewelry except for a wrist-watch. Her blouse was pale grey, the skirt a darker shade, and he noticed that her shoes didn't have high heels. Again he thought, *Sure, it's a bum steer*. But anyway, he said, "Are you Wilma Burnett?"

She nodded.

"Police," he said, turning his lapel to show her the badge.

She blinked a few times, but that was all. Then she stepped aside to let him enter the apartment. As he walked in, the quiet neatness of the place was impressed upon him. It was simply furnished. The color motif was subdued, and there wasn't the slightest sign of fast or loose living.

He frowned slightly, then got rid of it and put the official tone in his voice as he said, "All right, Miss Burnett. Let's have it."

She blinked again. "Let's have what?"

"Information," he said. "Where is he?"

"Who?" She spoke quietly; her expression was calm and polite. "Who are you talking about?"

"Dice." He said it softly.

It seemed she didn't get that. She said, "I don't know anyone by that name."

"Dice Nolan," he said.

For a moment she said nothing. Then, very quietly, "I know a Philip Nolan, if that's who you mean."

"Yes, that's him." And he thought, *Let's see if we can rattle her*. His voice became a jabbing blade, "I figured you'd know him. He pays your rent here, doesn't he?"

It didn't do a thing. There was no anger, not even annoyance. All she did was shake her head.

He told himself it wasn't going the way he wanted it to go. The thing to do was to hit her with something that would throw her off balance, and while he groped for an idea he heard her saying, "Won't you sit down?"

"No thanks," he said automatically. He folded his arms, looked at her directly and spoke a trifle louder. "You're doing very nicely, Miss Burnett. But it isn't good, it just can't work."

"I don't know what you mean."

"Yes you do." And he put the hard smile of law-enforcement on his lips. "You know exactly what I mean. You know he's wanted for robbery and murder and you're trying to cover for him."

That'll do it, he thought. *That'll sure enough break the ice*. But it didn't work that way, it didn't come anywhere near that. For a few moments she just stood there looking at him. Then she turned slowly and walked across the room. She settled herself in a chair near the window, folded her hands in her lap, and waited for his next remark. Her calm silence seemed to say, *You're getting nowhere fast.*

He said to himself, *Easy now, don't push it too hard.* Yet his voice was somehow gruff and impatient, more demand than query. "Where can I find him? Where?"

"I don't know."

"Not much you don't." He took a step toward her, his mouth tightening. "Come on, now. Let's quit playing checkers. Where's he hiding out?"

"Hiding?" Her eyebrows went up just a little. "I didn't know he was hiding."

"You're a liar."

She gazed past him. She said, "Tell me something. Is this the only way you can gather information? I mean, does your job require that you go around insulting people?"

He winced. He knew she had him there, and if this was really checkers, she'd scored a triple-jump. But then he thought, *It's only the beginning of the game, we can get her to talk if we take our time and play it careful—.*

Again he smiled at her. This time it was an easy pleasant smile, and his voice was soft. "I'm sorry, Miss Burnett. I shouldn't have said that. I apologize."

"That's quite all right, Mister—" she hesitated.

"Childers," he said. "Lieutenant Childers—Homicide." He pulled a chair toward hers, sat down and went on smiling at her. "It'll help both of us if you tell me the truth. I'm looking for a crook and a killer, and you're looking to stay out of prison."

"Prison?" Her eyebrows went up again. "But I haven't done anything—"

"I want to be sure about that. I'm hoping you can prove you're not an accessory."

"Meaning what?"

"Meaning if you're helping him to hide, you're an accessory after the fact. That's a very serious charge and I've known cases when they've been sent up for anywhere from three to five years."

She didn't say anything.

He leaned forward slightly and said, "Of course you understand that anything you say can be held against you."

"I'm not worried about that, Lieutenant. I haven't broken any laws."

"Well, let's check on it, just to be sure." His smile remained pleasant, his voice soft and almost friendly. "Tell me about yourself."

She told him she was a free-lance commercial artist. She said her age was twenty-seven and for the past several years she'd been a widow. Her husband and two children had died in an auto accident. There was no emotion in her voice as she talked about it, but he saw something in her eyes that told him this was genuine and she'd been through plenty of hell. He thought, *She's really been hit hard.*

* * *

Then all at once it occurred to him that she was something out of the ordinary. It wasn't connected with her looks, although her looks summed up as extremely attractive. It was more on the order of a feeling she radiated, a feeling that came from deep inside and hit him going in deep, causing him to frown because he had no idea what it was and it made him uncomfortable.

He heard himself saying, "I owe you another apology. That crack I made about Nolan paying the rent. I guess that wasn't a nice thing to say."

"No, it wasn't." She said it forgivingly. "But I know you didn't mean to be personal. You were only trying to find out—"

"I'm still trying," he reminded her. His manner became official again. "I want to know all about you and Nolan."

For a long moment she was quiet. Then, her voice level and calm, "I can't tell you where he is, Lieutenant. I really don't know."

"When'd you last see him?"

"A few nights ago."

"Where, exactly?"

"Here," she said. "He came here and we had dinner."

He leaned back in the chair. "You cooked dinner for him?"

"It wasn't the first time," she said matter-of-factly.

He pondered on the next question. He wasn't looking at her as he asked, "What is it with you and Nolan? How long have you known him?"

"About a month." And then, before he could toss another question, she volunteered, "We met in a cocktail lounge. I was alone, and I think I ought to explain about that. I don't usually go out alone. But that night I felt the need for company, and although I drink very little I really needed a lift. I'd been going with someone who disappointed me, one of those awfully nice gentlemen who leads you on until you happen to find out he's married—"

"Rough deal." He looked at her sympathetically.

She shrugged. "Well anyway, I must have looked very lonesome and unhappy. I don't know how we got to talking, but one word led to another and I didn't know where it was leading. But to be quite truthful about it, I really didn't care. He told me he'd just been released from prison and it had no effect on me, except that somehow I appreciated the blunt way he put it. Then he asked me for my phone number and I gave it to him. Since then we've been seeing each other steadily. And if you're curious as to whether I sleep with him—"

"I didn't ask you about that."

"I'll tell you anyway, Lieutenant." There was a certain quiet defiance in her voice, and it showed in her eyes along with all the pain and suffering that had been too much to take, that had led to the breaking-point where a woman grabs at almost anything that comes along.

She said, "Yes, I sleep with him. I sleep with the ex-convict you're looking for. I know what he is and I don't care. And if that makes me a criminal, you might as well put the handcuffs on me and take me in."

Childers stood up. He turned away from her and said, "You shouldn't have said all those things. It wasn't necessary."

She didn't reply. He waited for her to say something, but there was no sound in the room, and after some moments he moved toward the door. As he opened it, he glanced at her. She sat there bent far forward with her head in her hands. He murmured, "Goodbye, Miss Burnett," and walked out.

His wife and four children were looking at him and he could feel the pressure of their eyes. Their plates were empty and on his plate the pot roast and vegetables hadn't been touched. He gazed down at the food and wondered why he couldn't eat it. There was an empty feeling inside him but it wasn't the emptiness of needing a meal. It was something else, something unaccountable. The more he tried to understand it, the more it puzzled him.

"What's wrong with you?" his wife asked. It was the fifth or sixth time she'd asked it since he'd come home that evening. He couldn't remember what answers he'd given her.

Now he looked at her and said wearily, "I'm just not hungry, that's all."

The children began chattering, and the youngest, five-year-old Dotty, said, "Maybe Daddy ate some candy bars. Whenever I eat too much candy bars, I can't eat my supper."

"Grown-ups don't eat candy bars." It was Billy, aged nine.

And Ralph, who was seven, said, "Grown-ups can do anything they want to."

No they can't, Childers said without sound. *They sure as hell can't.*

Then he asked himself what he meant by that. The answer came in close, danced away, went off very far away and he knew there was no use trying to reach for it.

He heard six-year-old Agnes saying, "Mommie, what's the matter with Daddy?"

"You ask him, honey," his wife said. "He won't tell me."

"What's there to tell?" Childers said loudly, the irritation grinding through his voice.

"Don't shout, Roy. You don't have to shout."

"Then lay off me. You've said enough."

"Is that the way to talk in front of the children?"

His voice lowered. "I'm sorry, Louise." He tried to smile at her. But his mouth felt stiff and he couldn't manage the smile. He said lamely, "I've had a bad day. It's taken a lot out of me—"

"That's why you need a good meal," she said. And then, getting up and coming towards him, "Tell you what. I'll warm up your plate and—"

"No." He shook his head emphatically. "I don't feel like eating and that's all there is to it."

"I wonder," she murmured.

He looked at her. "You wonder what?"

"Nothing," she said. "Let's skip it—"

"No we won't." He heard the suspicion in his voice, couldn't understand why it was there, then felt it more strongly as he said, "You started to say something and you're gonna finish it."

She didn't say anything. Her head was inclined and she was regarding him with puzzlement.

"Come on, spill it," he demanded. He rose from the table, facing her. "Tell me what's on your mind."

"Well, all I wanted to say was—"

"Come on, come on, don't stall."

"Say, who're you yelling at?" Louise shot back at him. She put her hands on her somewhat wide hips. "You're not talking to some tramp they've dragged in for questioning. I'm your wife and this is your home. The least you can do is show some respect."

"Mommie and Daddy are fighting," little Agnes said.

"And maybe it's about time," Louise said. She kept her hands on her hips. "I knew we had a show-down coming. Well, all right then. You told me to say what's on my mind and I'll say it. I want you to drop this Nolan case."

He stared at her. "What's that you said?"

"You heard me. I don't have to repeat it. I know your work is important, but your health comes first."

She pointed to the untouched food on his plate. "I had a feeling it would come to that. I've seen you walking in at night looking as if you were ready to drop. I knew it would reach the point where you wouldn't be able to eat. First thing you know, you'll have an ulcer."

He felt a thickness in his throat, a wave of tenderness and affection came over him, and he reminded himself he was a very fortunate man. This woman he had was the genuine article, an absolute treasure. His health and happiness and welfare were her primary concern. In her eyes he was the only man in the world, and after more than a decade of marriage, the knowledge of her feeling for him was something priceless.

He looked at her plump figure that was now over-plump with pregnancy, looked at her disordered hair that seldom enjoyed the luxury of a beauty parlor because she was too busy taking care of four children. Then he looked at her hands, reddened and coarse from washing dishes and doing the laundry and scrubbing the floors. He said to himself, *She's the best, she's the finest*. And he wanted very much to put his arms around her.

But somehow he couldn't. He didn't know why, but he couldn't. He stood there paralyzed with the realization that she was waiting for his embrace and he could not respond.

All at once he felt a frantic need to get out of the house. He groped for an excuse, and without looking at her, he said, "I told the Captain I'd see him tonight. I'm going down to the Hall."

He turned quickly and walked toward the front door.

But his meeting was not with the Captain, his destination was not City Hall. He walked a couple of blocks, climbed into a taxi, and said to the driver, "Lakeside Apartments."

"Right you are," the driver said.

Am I? he asked without sound. *Am I right?* And there was no use trying to answer the question, his brain couldn't handle it. Yet somehow he knew that from a purely technical standpoint this move was the logical move, and he was making it according to the book. It amounted to a stakeout, going there to watch and wait for Dice Nolan. The thing to do, of course, was plant himself across the street from the apartment-house and keep an eye on the front-entrance.

Twenty minutes later he stood in the darkness under a thickly leafed tree diagonally opposite the Lakeside Apartments. A car was parking across the street and instinctively he reached inside his jacket to check his shoulder-holster. But there was nothing there to check. He'd forgotten to put on his holster and the .38 it carried.

You've never done that before, he thought. And then, with a slight quiver that went down from his chest to his stomach and up to his chest again, *What's the matter here? What the hell is happening to you?*

Across the street someone was getting out of the car. But it wasn't Nolan, it was just a tiny middle-aged woman with a tiny dog in her arms. She walked inside the apartment-house and the car moved away.

Childers leaned against the tree. For a moment he wished the tree-trunk were a pillow and he could sink into it and fall asleep. It had nothing to do with weariness. It was simply and acutely the need to get away from everything, especially himself. The thought brought a blast of anger, aimed at his own eyes, his own mind, and in that moment he fought to think only in terms of his badge and the job he had to do.

He glanced at his wristwatch. The hands pointed to seven forty-five. Assuming that Nolan would be coming to see her tonight, assuming further she'd be cooking dinner for Nolan, the chances were that Nolan hadn't yet arrived. In Nolan's line of business, dinnertime was anywhere from eight-thirty to midnight. So it figured he had time to hurry back home and get his gun and come back here and—

His brain couldn't take it past that. Before he fully realized what he was doing, he'd crossed the street and entered the apartment-house.

In the elevator, going up to the ninth floor, he wasn't thinking of Nolan at all. Somewhat absently, he straightened his tie and smoothed the hair along his temples. There was a small mirror in the elevator but he didn't look into it. He knew that if he looked at himself in the mirror, he'd see something that he didn't want to see.

The elevator was going up very fast, going up and up, and there was something paradoxical and creepy about that. Because it wasn't the way going up should seem or feel at all. It was more like falling.

He pressed the doorbell-button. A few moments passed and then the door of 907 opened and she stood there smiling at him. He wasn't surprised to see the smile. He had a feeling she'd been expecting him. It wasn't based on anything in particular. It was just a feeling that this was happening the way it had to happen, there was no getting away from it.

"Hello, Wilma," he said.

She went on smiling at him. She didn't say anything. But her hand came up in a beckoning gesture that told him to enter the apartment. In the instant before he stepped through the doorway, he noticed she was wearing a small apron. And then, as she closed the door behind him, he caught the smell of cooking.

"Excuse me a moment," she said, walking past him and into the kitchen. "I have something on the stove—"

He sat down on the sofa. He looked down at the carpet. It was a solid-color broadloom, a subdued shade of grey-green. But as he listened to her moving around in the kitchen, as he visualized her hands preparing a meal for Dice Nolan, the color he saw was an intense green, a furious green that seemed to blaze before his eyes.

Before he could hold himself back, he'd lifted himself from the sofa and walked into the kitchen. His voice was tight as he said, "When is he due here?"

She was pouring seasoning into a pot on the stove. "I'm not expecting him tonight."

He moved toward the stove. He looked into the pot and saw it was lamb stew and there was only enough for one person.

Again she was smiling at him. "You don't put much trust in me, do you, Lieutenant?"

"It isn't that," he said. "It's just—" He didn't know how to finish it. Then, without thinking, without trying to think, "I wish you'd call me Roy."

Her smile faded. She gave him a level look that almost seemed to have substance, hitting him in the face and going into him, drilling in deep. For a very long moment the only sound in the kitchen was the stew simmering in the pot.

And then, her voice down low near a whisper, she said, "Is that the way it is?"

He nodded slowly. His eyes were solemn.

"Are you sure?" she murmured. "I mean—"

"I know what you mean," he interrupted. "You mean it can't be happening this fast. You want to tell me it's impossible, we hardly know each other—"

"Not only that," she said, her eyes aiming down to the thin band of gold on his finger. "You're a married man."

"Yes," he said bluntly. "I'm married and I have four children and my wife will soon have another."

She looked past him. She seemed to be speaking aloud to herself as she murmured, "I think we'd better talk about something else—"

"No." He came near shouting it. "We'll talk about this. Can't you see the way it is? We've got to talk about this."

She shook her head. "We can't. We just can't, that's all. We'd better not start—"

"We've started already. It was started as soon as we met each other."

His voice became thick as he went on, "Listen to me, Wilma. I tried to fight it the same as you're fighting it now. But it's no use. It's a thing you can't fight. It's like a sickness and there's no cure. You know that as well as I do. If I thought for a minute it hasn't hit you the same as me, I wouldn't be saying this. But I know it's hit you. I can see it in your eyes."

She tried to shake her head again. She was biting her lip. "If only—" She couldn't get it out. "If only—"

"No, Wilma." He spoke slowly and distinctly. "We won't have any *ifs* or *buts*. A thing like this happens once in a lifetime. It's more important than anything else. It's—"

He hadn't heard the sound of the key turning in the lock. He hadn't heard the door opening, the footsteps coming toward the kitchen. But now he saw her staring eyes focused on something behind his back. He turned very slowly and the first thing he saw was the gun.

Then he was looking at the face of Dice Nolan.

Nolan said very softly, "Keep talking." His lips scarcely moved as he said it, and there was nothing at all in his eyes.

The prison pallor seemed to harmonize with the granite hardness of his features. Except for a deep scar that twisted its way from one eyebrow to the other, he was a good-looking man with the accent on strength and virility. He was only five-nine and weighed around one-sixty, but somehow he looked very big standing there. *Maybe it's the gun*, Childers thought in that first long moment. *Maybe that's what makes him look so big*.

But it wasn't the gun. Nolan held it loosely and didn't seem to attach much importance to it. Now he was looking at Wilma and his voice remained soft and relaxed as he said, "You fooled me, girl. You really fooled me."

"Maybe I fooled myself," she said.

"Could be," Nolan murmured. He shifted his gaze to Childers. "Hey you, I told you to keep talking."

"I guess you heard enough," Childers said. "Saying more would make no sense."

Nolan grinned with only one side of his mouth. "Yeah, I guess so." Then suddenly the grin became a frown and he said, "You look sorta familiar. Don't I know you from someplace?"

"From Third and Patton," Childers said. "From playing cops and bums when we were kids."

"And playing it for real when we grew up," Nolan murmured, his eyes sparked with recognition. "You put the pinch on me so many times I lost count. I guess ten years in stir does something to the memory. But now I remember you, Childers. I damn well oughta remember you."

"You're a bad boy, Dice. You were always a bad boy."

"And you?" Dice grinned again, his eyes flicking from Childers to Wilma and back to Childers. "You're the goodie-goodie—the Boy Scout who always plays it clean and straight."

Suddenly he chuckled. "Goddam, I'm getting a kick out of this. What're you gonna do when your wife finds out?"

Childers didn't reply. He wasn't thinking of his wife, nor of Wilma, nor of anything except the fact that he was a Detective Lieutenant attached to Homicide and he'd finally found the man he'd been looking for.

"Well? What about it?" Dice went on chuckling. "Tell me, Childers. How you gonna crawl outta this mess?"

"Don't let it worry you," Childers murmured. "You better worry about your own troubles."

The chuckling stopped. Nolan's eyes narrowed. The words seemed to drip from his lips. "Like what?"

"Like skipping parole. Like carrying a deadly weapon."

Nolan didn't say anything. He stood there waiting to hear more.

Childers let him wait, stretching the quiet as though it was made of rubber. And then, letting it out very slowly, very quietly, "Another thing you did, Dice. You pulled a job on the waterfront three weeks ago. You heisted warehouse number four and got away with fifteen thousand dollars. You murdered a night-watchman and the other one is permanently blinded. And that does it for you, bad boy. That puts you where you belong. In the chair."

"You—" Nolan choked on it. "You can't pin that rap on me. I didn't do it."

Childers smiled patiently. "Don't get excited, Dice. It won't help you to get excited."

"Now listen—" The sweat broke out on Nolan's face. "I swear to you, I didn't do it. Whoever engineered that deal, they fixed it so the Law would figure it was me. When I read about it in the papers, I knew what the score was. I knew that sooner or later you'd be looking for me—"

"It sounds weak, Dice. It's gonna sound weaker in the courtroom."

Nolan's features twisted and he snarled, "You don't hafta tell me how weak it sounds. I wracked my brains, trying to find an alibi. But all I got was zero. I knew if I was taken in for grilling, I wouldn't have a chance. That's why I skipped parole. That's why I'm carrying a rod. I ain't gonna let them burn me for something I didn't do."

Childers frowned slightly. For an instant he was almost ready to believe Nolan's statement. There was something feverishly convincing in the ex-con's voice and manner. But then, as he studied Nolan's face, he saw that Nolan's eyes were aimed at Wilma, and he thought, *It's not me he's talking to, it's her. He's trying to sell her a bill of goods. He wants her to think he's clean, so when he walks out of here she'll be going along with him.*

And then he heard himself saying through clenched teeth, "She won't buy it, Nolan. She knows you're a crook and a killer and no matter how many lies you tell, you can't make her think otherwise."

Nolan's eyes remained focused on Wilma. His face was expressionless as he said, "You hear what the man says?"

She didn't reply. Childers looked at her and saw she was gazing at the wall behind Nolan's head.

"I'm telling you I'm innocent," Nolan said to her. "Do you believe me?"

She took a deep breath, and before she could say anything, Childers grabbed her wrist and said, "Please—don't fall for his line, don't let him play you for a sucker. You walk out of here with him and you're ruined."

Her head turned slowly, her eyes were like blades cutting into Childers' eyes. She said, "Let go of my wrist, you're hurting me."

Childers winced as though she'd hit him in the face. He released his burning grip on her wrist. As his hand fell away, he was seized with a terrible fear that had no connection with Dice Nolan's presence or the gun in Nolan's hand. It was the fear of seeing her walking out of that room with Nolan and never coming back.

His brain was staggered with the thought, and again he had the feeling of falling, of plunging downward through immeasurable space that took him away from the badge he wore, the desk he occupied at Homicide in City Hall, his job and his home and his family. *Oh God*, he said without sound, and as the plunge became swifter he made a frantic try to get a hold on himself, to stop the descent, to face this issue and see it for what it was.

He'd fallen victim to a sudden blind infatuation, a maddened craving for this woman whom he'd never seen before today. And that didn't make sense, it wasn't normal behavior. It was a kind of lunacy and what he had to do here and now was—

But he couldn't do anything except stand there and stare at her, his eyes begging her not to leave him.

And just then he heard Dice Nolan saying, "You coming with me, Wilma?"

"Yes," she said. She walked across the kitchen and stood at Nolan's side.

Nolan had the gun aiming at Childers' chest. "Let's do this nice and careful," Nolan said. "Keep your hands down, copper. Turn around very slowly and lemme see the back of your head."

"Don't hurt him," Wilma said. "Please don't hurt him."

"This won't hurt much," Nolan told her. "He'll just have a headache tomorrow, that's all."

"Please, Philip—"

"I gotta do it this way," Nolan said. "I gotta put him to sleep so we'll have a chance to clear out of here."

"You might hit him too hard." Her voice quivered. "I'm afraid you might kill him—"

"No, that won't happen," Nolan assured her. "I'm an expert at this sort of thing. He won't sleep for more than ten minutes. That'll give us just enough time."

Childers had turned slowly so that now he stood with his back to them. He heard Nolan coming toward him and his nerves stiffened as he visualized the butt of the revolver crashing down on his skull. But in that same instant of anticipating the blow he told himself that Nolan would be holding the barrel instead of the butt, Nolan's finger would be away from the trigger.

In the next instant, as Nolan came up close behind him, he ducked going sideways, then pivoted hard and saw the gun-butt flashing down and hitting empty air. He saw the dismay on Nolan's face, and then, grinning at Nolan, he delivered a smashing right to the belly, a left hook to the side of the head, another right that came in short and caught Nolan on the jaw. Nolan sagged to the floor and the gun fell out of his hand.

As Childers leaned over to reach for the gun, Nolan grunted and lunged with what remaining strength he had. His shoulder made contact with Childers' ribs, and as they rolled over, Nolan's hands made a grab for Childers' throat. Childers raised his arm, hooked it, and bashed his elbow against Nolan's mouth. Nolan fell back, going flat and sort of sliding across the kitchen floor.

Childers came to his knees, and went crawling very fast, headed toward the gun. He picked it up and put his finger through the trigger-guard. As his finger came against the trigger with the weapon aiming at Nolan's chest, a voice inside him said, *Don't—don't—*. But another voice broke through and told him, *You want that woman and he's in the way, you gotta get rid of him.*

Yet even as he agreed with the second voice, even as the rage and jealousy blotted out all normal thinking, he was trying not to pull the trigger. So that even when he did finally pull it, when he heard the shot and saw Nolan instantly dead with a bullet through the heart, he thought dazedly, *I didn't really mean to do that.*

He lifted himself to his feet. He stood there, looking down at the corpse on the floor.

Then he heard Wilma saying, "Why did you kill him?"

He wanted to look at her. But somehow he couldn't. He forced the words through his lips, "You saw what happened. He was putting up a fight. I couldn't take any chances."

"I don't believe that," she said. And then, her voice dull, "It's too bad you didn't understand."

He stared at her. "Understand what?"

"When I agreed to go away with him—I was only pretending. It was the only way I could keep him from shooting you."

He felt a surge of elation. "You—you really mean that?"

"Yes," she said. "But it doesn't matter now." Her eyes were sad for a moment, and then the bitterness crept in as she pointed toward the parlor and said, "You'd better make a phone call, Lieutenant. Tell them you've found your man and you've saved the State the expense of a trial."

He moved mechanically, going past her and into the parlor. He picked up the phone and got the P.D. operator and said, "Get me Homicide—this is Childers."

The next voice on the wire was the Captain's, and before Childers could start talking, he heard the Captain saying, "I'm glad you called in, Roy. You can stop looking for Dice Nolan. We got something here that proves he's clean."

"Yeah?" Childers said. He wondered if it was his own voice, for it seemed to come from outside of himself.

"We got the man who did it," the Captain said. "Picked him up about an hour ago. We found him with the payroll money and the gun he used on those night-watchmen. He's already signed a confession."

Childers closed his eyes. He didn't say anything.

The Captain went on, "I phoned you at your home and your wife said you were on your way down here. Say, how come it's taking you so long?"

"I got sidetracked," Childers said. He spoke slowly. "I'm at the Lakeside Apartments, Captain. You better send some men up here. It's Apartment nine-o-seven."

"A murder?"

"You guessed it," Childers said. "It's a case of cold-blooded murder."

He hung up. In the corridor outside there was the sound of footsteps and voices and someone was shouting, "Is everything all right in there?" Another one called, "Was that a shot we heard?"

Wilma was standing near the door leading to the corridor and he said to her, "Go out and tell them it was nothing. Tell them to go away. And keep the door closed. I don't want anyone barging in here."

She went out into the corridor, closing the door behind her. Childers walked quickly to the door and turned the lock. Then he crossed to the nearest window and opened it wide. He climbed out and stood on the ledge and looked down at the street nine floors below.

I'm sorry, he said to Louise and the children, *I'm terribly sorry*. And then, to the Captain, *You'll find the gun on the kitchen table. His fingerprints and my fingerprints and I'm sure you'll believe her when she tells you how it happened, how someone who's tried so hard to be clean can slip and fall and get himself all dirty.*

But as he stepped off the ledge and plunged through empty darkness, he began to feel clean again.

MICKEY SPILLANE

Back in the fifties, when Americans were exulting in winning the war and moving into houses their parents could never have afforded, Mickey Spillane (1918–) took it upon himself to tell us that there was a darkness upon the land (see the opening page of *One Lonely Night* to see how well he describes this darkness) and that it had to be dealt with.

While his critics savaged him for the violence in his books and for his angry anti-Communism, they seemed to overlook the fact that most of Spillane's crime stories dealt with municipal corruption and thugs hired by quite respectable people. This was at a time when a record number of midsized cities were mobbed up. Only Spillane and a few others seemed concerned about this. His critics—who were sometimes embarrassingly overwrought—didn't seem to care.

Well, Spillane easily survived his critics (his most recent novel is *Black Alley*, 1996) and is acknowledged today as one of the true masters of the hard-boiled crime story. His groundbreaking Mike Hammer novels are now available in three-in-one editions for a whole new generation of readers to discover.

Tomorrow I Die

The noon train had pulled into Clarksdale at the hottest part of the day, an hour late. Twice a day that cross-country special stopped there for a thirty-minute layover giving the reporters a chance to photo and interview the celebs making the trip. The station even went so far as to set up a real deal for anybody who felt like stretching his legs. Local food and souvenirs.

Trouble was, the heat. The passengers preferred the air conditioning to the shimmering blasts of sunlight that waited outside. So only three of us got off.

One was met by a fat woman in a new Buick. The other guy and me headed straight across the street for the same thing . . . a fat draught beer.

Both of us half ran across the intersection, made the door at the same time and helped the other one in. Then the cold hit you. So cold it hurt, but it was wonderful.

At the bar the Sheriff smiled and asked, "Too hot for you gentlemen?"

When the beer came, I let it all go down, tasting every swallow.

My train buddy took longer and when I asked him to have one on me he shook his head sadly. "Thanks, but no go. The wife can't stand my breath." He threw a quarter on the bar and left.

"A shame, the way women run men," the Sheriff said.

"Awful. That guy isn't finished growing up."

"Well, that ain't always the case."

Before I could answer a low, rich voice laughed, "You better say that, Dad."

The tan brought out the grey in her eyes. The sun had made her blonde and riding too much had made her belly flat. The swell of her thighs showed right through the skirt and melted into lush curves that the blouse couldn't hide.

"My daughter Carol," the Sheriff said. "You look familiar, son."

"Rich Thurber," I grinned.

The dish frowned at me, then her face made up into a smile. "Certainly. Hollywood, post-war. One of the young up and comings. I remember you."

"Thanks," I said.

"What happened?"

I waved over my shoulder toward Hollywood. "The land of the gas pipe. All the good ones came home and replaced us. In simple, we had one thing in common. No talent."

The Sheriff fingered his hat back. Under it the hair was full and white. "Why do I know you? I never go to the movies, son."

Carol gave her pop an annoyed glance. "You didn't have to. He used to be on all the magazine covers." She smiled back at me. "You just don't quite look like yourself."

I put the beer down. "Sugar, let me remind you painfully. The war ended ten years ago. I'm not the same boy anymore."

The laugh came out of her like music. She threw back her head and let it dance out lightly. "I was fifteen then. You were one of my many heroes." She saw my face then and stopped the laugh. She looked at me through a woman's eyes and said, "I mean for real. You came out of the war and all that. I had a small girl's crush on you."

"I like big girls," I said.

"Uh-uh." She lifted those eyes toward the top of my head. "That hat. Who'd ever wear a hat like that."

"Our Mayor," her father answered.

"Except the Mayor," she answered.

I reached up and took the kady off. "I always wanted one. My old man wore one and I thought he looked like a million. So I got one." I put it back on, tapped it in place with a grin and finished my beer.

I ordered a refill, downed it and had another. The bartender pushed it across pretty fast. He seemed a little too anxious and kept watching the clock. I had one more and it was the pay-off one.

My stomach went into those warning motions and while there was still plenty of time to be casual about it, I walked off to the can in the back and tried to be quiet. I should have known better, but it was my own fault. The bartender came in and said, "Two minutes till train time, feller."

". . . hell with it."

"Okay . . ."

I was long past caring when the train left. I heard the whistle and the wheels and by the time I could face myself in the mirror again it was quiet outside with only the noise of the wind in the eaves. I went to the basin, doused my face with cold water and called myself some names.

Stupid. I was stupid. I wasn't drunk. Not on four quick beers. I'd just made myself sick as a slob on heat and thirst. I stayed there cooling down from the exertion, wondering why the bartender hadn't given me at least a second call when the door opened again and he walked in.

Or at least partly in. He was all shook up.

"Gotta come out, stranger. You gotta." His bottom lip quivered and under his pants his thighs were giving his bones a massage.

"What?"

"You . . . gotta. There's a man here . . ."

The man didn't wait to be introduced. He shoved the bartender against the door jamb and slid in so I could see him but all that I bothered watching was the rod in his fist. It was big and black with the grey noses of the slugs showing in the cylinder and the hammer cocked back to start them moving. There was another one in his belt at a ready angle and from the expression on his face he was looking for an excuse to shoot somebody.

He was crazy. Crazy as a loon. And he was a killer.

"You don' wanna come out here, mister?" His voice was too high.

I nodded quickly. "I'm coming. Right now."

He stepped back and let me go past with the bartender crowding my heels.

Whatever happened to make him go off I didn't see. There was just a grunt, then a sharp curse from the hood. The sound the gun made as it cracked against the bartender's skull had a nasty splitting note to it. He went down against my back, almost tumbled me, then his face hit the floor with a meaty smack. When I looked back, the gun pointed at my eyes and nudged me ahead. I kept right on going. Straight.

Since I left, the bar had filled up. At one of the tables two men sat quietly waiting, saying nothing, doing nothing. There was one more at the door with a shotgun in his hands and he kept watching out the window.

The Sheriff was at the other table. He had a welt over his eye and was just starting to wake up. Carol had a cloth pressed to his head and her lip between her teeth, trying hard to keep back the sobs.

I heard the gun boy say, "He was in the john, Mr. Auger."

Auger was the small fat one. He smiled and said, "Good boy, Jason."

"Please don't call me Jason, Mr. Auger." Something went wrong with the high voice. It had a warble to it and I wondered if the gun guy was asking or telling.

The fat one smiled even bigger and nodded solemnly. "I'm sorry, Trigger. I won't forget again."

"That's all right, Mr. Auger."

Then the fat one stared hard at me, his smile fading back into his cheeks again. "Who are you?"

"Just passing through, buddy. That's all."

Behind me gun-happy said, "Watch me make him talk, Mr. Auger," and I tightened up, hoping I'd pull away in the right direction when it came.

Before I had to Auger said, "He's telling the truth, Trigger. You can tell by his accent. He's no native." He looked back at me again. "You have a car outside?"

"No. I came in on the special."

"Why didn't you go out on it then?"

"I got sick and missed it."

"Uh-huh."

Someplace a clock ticked loudly and you could hear the ice settling in the cooler. Twice, somebody passed by the place on the sidewalk, but neither came in nor bothered to look in.

By rough estimation we stayed that way five minutes. The Sheriff opened his eyes and they were dull and hurt-looking. He moaned softly and put a hand to the lump that was turning a deep blue color.

Carol said, "Can I wet this rag again?"

Auger beamed paternally. "Certainly, my dear. But just wet the rag, nothing else." The smile turned to the one behind me. "If she takes out a gun . . . or anything dangerous, then shoot her—Trigger."

"Sure, Mr. Auger."

I heard the guy turn and take two steps. Carol went across the room with him behind her and I knew he was hoping for any excuse to put one in her back. There was a fever in the eyes of the Sheriff as he watched his daughter walk in front of that gun and all the hate in the world was in the set of his face.

All the hate, that is, except mine. I knew I was getting set to go when the small muscles in my shoulders began to jump. I was almost ready and close to where I couldn't stop if it came and it wasn't time. It wasn't the time! My gut was sucked in so far that my pants fell away loose and I had to swallow before I could talk. I had to get off it, damn it, I had to get off.

I said, "As long as you're doing favors . . . can I sit down, mister?"

Auger showed me his slow smile. "You are nervous?"

"Very nervous."

"That's good. It's good to be nervous. It keeps you from making mistakes."

He didn't know how right he was. He didn't know how big the mistake could have been. Someplace in back a faucet ran, then stopped. Carol came back with the wet cloth in her hand and laid it on her father's head. Auger pointed to their table. "You can sit with them. Just sit. I think you understand?"

"I couldn't miss, mister."

When I moved my feet, the feeling went away. My shoulders got still and I could feel my gut taking up the slack in my pants again. It was too close. I looked at Carol and for the first time in a long while felt scared down deep. Not so it showed. Just so I knew it.

Carol looked up at me and smiled when I reached the table. Two people in trouble together, her eyes said. Two people mixed up in a crazy impossible nightmare together.

The Sheriff's eyes were closed, but his hand on the table was clenching and unclenching. His chest moved deeply, but too slow, as if he were controlling it to keep back a sob. Carol reached out and covered his hand patting it gently, cradling his head against her cheek.

It was very quiet.

You know how it is when you feel somebody looking hard at your back? You get crawly all over like it's too cold and at the same time there's a funny burn that grows inside your chest cavity. The hairs on the back of your arms stand up and you don't know whether to look around fast or slow.

The voice was so deep a bass it almost growled. It said, "Turn around, you."

So I turned slow and looked at the dark one next to Auger. His face showed a hard anger and I knew that this was the bad one. This was the one who ran things when the chips were down. Trigger was only a killer, but this one was a murderer.

"I know this guy, Auger," he said.

Auger only smiled.

"Why should I know you, guy?"

My shrug was to work the jumps out of my shoulders again. I felt it starting but this time it wasn't so bad. "I was a movie actor," I told him.

"In what ones?"

I named three. I was lucky to remember the titles.

The guy's face was getting nasty edges to it. "I don't remember them. What's your name?"

Before I could answer him Auger said, "Thurber. Richard Thurber." He glanced at the dark guy with just a shade too much cunning. "You should leave these details to me, Allen."

The anger on Allen's face disappeared. He almost smiled, almost let his teeth match the look in his eyes, then he stopped and I knew if he had smiled all the way somebody would have died.

"Sorry, Mr. Auger. I just don't like to meet people I know. Not on a job, anyway. If I know them, then they know me. Oke?"

"A good thought, Allen. But actually, what difference would it have made?"

Carol didn't look up. She was crying inside and not for herself. She was crying for the old man against her cheek because we were all going to die and nobody could stop it. You could stop some things, but you couldn't stop this.

Auger's chair scraped as he swung around in it. The guy at the door pulled back a little and spoke over his shoulder. "Here comes Bernie, Mr. Auger."

"Whom does he have, Leo?"

"Short guy. Guy's got a gun on him. They're talking."

"No trouble?" Auger asked.

"Nothing so far. It's just like fishing. He's being suckered right in."

"Anything of Carmen?"

"Can't see him, Mr. Auger."

Auger leaned back in his chair. "Be nice when they come in, Leo."

Leo was big and he had teeth missing, three knuckles wide, but he still liked to grin. It was mostly all fun with a fat tongue in the middle. "I'll be real sweet to him, Mr. Auger," he said.

Then he stepped back and faced the bar like he was a customer as the two men came in the door. It was all very neat. The boy he called Bernie came in first, paused fast so the other bumped into him, and as Leo slid the gun out of the holster from behind, Bernie poked one into his middle section from in front.

The guy didn't know what was going on. Carol let out a stifled, "George!" the same time Leo belted him behind the ear with his own gun and as George was heading face into the sawdust, he got the idea.

George was a deputy.

Auger swung forward in the chair and peered at him. "Carry him over by the other, Bernie. He'll be all right. Did it come off as we planned?"

Bernie hefted the deputy and grunted, "Sure. He was eating in the back room alone."

"Find their car?"

"Around the corner." He threw the deputy into a chair. "This one didn't have the keys on him."

"We got the keys," Auger said, and nodded toward the Sheriff.

On the wall the clock whirred and a bent hammer tapped a muffled gong. Three times. For a brief instant every eye checked a watch and at the door Leo said, "I see Carmen, Mr. Auger. He's alone."

Allen's bass voice said something dirty.

"You're sure, Leo?"

"Positive, Mr. Auger. He's coming slow. No trouble. He's just alone."

Auger's fat little face showed its paternal smile again. He swung around the way fat men do and looked at us. At first I thought it was me he was going to speak to. Then I saw Carol flinch and go white around the mouth.

"The Mayor, Miss Whalen. Every day at exactly the same time he goes to his office to take care of his private practice. Every day. Without fail." There was something too pregnant in the pause that followed. He said, "Well?" and though his smile was still there, his eyes had a wetness of murder in them.

I was surprised at the calm in her voice. "He's out of town. He left Friday night to attend the State Bar Convention and is on this morning's program so he won't be home until tonight."

Trigger said, "You want me to make sure for you, Mr. Auger?"

"No, Trigger. She's telling the truth. People just can't make up a lie that fast and that sound." He stood up and the other two did the same. Allen was almost a foot taller so it seemed funny to hear Auger give the orders.

I said, "Any chance finding out what the hell's going on?"

"I was wondering when you'd ask," Auger laughed. "We're robbing the bank. Simple? You'll be the hostages. If followed, somebody is killed and thrown out the door. The chase will stop then. That is, if there will be a chase. We'll go in the Sheriff's car with lights, sirens and radio. However, we expect no chase."

"Then?"

"Then you'll all be shot. Very simple."

"That could urge a guy like me into making a break for it anytime."

His smile broadened. "No, it couldn't really. Everybody wants to hang right on to life. It's the most precious item. The minute you start to fuss—dead. It's all very simple."

"It's after three o'clock," I suggested.

"I know. The Sheriff will be our passport in. Two million dollars awaits. Pleasant thought?"

"From your angle. You'll get picked up," I said.

"Did they get the Brink's boys yet?"

"Nobody got shot on that job. It's different when somebody gets shot."

"So? You're familiar with criminology?"

"I read mystery books."

He smiled at my joke. He let everybody smile at my joke. Then he looked at his watch and the tension was back with all its implications when he said, "Go look at the bartender, Trigger."

The killer went back past the bar and skirted its edge. He bent out of sight for a second, then straightened. "Guy's dead, Mr. Auger."

"We'll lock the place up. You have the keys, Trigger?"

"I have them."

"Very well," Auger said. "Let us go then."

On the floor the deputy was coming up into a sitting position and he drooled. He knew what was happening and it was too big for him. Even Trigger's eyes were pointed at the corners like he was trying too hard to seem normal and beside Auger, the tall one called Allen was supressing something that wasn't quite a grin.

I said, "I want my hat."

The tension turned to surprised silence. Trigger's gun came up and his head cocked like a parrot's. Auger asked, "What?"

"My hat. I don't leave without my lid."

"Should I shoot him, Mr. Auger?"

My shoulders started in again. I could feel it beginning but this time I sat on it quickly enough and it went away.

"The fruitcake shoots me," I said, "and outside they pile in on you. Like somebody once said, 'the jig's up.' You know?"

I think Auger smiled for real this time. He said, "Let him go get his hat, Trigger." The fine line of his teeth showed under his lip. "Just go with him to be sure that's all he gets."

"Sure, Mr. Auger."

So I got up and walked back to the men's room. I went in with Trigger holding the door open and came out with my hat. When I was back beside Carol, I slapped the kady on, tapped the crown and said, "Okay, kids, put on the show."

I didn't quite expect the reaction I got. Allen's face was a dull mask and the other guy just stared at Auger. Our little fat friend looked like a pickpocket who got his pocket picked and for an instant a little shake ran right down his pudgy frame.

"Imagine that," he said. His eyes glinted at me. "You have nerve, our misnomered friend."

"You got took, Auger," Allen said softly.

"No . . . not took . . . just taken temporarily. His Honor is a shrewdy."

I started to squint when I got the picture. It came all at once and was so damn funny I almost started laughing right then.

Auger shook his head. "Don't laugh. It isn't appreciated. I've been fooled before and it's one thing I don't appreciate." His face flattened back into that smile again. "Though I do appreciate the humor of *his* situation, Allen. His Honor, whom we never saw up close, was to be identified as the only one in town who would forego a Stetson for a straw hat. He was also to be identified as a non-native. Whether he wanted to be or not, he was caught . . . and he wants to die with his hat on, so to speak."

Allen's voice held a stubborn tone. "The dame, Auger. She was lying."

His head bobbed. "Something our informants overlooked. They're in love. Lovers can think clearly when the loved one is in trouble."

"He's a movie actor, Auger?"

The smile went all the way to a laugh. "No . . . but so close a look-alike he can capitalize on it when he wants to."

This time I played it all the way. I said, "Do you blame me? So I was figuring. Maybe I could've had an out if you counted on survivors."

"Very smart. It's too bad you have to die."

"It is?"

"Me?"

I could see the back of his tongue now. "It is," he said. "Now let's go."

"Me?"

"That's right. You and the Sheriff. Our in and our out." He stopped a moment, smiled gently, then said, "Need I remind you that anyone sounding off will be shot? We're playing for big stakes. You can take your choice. Sheriff . . . I'll warn you that one peep from you and your daughter will be killed. Understood?"

I saw the Sheriff nod and his face showed each line deeper than ever.

Carol's face didn't seem so tan anymore. I grinned at her real big, almost as if the whole thing were funny and whatever she saw in that grin brought the tan back to her face and her eyes were grey again. She gave me a twisted little smile and one eyebrow had the slightest cock to it like she was trying to figure out the gimmick that should never have been there at all.

She looked and wondered, and our eyes were saying hello all over again. I tried to stop looking at her but couldn't make it and inside me a tight, hot little fire started to burn.

I wasn't grinning anymore. I was watching her, trying to say a soundless, "No . . . !" to both of us that something stifled before it could come out.

At the door Auger said, "Get the Sheriff's car, Carmen. Allen . . . are you ready to load the other?"

"I'm ready."

Carmen walked back to the deputy, his hand in one pocket palming a gun. He eased the deputy from his chair with, "Up, laddie boy. Let's make like an official."

Without a word, the deputy started toward the door. I thought he was going to be sick. Allen followed them out and the rest of us waited.

Nobody had tried to come in as yet. Nobody had even passed the place as yet. It was going to be an easy grab. A mark. A first-class creampuff.

The cars pulled in to the curb, a dark blue Olds sedan behind the black Ford with the whiplash aerial and blinker-siren combo. The Sheriff drove while I rode beside him. Auger and the killer stayed in the back seat. The deputy was unconscious on the floor again. All the others were behind us in the Olds and there was no way out. No way at all. It was all going nice and easy.

And that's the way it happened at the bank, too.

They robbed it at 3:22 with no complications at all because the Sheriff saw the only possible hitch in the deal and took the lead almost willingly. The guard opened the doors for him and seemed more hurt than mad when a gun covered him.

Auger walked us to the manager's cage and indicated us with his gun. "This is a holdup. Touch the alarm and you and these hostages die. Others outside will die too and since you are fully covered by insurance, don't try to be a hero."

The manager was almost cordial. "No . . . I won't."

It didn't need any more than that. They even did the work themselves. The cashier and two clerks brought it out stacked and packed while the killer's mouth worked wetly, hoping for a mistake. Auger's head bobbed like a satisfied customer and clucked at the killer to be patient. The mother-hen noises were a promise of better pickings later and his hands relaxed around the butt of the gun.

Quietly I asked, "What's the angle, Sheriff?"

Just as quietly he answered, "She's engaged to the Mayor. He'll get us out."

The vastness of the desert disappeared into the darkness closing in behind us, while ahead the last groping fingers of sunlight poked over the range of mountains to probe the gullys and ravines of the foothills with splashes of dull reds and oranges.

Beside me the Sheriff's face was as tight as his hands on the wheel, his eyes bloodshot and tired. His breath was harsh in nostrils dilated taut and I knew just what he was feeling. Right in the back of my head was a cold spot where the bullet would land if we moved too fast or too wrong. Behind us sat Auger and his gun boy and even over the sound of the engine I could hear the lazy fingering and cocking of the triggers on the two rods.

It was worse for the Sheriff. In the blue Olds behind us his daughter was on the end of another rod and whether she lived or died depended on what he did. Me too, in a way. Back there was the dough, a deputy and a daughter. Back there was a lot of reasons for playing it their way.

The Sheriff had inched up on the wheel until the bottom of it was in his belly. Without turning, he said, "Either we stop and get the dirt and bugs off this windshield or you better let me turn the lights on."

Auger's voice was totally calm. Completely without emotion. "You'll do neither."

"We'll wind up in a hole someplace then."

"I don't think so," Auger told him. "You have a reputation for knowing every inch of road to the border."

"Not the holes, mister."

He slowed for a turn, braked to ease over the sandy pot holes, then downshifted to get through the rubble of a rockslide. I saw the Olds jouncing in the ruts and almost run up our trunk. The Sheriff hit the go-pedal to get away from the sedan and his face got tighter than ever.

"You better let me put them dims on, mister."

For a second I thought Auger was going to agree when the radio suddenly kicked up a carrier-wave hum and a woman's high voice mouthed a call signal.

Auger said, "Turn it up!"

The gesture was automatic. The Sheriff's hand touched the knob and the voice came in, faint but clear. "The Marshall's call," he said before he was asked.

"Shut up!"

". . . using two cars, carrying Sheriff LaFont and several others. Sighted going west on ninety-two. High Section Six, can you report. Over."

Another hum was overlaid on the first, but there was no voice.

Auger's calm was still there. "Who is High Section Six?"

"Forestry Service. They send on another frequency. We can't pick them up."

"Mr. Auger . . ."

"Yes, Trigger?"

"We in trouble?"

Instead of answering, he spoke to the Sheriff. "You tell him," he said. The calm in his voice had turned deadly. I felt my shoulders hunching again.

I could see the Sheriff's teeth through his grimace. "No. Not yet. It'll be a while before they figure this road."

The hum went into a series of clicks, then, ". . . all sections report moving lights. Do not radio. Repeat, do not radio. Telephone all reports. Out."

"Neat," I said.

"Not for you," Auger told me.

I think I was reaching for a wise answer. I had it in my mouth when I stopped, just barely glancing at the Sheriff. The Ford was moving too fast and the car had a peculiar set to it. There was a trace of swoosh in the tail section and I knew the wheels were on the edge of a drift. The road ahead was barely outlined and seemed to have the slightest curve to it.

Right away I knew what he was playing for. He was setting up a dust storm behind us hoping the Olds would cut on its lights and maybe be spotted from one of those towers. He was doing it nice, but he did it wrong.

From back there came the raucous blast of a horn, a screaming of tires scraping rock and the smashing, tinny racket of a car going end over end.

The Sheriff didn't try to hit the brakes because two guns were right against our necks. He eased to a stop, horsed into reverse and backed through the dust. There was no way of seeing anything, and at the same time we heard the yells as the rear end of the Ford plowed into metal and glass and with a sickening jolt the Olds rolled once more.

Just once, then it toppled off the road into the ravine and you could have counted three before you heard it hit the bottom.

The horror of what had happened swept into the Sheriff's face and while he was starting to shrivel up and die inside, Carol's voice, sobbing quietly, carried through the settling dust.

Just as quickly, Allen was framed in the door with a gun in his fist pointing at me and his face twisted into a mad snarl. "You damn fool . . ."

"Put that gun down, Allen."

The big guy turned his snarl to Auger without moving the gun. "Carmen and Leo were in there. They were getting the money out!" His hand tightened on the rod. "Let's get that dough up here."

Auger moved slowly. He got out, then waved the Sheriff and me out and let Trigger stand behind us with the two guns at full cock. I could tell that Trigger was wearing his hoping smile. The big one.

Out of the side of my mouth I told the Sheriff, "She's okay. Just don't move, that's all."

He knew what I meant and nodded, never taking his eyes from Carol. She sat by the side of the road, dazed and crying but obviously unhurt. The deputy had a cut across his nose and was holding his ankle, his face twisting in pain.

Allen said, "What about the dough?"

There were just a few final snatches of light. Just enough to make out forms and vague shapes. The Sheriff moved to the edge of the ravine and peered over it. He shook his head. "Nobody gets down there until there's light. Even then you got to go in from the cut up yonder."

Allen and Auger looked at each other quickly. I knew damn well what they were thinking because I would have thought about it myself. The pie was going to be cut in bigger slices now. The grin I tried to hold back picked up my lip because when you start that stuff it keeps going on and on. The pie looks best whole. Carol saw the grin and her sobbing stopped. It probably was too dark for her to see it, but I made like a kiss and blew it her way. She did something with her mouth too, but I couldn't be quite sure just what.

It was Trigger who finally asked the question. "What are we going to do now, Mr. Auger?"

"You'll see, Jason."

Behind me I could feel the gun goon go cold, ice cold. "You said you wouldn't call me that anymore, Mr. Auger."

The fat man nodded solemnly. "I'm sorry, Trigger. I forgot." Then his face showed that he had all the answers and he pointed his finger at me. "You can start clearing away all bits of metal and glass you can find on the road. You and the girl both. Watch them, Trigger."

"Sure, Mr. Auger."

I didn't wait to be prodded. I walked to Carol, helped her up and wiped the dirt off her face. "You okay?"

She nodded briefly. “Shaken up a little, that’s all. George twisted his ankle, but I don’t think it’s broken.”

“You were lucky.”

“I guess so. The three of us were thrown clear when the car rolled. I . . . I think both the others were dead . . . before the car went over.”

“Don’t think about it. Let’s get this road cleared.”

I had to pull a handful of brush from the shoulder of the road to make a couple of sweeps. It took a while, but we got up what glass and odd bits that were around. When there wasn’t anything left on top to show there was an accident I took Carol’s hand and walked back to the car.

“That’s done. Now what?”

Auger smiled. “You seem awfully unconcerned for a man who will be dead shortly.”

“I don’t count on dying.”

“You have to, Mr. Mayor. You just have to.”

“That wasn’t what I asked.”

From the darkness Allen half whispered, “Stop talking to him. Damn . . . let’s roll.”

Trigger said, “We going, Mr. Auger?”

Carol’s hand was squeezing mine hard. Auger turned to the Sheriff, his face a pale oval in the dark. “This house you mentioned?”

The Sheriff waved toward the southwest. “Fourteen-fifteen miles maybe. Feller works a claim there.”

“Completely alone?”

“Don’t get to see folks for months.”

“You know what happens if you lead us into any trap?” The Sheriff didn’t answer. Auger said, “First your daughter gets it. Then you. Then the others. We’re far enough off to be able to make our way without help now.”

The Sheriff nodded. “There’s no trap.”

Allen came in closer, the gun in his hand held too tensely. “I don’t like it. We ought to go after it now. Right now.”

“And get ourselves killed, Allen? Don’t be silly. It’s too much to be clumsy about. We’ll do it the smart way.” He paused a moment, looking us over in that arrogant way he had. “Sheriff, you drive. Your daughter can sit between you and the Mayor. I want the deputy on the floor in the back with the rest of us.”

“We ought to dump the crip, Auger. That’s a big load.”

“Buzzards, Allen. They have them in this country. Why tip our hand? This time we’ll take it slowly, won’t we, Sheriff?”

“Without lights we got to.”

“And no mistakes.”

I saw the Sheriff glance at Carol. “Don’t reckon so,” he said.

The old man was big and angular, with arthritis. He had pale eyes that you knew had killed a dozen times and the type of face you wouldn’t have messed with even ten years ago. There was a leanness of age and of work in his hips and shoulders but over it all was the mantle of desert philosophy.

His time had come and he knew it.

He opened the door and in that single second he saw all of us there and knew what had happened. He saw the despair in the Sheriff's face and the anxiety in Carol's. He saw the abject fear of the deputy and the total lack of humanity in Auger. There was a touch of pity when he looked on Trigger and cold hatred for Allen.

I was last. He stared at me longest, the corner of his mouth twitching with a strange quirk, then he flipped the door wide and let us all come in. He smiled when Allen patted him down, and smiled again when Trigger jacked the shells out of the rifle on the wall. The smile even stayed there when they pulled the ancient .44s out of the gun belt and punched them out of the Colt.

Then he looked past the gunman and said, "Evenin' Sheriff . . . Miss Carol . . . George."

He saved the faintest of smiles for me and barely nodded. Yet he knew. *He knew damn well!*

Auger pulled a chair out with a wave to Allen and the gun boy. He sat down with a sigh and mopped his face with a clean folded handkerchief. "Old man . . . you seem to have gotten the picture here very rapidly."

The old boy nodded again.

"You know what happened?"

"I have a radio."

"Phone?"

"No telephone."

"Perhaps you expect visitors. A neighbor. Someone from the Forestry Service?"

"Nobody. Not until two weeks from now. Then Tillson comes with my trailer hitch for the Jeep. Then he can bury us all."

"Very perceptive. You're not afraid?"

"No."

"That's too bad. It's better to be afraid. You can stay alive just that much longer sometimes."

"I'm no kid."

"But you might be enjoying the twilight years."

"I am."

"For only a while. A pity."

He shouldn't have looked at me. I felt the crazy itch across my shoulders and the sudden hunching in my shoulders. The old man looked at me and grinned and he was the only one who found out. His eyes saw the creases and curves on the outside and the dips and contortions on the inside. His eyes were little feelers tipped with needles and they were on me.

"You can never tell," he said, "never."

Auger frowned at his tone. "I can tell."

It was Allen who broke the long stillness that followed. He leaned on the battered hand-carved table, the gun beside his hand and his voice filled with controlled rage. "Maybe you can tell me what we're going to do next?"

For the first time I saw the deadliness in Auger's character. It wasn't something added; it was something lacking and even deadlier than murder. It was some barbaric callousness that nullified human life or feeling and fed on the lusting that led to death and destruction. With the first word Allen drew back slowly, recognizing something that wasn't there by sight nor sound, seeing something that only I saw too.

Or maybe the old man. He knew about those things.

"Yes, Allen," Auger said quietly, "I can tell you."

Something was about to happen then. I didn't want to see it spelled out so I broke into it. I wasn't welcome because I put out the flame but if a fire started I wanted it to be one I started myself. I said, "Sure, tell us. Give us a clue."

And Auger looked at me a long time, long enough so I began to wonder if he knew too. My shoulders felt funny again and for the first time I looked down and saw my fingers splayed.

His character had a fault in it. A crack where the juice could leak out easy. He licked his lips until they shone wet. "I'll enjoy telling you," he said. "I think it's funny. Tomorrow the girl and the Mayor go back for the money. If there's any hitch her father is shot along with the others."

"You're nuts!"

"Allen . . ."

"They'll take off."

"It's her father, Allen."

"Okay, so the guy takes off . . ."

"They're in love. Remember?"

"Listen . . ."

"No, you listen, Allen. Listen very carefully and you'll know why this operation is mine, carefully conceived, planned and executed." He looked at all of us while he spoke, a dramatist watching his audience for each reaction.

"We picked that one town for its amazing cash wealth. We took their loved citizens as hostages knowing their incredible affection for each other, knowing that life is put above wealth. We selected an escape route impossible to trace." He smiled at us gently. "And tomorrow, the Mayor and his girl recover our wealth. If they are interrupted . . . they think. If they don't think, the Sheriff is dead."

"So what do they think?"

"How to cover the situation. How to stay alive, bring the cash back here and keep her father alive."

I grinned at him. "You already said we were as good as dead."

Auger's smile had the devil's benevolency in it. "And I say it again. You just forget that there's always that one chance."

"We might get out?"

"That's right," Auger told me. "That you might win the game. Hopeless, but a game."

Allen said something filthy and wiped his mouth with the back of his hand. Trigger was there too, the idiot's grin in his jaws. He watched Allen and both triggers were cocked on his guns. They were held idly, but ready.

I didn't feel that shaking anymore. I was away ahead of them all and being careful so it wouldn't show on my face. I was thinking of how easy it was going to be to get away from there, how that one chance Auger thought was an impossibility was a fat reality after all and how fast and slick I was going to take it.

Then I saw Carol's face and though I knew she couldn't see what I was thinking she was wondering about it just the same.

There was one other angle. The big one. The one only the old man got and his mouth was making faces at me because he knew for sure now. He was thinking what I was trying hard not to remember and I didn't want to look at him. His eyes went back too deep and penetrated too far into a guy's mind.

"Mr. Mayor . . ."

I grinned. "Yes, Mr. Auger?"

"Do you need any further explanation?"

"No."

"There is only one road. You'll be able to find the site?"

"I'll find it."

"The Sheriff will tell you how to get into the ravine."

"I know where it is," Carol said.

"Good," Auger beamed. "That makes it so much easier. And of course you realize the consequences of any nonsense, my dear?"

Carol simply nodded, not speaking.

"You'll bring the money up and come directly here. I'm going to estimate a time of twelve hours. If you have not appeared by then, your father, his deputy and this old man will be shot. That much is clear?"

We both nodded this time.

"If, then, there is any sign of any trickery . . . any at all, understand, they die and we figure another way out. Don't underestimate us. Don't think we won't do exactly as we say. That's clear?"

"Clear," I said.

"You take the road back in . . ." he checked his watch, "two hours. No lights. You travel slowly. Be sure not to raise a dust cloud or otherwise attract attention. You'll arrive at the site after daybreak and have ample time to do what is expected of you." He looked at Carol first then me. "Any questions?"

I nodded. "Yeah. What about the bodies in the car."

"Forget them."

"The buzzards might be up early."

That got to him. Something twitched in his cheek. "If they have fallen out of the car, put them back. Buzzards hunt on sight."

"Yeah."

He got that twitch again. "You're being awfully solicitous about our safety."

"Certainly," I said, "I wouldn't want anything to happen to my friends."

I smiled. A real easy one. Only the old man knew what it meant.

"You'll take the Jeep. Our aged friend here will check you out on it."

"I don't need checking out."

"Good, good. I'm expecting a whole lot of you, Mr. Mayor."

There wasn't a sound in the entire room. Outside the wind blew gently and whispered across the eaves. Carol shuddered gently then was still.

"Here's where we turn off," she said. "The road only goes down a few hundred feet then we'll have to walk."

I stopped the Jeep without turning and looked at her. The sun had washed her face with the first red light of morning and in its glow she looked tired. Tired and sorry. She hadn't spoken since we left the cabin and there was a peculiar apathy in her voice.

"Or do we?" she asked suddenly.

For some reason she smiled wanly and there was a wetness in her eyes that threw back the sun.

Then she turned her head and her smile grew a little twisted. "I guess we don't. I . . . can't blame you."

"You're scrambled, kid," I said.

"Why should you?"

"Why?" I shoved the straw kady back on my head and pawed the dirt out of my eyes. "Let's say I could go through with this out of common decency. My love for my fellow man."

"That's a lot of love. We take the money back and all get killed. It would be more sensible if you let me take it back while you went on."

"You'd still get bumped."

"But they'd be caught. It's something." She dropped her eyes when they got too wet. "This is none of your affair."

"It could be, sugar. It sure could be."

"What?" Her voice was tight in her chest.

"You forgot the other angle. There's a perfect crime involved." I let my grin stretch out into a short laugh. "I could bump you, take the cabbage and let the boys kill the others. I could put your body in the car with the other two and it'll all look legit. I could stash the dough for a year then come back and pick it up when all is cooled down. The law gets the boys, blames the deal on them, they cook and that's that."

"Would you?"

"I gave it some thought."

Carol looked at the road where we had stopped. There was a puzzle written in the set of her face and I saw her shoulders tighten and her fingers go white around each other.

"Would you?" she asked again.

I nodded. "I would."

But I didn't move. I sat there lazy-like, still grinning, hoping nothing was showing, wondering if she had the normal intuitive quality a woman was supposed to have, trying to figure what I'd do if she had.

Her face came back to mine slowly. "But *will* you?"

"No," I said, "I'll go back with you."

"Why?" Her eyes weren't wet any longer. They were curious now.

"Does there have to be a reason?"

"There are too many reasons why you shouldn't go back. You can only die back there."

"Maybe the future holds nothing better anyway," I told her quietly. "Maybe I already died someplace else and once more won't make any difference anyway."

"But that isn't why."

"No," I admitted. "It's you. I'm doing it for you. Something stupid has hold of me and when I look at you, I start to go fuzzy. I know it's you and the Mayor all the way but right now I feel like being noble and I don't feel like talking about it. Just take it for what it's worth. I'm going back with you."

"What then?"

"We'll think about it when it happens."

"Rich . . ."

Up ahead there was a speck in the sky.

"Rich." She touched my arm lightly. "Rich . . ."

I caught myself quickly reaching out for her hand.

"Thanks," she said.

"Forget it. We'll make out all right."

I started the Jeep up, snatched it into gear and started straight down the road. Carol grabbed my sleeve and pulled. "We can't . . . Rich, we have to go back down the road! We can't go over the cliff side!"

When I pulled my arm free, I pointed into the sun. "Plane up there. They could be looking for us. We drag the police in now there'll be trouble." Down toward the south a haze was rising into the morning sky. "Dust cloud. They're coming this way."

"What will we do?"

"We get out of here. The dust is coming from more than one car and I don't think the police will like the set of our plans."

"You think they know where we are?"

"I doubt it. They're just starting to fan out." I edged closer to the sheer rise of rock on my left and rode the hardpan, trying hard not to fly a dirt flag behind us.

Overhead, the plane came toward us, banked and headed back to the dust cloud. I tried to remember back through time and distance to where we turned off and when I thought I had it, stepped the Jeep up to beat the dust cloud to the intersection. I could be wrong, but I wasn't taking chances.

Carol licked the alkali from her lips and shouted, "What will we tell them, Rich?"

I had that one figured out too. "They don't know me, remember? So I picked you up. You were walking back the highway and I picked you up. You don't know where you came from or where the others are. Just give them that, no more."

"All right, Rich."

The plane spotted us first. It came down low, an old Army L-5 and I waved at the uniformed trooper in the rear seat. He looked at us hard, tapped the pilot and they both stared quickly before they pulled up and around for another pass. This time I gave them the okay sign and jerked my thumb at Carol.

That was all they needed. The L-5 pulled up, throttled back and started a glide ahead of us. It came down on the highway, stopped and I pulled up beside it. The trooper was out, his hand on the gun in his holster, taking big strides our way.

"You all right, Miss LaFont?"

"Yes, thanks."

"Who're you?"

I didn't have to answer. Carol did it for me. "He gave me a ride. I . . . got away from them and reached the highway."

"Glad to help," I said. "I heard the news."

"Where are they, Miss LaFont?"

Carol shook her head. The tears that went with it were real. "I don't know!" Her face went into her hands to muffle the sobbing.

I fanned myself with the straw kady. It was pretty dirty now. I said, "Lady told me she got away someplace in the hills. Must've walked ten miles across the brush fields before I picked her up. I can take you back and show you."

"Never mind. We can pick up her trail if she came across the brush. You can track a mouse in that sand."

Behind the plane the dust took shape, a brown plume like a cock's tail following the six cars driving abreast. They came up and disgorged the hunters, avid men with guns in their hands and identical expressions on their faces. They were all angry men. They were all intent and serious. They all had a touch of lust too. Blood lust.

The big guy in front ran to the Jeep and half lifted Carol out of the seat. "Honey, honey," he crooned to her, "you okay, baby?"

"I'm all right, Harold."

"You take it easy baby. I'll take care of you now. You just take it easy."

The trooper raised a finger to his hat brim. "Pardon me, Mr. Mayor, we better start backtracking Miss LaFont while her tracks are fresh. This feller here . . ." he nodded toward me, "picked her up about ten miles back coming across the brush."

"You can't miss it," I said. "There's a dead dog by the side of the road just where she came on."

The trooper gave me a funny look. "Dog? No dogs out here, feller. Must be a coyote. Where you from, boy?"

I didn't answer the question. I said, "A dog, officer. A black Scotty. Somebody probably tossed him from their car. He's got a collar on."

The trooper squinted his apology and nodded, then turned back to the Mayor. "Excuse me, sir, but do you want to stay with Miss LaFont or go with the posse?"

For the first time I had a good look at the big guy, and saw all the parts of him I didn't like. He was too big and too good-looking. He reeked of maleness and you could almost feel the destiny that rode his shoulders. He looked at the trooper quickly and you could see the momentary flash of lust and blood scent in his mouth and nostrils. Then something else followed just as briefly that I couldn't quite identify, but immediately hated.

He took Carol's hand in his and the other went around her waist. "Go ahead, officer. I'll be sure that Carol is all right then I'll follow you. Take my car along with you. We'll stay with the Jeep here."

"Yes, sir." The trooper saluted again, waved the pack of cars off the road and let the L-5 get back into the blue. It circled once, then paralleled the highway behind us. The rest piled back into the cars, the trooper in the first one, and went by with their wheels throwing up dust from the shoulder.

Ten miles, I thought. *I should have made it further. If I was lucky, they'd look for the dog and keep right on going.*

Maybe it was the way Carol looked at me. Maybe it was the drawn expression and the way her eyes seemed to slant up at the corners. The Mayor stopped his soft talk and his lips hardened into a tight line.

His voice was a soft hiss. "What is it, Carol?"

"Harold . . ."

"Tell me."

"We had to get rid of them. They would have spoiled it."

"We?" He watched me with a careful disdain for a moment, then: "Who are you, feller?"

"A victim, buster. Part of the *we* she mentioned."

"Go on."

It was better letting her tell it. I could watch his face then and make a play of getting out of the Jeep. When she got to the part about the money, that look came back on his face and stayed long enough for me to see the greed that was there.

When she finished, he forced the excitement from his face and pounded a fat fist into his palm. "Good heavens, Carol, you can't expect us to let you go through with a thing like that! You can't jeopardize your life by going back there!"

"What else can she do?" I put in.

"Do? I'll show you what we'll do! We'll go back to that cabin and shoot them out of there like they deserve. We'll kill every one of those thieving skunks. . . ."

"And the Sheriff, and the deputy, and the old man," I said.

Carol's face was white. Chalk-white. "You can't, Harold."

His tongue made a pass across his lips. "We have to. There are some things that must be done."

"Like being governor?"

He knew the greed had shown then. He knew I saw what was in his mind, the AP and UPI headlines. *Mayor recovers stolen millions. Leads fight on thieves' den*. In subheads they'd tell about the three who died with the thieves in line of civic duty.

"You're talking out of turn, mister." His grimace had a snarl in it.

He started to burn when I turned on the grin. "I don't think so. My hide's wrapped up in this mess too. You figure a way to pull it off and get the kid's dad out whole? You have an angle to snake out all three maybe?"

"Somebody is bound to get hurt. I could be myself, too."

"Harold . . ."

"Yes, Carol?"

"You can't do it. I won't let you." She had trouble getting the words out. She was looking at this guy she had never seen before and what she saw shook her bad. "You said you loved me, Harold . . ."

"I do, sugar. You know I do." He paused and sucked in his breath. "But I'm still the Mayor, honey. We can't let a thing like this happen."

"It means my father's life."

"And yours if you go back."

Slowly, very slowly, Carol turned her face to me. She smiled gently and I winked her a kiss and told myself that I was a sucker, a real, prime, first-class sucker who went up the pipe for a broad when the odds you were bucking were rigged from the very start.

The Mayor said, "I'm sorry, Carol," and this time all the hardness was there in his voice. It spelled out what he was going to do and he didn't have to say anything more to make it clear. "You two can wait here for the posse. I'll go in after that money and they can meet me there." He paused and looked at her as he would a pawn he willingly lost to gain a better position. "And Carol . . . I'm sorry. Truly sorry."

"So am I," I said.

"What?"

I grinned again. All the teeth this time. Then I splashed him. He turned blood all over and his jaw hung at a crazy angle and even before the dust had settled the flies were drifting down on his face. My knuckles went puffy before I could rub them but it was worth it. I picked him up, dumped him in the back of the Jeep and nodded for Carol to get aboard.

Almost out of sight down the highway was the thin brown plume. There was still time if we hurried but we'd have to make it fast. I spun the Jeep around, geared it up and floorboarded it to the cut off. This time I wasn't bothered about being followed and could make better time along the curves and switchbacks of the trail.

Carol was shouting for me to slow down and I braked the Jeep to a crawl. "The next turn and we can go down the ravine. Don't pass it!"

"How long will it take?" I shouted back.

"A half hour to reach the car." She leaned closer, squinting into the wind. "Can we do it?"

My fingers were crossed when I said it. "I think so. It'll be close, but we might just do it."

"What about Harold?"

"We'll leave him here. He'll come around. That posse won't have too much trouble tailing us in this dirt and our boy here will put them on the cabin right off."

She reached out and laid her hand on mine. It was warm and soft with a little burning place in the middle of her palm. Her thumb ran back and forth across my wrist lightly and all of a sudden a whole minute was yanked out of eternity and given to us for our own.

"Rich . . . we don't have much time any more . . . do we?"

"We can hurry. . . ."

"I mean . . . for us, Rich. There's only one answer if we go back."

"Perhaps. Why?"

Her smile was a beautiful thing. "I'm just finding out . . . certain things."

"I knew them right along," I said.

"Harold . . ."

"Greedy. Ambitious. Mean. He'll spoil anything to get what he wants."

"I thought he wanted me."

"He did for a while, kid. But just now he saw a little more he could have and he took his choice."

"Why are you so perceptive?"

My face felt tight and all I said was, "I've been around, kid."

"Rich . . ."

"What?"

She leaned toward me. I knew what she was going to say and I didn't let her. I could taste the dust through the wet of her mouth and feel the life and fire of her as she pressed against me. Everything inside me seemed to turn over suddenly. Then I pushed her away before it could get worse.

There were tears in her eyes, the path of one etching its way down her cheek. She frowned through them, watching me closely, her hand squeezing mine even tighter.

"There's something about you, Rich . . ."

"Don't look at it."

"We're only going back to die, aren't we?"

"Not you, kitten."

For a second it was like it was with the old man. For an instant she saw that one thing, but before she could hold it long enough it passed and left only the trace of a puzzle, barely long enough to get a glimmer of understanding.

But somehow it was enough. There was that change in her eyes and the taut way she held herself. The shadow of bewilderment was obscured in a moment of reality.

"Why are you doing it, Rich?"

"You'll never know," I said.

She brushed back her hair with one hand and looked past me into the ravine. "And when it's over?"

"I'll be gone. One way or another."

"And then there'll be no more."

"That's right."

"Rich . . ."

"Don't say it, kitten. Look at it and squeeze it with your hand, but don't say it."

"I love you, Rich."

"I told you, don't say it. It's because of the trouble. It's now, that's all. Maybe it will be gone tomorrow."

"Maybe there'll be no tomorrow."

"It always comes," I said. "I hate it too, but tomorrow always comes."

In the back the Mayor moaned softly. I said, "Let's get to it," and spun the wheel of the Jeep.

The road went down a quarter of a mile before the rock slide wiped it out. I used the tarp ropes to snag the Mayor to the seat backs and waved Carol out. Overhead the sun was tracing its arc through the sky too fast, too fast. By my watch we had only two hours more to go and if there was anything in the way we'd be too late.

Had I been alone I never would have made it, but Carol knew the path and could pick it up even when there was nothing to mark it. We skirted the stream in the belly of the gorge, climbed to the shoulder that was gouged and ripped by the roll of the dead Olds and tore open the metal corpse.

Both bodies were inside, huddled together like kids asleep in the same bed. But here there was a difference. Both of them wore their rods over their pajamas. They were better off the way they were. I took a quick look at Carol and there was nothing about her that was soft or afraid. She took the satchels I handed her, tossed them to the ground and helped me out of the wreck. I closed the door against the buzzards and waved her to go ahead, then picked up the bags and followed her.

The Mayor was awake when we got back. He was awake and mad but hurting too hard to set up a fuss. His eyes were little things that wanted to rip into me, and when they turned on Carol the hatred was there too. They saw the bags and the governorship going up in smoke at the same time and something like a sob caught in his throat.

Carol said, "So long, Harold."

He didn't answer. I untied his hands and feet, and while they were still numb, dragged him out of the Jeep. He lay there in the dirt looking up at me, watching the crazy smile I wore while I did all the things I did and I knew that he had found out too. Not a little bit like Carol . . . but like the old man. He knew too.

We had one hour left. One time around the clock before it was too late. I spun the heap in the dust, rode the gears up as high as I could in second and kept it there. Beside me Carol hung on to the seat back, one hand braced against the dash. Her hair was a blonde swirl in the wind and twice I heard her laugh over the howl of the engine.

There was only one straight in the road, one half-mile stretch that eased the pull on the shoulders and let the engine go into high.

I felt Carol's hand on my arm and looked over at her. There was a smile on her mouth and a lifetime in her eyes. "You're a great actor, Rich," she said. I sensed the words more than heard them.

This time I shook my head. "Hell, I'm no actor."

"You're a great one," she disagreed with another smile.

The laugh she heard was something that hadn't come out of me in a long time. It was a laugh that said everything was screwy funny because it never should have happened at all. Everything was all balled up like a madman's dream. It was giving a starving man a turkey dinner that was sure to kill him the minute he ate it.

When we reached the end of the stretch, I was glad. There in the distance was the cabin and the killers and I was glad. There was where the big bang would be and it would all be over. There would be a chance here and a chance there but in the end it would all be the same. You die. You catch the one you didn't expect and die.

Up ahead the dust sifted up from the hardpan and I braked easily before I hit it. I pulled in close to the uprise of rock and took out the bags.

Carol didn't get it. I winked and said, "Insurance. They're playing hostage with us. They got what we want. Friend Auger forgot we got what he wants too."

She didn't see where I went and I didn't want her to. I opened the bag, took out handsful at a time and laid the sacks of money beside definite markers, noting the location of each on the back of a hundred dollar bill. It wasn't a good job, but if anybody was in a big hurry, they were going to have trouble rounding it all up. When I finished with one, I took the other and did the same across the road. In each bag I left a thousand bucks, neatly-wrapped. Then I started the Jeep up and drove back to the cabin. Someplace behind us the Mayor was staggering to the highway to intercept the posse. It wouldn't be long now before they found him and followed our trail back.

There was very little time left at all.

The killer opened the door with his foot and pointed the one gun at me. He wore a stupid smile on his face and he had sucked on the unlit butt so long the paper was completely wet and starting to unfurl at the end. He said, "Here they are, Mr. Auger."

In the soft glow of the kerosene lamp the fat man looked like a little Buddha. "Show them in, Trigger," he smiled.

The stiff fingers of the gun muzzles prodded us in. The door was kicked shut again and Trigger mumbled, "Hold still." His hands did a professional job of patting me down from my chest to my legs. He took a little longer with Carol and kept grinning all the while.

I was thinking how nice it would be to kill him right there.

The guns probed the small of our backs again and pushed us forward. Trigger sounded puzzled this time. "They ain't loaded, Mr. Auger. They didn't take no guns from Carmen or Leo."

"I really didn't expect them to. It was merely a precaution, Trigger."

And in the back where it was dark I heard the Sheriff curse a wild one softly and mutter, "*Why didn't she stay away . . . why!*"

"You had twelve minutes more, Rich." Auger smiled gently. "You almost didn't come back?"

I grinned to him.

The dark blob on the cot came to his feet slowly and Allen mouthed his murderer's smile. "He's been thinking."

"That right?"

I shrugged. "For a while, maybe. It all came to a dead end, so to speak."

"You're a brave man, Rich. There aren't many left like you. Do you know why?"

"Sure," I nodded, "they're all dead."

"Yes."

In back of us the killer kicked the door shut. Someplace I heard George, the deputy, sobbing as he breathed.

Auger asked, "You met anyone?"

"We met everyone."

For a second there was no sound, not even that of someone breathing. Allen took a step forward into the light.

"So?"

"They're turning over every rock. They'll be here, but not for a while yet."

Very slowly, Auger came to his feet. "You told them anything?"

"I sent them looking for a dead dog," I said. Then I smiled back at the fat man and put my straw kady on and tapped it in place. I shouldn't have been so damned wise. Allen took a quick stride and rapped one across my jaw and I went down on the floor with the kady rolling over beside the chair the Sheriff was tied to.

He looked big, standing over me. He was bastard-mean and big and the cold murder in him was leaking out every pore. He was the methodical kind that looked at life and death with the same expression of contempt and used either to suit his own purpose. The gun came out of his pocket, the hammer was thumbed back and he was smiling . . . smiling hard, even bigger than Auger.

He stopped smiling when I kicked him across the shins and lost the rod when my other foot caught him in the belly. Trigger picked the gun up, laughed, and it wasn't at me.

Auger took the rod from Trigger and said, "All right. Enough, Allen."

It took a while for him to talk. It took a time that never seemed to end for him to tear his eyes away from Trigger who still laughed, silently.

"Enough?" He sucked his breath in deep. "I'm going to kill this boy."

"Not now."

"So later, Auger. Then I'm going to powder Jason here."

Everything got tight too fast. There was a chuckle in Trigger's throat and Auger said, "Keep it down, laddies. Way down. We have two million in front of us. When there's shooting to be done, let's do it right."

Money was the magic word. They all looked at the cases on the floor, and I didn't want them to look too long. I said, "Yeah, think of the loot. Two million bucks which you won't get without trouble."

Auger was the second one who got it. The old man caught it first and his eyes did the talking when they looked at me. They were funny eyes, eyes that had looked over guns, eyes that had looked over corpses, eyes that had seen too much and now they were watching me and laughing hard. They were eyes that had lived too long and didn't care anymore.

"Allen . . . open the bags."

He had to stoop down close to me and I was almost hoping he'd take another swipe my way. I could feel the tight feeling in my shoulders and down deep in the pit of my stomach unseen hands were tying me into a knot. They squeezed hard and the thing that coursed through me was like a voice saying to be quiet, be still, be patient, for soon it would be over. Soon it could all come out one way or another and then it would be over.

Allen's fingers fumbled open the catches, reached in and came out with an expression of disbelief across his face.

I said, "My hostage, Auger. My guarantee for a few minutes more of living."

His neck was livid with rage. It showed there and no place else. His voice was almost conversational. "A trade, perhaps?"

"Don't be silly."

"Of course not. You die anyway."

"But I got more minutes."

"Yes, you have that. Where is the money?"

I turned and looked outside. The sun was settling down into the west, the long fingers reaching out again to probe the hills and valleys that surrounded the cabin.

"Someplace there," I said. "You won't find it easily."

"Why, Mr. Mayor? Shall we squeeze the girl until you show us where you put it?"

"No." I laughed and pushed myself up, dusting the dirt off my pants. "I said all I wanted was minutes. I'm stalling."

Allen had started to breathe normally again. His face had a flat look and his thumbs were hooked in his belt. "I want to kill this guy, Auger."

"Not yet. He hasn't explained yet."

I reached up to my shirt pocket and flipped out the hundred buck bill with the lines and writing on it. I spread it open, folded it lengthwise and sailed it across to Auger. "There it is, friend. Two million bucks. Out there in the brush. You want it, go find it."

"He'll show us," Allen said.

Auger had that paternal smile again. "No . . . we really don't need him, Allen. He's telling the truth, can't you see? He wants us to go look for it to give him time. Oh, we'll be able to find it, but that's part of the game, see . . . like a treasure hunt. Each find stimulates us to go find the rest before it gets dark and not to go back to see whether or not they've broken loose or not. It's a very cute . . . and daring plan, Allen."

"He's nuts."

Auger put the bill in his pocket. "No . . . but shrewd. Not shrewd enough, but shrewd." He looked at me, his tongue making a wet smear of his lips. He had the stuff in his hands now and he knew it and all he had to do was pull out his ace card.

"I won't even bother tying you, Mr. Mayor. Allen and I shall go and leave you in the care and keeping of Trigger here. A pleasant prospect? Trigger . . . would you like that?"

"I'd like that, Mr. Auger."

"We'll take the patrol car back to the site, pick up the money and come back for you, Trigger. I expect you'll be alone by then?"

"I'll be alone, Mr. Auger."

"Take your time, Trigger. Don't hurry. Let them think some. Let them see how well they didn't make out after all. You know what I mean, Trigger?"

"I won't hurry none, Mr. Auger."

Very deliberately, Allen pulled his hand back and cut one across my jaw. My head rocked and I was on the floor again with the taste of blood in my mouth. I said, "Thanks."

"No trouble," Allen said. He bent down, picked up the cases and walked out.

For the second time I got up off the floor and watched the fat man. He put the gun in his coat pocket and looked up at me. "In a way I'm sorry that I can't kill you myself," he said, "but I promised Trigger here the pleasure."

"You expect to get away with it?"

His nod was serious, even to me. "I expect to get away with it."

"Want to bet?" I said.

He smiled for the last time and walked out. The car started, pulled around from the back and Trigger closed the door with his elbow.

There was a peculiar expression in his eyes. Like hunger.

Nobody noticed it until the sound of the car diminished into the distance, but there was a clock on the back wall. It was an old fashioned job and the works in it were worn thin. The walls were a sounding board and each *tick* was loud. There was something unnatural about the sound because it wasn't ticking us into the future, but bringing us closer to the end of the present.

Even Trigger noticed it and knew what we were thinking. He liked the idea. It made him king for a minute and gave him the power of life or death over his subjects. He watched the clock and us, his mouth working around the ruins of the cigarette.

The Sheriff sat there in his chair, roped tight, and I wondered what he had tried while we were gone to get him there. I wondered what happened to his deputy to make him cry like that.

Then I looked at Carol and wondered why it had to be like this at all. She seemed tired and even while I watched the tears welled up in her eyes.

"Carol . . ."

She looked up slowly.

Behind me Trigger said, "Why don'tcha go kiss her, Mac?"

"Yeah, thanks," I said. I crossed the room and held out my hand to her. All she did was touch it.

The end, I thought. *Everything was all gone now. It was over. Climax, anticlimax.*

I turned around and looked at Trigger. "You figure me for a screwball, don'tcha?" he asked me.

"That's right."

"I ain't dumb." He fiddled with the hammers on the guns. "You ain't the Mayor."

"No?" The clock sounded loud again. "Who am I?"

"You ain't the Mayor."

"I could have told you that."

"Nobody really asked, feller." His smile got real crooked then. "I got the play. Them guys . . ." he jerked his head toward the door, "They're too smart. They didn't get you quick like I did, Mac."

"No?"

"Un-uh. You're a cutie. You figure Allen and Auger, they go out there and get in a rumble about the money. You figure that, don't you? They rumble and somebody catches it. That it?"

I shook my head. "Not quite."

"That's good. You figure anything and you die real fast, feller. You and everybody else. Allen and Auger rumble and sure as hell I'll rumble everybody here. You'll get real rumbled, boy."

I said, "That's not what I figured."

You could hear the ropes creak as the Sheriff tightened his hands on the arm of the chair. His face was a hot white glow of hate, stiff with creases and marked by the slash of his eyes and mouth. "You fool," he said. "You young damn fool. You could've stayed off. You didn't have to bring her back here. Yourself either."

Very quietly Carol said, "He had to, Dad."

"Damn fool actor . . ."

"He's no actor," the old man laughed.

All of us looked at him and I shook my head. I tried to tell him no but he wouldn't have any part of it. He saw what was coming and wanted in.

"Pop . . ."

"You're no actor like he thinks, are you son? You're no mayor and no actor at all." He paused and let the corner of his mouth wrinkle up. "Or maybe you're an awfully good one."

The metallic clicking of the gun hammers was too loud. I turned to where Trigger was standing stiff against the door. "What you figger, man?"

I looked at my watch. It was about time. They could all know now. I said, "There's a posse out there, Jason. I made them mad at us and about now they'll have backtracked us and they can't miss seeing your pals poking around for that dough. They won't ask questions. They'll shoot and that's all for you."

In the back of his eyes a dawn of reason came through. "Not for me. The Jeep is outside. Not for me. Just for you." His eyes swept the room and the reason left him. He was hungry again. "For all of you."

The Sheriff was watching me avidly. There was something drawn about him I didn't like. "You're no actor, son?"

"That's right. No actor."

"Rich . . . ?"

The old man didn't let me answer. "He's not what you think he is, Carol."

"Rich . . ."

"I'm not Thurber, Carol." Her eyes were even more puzzled now. "I look like him, that's all. I'm no movie actor. Sometimes it helps to say so."

"Rich . . . I love you."

"Don't," the old man said simply.

"I'll always love you, Rich."

"Don't," the old man said again.

Across time and space there was just the two of us. Two people looking and saying silent words nobody else in the world could ever understand. There was love, and want, and understanding in that one meeting and a sudden revelation that was so shocking that her eyes could only widen imperceptibly, then go wet with tears.

It was quiet then. The clock sounded loud and alone until the killer at the door moved. He said, "You called me Jason, mister."

"That's right, Jason."

"You're crazy, mister."

"Not me, Jason. Just you. Just you."

His mouth made a tight oval. "I don't care what happens outside now, mister. You know?"

"It doesn't matter. It's over."

"Sure it's over. I can do it now. Like Mr. Auger said, you gimme a reason now." He licked his mouth, wiping it dry on his shoulder. "I can do it now like I want to and not wait for them to come back."

Like an echo from a tunnel the old man's voice said, "Why don't you warn the slob?"

And Jason smiled because he thought the old man was talking to him. "I warned him," he chuckled.

The clock ticked again, whirred a moment, then struck a quarter hour note on a muffled bell.

From outside, from someplace far off, came the flat continued cough of a Tommy gun. Another answered it and in agreement was the dull thunder of wide bore rifles and the sharp *splat* of small arms. It lasted through two minutes and I thought that even before we heard the guns the thing was over out there.

It was over in here too. All over. Everybody knew it, even Jason. Softly, almost so I didn't hear it, Carol said, "I love you, Rich . . ."

And I repeated it. "I love you, Carol."

I said it looking at the old man. He shook his head. "Don't . . ."

The killer looked at me with those crazy, fruity eyes and I knew we were right at the end. He was grinning real big with his face twisted like he was enjoying it and you could tell that he was all gone upstairs. All gone.

Carol was crying softly in the corner sitting there with her hands bunched in her lap, fear not even a part of her anymore. She had been afraid too long. There was nothing left except anticipation; dull, deadly anticipation. The killer looked at her, grinned and licked his lips. He didn't know whether to take her first or last . . . whichever would be better.

The Sheriff said nothing. There wasn't an expression on his face either. The ropes holding him down were too tight and his hands looked like white gloves. He was trying to hate the killer to death and it wasn't working.

His deputy was crying too. A dry cry like an idiot. With the empty holster on his belt he reminded me of a kid who had fallen down a well while playing cops and robbers.

Beside Carol the old man who had seen too much of life stood with his bony hands shoved under his belt and shook his head in pity at what was going on. He was neither afraid nor expectant. Death had passed him up too many times for him to be afraid of it when it came for certain. For some reason he was feeling sorry for the killer. There was abject pity in his face for the goon boy with the all-gone eyes and the two rods in his fists.

My straw hat was on the floor beside me and very slowly the killer snaked it back with his foot until he had it in front of him, then even slower still, stood on it.

There was something nasty and ominous in the act, in the sound of it. One old-fashioned straw kady mashed to nothing. Then the killer grinned at me and cocked the hammers on the two rods. I was to be the first.

I could tell that he didn't know why I was grinning too.

Outside was the Jeep and without too much trouble I could reach the border. It would be close, but I could still do it. If I stayed, the cops or papers would make me for sure and if they dusted for prints it would all come out in the wash.

Someday it was going to happen, but when it did it wouldn't be where Carol was. She could have her dream and I'd have mine and maybe she'd never find out.

Life, I thought.

The killer grinned again and brought the guns up and I knew that in the back the old man was waiting to see if he was right.

The grin got real wide, then stopped altogether and tried to see why I was grinning even bigger.

He didn't know why. He couldn't tell.

When I pulled the little .32 from the sleeve holster he knew, but by then it was too late and the Jeep and the border were outside and he was dying in a slow puddle of red on the floor.

The old man laughed because *he knew he had been right.*

I was a killer too!

DONALD E. WESTLAKE

What can one say about Donald E. Westlake (1933–) that hasn't been said 2,761 times before?

Yes, he virtually created the comic-caper novel. Yes, he has taken the crime novel into startling new directions, particularly with his recent novel *The Ax*, one of the most memorable and disturbing novels of the past twenty-five years. And yes, he wrote the Academy Award–nominated screenplay for the Jim Thompson adaptation *The Grifters*.

In the late sixties and early seventies, he wrote five novels about a disgraced cop named Mitch Tucker. The series never got its due. The books portray their particular era—the time of flower power as seen through middle-aged eyes—with precision and insight. Thankfully, they are being brought back, in hardcover, and are no less powerful than when they were written.

Then there's the Parker novels he writes as Richard Stark. Parker is a thief, a pro, and an unrepentant one. Two or three excellent films—including the original *Point Blank*—were made from the Parker novels. And after an absence of many years, he's back, Westlake as Stark giving us three fine new novels about Parker.

As one critic recently noted, Westlake is most likely the best crime fiction writer of his generation. Hard to argue with that.

Never Shake a Family Tree

Actually, I have never been so shocked in all my born days, and I am seventy-three my last birthday and eleven times a grandmother and twice a great-grandmother. But never in all my born days did I see the like, and that's the truth.

Actually, it all began with my interest in genealogy, which I got from Mrs. Ernestine Simpson, a lady I met at Bay Arbor, in Florida, when I went there three summers ago. I certainly didn't like Florida—far too expensive, if you ask me, and far too bright, and with just too many mosquitoes and other insects to be believed—but I wouldn't say the trip was a total loss, since it did interest me in genealogical research, which is certainly a wonderful hobby, as well as being very valuable, what with one thing and another.

Actually, my genealogical researches had been valuable in more ways than one, since they have also been instrumental in my meeting some very pleasant ladies and gentlemen, although some of them only by postal, and of course it was through this hobby that I met Mr. Gerald Fowlkes in the first place.

But I'm getting far ahead of my story, and ought to begin at the beginning, except that I'm blessed if I know where the beginning actually is. In one way of looking at things, the beginning is my introduction to genealogy through Mrs. Ernestine Simpson, who has since passed on, but in another way the beginning is really almost two hundred years ago, and in still another way the story doesn't really begin until the first time I came across the name of Euphemia Barber.

Well. Actually, I suppose, I really ought to begin by explaining just what genealogical research is. It is the study of one's family tree. One checks marriage and birth and death records, searches old family Bibles and talks to various members of one's family, and one gradually builds up a family tree, showing who fathered whom and what year, and when so-and-so died, and so on. It's really a fascinating work, and there are any number of amateur genealogical societies throughout the country, and when one has one's family tree built up for as far as one wants—seven generations, or nine generations, or however long one wants—then it is possible to write this all up in a folder and bequeath it to the local library, and then there is a *record* of one's family for all time to come, and I for one think that's important and valuable to have even if my youngest boy Tom does laugh at it and say it's just a silly hobby. Well, it *isn't* a silly hobby. After all, I found evidence of murder that way, didn't I?

So, actually, I suppose the whole thing really begins when I first came across the name of Euphemia Barber. Euphemia Barber was John Anderson's second wife. John Anderson was born in Goochland County, Virginia, in 1754. He married Ethel Rita Mary Rayborn in 1777, just around the time of the Revolution, and they had seven children, which wasn't at all strange for that time, though large families have, I notice, gone out of style today, and I for one think it's a shame.

At any rate, it was John and Ethel Anderson's third child, a girl named Prudence, who is in my direct line on my mother's father's side, so of course I had them in my family tree. But then, in going through Appomattox County records—Goochland County being now a part of Appomattox, and no longer a separate county of its own—I came across the name of Euphemia Barber. It seems that Ethel Anderson died in 1793, in giving birth to her eighth child—who also died—and three years later, 1796, John Anderson remarried, this time marrying a widow named Euphemia Barber. At that time, he was forty-two years of age, and her age was given as thirty-nine.

Of course, Euphemia Barber was not at all in my direct line, being John Anderson's second wife, but I was interested to some extent in her pedigree as well, wanting to add her parents' names and her place of birth to my family chart, and also because there were some Barbers fairly distantly related on my father's mother's side, and I was wondering if this Euphemia might be kin to them. But the records were very incomplete, and all I could learn was that Euphemia Barber was not a native of Virginia, and had apparently only been in the area for a year or two when she had married John Anderson. Shortly after John's death in 1798, two years after their marriage, she had sold the Anderson farm, which was apparently a somewhat prosperous location, and had moved away again. So that I had neither birth nor death records on her, nor any record of her first husband, whose last name had apparently been Barber, but only the one lone record of her marriage to my great-great-great-great-great-grandfather on my mother's father's side.

Actually, there was no reason for me to pursue the question further, since Euphemia Barber wasn't in my direct line anyway, but I had worked diligently and, I think, well, on my family tree, and had it almost complete back nine generations, and there was really very little left to do with it, so I was glad to do some tracking down.

Which is why I included Euphemia Barber in my next entry in the Genealogical Exchange. Now, I suppose I ought to explain what the Genealogical Exchange is. There are any number of people throughout the country who are amateur genealogists, concerned primarily with their own family trees, but of course family trees do interlock, and any one of these people is liable to know about just the one record which has been eluding some other searcher for months. And so there are magazines devoted to the exchanging of some information, for nominal fees. In the last few years, I had picked up all sorts of valuable leads in this way. And so my entry in the summer issue of the Genealogical Exchange read:

> BUCKLEY, Mrs. Henrietta Rhodes, 119A Newbury St., Boston, Mass. Xch data on *Rhodes, Anderson, Richards, Pryor, Marshall, Lord*. Want any info Euphemia *Barber*, m. John Anderson, Va. 1796.

Well. The Genealogical Exchange had been helpful to me in the past, but I never received anywhere near the response caused by Euphemia Barber. And the first response of all came from Mr. Gerald Fowlkes.

It was a scant two days after I received my own copy of the summer issue of the Exchange. I was still poring over it myself, looking for people who might be linked to various branches of my family tree, when the telephone rang. Actually, I suppose I was somewhat irked at being taken from my studies, and perhaps I sounded a bit impatient when I answered.

If so, the gentleman at the other end gave no sign of it. His voice was most pleasant, quite deep and masculine, and he said, "May I speak, please, with Mrs. Henrietta Buckley?"

"This is Mrs. Buckley," I told him.

"Ah," he said. "Forgive my telephoning, please, Mrs. Buckley. We have never met. But I noticed your entry in the current issue of the Genealogical Exchange—"

"Oh?"

I was immediately excited, all thought of impatience gone. This was surely the fastest reply I'd ever had to date!

"Yes," he said. "I noticed the reference to Euphemia Barber. I do believe that may be the Euphemia Stover who married Jason Barber in Savannah, Georgia, in 1791. Jason Barber is in my direct line, on my mother's side. Jason and Euphemia had only the one child, Abner, and I am descended from him."

"Well," I said. "You certainly do seem to have complete information."

"Oh, yes," he said. "My own family chart is almost complete. For twelve generations, that is. I'm not sure whether I'll try to go back farther than that or not. The English records before 1600 are so incomplete, you know."

"Yes, of course," I said. I was, I admit, taken aback. Twelve generations! Surely that was the most ambitious family tree I had ever heard of, though I had read sometimes of people who had carried particular branches back as many as fifteen generations. But to actually be speaking to a person who had traced his entire family back twelve generations!

"Perhaps," he said, "it would be possible for us to meet, and I could give you the information I have on Euphemia Barber. There are also some Marshalls in one branch of my family; perhaps I can be of help to you there, as well." He laughed, a deep and pleasant sound, which reminded me of my late husband, Edward, when he was most particularly pleased. "And, of course," he said, "there is always the chance that you may have some information on the Marshalls which can help me."

"I think that would be very nice," I said, and so I invited him to come to the apartment the very next afternoon.

At one point the next day, perhaps half an hour before Gerald Fowlkes was to arrive, I stopped my fluttering around to take stock of myself and to realize that if ever there were an indication of second childhood taking over, my thoughts and actions preparatory to Mr. Fowlkes' arrival were certainly it. I had been rushing hither and thither, dusting, rearranging, polishing, pausing incessantly to look in the mirror and touch my hair with fluttering fingers, all as though I were a flighty teenager before her very first date. "Henrietta," I told myself sharply, "you are seventy-three years old, and all that nonsense is well behind you now. Eleven times a grandmother, and just look at how you carry on!"

But poor Edward had been dead and gone these past nine years, my brothers and sisters were all in their graves, and as for my children, all but Tom, the youngest, were thousands of miles away, living their own lives—as of course they should—and only occasionally remembering to write a duty letter to Mother. And I am much too aware of the dangers of the clinging mother to force my presence too often upon Tom and his family. So I am very much alone, except of course for my friends in the various church activities and for those I have met, albeit only by postal, through my genealogical research.

So it *was* pleasant to be visited by a charming gentleman caller, and particularly so when that gentleman shared my own particular interests.

And Mr. Gerald Fowlkes, on his arrival, was surely no disappointment. He looked to be no more than fifty-five years of age, though he swore to sixty-two, and had a fine shock of gray hair above a strong and kindly face. He dressed very well, with that combination of expense and breeding so little found these days, when the well-bred seem invariably to be poor and the well-to-do seem invariably to be horribly plebeian. His manner was refined and gentlemanly, what we used to call courtly, and he had some very nice things to say about the appearance of my living room.

Actually, I make no unusual claims as a housekeeper. Living alone, and with quite a comfortable income having been left me by Edward, it is no problem at all to choose tasteful furnishings and keep them neat. (Besides, I had scrubbed the apartment from top to bottom in preparation for Mr. Fowlkes' visit.)

He had brought his pedigree along, and what a really beautiful job he had done. Pedigree charts, photostats of all sorts of records, a running history typed very neatly on bond paper and inserted in a looseleaf notebook—all in all, the kind of careful, planned, well-thought-out perfection so unsuccessfully striven for by all amateur genealogists.

From Mr. Fowlkes, I got the missing information on Euphemia Barber. She was born in 1765, in Salem, Massachusetts, the fourth child of seven born to John and Alicia Stover. She married Jason Barber in Savannah in 1791. Jason, a well-to-do merchant, passed on in 1794, shortly after the birth of their first child, Abner. Abner was brought up by his paternal grandparents, and Euphemia moved away from Savannah. As I already knew, she had then gone to Virginia, where she had married John Anderson. After that, Mr. Fowlkes had no record of her, until her death in Cincinnati, Ohio, in 1852. She was buried as Euphemia Stover Barber, apparently not having used the Anderson name after John Anderson's death.

This done, we went on to compare family histories and discover an Alan Marshall of Liverpool, England, around 1680, common to both trees. I was able to give Mr. Fowlkes Alan Marshall's birth date. And then the specific purpose of our meeting was finished. I offered tea and cakes, it then being four-thirty in the afternoon, and Mr. Fowlkes graciously accepted my offering.

And so began the strangest three months of my entire life. Before leaving, Mr. Fowlkes asked me to accompany him to a concert on Friday evening, and I very readily agreed. Then, and afterward, he was a perfect gentleman.

It didn't take me long to realize that I was being courted. Actually, I couldn't believe it at first. After all, at *my* age! But I myself did know some very nice couples who had married late in life—a widow and a widower, both lonely, sharing interests, and deciding to lighten their remaining years together—and looked at in that light it wasn't at all as ridiculous as it might appear at first.

Actually, I had expected my son Tom to laugh at the idea, and to dislike Mr. Fowlkes instantly upon meeting him. I suppose various fictional works that I have read had given me this expectation. So I was most pleasantly surprised when Tom and Mr. Fowlkes got along famously together from their very first meeting, and even more surprised when Tom came to me and told me Mr. Fowlkes had asked him if he would have any objection to his, Mr. Fowlkes', asking for my hand in matrimony. Tom said he had no objection at all, but actually thought it a wonderful idea, for he knew that both Mr. Fowlkes and myself were rather lonely, with nothing but our genealogical hobbies to occupy our minds.

As to Mr. Fowlkes' background, he very early gave me his entire history. He came from a fairly well-to-do family in upstate New York, and was himself now retired from his business, which had seen a stock brokerage in Albany. He was a widower these last six years, and his first marriage had not been blessed with any children, so that he was completely alone in the world.

The next three months were certainly active ones. Mr. Fowlkes— Gerald—squired me everywhere, to concerts and to museums and even, after we had come to know one another well enough, to the theater. He was at all times most polite and thoughtful, and there was scarcely a day went by but what we were together.

During this entire time, of course, my own genealogical researches came to an absolute standstill. I was much too busy, and my mind was much too full of Gerald, for me to concern myself with family members who were long since gone to their rewards. Promising leads from the Genealogical Exchange were not followed up, for I didn't write a single letter. And though I did receive many in the Exchange, they all went unopened into a cubbyhole in my desk. And so the matter stayed, while the courtship progressed.

After three months, Gerald at last proposed. "I am not a young man, Henrietta," he said. "Nor a particularly handsome man"—though he most certainly was very handsome, indeed—"nor even a very rich man, although I do have sufficient for my declining years. And I have little to offer you, Henrietta, save my own self, whatever poor companionship I can give you, and the assurance that I will be ever at your side."

What a beautiful proposal! After being nine years a widow, and never expecting even in fanciful daydreams to be once more a wife, what a beautiful proposal and from what a charming gentleman!

I agreed at once, of course, and telephoned Tom the good news that very minute. Tom and his wife, Estelle, had a dinner party for us, and then we made our plans. We would be married three weeks hence. A short time? Yes, of course, it was, but there was really no reason to wait. And we would honeymoon in Washington, D.C., where my oldest boy, Roger, has quite a responsible position with the State Department. After which, we would return to Boston and take up our residence in a lovely old home on Beacon Hill, which was then for sale and which we would jointly purchase.

Ah, the plans! The preparations! How newly filled were my so-recently empty days!

I spent most of the last week closing my apartment on Newbury Street. The furnishings would be moved to our new home by Tom, while Gerald and I were in Washington. But, of course, there was ever so much packing to be done, and I got at it with a will.

And so at last I came to my desk, and my genealogical researches lying as I had left them. I sat down at the desk, somewhat weary, for it was late afternoon and I had been hard at work since sunup, and I decided to spend a short while getting my papers into order before packing them away. And so I opened the mail which had accumulated over the last three months.

There were twenty-three letters. Twelve asked for information on various family names mentioned in my entry in the Exchange, five offered to give information, and six concerned Euphemia Barber. It was, after all, Euphemia Barber who had brought Gerald and me together in the first place, and so I took time out to read these letters.

And so came the shock. I read the six letters, and then I simply sat limp at the desk, staring into space, and watched the monstrous pattern as it grew in my mind. For there was no question of the truth, no question at all.

Consider: Before starting the letters, this is what I knew of Euphemia Barber: She had been born Euphemia Stover in Salem, Massachusetts, in 1765. In 1791, she married Jason Barber, a widower of Savannah, Georgia. Jason died two years later, in 1793, of a stomach upset. Three years later, Euphemia appeared in Virginia and married John Anderson, also a widower. John died two years thereafter, in 1798, of stomach upset. In both cases, Euphemia sold her late husband's property and moved on.

And here is what the letters added to that, in chronological order:

From Mrs. Winnie Mae Cuthbert, Dallas, Texas: Euphemia Barber, in

1800, two years after John Anderson's death, appeared in Harrisburg, Pennsylvania, and married one Andrew Cuthbert, a widower and a prosperous feed merchant. Andrew died in 1801, of a stomach upset. The widow sold his store, and moved on.

From Miss Ethel Sutton, Louisville, Kentucky: Euphemia Barber, in 1804, married Samuel Nicholson of Louisville, a widower and a well-to-do tobacco farmer. Samuel Nicholson passed on in 1807, of a stomach upset. The widow sold his farm, and moved on.

From Mrs. Isabelle Padgett, Concord, California: In 1808, Euphemia Barber married Thomas Norton, then Mayor of Dover, New Jersey, and a widower. In 1809, Thomas Norton died of a stomach upset.

From Mrs. Luella Miller, Bicknell, Utah: Euphemia Barber married Jonas Miller, a wealthy shipowner of Portsmouth, New Hampshire, a widower, in 1811. The same year, Jones Miller died of a stomach upset. The widow sold his property and moved on.

From Mrs. Lola Hopkins, Vancouver, Washington: In 1813, in southern Indiana, Euphemia Barber married Edward Hopkins, a widower and a farmer. Edward Hopkins died in 1816, of a stomach upset. The widow sold the farm, and moved on.

From Mr. Roy Cumbie, Kansas City, Missouri: In 1819, Euphemia Barber married Stanley Thatcher of Kansas City, Missouri, a river barge owner and a widower. Stanley Thatcher died, of a stomach upset, in 1821. The widow sold his property, and moved on.

The evidence was clear, and complete. The intervals of time without dates could mean that there had been other widowers who had succumbed to Euphemia Barber's fatal charms, and whose descendants did not number among themselves an amateur genealogist. Who could tell just how many husbands Euphemia had murdered? For murder it quite clearly was, brutal murder, for profit. I had evidence of eight murders, and who knew but what there were eight more, or eighteen more? Who could tell, at this late date, just how many times Euphemia Barber had murdered for profit, and had never been caught?

Such a woman is inconceivable. Her husbands were always widowers, sure to be lonely, sure to be susceptible to a wily woman. She preyed on widowers, and left them all a widow.

Gerald.

The thought came to me, and I pushed it firmly away. It couldn't possibly be true; it couldn't possibly have a single grain of truth.

But what did I know of Gerald Fowlkes, other than what he had told me? And wasn't I a widow, lonely and susceptible? And wasn't I financially well off?

Like father, like son, they say. Could it be also, like great-great-great-great-great-grandmother, like great-great-great-great-great-grandson?

What a thought! It came to me that there must be any number of widows in the country, like myself, who were interested in tracing their family trees. Women who had a bit of money and leisure, whose children were grown and gone out into the world to live their own lives, and who filled some of the empty hours with the hobby of genealogy. An unscrupulous man, preying on well-to-do widows, could find no better introduction than a common interest in genealogy.

What a terrible thought to have about Gerald! And yet, I couldn't push it from my mind, and at last I decided that the only thing I could possibly do was try to substantiate the autobiography he had given me, for if he had told the truth about himself, then he could surely not be a beast of the type I was imagining.

A stockbroker, he had claimed to have been, in Albany, New York. I at once telephoned an old friend of my first husband's, who was himself a Boston stockbroker, and asked him if it would be possible for him to find out if there had been, at any time in the last fifteen or twenty years, an Albany stockbroker named Gerald Fowlkes. He said he could do so with ease, using some sort of directory he had, and would call me back. He did so, with the shattering news that no such individual was listed!

Still I refused to believe. Donning my coat and hat, I left the apartment at once and went directly to the telephone company, where, after an incredible number of white lies concerning genealogical research, I at last persuaded someone to search for an old Albany, New York, telephone book. I knew that the main office of the company kept books for other major cities, as a convenience for the public, but I wasn't sure they would have any from past years. Nor was the clerk I talked to, but at last she did go and search, and came back finally with the 1946 telephone book from Albany, dusty and somewhat ripped, but still intact, with both the normal listings and the yellow pages.

No Gerald Fowlkes was listed in the white pages, or in the yellow pages under Stocks & Bonds.

So. It was true. And I could see exactly what Gerald's method was. Whenever he was ready to find another victim, he searched one or another of the genealogical magazines until he found someone who shared one of his own past relations. He then proceeded to effect a meeting with that person, found out quickly enough whether or not the intended victim was a widow, of the proper age range, and with the properly large bank account, and then the courtship began.

I imagined that this was the first time he had made the mistake of using Euphemia Barber as the go-between. And I doubted that he even realized he was following in Euphemia's footsteps. Certainly, none of the six people who had written to me about Euphemia could possibly guess, knowing only of one marriage and death, what Euphemia's role in life had actually been.

And what was I to do now? In the taxi, on the way back to my apartment, I sat huddled in a corner, and tried to think.

For this *was* a severe shock, and a terrible disappointment. And could I face Tom, or my other children, or any one of my friends, to whom I had already written the glad news of my impending marriage? And how could

I return to the drabness of my days before Gerald had come to bring gaiety and companionship and courtly grace to my days?

Could I even call the police? I was sufficiently convinced myself, but could I possibly convince anyone else?

All at once, I made my decision. And, having made it, I immediately felt ten years younger, ten pounds lighter, and quite a bit less foolish. For, I might as well admit, in addition to everything else, this had been a terrible blow to my pride.

But the decision was made, and I returned to my apartment cheerful and happy.

And so we were married.

Married? Of course. Why not?

Because he will try to murder me? Well, of course he *will* try to murder me. As a matter of fact, he has already tried, half a dozen times.

But Gerald is working at a terrible disadvantage. For he cannot murder me in any way that looks like murder. It must appear to be a natural death, or at the very worst, an accident. Which means that he must be devious, and he must plot and plan, and never come at me openly to do me in.

And there is the source of his disadvantage. For I am forewarned, and forewarned is forearmed.

But what, really, do I have to lose? At seventy-three, how many days on this earth do I have left? And how *rich* life is these days! How rich compared to my life before Gerald came into it! Spiced with the thrill of danger, the excitement of cat and mouse, the intricate moves and countermoves of the most fascinating game of all.

And, of course, a pleasant and charming husband. Gerald *has* to be pleasant and charming. He can never disagree with me, at least not very forcefully, for he can't afford the danger of my leaving him. Nor can he afford to believe that I suspect him. I have never spoken of the matter to him, and so far as he is concerned I know nothing. We go to concerts and museums and the theater together. Gerald is attentive and gentlemanly, quite the best sort of companion at all times.

Of course, I can't allow him to feed me breakfast in bed, as he would so love to do. No, I told him I was an old-fashioned woman, and believed that cooking was a woman's job, and so I won't let him near the kitchen. Poor Gerald!

And we don't take trips, no matter how much he suggests them.

And we've closed off the second story of our home, since I pointed out that the first floor was certainly spacious enough for just the two of us, and I felt I was getting a little old for climbing stairs. He could do nothing, of course, but agree.

And, in the meantime, I have found another hobby, though of course Gerald knows nothing of it. Through discreet inquiries, and careful perusal of past issues of the various genealogical magazines, the use of the family names in Gerald's family tree, I am gradually compiling another sort of tree. Not a family tree, no. One might facetiously call it a hanging tree. It is a list of Gerald's wives. It is in with my genealogical files, which I have willed to the Boston library. Should Gerald manage to catch me after all, what a surprise is in store for the librarian who sorts out those files of mine! Not as big a surprise as the one in store for Gerald, of course.

Ah, here comes Gerald now, in the automobile he bought last week. He's going to ask me again to go for a ride with him.

But I shan't go.

TALMAGE POWELL

Talmage Powell (1920–2000) did some of the best pure storytelling to be found in the pulps of the forties and fifties. Like most pulpsters, he had to work in a variety of genres to pay the bills. But unlike most pulpsters, he was as good at horror as he was at crime, and his Western stuff was damned fine, too. Editors could rely on him. He had a forty-year run as a freelancer, something few can claim.

While he wrote a number of excellent books (including a nice, tight puzzler called *The Smasher*), his best crime work was probably the Ed Rivers private eye series. Powell created a different kind of character for his lead man, working against most of the genre's clichés, finding a fresh if sometimes grumpy voice for his hero and cases that each had a nice new twist.

Somebody Cares

Being teamed with Odus Martin wasn't an inviting prospect, but I didn't intend to let it blight the pleasure of my promotion to plainclothes.

His own reaction was buried deep in his personal privacy. I, the greenie fresh out of uniform, was accepted as just another chore. Martin volunteered no helpful advice; neither did he pass judgment on me. I suspected that he would be slow to praise and reluctant to criticize.

If my partner's almost inhuman taciturnity made him a poor companion, I had compensations. A ripple of pleasure raced through me each time I entered the squadroom. To me it was not a barren bleak place of scarred desks, hard chairs, dingy walls, and stale tobacco.

My first days as Martin's partner were busy ones. We rounded up suspects in a knifing case. Martin questioned them methodically and dispassionately. He decided a man named Greene was lying. He had Greene brought back and after seven hours and fifteen minutes of additional questioning by Martin, Greene signed a statement attesting his guilt.

Martin's attitude irritated me. A man's life had been cut short with a knife. Another man would spend his best years behind bars. Wives, mothers, children, brothers, sisters were affected. Their lives would never again be quite the same, no matter how strong they were or how much they managed to forget.

But to Odus Martin it was all a chore, nothing more. A small chore at that, one of many in an endless chain.

When I mentioned the families, Martin looked at me as if I were a truant and not-too-bright schoolboy. "Everybody in this world has someone," he said. "Accept that—and quit worrying about it."

"I'm not necessarily worrying," I said, an edge creeping into my voice.

He shrugged and bent over some paper work on his desk. His manner was a dismissal—a reduction of me to a neuter, meaningless zero.

"Since you put it that way," I said argumentatively, "how about the nameless tramp the county has to bury?"

He looked up at me slowly. "Somewhere, Jenks, somebody misses that tramp. You take my word for it. There are no total strangers in this world. Somebody cares—somebody always cares."

I hadn't expected this bit of philosophy from him. It caused me to give him a second glance. But he still reminded me of a slab of silvery-gray casting in iron.

As the weeks passed, I learned to get along with Martin. I adopted a cool manner toward him, but only as a protective device. I told myself I'd never let a quarter of a century of violence and criminals turn me into an unsmiling robot, as had happened to Odus Martin.

I paid him the respect due a first-rate detective. His movements, mental as well as physical, were slow, thorough, and objective. He made colorless—hence, uninteresting—newspaper copy. This, coupled with his close-mouthed habits, caused most reporters to dislike him. Martin didn't mind in the least.

But when it came to criminals he had the instincts of a stalking leopard. As I became better acquainted with him, I realized these were not natural endowments—they were the cumulative conditioning and results of twenty-five years. He seemed never to have forgotten the smallest trick that experience had taught him.

The day Greene was arraigned, I put a question to Martin that had been bothering me. "You decided Greene was lying when he told us his alibi. Why? How could you be sure?"

"He looked me straight and forthrightly in the eye with every word he spoke," Martin explained.

This drew a complete blank with me.

Martin glanced at me and said patiently, "Greene *normally* was a very shifty-eyed character."

Well, I knew I could learn a lot from this guy, if I were sufficiently perceptive and alert myself. He didn't regard it as his place to teach. He was a cop.

As usual, I was fifteen minutes early to work the morning after the murder of Mary Smith. Martin was coming from the squadroom when I arrived. He was moving with the slow-motion, elephantine gait that covered distance like a mild sprint. It was clear he'd just got in and had intended to leave without waiting for me.

I fell in step beside him. "What's up?"

"Girl been killed."

"Where?"

"In Hibernia Park."

She lay as if sleeping under some bushes where she'd been dragged and hurriedly and ineffectually hidden. It was a golden day, filled with the freshness of morning, the grass and trees of the park dewy and vividly green.

Squad cars and uniformed men had already cordoned off the area. Men from the lab reached the scene about the same time as Martin and I. Efficiently, they started the routine of photography and footprint moulage.

I had not, as yet, the objectivity of the rest of them. The girl drew and held my attention. She was small, fine of bone, and sparsely fleshed. Her face had a piquant quality. She might have been almost pretty, if she'd known how to fix herself up.

As it was, she lay drab and colorless in her cheap, faded cotton dress, dull brown hair framing her face.

Her attitude of sleep, face toward the sky, became a horror when my eyes followed the lines her dragging heels had made. The lines ended beyond a flat stone. The stone was crusted with dark, dried blood. It was obvious that she'd been knocked down there, as she came along the walkway. The back of her head had struck the stone. Perhaps she'd died instantly. Her assailant had dragged her quickly to the bushes, concealing the body long enough for him to get far away from the park.

Looking again at her, I shivered slightly. What in your nineteen or twenty years, I asked silently of her, brought you to this?

The murder scene yielded little. Her purse, if she'd had one, was gone. She wore no jewelry, although she might have had a cheap watch or ID bracelet. The golden catch from such an item was found near the flat stone by one of the lab men.

Later in the squadroom, Martin and I sat and looked at the golden clasp.

"Mugged, robbed, murdered," Martin decided. "I wonder how much she was carrying in her purse. Five dollars? Ten?"

He held the catch so that it caught the light. "We'll check the pawnshops. A hoodlum this cheap will try to pawn the watch. Nothing from Missing Persons?"

I'd just finished the routine in that department. I shook my head.

"Nothing from the lab, either," Martin said. "Her clothes came from any bargain basement. No laundry marks. Washed them herself. No scars or identifying marks. No bridgework in the mouth. We'll run the fingerprints, but I'm not hopeful. The P.M. will establish the cause of death as resulting from compound fracture of the skull, probably late last night."

"None of it will tell us who she is," I said.

"That's what I'm saying. But somebody will turn up, asking for her. Somebody will claim her. Girl that young—she can't die violently and disappear without it affecting someone. Meantime, all we got is this clasp."

We took it to all the pawnshops in the city. No watch with such a clasp missing had been pawned.

Martin next picked up every punk who had a mugging or mugging attempt on his record. We questioned each one of them. The task ate up two days, and when it was over we had placed nobody near Hibernia Park at the right time.

The girl's body remained in the morgue. No one inquired about her. She wasn't reported missing. She continued to be an unclaimed Jane Doe.

"It means," Martin said, "that she has no family here. She must have come here to work, maybe from a farm upstate. Lucky for us that we live in a reasonably small city. We'll check all the rooming houses—places where such a girl might have lived."

We did it building by building, block by teeming block, from landlord to landlady to building super.

Martin would take one side of the street, I the other. Our equipment was a picture of the girl, and the question was always the same. So were all the answers.

We spent two fatiguing, monotonous days of this. Then about midafternoon the third day, I came disconsolately from a cheaper apartment building and saw Martin waving to me from a long porch across the street.

I waited for a break in traffic and crossed over. The rooming house was an old gables-and-gingerbread monstrosity, three stories, a mansion in its day, but long since chopped into small apartments and sleeping rooms.

A small, gray, near-sighted woman hovered in the hallway behind Odus Martin.

"This is Mrs. Carraway," Martin said.

The landlady and I nodded our new acquaintance.

"May we see Mary Smith's room?" Martin asked.

Mary Smith, I thought. I'd begun to think you'd remain Jane Doe forever, Mary Smith.

"Since you're police officers I guess it's all right," Mrs. Carraway said.

"You've seen my credentials," Martin said. "We'll take full responsibility."

We followed Mrs. Carraway to a small clean room at the end of the hallway. She stood in the open doorway while we examined the room.

The furnishings were typical—mismatched bed, bureau, chest of drawers, and worn carpet, faded curtains.

A neat person, Mary Smith. The few items of clothing she'd owned were pressed and properly placed in the closet and chest of drawers.

The room reflected a lonely life. There were no photos, no letters. Nothing of a personal nature except the clothing and a few magazines on a bedside table.

"How long she lived with you?" Martin asked.

"A little over two months," Mrs. Carraway said in her cautious, impersonal voice.

"When did you see her last?"

"A week ago Thursday when she paid a month's rent."

"She have any callers?"

"Callers?"

"Boy friend, perhaps."

"Not that I know of." Mrs. Carraway pursed her lips. "I'm not a nosy landlady. She seemed like a quiet, nice girl. So long as they pay their rent and don't raise a disturbance—that's all I'm concerned with."

"Know where she came from?"

"No. She came and looked at the room and said she'd take it. She said she was employed. I checked, to make sure."

"Where was that?"

"At the Cloverleaf Restaurant. She's a waitress."

Martin thanked her, and we started from the room.

Mrs. Carraway said, "Is she in serious trouble?"

"Pretty much," Martin said. "I'm sure she won't be coming back."

"What'll I do with her things?"

"We'll let you know."

Mrs. Carraway followed us to the front door. "I've told you everything I know. I'm not an unkind person. But whatever she's done is none of my business. You'd just be wasting my time to be calling me in as a witness."

"We'll trouble you no more than we have to," Martin said.

We returned to the unmarked police car parked in the middle of the block. Martin got behind the wheel and drove in silence.

"Any doubt of her identity?" I asked.

"I don't think so. We'll check fingerprints in the room against the Jane Doe to be sure. But the landlady showed no hesitation when she saw the picture. She was Mary Smith, right enough."

Hello, Mary Smith, I thought. Hello, stranger. Who were you?

A man named Blakeslee was the owner of the Cloverleaf, a large drive-in on the south side of town. He was a slender, dark, harried-looking fellow, about forty.

He was checking the cash register when we arrived. We showed him our credentials, and with a gesture of annoyance he led us to a small office off the kitchen.

"Well," he said, closing the door, "what's this all about?"

"Got a Mary Smith on your payroll?" Martin asked.

"I did have. She quit without notice. A lot of them do. You've no idea what it is to keep help nowadays."

"What were the circumstances?"

"Circumstances?" He shrugged. "She didn't show up for a couple of days, so I put another girl on. There weren't any circumstances, as you put it."

"Did you wonder if maybe she was sick?"

"I figured she'd have called in. She's not the first to quit like that. I haven't time to be running around checking on them. What's your interest in her?"

"She's dead."

"What's that?" After his initial start, Blakeslee raised his hand and stroked his chin. "Why, that's too bad," he said in a tone without real meaning.

"The papers carried a story," Martin said. "Unidentified girl murdered."

"I don't recall seeing it. Probably wouldn't have connected it with Mary Smith anyway. How did it happen?"

"She was apparently on her way home. We think she was knocked down for whatever of value she was carrying."

"It couldn't have been much."

"Can you tell us anything about her?"

"Only that she came to work here. She seemed nice enough, always on time. Too quiet to make many friends."

"Where did she work formerly?"

"She came here from Crossmore." Blakeslee spread his hands. "I wish I could help. But after all, what was she to me?"

Martin and I took the expressway out of town. The drive to Crossmore, a small town in the next county, required only forty minutes.

I wondered how many restaurants there were in Crossmore. Very few, I guessed. We had at least that much in our favor.

However, Martin drove right on through the village.

"I'm playing a hunch," he said.

Just beyond Crossmore, overlooking the busy highway, were the rolling hills and meadows and buildings of the county-supported orphanage.

Martin turned into a winding driveway which was shaded by tall pines. He stopped before an old colonial-type home that had been converted into an administration building. More recent structures of frame and brick housed dorms and classrooms. Beyond there were barns and workshops.

A few minutes later we were in the office of Dr. Spreckles, the superintendent. A wiry, sandy man, Spreckles struck me as being a pleasant individual who nevertheless knew how to run things.

He looked at the picture of Mary Smith that the lab boys had made.

"Yes," he said. "She was one of our girls." His lips tightened slightly. "We hope she has done nothing to reflect on the training she received here."

"She hasn't," Martin assured him. "Who were her people?"

Spreckles went behind his desk and sat down. "She had none. She was born out of wedlock in the county hospital to a woman who gave her name only as Mary Smith. As soon as she was able to get about, the mother abandoned the child."

"The girl grew up here?"

"Yes."

"Never adopted?"

"No," Spreckles said slowly, resting his elbows on his desk and steepling his fingers. "As a child, she was quite awkward, too quiet, too shy. She lived here until she was eighteen."

"Who were her friends?"

"Strangely enough," Spreckles frowned, "I can't say. I don't think she had any really close ones. She was a face in a crowd, you might say. Never precocious. Not at the bottom of her classes, you understand, but not at the top. I do wish you'd tell me what difficulty she's in."

"She's dead," Martin said. "A mugger killed her during a robbery attempt."

"How terrible!" Spreckles made an honest attempt to muster genuine grief, but he simply didn't have it. He was shocked and upset by the passing forever of an impersonal image, but that was all . . .

As we drove back through Crossmore, Martin broke his silence—with a single utterance. It was softly spoken but the most vicious oath I'd ever heard. It was so unlike Martin that I stared at him out of the corner of my eyes.

But I let the silence return and stay that way. Right then, he had the look about him of a heavy-chested, steel-gray tomcat whose wounds have been rubbed with turpentine and salt.

We returned to grinding routine. The pawnshops. Still no watch. The vicinity of Hibernia Park—questioning all the people, one by one, who lived in the area. No one had glimpsed a man coming from the park about the time she was killed.

At night I was too tired to sleep. I wondered what this was getting us, if we'd ever catch the man. Yet there wasn't the slightest letdown in Martin's determination. I only wished I shared it . . .

Martin and I returned to the squadroom late Wednesday afternoon. A few minutes afterward, a uniformed policeman walked in and handed Martin an inexpensive woman's watch.

My scalp pulled tight. I crossed to Martin's desk as he opened a drawer. He shook the golden clasp from a small manila envelope. The clasp matched the broken band of the watch perfectly.

Martin stood up. His nostrils were flaring. "Where'd this come from?"

"The personal effects of a guy named Biddix," the man in uniform said. "He was in a poker game we just broke up in an old loft. The desk sergeant said you'd want to see the watch."

Martin's big hand closed over the tiny timepiece. I followed him out of the office.

Biddix was a dried-up, seedy little fellow in his late sixties. He'd been separated from the other poker players and put in a solitary cell.

When the cell door opened, Biddix took one look at Martin's face and backed against the wall.

Martin held out his hand and opened it. "Where'd you get this?"

"Look . . ." Biddix swallowed. "If it's stolen, I swear I had nothing to do with it."

"It was torn from a murdered girl's wrist," Martin said.

The dead-gray of Biddix's beard stubble suddenly blended exactly with the color of his skin.

"A guy put the watch in the game," Biddix said. "And that's the truth, so help me!"

"Which one?"

"He left before he was raided."

"What's his name?"

"Edgar Collins."

"Know where he lives?"

"Sure. In a flop on East Maple Street, number 311."

We went out. The cell door clanged behind us. Biddix came over and stood holding the bars. "I didn't know anything about the watch."

"Sure," Martin said.

"You'll put me in with the others now, won't you?"

"No," Martin said. "Not yet."

We got the location of Edgar Collins's room from the building super, went up one flight, and eased to the door.

The house was hot and the hallway smelled of age and many people. We listened. After a little, we heard a bedspring creak.

We put our shoulders to the door, and it flew open. A stringy, big-boned, bald-headed man sprang off the bed and dropped the tabloid he'd been reading. He was tall and stooped. He wore dirty khaki pants and a dirty undershirt.

"What's the big idear?" he demanded.

"Your name Edgar Collins?" Martin asked.

"So what if it is?"

"We're police officers. We want to talk to you."

"Yeah? What about?"

"A girl who was killed in Hibernia Park. If you're innocent, you got nothing to worry about. If not . . . We've got a shoe-track moulage to start. We'll find plenty of other things with the help of the lab boys, once we know where to start looking."

Collins stared at us. An explosion took place behind his pale eyes. He lunged toward the open window.

Martin got between me and Collins and grabbed the man first. He dragged Collins back in the room. Collins threw punches at Martin in blind panic.

Martin hit him three times in the face. Collins fell on the floor, wrapped his arms about his head, and began rolling back and forth.

"I didn't mean it," he said, babbling. "She fell on the stone. She was a stranger, nothing to me. It was an accident . . . please . . . give me a break! I didn't mean it, I tell you."

For a moment I thought Odus Martin was going to start hitting the man again.

A volunteer minister performed graveside rites the next morning. Martin and I stood with our hats in our hands.

I looked at the casket and thought: Good-bye, Mary Smith—that name will do as well as any. No father, no mother, no one. Killed by a man who never saw you before.

The sun was shining, but the day felt bleak and dismal.

Then, as we returned to headquarters, it came to me that Odus Martin had been right. There are no absolute strangers in this world, no zeros.

The death of Mary Smith had affected Odus Martin. Because I was his partner, it had affected me. Through us, it seemed to me, the human race had recognized the importance of her and expressed its unwillingness to let her die as an animal dies.

Mary Smith had lived and died in loneliness, but she had not been alone.

I didn't say anything of this to Odus Martin. He was a hard man to talk to. Anyhow, I felt that he understood it already, probably much more deeply than I ever could.

DOROTHY B. HUGHES

Dorothy B. Hughes (1904–1993) had a number of films made from her novels, the best of which, the Humphrey Bogart–Gloria Grahame picture *In a Lonely Place,* is a genuine suspense classic.

Hughes was an incisive book critic without ever being mean-spirited and wrote ticking-bomb crime stories without ever giving up the clean, controlled style that made her, as an undergraduate, a Yale Young Poet.

Hughes fused elements of the thriller with elements of the traditional mystery in most of her novels. Odd that Hitchcock never bought one for the screen. They were exactly the sort of material he favored.

The Collected Stories of Dorothy B. Hughes (a book that needs to be published) would span four decades and show how artists both use and transcend their time. The Grand Master award she received from the Mystery Writers of America in 1978 was deserved indeed.

The Granny Woman

They was waiting for him, the three of them, setting there on the stoop of Aunt Miney's cabin. I remember like it was yesterday. Old Cephus wasn't rightly on the stoop, he was on the gallery in Uncle Dauncy's rocking chair. He wa'nt rocking. He was setting tall and upright as the silver-mounted Old Betsey he was holding aside him. Ol Cephus must of been eighty year then, gaunt and gray as an old goose, but strong not weak in his age.

Orville was setting on the top of the stoop. He wasn't doing anything, just setting there chawing, looking mean and sloppy and dirty like always.

You'd find it hard to believe Orville was Old Cephus' son. There wa'nt nothing like in them.

Down on the low step was Toll, Cousin Tolliver Sorkin, another mean one, though he wa'nt no more than twenty year to Orville's fifty. Toll was whittling nothing like he'd do when he was waiting. Some men whittle something, a dog or a bird, or maybe a doll poppet, but Toll never whittled nothing.

I knowed the man wasn't coming friendly because none of them was fixed for company. They was wearing their working pants and shirts, dusty boots, and their old sweaty-stained hats. None of them appeared to be looking down the road, but they was seeing without looking. They didn't know I was there, hiding up in the old crabapple tree aslant of the house. I'd sneaked up in the tree afore they come out on the stoop. If'n they'd knowed, they'd of sent me packing. They wa'nt meaning no good to the man.

You could see him coming over the hill afore he was in sight. You could see him when he wa'nt no more than a twig of a man, down there below. It could of been that Toll, when he took his maw and paw down to Middle Piney that morning, heerd about him coming. But I think they'd knowed it afore then, the way a body does know things in these hills. Knowing don't come from smoke signals like the Indians made when they lived here afore the war, leastways the Granny Woman used to claim she'd seed smoke signals when first she come to the Ozarks. Knowing is just knowing something afore you been told. It whispers out of the town and up into the hills some way or tuther.

I could hear everything the menfolks was saying, not that it was much. The man was big enough to reckanize as a man when Cephus asked for about the hundredth time, "Is he still a-coming?"

"He's a-coming all right," Orville grunted.

"Purty nigh here." Toll had that sly mouth on him, like he was itching for trouble.

"What-all's he coming up here for anyway?" Cephus complained.

"You know what for," Toll said.

"You best keep your mouth shet, Toll." When Orville had that real ugly look, it'd fair give you the shivers.

"Sure, Orville. You don't need to worry none about me."

Cephus' voice sounded again. "Where's he at now?"

"Cain't you see for yourself, Paw?"

"The sun gits in my eyes. How nigh is he?"

Toll said real quiet, "Not more'n six or seven paces."

I'd been watching my kin for a time, not the road, so I'd missed him approaching that night. Now I looked down at him, a nice clean-appearing man, older'n Toll, not so old as Orville. He was wearing jeans and a blue shirt, too, but they wasn't all begaumed, the shirt had been clean afore he sweated it out clumbing up the hill. A woman can tell these things. He stopped there out in the road, keeping his distance until he was invited in, like was the custom. When he commenced talking, he talked somewhat like he was a native. Young as I was then, I figgered out he was Ozark born but had been gone long enough to be a furriner.

"Howdy," he said.

None of the menfolks said anything for what seemed an awful long time. Finally Toll spoke up. "Howdy."

"Mighty hot day."

"Yeh." Toll took his time responding. "Hotter'n the cinders of hell." He gave a sidelong look at the stranger. "You come far?"

"From Middle Piney."

"A far piece," Toll allowed. "Mighty hot day to clumb all the way up here." Middle Piney was about seven mile uphill to Tall Piney.

"I found that out," the man said rueful-like.

Toll throwed away his whittling stick. "Light down and set a spell," he said like he was natural neighborly. "You must be plumb tuckered out."

"Thanks." The man walked over towards the stoop. "Could I trouble you first for a drink of water?"

"Help yourself." Toll pointed with his knife. "Bucket's around yander."

I didn't dast move a muscle when the man walked under the tree to the water bucket. First he drunk a full dipper of water, then he took off his hat and poured a little water onto his head. I didn't blame him none. No place in the world hotter'n Missouri in August. He shook off the water and took another drink from the dipper afore going back to the stoop. He set hisself down at the far end of the second step. This way he could be looking at all three menfolks while he visited, and them at him.

Orville said, "You must of had some extry special purpose to clumb all the way up here today."

The stranger seemed to think about it. Before he had a chanct to answer, Toll cut him off like as if he was suddenly reckanizing him.

"Ain't you the Perfessor been stopping down to Little Piney?"

You could tell by the Perfessor's face that he'd knowed all along the three of them knowed who he was. But he feigned he didn't know. He said, "That's right. I'm Professor James. From the University up at Columbia."

"Pleased to make your acquaintance, Perfessor." Toll put out his hand and shook the Perfessor's. If I hadn't seed how they was waiting for him, I'd of thought Toll was right friendly. "I'm Tolliver Sorkin, mostly known as Toll. This here's my cousin, Orville. That's old Cephus up there on the gallery. He's my cousin also." That's the way the kinship was. Toll wasn't a close cousin to us, he was removed.

The Perfessor reared up and shook hands with Orville. He stretched for to shake old Cephus' hand, but Cephus wa'nt letting go of Old Betsey. That meant plain that the Perfessor was no friend so far as Cephus was concerned. Cephus wasn't no sly one like Toll nor a bully like Orville. He was straight out what he was.

"Pleased to meet you all," the Perfessor said, setting again.

Toll took up another stick to whittle. He went on talking, reasonable, if you hadn't knowed he was up to something. "I thought I reckanized you. You're the ballut man."

"That's what folks call me down at Little Piney." Little Piney was ten mile downhill from Middle Piney. It was the County Seat.

"This is the second summer I've been around, looking for old ballads."

"We'n got no ballut singers at Tall Piney," Orville said, real hostile.

"Down at Little Piney I heard different."

"Like to hear anything down Little Piney." Orville spat through the railing slats.

Toll said, sort of cautious, "What might they been telling you down there?"

"They said if I was to go up to Tall Piney, I might get some real good ballads off the Granny Woman."

"Reckon you won't."

"Why not?"

Orville said it blunt. "She's dead."

"She's dead?" He was just pretending to be surprised. I knowed it and I'm sure the menfolks knowed it, too. But they went on feigning they didn't.

"Deader'n a doornail," Toll said.

"Been dead nigh on two weeks now," Orville went on. "Kind of peculiar they wouldn't know bout that down to Little Piney. Who all you been visiting with there?"

"I've been stopping with the Preacher," the Perfessor said. "He didn't say he'd done any preaching over the Granny Woman."

"She didn't hold with preaching." Orville spat again.

And Toll asked, "Didn't the Reverint tell you that?"

When the Perfessor answered, it was almost like hearing preaching about her. It was like he'd been fond of her the same as I, although he hadn't ever knowed her. "He told me if anyone would know the old, old ballads, she would. He told me she was the oldest woman in the Pineys. She could remember coming by wagon from Virginny when she was a young maid, before the war. Folks say she might be a hundred years old."

Suddenly Cephus shouted out in his loud old voice, "She's dead!"

Orville acted like nobody had heerd his paw. "We give her a proper burial."

Toll elaborated, "We didn't have no preachment because she didn't hold with preaching, but we buried her proper."

"That her cabin up yonder?" the Perfessor asked, looking up to where it stood on the tiptop of the hill.

"Now, how'd you know that?" Toll asked him.

"The Preacher told me she lived on top of Tall Piney. Is that hers?"

"It's hern," Orville admitted.

"Might be her ballad book is still there."

"There ain't no ballut books there," Orville said flatly.

"What did you do about her belongings?"

Toll was quick to defend himself just in case. "We didn't touch nothing of hern."

"There wa'nt no ballut book," Orville repeated ugly. "There never was none."

Toll of a sudden looked right up into the tree I was in. I was so still I twinged but even so I was scairt he might of seen me. Sometimes it 'pears he has eyes like a chicken hawk. He didn't say nothing, he just turned hisself round to the Perfessor.

"Orville's right, Perfessor." He snapped his knife shut and put it in his pocket. "Now, if it's a ballut you're hankering for, reckon I can give you one myself." He began to sing in that scrawny voice of his:

"There onct was a mountain girl, Bonnie Bluebell,
She lived on Tall Piney or so I've heerd tell,
She didn't know naught cause she'd never been taught,
Oh, hark to my story . . ."

I didn't let him finish his silly old song. I didn't care that I was discovered. I yelled at him, "You stop that, Tolliver," and I jumped down out of that tree and run over to him.

He grinned, singing up high like a woman, "Oh, hark to my story of Bonnie Bluebell."

He was twict as tall as I, and though he looked skinny enough for the wind to blow away, he was strong. I didn't care. I pounded on him. "You stop that right this minute. If'n you don't, I'll fix you so's you . . ."

He held me off. "You'll do what?" He begun louder.

"She run with the hounds and she run with the hare . . ."

All at onct I realized what I must appear like to the stranger man, my face and hands all gaumed from climbing the tree, and my feet even dirtier, and my old house dress ripped in the arms. I pushed Toll away and said dignified, "That ain't no ballut-song. You're just making that up."

Orville yelled at me, "Git home, Bluebell."

"You make him stop that fool singing."

"Git home." Orville got on his feet and started down the step towards me.

I didn't move far, I just backed up a bit. "I come over to fetch Grampaw. When I seed you had company—"

"Git home and git the supper."

"Supper's ready." The stew pot had been on all afternoon and I'd mixed the johnnycake afore I sneaked over to see what they was up to.

"Dish it up," Orville said. "I'll fetch Paw. Git now."

From the look in his eyes I decided might be I'd better git afore he whaled at me. But I knew I wasn't going to have a chanct to warn the perfessor man about them unless I made sure right now that he'd be invited to sup. Orville was too mean and stingy to invite anyone in on his own. "You ast the stranger to supper, Paw?" I said real innocent like. I was still calling him Paw then.

He scowled at me, but he had to make the invitation being as I'd brought it up. "You kin sup with us," he told the Perfessor.

"I'd appreciate that."

"I'm a-coming, too, Bluebell," Toll said.

I'd knowed he'd invite hisself. "Won't your Maw and Paw feed you no more?" I put my head up high and walked away.

He hollered after me, "You know dern well Maw and Paw are down to Middle Piney—"

I didn't linger to hear no more from him. Onct I was across the road I scatted down to our cabin. I wanted time to wash up and comb out the tangles of my hair and put on a fresh dress afore the Perfessor arrived. We didn't have company often. First I slammed the johnnycake into the oven and I opened a big jar of my best plum sass. I washed quick, but I used soap and I went behind the curtain to pull off that old dress and put on my sprigged blue, the one I wore to wedding frolics and buryings. When Orville and Cephus come in, I was trying to get a comb through my hair, standing out in front of the looking glass I'd hung over the wash bench. The Perfessor wasn't with them.

For a moment I was anxious. "Ain't he a-coming?"

Orville said, "He's follering after us. He's washing up at Toll's." He went over to the wash bench and splattered a little bit of water on his hands. "City fellers are allus hankering after soap and water. I remember when I was in the War." He wasn't talking about the real War but about when they'd fit the Kaiser four years back. "Should think they'd have the skin clean washed off afore they're old enough to spit."

"It don't seem to hurt them none," I told him.

Cephus had walked to the hearth to place Old Betsey up over the fireplace where he kept her. She was a beautiful long rifle with her silver mountings. He took better care of her than he did of himself. After he'd put her up, he set down in his rocking chair.

Orville went over to him, wiping dirt on the towel.

"What's he want to come up here for?" Cephus asked him. "What's he want anyhow?"

"It ain't no ballut book, Paw."

Cephus shook his head from side to side, trying to figger things. Finally he burst out, "The Granny Woman's dead. Ain't no call for him to come up here trying to rise the dead."

Orville said real calm, "Ain't no one's going to riz her up, Pappy. Not till the Last Judgment." He walked back with the towel and hung it on the drying rack. Like he didn't know that nobody but a pig would want to use it again until it was washed and biled. "Be careful what you say, Paw. Don't say nothing the Perfessor can carry tales about." He didn't pay no heed to what I was hearing. "One thing's for sartin, Paw. He was lying when he said he hadn't knowed the Granny Woman was dead. He knowed it all right."

I wouldn't of thought Orville was that smart. He must of been doing a deal of thinking today. Or Toll had been filling his mind up with what-for.

"How'd you figger that, Orvy?"

"Figger it yourself. When Toll was down to Middle Piney last week, he told that the Granny Woman was dead. What you tell in Middle Piney runs downhill to Little Piney afore you can blink an eye. And who gits the first word in Little Piney about deaths and so forth? The preacher man, that's who. The preacher man what the Perfessor's been a-visiting with. So he knowed."

Cephus nodded over it. "Reckon you're right, Orvy. What you aim to do about it?"

"We'll give him his vittles and after that—" He thumped his fist and rattled the table. "After that we'll see if he wants to go peaceful back down to Little Piney. If'n he don't . . ."

He didn't finish what he had to say because right then we heard Toll tittering to the Perfessor out on the path. My hair was combed out tolerably well. I was tying it back, with an old piece of blue ribbon the Granny Woman had give me, when Orville come over and put his hand on my arm.

"Don't you let me catch you talking to that there Perfessor man," he said.

"I won't."

"You keep your mouth shet, hear me?"

His hand squeezed until I couldn't help crying out. "You're hurting me!"

"I'll hurt you worse'n that if you don't keep your mouth shet."

The Perfessor and Toll was at the door by then so Orville let go of me. He went to table, set hisself down, and commenced dishing up his plate. "Fetch me some johnnycake, Bluebell," he hollered at me.

My arm hurt worse'n it had been hit by a stick, but I went right ahead tying my ribbon until I made a bow. Toll set down at the table with Orville and begun dishing his plate also. The Perfessor stood waiting.

Orville hollered again. "You hear me, fetch the johnnycake."

I opened the oven door. "Some folks wait for the company to set before they commence eating."

It was Toll who took care of the inviting. "Come on, Perfessor, set down and dig in. Bluebell ain't the best cook in the Ozarks, but there' allus a-plenty on Old Cephus' table. Come on, Cephus, you're getting left."

The Perfessor waited to set until Cephus come to the table. He must of seen by then that Ozark ladies don't eat with the gentlemen. He took the only chair left.

I dished up a big platter of johnnycake and I toted it right over to the Perfessor to make sure he got the best piece. Then I passed him the other dishes real polite, like I'd been larned by the Granny Woman. "Try this rabbitmeat stew, Perfessor. It's real fresh." It was, too. Cephus had skun the rabbit only this morning. "Some wild sallet?" The greens had stewed just long enough, not too long to be bitter. "Have some plum sass, too, it goes good with johnnycake."

"Plum sass!" Toll exclaimed greedy-like. "You must of knowed there was company coming."

I ignored him, bringing the pitcher of milk and inquiring, "Can I help you to milk, Perfessor? Or maybe you'd prefer sweet milk?"

Orville grunted with his mouth full, "Leave the Perfessor eat his vittles, Bluebell. Stop urging him." He took another piece of johnnycake and pushed half of it into his mouth. He should have et with the pigs.

The Perfessor give me a big smile. He had the nicest smile you ever did see and he give it right at me, like I was a lady. He held up his glass. "This is just fine, Bluebell. Everything's fine. I'll bet you are the best cook in the Ozarks."

I retired to the stove, sort of flustered. I knew Toll would be mocking me and the Perfessor later on, but I just didn't care. It was worth it being treated like a lady for onct. There wasn't any talk while they was eating, Orville didn't hold with talk at table. But when he'd stuffed hisself to the busting point, he pushed back his chair and come right out with it.

"Seems a mite peculiar the preacher'd be sending you up here now the old woman's gone."

"Seems like he didn't know she was gone," the Perfessor said, filling up his pipe.

"Mighty peculiar he wouldn't know."

"Had she been ill?"

"No, sir!" Toll spoke up. "She was right as rain one day and the next she was dead." He dropped his voice. "Could have been that old screech owl what she heerd outside her door round about that time."

The Perfessor looked up, real interested. "It scared her?"

Toll peered over his shoulder. "Nobody's going to feel easy if he hears a screech owl on his doorstep. It's a sign of death for sure."

"At her age, a fright like that could cause a heart attack." The Perfessor puffed on his pipe.

"Not the Granny Woman! She come out with her old sweeping broom and shooed that owl off in a hurry." Real quick Toll added, "I just happened to be passing by when she done it. Might be she give that old owl a heart attack." He snickered behind his hand.

"I'm sorry I came too late to meet her," the Perfessor said.

"Wouldn't of done you no good," Toll told him. "She couldn't of sung you no balluts. She was crazy as a wild mule."

I wanted to shout out that she was not, but I was afeared if I said anything Orville might tell me to git.

"She was crazy all right," Orville yawned out loud. "Reckon you'll want to be gitting back to Middle Piney. It's a far walk. Even going downhill."

"I don't think I'll go back tonight," the Perfessor said. "As long as I'm here I might as well have a look at her cabin."

Orville started to rise up, but Toll had a hold of his arm. "Seems like you won't take our word there ain't no ballut books there," Toll said.

"I'd sort of like to look around for myself." The Perfessor got up from the table then, moving slow, like the menfolks was strange dogs what might spring at him if he moved rapid. He wasn't no more than a step away when Toll was aside him.

"If'n I was you, I'd consider it real careful afore going inside her cabin. It mightn't be safe."

The Perfessor wasn't afeared. He looked straight at Toll. "Why not?"

Toll almost whispered it. "You might be witched."

This sure enough surprised the Perfessor. His mouth went open and he had to grab for his pipe. "You mean you think she was a witch?"

Cephus hadn't said a word up till then. Now he started sing-songing real loud, the way he used to do afore the Granny Woman died. Though we-uns was used to it, it always made me jump. It almost made the Perfessor jump out of his skin.

"She witched the cow out of her milk! She witched away my little girl, my little Rosebud! She witched my old hound dog! Howling into the woods he went and he never come back no more."

Orville said, "Now, Paw—"

"She won't lay no more spells on me and mine," Old Cephus declared. "She's dead. Dead and buried deep."

The Perfessor seemed sorry for Cephus. He turned away from him and he asked Toll, "Do you honestly believe she was a witch?"

Toll nodded his head solemn and slow. "She was a real Granny Woman, Perfessor. Not the kind you hear tell of nowadays, the kind that births the babies. *A real Granny Woman*."

I was surprised that the Perfessor knew what Toll was talking about, but he did. He said kind of to hisself, "The old kind. The witch."

I couldn't keep quiet no more. I cried out, "She wa'nt no witch!"

"She was witching you," Orville hollered back at me. "You just didn't know it."

Toll reached inside his shirt and hung out the carved hickory nut on a string which he always wore. "You see that?" he said to the Perfessor. "Onct when I was a little shaver, the Granny Woman tried to take aholt of me in the woods. I skun home so fast you couldn't see my dust and my maw tied this to me. So's that old witch would never put a spell on me."

"If she's dead," the Perfessor asked him, "why do you still wear it?"

Toll stuck it back under his shirt. "It don't do no harm," he muttered.

Old Cephus burst out loud again, "There ain't but one way to kill a witch! With a silver bullet!"

Orville come quick to him, helping him up from the chair. "Now, Paw, no use gitting het up. She cain't witch you no more." He headed Cephus toward the hearth. "Git him his snuff stick, Bluebell."

When he had his snuff stick, Old Cephus would almost always quieten down. But this time he kept right speaking. "She was the purtiest girl in the Pineys. I promised her maw I'd care for her."

Toll said offside, "He gits to wandering some, Perfessor. He was mighty partial to Rosebud. She was his youngest. She run off to the city." He snickered, "He claims it was the Granny Woman witched her away, but I don't see as how you can blame her for that."

The Perfessor picked up his hat from the bench. "I'm obliged for the supper." He looked at me and sort of made a bow. "I've never had a better one in the Ozarks, Miss Bluebell."

When he turned round to the door, Orville was in his way. "Where you going at?"

"Like I told you, I'm going to the Granny Woman's cabin. I've never been afraid of witches. And I'm not trespassing. I have permission from Deputy Clegg to visit it." He took a folded piece of paper out of his pocket and passed it to Orville.

Orville studied it when he passed it to me. "Speak it out loud, Bluebell. You've had more book larning than we-uns."

I read it oral, like he told me. I had to go slow on the big words, but I sounded them out like the teacher had larned me at the school house. "To whom it may concern: This gives permission for Professor Richard James to visit the Granny Woman's cabin at Tall Piney. Signed, Deputy Jim Clegg."

Orville and Toll never said no word. I reckon they was too overcome right then. The Perfessor took back the paper from me and said, "Good night, Miss Bluebell. Good night, Old Cephus. Good night, Orville and Toll."

With that he walked plumb out the door, Orville moving out of his way like in a daze. When he was gone, Orville sunk down in a chair. "Jim Clegg had no business writing them words on the paper. He'd no business letting a furriner rummage and root through the Granny Woman's belongings."

Old Cephus didn't appear to be listening, but he heerd. He set his mouth tight. "You aim to let him do that, Orvy?"

Orville said, "No, Paw." He walked to the corner where he kept his rifle and he took it up.

Toll run over to him. "Look here, Orvy! Scaring him out is one thing, but you got no call to take a gun after him. We don't want no trouble with the law."

"If Jim Clegg wants to let a furriner snoop around our property, I reckon it'll be his fault if trouble comes of it."

"I ain't talking about Deppity Jim's law," Toll argufied. "I'm talking about city law, Orville. This here feller's a college perfessor from the University. If you was to harm him . . ."

"Leave me be, Toll. I know what I'm at." I'd never seen Orville so mean and determined.

"Wait a minute, Orvy." Toll hung on his arm. "We got to talk this over. He ain't going to run away. He's going to snoop through that there cabin first. But he ain't going to do no harm there."

Orville didn't put down his rifle but he did set hisself down again. "How do you know he ain't?"

"There's nothing there for him to find out. So ain't it best to let him do his snooping there? Instead of certain other places?"

Orville wasn't convinced. "That property's ourn now. He's got no call to set foot on our property."

I'd been working at the dishes while they was talking. I had to warn the Perfessor man that Orville was coming after him with a load of buckshot. But I didn't know how I was going to get away to do it. Old Cephus give me my chanct. All at onct he reared up from his rocking chair and reached for his Old Betsey. His voice was like thunder. "It takes a silver bullet to kill a witch!"

Toll and Orville both hurried over to calm him. I took up the dish pan of water, just in case they should ask where I was going, and I skun on outside. I dumped the water and I run like a hare through the trees towards the special path to the cabin that only the Granny Woman and I ever used. The menfolks knowed about it, but they never set foot on it. They called it the Witch's Path.

I got the edge of the clearing before the Perfessor did. I could hear him coming, strangers can't move soft-footed through the brush like we'ns can. And I could smell his pipe. It was dark of the moon, but I didn't want to step out into the open for fear Orville and Toll might already have set out. When the Perfessor was nearby, I whispered, "Perfessor man!"

He jumped like I was a bobcat. "Who is it?"

I stepped out where he could see me.

"What are you doing here?"

"I come to warn you. Orville's got his rifle. He means to stop you."

He sort of smiled. "I'm not afraid, Bluebell."

"But you got to be afraid!" I told him. "Orville won't let nobody up there. Not even me."

He said, meaning to be kind, "Then you better get back to the cabin before your Paw misses you. I wouldn't want any trouble to come to you from me."

"He ain't my Paw." I up and told him like I'd never told nobody before. "He states he is but he ain't. My Paw was a Joplin man."

He seemed real surprised. "Then you're Rosebud's daughter."

"What if I am? It ain't true all them lies they tell about her. She didn't run off to the city. The Granny Woman helped her to git away. She saved up her yarb money to help her. Afore she died she was saving her yarb money for me to get away, too."

"And so they killed her."

I couldn't explain it all to him then, there wasn't time. "She died natural. In her bed."

"Then what are they afraid of, Bluebell? Why don't they want me to go to her cabin?"

I told him part of the truth. "They promised Cephus. He's afeered of stirring her up. He's afeered she might come back."

"Is that it?" He puffed on his pipe and then he smiled at me again. "Well, I'm not afraid of ghosts or ghoulies or Sorkinses. You scat home now, Bluebell. I don't want you following me to the cabin, just in case trouble should develop."

He set off. The only way I could of stopped him was to run after him, and I was scairt they'd be missing me if I was away longer. I run all the way home. After I'd caught my breath, I picked up the dishpan and come back in.

"Where you been?" Orvy asked right away.

"I been out back," I said. I carried the pan over to where I kept it by the stove. Then I noticed that Toll was loading a rifle, too. I rushed over to him. "What you doing with that gun, Tolliver Sorkin?"

"Orvy and me aim to do a little hunting tonight."

I could scarce believe my ears. Instead of him talking Orville around, it was the other way.

"You're going to the Granny Woman's cabin!"

"It's nary of your business where we're going." Orville got up on his feet. "You stay put and tend to your knitting. And see to it that Grampaw don't foller us."

"You cain't shoot the Perfessor! He don't know nothing about what you done." I clamped my hand over my mouth, but I'd said it.

Orville come advancing to me and I backed up fast, nigh to Old Cephus by the fire.

"You been spying on us."

"No, I ain't. Swear to God, I ain't!"

"You swear to a lie, you'll burn in hellfire."

"I ain't swearing to no lie!"

Orville didn't stop for Grampaw being there. He grabbed my wrist and pulled me out to him. "You follered us to the grave."

"I didn't!" I screamed it because he was hurting me bad. "I swear—"

"Leave her be," Toll shouted over my screaming. "We're wasting time. You can take keer of her later."

Orville give me a shove as he let go. I fell down to the floor. He stumped out the door after Toll. Every bone in my body was bruised. When I leaned on my wrist trying to get up, it felt like it was broken though it wa'nt.

Cephus asked, "Where they going? Why don't they want me to go with them?"

I was mad enough to tell him, "They're going hunting."

"Whyn't they wait for me? I can outhunt both of them." He commenced to rise up from his chair.

"It's night times, Grampaw." I managed to push myself up from the floor, favoring my bad wrist. "You cain't hunt at night no more. You don't see no good."

"I can see further than both of them together. Me and my old hound dog—" He remembered and sank back sorrowing. "My old hound dog. He never come back. She witched him away."

"She didn't have naught to do with it, Grampaw. It was Orville's meanness druv him away."

"It was her done it." He was starting to meander into the past again. "If'n I'd knowed she was a witch, she couldn't of witched me with her daughter like she done. When I first seen Amarylly, she didn't look like no witch's brat. She had yellowy hair and rosebud in her cheeks. Rosebud! That's the name she give our own little one." He come back from his meandering. "She witched Rosebud away from me."

"My maw." I don't know why I said it to him then, I never had before.

"Who's been telling you sech things?"

"The Granny Woman told me."

"What else did she tell you?"

"Nothing wrong. She said you was the strongest man in the Pineys onct. You stood so straight and tall, there wa'nt a man could match up to you."

He recollected, "I was felling a big old pine tree when she and her child come on me. They was gathering yarbs."

"After her child was dead, you took Rosebud away from the Granny Woman."

"I wa'nt going to let my little Rosebud grow up a witch's child. My old woman never knowed why I took the little one." Without any warning, he stood up, roaring mad. He towered over me. "What else did she tell you? How to dry up the old cow? How to sour the milk?"

"No!" I tried to inch away. I'd never seed him like this before.

"Did she tell you how to witchride a man all night through the brambles? Did she tell you how to set a pure young gal to lallygagging in the woods? Did she tell you how she witched Rosebud into running away from her own Paw? Did she tell you how to drive a man's faithful old hound howling into the night?"

I kept saying No and No and inching, but I couldn't get clear to make it to the door. When he reached to take down Old Betsey, I tried to stop him. But he brushed me aside, not mean like Orville, just like I was nothing, a pine branch in his path.

"She didn't know I was a witchkiller like my pappy afore me. She didn't know he larned me to kill witches same as him. You got to have a silver gun and a silver bullet to kill a witch."

"No, Grampaw, no!" I screamed it at him. He had that rifle pointed right to my heart. Somehow he'd made hisself believe she'd passed her witching on to me, that I was a witch child. And then I remembered. "You got no silver bullet," I hollered. "You used it on the Granny Woman."

Slowly he lowered the rifle. The spirit went out of him. "It takes a long time to git enough silver to make a bullet."

"Set down, Grampaw," I said to him kindly. "I swear she didn't larn me no witching. She was good to me."

He stood there holding fast to the long rifle. "Nigh on to fifteen years it took me to git enough silver. Pure silver it's got to be."

I freshened up his snuff stick and held it out to him. "Just rest yourself, Grampaw. Rock a bit."

Instead of setting down, he started to the door. I run after him. "No, Grampaw. Orvy don't want you to foller him. It's dark of the moon." You see, I knowed his intent. He was going after his silver bullet.

He paid me no heed. He kept right on walking. I didn't hardly wait until he was out of sight. I tore out of there and over to the Witch's Path. The only chanct I had was to get the Perfessor to protect me. I knew what Old Cephus meant to do. And Orville and Toll wouldn't stop him if'n they could. They'd be a-feared he was right.

I didn't reckon Orville and Toll would be at the Granny Woman's cabin yet. First they'd have gone down to the stump, where their mountain dew was hid out, to get some courage in them. They was shy of her cabin even in daylight.

I run like I never run before and when I come to the cabin I didn't knock on the door, I busted right in. The Perfessor man looked up real surprised to see me. He'd lit her table lamp and he was rummaging through her old horsehair trunk. He'd already took out the face fan she'd carried back in Virginny when she was a girl. And the silk and satin baby bonnet, so tiny you wouldn't think it would fit a poppet, but it had been my maw's. He was holding her papers, the ones she kept tied with a blue ribbon, when I busted in.

He said, "I told you not to come here, Bluebell."

"I had to. Old Cephus is out gitting him a silver bullet to kill me with."

"To kill you?" His eyes most popped out of his head. "Why would he want to kill you?"

"Because . . ." I didn't want to tell him. "Because he thinks she made me into a witch."

Just then I heerd someone outside the door and I run over and crouched down behind the Perfessor. Maybe I was daft thinking he could protect me without no gun nor nothing, but I did think so. I reckon it was because he wa'nt afraid. He didn't even put down the papers.

I closed my eyes when the door started to open. And I heered him say, "Come in, Jim." So I opened up my eyes and there was Deputy Jim Clegg closing the door.

Deputy Jim said, "Looks like you got you some company, Rick." Deputy Jim was as big as Orville, but he wa'nt nothing like him otherwise. He was clean and strong and I never in my life seed him do a mean thing to man or beast. He was born and raised right here in the Ozarks, but he'd gone to school up at Columbia and knowed how to talk good. He said to me, "What you doing here, Bluebell?"

I told him, "Orville and Toll are hunting the Perfessor man and Old Cephus is hunting me. He's got in his mind that the Granny Woman made a witch of me."

"So he's going to kill you like he killed the Granny Woman?"

The Perfessor spoke up. "Bluebell says she died natural, in her bed."

Deputy Jim said, "A witch killer doesn't have to kill you to make you die, Rick."

Because he understood, I told him, "Orvy stuck the pins in the dishrag and burnt it. Toll trapped the screech owl to set outside her door. Old Cephus molded the silver bullet and feathered it into the tree. And she died."

The Perfessor looked across at Deputy Jim. Deputy Jim put his hand in his pocket and brought out what looked like a ball of silver. He said, "I found the silver bullet. In the tree, not in her heart."

"You don't have to put the bullet in a witch's heart," I told them. "You can peel the bark off the tree and sketch her shape there. Then you can feather the bullet into her on the tree."

Deputy Jim put the bullet back into his pocket. "Thanks to you keeping them busy, Rick, we found the grave, down by Piney Run. And we didn't have any interruptions at the exhumation. Doc's taking her down to Little Piney for an autopsy, but it looks like she died what you'd call natural. So I was wrong. I'm going down to their cabin now. Want to come?"

I didn't know much what he was talking about, but I knowed I didn't want to go back to the cabin again. Not even with Deputy Jim and the Perfessor for protection. I was readying to say so when we heard Orville roaring outside, "Come out of there, Perfessor. If'n you don't . . ." He shot off his gun for a warning.

Deputy Jim walked over and swung open the door wide. When Orville and Toll saw who it was, they let their rifles down. Deputy Jim asked them, "Could it be you're hunting witches?"

Orville said, "We come to protect our property."

"It's not your property," Deputy Jim said. "It's Bluebell's. By direct descent from the Granny Woman." He shook his head and sighed. "Seems like there ought to be something I could arrest you for, Orvy, but blamed if I know what it could be this time. You might better watch your Paw closer, however, before he gets in some trouble I might have to arrest him for."

You mightn't think Orville set store by anything, but he did by his Paw. "I will," he vowed. Then he noticed me and he hollered, "Where is Paw? You was supposed to be caring for him, Bluebell."

"I couldn't hold him," I said. "He took old Betsey and he—"

They didn't wait for me to finish. Orville and Toll both set out running down the hill, hollering, "Paw" and "Old Cephus."

Deputy Jim said, "Come on."

I hung back until the Perfessor took me by the hand. "You needn't be afraid, Bluebell. Jim and I will take care of you."

By my path we got to the cabin almost as soon as Orville and Toll. Old Cephus was already back inside. He was tearing up the almanac and scattering the writing around on the floor. He already had the feathers spread around in the fireplace and under the windows and on the doorsill. When he saw us all standing there, he thundered, "She's riz up! There ain't no time to make a fire ring, we got to git her shet out of here afore she comes trying to sneak in. Help me, Orvy." He pushed the book into Orville's hands. "Git the dishrag, Tolliver, and stick them pins in it for the burning. They's up on Bluebell's shelf in the matchbox."

"Them pins been burnt onct, Cephus," Toll said. "The time the dog run off."

"They's all we have, we'll have to make use of them again."

Toll was about to do like Cephus said when Deputy Jim spoke up. "By the time that old witch picks up all these feathers and reads all that writing, it'll be cockcrow and she can't do you no harm tonight, Cephus." He dipped his hand in his pockets like he had afore and brought out the silver bullet on his palm.

Cephus picked it out of his hand, looked at the markings and he shook his head like he couldn't believe it. "No wonder she riz up," he whispered. "The silver bullet come out of her heart." He set down heavy in the rocking chair. "I'm too old. I've lost my powers to kill witches."

Deputy Jim said, "You feather it back into the tree tomorrow, Old Cephus. Maybe it'll go deep enough this time." He turned round to me. "Get your things together, Bluebell."

"What for?" Toll spoke up though it wasn't his business.

"She's coming down to Little Piney with us," Deputy Jim told him. "I'll find a place for her to board and maybe fix it up for her to go back to school. It's better she stays off of Tall Piney for a time."

Orville asked, "And who's going to cook for me and Paw while she's gone away?"

"If you weren't so mean, Orvy," Deputy Jim answered him, "you could find a wife to cook for you."

That was how it come about I went down to Little Piney for my education, not that it took on me much. I didn't go back to Tall Piney until after Toll and me was married. Onct Toll got away from Orville's influence, he stopped being so mean. Fact is, Orville wasn't so dirty and mean hisself after the Widder Claggett married up with him. She wouldn't put up with a pig in her cabin.

Old Cephus was dead by then, peaceful. He fell asleep in his rocking chair one afternoon and never woke up. The Perfessor bought his Old Betsey off'n Orville and give it to the Historical Society. You can see it up at their museum.

The Granny Woman was buried again, this time on the hill nearby her cabin, where Toll and me live. The Perfessor put up a headstone for her: Mary Virginia Piper, born in Roanoke, Virginia, 1823; died on Tall Piney, Missouri, 1924.

The silver bullet is still in the tree by Piney Run where Old Cephus feathered it twict. Nobody in the Pineys would dast prize it out.

STEPHEN MARLOWE

Stephen Marlowe (1928–   ) wrote some of the best paperback originals of the fifties and sixties. His most popular novels dealt with Chet Drum, former FBI agent turned independent gumshoe who managed, in the span of nineteen novels and a number of short stories, to deal with most of the important concerns and issues of the time.

Marlowe was always the real thing. Even his earliest material—done primarily for the science fiction pulps of the early fifties—has a deftness not often found in beginners. Not that the Nobel Committee pestered him for any copies of this stuff, but by 1955 when he began selling to Gold Medal, Ace, and Avon, he was writing books with real style and pith. The opening chapter of *Violence Is My Business*, Chet Drum number six, should be force-fed to anybody who is even thinking of writing suspense fiction. It's a masterpiece of atmosphere, plot, and genuine anxiety as a man tries to decide whether to jump off the foggy ledge of a college administration building.

Though Marlowe never got the recognition he deserves for his crime novels, he wrote a fine literary novel in 1995, *The Lighthouse at the End of the World*, which at the time was being touted as a National Book Award nominee.

Wanted—Dead and Alive

(Chester Drum)

I was drinking an ouzo-and-water on the aft deck of the car ferry *Hellas* and watching the lights of Brindisi fade into the Mediterranean darkness when a stocky figure came toward me, lurching slightly with the ship's roll.

"What the hell are you doing aboard?" I said.

"Did I ever say I wouldn't be?"

"Wife see you yet?" I asked.

"In the lounge. A real touching scene. She was looped. As usual."

That made two of them, I thought. Sebastian Spinner's lurch hadn't been all ship's roll. He was gripping the rail hard with both hands to keep the deck from tilting.

"What about the hired gun?"

"Christ, no. If he's aboard, I haven't made him." Spinner sighed ruefully. "Provided I remember what the sonofabitch looks like." A foghorn tooted in the bay, sounding derisive.

Sebastian Spinner was producer-director of *Lucrezia Borgia*, which was being filmed on location all over Italy. Twenty-five million bucks, not Spinner's money, had been pumped into it so far. The studio was near bankruptcy, the picture still wasn't finished and never would be if Spinner's wife kept wandering all over the map, with or without whatever stud struck her fancy at the moment.

It seemed even less likely that the picture would be finished if Spinner's wife, Carole Frazer, who was playing La Lucrezia, wound up dead on the twenty-six-hour steamer trip between Brindisi, Italy, and Patras, Greece. Neither Spinner nor I would make book that she wouldn't. Spinner had hired a Neapolitan killer to hit her in the head.

I'd first bumped into Sebastian Spinner in Rome a couple of weeks ago, when I'd blown myself to a vacation after the Axel Spade case. It was a party, the kind they throw in Cinecittà or Hollywood, where somebody dressed to the earlobes always gets tossed into the pool, where an unknown starlet named Simonetta or something like that peels to the waist to prove her astonishing abundancy and where guys like me, if their luck is running bad, get hired by guys like Sebastian Spinner.

"Drum?" he'd said, scooping a couple of martinis off a tray and handing me one. "That wouldn't be Chester Drum?"

I admitted my guilt.

"The private dick?"

"Not very private if you keep shouting it like that."

Spinner laughed phlegmily and clamped my arm with a small, soft hand. He was a stocky bald man, and his face and pate were shiny with sweat.

"They say you're the best in the business," he said, and added modestly: "I'm the best in my business. Sweetheart, if we get together it could be you're gonna save my life. Though sometimes I ain't too sure it's worth the trouble." Spinner was alternately egotistic and self-deprecating, a typical Hollywood type who made me glad I usually worked out of Washington, D.C.

He steered me outside and we drove off into the hot Roman night in his low-slung Facel Vega. He said nothing until we'd parked on the Via Veneto and took a curb-side table at Doney's.

"Somebody's gonna hit my wife in the head," he said then. "Christ, they kill her and there goes *Lucrezia Borgia*, not to mention twenty-five million bucks of Worldwide Studio money. If that happens, they wouldn't give me a job sweeping out the latrine of the second unit of one of those goddam grade Z epics made with the Yugoslav army."

I asked: "How do you know somebody's going to kill your wife, Mr. Spinner?" I asked it politely, the way you do with a loquacious drunk.

Spinner recognized my point of view and didn't like it. "On account of I hired the guy," he said indignantly, and then I was all ears.

A few days before, while they were shooting on location outside of Naples, Spinner had gone up to Vomero on a bat. You couldn't blame him. His wife was sleeping with Philip Stanley, her leading man, and everybody knew it.

"I was sitting in this trattoria in Vomero," Spinner said. "I was gassed to the eyeballs, and all of a sudden it was like that Hitchcock gimmick where two guys meet on a train and . . . You remember the film, don't you?

"Well, I met me a mafiosa type and we started in to talking. I ain't usually the jealous type. Merde, I been married six times, what's an extra-curricular roll in the hay more or less matter, it's a free country, I get yens too. But Carole's been spreading it around and her middle name ain't exactly discretion and this Stanley bastard practically rubs my face in it. No dame's gonna make Sebastian Spinner wear neon horns.

"That's what I tell the mafiosa type, and he nods his head and listens, and pretty soon, like, I'm foaming at the mouth, and finally I shut up. That's when he says, 'For five thousand dollars American I will kill her,' and that's when I say, 'For five thousand dollars American you got yourself a deal,' and he swifty cons me into giving him half of it in advance, walks out of the trattoria after I tell him when the best time to hit Carole in the head would be."

"When would it be?"

He told me about her up-coming trip to Greece. "On the boat," he said. "They got a ferry that runs from Brindisi to Patras. Carole hates to fly."

I watched the traffic swarming along the Via Veneto and being swallowed by the Pinciana Gate. "I take it you sort of changed your mind."

"You bet your sweet life I did. What goes with *Lucrezia Borgia* if Carole gets hit in the head? You tell me that, pal."

"Okay, call your gun off. What do you need me for?"

"I can't call him off."

That got a raised eyebrow from me.

"I don't even know his goddam name, I'm not sure what trattoria in Vomero it was and he had a face like all the other little swifties who'll sell their own sisters for a thousand lire in Naples. Kee-rist, I need a drink."

"Maybe he just let you talk yourself out of twenty-five hundred bucks," I suggested. "What makes you so sure he intends to go through with it?"

"Nothing, sweetheart," Spinner admitted with a slightly sick smile. "Nothing at all. Maybe he *is* laughing up his sleeve down in Vomero. Don't you think I know that?"

"So?"

"So maybe on the other hand he ain't."

I went down to Naples for a few days and prowled all the dives in Vomero without any luck. I got to Brindisi half an hour before the *Hellas* sailed. Now, on the aft deck of the car ferry, I told Spinner: "Look. Sober up and stay that way. I'll watch your wife, but if the guy's aboard maybe you'll recognize him."

A voice, not Spinner's, said: "I say, old man, don't you feel a bit of a horse's ass following us?" and a man joined us at the rail. In the light streaming through the portholes of the lounge, I recognized Philip Stanley. He was a big guy, about my size, in a navy blue blazer with gold buttons and a pair of gray flannel slacks. He had a hard, handsome face going a little heavy in the jowls, and his eyes held that look of smug, inbred self-satisfaction they seem to give out along with the diplomas at Eton and Harrow and the other public schools that turn out the members of the British Establishment. Actually, he had grown up in a Birmingham slum, and it had taken him all his life to cultivate that look of supercilious disdain.

"Sweetheart," Spinner said, "I never dreamed Carole would pack her playmate for the trip. Maybe she's slipping if she don't think she can do better in Greece. A lot better. They're pretty torrid in the sack, those Greeks, what I hear."

Stanley laughed. "Better than you she can always do, at any rate. But tell me, old boy," he asked dryly, "would you be speaking about those Greeks from personal experience?"

Spinner took a drunken, clumsy swing at him. Evading it easily, Stanley grabbed his wrist and levered the plump man a few staggering steps along the deck before letting go. Spinner fell down and leaped up again as if he had springs in his shoes.

I got between them, and Spinner said gratefully, "Hold me back, Drum. Hold me back, sweetheart. Every mark I put on his face'll cost Worldwide half a million bucks."

Stanley snickered, and neatly turned his broad back, and walked away along the rail. Spinner shuffled toward the door to the lounge. I lit a cigarette and followed the Englishman. A few more minutes away from Carole Frazer wouldn't hurt. Spinner would have the sense to keep an eye on her until I showed up.

"Got a few minutes?" I asked Stanley.

"Twenty-five hours to Patras," he said, leaning both elbows on the rail and staring down at the frothy white wake. "But just who are you?"

"Drum," I said crisply. "Worldwide front office."

"I never heard of you."

"You're not supposed to—until I land on you with both feet."

"Meaning?"

"Meaning if I can't get some assurance *Lucrezia*'ll be in the cutter's room inside of six months, the front office is half-inclined to chuck the whole works."

Stanley straightened and turned suddenly in my direction. He looked worried. "Are you serious?"

"Sure I am," I said. Though with his rugged Anglo-Saxon good looks Philip Stanley was about as far from a hungry little Neapolitan killer as you could get, the more I knew about the principals in the case the better I'd be able to handle whatever developed. "The director's been throwing a bat all the way from the Italian Alps to Calabria and between takes the stars go hop-scotching from bed to bed all over Europe. You think maybe Worldwide's wild about that?"

"I'll admit I've slept with Carole," Stanley said, "but—"

"Admit it? Hell, everybody knows it."

"But I had hoped to keep her somewhat closer to the set by doing it."

"That's what I like about you box-office big-shots. Your modesty."

"I am afraid you misunderstand," Stanley said, and a tortoni wouldn't have melted in his mouth. "Naturally I've gotten a certain amount of publicity as Carole's leading man, but I am not, as you put it, a box-office big-shot. I will be, if we ever finish *Lucrezia*. Otherwise I'll just be another not-quite-matinee-idol knocking at the back doors of Cinecittà for work."

Him and Sebastian Spinner both, I thought. The only one who didn't seem to mind was Carole Frazer.

"Damn it all," he went on, "why d'you think we're languishing a year behind schedule? Because I've slept with Carole? That's nonsense, old boy. I don't have to tell you the woman's a nymphomaniac, if a lovely one. But if it isn't me then it's someone else, and that's only the half of it. Carole was rushed to London three times for emergency medical treatment, and each time as I also don't have to tell you it was some psychosomatic foolishness. Why, she's only appeared in half a dozen crucial scenes so far, close-ups, and virtually every far shot's been done by her stand-in. We have a great deal more footage of the stand-in than we do of Carole. If you doubt my word, ask Spinner. And Dawn Sibley's no mere double, she's a fine actress in her own right. Sometimes I think it would be simpler all around if we were to chuck Carole and let Dawn do *Lucrezia*. I don't stand alone. Ask around, old boy, and then tell *that* to the front office. Most of us want to see this film completed as much as you do. But unfortunately it was conceived as a vehicle for Carole."

After that long tirade, he had nothing else to say. I watched him walk across the deck and inside. For a little while I listened to the rush of water under the hull-plates. Brindisi was a faint and distant line of light. Overhead a gull, nailed in silhouette against the starlit sky, screamed and flapped its wings once. When I looked again, only a glow remained on the horizon in the direction of Brindisi. I carried my empty ouzo glass to the lounge.

At a big table near the bar, Carole Frazer was holding court. She was wearing black tapered slacks and a paisley blouse that fondled her high breasts without hugging them lasciviously. A casual lock of her blond hair had fallen across her right eye and right cheek. A languid smile that did not quite part her moist red lips was the reward her suitors got.

There were about a dozen of them, most of them dark and slender Italians and Greeks with intense eyes and gleaming teeth. Any one of them, I realized, could have been Sebastian Spinner's little swifty from Vomero. He'd be as easy to single out as a fingerling in a fish hatchery.

"Ouzo," I told the barman, and he poured the anise-flavored liqueur and added enough water to turn it milky. His hand was not steady on the carafe, and he sloshed a little water on the bar. In the world that Hollywood made, Carole Frazer was an institution. He was staring at her bugeyed. I couldn't blame him. Seen close, her blond beauty was really scorching.

Spinner sat alone at a table nearby. He was drinking Scotch and darting small, anxious glances at the men clustered around his wife. Each time he'd shake his head slightly, and his eyes would flick on like a snake's tongue. He had trouble keeping his head off the table. He was very drunk.

I went over to him and sat down. "Any luck?"

"Nope. Maybe he's here. Maybe not. I can't tell them apart, bunch a goddam Chinamen."

"Lay off the sauce," I suggested, "and you won't see double."

Carole Frazer called across to us in her throaty purr of a voice. "Mister, if you can make him do that, you're a better man than his psychiatrist. Who are you?"

"I'm his new psychiatrist," I said, and she laughed, and then she lost interest in us as the dark heads bobbed and the white teeth flashed all around her. She lapped up male adulation the way a thirsty kitten laps up milk.

Pretty soon Spinner told me, "Gonna hit the sack. It's no use. You'll keep an eye on her?"

I said that was why I was here, and he lurched across the lounge toward the companionway that led to the *Hellas* de luxe staterooms. A while later Carole Frazer got up and stretched like a cat, every muscle of her lithe body getting into the act. The Italians and Greeks went pop-eyed, watching. She patted the nearest dark head, said, "Down, boy," and, "Arrivederci" and went in the direction her husband had gone. But that didn't necessarily mean she was going to find him. After all, her leading man Philip Stanley was aboard too.

Finishing my ouzo, I went in search of the purser's office. It was located in the first class entrance foyer. A kid in a white uniform sat there reading a letter and sighing.

"What's the number of Carole Frazer's stateroom?" I asked him.

"Kyros," he said smoothly, "the next time you see the lady, why not ask her?"

He smiled. I smiled and studied half a dozen travel brochures spread out on the counter. I picked one of them up. In English, French and Italian it described the delights of a motor trip that could be made from Athens to Delphi and back in a day.

"How much?" I asked.

"Depending on whether you wish a chauffeur or a self-drive car, kyros—"

"No. I mean the brochure."

"That is free, kyros, compliments of the Adriatic Line."

I pocketed the folder and dropped a fifty drachma note on the counter. "Fifty?" I said. "That seems fair enough."

"But I just—" he began, and then his eyes narrowed and his lips just missed smiling. "De Luxe Three, starboard side," he said without moving his mouth, and returned to his letter.

The starboard de luxe companionway ended at a flight of metal stairs going up. At the top was a door and beyond that a narrow deck above the boat-deck, with three doors numbered one, two and three spaced evenly along it. There were wide windows rather than portholes, all of them curtained and two of them dark. Faint light seeped through the third. It was Carole Frazer's cabin.

Looking at it, I liked the setup. Door and window both outside, on this deck. If I spent the night here, nobody could reach Carole Frazer without me knowing it. I listened to the throb of the ship's engines and looked at my watch. It was a quarter to one. I sat down between the door and the window of Carole Frazer's stateroom. The bulk of the Magnum .44 in its clam-shell rig under my left arm was uncomfortable. I shifted the holster around a little, but that didn't help. No one has ever invented a shoulder holster that is comfortable, just as no one has ever invented any other way of wearing a revolver the size of a Magnum and hiding it when what else you are wearing is a light-weight seersucker suit.

For about an hour I kept a silent vigil. Nobody screamed, no Vomero swiftly came stalking up stairs, nothing happened except that the *Hellas* covered another twenty-five miles of Adriatic Sea.

And then I heard voices. The only thing that wasn't de luxe about the half-dozen de luxe state rooms aboard the *Hellas* was the sound-proofing. Well, you couldn't have everything.

"Awake?" a man asked.

"Uh-huh."

"Like another drink?"

"My head's spinning right now."

"Just one more? With me?"

"All right."

Silence while Philip Stanley and Carole Frazer had a post-nightcap nightcap. Like any private dick, I'd been called a peeper more than once. Like any private dick, I'd never liked it. I'd done my share of peeping—or anyway listening—but never outside a woman's bedroom. The one kind of work I don't do is divorce work. But if the hired gun was going to make his move, it figured to be during the night. "Peeper," I muttered sourly under my breath, and remained where I was.

"Oh, Phil," Carole Frazer said, and her voice was more throaty than it had been in the lounge. "When you do that—"

"What's wrong, don't you like it?"

"You know I do. I love it. But I'm so—drunky. Head going around and 'round."

Another silence. Then he laughed, and she laughed and said: "Phil, you amaze me." She called him a brief Anglo-Saxon word that is usually not a term of endearment, but her voice made it sound endearing. Then she laughed again, deep in her throat, and then she said, "You keep this up, you're going to screw yourself right into the wall," and then after that there was silence for a long time.

I must have half-dozed. I blinked suddenly and realized that the night had grown cooler and I had grown stiff from sitting in one position for so long. I glanced at the luminous dial of my watch. After three o'clock. It would be dawn before long, and still no sign of the Vomero swifty.

There was a faint click, and the stateroom door opened enough for Philip Stanley to poke his head out and take a quick look to left and right. The one way he didn't look was down, where I was sitting. His head popped back inside, and the door shut softly. I remained where I was.

The door opened again. This time Stanley came out. He was carrying a suitcase, and from the way his shoulder slumped it looked heavy. He took it to the rail, set it down and placed a coil of rope on top of it. I froze, absolutely still. If he turned right on his way back to the stateroom he would see me. If he turned left, he wouldn't.

He turned left and went inside again. What the hell was he up to?

In a few seconds he reappeared with Carole Frazer cradled in his arms. He was fully dressed. She wasn't dressed any way at all. She mumbled against his ear. He set her down, gently, next to the suitcase. For a while longer I sat there like someone who had walked in on the middle of a movie and didn't know what the hell was happening on the screen or why. Stanley tied the rope to the handle of the suitcase, uncoiled the rest of it, took two turns around the suitcase, passed the rope through the handle once more, took four or five turns around Carole Frazer's body under the arms, passed the rope through the handle a third time and knotted it.

Carole Frazer mumbled again, faintly complaining. She was as drunk as Bacchus. He ignored her until she said, "It's cold out here. I'm cold. What's the matter with you? I don't—"

He clipped her once, behind the left ear, with his fist, just as I started to get up in a hurry. I had the Magnum in my hand.

"Need some help with your package?" I said. "Kind of heavy for one man to get over the rail."

The gun meant nothing to him. He cried out once, hoarsely, and came for me. The big Magnum could have ripped a hole the size of a saucer in him, but I didn't fire. When you get trigger happy you're not long for my line of work, despite any evidence to the contrary on TV.

Stanley lunged as a bull lunges, horns and head down, going for the muleta. I took his head in chancery under my arm, and his weight slammed us both against the wall. I jarred him loose. I was stiff from my long vigil, and he was fighting for his life. What I'd seen was attempted murder, and he knew it. He butted me. My teeth clicked and my head jolted the wall a second time. He stepped back, almost gracefully, and kicked me in the gut. Right around there I began to wish I had used the gun.

But by then it was too late. We hit the deck together, Stanley on top, me trying my best to remember how to breathe and Stanley clamping a hand like a Stilson wrench on my right wrist so I couldn't use the Magnum. I cuffed his head, somewhat indolently, with my left hand. He cuffed mine, harder, with his right. I tasted blood in my mouth. At least I had begun to breathe again, and that was something.

All of a sudden the Magnum went off. The big slug hit the window of Carole Frazer's stateroom, and glass crashed down all around us. I judo-chopped the side of Stanley's neck. His weight left me as he went over sideways. I got up before he did, but not by much. His eyes were wild. He knew that shot was going to bring company.

He swung a right that sailed past my ear, and I hooked a left that hit bone somewhere on his face. He dropped to his knees and got up and dropped to them again.

I heard footsteps pounding up the metal staircase. Stanley heard them too. Two faces and two white, black-visored caps appeared. Stanley did not try to get up again right away. There was a dark and glistening stain on the deck below him. He stared down at it, fascinated. He touched his throat. Blood pumped, welling through his fingers.

The two ship's officers saw the gun in my hand and remained where they were.

A shard of flying glass had hit Stanley in the throat. The way the blood pumped, an artery had to be severed.

"There a doctor aboard?" I said, going to Stanley. "This man needs help in a hurry."

But he got to his feet and backed away from me. Who knows what a guy will do when he's little drunk, and half-crazy with fear, and in danger of bleeding to death?

"Keep away from me," he said.

"You crazy? You won't last ten minutes bleeding like that."

Smiling faintly he said, "I'm afraid I wouldn't come on very well as a convict, old boy."

Then he took a single step to the rail and went over.

They stopped the ship. They always do, but it rarely helps. We covered another mile, and turned sharp to port, and came back. Three life-preservers were floating in the water, where the ship's officers had thrown them. But Philip Stanley was gone.

On deck after lunch and after I'd made and signed a deposition for the *Hellas'* captain, Spinner said: "I don't get it. You think I'm nuts or something? There was this little swifty in Vomero. I know there was."

"Sure," I said. "Stanley hired him, but his job ended in Vomero."

"Stanley hired him?"

"To make you think you'd hired yourself a killer. If your wife had disappeared during the crossing, you'd have kept your mouth shut about the possibility of foul play if you thought your own man had done it."

"Why did Stanley want her dead?" Skinner squealed.

"Because the picture was more important to him. He got scared they'd never finish it, the way Carole was carrying on." I lit a cigarette. "Hell, he told me last night how he wanted Carole's understudy to take over. She almost did."

Carole Frazer joined us on deck. She was wearing a bikini and stretched out languidly in the bright, hot sun. She didn't look at all like a girl who'd almost been murdered a few hours ago.

"Watch the sun," Spinner warned her. "La Lucrezia's pale, baby." He sighed. "That is, if you're gonna do the picture after what you been through."

"Do it?" Carole asked sleepily. "But of course I'll do it, darling. The publicity will be marvelous."

It was, and after our night aboard the *Hellas,* Carole Frazer settled down to work. They made *Lucrezia Borgia* with a new leading man. Carole Frazer's up for an Oscar.

RICHARD S. PRATHER

Richard S. Prather (1921–) was one of the great pulp treasures of the fifties and early sixties. Sensing that the private eye form was ripe for spoofing, he created L.A. gumshoe Shell Scott. Where most fictional private eyes lived by Raymond Chandler's naive code—justice, bourbon, and self-pity—ole Shell had dedicated his life to the other things—chicks, broads, and tomatoes. Yes, he would eventually get around to solving the crime, but the fun was watching Shell sleep his way through a couple dozen girls per book (or so it seemed). There's been an attempt, in these politically correct times, to denigrate his contribution. But the Scott novels are first-rate stories and first-rate fun, even despite Shell's sometimes wearying right-wing politics. Prather is the forgotten superstar of the first wave of "paperback original" novels.

The Double Take

This was a morning for weeping at funerals, for sticking pins in your own wax image, for leaping into empty graves and pulling the sod in after you. Last night I had been at a party with some friends here in Los Angeles, and I had drunk bourbon and Scotch and martinis and maybe even swamp water from highball glasses, and now my brain was a bomb that went off twice a second.

I thought thirstily of Pete's Bar downstairs on Broadway, right next door to this building, the Hamilton, where I have my detective agency, then got out of my chair, left the office, and locked the door behind me. I was Shell Scott, the Bloodshot Eye, and I needed a hair of the horse that bit me.

Before I went downstairs I stopped by the PBX switchboard at the end of the hall. Cute little Hazel glanced up.

"You look terrible," she said.

"I know. I think I'm decomposing. Listen, a client just phoned me and I have to rush out to the Hollywood Roosevelt. I'll be back in an hour or so, but for the next five minutes I'll be in Pete's. Hold down the fort, huh?"

"Sure, Shell. Pete's?" She shook her head.

I tried to grin at her, whereupon she shrank back and covered her eyes, and I left. Hazel is a sweet kid, tiny, and curvy, and since mine is a one-man agency with no receptionist or secretary, the good gal tries to keep informed of my whereabouts.

I tottered down the one flight of stairs into bright June sunshine on Broadway, thinking that my client would have to wait an extra five minutes even though he'd been in a hell of a hurry. But he'd been in a hurry the last time, too, and nothing had come of it. This Frank Harrison had first called me on Monday morning, three days ago, and insisted I come right out to his hotel in Hollywood. When I got there he explained that he was having marital troubles and wanted me to tail his wife and see if I could catch her in any indiscretions. When I told him I seldom handled that kind of job, he'd said to forget it, so I had. The deal seemed screwy; he'd not only been vague, but hadn't pressed me much to take the case. It had added up to an hour wasted, and no fee.

But this morning when I'd opened the office at nine sharp the phone had been ringing and it was Harrison again. He wanted me right away this time, too, but he had a real case for me, he said, not like last time, and it wasn't tailing his wife. He was in a sweat to get me out to the Roosevelt's bar, the Cinegrill where we were to meet, and was willing to pay me fifty bucks just to listen to his story. I still didn't know what was up, but it sounded like a big one. I hoped it was bigger than the last "job," and, anyway, it couldn't be as big as my head. I went into Pete's.

Pete knew what I wanted as soon as I perched on a stool and he got a good look at my eyeballs, so he immediately mixed the ghastly concoction he gives me for hangovers. I was halfway through it when his phone rang.

He listened a moment, said, "I'll tell him," then turned to me. "That was Hazel," he said. "Some dame was up there looking for you. A wild woman—"

That was as far as he got. I heard somebody come inside the front door, and high heels clicked rapidly over the floor and stopped alongside me. A woman's voice, tight and angry, said, "There you are, you, you—you crook!" and I turned on my stool to look at the wild woman.

I had never seen her before, but that was obviously one of the most unfortunate omissions of my life, because one look at her and I forgot my hangover. She was an absolutely gorgeous little doll, about five feet two inches tall, and any half-dozen of her sixty-two delightful inches would make any man stare, and all of her at once was enough to knock a man's eyes out through the back of his head.

"Oh!" she said. "You ought to be tarred and feathered."

I kept looking. Coal black hair was fluffed around her oval face, and though she couldn't have been more than twenty-four or twenty-five years old, a thin streak of gray ran back from her forehead through that thick glossy hair. She was dressed in light blue clam-diggers and a man's white shirt which her chest filled out better than any man's ever did, and her eyes were an incredibly light electric blue—shooting sparks at me.

She was angry. She was so hot she looked ready to melt. It seemed, for some strange reason, she was angry with me. This lovely was not one I wanted angry with me; I wanted her happy, and patting my cheek, or perhaps even chewing on my ear.

She looked me up and down and said, "Yes. Yes, you're Shell Scott."

"That's right. Certainly. But—"

"I want that twenty-four thousand dollars and I'm going to get it if I—if I have to *kill* you! I mean it!"

"Huh?"

"It's just money to you, you crook! But it's all he had, all my father's saved in years and years. Folsom's Market, indeed! I'll kill you, I *will*! So give me that money. I know you're in with them."

My head was in very bad shape to begin with, but now I was beginning to think maybe I had mush up there. She hadn't yet said a single word that made sense.

"Take it easy," I said. "You must have the wrong guy."

If anything, that remark made her angrier. She pressed white teeth together, and made noises in her throat, then she said, "I suppose you're not Shell Scott."

"Sure I am, but I don't know what you're babbling about."

"Babbling! *Babbling!* Ho, that's the way you're going to play it, are you? Going to deny everything, pretend it never happened! I knew you would! Well—"

She backed away from me, fumbling with the clasp of a big handbag. I looked at her thinking that one of us was completely mad. Then she dug into her bag and pulled out a chromed pistol, probably a .22 target pistol, and pointed it at me. She was crying now, her face twisted up and tears running down her cheeks, but she still appeared to be getting angrier every second, and slowly the thought seeped into my brain: this tomato is aiming a real gun at me.

She backed away toward the rear of Pete's, but she was still too close to suit me, and close enough so I could see her eyes squeeze shut and her finger tighten on the trigger. I heard the crack of the little gun and I heard a guy who had just come in the door let out a yelp behind me, and I heard a little tinkle of glass. And then I heard a great clattering and crashing of glass because by this time I was clear over behind the bar with Pete, banging into bottles and glasses on my way down to the floor. I heard the gun crack twice more and then high heels clattered away from me and I peeked over the bar just in time to see the gal disappearing into the ladies' room.

A man on my left yelled, "Janet! *Jan!*" I looked at him just as he got up off the floor, and I remembered the guy who had yelped right after that first shot. He didn't seem to be hurt, though, because he got to his feet and started after the beautiful crazy gal.

He was a husky man, about five-ten, wearing brown slacks and a T-shirt which showed off his impressive chest. Even so, it wasn't as impressive as the last chest I'd seen, and although less than a minute had elapsed since I'd first seen the gal who'd been behind it, I was already understandably curious about her. I vaulted over the bar and yelled at the man, "Hey, you! Hold it!"

He stopped and jerked his head around as I stepped up in front of him. His slightly effeminate face didn't quite go with the masculine build, but many women would probably have called him "handsome" or even "darling." A thick mass of black curly hair came down in a sharp widow's peak on his white forehead. His mouth was full, chin square and dimpled, and large black-lashed brown eyes blinked at me.

"Who the hell was that tomato?" I asked him. "And what's happening?"

"You tell me," he said. And then an odd thing happened. He hadn't yet had time to take a good look at me, but he took it now. He gawked at my white hair, my face, blinked, and his mouth dropped open. "Oh, *Christ*!" he said, and then he took off. Naturally he ran into the ladies' room. It just wouldn't have seemed right at that point if he'd gone anyplace else.

I looked over my shoulder at Pete, whose mouth was hanging completely ajar, then I went to the ladies' room and inside. Nobody was there. A wall window was open and I looked out through it at the empty alley, then looked all around the rest room again, but it was still empty.

I went back to the bar and said, "Pete, what the hell did you put in that drink?"

He stared at me, shaking his head. Finally he said, "I never seen nothing like that in my life. Thirteen years I've run this place, but—" He didn't finish it.

My hand was stinging and so was a spot on my chin. Going over the bar I had broken a few bottles and cut my left hand slightly, and one of those little slugs had apparently come close enough to nick my chin. I had also soaked up a considerable amount of spilled whiskey in my clothes and I didn't smell good at all. My head hadn't been helped, either, by the activity.

Pete nodded when I told him to figure up the damage and I'd pay him later, then I went back into the Hamilton Building. It appeared Frank Harrison would have to wait. Also, the way things were going, I wanted to get the .38 Colt Special and harness out of my desk.

At the top of the stairs I walked down to the PBX again. Hazel, busy at the switchboard, didn't see me come up but when I spoke she swung around. "What's with that gal you called Pete's about?" I asked her.

"She find you? Wasn't she a beautiful little thing?"

"Yeah. And she found me."

Hazel's nose was wrinkling. "You *are* decomposing," she said. "Into bourbon. How many shots did you have?"

"Three, I think. But they all missed me."

"Missed you, ha—"

"Shots that beautiful little thing took at me, I mean. With a gun."

Hazel blinked. "You're kidding." I shook my head and she said, "Well, I—she did seem upset, a little on edge."

"She was clear the hell over the edge. What did she say?"

"She asked for you. As a matter of fact, she said, 'Where's the dirty Shell Scott?' I told her you'd gone to Pete's downstairs"—Hazel smiled sweetly—"for some medicine, and she ran away like mad. She seemed very excited."

"She was."

"And a man came rushing up here a minute or two after the girl and asked about her. I said I'd sent her to Pete's—and *he* ran off." She shook her head. "I don't know. I'm a little confused."

That I could understand. Maybe it was something in the L.A. air this morning. I thanked Hazel and walked down to the office, fishing out my keys, but when I got there I noticed the door was already cracked. I shoved it open and walked inside. For the second or third time this morning my jaw dropped open. A guy was seated behind my desk, fussing with some papers on its top, looking businesslike as all hell. He was a big guy, husky, around thirty years old, with white hair sticking up into the air about an inch.

Without looking up, he said, "Be right with you."

I walked to the desk and sank into one of the leather chairs in front of it, a chair I bought for clients to sit in. If the chair had raised up and floated me out of the window while violins played in the distance, my stunned expression would not have changed one iota. In a not very strong voice I said, "Who are you?"

"I'm Shell Scott," he said briskly, glancing up at me.

Ah, yes. That explained it. He was Shell Scott. Now I knew what was wrong. I had gone crazy. My mind had snapped. For a while there I'd thought *I* was Shell Scott.

But slowly reason filtered into my throbbing head again. I'd had all the mad episodes I cared for this morning, and here was a guy I could get my hands on. He was looking squarely at me now, and if ever a man suddenly appeared scared green, this one did. Except for the short white hair and the fact that he was about my size, he didn't resemble me much, and right now he looked sick. I got up and leaned on the desk and shoved my face at him.

"That's interesting," I said pleasantly. "I, too, am Shell Scott."

He let out a grunt and started to get up fast, but I reached out and grabbed a bunch of shirt and tie and throat in my right fist and I yanked him halfway across the desk.

"O.K., you smart sonofabitch," I said. "Let's have a lot of words. Fast, mister, before I break some bones for you."

He squawked and sputtered and tried to jerk away, so I latched onto him with the other hand and started to haul him over the desk where I could get at him good. I only started to though, because I heard someone behind me. I twisted my head around just in time to see the pretty boy from Pete's, the guy who'd left the ladies' room by the window. Just time to see him, and the leather-wrapped sap in his hand, swinging down at me. Then another bomb, a larger one this time, went off in my head and I could feel myself falling, for miles and miles, through deepening blackness.

I came to in front of my desk, and I stayed there for a couple of minutes, got up, made it to the desk chair, and sat down on it. If I had thought my head hurt before, it was nothing to the way it felt now. It took me about ten seconds to go from angry to mad to furious to raging, then I grabbed the phone and got Hazel.

"Where'd those two guys go?"

"What guys?"

"You see anybody leave my office?"

"No, Shell. What's the matter?"

"Plenty." I glanced at my watch. Nine-twenty. Just twenty minutes since I'd first opened the office door this morning and answered the ringing phone. I couldn't have been sprawled on the floor more than a minute or two, but even so my two pals would be far away by now. Well, Harrison was going to have a long wait because I was taking no cases but my own for a while. What with people shooting at me, impersonating me, and batting me on the head, this was a mess I had to find out about fast.

"Hazel," I said, "get me the Hollywood Roosevelt."

While I waited I calmed down a little and, though the throbbing in my head made it difficult, my thoughts got a little clearer. It seemed a big white-haired ape was passing himself off as me, but I didn't have the faintest idea why. He must have been down below on Broadway somewhere, waited till he saw me leave, then come up. What I couldn't figure was how the hell he'd known I'd be leaving my office. He certainly couldn't have intended hanging around all day just in case I left, and he couldn't have known I'd be at Pete's—

I stopped as a thought hit me. "Hazel," I said. "Forget that call." I hung up, thinking. Whitey couldn't have known I'd show up with a hangover, but he might have known I'd be out of here soon after I arrived. All it takes to get a private detective out of his office is—a phone call. An urgent appointment to meet somebody somewhere, say, maybe somebody like Frank Harrison. Could be I was reaching for that one, but I didn't think so. I'd had only the one call this morning, an urgent call that would get me out of the office—and from the very guy who'd pulled the same deal last Monday. And all I'd done Monday was waste an hour. The more I thought about it the more positive I became.

Harrison might still be waiting in the Cinegrill—and he might not. If

Harrison were in whatever this caper was with Whitey and Pretty Boy, they'd almost surely phone him soon to let him know I hadn't followed the script; perhaps were even phoning him right now. He'd know, too, that unless I was pretty stupid, I'd sooner or later figure out his part in this.

Excitement started building in me as I grabbed my gun and holster and strapped them on; I was getting an inkling of what might have been wrong with that black-haired lovely. Maybe I'd lost Whitey and Pretty Boy, but with luck I could still get my hands on Harrison. Around his throat, say. I charged out of the office. My head hurt all the way, but I made it to the lot where I park my convertible Cadillac, leaped in, and roared out onto Broadway. From L.A. to downtown Hollywood I broke hell out of the speed limit, and at the hotel I found a parking spot at the side entrance, hurried through the big lobby and into the Cinegrill.

I remembered Harrison was a very tall diplomat-type with hair graying at the temples and bushy eyebrows over dark eyes. Nobody even remotely like him was in the bar. I asked the bartender, "You know a Frank Harrison?"

"Yes, sir."

"He been in here?"

"Yes, sir. He left just a few minutes ago."

"Left the hotel?"

"No, he went into the lobby."

"Thanks." I hustled back into the lobby and up to the desk. A tall, thin clerk in his middle thirties, wearing rimless glasses, looked at me when I stopped.

"I've got an appointment with Mr. Frank Harrison," I said. "What room is he in?"

"Seven-fourteen, sir." The clerk looked a little bewildered. "But Mr. Harrison just left."

"Where'd he go? How long ago?"

The clerk shook his head. "He was checking out. I got his card, and when I turned around I saw him going out the door. Just now. It hasn't been a minute. I don't—"

I turned around and ran for the door swearing under my breath. The bastard would have been at the desk when I came in through the side entrance and headed for the Cinegrill. He must have seen me, and that had been all; he'd powdered. He was well powdered, too, because there wasn't a trace of him when I got out onto Hollywood Boulevard.

Inside the hotel again I checked some more with the bartender and desk clerk, plus two bellboys and a dining-room waitress. After a lot of questions I knew Harrison had often been seen in the bar and dining room with two other men. One was stocky, with curly black hair, white skin, cleft chin, quite handsome—Pretty Boy; the other was bigger and huskier and almost always wore a hat. A bellhop said he looked a bit like me. I told him it *was* me, and left him looking bewildered. Two bellboys and the bartender also told me that Harrison was seen every day, almost *all* of every day, with a blond woman a few years under thirty whom they all described as "stacked." The three men and the blonde were often a foursome. From the bartender I learned that Harrison had gotten a phone call in the Cinegrill about five minutes before I showed up. That would have been from the other two guys on my list, and fit with Harrison's checking out fast—or starting to. I went back to the desk and chatted some more with the thin clerk after showing him the photostat of my license. Pretty Boy—Bob Foster—was in room 624; Whitey—James Flagg—was in 410; Frank Harrison was in 714.

I asked the clerk, "Harrison married to a blonde?"

"I don't believe he is married, sir."

"He's registered alone?" He nodded, and I said, "I understand he's here a lot with a young woman. Right?"

"Yes, sir. That's Miss Willis."

"A blonde?"

"Yes, Quite, ah, curvaceous."

"What room is she in?"

He had to check. He came back with the card in his hand and said, "Isn't this odd? I had never noticed. She's in seven-sixteen."

It wasn't at all odd. I looked behind him to the slots where room keys were kept. There wasn't any key in the slot for 714. Nor was there any key in the 716 slot. I thanked the clerk, took an elevator to the seventh floor, and walked to Harrison's room. There were two things I wanted to do. One was look around inside here to see if maybe my ex-client had left something behind which might help me find him; and the other was to talk with the blonde. As it turned out, I killed two birds with one stone.

The door to 714 was locked, and if I had to I was going to bribe a bellboy to let me in. But, first, I knocked.

It took quite a while, and I had almost decided I'd have to bribe the bellhop, but then there was the sound of movement inside, a muffled voice called something I couldn't understand, and I heard the soft thud of feet coming toward the door. A key clicked in the lock and the door swung open. A girl stood there, yawning, her eyes nearly closed, her head drooping as she stared at approximately the top button of my coat.

She was stark naked. Stark. I had seldom seen *anything* so stark. She had obviously just gotten out of bed, and just as obviously had been sound asleep. She still wasn't awake, because blinking at my chest she mumbled, "Oh, dammit to hell, John."

Then she turned around and walked back into the room. I followed her, as if hypnotized, automatically swinging the door shut behind me. She was about five-six and close to 130 pounds, and she was shaped like what I sometimes muse about after the third highball. Everybody who had described the blonde, and she was a blonde, had been correct: she was not only "stacked" but "ah, curvaceous." There was no mistaking it, either;

the one time a man can be positive that a woman's shape is her own is when she is wearing nothing but her shape, and this gal was really in *dandy* shape. She walked away from me toward a bedroom next to this room, like a gal moving in her sleep. She walked to the bed and flopped onto it, pulling a sheet up over her, and I followed her clear to the bed, still coming out of shock, my mind not yet working quite like a well-oiled machine. I managed to figure out that my Frank Harrison was actually named John something. Then she yawned, blinked up at me and said, "Well, dammit to hell, John, stop staring."

And then she stopped suddenly with her mouth stretching wider and wider and her eyes growing enormous as she stared at me. Then she screamed. Man, she screamed like a gal who had just crawled into bed with seventeen tarantulas. I was certainly affecting people in peculiar fashion this morning. She threw off the sheet, leaped to the floor, and lit out for an open door in the far wall, leading into the bathroom, and by now that didn't surprise me a bit.

She didn't make it though. She was only a yard from me at the start, and I took one step toward her, grabbed her wrist and hung on. She stopped screaming and slashed long red fingernails at my face, but I grabbed her hand and shoved her back onto the bed, then said, "Relax, sister. Stop clawing at me and keep your yap closed and I'll let go of you."

She was tense, jerking her arms and trying to get free, but suddenly she relaxed. Her face didn't relax, though: she still glared at me, a mixture of hate, anger, and maybe fright, staining her face. She didn't have makeup on, but her face had a hard, tough-kid attractiveness.

I let go of her and she grabbed the sheet, pulled it up in front of her body. "Get the hell out of here," she said nastily. There was a phone on a bedside stand and her eyes fell on it. She grabbed it, pulled it off the hook. "I'm calling the cops."

I pulled a chair over beside the bed and sat down. Finally she let go of the phone and glared some more at me.

"I didn't think you'd call any cops, sweetheart," I said. "Maybe I will, but you won't. Quite a shock seeing me here, isn't it? I was supposed to meet Frank—I mean, John—in the Cinegrill, not up here. You're in trouble, baby."

"I don't know what you're talking about."

"Not much. You know who I am."

"You're crazy."

"Shut up, Miss Willis. I got a call from your boyfriend at nine sharp this morning. I was supposed to rush out here for an important job; only there isn't any important job. Your John, the guy I know as Frank Harrison, just wanted me out of my office for an hour or so. Right?"

She didn't say anything.

"So another guy could play Shell Scott for a while. Now you tell me why."

Her lips curled and she swore at me.

I said, "Something you don't know. You must have guessed the caper's gone sour, but you probably don't know John has powdered. Left you flat, honey."

She frowned momentarily, then her face smoothed and got blank. It stayed blank.

She was clammed good. Finally I said, "Look, I know enough of it already. There's John, and Bob Foster, and a big white-haired slob named Flagg who probably got his peroxide from you. And don't play innocent because I know you're thick with all of them, especially John. Hell, this is his room. So get smart and—"

The phone rang. She reached for it, then stopped.

I yanked the .38 out from under my coat and said, "Don't get wise; say hello." I took the phone off the hook and held it for her. She said, "Hello," and I put the phone to my ear just in time to hear a man's voice say, "John, baby. I had to blow fast, that bastard was in the hotel. Pack and meet me at Apex." He stopped.

I covered the mouthpiece and told the blonde, "Tell him O.K. Just that, nothing else."

I stuck the phone up in front of her and she said, "The panic's on. Fade out." I got the phone back to my ear just in time to hear the click as he hung up.

The blonde was smiling at me. But she stopped smiling when I stuck my gun back in its holster, then juggled the receiver and said, "Get me the Hollywood Detective Division."

"Hey, wait a minute," the blonde said. "What you calling the cops for?"

"You can't be that stupid. Tehachapi for you, sweetheart. You probably have a lot of friends there. It won't be so bad. Just horrible."

She licked her lips. When the phone was answered I said, "Put Lieutenant Bronson on, will you?"

The gal said, "Wait a minute. Hold off on that call. Let's . . . talk about it."

I grinned. "Now you want to talk. No soap. You can talk to the cops. And don't tell me there isn't enough to hold you on."

"Please. I—call him later if you have to." She let go of the sheet and it fell to her waist. I told myself to be strong and look away, but I was weak.

"You got it all wrong," she said softly. "Let's—talk." She tried to smile, but it didn't quite come off. I shook my head.

She threw the sheet all the way back on the bed then, stood up, holding her body erect, and stepped close to me. "Please, honey. We can have fun. Don't you like me, honey?"

"What's with that white-haired ape in my office? And what's Apex?"

"I don't know. I told you before. Honest, honey, look at me."

That was a pretty silly thing to say, because I sure wasn't looking at the wallpaper. Just then Lieutenant Bronson came on and I said, "Shell Scott here, Bron. Hollywood Roosevelt, room seven-fourteen."

The blonde stepped closer, almost touching me, then picked up my free hand and passed it around her waist. "Hang up," she said. "You won't be sorry." Her voice dropped lower, became a husky murmur as she pressed my fingers into the warm flesh. "Forget it, honey. I can be awfully nice."

Bronson was asking me what was up. I said, "Just a second, Bron," then to the girl, "Sounds like a great kick. Just tell me the story, spill your guts—"

She threw my hand away from her, face getting almost ugly, and then she took a wild swing at me. I blocked the blow with my right hand, put my hand flat on her chest and shoved her back against the bed. She sprawled on it, saying some very nasty things.

I said into the phone, "I've got a brassy blonde here for you."

"What's the score?"

"Frankly, I'm not sure. But I'll sign a complaint. Using foul language, maybe."

"That her? I can hear her."

"Or maybe attempted rape." I grinned at the blonde as she yanked the sheet over her and used some more foul language. I said to Bronson, "Actually, it looks like some kind of confidence game—with me a sucker. I don't know the gal, but you guys might make her. Probably she's got a record." I saw the girl's face change as she winced. "Yeah," I added, "she's got a record. Probably as long as her face is right now."

"I'll send a man up."

"Make it fast, will you? I've got to get out of here, and this beautiful blonde hasn't a stitch of clothes on."

"Huh? She—I'll be right there."

It didn't take him long. By ten-forty-five Bronson, who had arrived grinning—and the three husky sergeants who came with him—had taken the blonde away, and I was back in the hotel's lobby. I had given Bronson a rundown on the morning's events, and he'd said they'd keep after the blonde. Neither of us expected any chatter from her, though. After that soft, "I can be awfully nice," she hadn't said anything except swear words and: "I want a lawyer, I know my rights, I want a lawyer." She'd get a lawyer. Tomorrow, maybe.

I went into the Cinegrill and had a bourbon and water while I tried to figure my next move. Bron and I had checked the phone book and city directory for an "Apex" and found almost fifty of them, from Apex Diaper Service to an Apex Junk Yard, which was no help at all, though the cops would check. That lead was undoubtedly no good now that the blonde had warned Harrison. I was getting more and more anxious to find out what the score was, because this was sure shaping up like some kind of con, and I wasn't a bit happy about it.

The confidence man is, in many ways, the elite of the criminal world. Usually intelligent, personable, and more persuasive than Svengali, con-men would be the nicest guys in the world except for one thing: they have no conscience at all. I've run up against con-men before, and they're tricky and treacherous. One of my first clients was an Englishman who had been taken on the rag, a stock swindle, for $140,000. He'd tried to find the man, with no luck, then came to me; I didn't have any luck, either. But when he'd finally given up hope of ever seeing his money again, he'd said to me, of the grifter who had taken him, "I shall always remember him as an extrah-dn'rly chahming chap. He was a pleasant bahstahd." Then he'd paused, thought a bit, and added, "But, by God, he *was* a bahstahd!"

The Englishman was right. Confidence men are psychologists with diplomas from sad people: the suckers, the marks, that the con-boys have taken; and there's not a con-man worthy of the name who wouldn't take a starving widow's last penny or a bishop's last C-note, with never a twinge of remorse. They are the pleasant bastards, the con-men, and they thrive because they can make other men believe that opportunity is not only knocking but chopping the door down—and because of men's desire for a fast, even if dishonest, buck, or else the normal greed that's in most of us. They are the spellbinders, and ordinarily don't resort to violence, or go around shooting holes in people.

And it looked as if three of them, or at least two, were up against me. The other one, Pretty Boy Foster, was a bit violent, I remembered, and swung a mean sap. My head still throbbed. All three men, now that the blonde had told Harrison there was big trouble, would probably be making themselves scarce.

But there was still the girl. The gorgeous little gal with black hair and light blue eyes and the chrome-plated pistol. I thought back over what she'd said to me. There'd been a lot of gibberish about $24,000 and my being a crook and—something else. Something about Folsom's Market. It was worth a check. I looked the place up in the phone book, found it listed on Van Ness Avenue, finished my drink, and headed for Folsom's Market.

It was on Van Ness near Washington. I parked, went inside, and looked around. Just an ordinary small store; the usual groceries and a glass-faced meat counter extending the length of the left wall. The place was doing a good business. I walked to the single counter where a young red-haired girl about twenty was ringing up a customer's sales on the cash register, and when she'd finished I told her I wanted to speak with the manager. She smiled, then leaned forward to a small mike and said, "Mr. Gordon. Mr. Gordon, please."

In a few seconds a short man in a business suit, with a fleshy pink face and a slight potbelly walked up to me. I told him my name and business, showed him my credentials, then said, "Actually, Mr. Gordon, I don't know if you can help me or not. This morning I talked briefly with a young lady who seemed quite angry with me. She thought I was some kind of crook and mentioned this place, Folsom's Market. Perhaps you know her." I described the little doll, and she was easy enough to describe, particularly with the odd gray streak in her dark hair. That gal was burned into my memory and I remembered every lovely thing about her, but when I finished the manager shook his head.

"Don't remember anything like her around here," he said.

"She mentioned something about her father, and twenty-four thousand dollars. I don't—"

I stopped, because Mr. Gordon suddenly started chuckling. The cashier said, "Oh, it must be that poor old man."

The manager laughed. "This'll kill you," he said. "Some old foreigner about sixty years old came in here this morning, right at eight when we opened up. Said he just wanted to look his store over. *His* store, get that, Mr. Scott. Claimed he'd bought the place, and—this'll kill you—for twenty-four thousand dollars. Oh, boy, a hundred grand wouldn't half buy this spot."

He was laughing every third word. It had been very funny, he thought. Only it wasn't a bit funny to me, and I felt sick already. The way this deal was starting to figure, I didn't blame the little cutey for taking a few shots at me.

I said slowly, "Exactly what happened? What else did this . . . this foreigner do?"

The manager's potbelly shook a little. "Ah, he gawked around for a while, then I talked to the guy. I guess it must of taken me half an hour to convince him Mr. Borrage owns this place—you know Borrage, maybe, owns a dozen independent places like this, real rich fellow—anyway this stupid old guy swore he'd bought the place. For the money and his little grocery store. You imagine that? Finally I gave him Borrage's address and told him to beat it. Hell, I called Borrage, naturally. He got a chuckle out of it, too, when I told him."

Anger was beginning to flicker in me. "Who was this stupid old man?" I asked him.

He shrugged. "Hell, I don't know. I just told him finally to beat it. I couldn't have him hanging around here."

"No." I said. "Of course not. He was a foreigner, huh? You mean he wasn't an Indian?"

Mr. Gordon blinked at me, said, "Hey?" then described the man as well as he could. He told me he'd never seen the guy before, and walked away.

The cashier said softly, "It wasn't like that at all, Mr. Scott. And he left his name with me."

"Swell, honey. Can you give it to me?"

Her face was sober, unsmiling as she nodded. "I just hate that Mr. Gordon," she said. "The way it was, this little man came in early and just stood around, looking pleased and happy, kind of smiling all the time. I noticed he was watching me for a while, when I checked out the customers, then he came over to me and smiled. 'You're a fast worker,' he said to me. 'Very good worker, I'm watching you.' Then he told me I was going to be working for him, that he'd bought this place and was going to move in tomorrow." She frowned. "I didn't know any better. For all I knew, he might have bought the store. I wish he had." She glanced toward the back of the store where Mr. Gordon had gone. "He was a sweet little man."

"What finally happened?"

"Well, he kept standing around, then Mr. Gordon came up here and I asked him if the store had been sold. He went over and talked to the old man a while, started laughing, and talked some more. The old man got all excited and waved his arms around and started shouting. Finally Mr. Gordon got a little sharp—he's like that—and pointed to the door. In a minute the little guy came over to me and wrote his name and address down. He said there was some kind of mistake, but it would be straightened out. Then he left." She paused. "He looked like he was going to cry."

"I see. You got that name handy?"

"Uh-huh." She opened the cash register and took a slip of paper out of it. "He wanted us to be able to get in touch with him; he acted sort of dazed."

"He would have," I said. She handed me the note. On it, in a shaky, laboriously scrawled script, was written an address and: *Emil Elmlund, Elmlund's Neighborhood Grocery, Phone WI2-1258*.

"Use your phone?" I asked.

"Sure."

I dialed WI 2-1258. The phone rang several times, then a girl's voice answered, "Hello."

"Hello. Who is this, please?"

"This is Janet Elmlund."

That was what Pretty-Boy had called the girl in Pete's; Janet, and Jan. I said, "Is Mrs. McCurdy there?"

"McCurdy? I—you must have the wrong number."

I told her I wanted WI 2-1259, apologized, and hung up. I didn't want her to know I was coming out there. This time she might have a rifle. Then I thanked the cashier, went out to the Cad, and headed for Elmlund's Neighborhood Grocery.

It was a small store on a tree-lined street, the kind of "Neighborhood Grocery" you used to see a lot of in the days before supermarkets sprang up on every other corner. A sign on the door said, "Closed Today." A path had been worn in the grass alongside the store's right wall, leading to a small house in the rear. I walked along the path and paused momentarily before the house. It was white, neat, with green trim around the windows, a porch along its front. A man sat on the porch in a wooden chair, leaning forward, elbows on his knees, hands clasped. He was looking right at me as I walked toward him, but he didn't give any sign that he'd noticed me, and his face didn't change expression.

I walked up onto the porch. "Mr. Elmlund?"

He slowly raised his head and looked at me. He was a small man, with a lined brown face and very light blue eyes. Wisps of gray hair still clung to his head. He looked at me and blinked, then said, "Yes."

He looked away from me then, out into the yard again. It was as if I weren't there at all. And, actually, my presence probably didn't mean a thing to him. It was obvious that he had been taken in a confidence game, taken for $24,000 and maybe a dream. I couldn't know all of it yet, but I knew enough about how he must feel now, still shocked, dazed, probably not yet thinking at all.

I squatted beside him and said, "Mr. Elmlund, my name is Shell Scott."

For a minute nothing happened, then his eyebrows twitched, pulled down. Frowning, he looked at me. "What?" he said.

I heard the click of high heels, the front door was pushed open, and a girl stood there, holding a tray before her with two sandwiches on it. It was the same little lovely, black hair pulled back now and tied with a blue ribbon. She still wore the blue clam-diggers and the man's shirt.

I stood up fast. "Hold everything," I said to her. "Get this through your head—there's a guy in town about my size, with hair the same color as mine, and he's pretending to be me. He's taken my name, and he's used my office. But I never heard of you, or Mr. Elmlund, or Folsom's Market until this morning. Now don't throw any sandwiches at me and for Pete's sake don't start shooting."

She had been staring at me open-mouthed ever since she opened the door and spotted me. Finally her mouth came shut with a click and her hands dropped. The tray fell clattering to the porch and the sandwiches rolled almost to my feet. She stared at me for another half-minute without speaking, comprehension growing on her face, then she said, "Oh, no. Oh, no."

"Oh, yes," I said. "Now suppose we all sit down and get to the bottom of this mess."

She said. "Really? Please—you wouldn't—"

"I wouldn't." I showed her several different kinds of identification from my wallet, license, picture, even a fingerprint, and when I finished she was convinced. She blinked those startling blue eyes at me and said, "How awful. I'm so sorry. Can you ever forgive me?"

"Yes. Yes, indeed. Right now, I forgive you."

"You don't. You can't." For the first time since I'd seen her, she wasn't looking furious or shocked, and for the moment at least she seemed even to have forgotten about the money they'd lost. I had, I suppose, spoken with almost frantic eagerness, and now she lowered her head slightly and blinked dark lashes once, and her red lips curved ever so slightly in a soft smile. At that moment I could have forgiven her if she'd been cutting my throat with a hack saw. She said again, "You can't."

"Oh, yes, I can. Forget it. Could have happened to anybody."

She laughed softly, then her face sobered as she apparently remembered why I was here. I remembered, too, and started asking questions. Ten minutes later we were all sitting on the porch eating picnic sandwiches and drinking beer, and I had most of the story. Mr. Elmlund—a widower, and Janet's father—had run the store here for more than ten years, paid for it, saved $24,000. He was looking for a larger place and had been talking about this to a customer one day, a well-dressed man, smooth-talking, very tall, graying at the temples. The guy's name was William Klein, but he was also apparently my own Frank Harrison. It seemed Harrison was a real-estate broker and had casually mentioned that he'd let Mr. Elmlund know if he ran across anything that looked good.

Mr. Elmlund sipped his beer and kept talking. Elmlund said to me, "He seemed like a very nice man, friendly. Then when he come in and told me about this place it sounded good. He said this woman was selling the store because her husband had died not long ago. She was selling the store and everything and going back East, wasn't really much interested in making a lot of money out of it. She was rich, had a million dollars or more. She just wanted to get away fast, he said, and would sell for sixty-thousand cash. Well, I told him that was too much, but he asked me to look at it—that was Folsom's Market—maybe we could work a deal, he said. So the next Sunday we went there; I didn't think it would hurt none to look."

"Sunday? Was the store open?"

"No, it was closed, but he had a key. That seemed right because he was—he said he was agent for it. Well, it was just like I'd always wanted, a nice store. Nice market there, and plenty of room, good location—" He let the words trail off.

The rest of it was more of the same. The old con play; give the mark a glimpse of something he wants bad, then make him think he can have it for little or nothing, tighten the screws. A good con-man can tie up a mark so tight that normal reasoning powers go out the window. And getting a key which would open the store wouldn't have been any more trouble than getting the one which opened my office.

Last Sunday, a week after they'd looked over the store, Harrison had come to Elmlund all excited, saying the widow was anxious to sell and was going to advertise the store for sale in the local papers. If Elmlund wanted the place at a bargain price he'd have to act fast. Thursday—today, now—the ads would appear and the news would be all over town; right then only the widow, Harrison, and Elmlund himself knew about it. So went Harrison's story. After some more talk Harrison had asked how much cash Elmlund could scrape together. When Harrison learned $24,000 was tops, why naturally that was just enough cash—plus the deed to Elmlund's old store—to maybe swing a fast deal. All con-men are actors, expert at making their lines up as they go along, and Harrison must have made up the bit about throwing the deed in merely to make Elmlund think he was paying a more legitimate price; no well-played mark would think of wondering why a widow getting rid of one store so she could blow would take another as part payment.

Janet broke in, looking at me. "That was when Dad thought about having the transaction investigated. He talked to me about it and decided to see you, have you look into it. You see, he thought the sale was still secret, and you could check on it before the ads came out in the papers. And—he just couldn't believe it. He intended originally to invest only about ten thousand above what we'd get out of our store, but, well, it seemed like such a wonderful chance for him, for us. We were both a little suspicious, though."

"Uh-huh." I could see why Elmlund might want the deal checked, and I could even understand why he'd decided to see me instead of somebody else. The last six months I'd been mixed up in a couple cases that got splashed all over the newspapers, and my name was familiar to most of Los Angeles. But another bit puzzled me.

I said, "Janet, this morning in Pete's"—she made a face—"who was the man who charged in and yelled at you? Just as you were leaving."

"Man? I didn't see any man. I—lost my head." She smiled slightly. "I guess you know. And after—afterwards, I got scared and ran, just wanted to get away. I thought maybe I'd killed somebody."

"I thought maybe you had, myself."

She said. "I was almost crazy. Dad had just told me what had happened, and I was furious. And you'd told Dad everything was fine, that the transaction was on the level—I mean *he* had, the other Shell Scott—you know."

"Yeah. What about that?" I turned to Mr. Elmlund. "When did you see this egg in my office?" I already knew, but I wanted to be sure.

"At nine-thirty on Monday morning, this last Monday. I went in right at nine-thirty, there in the Hamilton Building, and talked to him. He said he'd investigate it for me. Then yesterday morning he came out to the store here and said it was all right. It cost me fifty dollars."

"Sure. That made the con more realistic. You'd have thought it was funny if you weren't soaked a little for the job."

He shrugged and said, "Then right after I talked yesterday to the detective—that one—he drove me and Janet from here to the real estate office, the Angelus Realty. Said he was going by there. Well, I stopped at the bank—those ads were supposed to come out in the papers today, you know—and got the money. Then at that office I gave him the money and signed all the papers and things and—that was all. I wasn't supposed to go to the store till tomorrow, but I couldn't wait."

Janet told me where the "real estate office" was, on Twelfth Street, but I knew that info was no help now. She said that this morning, before she'd come charging in at me, she'd first gone to the Angelus Realtors—probably planning to shoot holes in Harrison, though she didn't say so. But the place had been locked and she'd then come to the Hamilton Building. She remembered the sign. "Angelus Realtors" had still been painted on the door, but I knew, sign or no sign, that office would be empty.

I looked at Janet. "This guy I was talking about, the one in Pete's bar this A.M., was about five-ten, stocky; I suppose you'd say he was damned good looking. Black hair, even features."

"That sounds like Bob Foster. Cleft chin and brown eyes?"

"That's him. Did you meet him before or after this deal came up?"

"Bob? Why, you can't think he—"

"I can and do. I'm just wondering which way it was; did he set up the con, or did he come in afterwards."

"Why, I met Bob a month before the realtor showed up. Bob and I went out several times."

"Then dear Bob told him to come around, I imagine. I suppose Bob knew your father was thinking about a new store."

"Yes, but—"

"And after you and your father talked about hiring me to make sure the deal was square, did Bob happen to learn about it?"

"Why—he was here when we discussed it. He—" She stopped, eyes widening. "I'd forgotten it until now, but *Bob* suggested that Dad engage an investigator. When we told him we couldn't believe it, that there just had to be something wrong or dishonest about the sale for the price to be so low, *he* suggested we hire a detective to investigate the man and all the rest of it." She paused again. "He even suggested your name, asked us if we'd heard of you or met you. We hadn't met you, but of course we'd read about you in the papers, and told Bob so. He said he knew you, that you were capable and thoroughly honest—and he—made the appointment with you for nine-thirty Monday."

"Good old Bob," I said. "That made it perfect. That would get rid of the last of your doubts. Janet, Bob Foster is probably no more his right name than Harrison is a real estate dealer. The guy I know as Harrison, you know as Klein; his girl friend calls him John, and his real name is probably Willie Zilch. And I'm not getting these answers by voodoo. Harrison, Foster, and the guy who said he was Shell Scott all stay at the same hotel. They're a team, with so many fake names they sound like a community."

"But Bob—I thought he was interested in me. He was always nice."

"Yeah, pleasant. So you saw him a few times, and then he learned your dad was ripe for a swindle. He tipped Harrison, the inside-man, and they set up the play. The detective angle just tied it tighter. It was easy enough. A phone call to me to get me out of the office, another guy bleaches his hair, walks in, and waits for your dad to show, then kills a couple days and reports all's well."

It was quiet for a minute, then I said, "The thing I don't get is how he happened to show up at Pete's right after you did?"

Mr. Elmlund answered that one. "He and Jan were going on a picnic today. When I told her about—about losing my money she ran to the car and drove away. Right after, Bob come in and asked for Janet. I told him what happened. Said she mentioned going to see that Klein and you. Now I think of it, he got a funny look and run off to his car."

"I hate to say it, Janet," I said, "but Bob was probably less interested in the picnic—under the circumstances—than in finding out if everything was still under control."

I thought a minute. The white-haired egg had probably been planted outside waiting for me to leave; when I did, he went up to the office. Bob must have showed up and checked with Hazel, reached Pete's just as Janet started spraying bullets around, chased her but couldn't find her or else knew he'd better tip Whitey fast. So he'd charged to the office just in time to sap me. Something jarred my thoughts there. It bothered me but I couldn't figure out what it was.

I said, "Have you been to the police yet?"

Janet said, "No. We've been so—upset. We haven't done anything since I got back home."

"I'll take care of it, then." I got up. "That's about it, I guess. I'll try running the men down, but it's not likely they'll be easily found. I'll do what I can."

Janet had been sitting quietly, looking at me. Now she got up, took my hand, and pulled me after her into the front room of the house. Inside, she put a hand on my arm and said softly, "You know how sorry I am about this morning. I was a little crazy for a while there. But I want to thank you for coming out, saying you'll help."

"I'll be helping myself, too, Janet."

"I get sick when I think I might actually have shot you." She looked at the raw spot on my chin. "Did I—shoot you there?"

I grinned at her. "It might have been a piece of glass. I landed in some."

"Just a minute." She went away and came back with a bit of gauze and a piece of tape. She pressed it gently against the "wound," as she called it, her fingers cool and soft against my cheek. Her touch sent a tingle over my skin, a slight shiver between my shoulder blades. Then she stretched up and gently pressed her lips against my cheek.

"That better?"

It's funny; some women can leap into your lap, practically strangle you, mash their mouth all over you, kiss you with their lips and tongues and bodies, and leave you cold—I'm talking about *you* of course. But just the gentle touch of this gal's lips on my cheek turned my spine to spaghetti. That was the fastest fever I ever got; a thermometer in my mouth would have popped open and spouted mercury every which way.

I said, "Get your .22. I'm about to shoot myself full of holes."

She laughed softly, her arms going around my neck, then she started to pull herself up but my head was already on its way down, and when her lips met mine it was a new kind of shock. The blonde back there in the hotel room had been fairly enjoyable, but Janet had more sex and fire and hunger in just her lips than the blonde had in her entire stark body. When Jan's hands slid from my neck and she stepped back I automatically moved toward her, but she put a hand on my chest, smiling, glanced toward the porch, then took my arm and led me outside again.

When my breathing was reasonably normal I said, "Mr. Elmlund, I'm leaving now but if I get any news at all, I'll hurry back—I mean, ha, come back."

Janet chuckled. "Hurry's all right," she said.

Mr. Elmlund said, "Mr. Scott, if you can get our money again I'll pay you anything—half of it—"

"Forget that part. I don't want any money. If I should miraculously get it back, it's all yours."

He looked puzzled. "Why? Why should you help me?"

I said, "Actually, Mr. Elmlund, this is just as important to me. I don't like guys using my name to swindle people; I could get a very nasty reputation that way. Not to mention my dislike for being conned myself and getting hit over the head. For all I know there are guys named Shell Scott all over town, conning people, maybe shooting people. The con worked so well for these guys once, they'll probably try the same angles again—or would have if I hadn't walked in—on—" I stopped. That same idea jarred my thoughts as it had before when I'd been thinking about the guy in my office. It was so simple I should have had it long ago. But now a chill ran down my spine and I leaned toward Mr. Elmlund.

"You weren't supposed to see me—the detective—this morning, were you?"

"Why, no. Everything was finished, he already give me his report."

I didn't hear the rest of what he said. I was wondering why the hell Harrison had called me again, why Whitey had needed my office again, if not for Mr. Elmlund.

I swung toward Janet. "Where's your phone? Quick."

She blinked at me, then turned and went into the house. I followed, right on her heels.

"Show me. Hurry."

She pointed out the phone on a table and I grabbed it, dialed the Hamilton Building. There was just a chance—but it was already after noon.

Hazel came on. "This is Shell. Anyone looking for me?"

"Hi, Shell. How's your hangover—"

"This is important, hell with the hangover. Anybody there right after I took off?"

Her voice got brisk. "One man, about fifty, named Carl Strossmin. Said he had an appointment for nine-thirty."

"He say what about?"

"No. I took his name and address. Thirty-six, twenty-two Gramercy. Said he'd phone back; he hasn't called."

"Anything else?"

"That's all."

"Thanks." I hung up. I said aloud, "I'll be damned. They've got another mark."

Jan said, "What?" but I was running for the door. I leaped into the Cad, gunned the motor, and swung around in a U-turn. It was clear enough. Somewhere the boys had landed another sucker, and the "investigation" by Shell Scott had worked so well once that they must have used the gimmick again. They would still be around, but if they made this score they'd almost surely be off for Chicago, or Buenos Aires, or no telling where.

Carl Strossmin—I remembered hearing about him. He'd made a lot of money, most of it in deals barely this side of the law; he'd be the perfect mark because he was always looking for the best of it. Where Elmlund had thought he was merely getting an amazing piece of good fortune, Strossmin might well think he was throwing the blocks to somebody else. I didn't much like what I'd heard about Strossmin, but I liked not at all what I knew of Foster and Whitey and Harrison.

When I spotted the number I wanted on Gramercy I slammed on the brakes, jumped out, and ran up to the front door of 3622. I rang the bell and banged on the door until a middle-aged woman looked out at me, frowning.

"Say," she said. "What is the matter with you?"

"Mrs. Strossmin?"

"Yes."

"Your husband here?"

Her eyes narrowed. "No. Why? What do you want him for?"

I groaned. "He isn't closing any business deal, is he?"

Her eyes were slits now. "What are you interested for?" She looked me up and down. "They told us there were other people interested. You—"

"Lady, listen. He isn't buying a store, or an old locomotive or anything, is he?"

She pressed her lips together. "I don't think I'd better say anything till he gets back."

"That's fine," I said. "That's great. Because the nice businessmen are crooks. They're confidence men, thieves, they're wanted by police of seventy counties. Kiss your cabbage good-bye, lady—or else start telling me about it fast."

Her lips weren't pressed together anymore. They peeled apart like a couple of liver chunks. "Crooks?" she groaned. *"Crooks?"*

"Crooks, gyps, robbers, murderers. Lady, they're dishonest."

She let out a wavering scream and threw her hands in the air. "Crooks!" she wailed. "I told him they were crooks. Oh, I told the old fool, you can bet—!" She fainted.

I swore nastily, jerked the screen door open, and picked her up, then carried her to a couch. Finally she came out of it and blinked at me. She opened her mouth.

I said, "If you say 'crooks' once again I'll bat you. Now where the hell did your husband go?"

She started babbling, not one word understandable. But finally she got to her feet and started tottering around. "I wrote it down," she said. "I wrote it down. I wrote—"

"What did you write down?"

"Where he was going. The address." She threw up her hands. "Forty-one thousand dollars! Crooks! Forty-one—"

"Listen," I said. "He have that much money on him?"

"No. He had to go to the bank."

"What bank?" By the time she answered I'd already spotted the phone and was dialing. A bank clerk told me that Carl Strossmin had drawn $41,000 out of his account only half an hour ago. He'd been very excited, but he'd made no mention of what he wanted the money for. I hung up. I knew why Carl hadn't mentioned anything about it: it was a secret.

Mrs. Strossmin was still puttering around, pulling out drawers, and occasionally throwing her hands up into the air and screeching. Gradually I got her story and, with what I already knew, put the pieces together. Her husband's appointment with "Shell Scott" had been made two days ago by real estate dealer "Harrison" himself, here in Strossmin's home. After suggesting that since Strossmin seemed a bit undecided he might feel safer if he engaged a "completely honest" detective, Harrison had dialed a number, chatted a bit, and handed Strossmin the phone. Finally an appointment had been made for nine-thirty this A.M. Strossmin had been talking, of course, to Whitey who most likely was in a phone booth or bar.

Harrison probably wouldn't have suggested me *by name* to Strossmin, expecting the mark to accept his, the realtor's suggestion, except for one thing, which was itself important to the con: my reputation in L.A. A lot of people here believe I'm crazy, others think I'm stupid, and many, particularly old maids, are sure I'm a fiendish lecher; but there's never been any question about my being honest. This phase of the con was based on making Strossmin—and Elmlund before him—think he was really talking to me when he met Whitey, the Shell Scott of the con, in my office. However, when I popped back into the office and messed up that play this morning, the boys had to change their plans fast.

At eleven-thirty, about the time I was driving to Elmlund's, Whitey had come here to Strossmin's home, apologized for not being in his office when Strossmin had arrived this A.M., and said he'd come here to spare Strossmin another trip downtown. After learning what Strossmin wanted investigated, Whitey had pretended surprise and declared solemnly that this was a strange coincidence indeed, because Strossmin was the second man to ask for the identical investigation. Oh, yes, he'd already investigated—for this other eager buyer—and told him that the deal was on the level. No doubt about it, this was the opportunity of the century—and time, sad to say, was terribly short. Apparently, said Whitey, negotiations were going on with dozens of other people—and so on, until Strossmin had been in a frenzy of impatience.

Finally Mrs. Strossmin found her slip of paper and thrust it at me. An address was scribbled on it: Apex Realtors, 4870 Normandie Avenue. I grabbed the paper and ran to the Cad.

Apex Realtors was, logically enough, no more than an ordinary house with a sign in the window: Apex Realtors. When I reached it and parked, a small, well-dressed man with a thick mustache was just climbing into a new Buick at the curb. I ran from the Cad to his Buick and stopped him just as he started the engine.

"Mr. Strossmin?"

He was just like his wife. His eyes narrowed. "Yes."

I took a deep breath and blurted it out, "Did you just buy Folsom's Market?"

He grinned. "Beat you, didn't I? You're too late—"

"Shut up. You bought nothing but a headache. How many men inside there?"

About ready to flip, I yanked out my gun and pointed it at him. *"How many men in there?"*

I thought for a minute he was going to faint, too, but he managed to gasp, "Three."

I said, "You wait here," then turned and ran up to the house. The door was partly ajar, and I hit it and charged inside, the gun in my right hand. There wasn't anybody in sight, but another door straight ahead of me had a sign, "Office," on it. As I went through the door a car motor growled into life behind the house. I ran for the back, found a door standing wide open, and jumped through it just as a sky-blue Oldsmobile sedan parked in the alley took off fast. I barely got a glimpse of it, but I knew who was in it. The three con-men were powdering now that they had all the dough they were after. There was a chance they'd seen me, but it wasn't likely. Probably they'd grabbed the dough and left by the back way as soon as Strossmin stepped through the front door.

I race out front again and sprinted for the Cad, yelling to Strossmin, "Call the police!" He sat there, probably feeling pleased at the coup he'd just put over. He'd call the cops, next week, maybe. I ripped the Cad into gear and roared to the corner, took a right, and stepped on the gas. I had to slow at the next intersection, looked both directions and caught a flash of blue two blocks away on my right, swung in after them, and pushed the accelerator to the floorboards. I was gaining on them rapidly, and now I had a few seconds to try figuring out how to stop them. Up close I could see the Olds sedan, and the figures of three men inside it, two in the front seat and one in back. Con-men don't usually carry guns, but these guys operated a little differently from most con-men. In the first place they usually make the mark think he's in on a crooked deal, and in the second they almost always try to cool the mark out, allay his suspicions so he doesn't know, at least for a long time, that he's been taken. The boys ahead of me had broken both those rules, and there was a good chance they'd also broken the rule about guns.

But I was less than half a block behind them now and they apparently hadn't tumbled. They must figure they were in the clear, so I had surprise on my side. Well, I'd surprise them.

We were a long way from downtown here, but still in the residential section. I caught up with their car, pulled out on their left and slightly ahead, then as we reached an intersection I swung to my right, cutting them off just as I heard one of the men in the blue Olds yell loudly.

The driver did the instinctive thing, jerked his steering wheel to the right, and they went clear up over the curb and stalled on a green lawn before a small house. I was out of my Cad and running toward them, the Colt in my fist, before their car stopped moving twenty feet from me. And one of them *did* have a gun.

They sure as hell knew who I was by now, and I heard the gun crack. A slug snapped past me as I dived for the lawn, skidded a yard. Doors swung open on both sides of the blue Olds. Black-haired Pretty Boy jumped from the back and started running away from me, lugging a briefcase.

I got to my knees, and yelled, "Stop! Hold it or you get it, Foster."

He swung around, crouching, and light gleamed on the metal of a gun in his hand. He fired once at me and missed, and I didn't hold back any longer. I snapped the first shot from my .38, but I aimed the next two times, and he sagged slowly to his knees, then fell forward on his face.

Gray-haired Harrison was a few steps from the car, standing frozen, staring at Foster's body, but Whitey was fifty feet beyond him running like mad. I took out after him, but as I went by Harrison I let him have the full weight of my .38 on the back of his skull. I didn't even look back; he'd keep for a while.

I jammed my gun into its holster and sprinted down the sidewalk, Whitey half a block ahead but losing ground. He wasn't in very good shape, apparently, and after a single block he was damn near staggering. He heard my feet splatting on the pavement behind him and for a moment he held his few yards' advantage, then he slowed again. He must have known I had him; because he stopped and whirled around to face me, ready to go down fighting.

He went down, all right, but not fighting. When he stopped I had been less than ten feet from him, traveling like a fiend, and he spun around just in time to connect his face with my right fist. I must have started the blow from six feet away, just as he began turning, and what with my speed from running, and the force of the blow itself, my fist must have been traveling fifty miles an hour.

It was awful what I did to him. I caught only a flashing glimpse of his face as he swung around, lips peeled back and hands coming up, and then my knuckles landed squarely on his mouth and his lips really peeled back and he started going the same direction I was going and almost as fast. I ran several steps past him before I could stop, but when I turned around he was practically behind me and there was a thin streak of blood for two yards on the sidewalk. He was all crumpled up, out cold, and for a minute I thought he was out for good. But I felt for his heartbeat and found it.

So I squatted by him and waited. Before he came out of it, a little crowd gathered: half a dozen kids and some housewives, one young guy about thirty who came running from half a block away. I told him to call the cops and he phoned. Whitey was still out when the guy came back and said a car was on its way.

Finally Whitey stirred, moaned. I looked around and said to the women, "Get the kids out of here. And maybe you better not stick around yourselves."

The women frowned, shifted uneasily, but they shooed the kids away. Whitey shook his head. Finally he was able to sit up. His face wasn't pretty at all. I grabbed his coat and pulled him close to me.

I said, "Shell Scott, huh? I hear you're a tough baby. Get up, friend."

I stood up and watched him while he got his feet under him. It took him a while, and all the time he didn't say a word. I suppose the decent thing would have been to let him get all the way up, but I didn't wait. When he was halfway up I balled my left fist and slammed it under his chin. It straightened him just enough so I could set myself solidly, and get him good with my right fist. It landed where I wanted it to, on his nose, and he left us for a while longer. He fell onto the grass on his back, and perhaps he had looked a bit like me at one time, but he didn't anymore.

The guy who had called the cops helped me carry Whitey back to the blue Oldsmobile. We dumped him and Harrison inside and I climbed in back with them—and with the briefcase—while he went out to the curb and waited for a prowl car. I got busy. When I finished, these three boys had very little money in their wallets and none was in the briefcase. It added up to $67,500. There was Elmlund's $24,000, I figured, plus Strossmin's $41,000, plus my $2,500. I lit a cigarette and waited for the cops.

It was two P.M. before I got away. Both cops in the patrol car were men I knew well; Borden and Lane. Lane and I especially were good friends. I gave my story and my angles to Lane, and finally he went along with what I wanted.

I finished it with, "This Strossmin is still so wound up by these guys he'll probably figure it out about next week, but when he does, he should have a good witness. No reason why Elmlund can't be left out of it."

Lane shook his head and rubbed a heavy chin where bristles were already sprouting. "Well . . . if this Strossmin doesn't come through in court, we'll need Elmlund."

"You'll get him. Besides, I'll be in court, remember. Enjoying myself."

He nodded. "O.K., Shell."

I handed him the briefcase with $41,000 inside it, told him I'd come to headquarters later, and took off. I'd given Lane the address where I'd left Strossmin, as well as his home address, but Strossmin hadn't waited. I drove to his house.

I could hear them going at it hammer and tongs. Mrs. Strossmin didn't even stop when I rang the bell, but finally her husband opened the door. He just stood there glowering at me. "Well?" he said.

"I just wanted to let you know, Mr. Strossmin, that the police have caught the men who tricked you."

I was going on, but he said, "Trick me? Nobody tricked me. *You're* trying to trick me."

"Look, mister, I just want you to know your money's safe. The cops have it. My name is Shell Scott—"

"Ha!" he said. "It is, hey? No, it's not, that's not your name, can't fool me. You're a crook, that's what you are."

His wife was in the door.

She screeched in his ear, "What did I say? Old fool, I warned you."

"Mattie," he said. "If you don't sit down and shut up—"

I tried some more, but he just wouldn't believe me. A glowing vision could have appeared in the sky crying, "You been tricked, Strossmin!" and the guy wouldn't have believed it. There are marks like him, who beg to be taken.

So finally I said, "Well, you win."

"What?"

"You win. Nothing I can do about it now. Store's yours." I put on a hangdog look. He cackled.

I said, "You can take over the place today, you know. Well, good-bye—and the better man won."

"Today?"

"Yep. Folsom's Market, isn't it?"

"Yes, yes."

"Well, you go right down there. Ask for Mr. Gordon."

"Mr. Gordon?"

"Yep." I shook his hand. He cackled, and Mrs. Strossmin screeched at him, and he told her to shut up and I left. They were still going at it as I drove away to the Elmlunds.

Mr. Elmlund didn't quite know what to do when I dropped the big packet of bills on his table and said the hoods were in the clink. He stared at the money for a long time. When finally he did speak it was just, "I don't know what to say."

Jan came out onto the porch and I told them what happened and I thought they were going to crack up for a while, and then I thought they were going to float off over the trees, but finally Mr. Elmlund said, "I must pay you, Mr. Scott. I must."

I said, "No. Besides I got paid."

Jan was leaning against the side of the door, smiling at me. She'd changed clothes and was wearing a smooth, clinging print dress now, and the way she looked I really should have had on dark glasses. She looked happy, wonderful, and her light blue eyes were half-lidded, her gaze on my mouth.

"No," she said. "You haven't been paid."

Her tongue traced a smooth, gleaming line over her lower lip, and I remembered her fingers on my cheek, her lips against my skin.

"You haven't been paid, Shell."

I had a hunch she was right.

JOHN LUTZ

When John Lutz (1939–) won the Edgar for best short story, a number of critics pointed out that such recognition was long overdue. Whether writing his Fred Carver or Alo Nudger books—or his suspense novels, one of which, *SWF Seeks Same*, was the basis for the hit movie *Single White Female*—Lutz brings to the noir school of writing a sympathy for the average man rarely seen in contemporary fiction of any kind.

Lutz knows how most of us live and manages to give engaging (and sometimes sad, sometimes violent) portraits of life lived here in the cities and suburbs of the United States at the start of the new millennium. Novels such as *The Ex*, recently produced as a made-for-cable movie, illustrate how characters and situations, in his skillful hands, can come back to haunt you.

His quiet, elegant prose stays with you far longer than the bestseller bombast so much in fashion these days.

The Real Shape of the Coast

Where the slender peninsula crooks like a beckoning finger in the warm water, where the ocean waves crash in umbrellas of foam over the low-lying rocks to roll and ebb on the narrow white-sand beaches, there squats in a series of low rectangular buildings and patterns of high fences the State Institution for the Criminal Incurably Insane. There are twenty of the sharp-angled buildings, each rising bricked and hard out of sandy soil like an undeniable fact. Around each building is a ten-foot redwood fence topped by barbed wire, and these fences run to the sea's edge to continue as gossamer networks of barbed wire that stretch out to the rocks.

In each of the rectangular buildings live six men, and on days when the ocean is suitable for swimming it is part of their daily habit—indeed, part of their therapy—to go down to the beach and let the waves roll over them, or simply to lie in the purging sun and grow beautifully tan. Sometimes, just out of the grasping reach of the waves, the men might build things in the damp sand, but by evening those things would be gone. However, some very interesting things had been built in the sand.

The men in the rectangular buildings were not just marking time until their real death. In fact, the "Incurably Insane" in the institution's name was something of a misnomer; it was just that there was an absolute minimum of hope for these men. They lived in clusters of six not only for security's sake, but so that they might form a more or less permanent sensitivity group—day-in, day-out group therapy, with occasional informal gatherings supervised by young Dr. Montaign. Here under the subtle and skillful probings of Dr. Montaign the men bared their lost souls—at least, some of them did.

Cottage D was soon to be the subject of Dr. Montaign's acute interest. In fact, he was to study the occurrences there for the next year and write a series of articles to be published in influential scientific journals.

The first sign that there was something wrong at Cottage D was when one of the patients, a Mr. Rolt, was found dead on the beach one evening. He was lying on his back near the water's edge, wearing only a pair of khaki trousers. At first glance it would seem that he'd had a drowning accident, only his mouth and much of his throat turned out to be stuffed with sand and with a myriad of tiny colorful shells.

Roger Logan, who had lived in Cottage D since being found guilty of murdering his wife three years before, sat quietly watching Dr. Montaign pace the room.

"This simply won't do," the doctor was saying. "One of you has done away with Mr. Rolt, and that is exactly the sort of thing we are in here to stop."

"But it won't be investigated too thoroughly, will it?" Logan said softly. "Like when a convicted murderer is killed in a prison."

"May I remind you," a patient named Kneehoff said in his clipped voice, "that Mr. Rolt was not a murderer." Kneehoff had been a successful businessman before his confinement, and now he made excellent leather wallets and sold them by mail order. He sat now at a small table with some old letters spread before him, as if he were a chairman of the board presiding over a meeting. "I might add," he said haughtily, "that it's difficult to conduct business in an atmosphere such as this."

"I didn't say Rolt was a murderer," Logan said, "but he is—was—supposed to be in here for the rest of his life. That fact is bound to impede justice."

Kneehoff shrugged and shuffled through his letters. "He was a man of little consequence—that is, compared to the heads of giant corporations."

It was true that Mr. Rolt had been a butcher rather than a captain of industry, a butcher who had put things in the meat—some of them unmentionable. But then Kneehoff had merely run a chain of three dry-cleaning establishments.

"Perhaps you thought him inconsequential enough to murder," William Sloan, who was in for pushing his young daughter out of a fortieth-story window, said to Kneehoff. "You never did like Mr. Rolt."

Kneehoff began to splutter. "You're the killer here, Sloan! You and Logan!"

"I killed no one," Logan said quickly.

Kneehoff grinned. "You were proved guilty in a court of law—of killing your wife."

"They didn't prove it to me. I should know whether or not I'm guilty!"

"I know your case," Kneehoff said gazing dispassionately at his old letters. "You hit your wife over the head with a bottle of French Chablis wine, killing her immediately."

"I warn you," Logan said heatedly, "implying that I struck my wife with a wine bottle—and French Chablis at that—is inviting a libel suit!"

Noticeably shaken, Kneehoff became quiet and seemed to lose himself in studying the papers before him. Logan had learned long ago how to deal with him; he knew that Kneehoff's "company" could not stand a lawsuit.

"Justice must be done," Logan went on. "Mr. Rolt's murderer, a real murderer, must be caught and executed."

"Isn't that a job for the police?" Dr. Montaign asked gently.

"The police!" Logan laughed. "Look how they botched my case! No, this is a job for *us*. Living the rest of our lives with a murderer would be intolerable."

"But what about Mr. Sloan?" Dr. Montaign asked. "You're living with him."

"His is a different case," Logan snapped. "Because they found him guilty doesn't mean he is guilty. He says he doesn't remember anything about it, doesn't he?"

"What's your angle?" Brandon, the unsuccessful mystery bomber, asked. "You people have always got an angle, something in mind for yourselves. The only people you can really trust are the poor people."

"My angle is justice," Logan said firmly. "We must have justice!"

"Justice for all the people!" Brandon suddenly shouted, rising to his feet. He glanced about angrily and then sat down again.

"Justice," said old Mr. Heimer, who had been to other worlds and could listen to and hear metal, "will take care of itself. It always does, no matter where."

"They've been waiting a long time," Brandon said, his jaw jutting out beneath his dark mustache. "The poor people, I mean."

"Have the police any clues?" Logan asked Dr. Montaign.

"They know what you know," the doctor said calmly. "Mr. Rolt was killed on the beach between nine-fifteen and ten—when he shouldn't have been out of Cottage D."

Mr. Heimer raised a thin speckled hand to his lips and chuckled feebly. "Now, maybe that's justice."

"You know the penalty for leaving the building during unauthorized hours," Kneehoff said sternly to Mr. Heimer. "Not death, but confinement to your room for two days. We must have the punishment fit the crime and we must obey the rules. Any operation must have rules in order to be successful."

"That's exactly what I'm saying," Logan said. "The man who killed poor Mr. Rolt must be caught and put to death."

"The authorities are investigating," Dr. Montaign said soothingly.

"Like they investigated my case?" Logan said in a raised and angry voice. "They won't bring the criminal to justice! And I tell you we must not have a murderer here in Compound D!"

"Cottage D," Dr. Montaign corrected him.

"Perhaps Mr. Rolt was killed by something from the sea," William Sloan said thoughtfully.

"No," Brandon said, "I heard the police say there was only a single set of footprints near the body and it led from and to the cottage. It's obviously the work of an inside subversive."

"But what size footprints?" Logan asked.

"They weren't clear enough to determine the size," Dr. Montaign said. "They led to and from near the wooden stairs that come up to the rear yard, then the ground was too hard for footprints."

"Perhaps they were Mr. Rolt's own footprints," Sloan said.

Kneehoff grunted. "Stupid! Mr. Rolt went to the beach, but he did not come back."

"Well—" Dr. Montaign rose slowly and walked to the door. "I must be going to some of the other cottages now." He smiled at Logan. "It's interesting that you're so concerned with justice," he said. A gull screamed as the doctor went out.

The five remaining patients of Cottage D sat quietly after Dr. Montaign's exit. Logan watched Kneehoff gather up his letters and give their edges a neat sharp tap on the table top before slipping them into his shirt pocket. Brandon and Mr. Heimer seemed to be in deep thought, while Sloan was peering over Kneehoff's shoulder through the open window out to the rolling sea.

"It could be that none of us is safe," Logan said suddenly. "We must get to the bottom of this ourselves."

"But we are at the bottom," Mr. Heimer said pleasantly, "all of us."

Kneehoff snorted. "Speak for yourself, old man."

"It's the crime against the poor people that should be investigated," Brandon said. "If my bomb in the Statue of Liberty had gone off . . . And I used my whole week's vacation that year going to New York."

"We'll conduct our own investigation," Logan insisted, "and we might as well start now. Everyone tell me what he knows about Mr. Rolt's murder."

"Who put you in charge?" Kneehoff asked. "And why should we investigate Rolt's murder?"

"Mr. Rolt was our friend," Sloan said.

"Anyway," Logan said, "we must have an orderly investigation. Somebody has to be in charge."

"I suppose you're right," Kneehoff said. "Yes, an orderly investigation."

Information was exchanged, and it was determined that Mr. Rolt had said he was going to bed at nine-fifteen, saying good night to Ollie, the attendant, in the TV lounge. Sloan and Brandon, the two other men in the lounge, remembered the time because the halfway commercial for "Monsters of Main Street" was on, the one where the box of detergent soars through the air and snatches everyone's shirt. Then at ten o'clock, just when the news was coming on, Ollie had gone to check the beach and discovered Mr. Rolt's body.

"So," Logan said, "the approximate time of death has been established. And I was in my room with the door open. I doubt if Mr. Rolt could have passed in the hall to go outdoors without my noticing him, so we must hypothesize that he did go to his room at nine-fifteen, and sometime between nine-fifteen and ten he left through his window."

"He knew the rules," Kneehoff said. "He wouldn't have just walked outside for everyone to see him."

"True," Logan conceded, "but it's best not to take anything for granted."

"True, true," Mr. Heimer chuckled, "take nothing for granted."

"And where were *you* between nine and ten?" Logan asked.

"I was in Dr. Montaign's office," Mr. Heimer said with a grin, "talking to the doctor about something I'd heard in the steel utility pole. I almost made him understand that all things metal are receivers, tuned to different frequencies, different worlds and vibrations."

Kneehoff, who had once held two of his accountants prisoner for five days without food, laughed.

"And where were *you?*" Logan asked.

"In my office, going over my leather-goods vouchers," Kneehoff said. Kneehoff's "office" was his room, toward the opposite end of the hall from Logan's room.

"Now," Logan said, "we get to the matter of motive. Which of us had reason to kill Mr. Rolt?"

"I don't know," Sloan said distantly. "Who'd do such a thing—fill Mr. Rolt's mouth with sand?"

"You were his closest acquaintance," Brandon said to Logan. "You always played chess with him. Who knows what you and he were plotting?"

"What about you?" Kneehoff said to Brandon. "You tried to choke Mr. Rolt just last week."

Brandon stood up angrily, his mustache bristling. "That was the week *before* last!" He turned to Logan. "And Rolt always beat Logan at chess—that's why Logan hated him."

"He didn't *always* beat me at chess," Logan said. "And I didn't hate him. The only reason he beat me at chess sometimes was because he'd upset the board if he was losing."

"You don't like to get beat at anything," Brandon said, sitting down again. "That's why you killed your wife, because she beat you at things. How middle class, to kill someone because of that."

"I didn't kill my wife," Logan said patiently. "And she didn't beat me at things. Though she was a pretty good businesswoman," he added slowly, "and a good tennis player."

"What about Kneehoff?" Sloan asked. "He was always threatening to kill Mr. Rolt."

"Because he laughed at me!" Kneehoff spat out. "Rolt was a braggart and a fool, always laughing at me because I have ambition and he didn't. He thought he was better at everything than anybody else—and you, Sloan—Rolt used to ridicule you and Heimer. There isn't one of us who didn't have a motive to eliminate a piece of scum like Rolt."

Logan was on his feet, almost screaming. "I won't have you talk about the dead like that!"

"All I was saying," Kneehoff said, smiling his superior smile at having upset Logan, "was that it won't be easy for you to discover Rolt's murderer. He was a clever man, that murderer, cleverer than you."

Logan refused to be baited. "We'll see about that when I check the alibis," he muttered, and he left the room to walk barefoot in the surf.

On the beach the next day Sloan asked the question they had all been wondering.

"What are we going to do with the murderer if we do catch him?" he asked, his eyes fixed on a distant ship that was just an irregularity on the horizon.

"We'll extract justice," Logan said. "We'll convict and execute him—eliminate him from our society!"

"Do you think we should?" Sloan asked.

"Of course we should!" Logan snapped. "The authorities don't care who killed Mr. Rolt. The authorities are probably glad he's dead."

"I don't agree that it's a sound move," Kneehoff said, "to execute the man. I move that we don't do that."

"I don't hear anyone seconding you," Logan said. "It has to be the way I say if we are to maintain order here."

Kneehoff thought a moment, then smiled. "I agree we must maintain order at all costs," he said. "I withdraw my motion."

"Motion, hell!" Brandon said. He spat into the sand. "We ought to just find out who the killer is and liquidate him. No time for a motion—time for action!"

"Mr. Rolt would approve of that," Sloan said, letting a handful of sand run through his fingers.

Ollie the attendant came down to the beach and stood there smiling, the sea breeze rippling his white uniform. The group on the beach broke up slowly and casually, each man idling away in a different direction.

Kicking the sun-warmed sand with his bare toes, Logan approached Ollie.

"Game of chess, Mr. Logan?" Ollie asked.

"Thanks, no," Logan said. "You found Mr. Rolt's body, didn't you, Ollie?"

"Right, Mr. Logan."

"Mr. Rolt was probably killed while you and Sloan and Brandon were watching TV."

"Probably," Ollie agreed, his big face impassive.

"How come you left at ten o'clock to go down to the beach?"

Ollie turned to stare blankly at Logan with his flat eyes. "You know I always check the beach at night, Mr. Logan. Sometimes the patients lose things."

"Mr. Rolt sure lost something," Logan said. "Did the police ask you if Brandon and Sloan were in the TV room with you the whole time before the murder?"

"They did and I told them yes." Ollie lit a cigarette with one of those transparent lighters that had a fishing fly in the fluid. "You studying to be a detective, Mr. Logan?"

"No, no," Logan laughed. "I'm just interested in how the police work, after the way they messed up my case. Once they thought I was guilty I didn't have a chance."

But Ollie was no longer listening. He had turned to look out at the ocean. "Don't go out too far, Mr. Kneehoff!" he called, but Kneehoff pretended not to hear and began moving in the water parallel with the beach.

Logan walked away to join Mr. Heimer who was standing in the surf with his pants rolled above his knees.

"Find out anything from Ollie?" Mr. Heimer asked, his body balancing slightly as the retreating sea pulled the sand and shells from beneath him.

"Some things," Logan said, crossing his arms and enjoying the play of the cool surf about his legs. The two men—rather than the ocean—seemed to be moving as the tide swept in and out and shifted the sand beneath the sensitive soles of their bare feet. "It's like the ocean," Logan said, "finding out who killed Mr. Rolt. The ocean works and works on the shore, washing in and out until only the sand and rock remain—the real shape of the coast. Wash the soil away and you have bare rock; wash the lies away and you have bare truth."

"Not many can endure the truth," Mr. Heimer said, stooping to let his hand drag in an incoming wave, "even in other worlds."

Logan raised his shoulders. "Not many ever learn the truth," he said, turning and walking through the wet sand toward the beach. Amid the onwash of the wide shallow wave he seemed to be moving backward, out to sea . . .

Two days later Logan talked to Dr. Montaign, catching him alone in the TV lounge when the doctor dropped by for one of his midday visits. The room was very quiet; even the ticking of the clock seemed slow, lazy, and out of rhythm.

"I was wondering, doctor," Logan said, "about the night of Mr. Rolt's murder. Did Mr. Heimer stay very late in your office?"

"The police asked me that," Dr. Montaign said with a smile. "Mr. Heimer was in my office until ten o'clock, then I saw him come into this room and join Brandon and Sloan to watch the news."

"Was Kneehoff with them?"

"Yes, Kneehoff was in his room."

"I was in my room," Logan said, "with my door open to the hall, and I didn't see Mr. Rolt pass to go outdoors. So he must have gone out through his window. Maybe the police would like to know that."

"I'll tell them for you," Dr. Montaign said, "but they know Mr. Rolt went out through his window because his only door was locked from the inside." The doctor cocked his head at Logan, as was his habit. "I wouldn't try to be a detective," he said gently. He placed a smoothly manicured hand on Logan's shoulder. "My advice is to forget about Mr. Rolt."

"Like the police?" Logan said.

The hand patted Logan's shoulder soothingly.

After the doctor had left, Logan sat on the cool vinyl sofa and thought. Brandon, Sloan and Heimer were accounted for, and Kneehoff couldn't have left the building without Logan seeing him pass in the hall. The two men, murderer and victim, might have left together through Mr. Rolt's window—only that wouldn't explain the single set of fresh footprints to and from the body. And the police had found Mr. Rolt's footprints where he'd gone down to the beach farther from the cottage and then apparently walked up the beach through the surf to where his path and the path of the murderer crossed.

And then Logan saw the only remaining possibility—the only possible answer.

Ollie, the man who had discovered the body—Ollie alone had had the opportunity to kill! And after doing away with Mr. Rolt he must have noticed his footprints leading to and from the body; so at the wooden stairs he simply turned and walked back to the sea in another direction, then walked up the beach to make his "discovery" and alert the doctor.

Motive? Logan smiled. Anyone could have had motive enough to kill the bragging and offensive Mr. Rolt. He had been an easy man to hate.

Logan left the TV room to join the other patients on the beach, careful not to glance at the distant white-uniformed figure of Ollie painting some deck chairs at the other end of the building.

"Tonight," Logan told them dramatically, "we'll meet in the conference room after Dr. Montaign leaves and I promise to tell you who the murderer is. Then we'll decide how best to remove him from our midst."

"Only if he's guilty," Kneehoff said. "You must present convincing, positive evidence."

"I have proof," Logan said.

"Power to the people!" Brandon cried, leaping to his feet.

Laughing and shouting, they all ran like schoolboys into the waves.

The patients sat through their evening session with Dr. Montaign, answering questions mechanically and chattering irrelevantly, and Dr. Montaign sensed a certain tenseness and expectancy in them. Why were they anxious? Was it fear? Had Logan been harping to them about the murder? Why was Kneehoff not looking at his letters, and Sloan not gazing out the window?

"I told the police," Dr. Montaign mentioned, "that I didn't expect to walk up on any more bodies on the beach."

"You?" Logan stiffened in his chair. "I thought it was Ollie who found Mr. Rolt."

"He did, really," Dr. Montaign said, cocking his head. "After Mr. Heimer left me I accompanied Ollie to check the beach so I could talk to him about some things. He was the one who saw the body first and ran ahead to find out what it was."

"And it was Mr. Rolt, his mouth stuffed with sand," Sloan murmured.

Logan's head seemed to be whirling. He had been so sure! Process of elimination. It had to be Ollie! Or were the two men, Ollie and Dr. Montaign, in it together? They had to be! But that was impossible! There had been only one set of footprints.

Kneehoff! It must have been Kneehoff all along! He must have made a secret appointment with Rolt on the beach and killed him. But Rolt had been walking alone until he met the killer, who was also alone! And *someone* had left the fresh footprints, the single set of footprints, to and from the body.

Kneehoff must have seen Rolt, slipped out through his window, intercepted him, and killed him. But Kneehoff's room didn't have a window! Only the two end rooms had windows, Rolt's room and Logan's room!

A single set of footprints—they could only be his own! *His own!*

Through a haze Logan saw Dr. Montaign glance at his watch, smile, say his good-byes and leave. The night breeze wafted through the wide open windows of the conference room with the hushing of the surf, the surf wearing away the land to bare rock.

"Now," Kneehoff said to Logan, and the moon seemed to light his eyes, "who exactly is our man? Who killed Mr. Rolt? And what is your evidence?"

Ollie found Logan's body the next morning, face down on the beach, the gentle lapping surf trying to claim him. Logan's head was turned and half buried and his broken limbs were twisted at strange angles, and around him the damp sand was beaten with, in addition to his own, four different sets of footprints.

EVAN HUNTER

There are careers and then there are careers.

Consider these facts: Evan Hunter (1926–), the same man who wrote *The Blackboard Jungle*, a serious novel about juvenile delinquency that had a seminal effect on the popular culture of the 1950s, also wrote the screenplay for *The Birds*, which of course was filmed by Alfred Hitchcock. Under the name Ed McBain, he also wrote (and is still writing) one of the most popular detective series of all time, the police procedurals known as the 87th Precinct books.

Whether you read him as Evan Hunter or Ed McBain, you are reading one of the most skilled storytellers of our time. And that time, in Hunter-McBain years, now spans better than fifty years of not only writing, but staying on the cutting edge.

With all this activity, you might not think that he'd have time to develop his talents as a short story writer. But he's one of the best with the shorter form, too, his range of style, mood, and form showing him to be every bit the virtuoso that he is with novels.

Here is "Curt Cannon" (the byline he used on this story when it first appeared) at his cleverest and most hard-boiled. There were two Cannon books, if you care to read more: a collection of short stories called *I Like 'Em Tough*, and a novel about the same gumshoe, *I'm Cannon—for Hire*. This tale of Hunter's down-and-out dick was adapted for the 1958 *Mike Hammer* TV series starring McGavin.

Dead Men Don't Dream

The old neighborhood hadn't changed much. I was standing near the window in Charlie Dagerra's bedroom looking out at the tenements stretched across the cold winter sky like a gray smear. There was no sun.

The day was cold and gloomy and somehow forbidding, and that was as it should be because Charlie Dagerra lay in a casket in the living room.

The undertaker had skillfully adjusted Charlie's collar so that most of the knife slash across his neck was covered. He'd disguised the rest with heavy make-up and soft lights, but everyone knew what lay under the make-up. Everyone knew, and no one was talking about it.

They passed the bottle, and I poured myself a stiff hooker. Charlie and I had been kids together, hitching rides on the trolley that used to run along First Avenue. That was a long time ago, though, and I hadn't seen Charlie since long before I'd lost my license. I probably would never have seen Charlie again, dead or alive, if I hadn't run into The Moose down on Fourteenth Street. He'd told me about Charlie, and asked me to come pay my respects. He didn't mention the fact that I had a three-day growth on my face or that my eyes were rimmed with red. His glance had traveled briefly over my rumpled suit. He ignored all that and asked me to come pay my respects to a dead childhood friend, and I'd accepted.

"So how you been?" The Moose asked now. He was holding a shot glass between two thin fingers. The Moose is a very small man, his hair thinning in an oval on the back of his head. He'd been a small kid, too, which was why we tagged him with a virile nickname.

"So-so," I told him. I tossed off the drink and held out my glass. One of Charlie's relatives filled it, and I nodded my thanks.

"I read all about it in the paper," The Moose said.

"Oh?"

"Yeah." The Moose shook his head sadly. "She was a bitch, Curt," he said. "You should have killed that guy."

He was talking about my wife Toni. He was referring to the night I'd found her in my own bedroom, after four months of crazy-in-love marriage, with a son of a bitch named Parker. He was recalling the vivid newspaper accounts of how I'd worked Parker over with the butt end of my .45, of how the police had tagged me with an ADW charge—assault with a deadly weapon. They'd gotten my license, and Parker had gotten my wife, but not until I'd ripped a trench down the side of his face and knocked half his goddam teeth out.

"You should have killed him," The Moose repeated.

"I tried to, Moose. I tried damn hard." I didn't like remembering it. I'd been putting in a lot of time forgetting. Whisky helps in that category.

"The good ones die," he said, shaking his head, "and the bad ones keep living." He looked toward the living room, where the flowers were stacked on either side of the coffin. I looked there, too, and I saw Charlie's mother weeping softly, a big Italian woman in a black dress.

"What happened?" I asked. "Who gave Charlie the knife slash?"

The Moose kept nodding his head as if he hadn't heard me. I looked at him over the edge of my glass, and finally his eyes met mine. They were veiled, clouded with something nameless.

"What happened?" I asked again.

The Moose blinked, and I knew what the something nameless was then. Fear. Cold, stark, unreasoning fear.

"I don't know," he said. "They found him outside his store. He ran a tailor shop, you know. You remember Charlie's father, don't you, Curt? Old Joe Dagerra? When Joe died, Charlie took over the shop."

"Yeah," I said. The whisky was running out, and the tears were running in all over the place. It was time to go. "Moose," I said, "I got to be running. I want to say good-by to the old lady, and then I'll be . . ."

"Sure, Curt. Thanks for coming up. Charlie would have appreciated it."

I left The Moose in the bedroom and said good-by to Mrs. Dagerra. She didn't remember me, of course, but she took my hand and held it tightly. I was a friend of her dead son, and she wanted to hold everything he'd known and loved for as long as she could. I stopped by the coffin, knelt, and wished Charlie well. He'd never harmed a fly as far as I could remember, and he deserved a soft journey and maybe a harp and a halo or whatever they gave them nowadays.

I got to my feet and walked to the door, and another of Charlie's relatives said, "He looks like he's sleeping, doesn't he?"

I looked at the coffin and at the red, stitched gash on Charlie's neck where it was already beginning to show through the make-up. I felt sick all of a sudden. "No," I said harshly. "He looks dead."

Then I went downstairs.

The neighborhood looked almost the same, but not quite. There was still the candy store huddling close to the building on the left, and the bicycle rental shop on the right. The iceman's wagon was parked in the gutter, and I remembered the time I'd nearly smashed my hand fooling with the wagon, tilting it until a sliding piece of ice sent the wagon veering to the gutter, pinning my hand under the handle. I'd lost a nail, and it had been tragic at the time. It got a smile from me now. The big white apartment house was across the street, looking worn and a little tired now. The neighborhood had changed from Italian-Irish to Italian-Irish-Puerto Rican. It was the same neighborhood, but different.

I shrugged and walked into the candy store. The guy behind the counter looked up when I came in, squinting at my unfamiliar face.

"Pall Mall," I said. I fished in my pocket for change, and his eyes kept studying me, looking over my clothes and my face. I knew I was no Mona Lisa, but I didn't like the guy's scrutiny.

"What's with you?" I snapped.

"Huh? I . . ."

"Give me the goddam cigarettes and cut the third degree."

"Yes, sir. I . . . I'm sorry, sir."

I looked into his eyes and saw the same fear that had been on Moose's face. And then I recalled that the guy had just called me "sir." Now who the hell would call a bum "sir"? He put the cigarettes on the counter and I shoved a fifty-cent piece at him. He smiled thinly and pushed the coin back at me. I looked at it and back into his eyes. In the days when I'd been a licensed private eye, I'd seen fear on a lot of faces. I got so I could smell fear. I could smell it now, and the odor was overpowering.

I pushed the fifty-cent piece across the counter once more and said, "My change, mac."

The guy picked up the money quickly, rang it up, and gave me my change. He was sweating now. I shrugged, shook my head, and walked out of the store.

Well, Cannon, I told myself, where now?

"Curt?"

The voice was soft, inquisitive. I turned and found its owner. She was soft, too, bundled into a thin coat that swelled out over the curves of her body. Her hair was black, as black as night, and it curled against the oval of her face in soft wisps that didn't come from a home permanent kit. Her eyes were brown, and wide; her lips looked as if they'd never been kissed—but wanted to be.

"I don't think I know you," I said.

"Kit," she said. "Kit O'Donnell."

I stared at her hard. "Kit O'Donn . . ." I took another look. "Not Katie O'Donnell? I'll be damned."

"Have you got a moment, Curt?"

I still couldn't get over it. She'd been a dirty faced kid when last I'd seen her. "Sure," I said. "Plenty of time. More than I need."

"There's a bar around the corner," she said. "We can talk there."

I grinned and pulled up the collar of my coat. "That's just where I was heading anyway."

The bar was like all bars—it had whisky and the people who drink whisky. It also had a pinball machine and two tables set against the long front window. We sat at one of the tables, and she shrugged out of her coat. She shrugged very nicely. She was wearing a green sweater and a loose bra, and when she shrugged I leaned closer to the table and the palms of my hands itched.

She didn't bother with a preamble. "Curt," she said, "my father is in trouble."

"Well, I'm sorry to hear that," I said.

"You're a private detective. I'd like you to help."

I grinned. "Katie . . . Kit . . . I'm not practicing any more. The Law took my ticket."

"That doesn't matter."

"Oh, doesn't it?"

"Curt, it's the whole neighborhood, not just my father. Charlie . . . Charlie was one of them. He . . . they . . ."

She stopped talking, and her eyes opened wide. Her voice seemed to catch in her throat, and she lowered her head slightly. I turned and looked at the bar. A tall character in a belted camel's-hair coat was leaning on the bar, a wide grin on his face. I stared at him and the grin got bigger. Briefly, I turned back to Kit. She raised her eyes, and I was treated to my third look at fear in the past half-hour.

"Now what the hell?" I said.

"Curt, please," she whispered.

I shoved my chair back and walked toward the bar. The tall character kept grinning, as if he were getting a big kick out of watching a pretty girl with a stumblebum. He had blond hair and sharp blue eyes, and the collar of his coat was turned up in the back, partially framing his narrow face.

"Is something wrong, friend?" I asked.

He didn't answer. He kept grinning, and I noticed that one hand was jammed into a pocket of the coat. There was a big lump in that jacket, and unless the guy had enormous hands, there was something besides the end of his arm there.

"You're staring at my friend," I said.

His eyes flicked from the swell of Kit's breasts where they heaved in fright beneath the green sweater.

"So I am," he said softly.

"So cut it out."

The grin appeared on his face again. He turned his head deliberately, and his eyes stripped Kit's sweater off.

I grabbed the collar of his coat, wrapped my hand in it, and yanked him off the bar.

He moved faster than I thought he would. He brought up a knee that sent a sharp pain careening up from my groin. At the same time, his hand popped out of the pocket and a snub-nosed .38 stared up at my face.

I didn't look at the gun long. There are times when you can play footsie, and there are times when you automatically sense that a man is dangerous and that a fisted gun isn't a bluff but a threat that might explode any second. The knee in my groin had doubled me over so that my face was level with the .38. I started to lift my head, and I smashed my bunched fist sideways at the same time. I caught him on the inside of his wrist, and the gun jerked to one side, its blast loud in the small bar. I heard the front window shatter as the bullet struck it, and then I had his wrist tightly in my fingers, and I was turning around and pulling his arm over my shoulder. I gave him my hip, and he left his feet and yelped hoarsely.

And then he was in the air, flipping over my shoulder, with his gun still tight in my closed fist. My other hand was cupped under his elbow. He started coming down bottoms up and the gun blasted again, ripping up six inches of good floor. He started to swear and the swear erupted into a scream as he felt the bone in his arm splinter. I could have released my grip when I had him in the air. I could have just let him drop to the floor like an empty sack. Instead, I kept one hand on his wrist and the other under his elbow, and his weight pushed down against his stiffened arm.

The bone made a tiny snap, like someone clicking a pair of castanets. He dropped the gun and hit the floor with a solid thump that rattled some glasses on the bar. His hand went instantly to his arm, and his face turned gray when he saw the crooked dangle of it. The grayness turned to a heavy flush that mingled with raw pain. He dove headlong on the floor, reaching for the gun with his good arm.

I did two things, and I did them fast. I stepped on his hand first. I stepped on it so hard that I thought I heard some more bones crush. And then, while he was pulling his hand back in pain, I brought my foot back and let it loose in a sharp swing that brought my toe up against his jaw. His teeth banged together and he came up off the floor as if a grenade had exploded under him, collapsing against the wood flat on his face a second later.

"Get your broom," I said to the bartender. I walked back to Kit and helped her on with her coat.

"Curt, you shouldn't have," she mumbled. "You shouldn't have."

"Let's get out of here," I said.

She huddled close against me in the street. A sharp wind had come up, and it drove the newspapers along in the gutter like sailboats in a furious hurricane. I kept my arm around her, and it felt good to hold a woman once more. Subconsciously my hand tightened and then started to drop. She reached up with one hand and pulled my fingers away, staring up into my face.

"I'm sorry," I said. "I sometimes forget."

A sort of pity came into her eyes. "Where are you living now, Curt?" she asked.

"A charming little spot called The Monterey. It's in the Bowery. I don't suppose you've ever been there."

"No. I . . ."

"Who was the joker?"

"What joker?"

"The one who's picking up his arm."

"His name's Lew. He's one of them. They've been . . . we've been paying them, Curt. All the storekeepers. My father with his grocery, and Charlie—everybody. That's why he was killed. Charlie, I mean. And now my father, Curt, he's refused to pay them any more. He told them they could . . . Curt, I'm frightened. That's why I want your help." It all came out in a rush, as if she were unloading a terrible burden.

"Honey," I said, "I have no license. I told you before. I'm not a real eye any more. I'm more a . . . a glass eye. Do you understand?"

She turned her face toward mine. "You won't help?"

"What could I do?"

"You could . . . scare them. You could make them afraid to take any more money."

"Me?" I laughed out loud. "Who'd be afraid of me? Honest, Kit, I'm just a . . ."

"What do you want, Curt?" she asked. "I haven't any money but I'll give you . . . whatever else you want."

"What!"

"They'll kill my father, Curt. As sure as we're standing here, they'll kill him. I'll do anything." She paused. "Anything you say."

I grinned, but only a bit. "Do I look that way, Kit? Do I really look that way?"

She lifted her face, and her eyes were puzzled for a moment. I shook my head and left her standing there on the corner, with the wind whipping her coat around her long, curving legs.

I walked for a long while, past the public school, past the *Latticini*, past the bars and the coal joint and the butcher and all the places I'd known since I was old enough to crawl. I saw kids with glazed eyes and the heroin smell about them, and I saw young girls with full breasts in tight brassières. I saw old women shuffling along the streets with their heads bent against the wind, and old men puffing pipes in dingy doorways.

This was the beginning. Curt Cannon had started here. It had been a long way up out of the muck. I had had four men working for me in my agency. I had gone a long way from First Avenue. And here I was back again, back in the muck, only the muck was thicker, and it was contaminated with a bunch of punks who thought a .38 was a ticket on the gravy train. And guys like Charlie Dagerra got their throats slit for not liking the scheme of things.

Well, that was tough, but that wasn't my problem. I had enough troubles of my own. Charlie Dagerra was dead, and the dead don't dream. The living do. They dream a lot. And their dreams are full of blonde beauties with laughing eyes and mocking lips. And all the blondes are called Toni.

She startled me. She was almost like the dream come to life. I almost slammed into her, and I started to walk around her when she took a step to one side, blocking my path.

She had long blonde hair, and blue eyes that surveyed me speculatively now. Her mouth was twisted in a small grin, her lips swollen under their heavy lipstick. She wore a leather jacket, the collar turned up, and her hands were rammed into her pockets.

"Hello," she said. Her voice rose on the last syllable and she kept staring at me. It was getting dark now, and the wind was brisk on the back of my neck. I looked at her and at the way her blonde hair slapped at her face.

"What do you want, sister?" I asked.

"It's what you want that counts," she said.

I looked her over again, starting with the slender, curving legs in the high heels, up the full rounded thighs that pressed against her skirt.

When my eyes met hers again, she looked at me frankly and honestly. "You like?"

"I like."

"It's cheap, mister. Real cheap."

"How cheap?"

She hooked her arm through mine, pressing her breasts against my arm. "We'll talk price later," she said. "Come on."

We began walking, and the wind started in earnest now, threatening to tear the gray structures from the sky.

"This way," she said. We turned down 119th Street, and we walked halfway up the street toward Second Avenue. "This house," she said. I didn't answer. She went ahead of me, and I watched her hips swinging under her skirt, and I thought again of Toni, and the blood ran hotly in my veins.

She stepped into the dark vestibule of the house, and I walked in after her. She walked toward the end of the hall on the ground floor, and I realized too late that there were no apartments on that floor except at the front of the building. She swung around suddenly, thrusting a nickel-plated .22 at me, shoving me back against the garbage cans that were lined up underneath the stairway.

"What is this?" I asked. "Rape?"

"It's rape, mister," she answered. She flicked her head, lashing the blonde hair back over her shoulder. Her eyes narrowed and then she lifted the .22 and brought it down in a slashing arc that sent blood spurting from my cheek.

"This is for Lew," she said. She brought the small gun back and down again, and this time I could feel the teeth rattling in my mouth. "And this is for Lew's broken arm!"

The gun went back, slashing down in a glinting arc. I reached up and grabbed her wrist, pulling the gun all the way over to one side. With my other hand, I slapped her across the face. I tightened my grip on her wrist until she let the gun clatter onto the garbage cans, a small scream coming out of her mouth. I slapped her again, backhanded, and she flew up against the wall, her mouth open in surprise and terror.

"We came here for something," I told her.

"You lousy son of a bitch. I wouldn't if you were the last man on earth."

I slapped her harder this time, and I pulled the zipper down on her leather jacket and ripped her blouse down the front. My fingers found her bra, and I tore it in two. I pulled her to me and mashed my mouth down against hers. She fought and pulled her mouth away, and I yanked her to me, my hand against her. She stopped struggling after a while.

The wind kept howling outside. I left her slumped against the wall. I threw a five-dollar bill into the garbage cans, and I said, "Tell Lew to keep his bait at home. I'll break his other arm if he sends another slut after me. You understand?"

"You didn't seem to mind, you bastard," she mumbled.

"Just tell him. Just tell him what I said."

I walked out of the building. I was sore, very sore. I didn't like being suckered. I was ready to find this Lew character and *really* break his other arm. I was ready to rip it off and stuff it down his God-damned mouth. That's the way I felt. The old neighborhood made it only tougher to bear. You go to a funeral, you don't expect a boxing match. You don't expect punks shaking down a poor neighborhood. It was like rattling pennies out of a gum machine. It was that cheap. It stank, and the smell made me sick, and I wanted to hold my nostrils.

I kept burning, and before I knew it, I was standing in front of O'Donnell's grocery. I walked in when I spotted Kit behind the counter.

"I'll take take six cans of beer," I told her.

Her head jerked up when she heard my voice. "Curt," she said, "one of them was just here!"

"What? Where is he?"

"He just left. He said we'd better have the money by tomorrow or . . ."

"Which way did he go?" I was halfway to the door.

"Toward Pleasant Avenue," she said. "He was wearing a tan fedora and a green coat."

I didn't wait for more. I headed out of the store and started walking down toward Pleasant. I caught up with him about halfway down the block. He was big from the back, a tall guy with shoulders that stretched against the width of his coat. I walked up behind him and grabbed one arm, yanking it up behind his back.

"Hello," I said. "My name is Curt Cannon."

"Hey, man, you nuts or something?" He tried to pull his arm away but I held it tightly.

"Take me to the cheese," I said. "The head punk."

"Man, you've flipped," he whined. I still couldn't see his face, but it sounded like a kid talking, a big kid who'd once lifted weights.

"You want to carry your arm away?" I asked.

"Cool it, man. Cool it." He tried to turn but I held him tightly. "What's your gripe?" he asked at last.

"I don't like shakedowns."

"Who does? Man, we see eye to eye. Loosen the flipper."

I yanked up on it and he screamed. "Cut the jive," I shouted. "Take me to the son of a bitch behind all this or I'll leave a stump on your shoulder."

"Easy, easy, man. Easy. I'm walking. I'm walking."

He kept walking toward Pleasant, and I stayed behind him, ready to tear his arm off if I had to.

"He ain't gonna cut this nohow," the weight-lifter said. "He ain't gonna cut this at all."

"He's done enough cutting," I said. "He cut Dagerra's throat."

"You don't dig me, Joe," the weight-lifter said. "You don't dig me at all."

"Just keep walking."

He kept walking, and then he stopped suddenly. "Up there," he said, gesturing with his head. "He's up there, but he ain't gonna cut this . . ."

"At all, I know."

"Just don't drag me in, man. Just leave me be. I don't want no headaches, thanks."

I shoved him away from me, and he almost fell on his face on the side-walk. "Keep your nose clean," I said. "Go listen to some of Dizzy's records. But keep your nose clean or I'll break it for you."

I saw his face for the first time. He was a young kid, no more than twenty-one, with wide blue eyes and pink cheeks. "Sure, man, sure." He scrambled to his feet and ran down the street.

I looked up at the red-fronted building, saw one light burning on the top floor, the rest of the windows boarded up. I climbed the sandstone steps and tried the door. When it didn't open on the second try, I pitted my shoulder against it, and it splintered in a hundred rotting pieces. The hall-way was dark.

I started up the steps, making my way toward the light on the top landing. I was winded when I reached it, and I stopped to catch my breath. A thin slice of amber light spilled onto the floor from under a crack in one of the doors. I walked up to the door and tried the knob. It was locked.

"Who is it?" a voice called.

"Me, man," I answered.

"Zip?"

"Yeah. Come on, man."

The door opened a crack, and I shoved it all the way open. It hit against something hard, and I kicked it shut and put my back against it. All I saw, at first, was Lew with his arm in a plaster cast hanging in a sling above his waist.

His eyes narrowed when he saw who it was, and he took one step to-ward me.

"I wouldn't," I told him. My voice was soft. "I wouldn't, Lew."

"He's right," another voice said. There was only one bulb burning in the room, and the corners were in shadow. I peered into one corner, made out an old sofa and a pair of blue slacks stretched the length of it. I fol-lowed the slacks up the length of the body, up to a hatchet face with glit-tering eyes, down again to the open switchblade that was paring the nails of one hand.

"Are you Mr. Punk himself?" I asked.

The long legs swung over the side of the sofa, and the face came into the light. It was a cruel face, young-old, with hard lines stretching from the nose flaps to the thinly compressed lips.

"The name's Jackie," he said. "Jackie Byrne. What's your game, mister?"

"How old are you, Jackie? Twenty-two? Twenty-three?"

"Old enough," he said. He took another step toward me, tossing the knife into the air and catching it on his palm. "How old are *you*, mister?"

"I'm really old, punk. I'm all of thirty. Really old."

"Maybe you won't get any older. You shouldn't complain."

"Charlie Dagerra was about thirty, too," I said. "He didn't get any older, either."

"Yeah," Byrne said. "That's just what I meant."

"How long you been shaking down the local merchants, Jackie?"

He grinned. "I don't know what you're talking about. The merchants donate money to me. I'm their favorite charity. They like to give me money. I make sure no snotnosed kids throw stink bombs in their stores or break their windows. I'm good to them."

"You think you've got a new dodge, don't you?"

"What?"

"You heard me. You've stumbled onto a real easy game. Just point your knife and the storekeepers wet their pants. It's been done before, Jackie. By bigger punks than you."

"You don't have to take that, Jackie," Lew said. "You don't have to take that from this bum."

"You'll find your girl on a garbage can in one of the hallways," I told him. "She was missing some clothes when I left her."

"Why, you son of a—" He lunged toward me and I whirled him around and shoved him across the room toward the sofa. His head clunked against the wall, making a hollow sound.

"All right, pop," Byrne said. "Enough playing around."

"I'm not playing, Jackie-boy."

"Get the hell out of this neighborhood," he said. "You got a long nose, and I don't like long noses."

"And what makes you think you can do anything about my nose, Jackie-boy?"

"A wise guy," he said disgustedly. "A real wise guy." He squeezed the knife shut and then pressed a button on its handle. The knife snapped open with a whistling noise.

"Very effective," I said. "Come on and use it."

"Nerves of steel, huh?" he asked, a small smile forming on his thin lips.

"No, sonny," I said. "I just don't give a damn, that's all. Come on." He hesitated, and I shouted, "Come on, you simple bastard!"

He lunged at me, the knife swinging in a glistening arc. I caught his arm and yanked it up, and we struggled under the bare bulb like two ballet dancers. I twisted his arm all the way up then, bringing up my foot at the same time. I kicked him right in the butt, hard, and he went stumbling across the room, struggling for his balance. He turned with a vicious snarl on his face, and then did something no expert knifeman would ever do.

He threw the knife.

I moved to one side as the blade whispered past my head. I heard it bury itself into the doorjamb behind me. I smiled then. "Well! It does appear we're even."

I took one step toward him, remembering Lew when it was too late.

"Not exactly, pop," Lew said.

I didn't bother turning around because I knew sure as hell that Lew would be holding the .38 I'd taken from him once today. Instead, I dove forward as the gun sounded, the smell of cordite stinking up the small room. My arms wrapped around Byrne's skinny legs, and we toppled to the floor in a jumble of twisting limbs.

The gun sounded once more, tearing into the plaster wall, and Byrne shouted, "You dumb mug! Knock it off!"

He didn't say anything else just then because my fist was in his mouth and he was trying hard to swallow it. I picked him up off the floor, keeping him in front of me. I lifted him to his feet and kept him ahead of me, moving toward Lew on the couch.

"Go ahead, Lew," I said. "Shoot. Kill your buddy and you'll get me, too."

"Don't move," he said.

I kept crossing the room, holding Byrne's limp body ahead of me.

"I said don't move!"

"Shoot, Lew! Fill Jackie-boy with holes. Go ahead!"

He hesitated a moment and that was all I needed. I threw Byrne like a sack of potatoes and Lew moved to one side just as I jumped. I hit him once in the gut and once in the Adam's apple, almost killing him. Then I grabbed Lew by his collar and Jackie by his, and I dragged them out of the room, and down the stairs, and out on the sidewalk. I found the cop not far from there.

I told Kit all about it later.

Her eyes held stars, and they made me think of a time when I'd roamed the neighborhood as a kid, a kid who didn't know the meaning of pain or the meaning of grief.

"Come see me, Curt," she said. "When you get the time, come see me. Please remember, Curt."

"I will, Kit," I lied.

I left the grocery store and walked over to Third Avenue. I grabbed the bus there, and I headed for home.

Home . . .

If I hurried, I might still find a liquor store open.

The bus rumbled past 120th Street, and I looked out of the window and up the high walls of the tenement cliffs. And then 120th Street was gone, and with it Curt Cannon's boyhood.

I slumped against the seat, pulling my collar high, smiling a little when the woman next to me got up and changed her seat.

LOREN D. ESTLEMAN

Loren D. Estleman (1952–) is a highly regarded crime novelist walking the mean streets of Raymond Chandler's America. He has borrowed from Chandler, but made his own detective more real, more contemporary, and much less a B-movie gumshoe. Along the way—Estleman was very young when he was first published—he also established himself as perhaps the best contemporary writer of Westerns in this country.

Estleman brings style and serious purpose to the mystery genre. People as different as John D. MacDonald and Robert B. Parker have praised Estleman's Amos Walker novel series. And deservedly so.

The Used

"But I never been to Iowa!" Murch protested.

His visitor sighed. "Of course not. No one has. That's why we're sending you there."

Slouched in the worn leather armchair in the office Murch kept at home, Adamson looked more like a high school basketball player than a federal agent. He had baby-fat features without a breath of whisker and collar-length sandy hair and wore faded Levi's with a tweed jacket too short in the sleeves and a paisley tie at three-quarter mast. His voice was changing, for God's sake. The slight bulge under his left arm might have been a sandwich from home.

Murch paced, coming to a stop at the basement window. His lawn needed mowing. The thought of it awakened the bursitis in his right shoulder. "What'll I do there? Don't they raise wheat or something like that? What's a wheat farmer need with a bookkeeper?"

"You won't be a bookkeeper. I explained all this before." The agent sat up, resting his forearms on his bony knees. "In return for your testimony regarding illegal contributions made by your employer to the campaigns of Congressmen Disdale and Reicher and Senator Van Horn, the Justice Department promises immunity from prosecution. You will also be provided with protection during the trial, and afterwards a new identity and relocation to Iowa. When you get there, you'll find a job waiting for you selling hardware, courtesy of Uncle Sam."

"What do I know about hardware? My business is with numbers."

"An accounting position seemed inadvisable on the off chance Redman's people traced you west. They'd never think of looking for you behind a sales counter."

"You said he wouldn't be able to trace me!" Murch swung around.

Adamson's lips pursed, lending him the appearance of a teenage Cupid. "I won't lie and say it hasn't happened. But in those cases there were big syndicate operations involved, with plenty of capital to spend. Jules Redman is light cargo by comparison. It's the senator and the congressmen we want, but we have to knock him down to get to them."

"What's the matter, they turn you down?"

The agent looked at him blankly.

Murch had to smile. "Come on, I ain't been in this line eighteen years I don't see how it jerks. Maybe these guys giving your agency a hard time on appropriations, or—" He broke off, his face brightening further. "Say, didn't I read where this Van Horn is asking for an investigation into clandestine operations? Yeah, and maybe the others support him. So you sniff around till something stinks and then tell them if they play ball you'll scratch sand over it. Only they don't feel like playing, so now you go for the jugular. Am I close?"

"I'm just a field operator, Mr. Murch. I leave politics to politicians." But the grudging respect in the agent's tone was enlightening.

"What happens if I decide not to testify?"

"Then you'll be wearing your numbers on your shirt. For three counts of conspiracy to bribe a member of the United States Congress."

They were watching each other when the doorbell rang upstairs. Murch jumped.

"That'll be your escort," Adamson suggested. "I've arranged for a room at a motel in the suburbs. The local police are lending a couple of plainclothesmen to stay there with you until the trial Monday. It's up to you whether I ask them to take you to jail instead."

"One room?" The bookkeeper's lip curled.

"There's an economy move on in Washington." Adamson got out of the chair and stood waiting. The doorbell sounded again.

"I want a color TV in the room," said Murch. "Tell your boss no color TV, no deal."

The agent didn't smile. "I'll tell him." He went up to answer the door.

* * *

He shared a frame bungalow at the motel between the railroad and the river with a detective sergeant named Kirdy and his relief, a lean, chinless officer who watched football all day with the sound turned down. He held a transistor radio in his lap; it was tuned in to the races. Kirdy looked smaller than he was. Though his head barely reached the bridge of Murch's nose, he took a size forty-six jacket and had to turn sideways to clear his shoulders through doorways. He had kind eyes set incongruously in a slab of granite. No-Chin never spoke except to warn his charge away from the windows. Kirdy's conversation centered around his granddaughter, a blonde tyke of whom he had a wallet full of photos. The bathroom was heated only intermittently by an electric baseboard unit and the building shuddered whenever a train went past. But Murch had his color TV.

At half past ten Monday morning, he was escorted into the court by Adamson and another agent who looked like a rock musician. Jules Redman sat at the defense table with his attorney. Murch's employer was small and dark, with an old-time gunfighter's handlebar mustache and glossy black hair combed over a bald spot. Their gazes met while the bookkeeper was being sworn in, and from then until recess was called at noon Redman's tan eyes remained on the man in the witness chair.

Charles Anthony Murch—his full name felt strange on his tongue when the court officer asked him for it—was on the stand two days. His testimony was complicated, having to do with dates and transactions made through dummy corporations, and he consulted his notebook often while the jurors stifled yawns and the spectators fidgeted and inspected their fingernails. After adjournment the first day, the witness was whisked along a circuitous route to a hotel near the airport, where Kirdy and his partner awaited their duty. On the way Adamson was talkative and in good spirits. Already he spoke of how his agency would proceed against the congressmen and Senator Van Horn after Redman was convicted. Murch was silent, remembering his employer's eyes.

The defense attorney, white-haired and grandfatherly behind a pair of half-glasses, kept his seat during cross-examination the next morning, reading from a computer printout sheet on the table in front of him while the government's case slowly fell to pieces. Murch had thought that his dismissal from that contracting firm upstate was off the books, and he was surprised to learn that someone had penetrated his double-entry system at the insurance company he had left in Chicago. Based on this record, the lawyer accused the bookkeeper of entering the so-called campaign donations into Redman's ledger to cover his own thefts. The jurors' faces were unreadable, but as the imputation continued Murch saw the corners of the defendant's mustache rise slightly and watched Adamson's eyes growing dull.

The jury was out twenty-two hours, a state record for that kind of case. Jules Redman was found guilty of resisting arrest, reduced from assaulting a police officer (he had lost his temper and knocked down a detective during an unsuccessful search of his office for evidence), and was acquitted on three counts of bribery. He was fined a hundred dollars.

Adamson was out the door on the reporters' scurrying heels. Murch hurried to catch up.

"You just don't live right, Charlie."

The bookkeeper held up at the hissed comment. Redman's diminutive frame slid past him in the aisle and was swallowed up by a crowd of well-wishers gathered near the door.

The agent kept a twelve-by-ten cubicle in the federal building two floors up from the courtroom where Redman had been set free. When Murch burst in, Adamson was slumped behind a gray steel desk deep in conversation with his rock musician partner.

"We *had* a deal," corrected the agent, after Murch's panicky interruption. His colleague stood by brushing his long hair out of his eyes. "It was made in good faith. We gave you a chance to volunteer any information from your past that might put our case in jeopardy. You didn't take advantage of it, and now we're all treading water in the toilet."

"How was I to know they was gonna dig up that stuff about those other two jobs? You investigated me. *You* didn't find nothing." The ex-witness's hands made wet marks on the desk top.

"Our methods aren't Redman's. It takes longer to subpoena personnel files than it does to screw a magnum into a clerk's ear and say gimme. Now I know why he didn't try to take you out before the trial." He paused. "Is there anything else?"

"Damn right there's something else! You promised me Iowa, win or lose."

Adamson reached inside his jacket and extracted a long narrow folder like the airlines use to put tickets in. Murch's heart leaped. He was reaching for the folder when the agent tore it in half. He put the pieces together and tore them again. Again, and then he let the bits flutter to the desk.

For a numb moment the bookkeeper goggled at the scraps. Then he lunged, grasping Adamson's lapels in both hands and lifting. "Redman's a killer!" He shook him. The agent clawed at his wrists, but Murch's fingers were strong from their years spent cramped around pencils and the handles of adding machines. Adamson's right hand went for his underarm holster, but his partner had gotten Murch in a bearhug and pulled. The front of the captive agent's coat tore away in his hands.

Adamson's chest heaved. He gestured with his revolver. "Get him the hell out of here." His voice cracked.

Murch struggled, but his right arm was yanked behind him and twisted. Pain shot through his shoulder. He went along, whimpering. Shoved out into the corridor, he had to run to catch his balance and slammed into the opposite wall, knocking a memo off a bulletin board. The door exploded shut.

A group of well-dressed men standing nearby stopped talking to look at him. He realized that he was still holding pieces of Adamson's jacket. He let them fall, brushed back his thinning hair with a shaky hand, adjusted his suit, and moved off down the corridor.

Redman and his lawyer were being interviewed on the courthouse steps by a television crew. Murch gave them a wide berth on his way down. He overheard Redman telling the reporters he was leaving tomorrow morning for a week's vacation in Jamaica. Ice formed in the bookkeeper's stomach. Redman was giving himself an alibi for when Murch's body turned up.

Anyway, he had eighteen hours' grace. He decided to write off the stuff he had left back at the hotel and took a cab to his house on the west side. For years he had kept two thousand dollars in cash there in case he needed a getaway stake in a hurry. By the time he had his key in the front door lock he was already breathing easier; Redman's men wouldn't try anything until their boss was out of the country, and a couple of grand could get a man a long way in eighteen hours.

His house had been ransacked.

They had overlooked nothing. They had torn up the rugs, pulled apart the sofa and easy chairs and slit open the cushions, taken pictures down from the wall and dismantled the frames, removed the back panel from the TV set, dumped out the flour and sugar canisters in the kitchen. Even the plates had been unscrewed from the wall switches. The orange juice can in which he had kept the rolled bills in the freezer compartment of the refrigerator lay empty on the linoleum.

The sheer cold logic of the operation dizzied Murch. Even after they had found the money they had gone on to make sure there were no other caches. His office alone, its contents smeared out into the passage that led to the stairs, would have taken hours to reduce to its present condition. The search had to have started well before the verdict was in, perhaps even as early as the weekend he had spent in that motel by the railroad tracks. Redman had been so confident of victory he had moved to cut off the bookkeeper's escape while the trial was still in progress.

He couldn't stay there. Probably he was already being watched, and the longer he remained the greater his chances of being kept prisoner in his own home until the word came down to eliminate him. He stepped outside. The street was quiet except for some noisy kids playing basketball in a neighbor's driveway and the snort of a power mower farther down the block. He started walking toward the corner.

Toward the bank. They'd taken his passbook, too, but he had better than six thousand in his account and he could borrow against that. Buy a used car or hop a plane. Maybe even go to Jamaica, stretch out on the beach next to Redman, and wait for his reaction. He smiled at that. Confidence warmed him, like whiskey in a cold belly. He mounted the bank steps, grasped the handle on the glass door. And froze.

He was alerted by the one reading a bank pamphlet in a chair near the door. There were no lines at the tellers' cages and no reason to wait. He spotted the other standing at the writing table, pretending to be making out a deposit slip. Their eyes wandered the lobby from time to time, casually. Murch didn't recognize their faces, but he knew the type: early thirties, jackets tailored to avoid telltale bulges. He reversed directions, moving slowly to keep from drawing attention. His heart started up again when he cleared the plate glass.

It was quarter to five, too late to reach another branch before closing, and even if he did he knew what would be waiting for him. He knew they had no intention of molesting him unless he tried to borrow money. They were running him like hounds, keeping him within range while they waited for the go-ahead. He was on a short tether with Redman on the other end.

But a man who juggled figures the way Murch did had more angles than the Pentagon. He hailed a cruising cab and gave the driver Bart Morgan's address on Whitaker.

Morgan's laundromat was twice as big as the room in back where the real business was conducted, with a narrow office between to prevent the ringing of the telephones from reaching the housewives washing their husbands' socks out front. Murch found the proprietor there counting change at the card table he used for a desk. Muscular but running to fat, Morgan had crewcut steel-gray hair and wore horn-rimmed glasses with a hearing aid built into one bow. His head grew straight out of his T-shirt.

"How they running, Bart?"

"They need fixing." He reached across the stacked coins to shake Murch's hand.

"I meant the horses, not the machines."

"So did I."

They laughed. When they were through, Murch said, "I need money, Bart."

"I figured that." The proprietor's eyes dropped to the table. "You caught me short, Charlie. I got bit hard at the Downs Saturday."

"I don't need much, just enough to get out of the city."

"I'm strapped. I wish to hell I wasn't but I am." He took a quarter from one stack and placed it atop another. "You know I'd do it if I could."

The bookkeeper seized his wrist gently. "You owe me, Bart. If I didn't lend you four big ones when the Dodgers took the Series, you'd be part of an off-ramp somewhere by now."

"I paid back every cent."

"It ain't the money, it's doing what's needed."

Morgan avoided his friend's eyes.

"Redman's goons been here, ain't they?"

Their gazes met for an instant, then Morgan's dropped again. "I got a wife and a kid that can't stay out of trouble." He spoke quietly. "What they gonna do I don't come home some night, or the next or the next?"

"You and me are friends."

"You got no right to say that." The proprietor's face grew red. "You got no right to come in here and ask me to put my chin on the block."

Murch tightened his grip. "If you don't give it to me I'll take it."

"I don't think so." Morgan leaned back, exposing a curved black rubber grip pressing into his paunch above the waistband of his pants.

Murch said, "You'd do Redman's job for him?"

"I'll do what I got to to live, same as you."

Telephones jangled in back, all but drowned out by the whooshing of the machines out front. The bookkeeper cast away his friend's wrist. "Tell your wife and kid Charlie said goodbye." He went out, leaving the door open behind him.

"You got no right, Charlie."

Murch kept going. Morgan stood up, shouting to be heard over the racket of the front-loaders. "You should of come to me before you went running to the feds! I'd of give you the odds!"

His visitor was on the street.

Dusk was gathering when he left the home of his fourth and last friend in the city. His afflicted shoulder, inflamed by the humid weather and the rough treatment he had received at Adamson's office, throbbed like an aching tooth. His hands were empty. Like Bart Morgan, Gordy Sharp and Ed Zimmer pleaded temporary poverty, Zimmer stepping out onto the porch to talk while his family remained inside. There was no answer at Henry Arbogast's, yet Murch swore he had seen a light go off in one of the windows on his way up the walk.

Which left Liz.

He counted the money in his wallet. Forty-two dollars. He had spent almost thirty on cabs, leaving himself with just enough for a room for the night if he failed to get shed of the city. Liz was living in the old place two miles uptown. He sighed, put away the billfold, and planted the first sore foot on concrete.

Night crept out of the shadowed alleys to crouch beyond the pale rings cast by the street lights. He avoided them, taking his comfort in the invisibility darkness lent him. Twice he halted, breathing shallowly, when cars crawled along the curb going in his direction, then he resumed walking as they turned down side streets and picked up speed. His imagination flourished in the absence of light.

The soles of his feet were sending sharp pains splintering up through his ankles by the time he reached the brickfront apartment house and mounted the well-worn stairs to the fourth floor. Outside 4C he leaned against the wall while his breathing slowed and his face cooled. Straightening, he raised his fist, paused, and knocked gently.

A steel chain prevented the door from opening beyond the width of her face. Her features were dark against the light behind her, sharper than before, the skin creased under her eyes and at the corners of her mouth. Her black hair was streaked in mouse-color and needed combing. She had aged considerably.

"I knew you'd show up," she snapped, cutting his greeting in half. "I heard all about the verdict on the six o'clock news. You want money."

"I'm lonesome, Liz. I just want to talk." He'd forgotten how quick she was. But he had always been able to soften her up in the past.

"You never talked all the time we was married unless you wanted something. I can't help you, Charlie." She started to close the door.

He leaned on it. His bad shoulder howled in outrage. "Liz, you're my last stop. They got all the other holes plugged." He told her about Adamson's broken promise, about the bank and his friends. "Redman'll kill me just to make an example."

She said, "And you're surprised?"

"What's that supposed to mean?" He controlled his anger with an effort. That had always been her chief weapon, her instinct for the raw nerve.

"There's two kinds in this world, the ones that use and the ones that get used." Her face was completely in shadow now, unreadable. "Guys like Redman and Adamson squeeze all the good out of guys like you and then throw you away. That's the real reason I divorced you, Charlie. You was headed for the junkpile the day you was born. I just didn't want to be there to see it."

"Christ, Liz, I'm talking about my life!"

"Me too. Just a second." She withdrew, leaving the door open.

He felt the old warmth returning. Same old Liz: Deliver a lecture, then turn around and come through after all. It was like enduring the sermon at the Perpetual Mission in return for a hot meal and roof for the night.

"Here." Returning, she thrust a fistful of something through the opening. He reached for it eagerly. His fingers closed on cold steel.

He recoiled, tried to give back the object, but she'd dropped her hand. "You nuts?" he demanded. "I ain't fired a gun since the army!"

"It's all I got to give you. Don't let them find out where it came from."

"What good is it against a dozen men with guns?"

"No good, the way you're thinking. I wait tables in Redman's neighborhood, I hear things. He likes blow-torches. Don't let them burn you alive, Charlie."

He was still staring, holding the .38 revolver like a handful of popcorn, when she shut the door. The lock snapped with a noise like jaws closing.

It was a clear night. The Budweiser sign in the window of the corner bar might have been cut with an engraving tool out of orange neon. Someone gasped when he emerged from the apartment building. A woman in evening dress hurried past on a man's arm, her face tight and pale in the light coming out through the glass door, one brown eye rolling back at Murch. He'd forgotten about the gun. He put it away.

His subsequent pounding had failed to get Liz to open her door. If he'd wanted a weapon he'd have gotten it himself; the city bristled with unregistered iron. He fingered the unfamiliar thing in his pocket, wondering where to go next. His eyes came to the bright sign in the bar window.

Blood surged in his ears. Murch's robberies had all been from company treasuries, not people, his weapons figures in ledgers. Demanding money for lives required a steady hand and the will to carry out the threat. It was too raw for him, too much like crime. He started walking away from the bar. His footsteps slowed halfway down the block and stopped twenty feet short of the opposite corner. The pedestrian signal changed twice while he was standing there. He turned around and retraced his steps. He was squeezing the concealed revolver so hard his knuckles ached.

The establishment was quiet for that time of the evening, deserted but for a young bartender in a red apron standing at the cash register. The jukebox was silent. As Murch approached, the employee turned unnaturally bright eyes on him. The light from the beer advertisement reflecting off the bar's cherrywood finish flushed the young man's face. "Sorry, friend, we're—"

Murch aimed the .38. His hand shook.

The bartender smiled weakly.

"This ain't no joke! Get 'em up!" He tried to make his voice tough. It came out high and ragged.

Slowly the young man raised his hands. He was still smiling. "You're out of luck, friend."

Murch told him to shut up and open the cash register drawer. He obeyed. It was empty.

"Someone beat you to it," explained the bartender. "Two guys with shotguns came in an hour ago, shook down the customers, and cleaned me out. Didn't even leave enough to open up with in the morning. You just missed the cops."

His smile burned. Murch's finger tightened on the trigger and the expression was gone. The bookkeeper backed away, bumped into a table. The gun almost went off. He turned and stumbled toward the door. He tugged at the handle; it didn't budge. The sign said PUSH. He shoved his way through to the street. Inside, the bartender was dialing the telephone.

The night air stung Murch's face, and he realized there were tears on his cheeks. His thoughts fluttered wildly. He caught them and sorted them into piles with the discipline of one trained to work with assets and debits. Redman couldn't have known he would pick this particular place to rob, even had he suspected the bookkeeper's desperation would make him choose that course. Blind luck had decided whom to favor, and as usual it wasn't Charlie Murch.

A distant siren awakened him to practicalities. Soon he would be a fugitive from the law as well as from Redman; he wasn't cold enough to go back and kill the bartender to keep him from giving the police his description. He pocketed the gun and ran.

His breath was sawing in his throat two blocks later when he spotted a cab stopped at a light. He sprinted across to it, tore open the back door, and threw himself into a seat riddled with cigarette burns.

"Off duty, bub," announced the driver, hanging a puffy, stubbled face over the back of his seat. "Oil light's on. I'm on my way back to the garage to see what's wrong."

There was no protective panel between the seats. His passenger thrust the handgun in his face and thumbed back the hammer.

The driver sighed heavily. "All I got's twelve bucks and change. I ain't picked up a fare yet."

He was probably lying, but the light was green and Murch didn't want to be arrested arguing with a cabbie. "Just drive."

They passed a prowl car on its way toward the bar, its siren gulping, its lights flashing. Murch fought the urge to duck, hiding the gun instead. The county lock-up was full of men who would ice him just to get in good with Redman.

He got an idea that frightened him. He tried pushing it away, but it kept coming back.

"Mister, my engine's overheating."

Murch glanced up. The cab was making clunking noises. The warning light on the dash glowed angry red. They had gone nine blocks. "All right, pull over." The driver spun the wheel. As he rolled to a stop next to the curb the motor coughed, shuddered, and died. Steam rolled out from under the hood.

"Start counting." The passenger reached across the front seat and tore the microphone free of the two-way radio. "Don't get out till you reach a thousand. If you do, you won't have time to be sorry you did. You'll be dead." He slid out and slammed the door on six.

He caught another cab four blocks over, this time without having to use force. It was a twenty-dollar ride out to the posh residential district where Jules Redman lived. He tipped the cabbie five dollars. He had no more use for money.

The house was a brick ranch-style in a quiet cul-de-sac studded with shade trees. Murch found the hike to the front door effortless; for the first time in hours he was without pain. On the step he took a deep breath, let half of it out, and rang the bell. He took out the gun. Waited.

After a lifetime the door was opened by a very tall young man in a tan jacket custom-made to contain his enormous chest. It was Randolph, Redman's favorite bodyguard. His eyes flickered when he recognized the visitor. A hand darted inside his jacket.

The reports were very loud. Murch fired a split-second ahead of Randolph, shattering his sternum and throwing off his aim so that the second bullet entered the bookkeeper's left thigh. He had never been shot before; it was oddly sensationless, like the first time he had had sex. The bodyguard crumpled.

Murch stepped across him. He could feel the hot blood on his leg, nothing else. Just then Redman appeared in an open doorway beyond the staircase. When he saw Murch he froze. He was wearing a maroon velour robe over pajamas and his feet were in slippers.

The bookkeeper was motionless as well. What now? He hadn't expected to get this far. He had shot Randolph in self-defense; he couldn't kill a man in cold blood, not even this one, not even when that was the fate he had planned for Murch.

Redman understood. He smiled under his mustache. "Like I said before, Charlie, you just don't live right."

Another large man came steadily through a side door, towed by an automatic pistol. He was older than Randolph and wore neither jacket nor necktie, his empty underarm holster exposed. This was the other bodyguard. He held up before the sight that met his eyes.

"Kill him, Ted," Redman said calmly.

Murch's bullet splintered one of the steps in the staircase. He'd aimed at the banister, but that was close enough. "Next one goes between your boss's eyes," he informed the bodyguard.

Ted laid his gun on the floor and backed away from it, raising his hands.

The bookkeeper felt no triumph. He wondered if it was fear that was making him numb or if he just didn't care. To Redman: "Over here."

Redman hesitated. Murch cocked the revolver. The racketeer approached cautiously.

"Pick that up." Murch indicated Randolph's gun lying where he had dropped it when he fell. "Slow," he added, as Redman stooped to obey.

He accepted the firearm between the thumb and forefinger of his free hand and dropped it carefully into a pocket to avoid smearing the fingerprints. To Ted: "Get the car."

Murch was waiting in front with his hostage when the bodyguard drove the Cadillac out of the garage. "Okay, get out," he told Ted.

He made Redman get behind the wheel and climbed in on the passenger's side. "Start driving. I'll tell you what turns to make." He spoke through clenched teeth. His leg was starting to ache and he was feeling light-headed from the blood loss.

The bodyguard watched them until they reached the end of the driveway. Then he swung around and sprinted back inside.

"He'll be on the phone to the others in two seconds," jeered Redman. "How far you think you'll get before you bleed out?"

"Turn right," Murch directed.

The big car took the bumps well. Even so, each one was like a red-hot knife in the bookkeeper's thigh. He made himself as comfortable as possible without taking his eyes off the driver, the revolver resting in his lap with his hand on the butt. He welcomed Redman's taunts. They distracted him from his pain, kept his mind off the drowsiness welling up inside him like warm water filling a tub. He wasn't so far from content.

The dead bodyguard would take explaining. But a paraffin test would reveal that he'd fired a weapon recently, and the gun in Murch's pocket was likely registered to Randolph. Redman's prints on the butt and the fact that Randolph worked for him, together with the bullet in Murch's leg and a clear motive in his testimony in the bribery trial, would put his old boss inside for a long time for attempted murder. "Left here."

The lights of the 14th Precinct were visible down the block. Detective Sergeant Kirdy's precinct, the home of the kind, proud grandfather who had protected Murch during the trial. Murch told Redman to stop the car. It felt good to give him that last order. Charlie Murch had stopped being one of the used.

He recognized Kirdy's blocky shape hastily descending the front steps as he was following Redman out the driver's side and called to him. The sergeant shielded his eyes with one hand against the glare of the headlamps, squinted at the two figures coming toward him, one limping, the other in a bathrobe being pushed out ahead. He drew his magnum from his belt holster. Murch gestured to show friendship. The noise the policeman's gun made was deafening, but Murch never heard it.

"That was quick thinking, sergeant." Hands in the pockets of his robe, Redman looked down at his late captor's body spread-eagled in the gutter. A crowd was gathering.

"We got the squeal on your kidnapping a few minutes ago," Kirdy said. "I was just heading out there when you two showed."

"You ought to make lieutenant for this."

The sergeant's kind eyes glistened. "That'd be great, Mr. Redman. The wife and kids been after me for years to get off the street."

"You will if there's any justice. How's that pretty granddaughter of yours, by the way?"

STUART M. KAMINSKY

Stuart M. Kaminsky (1934–) made his first reputation as the author of the fast, furious, and funny Toby Peters series set in Hollywood of the forties.

He made his second and third reputations as the writer of the Porfiry Petrovich Bostnikov books set in contemporary Moscow and the Abe Lieberman novels set in contemporary Chicago.

Series seem to be his speciality. He knows how to keep them vital, even after a long sequence of novels. The Tobys, for example, are up to twenty now, and each one gets better and better.

He may be slightly undervalued (despite winning the Edgar for best novel) because he works quickly and prolifically. We all know that's a no-no, right?

But his books are consistently inventive, human, humane, and page-turning good. And he deserves to be held in higher regard than he sometimes is. His work will endure long beyond that of many flavors of the month.

Busted Blossoms

(Toby Peters)

Darkness. I couldn't see, but I could hear someone shouting at me about Adolf Hitler. I opened my eyes. I still couldn't see. Panic set in before memory told me where I was. I pushed away the jacket covering my head. After a good breath of stale air, I realized where I was, who I was, and what I was doing there.

It was 1938, February, a cool Sunday night in Los Angeles, and I was Toby Peters, a private investigator who had been hired to keep an eye on a washed-up movie director who had come in from out of town and picked up a few death threats. I was getting fifteen dollars a day, for which I was expected to stay near the target and put myself in harm's way if trouble came up. I was not being paid to fall asleep.

My mouth tasted like ragweed pollen. I reached over to turn off the radio. When I had put my head back to rest on the bed and pulled my suede zipped jacket over me, Jeanette MacDonald had been singing about Southern moons. I woke up to the news that Reichsführer Hitler had proclaimed himself chief of national defense and had promoted Hermann Wilhelm Göring, minister of aviation, to field marshal. I was just standing when the door opened and D. W. Griffith walked in.

"Mr. Peters," he said, his voice deep, his back straight, and, even across the room, his breath dispensing the Kentucky fumes of bourbon.

"I was on my way down," I said. "I was listening to the news."

Griffith eyed me from over his massive hawk of a nose. He was about five-ten, maybe an inch or so taller than me, though I guessed he weighed about 180, maybe twenty pounds more than I did. We both seemed to be in about the same shape, which says something good for him or bad for me. I was forty-one, and he was over sixty. He was wearing a black suit over a white shirt and thin black tie.

"I have something to tell you," Griffith said.

So, I was canned. It had happened before, and I had a double sawbuck in my wallet.

"I really was coming down," I said, trying to get some feeling in my tongue.

"You were not," Griffith said emphatically. "But that is of little consequence. A man has been murdered."

"Murdered?" I repeated.

I am not the most sophisticated sight even when I'm combed, shaved, and operating on a full stomach. My face is dark and my nose mush, not from business contacts, but from an older brother who every once in a while thought I needed redefinition. I sold that tough look to people who wanted a bodyguard. Most of my work was for second-rate clothing stores that had too much shoplifting, hard-working bookies whose wives had gone for Chiclets and never came back, and old ladies who had lost their cats, who were always named Sheiba. That's what I usually did, but once in a while I spent a night or a few days protecting movie people who got themselves threatened or were afraid of getting crushed in a crowd. D. W. had no such fears. No one was looking for his autograph anymore. No one was hiring him. He seemed to have plenty of money and a lot of hope; that was why he had driven up from Louisville. He hoped someone would pick up the phone and call him to direct a movie, but in the week I had worked for him, no one had called, except the guy who threatened to lynch him with a Ku Klux Klan robe. D. W. had explained that such threats had not been unusual during the past two decades since the release of *Birth of a Nation*, which had presented the glories of the Ku Klux Klan. D. W. had tried to cover his prejudice with *Intolerance* and a few more films, but the racism of *Birth* wouldn't wash away.

"Mr. Peters." He tried again, his voice now loud enough to be heard clearly in the back row if we were in a Loews theater. "You must rouse yourself. A man has been murdered downstairs."

"Call the police," I said brilliantly.

"We are, you may recall, quite a distance from town," he reminded me. "A call has been placed, but it will be some time before the constabulary arrives."

Constabulary. I was in a time warp. But that was the way I had felt since meeting Griffith, who now touched his gray sideburns as if he were about to be photographed for *Click* magazine.

"Who's dead?" I asked.

"Almost everyone of consequence since the dawn of time," Griffith said, opening the door. "In this case, the victim is Jason Sikes. He is sitting at the dinner table with a knife in his neck."

"Who did it?" I began.

"That, I fear, is a mystery," Griffith said. "Now let us get back to the scene."

I walked out the door feeling that I was being ushered from act one to act two. I didn't like the casting. Griffith was directing the whole thing, and I had the feeling he wanted to cast me as the detective. I wanted to tell him that I had been hired to protect his back, not find killers. I get double time for finding killers. But one just didn't argue with Dave Griffith. I slouched ahead of him, scratched an itch on my right arm, and slung my suede jacket over my shoulder so I could at least straighten the wrinkled striped tie I was wearing.

What did I know? That I was in a big house just off the California coast about thirty miles north of San Diego. The house belonged to a producer named Korites, who Griffith hoped would give him a directing job. Korites had gathered his two potential stars, a comic character actor, and a potential backer, Sikes, to meet the great director. I had come as Griffith's "associate." D. W. had left his young wife back at the Roosevelt Hotel in Los Angeles, and we had stopped for drinks twice on the way in his chauffeur-driven Mercedes. In the car Griffith had talked about Kentucky, his father, his mother, who had never seen one of his films—"She did not approve of the stage," he explained—and about his comeback. He had gone on about his youthful adventures as an actor, playwright, boxer, reporter, and construction worker. Then, about ten minutes before we arrived, he had clammed up, closed his eyes, and hadn't said another word.

Now we were going silently down the stairs of the house of Marty Korites, stepping into a dining room, and facing five well-dressed diners, one of whom lay with his face in a plate of Waldorf salad with a knife in his back.

The diners looked up when we came in. Korites, a bald, jowly man with Harold Lloyd glasses, was about fifty and looked every bit of it and more. His eyes had been resting angrily on the dead guest, but they shot up to us as we entered the room. On one side of the dead guy was a woman, Denise Giles, skinny as ticker tape, pretty, dark, who knows what age. I couldn't even tell from the freckles on her bare shoulders. On the other side of the dead guy was an actor named James Vann, who looked like the lead in a road-show musical, blond, young, starched, and confused. He needed someone to feed him lines. Griffith was staring at the corpse. The great director looked puzzled. The last guest sat opposite the dead man. I knew him, too, Lew Dollard, a frizzy-haired comedian turned character actor who was Marty Korites' top name, which gives you an idea of how small an operator Marty was and what little hope Griffith had if he had traveled all the way here in the hope of getting a job from him.

"Mr. Griffith says you're a detective, not a film guy," Korites said, his eyes moving from the body to me for an instant and then back to the body. I guessed he didn't want the dead guy to get away when he wasn't looking.

"Yeah, I'm a detective," I said. "But I don't do windows and I don't do corpses."

Dollard, the roly-poly New York street comic in a rumpled suit, looked up at me.

"A comedy writer," he said with a smile showing big teeth. I had seen one of Dollard's movies. He wasn't funny.

"Someone killed Sikes," Korites said with irritation.

"Before the main course was served, too," I said. "Some people have no sense of timing. Look. Why don't we just sit still, have a drink or two, and wait till the police get here. We can pass the time by your telling me how someone can get killed at the dinner table and all of you not know who did it. That must have been some chicken liver appetizer."

"It was," said Griffith, holding his open palm toward the dead man, "like a moment of filmic chicanery, a magic moment from Méliès. I was sipping an aperitif and had turned to Miss Giles to answer a question. And then, a sound, a groan. I turned, and there sat Mr. Sikes."

We all looked at Sikes. His face was still in the salad.

"Who saw what happened?" I asked.

They all looked up from the corpse and at each other. Then they looked at me. Dollard had a cheek full of something and a silly grin on his face. He shrugged.

"A man gets murdered with the lights on with all of you at the table and no one knows who did it?" I asked. "That's a little hard to believe. Who was standing up?"

"No one," said Vann, looking at me unblinking.

"No one," agreed Griffith.

There was no window behind the body. One door to the room was facing the dead man. The other door was to his right. The knife couldn't have been thrown from either door and landed in his back. The hell with it. I was getting paid to protect Griffith, not find killers. I'd go through the motions till the real cops got there. I had been a cop back in Glendale before I went to work for Warner Brothers as a guard and then went into business on my own. I knew the routine.

"Why don't we go into the living room?" Korites said, starting to get up and glancing at the corpse. "I could have Mrs. Windless—"

"Sit down," I said. "Mrs. Windless is . . . ?"

"Housekeeper," Korites said. "Cook."

"Was she in here when Sikes was killed?"

I looked around. All heads shook no.

"Anyone leave the room before or after Sikes was killed?" I went on.

"Just Mr. Griffith," said Vann. The woman still hadn't said anything.

"We stay right here till the police arrive. Anyone needs the toilet, I go with them, even the dragon lady," I said, trying to get a rise out of Denise Giles. I got none.

"What about you?" said Dollard, rolling his eyes and gurgling in a lousy imitation of Bert Lahr.

"I wasn't in the room when Sikes took his dive into the salad," I said. "Look, you want to forget the whole thing and talk about sports? Fine. You hear that Glenn Cunningham won the Wanamaker mile for the fifth time yesterday?"

"With a time of 4:11," said Denise Giles, taking a small sip of wine from a thin little glass.

I looked at her with new respect. Griffith had sat down at the end of the table, the seat he had obviously been in when murder interrupted the game. Something was on his mind.

"Who was Sikes?" I asked, reaching down for a celery stick.

"A man of means," said Griffith, downing a slug of bourbon.

"A backer," said Korites. "He was thinking of bankrolling a movie D. W. would direct and I would produce."

"With Vann here and Miss Giles as stars?" I said.

"Right," said Korites.

"Never," said Griffith emphatically.

"You've got no choice here," Korites shouted back. "You take the project the way we give it to you or we get someone else. Your name's got some curiosity value, right, but it doesn't bring in any golden spikes."

"A man of tender compassion," sighed Griffith, looking at me for understanding. "It was my impression that the late Mr. Sikes had no intention of supplying any capital. On the contrary, I had the distinct impression that he felt he was in less than friendly waters and had only been lured here with the promise of meeting me, the wretched director who had once held the industry in his hand, had once turned pieces of factory-produced celluloid into art. As I recall, Sikes also talked about some financial debt he expected to be paid tonight."

"You recall?" Korites said with sarcasm, shaking his head. "You dreamed it up. You're still back in the damn nineteenth century. Your movies were old-fashioned when you made them. You don't work anymore because you're an anachronism."

"Old-fashioned?" said Griffith with a smile. "Yes, old-fashioned, a romantic, one who respects the past. I would rather die with my Charles Dickens than live with your Hemingway."

Dollard finished whatever he had in his mouth and said, "You think it would be sacrilegious to have the main course? Life goes on."

"Have a celery stick," I suggested.

"I don't want to eat a celery stick," he whined.

"I wasn't suggesting that you put it in your mouth," I said.

This was too much for Dollard. He stood up, pushing the chair back.

"I'm the comic here," he said. "Tell him."

He looked around for someone to tell me. The most sympathetic person was Sikes, and he was dead.

"So that's the way it is," Dollard said, looking around the room. "You want me to play second banana."

"This is a murder scene," shouted Korites, taking his glasses off, "not a night club, Lew. Try to remember that." His jowls rumbled as he spoke. He was the boss, but not mine.

"Someone in this room murdered the guy in the salad," I reminded them.

"My father," said Griffith.

"Your father killed Sikes?" I asked, turning to the great director. Griffith's huge nose was at the rim of his almost empty glass. His dark eyes were looking into the remaining amber liquid for an answer.

"My father," he said without looking up, "would have known how to cope with this puzzle. He was a resourceful man, a gentleman, a soldier."

"Mine was a grocer," I said.

"This is ridiculous," said Denise Giles, throwing down her napkin.

"Not to Sikes," I said. Just then the door behind me swung open. I turned to see a rail of a woman dressed in black.

"Are you ready for the roast?" she asked.

"Yes," said Dollard.

"No," said Korites, "we're not having any more food."

"I have rights here," Dollard insisted.

Now I had it. This was an Alice in Wonderland nightmare and I was Alice at the Mad Hatter's tea party. We'd all change places in a few seconds and the Dormouse, Sikes, would have to be carried.

"What," demanded Mrs. Windless, "am I to do with the roast?"

"You want the punch line or can I have it?" Dollard said to me.

"Sikes already got the punch line," I reminded him.

Mrs. Windless looked over at Sikes for the first time.

"Oh my God," she screamed. "That man is dead."

"Really?" shouted Dollard leaping up. "Which one?"

"Goddamn it," shouted Korites. "This is serious." His glasses were back on now. He didn't seem to know what to do with them.

Griffith got up and poured himself another drink.

"We know he's dead, Mrs. Windless," Korites said. "The police are on the way. You'll just have to stick all the food in the refrigerator and wait."

"What happened?" Mrs. Windless asked, her voice high, her eyes riveted on Sikes. "Who did this? I don't want anything to do with murder."

"You don't?" said Dollard. "Why didn't you tell us that before we killed him? We did it for you." He crossed his eyes but didn't close them in time to block out the wine thrown in his face by the slinky Denise.

Dollard stood up sputtering and groped for a napkin to wipe his face. Purple tears rolled down his cheeks.

"Damn it," he screamed. "What the hell? What the hell?"

His hand found a napkin. He wiped his eyes. The stains were gone, but there was now a piece of apple from the Waldorf salad on his face.

"Mrs. Windless," said D. W., standing and pointing at the door. "You will depart and tell my driver, Mr. Reynolds, that Mr. Peters and I will be delayed. Mr. Dollard. You will sit down and clean your face. Miss Giles, you will refrain from outbursts, and Mr. Vann, you will attempt to show some animation. It is difficult to tell you from Mr. Sikes. Mr. Peters will continue the inquiry."

Vann stood up now, kicking back his chair. Griffith rose to meet him. They were standing face to face, toe to toe. Vann was about thirty years younger, but Griffith didn't back away.

"You can't tell us what to do. You can't tell anyone what to do. You're washed up," Vann hissed.

"As Bluebeard is rumored to have said," whispered Griffith, "I'm merely between engagements."

"See, see," grouched Dollard, pointing with his fork at the two antagonists. "Everyone's a comic. I ask you."

I sighed and stood up again.

"Sit down," I shouted at Vann and Griffith. The room went silent. The mood was ruined by my stomach growling. But they sat and Mrs. Windless left the room. "Who called the police?"

"I did," said Korites.

"I thought no one left the room but Griffith?" I said.

"Phone is just outside the door, everyone could see me call. I left the door open," Korites said. He pushed his dirty plate away from him and then pulled it back. "What's the difference?"

"Why didn't you all start yelling, panic, accuse each other?" I asked.

"We thought it was one of Jason's practical jokes," said Denise Giles. "He was fond of practical jokes."

"Rubber teeth, joy buzzers, ink in the soup," sighed Dollard. "A real amateur, a putz. Once pretended he was poisoned at a lunch in . . ."

"Lew," shouted Korites. "Just shut up."

"All right you people," I said. "None of you like Sikes, is that right?"

"Right," Korites said, "but that's a far cry from one of us . . ."

"How about hate?" I tried. "Would hate be a good word to apply to your feelings about the late dinner guest?"

"Maybe," said Korites, "there was no secret about that among our friends. I doubt if anyone who knew Jason did anything less than hate him. But none of us murdered him. We couldn't have."

"And yet," Griffith said, "one of you had to have done the deed. In *The Birth of a Nation*—"

"This is death, not birth," hissed Vann. "This isn't a damn movie."

Griffith drew his head back and examined Vann over his beak of a nose.

"Better," said Griffith. "Given time I could possibly motivate you into a passable performance. Even Richard Barthelmess had something to learn from my humble direction."

There was a radio in the corner. Dollard had stood up and turned it on. I didn't stop him. We listened to the radio and watched Sikes and each other while I tried to think. Griffith was drawing something on the white tablecloth with his fork.

Dollard found the news, and we learned that Hirohito had a cold but was getting better, King Farouk of Egypt had just gotten married, Leopold Stokowski was on his way to Italy under an assumed name, probably to visit Greta Garbo, and a guy named Albert Burroughs had been found semi-conscious in a hotel room in Bloomington, Illinois. The room was littered with open cans of peas. Burroughs managed to whisper to the ambulance driver that he had lived on peas for nine days even though he had $77,000 in cash in the room.

I got up and turned off the radio.

"You tell a story like that in a movie," said Korites, "and they say it isn't real."

"If you tell it well, they will believe anything," said Griffith, again doodling on the cloth.

The dinner mess, not to mention Sikes' corpse, was beginning to ruin the party.

"Things are different," Griffith said, looking down at what he had drawn. He lifted a long-fingered hand to wipe out the identations in the tablecloth.

"Things?" I asked, wondering if he was going to tell us tales about his career, his father, or the state of the universe.

"I am an artist of images," he explained, looking up, his eyes moving from me to each of the people around the table. "I kept the entire script of my films, sometimes 1,500 shots, all within my head." He pointed to his head in case we had forgotten where it was located.

"This scene," he went on, "has changed. When I left this room to find Mr. Peters, Mr. Sikes had a knife in his neck, not his back, and it was a somewhat different knife."

"You've had three too many, D. W.," Dollard said with a smile.

I got up and examined Sikes. There was no hole in his neck or anywhere else on his body that I could find.

"No cuts, bruises, marks . . ." I began, and then it hit me. My eyes met Griffith's. I think it hit him at the same moment.

"We'll just wait for the police," Korites said, removing his glasses again.

"Go on, Mr. G.," I said. "Let's hear your script."

Griffith stood again, put down his glass, and smiled. He was doing either Abe Lincoln or Sherlock Holmes.

"This scene was played for me," he said. "I was not the director. I was the audience. My ego is not fragile, at least not too fragile to realize that I have witnessed an act. I can see each of you playing your roles, even the late Mr. Sikes. Each of you in an iris, laughing, silently enigmatic, attentive. And then the moment arrives. The audience is distracted by a pretty face in close-up. Then a cut to body, or supposed body, for Sikes was not dead when I left this room to find Mr. Peters."

"Come on . . ." laughed Dollard.

"Of all . . ." sighed Denise Giles.

"You're mad . . ." counterpointed Vann.

But Korites sat silent.

"He wasn't dead," I said again, picking up for Griffith, who seemed to have ended his monologue. All he needed was applause. He looked good, but he had carried the scene as far as he could. It was mine now.

"Let's try this scenario," I said. "Sikes was a practical joker, right?"

"Right," Dollard agreed, "but—"

"What if you all agreed to play a little joke on D. W.? Sikes pretends to be dead with a knife in his neck when Denise distracts Griffith. Sikes can't stick the fake knife in his back. He can't reach his own back. He attaches it to his neck. Then you all discover the body, Griffith comes for me, Sikes laughs. You all laugh, then one of you, probably Korites, moves behind him and uses a real knife to turn the joke into fact. You're all covered. Someone did it. The police would have a hell of a time figuring out which one, and meanwhile, it would make a hell of a news story. Griffith a witness. All of you suspects. Probably wind up with a backer who'd cash in on your morbid celebrity."

"Ridiculous," laughed Korites.

"I was the audience," Griffith repeated with a rueful laugh.

"Even if this were true," said Denise Giles, "you could never prove it."

"Props," I said. "You didn't have time to get rid of that fake knife, at least not to get it hidden too well. D. W. was with me for only a minute or two, and you didn't want to get too far from this room in case we came running back here. No, if we're right, that prop knife is nearby, where it can be found, somewhere in this room or not far from it."

"This is ridiculous," said Vann, standing up. "I'm not staying here for any more of this charade." He took a step toward the door behind Griffith, giving me a good idea of where to start looking for the prop knife, but the director was out of his chair and barring his way.

"Move," shouted Vann.

"Never," cried Griffith.

Vann threw a punch, but Griffith caught it with his left and came back with a right. Vann went down. Korites started to rise, looked at my face, and sat down again.

"We can work something out here," he said, his face going white.

A siren blasted somewhere outside.

"Hell of a practical joke," Dollard said, dropping the radish in his fingers. "Hell of a joke."

No one moved while we waited for the police. We just sat there, Vann on the floor, Griffith standing. I imagined a round iris closing in on the scene, and then a slow fade to black.

WILLIAM CAMPBELL GAULT

William Campbell Gault (1910–1995) supported himself for three decades by writing books for high school boys. They featured sports or cars and were second only to the juvenile novels of Robert A. Heinlein in popularity.

He was the perfect man to write for teenagers. He'd developed a style in the pulps of the thirties and forties that was so simple and easygoing it was almost like direct address.

It was this style that won him the Edgar for *Don't Cry for Me*, one of the most remarkable private eye novels ever written. Take a Midwestern Republican, transplant him to the West Coast, make him start thinking in terms of gray rather than black and white—and you have a charmingly (and somewhat sadly) confused man who is no longer sure which set of values to apply to the world he encounters every day.

Because Gault spent so much time and effort on his teenager books, his crime career never quite got the recognition it deserved, even though both Raymond Chandler and Ross Macdonald praised him and the Private Eye Writers made him a Grand Master.

The Kerman Kill

"Pierre?" my Uncle Vartan asked. "Why Pierre? You were Pistol Pete Apoyan when you fought."

Sixteen amateur fights I'd had and won them all. Two professional fights I'd had and painfully decided it would not be my trade. I had followed that career with three years as an employee of the Arden Guard and Investigative Service in Santa Monica before deciding to branch out on my own.

We were in my uncle's rug store in Beverly Hills, a small store and not in the highest rent district, but a fine store. No machine-made imitation orientals for him, and *absolutely* no carpeting.

"You didn't change your name," I pointed out.

"Why would I?" he asked. "It is an honorable name and suited to my trade."

"And Pierre is not an honorable name?"

He signed. "Please do not misunderstand me. I adore your mother. But Pierre is a name for hairdressers and perfume manufacturers and those pirate merchants on Rodeo Drive. Don't your friends call you Pete?"

"My odar friends," I admitted. "Odar" means (roughly) non-Armenian. My mother is French, my father Armenian.

"Think!" he said. "Sam Spade. Mike Hammer. But Pierre?"

"Hercule Poirot," I said.

"What does that mean? Who is this Hercule Poirot? A friend?" He was frowning.

It was my turn to sigh. I said nothing. My Uncle Vartan is a stubborn man. He had four nephews, but I was his favorite. He had never married. He had come to this country as an infant with my father and their older brother. My father had sired one son and one daughter, my Uncle Sarkis three sons.

"You're so stubborn!" Uncle Vartan said.

The pot had just described the kettle. I shrugged.

He took a deep breath. "I suppose I am, too."

I nodded.

"Whatever," he said, "the decision is yours, no matter what name you decide to use."

The decision would be mine but the suggestion had been his. Tough private eye stories, fine rugs, and any attractive woman under sixty were what he cherished. His store had originally been a two-story duplex with a separate door and stairway to the second floor. That, he had suggested, would be a lucrative location for my office when I left Arden.

His reasoning was sound enough. He got the carriage trade; why wouldn't I? And he would finance the remodeling.

Why was I so stubborn?

"Don't sulk," he said.

"It's because of my mother," I explained. "She didn't like it when I was called Pistol Pete."

His smile was sad. "I know. But wouldn't Pistol Pierre have sounded worse?" He shook his head. "Lucky Pierre, always in the middle. I talked with the contractor last night. The remodeling should be finished by next Tuesday."

The second floor was large enough to include living quarters for me. Tonight I would tell my two roomies in our Pacific Palisades apartment that I would be deserting them at the end of the month. I drove out to Westwood, where my mother and sister had a French pastry shop.

My sister, Adele, was behind the counter. My mother was in the back, smoking a cigarette. She is a chain smoker, my mother, the only nicotine addict in the family. She is a slim, trim, and testy forty-seven-year-old tiger.

"Well—?" she asked.

"We won," I told her. "It will be the Pierre Apoyan Investigative Service."

"*You* won," she corrected me. "You and Vartan. It wasn't *my* idea."

"Are there any croissants left?" I asked.

"On the shelf next to the oven." She shook her head. "That horny old bastard! All the nice women I found for him—"

"Who needs a cow when milk is cheap?" I asked.

"Don't be vulgar," she said. "And if you do, get some new jokes."

I buttered two croissants, poured myself a cup of coffee, and sat down across from her. I said, "The rumor I heard years ago is that Vartan came on to you before you met Dad."

"The rumor is true," she admitted. "But if I wanted to marry an adulterer I would have stayed in France."

"And then you never would have met Dad. You did okay, Ma."

"I sure as hell did. He's *all* man."

The thought came to me that if he were all man, the macho type, my first name would not be Pierre. I didn't voice the thought; I preferred to drink my coffee, not wear it.

She said, "I suppose that you'll be carrying a gun again in this new profession you and Vartan dreamed up?"

"Ma, at Arden, I carried a gun only when I worked guard duty. I *never* carried one when I did investigative work. This will not be guard duty."

She put out her cigarette and stood up. "That's something, I suppose. You're coming for dinner on Sunday, of course?"

"Of course," I said.

She went out to take over the counter. Adele came in to have a cup of coffee. She was born eight years after I was; she is twenty and romantically inclined. She has our mother's slim, dark beauty and our father's love of the theater. She was currently sharing quarters with an aspiring actor. My father was a still cameraman at Elysian Films.

"Mom looks angry," she said. "What did you two argue about this time?"

"My new office. Uncle Vartan is going to back me."

She shook her head. "What a waste! With your looks you'd be a cinch in films."

"Even prettier than your Ronnie?"

"Call it a tie," she said. "You don't like him, do you?"

Her Ronnie was an aspiring actor who called himself Ronnie Egan. His real name was Salvatore Martino. I shrugged.

"He's got another commercial coming up next week. And his agent thinks he might be able to work me into it."

"Great!" I said.

That gave him a three-year career total of four commercials. If he worked her in, it would be her second.

"Why don't you like him?"

"Honey, I only met him twice and I don't dislike him. Could we drop the subject?"

"Aagh!" she said. "You and Vartan, you two deserve each other. Bullheads!"

"People who live in glass houses," I pointed out, "should undress in the cellar."

She shook her head again. "You and Papa, you know all the corny old ones, don't you?"

"Guilty," I admitted. "Are you bringing Ronnie to dinner on Sunday?"

"Not this Sunday. We're going to a party at his agent's house. Ronnie wants me to meet him."

"I hope it works out. I'll hold my thumbs. I love you, sis."

"It's mutual," she said.

I kissed the top of her head and went out to my ancient Camaro. On the way to the apartment I stopped in Santa Monica and talked with my former boss at Arden.

I had served him well; he promised that if they ever had any commercial reason to invade my new bailiwick, and were short-handed, I would be their first choice for associate action.

The apartment I shared with two others in Pacific Palisades was on the crest of the road just before Sunset Boulevard curves and dips down to the sea.

My parents had bought a tract house here in the fifties for an exorbitant twenty-one thousand dollars. It was now worth enough to permit both of them to retire. But they enjoyed their work too much to consider that.

I will not immortalize my roomies' names in print. One of them was addicted to prime-time soap operas, the other changed his underwear and socks once a week, on Saturday, after his weekly shower.

When I told them, over our oven-warmed frozen TV dinners, that I would be leaving at the end of the month, they took it graciously. Dirty Underwear was currently courting a lunch-counter waitress who had been hoping to share an apartment. She would inherit my rollout bed—when she wasn't in his.

On Thursday morning my former boss phoned to tell me he had several credit investigations that needed immediate action and two operatives home with the flu. Was I available? I was.

Uncle Sarkis and I went shopping on Saturday for office and apartment furniture. Wholesale, of course. "Retail" is an obscene word to my Uncle Sarkis.

The clan was gathered on Sunday at my parents' house, all but Adele. Uncle Vartan and my father played tavlu (backgammon to you). My mother, Uncle Sarkis, his three sons, and I played twenty-five-cent-limit poker out on the patio. My mother won, as usual. I broke even; the others lost. I have often suspected that the Sunday gatherings my mother hosts are more financially motivated than familial.

My roommates told me Monday morning that I didn't have to wait until the end of the month; I could move anytime my place was ready. The waitress was aching to move in.

The remodeling was finished at noon on Tuesday, the furniture delivered in the afternoon. I moved in the next morning. All who passed on the street below would now be informed by the gilt letters on the new wide front window that the Pierre Apoyan Investigative Service was now open and ready to serve them.

There were many who passed on the street below in the next three hours, but not one came up the steps. There was no reason to expect that anyone would. Referrals and advertising were what brought the clients in. Arden was my only doubtful source for the first; my decision to open this office had come too late to make the deadline for an ad in the phone book yellow pages.

I consoled myself with the knowledge that there was no odor of sour socks in the room and I would not be subjected to the idiocies of prime-time soap opera. I read the *L.A. Times* all the way through to the classified pages.

It had been a tiring two days; I went into my small bedroom to nap around ten o'clock. It was noon when I came back to the here and now. I turned on my answering machine and went down to ask Vartan if I could take him to lunch.

He shook his head. "Not today. After your first case, you may buy. Today, lunch is on me."

He had not spent enough time in the old country to develop a taste for Armenian food. He had spent his formative years in New York and become addicted to Italian cuisine. We ate at La Famiglia on North Canon Drive.

He had whitefish poached in white wine, topped with capers and small bay shrimp. I had a Caesar salad.

Over our coffee, he asked, "Dull morning?"

I nodded. "There are bound to be a lot of them for a one-man office. I got in two days at Arden last week. I might get more when they're short-handed."

He studied me for a few seconds. Then, "I wasn't going to mention this. I don't want to get your hopes up. But I have a—a customer who might drop in this afternoon. It's about a rug I sold her. It has been stolen. For some reason, which she wouldn't tell me, she doesn't want to go to the police. I gave her your name."

He had hesitated before he had called her a customer. With his history, she could have been more than that. "Was it an expensive rug?" I asked.

"I got three thousand for it eight years ago. Only God knows what it's worth now. That was a sad day for me. It's an antique Kerman."

"Wasn't it insured?"

"Probably. But if she reported the loss to her insurance company they would insist she go to the police."

"Was anything else stolen?"

"Apparently not. The rug was all she mentioned."

That didn't make sense. A woman who could afford my uncle's antique oriental rugs must have some jewelry. That would be easier and safer to haul out of a house than a rug.

"I'd better get back to the office," I said.

"Don't get your hopes up," he warned me again. "I probably shouldn't have told you."

I checked my answering machine when I got back to the office. Nothing. I took out my contract forms and laid them on top of my desk and sat where I could watch the street below.

I decided, an hour later, that was sophomoric. The ghost of Sam Spade must have been sneering down at me.

She opened the door about twenty minutes later, a fairly tall, slim woman with jet-black hair, wearing black slacks and a white cashmere sweater. She could have been sixty or thirty; she had those high cheekbones which keep a face taut.

"Mr. Apoyan?" she asked.

I nodded.

"Your uncle recommended you to me."

"He told me. But he didn't tell me your name."

"I asked him not to." She came over to sit in my client's chair. "It's Bishop, Mrs. Whitney Bishop. Did he tell you that I prefer not to have the police involved?"

"Yes. Was anything else stolen?"

She shook her head.

"That seems strange to me," I said. "Burglars don't usually carry out anything big, anything suspicious enough to alert the neighbors."

"Our neighbors are well screened from view," she told me, "and I'm sure this was not a burglar." She paused. "I am almost certain it was my daughter. And *that* is why I don't want the police involved."

"It wasn't a rug too big for a woman to carry?"

She shook her head. "A three-by-five-foot antique Kerman."

I winced. "For three thousand dollars—?"

Her smile was dim. "You obviously don't have your uncle's knowledge of rugs. I was offered more than I care to mention for it only two months ago. My daughter is—adopted. She has been in trouble before. I have *almost* given up on her. We had a squabble the day my husband and I went down to visit friends in Rancho Santa Fe. When we came home the rug was gone and so was she."

I wondered if it was her daughter she wanted back or the rug. I decided that would be a cynical question to ask.

"We have an elaborate alarm system," she went on, "with a well-hidden turnoff in the house. It couldn't have been burglars." She stared bleakly past me. "She knows how much I love that rug. I feel that it was simply a vindictive act on her part. It has been a—troubled relationship."

"How old is she?" I asked.

"Seventeen."

"Does she know who her real parents are?"

"No. And neither do we. Why?"

"I thought she might have gone back to them. How about her friends?"

"We've talked with all of her friends that we know. There are a number of them we have never met." A pause. "And I am sure would not want to."

"Your daughter's—acceptable friends might know of others," I suggested.

"Possibly," she admitted. "I'll give you a list of those we know well."

She told me her daughter's name was Janice and made out a list of her friends while I filled in the contract. She gave me a check, her unlisted phone number, and a picture of her daughter.

When she left, I went to the window and saw her climb into a sleek black Jaguar below. My hunch had been sound; this was the town that attracted the carriage trade.

I went downstairs to thank Vartan and tell him our next lunch would be on me at a restaurant of his choice.

"I look forward to it," he said. "She's quite a woman, isn't she?"

"That she is. Was she ever more than a customer to you?"

"We had a brief but meaningful relationship," he said coolly, "at a time when she was between husbands. But then she started talking marriage." He sighed.

"Uncle Vartan," I asked, "haven't you *ever* regretted the fact that you have no children to carry on your name?"

"Never," he said, and smiled. "You are all I need."

Two elderly female customers came in then and I went out with my list of names. It was a little after three o'clock; some of the kids should be home from school.

There were five names on the list, two girls and three boys, all students at Beverly Hills High. Only one of the girls was home. She had seen Janice at school on Friday, she told me, but not since. But that didn't mean she hadn't been at school Monday and Tuesday.

"She's not in any of my classes," she explained.

I showed her the list. "Could you tell me if any of these students are in any of her classes?"

"Not for sure. But Howard might be in her art appreciation class. They're both kind of—you know—"

"Artistic?" I asked.

"I suppose. You know—that weird stuff—"

"Avant-garde, abstract, cubist?"

She shrugged. "I guess, whatever *that* means. Janice and I were never really close."

From the one-story stone house of Miss Youknow, I drove to the two-story Colonial home of Howard Retzenbaum.

He was a tall thin youth with horn-rimmed glasses. He was wearing faded jeans and a light gray T-shirt with a darker gray reproduction of Pablo Picasso's *Woman's Head* emblazoned on his narrow chest.

Janice, he told me, had been in class on Friday, but not Monday or yesterday. "Has something happened to her?"

"I hope not. Do you know of any friends she has who don't go to your school?"

Only one, he told me, a boy named Leslie she had introduced him to several weeks ago. He had forgotten his last name. He tapped his forehead. "I remember she told me he worked at some Italian restaurant in town. He was a busboy there."

"La Famiglia?"

"No, no. That one on Santa Monica Boulevard."

"La Dolce Vita?"

He nodded. "That's the place. Would you tell her to phone me if you find her?"

I promised him I would and thanked him. The other two boys were not at home; they had baseball practice after school. I drove to La Dolce Vita.

They serve no luncheon trade. The manager was not in. The assistant manager looked at me suspiciously when I asked if a boy named Leslie worked there.

"Does he have a last name?"

"I'm sure he has. Most people do. But I don't happen to know it."

"Are you a police officer?"

I shook my head. "I am a licensed and bonded private investigator. My Uncle Vartan told me that Leslie is an employee here."

"Would that be Vartan Apoyan?"

"It would be and it is." I handed him my card.

He read it and smiled. "That's different. Leslie's last name is Denton. He's a student at UCLA and works from seven o'clock until closing." He gave me Leslie's phone number and address, and asked, "Is Pierre an Armenian name?"

"Quite often," I informed him coldly and left without thanking him.

The address was in Westwood and it was now almost five o'clock. I had no desire to buck the going-home traffic in this city of wheels. I drove to the office to phone Leslie.

He answered the phone. I told him I was a friend of Howard Retzenbaum's and we were worried about Janice. I explained that she hadn't been in school on Monday or Tuesday and her parents didn't know where she was.

"Are you also a friend of her parents?" he asked.

"No way!"

She had come to his place Friday afternoon, he told me, when her parents had left for Rancho Santa Fe. She had stayed over the weekend. But when he had come home from school on Tuesday she was gone.

"She didn't leave a note or anything?"

"No."

"She didn't, by chance, bring a three-foot-by-five-foot Kerman rug with her, did she?"

"Hell, no! Why?"

"According to a police officer I know in Beverly Hills, her parents think she stole it from the house. Did she come in a car?"

"No. A taxi. What in hell is going on? Are those creepy parents of hers trying to frame her?"

"Not if I can help it. Did she leave your place anytime during the weekend?"

"She did not. If you find her, will you let me know?"

I promised him I would.

I phoned Mrs. Whitney Bishop and asked her if Janice had been in the house Friday when they left for Rancho Santa Fe.

"No. She left several hours before that. My husband didn't get home from the office until five o'clock."

"Were there any servants in the house when you left?"

"We have no live-in servants, Mr. Apoyan."

"In that case," I said, "I think it is time for you to call the police and file a missing persons report. Janice was in Westwood from Friday afternoon until some time on Tuesday."

"Westwood? Was she with that Leslie Denton person?"

"She was. Do you know him?"

"Janice brought him to the house several times. Let me assure you, Mr. Apoyan, that he is a doubtful source of information. You know, of course, that he's gay."

That sounded like a non sequitur to me. I didn't point it out. I thought of telling her to go to hell. But a more reasonable (and mercenary) thought overruled it; rich bigots should pay for their bigotry.

"You want me to continue, then?" I asked.

"I certainly do. Have you considered the possibility that one of Leslie Denton's friends might have used her key and Janice told him where the turnoff switch is located?"

I hadn't thought of that.

"I thought of that," I explained, "but if that happened, I doubt if we could prove it. I don't want to waste your money, Mrs. Bishop."

"Don't you worry about that," she said. "You find my rug!"

Not her daughter; her rug. First things first. "I'll get right on it," I assured her.

I was warming some lahmajoons Sarkis's wife had given me last Sunday when I heard my office door open. I went out.

It was Cheryl, my current love, back from San Francisco, where she had gone to visit her mother.

"Welcome home!" I said. "How did you know I moved?"

"Adele told me. Are those lahmajoons I smell?"

I nodded. She came over to kiss me. She looked around the office, went through the open doorway, and inspected the apartment.

When she came back, she said, "And now we have this. Now we won't have to worry if your roommates are home, or mine. Do you think I should move in?"

"We'll see. What's in the brown bag?"

"Potato salad, a jar of big black olives, and two avocados."

"Welcome home again. You can make the coffee."

Over our meal I told her about my day, my lucky opening day in this high-priced town. I mentioned no names, only places.

It sounded like a classic British locked-room mystery, she thought and said. She is an addict of the genre.

"Except for the guy in Westwood," I pointed out. "Maybe one of his friends stole the rug."

Westwood was where she shared an apartment with two friends. "Does he have a name?" she asked.

I explained to her that that would be privileged information.

"I was planning to stay the night," she said, "until now."

"His name is Leslie Denton."

"Les Denton?" She shook her head. "Not in a zillion years! He is integrity incarnate."

"You're thinking of your idol, Len Deighton," I said.

"I am not! Les took the same night-school class that I did in restaurant management. We got to be very good friends. He works as a busboy at La Dolce Vita."

"I know. Were you vertical or horizontal friends?"

"Don't be vulgar, Petroff. Les is not heterosexual."

"Aren't you glad I am?"

"Not at the moment."

"Let's have some more wine," I suggested.

At nine o'clock she went down to her car to get her luggage. When she came back, she asked, "Are you tired?"

"Nope."

"Neither am I," she said. "Let's go to bed."

I was deep in a dream involving my high school sweetheart when the phone rang in my office. My bedside clock informed me that it was seven o'clock. The voice on the phone informed me that I was a lying bastard.

"Who is speaking, please?" I asked.

"Les Denton. Mr. Randisi at the restaurant gave me your phone number. You told me you were a friend of Howard Retzenbaum's. Mr. Randisi told me you were a stinking private eye. You're working for the Bishops, aren't you?"

"Leslie," I said calmly, "I have a very good friend of yours who is here in the office right now. She will assure you that I am not a lying bastard and do not stink. I have to be devious at times. It is a requisite of my trade."

"What's her name?"

"Cheryl Pushkin. Hold the line. I'll put her on."

Cheryl was sitting up in bed. I told her Denton wanted to talk to her.

"Why? Who told him I was here?"

"I did. He wants a character reference."

"What?"

"Go!" I said. "And don't hang up when you're finished. I want to talk with him."

I was half dressed when she came back to tell me she had calmed him down and he would talk to me now.

I told him it was true that I was working for Mrs. Bishop. I added that getting her rug back was a minor concern to me; finding her daughter was my major concern and should be his, too. I told him I would be grateful for any help he could give me on this chivalrous quest.

"I shouldn't have gone off half-cocked," he admitted. "I have some friends who know Janice. I'll ask around."

"Thank you."

Cheryl was in the shower when I hung up. I started the coffee and went down the steps to pick up the *Times* at my front door.

A few minutes after I came back, she was in her robe, studying the contents of my fridge. "Only two eggs in here," she said, "and two strips of bacon."

"There are some frozen waffles in the freezer compartment."

"You can have those. I'll have bacon and eggs." I didn't argue.

"You were moaning just before the phone rang," she said. "You were moaning 'Norah, Norah.' Who is Norah?"

"A dog I had when I was a kid. She was killed by a car."

She turned to stare at me doubtfully, but made no comment. Both her parents are Russian, a suspicious breed. Her father lived in San Diego, her mother in San Francisco, what they had called a trial separation. I suspected it was messing-around time in both cities.

She had decided in the night, she told me, to reside in Westwood for a while. I had the feeling she doubted my fidelity. She had suggested at one time that I could be a younger clone of Uncle Vartan.

She left and I sat. I had promised Mrs. Bishop that I would "get right on it." Where would I start? The three kids I had not questioned yesterday were now in school. And there was very little likelihood that they would have any useful information on the present whereabouts of Janice Bishop. Leslie Denton was my last best hope.

I took the *Times* and a cup of coffee out to the office and sat at my desk. Terrible Tony Tuscani, I read in the sports page, had outpointed Mike (the Hammer) Mulligan in a ten-round windup last night in Las Vegas. The writer thought Tony was a cinch to cop the middleweight crown. In my fifth amateur fight I had kayoed Tony halfway through the third round. Was I in the wrong trade?

And then the thought came to me that an antique Kerman was not the level of stolen merchandise one would take to an ordinary fence. A burglar sophisticated enough to outfox a complicated alarm system should certainly know that. He would need to find a buyer who knew about oriental rugs.

Uncle Vartan was on the phone when I went down. When he had finished talking I voiced the thought I'd had upstairs.

"It makes sense," he agreed. "So?"

"I thought, being in the trade, you might know of one."

"I do," he said. "Ismet Bey. He has a small shop in Santa Monica. He deals mostly in imitation orientals and badly worn antiques. I have reason to know he has occasionally bought stolen rugs."

"Why don't you phone him," I suggested, "and tell him you have a customer who is looking for a three-by-five Kerman?"

His face stiffened. "You are asking *me* to talk to a Turk?"

I said lamely, "I didn't know he was a Turk."

"You know now," he said stiffly. "If you decide to phone him use a different last name."

I looked him up in the phone book and called. A woman answered. I asked for Ismet. She told me he was not in at the moment and might not be in until this afternoon. She identified herself as his wife and asked if she could be of help.

"I certainly hope so," I said. "My wife and I have been scouring the town for an antique Kerman. We have been unsuccessful so far. Is it possible you have one?"

"We haven't," she said. "But I am surprised to learn you haven't found one. There must be a number of stores that have at least one in stock. The better stores, I mean, of course."

An honest woman married to a crooked Turk. I said, "Not a three-by-five. We want it for the front hall."

"That might be more difficult," she said. "But Mr.—"

"Stein," I said. "Peter Stein."

"Mr. Stein," she continued, "my husband has quite often found hard-to-find rugs. Do you live in Santa Monica?"

"In Beverly Hills." I gave her my phone number. "If I'm not here, please leave a message on my answering machine."

"We will. I'll tell my husband as soon as he gets here. If you should find what you're looking for in the meantime—"

"I'll let you know immediately," I assured her.

I temporarily changed the name on my answering machine from Pierre Apoyan Investigative Service to a simple Peter. Both odars and kinsmen would recognize me by that name.

Back to sitting and waiting. I felt slightly guilty about sitting around when Mrs. Bishop was paying me by the hour. But only slightly. Mrs. Whitney Bishop would never make my favorite-persons list.

Uncle Vartan was born long after the Turkish massacre of his people. But he knew the brutal history of that time as surely as the young Jews know the history of the holocaust—from the survivors.

I read the rest of the news that interested me in the *Times* and drank another cup of coffee. I was staring down at the street below around noon when my door opened.

It was Cheryl. She must have been coming up as I was looking down. She had driven in for a sale at I. Magnin, she told me. "And as long as I was in the neighborhood—"

"You dropped in on your favorite person," I finished for her. "What's in the bag, something from Magnin's?"

"In a brown paper bag? Lox and bagels, my friend, and cream cheese. I noticed how low your larder was this morning. Did Les Denton phone you?"

I shook my head.

"I bumped into him in front of the UCLA library this morning," she said, "and gave him the old third degree. He swore to me that he and Janice were alone over the weekend, so she couldn't have given her house key to *anybody*. I was right, wasn't I?"

"I guess you were, Miss Marple. Tea or coffee?"

"Tea for me. I can't stay long. Robinson's is also having a sale."

"How exciting! Your mama must have given you a big fat check again when you were up in San Francisco."

"Don't be sarcastic! I stopped in downstairs and asked your uncle if you'd ever had a dog named Norah."

"And he confirmed it."

"Not quite. He said he thought you had but he wasn't sure. Of course, he probably can't even remember half the women he's—he's courted."

"Enough!" I said. "Lay off!"

"I'm sorry. Jealousy! That's adolescent, isn't it? It's vulgar and possessive."

"I guess."

"You're not very talkative today, are you?"

"Cheryl, there is a young girl out there somewhere who has run away from home. That, to me, is much more important than a sale at Robinson's or whether I ever had a dog named Norah. This is a dangerous town for seventeen-year-old runaways."

"You're right." She sighed. "How trivial can I get?"

"We all have our hang-ups," I said. "I love you just the way you are."

"And I you, Petroff. Do you think Janice is in some kind of danger? Why would she leave Les's place without even leaving him a note?"

"*That* I don't know. And it scares me."

"You don't think she's—" She didn't finish.

"Dead? I have no way of knowing."

Five minutes after she left, I learned that Janice had still been alive yesterday. Les Denton phoned to tell me that a friend of his had seen her on the Santa Monica beach with an older man, but had not talked with her. According to the friend, the man she was with was tall and thin and frail, practically a skeleton.

"Thanks," I said.

"It's not the first time she's run away," he told me. "And there's a pattern to it."

"What kind of pattern?"

"Well, I could be reading more into it than there is. But I noticed that it was usually when her mother was out of town. Mrs. Bishop is quite a gadabout."

"Are you suggesting child molestation?"

"Only suggesting, Mr. Apoyan. I could be wrong."

And possibly right. "Thanks again," I said.

A troubled relationship is what Mrs. Bishop had called it. Did she know whereof she spoke? Mothers are often the last to know.

Ismet Bey phoned half an hour later to tell me he had located a three-by-five Kerman owned by a local dealer and had brought it to his shop. Could I drop in this afternoon?

I told him I could and would.

And now what? How much did I know about antique Kermans? Uncle Vartan would remember the rug he had sold, but he sure as hell wouldn't walk into the shop of Ismet Bey.

Maybe Mrs. Bishop? She could pose as my wife. I phoned her unlisted number. A woman answered, probably a servant. Mrs. Bishop, she told me, was shopping and wouldn't be home until six o'clock.

I did know a few things about rugs. I had worked for Uncle Vartan on Saturdays and during vacations when I was at UCLA.

I took the photograph of Janice with me and drove out to Santa Monica. Bey's store, like the building Vartan and I shared, was a converted house on Pico Boulevard, old and sagging. I parked in the three-car graveled parking lot next to his panel truck.

The interior was dim and musty. Mrs. Bey was not in sight. The fat rump of a broad, short, and bald man greeted me as I came in. He was bending over, piling some small rugs on the floor.

He rose and turned to face me. He had an olive complexion, big brown eyes, and the oily smile of a used-car salesman. "Mr. Stein?" he asked.

I nodded.

"This way, please," he said, and led me to the rear of the store. The rug was on a display rack, a pale tan creation, sadly thin and about as tightly woven as a fisherman's net.

"Mr. Bey," I said, "that is not a Kerman."

"Really? What is it, then?"

"It looks like an Ispahan to me, a cheap Ispahan."

He continued to smile. "It was only a test."

"I'm not following you. A test for what?"

He shrugged. "There have been some rumors around town. Some rumors about a very rare and expensive three-by-five Kerman that has been stolen. I thought you may have heard them."

What a cutie. "I haven't heard them," I said. And added, "But, of course, I don't have your contacts."

"I'm sure you don't. Maybe you should have. How much did you plan to spend on this rug you want, Mr. Stein?"

"Not as much as the rug you described would cost me. But I have a rich friend who might be interested. He is not quite as—as ethical as I try to be."

"Perhaps that is why he is rich. All I can offer now is the hope that this rug will find its way to me. Could I have the name of your friend?"

I shook my head. "If the rug finds its way to you, phone me. I'll have him come here. I don't want to be involved."

"You won't need to be," he assured me. "And I'll see that you are recompensed. You were right about this rug. It is an Ispahan. If you have some friends who are not rich, I hope you will mention my name to them."

That would be the day. "I will," I said.

I drove to Arden from there, and the boss was in his office. I told him about my dialogue with Bey and suggested they keep an eye on his place. I pointed out that they could make some brownie points with the Santa Monica Police Department.

"Thank you, loyal ex-employee. We'll do that."

"In return, you might make some copies of this photograph and pass them out among the boys. She is a runaway girl who was last seen here on your beach."

"You've got a case already?"

"With my reputation, why not?"

"Is there some connection between the missing girl and the rug?"

"That, as you are well aware, would be privileged information."

"Dear God," he said, "the kid's turned honest! Wait here."

He went out to the copier and came back about five minutes later. He handed me the photo and a check for the two days I had worked for him last week and wished me well. The nice thing about the last is that I knew he meant it.

From there to the beach. I sat in the shade near the refreshment stand with the forlorn hope that the skeleton man and the runaway girl might come this way again.

Two hours, one ice cream cone, and two Cokes later I drove back to Beverly Hills. Uncle Vartan was alone in the shop. I went in and related to him my dialogue with Ismet Bey.

"That tawdry Turk," he said, "that bush-leaguer! He doesn't cater to that class of trade. He's dreaming a pipe dream."

"How much do you think that rug would bring today?" I asked.

"Pierre, I do not want to discuss that rug. As I told you before, that was a sad day, maybe the saddest day of my life."

Saddest to him could be translated into English as least lucrative. A chauffeured Rolls-Royce pulled up in front of the shop and an elegantly dressed couple headed for his doorway. I held the door open for them and went up my stairs to sit again.

I typed it all down in chronological order, the history of my first case in my own office, from the time Mrs. Whitney Bishop had walked in to my uncle's refusal to talk about the Kerman.

There had to be a pattern in there somewhere to a discerning eye. Either my eye was not discerning or there was no pattern.

Cheryl had called it right; my larder was low. I heated a package of frozen peas and ate them with two baloney sandwiches and the cream cheese left over from lunch.

There was, as usual, nothing worth watching on the tube. I went back to read again the magic of the man my father had introduced me to when I was in my formative years, the sadly funny short stories of William Saroyan.

Where would I go tomorrow? What avenues of investigation were still unexplored? Unless the unlikely happened, a call from Ismet Bey, all I had left was a probably fruitless repeat of yesterday's surveillance of the Santa Monica beach.

I went to bed at nine o'clock, but couldn't sleep. I got up, poured three ounces of Tennessee whiskey into a tumbler, added a cube of ice, and sat and sipped. It was eleven o'clock before I was tired enough to sleep.

I drank what was left of the milk in the morning and decided to have breakfast in Santa Monica. I didn't take my swimming trunks; the day was not that warm.

Scrambled eggs and pork sausages, orange juice, toast, and coffee at Barney's Breakfast Bar fortified me for the gray day ahead.

Only the hardy were populating the beach. The others would come out if the overcast went away. I sat again on the bench next to the refreshment stand and reread Ralph Ellison's *Invisible Man*. It had seemed appropriate reading for the occasion.

I had been doing a lot of sitting on this case. I could understand now why my boss at Arden had piles.

Ten o'clock passed. So did eleven. About fifteen minutes after that a tall, thin figure appeared in the murky air at the far end of the beach. It was a man and he was heading this way.

Closer and clearer he came. He was wearing khaki trousers, a red-and-tan-checked flannel shirt, and a red nylon windbreaker. He nodded and smiled as he passed me. He bought a Coke at the stand and sat down at the other end of the bench.

I laid down my book.

"Ralph Ellison?" he said. "I had no idea he was still in print."

He was thin, he was haggard, and his eyes were dull. But skeleton had been too harsh a word. "He probably isn't," I said. "This is an old Signet paperback reprint. My father gave it to me when I was still in high school."

"I see. We picked a bad day for sun, didn't we?"

"That's not why I'm here," I told him. "I'm looking for a girl, a runaway girl. Do you come here often?"

He nodded. "Quite often."

I handed him the photograph of Janice. "Have you ever seen her here?"

He took a pair of wire-rimmed glasses from his shirt pocket and put them on to study the picture. "Oh, yes," he said. "Was it yesterday? No—Wednesday." He took a deep breath. "There are so many of them who come here. I talked with her. She told me she had come down from Oxnard and didn't have the fare to go home. I bought her a malt and a hot dog. She told me the fare to Oxnard was eight dollars and some cents. I've forgotten the exact amount. Anyway, I gave her a ten-dollar bill and made her promise that she would use it for the fare home."

"Do you do that often?"

"Not often enough. When I can afford it."

"She's not from Oxnard," I told him. "She's from Beverly Hills."

He stared at me. "She couldn't be! She was wearing a pair of patched jeans and a cheap, flimsy T-shirt."

"She's from Beverly Hills," I repeated. "Her parents are rich."

He smiled. "That little liar! She conned me. And what a sweet young thing she was."

"I hope 'was' isn't the definitive word," I said.

He closed his eyes and took another deep breath. He opened them and stared out at the sea.

I handed him my card. "If you see her again, would you phone me?"

"Of course. My name is Gerald Hopkins. I live at the Uphan Hotel. It's a—a place for what are currently called senior citizens."

"I know the place," I told him. "Let's hold our thumbs."

"Dear God, yes!" he said.

From there I drove to the store of the tawdry Turk. He was not there but his wife was, a short, thin, and dark-skinned woman. I told her my name.

She nodded. "Ismet told me you were here yesterday." Her smile was sad. "That man and his dreams! What cock-and-bull story did he tell you?"

"Some of it made sense. He tried to sell me an Ispahan."

"He didn't tell *me* that!"

"He also told me about some rumors he heard."

"Oh, yes! Rumors he has. Customers is what we need. Tell me, Mr. Stein, how can a man get so fat on rumors?"

"He's probably married to a good cook."

"*That* he is. Take my advice, and a grain of salt, when you listen to the rumors of my husband, Mr. Stein. He is a dreamer. It is the reason I married him. I, too, in my youth, was a dreamer. It is why we came to America many years ago."

Send these, the homeless, tempest-tost to me. I lift my lamp beside the golden door . . .

I smiled at her. "Keep the faith!" I went out.

My next stop was the bank, where I deposited the checks from Mrs. Bishop and Arden and cashed a check for two hundred dollars.

From there to Vons in Santa Monica, where I stocked up on groceries, meat, and booze. Grocery markups in Beverly Hills, my mother had warned me, were absurd. Only the vulgar rich could afford them.

Mrs. Bey might believe that all the rumors her husband heard were bogus. But the rumor he had voiced to me was too close to the truth to qualify as bogus. It was logical to assume that there were shenanigans he indulged in in the practice of his trade that he would not reveal to her. To a man of his ilk the golden door meant gold, and he was still looking for the door.

I put the groceries away when I got home and went out to check the answering machine. Zilch. I typed the happenings of the morning into the record. Nothing had changed; no pattern showed.

There was a remote chance that Bey might learn where the rug was now. That was what I was being paid to find. But, as I had told Les Denton, the girl was my major concern.

It wasn't likely that she was staying at the home of any of her classmates. Their parents certainly would have phoned Mrs. Bishop by now if she hadn't phoned them.

Which reminded me that I had something to report. I phoned the Bishop house and the lady was home. I told her Janice had been seen on the Santa Monica beach on Wednesday and that a man there had told me this morning that he had talked with her. She had lied to him, telling him that she lived in Oxnard.

"She's very adept at lying. Did you learn anything else?"

"Well, there was a rug dealer in Santa Monica who told me he had heard rumors about a three-by-five Kerman that had been stolen. I have no idea where he heard them."

"There could be a number of sources. My husband has been asking several dealers we know if they have seen it. And, of course, many of my friends know about the loss."

"Isn't it possible they might inform the police?"

"Not if they want to remain my friends. And the dealers, too, have been warned. If Janice has been seen on the Santa Monica beach, the rug could also be in the area. I think that is where you should concentrate your search."

It was warm and the weatherman had promised us sunshine for tomorrow. Cheryl and I could spend a day on the beach at Mrs. Bishop's expense.

"I agree with you completely," I said.

I phoned her apartment and Cheryl was there. I asked her if she'd like to spend a day on the beach with me tomorrow.

"I'd love it!"

I told her about the groceries I had bought and asked if she'd like to come and I'd cook a dinner for us tonight.

"Petroff, I can't! We're going to the symphony concert at the pavilion tonight."

"Who is *we*?"

"My roommates and I. Who else? Would you like to interrogate one of them?"

"Of course not! Save the program for me so I can see what I missed."

"I sure as hell will, you suspicious bastard. What time tomorrow?"

"Around ten."

"I'll be waiting."

I made myself a martini before dinner and then grilled a big T-bone steak and had it with frozen creamed asparagus and shoestring potatoes (heated, natch) and finished it off with lemon sherbet and coffee.

I had left *Invisible Man* in the car. I reread my favorite novel, *The Great Gatsby,* after dinner, along with a few ounces of brandy.

And then to my lonely bed. All the characters I had met since Wednesday afternoon kept running through my mind. All the chasing I had done had netted me nothing of substance. Credit investigations were so much cleaner and easier. But, like my Uncle Vartan, I had never felt comfortable working under a boss.

Cheryl was waiting outside her apartment building next morning when I pulled up a little after ten. She climbed into the car and handed me a program.

"Put it away," I said. "I was only kidding last night."

"Like hell you were!" She put it in the glove compartment. "And how was your evening?"

"Lonely. I talked with the man Denton's friend saw with Janice on the beach. She told him she had come down from Oxnard. He gave her the bus fare to go back."

"To Oxnard? Why would anybody want to go back to *Oxnard*?"

"She claimed she lived there. Don't ask me why."

"Maybe the man lied."

"Why would he?"

"Either he lied or she lied. It's fifty-fifty, isn't it?"

"Cheryl, he had no reason to lie. He told me the whole story and he has helped other kids to go home again. He gave me his name and address. Mrs. Bishop told me yesterday afternoon that Janice was—she called her an adept liar."

"And she is a creep, according to Les. Maybe Janice had reason to lie to the old bag."

"A creep she is. A bag she ain't. Tell me, what are you wearing under that simple but undoubtedly expensive charcoal denim dress?"

"My swimsuit, of course. Don't get horny. It's too early in the day for that."

It was, unfortunately, a great day for the beach; the place was jammed. They flood in from the San Fernando Valley and Hollywood and Culver City and greater Los Angeles on the warm days. Very few of them come from Beverly Hills. Most of those people have their own private swimming pools. Maybe all of them.

We laughed and splashed and swam and built a sand castle, back to the days of our adolescence. We forgot for a while the missing Janice Bishop and the antique Kerman.

After the fun part we walked from end to end on the beach, scanning the crowd, earning my pay, hoping to find the girl.

No luck.

Cheryl said, "I'll make you that dinner tonight, if you want me to."

"I want you to."

"We may as well go right to your place," she said. "You can drop me off at the apartment tomorrow when you go to the weekly meeting of the clan. It won't be out of your way."

"Sound thinking," I agreed.

What she made for us was a soufflé, an entree soufflé, not a dessert soufflé. But it was light enough to rest easily on top of the garbage we had consumed at the beach.

The garbage on the tube, we both agreed, would demean our day. We went to bed early.

The overcast was back in the morning, almost a fog. We ate a hearty breakfast to replace the energy we had lost in the night.

I dropped her off at her apartment a little after one o'clock, and was the first to arrive at my parents' house. Adele was the second. She had brought her friend with her, Salvatore Martino, known in the trade as Ronnie Egan.

It was possible, I reasoned, that I could be as wrong about him as Mrs. Whitney Bishop had been about Leslie Denton. I suggested to him that we take a couple of beers out to the patio while my mother and Adele fussed around in the kitchen.

We yacked about this and that, mostly sports, and then he said, "I saw three of your amateur fights and both your pro fights. How come you quit after that?"

"If you saw my pro fights, you should understand why."

"Jesus, man, you were *way* overmatched! You were jobbed. I'll bet Sam made a bundle on both of those fights."

Sam Batisto had been my manager. I said, "I'm not following you. You mean you think Sam is a crook?"

He nodded. "And a double-crossing sleazeball. Hell, he's got Mafia cousins. He'd sell out his mother if the price was right."

That son of a bitch . . .

"Well, what the hell," he went on, "maybe the bastard did you a favor. That's a nasty, ugly game, and people are beginning to realize it. Have you noticed how many big bouts are staged in Vegas?"

"I've noticed." I changed the subject. "How did you make out with the commercial?"

"Great! My agent worked Adele into it. And the producer promised both of us more work. We're going to make it, Adele and I. But we can't get married until we do. You understand that, don't you?"

"Very well," I assured him. "Welcome to the clan."

My mother had gone Armenian this Sunday, chicken and pilaf. One of Sarkis's boys hadn't been able to attend; Salvatore took his place at the poker session.

That was a red-letter day! Salvatore was the big winner. And for the first time in history Mom was the big loser. I would like to say she took it graciously, but she didn't. We are a competitive clan.

"Nice guy," I said, when Adele and he had left.

She sniffed. "When he marries Adele, *then* he might be a nice guy."

"He told me they're going to get married as soon as they can afford to."

"We'll see," she said. "He could be another Vartan."

The day had stayed misty; the traffic on Sunset Boulevard was slow. I dawdled along, thinking back on the past few days, trying to find the key to the puzzle of the missing girl and the stolen Kerman. The key was the key; who had the key to the house and why had only the rug been stolen?

One thing was certain, the burglar knew the value of antique oriental rugs. But how would he know that particular rug was in the home of Whitney Bishop?

It was a restless night, filled with dreams I don't remember now. I tossed and turned and went to the toilet twice. A little after six o'clock I realized sleep was out of the question. I put the coffee on to perc and went down the steps to pick up the morning *Times*.

The story was on page one. Whitney Bishop, founder and senior partner of the brokerage firm of Bishop, Hope, and Nystrom, had been found dead in a deserted Brentwood service station. A local realtor had discovered the body when he had brought a potential buyer to the station on

Sunday morning. Bishop had been stabbed to death. A loaded but unfired .32 caliber revolver had been found near the body.

According to his wife, Bishop had been nervous and irritable on Friday night. His secretary told the police that he had received a phone call on Friday afternoon and appeared agitated. On Saturday night, he had told his wife he was going to a board meeting at the Beverly Hills Country Club. When he hadn't come home by midnight, Mrs. Bishop had phoned the club. The club was closed; receiving no answer there, she had phoned the police.

When questioned about the revolver, she had stated that she remembered he had once owned a small-caliber pistol but she was almost sure it had been lost or stolen years ago.

A murdered husband. . . . And there was no mention in the piece about a missing daughter or a stolen rug. Considering how many of her friends knew about both, that was bound to come out.

When it did I could be in deep trouble for withholding information about the rug and the girl. But so could she for the same reason. And spreading those stories to the media could alert and scare off any seasoned burglar who had been looking forward to a buy-back deal. That was the slim hope I tried to hang on to.

I put the record of my involvement in the case under the mattress in my bedroom. I showered and shaved and put on my most conservative suit after breakfast and sat in my office chair, waiting for the police to arrive.

They didn't.

I thought back to all the people I had questioned in the past week. And then I realized there was one I hadn't.

I went down the stairs and asked Uncle Vartan if he had heard the sad news.

He nodded and yawned. He had heard it on the tube last night, he told me. I had the feeling that he would not mourn the death of Whitney Bishop.

"You told me you went with Mrs. Bishop when she was between husbands. Who was her first?"

"A man named Duane Pressville, a former customer of mine."

"Do you have his address?"

"Not anymore. It has been years since I've seen him. What is this all about, Pierre?"

"I was thinking that it was possible he still had the key to the house they shared and would know where the alarm turnoff switch was hidden."

He stared at me. "And you think he stole the rug? That's crazy, Pierre! He was a very sharp buyer but completely honest." He paused. "And now you are thinking that he might be a murderer?"

"The murder and the rug might not be connected," I pointed out. "Tell me, is he the man who bought the Kerman from you?"

"Yes," he said irritably. "And that's enough of this nonsense! I have work to do this morning, Pierre."

"Sorry," I said, and went up the stairs to look up Duane Pressville in the phone book. There were several Pressvilles in the book but only one Duane. His address was 332 Adonis Court.

I knew the street, a short dead-ender that led off San Vicente Boulevard. Into the Camaro, back on the hunt.

Adonis Court was an ancient neighborhood of small houses. It had resisted the influx of demolitions that had invaded the area when land prices soared. These were the older residents who had no serious economic pressures that would force them to sell out.

332 was a small frame house with a shingled roof and a small low porch in front of the door.

I went up to the porch and turned the old-fashioned crank that rang the bell inside the house.

The man who opened the door was tall and thin and haggard, the same man who had called himself Gerald Hopkins on the beach.

He smiled. "Mr. Apoyan! What brings you to my door?"

"I'm looking for a rug," I said. "An antique Kerman."

He frowned. "Did Victoria send you here?"

"Who is Victoria?"

"My former wife. What vindictive crusade is she on now? No matter what she might have told you, I bought that rug with my own money. It was *my* rug, until the divorce settlement."

"Why," I asked, "did you lie to me on the beach?"

He looked at me and past me. He sighed and said, "Come in."

The door opened directly into the living room. It was a room about fourteen feet wide and eighteen feet long. It was almost completely covered by a dark red oriental rug. It looked like a Bokhara to me.

The furniture was mostly dark mahogany, brightly polished, upholstered in well-worn velour.

"Sit down," he said.

I sat in an armchair, he on the sofa.

"Have you ever heard of Maksoud of Kashan?" he asked.

"I think so. Wasn't he a famous oriental rug weaver?"

He nodded. "The finest in all of Persia, now called Iran. But in his entire career, with all the associates he had working under him, he wove his name into only two of his rugs. One of them is in the British Museum. The other is the small Kerman I bought from your uncle. I remember now—you worked in his store on Saturdays, didn't you?"

I nodded.

"You weren't in the store that day this—this *peddler* brought in the Kerman. It was filthy! But far from being worn out. My eyes must be sharper than your uncle's. I saw the signature in the corner. I made the mistake of overplaying my hand; I offered him a thousand dollars for it, much more than it appeared to be worth. That must have made him suspicious. We dickered. When I finally offered him three thousand dollars he sold it to me."

"And I suppose he has resented you ever since that day."

He shrugged. "Probably. To tell you the truth, after he learned about the history of the rug I was ashamed to go back to the store."

"To tell the truth once again," I said, "where is your daughter? Where is Janice?"

"She is well and safe and far from here. She is back with her real parents, the parents who were too poor to keep her when she was born. I finally located them."

"You wouldn't want to tell me their name?"

"Not you, or anybody else. Not with the legal clout Victoria can afford. Do you want Janice to go back to that woman she complained to when her third father tried to molest her, that woman who called her a liar? I did some research on Bishop, too. He was fired by a Chicago brokerage firm for churning. He had one charge of child molestation dropped for insufficient evidence there. So he came out here and married money and started his own firm."

"And was stabbed to death Saturday night not far from here."

"I heard that on the radio this morning." His smile was cynical. "Are you going to the funeral?"

I shook my head. "According to the morning paper he must have been carrying a gun. But he didn't fire it."

"The news report on this morning's radio station explained that," he told me. "The safety catch was on."

"I didn't hear it. What do you think that Kerman would bring today?"

"Fifty thousand, a hundred thousand, whatever the buyer would pay." He studied me. "Are you suggesting that the murder and the rug are connected?"

"You know I am. My theory is that Bishop got the call from the burglar on Friday and decided not to buy the rug, but to shoot the burglar."

"An interesting theory. Is there more to it?"

"Yes. The burglar then stabbed him—and found another buyer. Bishop might have reason other than penuriousness. He might have known the burglar knew his history."

He said wearily, "You're zeroing in, aren't you? You're beginning to sound like a detective."

"I am. A private investigator. I just opened my own office over Uncle Vartan's store."

"You should have told me that when you came."

"You must have guessed that I was an investigator when we met on the beach. Why else would you have lied?"

He didn't answer.

"If Janice's real parents are still poor," I said, "fifty or a hundred thousand dollars should help to alleviate it."

He nodded. "If the burglar has found the right buyer. It should certainly help to send her to a first-rate college. And now I'm getting tired.

It's time for my nap. I have leukemia, Pierre. My doctor has told me he doesn't know how many days I have before I sleep the big sleep. I know what you are thinking, and it could be true. I'm sure you are honor bound to take what I have told you to the police. I promise I will bear you no malice if you do. But you had better hurry."

"There is no need to hurry," I said. "Thank you for your cooperation, Mr. Pressville."

"And thank you for your courtesy," he said. "Give my regards to Vartan."

I didn't give his regards to Uncle Vartan. I didn't even tell him I had talked with his former customer. I had some thinking to do.

For three days I thought and wondered when the police would call. They never came. Mrs. Bishop sent me a check for the balance of my investigation along with an acerbic note that informed me she would certainly tell her many friends how unsuccessful I had been in searching for both her rug and her daughter.

I had no need to continue thinking on the fourth day. Duane Pressville was found dead in his house on Adonis Court by a concerned neighbor. I burned the records of that maiden quest.

MARCIA MULLER

Whenever you mention Marcia Muller (1944–), you're duty-bound to stake her claim as the first writer to ever write seriously about the female private eye.

What gets overlooked in this statement, however, is the work itself, as if simply being first is justification enough to be honored at every mystery gathering she attends.

Not so. Marcia is honored because she's so good. While her early books are solid and technically sound, they don't even hint at the way her talent would bloom just a few years later. The writing lost all traces of genre cliché; the characters became truer, deeper, richer; and the social landscape began to encompass a good amount of contemporary America.

Many writers of her generation are reshaping the crime form in exciting new ways. And Marcia Muller—the first writer to create a believable female private eye series—is in the forefront with the best of them.

Deceptions

San Francisco's Golden Gate Bridge is deceptively fragile-looking, especially when fog swirls across its high span. But from where I was standing, almost underneath it at the south end, even the mist couldn't disguise the massiveness of its concrete piers and the taut strength of its cables. I tipped my head back and looked up the tower to where it disappeared into the drifting grayness, thinking about the other ways the bridge is deceptive.

For one thing, its color isn't gold, but rust red, reminiscent of dried blood. And though the bridge is a marvel of engineering, it is also plagued by maintenance problems that keep the Bridge District in constant danger of financial collapse. For a reputedly romantic structure, it has seen more than its fair share of tragedy: Some eight hundred-odd lost souls have jumped to their deaths from its deck.

Today I was there to try to find out if that figure should be raised by one. So far I'd met with little success.

I was standing next to my car in the parking lot of Fort Point, a historic fortification at the mouth of San Francisco Bay. Where the pavement stopped, the land fell away to jagged black rocks; waves smashed against them, sending up geysers of salty spray. Beyond the rocks the water was choppy, and Angel Island and Alcatraz were mere humpbacked shapes in the mist. I shivered, wishing I'd worn something heavier than my poplin jacket, and started toward the fort.

This was the last stop on a journey that had taken me from the toll booths and Bridge District offices to Vista Point at the Marin County end of the span, and back to the National Parks Services headquarters down the road from the fort. None of the Parks Service or bridge personnel—including a group of maintenance workers near the north tower—had seen the slender dark-haired woman in the picture I'd shown them, walking south on the pedestrian sidewalk at about four yesterday afternoon. None of them had seen her jump.

It was for that reason—plus the facts that her parents had revealed about twenty-two-year-old Vanessa DiCesare—that made me tend to doubt she actually had committed suicide, in spite of the note she'd left taped to the dashboard of the Honda she'd abandoned at Vista Point. Surely at four o'clock on a Monday afternoon *someone* would have noticed her. Still, I had to follow up every possibility, and the people at the Parks Service station had suggested I check with the rangers at Fort Point.

I entered the dark-brick structure through a long, low tunnel—called a sally port, the sign said—which was flanked at either end by massive wooden doors with iron studding. Years before I'd visited the fort, and now I recalled that it was more or less typical of harbor fortifications built in the Civil War era: a ground floor topped by two tiers of working and living quarters, encircling a central courtyard.

I emerged into the court and looked up at the west side; the tiers were a series of brick archways, their openings as black as empty eyesockets, each roped off by a narrow strip of yellow plastic strung across it at waist level. There was construction gear in the courtyard; the entire west side was under renovation and probably off limits to the public.

As I stood there trying to remember the layout of the place and wondering which way to go, I became aware of a hollow metallic clanking that echoed in the circular enclosure. The noise drew my eyes upward to the wooden watchtower atop the west tiers, and then to the red arch of the bridge's girders directly above it. The clanking seemed to have something to do with cars passing over the roadbed, and it was underlaid by a constant grumbling rush of tires on pavement. The sounds, coupled with the soaring height of the fog-laced girders, made me feel very small and insignificant. I shivered again and turned to my left, looking for one of the rangers.

The man who came out of a nearby doorway startled me, more because of his costume than the suddenness of his appearance. Instead of the Parks Service uniform I remembered the rangers wearing on my previous visit, he was clad in what looked like an old Union Army uniform: a dark blue frock coat, lighter blue trousers, and a wide-brimmed hat with a red plume. The long saber in a scabbard that was strapped to his waist made him look thoroughly authentic.

He smiled at my obvious surprise and came over to me, bushy eyebrows lifted inquiringly. "Can I help you, ma'am?"

I reached into my bag and took out my private investigator's license and showed it to him. "I'm Sharon McCone, from All Souls Legal Cooperative. Do you have a minute to answer some questions?"

He frowned, the way people often do when confronted by a private detective, probably trying to remember whether he'd done anything lately that would warrant investigation. Then he said, "Sure," and motioned for me to step into the shelter of the sally port.

"I'm investigating a disappearance, a possible suicide from the bridge," I said. "It would have happened about four yesterday afternoon. Were you on duty then?"

He shook his head. "Monday's my day off."

"Is there anyone else here who might have been working then?"

"You could check with Lee—Lee Gottschalk, the other ranger on this shift."

"Where can I find him?"

He moved back into the courtyard and looked around. "I saw him start taking a couple of tourists around just a few minutes ago. People are crazy; they'll come out in any kind of weather."

"Can you tell me which way he went?"

The ranger gestured to our right. "Along this side. When he's done down here, he'll take them up that iron stairway to the first tier, but I can't say how far he's gotten yet."

I thanked him and started off in the direction he'd indicated.

There were open doors in the cement wall between the sally port and the iron staircase. I glanced through the first and saw no one. The second led into a narrow dark hallway; when I was halfway down it, I saw that this was the fort's jail. One cell was set up as a display, complete with a mannequin prisoner; the other, beyond an archway that was not much taller than my own five-foot-six, was unrestored. Its water-stained walls were covered with graffiti, and a metal railing protected a two-foot-square iron grid on the floor in one corner. A sign said that it was a cistern with a forty-thousand-gallon capacity.

Well, I thought, that's interesting, but playing tourist isn't helping me catch up with Lee Gottschalk. Quickly I left the jail and hurried up the iron staircase the first ranger had indicated. At its top, I turned to my left and bumped into a chain link fence that blocked access to the area under renovation. Warning myself to watch where I was going, I went the other way, toward the east tier. The archways there were fenced off with similar chain link so no one could fall, and doors opened off the gallery into what I supposed had been the soldiers' living quarters. I pushed through the first one and stepped into a small museum.

The room was high-ceilinged, with tall, narrow windows in the outside wall. No ranger or tourists were in sight. I looked toward an interior door that led to the next room and saw a series of mirror images: one door within another leading off into the distance, each diminishing in size until the last seemed very tiny. I had the unpleasant sensation that if I walked along there, I would become progressively smaller and eventually disappear.

From somewhere down there came the sound of voices. I followed it, passing through more museum displays until I came to a room containing an old-fashioned bedstead and footlocker. A ranger, dressed the same as the man downstairs except that he was bearded and wore granny glasses, stood beyond the bedstead lecturing to a man and a woman who were bundled to their chins in bulky sweaters.

"You'll notice that the fireplaces are very small," he was saying, motioning to the one on the wall next to the bed, "and you can imagine how cold it could get for the soldiers garrisoned here. They didn't have a heated employees' lounge like we do." Smiling at his own little joke, he glanced at me. "Do you want to join the tour?"

I shook my head and stepped over by the footlocker. "Are you Lee Gottschalk?"

"Yes." He spoke the word a shade warily.

"I have a few questions I'd like to ask you. How long will the rest of the tour take?"

"At least half an hour. These folks want to see the unrestored rooms on the third floor."

I didn't want to wait around that long, so I said, "Could you take a couple of minutes and talk with me now?"

He moved his head so the light from the windows caught his granny glasses and I couldn't see the expression in his eyes, but his mouth tightened in a way that might have been annoyance. After a moment he said, "Well, the rest of the tour on this floor is pretty much self-guided." To the tourists, he added, "Why don't you go on ahead and I'll catch up after I talk with this lady."

They nodded agreeably and moved on into the next room. Lee Gottschalk folded his arms across his chest and leaned against the small fireplace. "Now what can I do for you?"

I introduced myself and showed him my license. His mouth twitched briefly in surprise, but he didn't comment. I said, "At about four yesterday afternoon, a young woman left her car at Vista Point with a suicide note in it. I'm trying to locate a witness who saw her jump." I took out the photograph I'd been showing to people and handed it to him. By now I had Vanessa DiCesare's features memorized: high forehead, straight nose, full lips, glossy wings of dark-brown hair curling inward at the jawbone. It was a strong face, not beautiful but striking—and a face I'd recognize anywhere.

Gottschalk studied the photo, then handed it back to me. "I read about her in the morning paper. Why are you trying to find a witness?"

"Her parents have hired me to look into it."

"The paper said her father is some big politician here in the city."

I didn't see any harm in discussing what had already appeared in print. "Yes, Ernest DiCesare—he's on the Board of Supes and likely to be our next mayor."

"And she was a law student, engaged to some hotshot lawyer who ran her father's last political campaign."

"Right again."

He shook his head, lips pushing out in bewilderment. "Sounds like she had a lot going for her. Why would she kill herself? Did that note taped inside her car explain it?"

I'd seen the note, but its contents were confidential. "No. Did you happen to see anything unusual yesterday afternoon?"

"No. But if I'd seen anyone jump, I'd have reported it to the Coast Guard station so they could try to recover the body before the current carried it out to sea."

"What about someone standing by the bridge railing, acting strangely, perhaps?"

"If I'd noticed anyone like that, I'd have reported it to the bridge offices so they could send out a suicide prevention team." He stared almost combatively at me, as if I'd accused him of some kind of wrongdoing, then seemed to relent a little. "Come outside," he said, "and I'll show you something."

We went through the door to the gallery, and he guided me to the chain link barrier in the archway and pointed up. "Look at the angle of the bridge, and the distance we are from it. You couldn't spot anyone standing at the rail from here, at least not well enough to tell if they were acting upset. And a jumper would have to hurl herself way out before she'd be noticeable."

"And there's nowhere else in the fort from where a jumper would be clearly visible?"

"Maybe from one of the watchtowers or the extreme west side. But they're off limits to the public, and we only give them one routine check at closing."

Satisfied now, I said, "Well, that about does it. I appreciate your taking the time."

He nodded and we started along the gallery. When we reached the other end, where an enclosed staircase spiraled up and down, I thanked him again and we parted company.

The way the facts looked to me now, Vanessa DiCesare had faked this suicide and just walked away—away from her wealthy old-line Italian family, from her up-and-coming liberal lawyer, from a life that either had become too much or just hadn't been enough. Vanessa was over twenty-one; she had a legal right to disappear if she wanted to. But her parents and her fiancé loved her, and they also had a right to know she was alive and well. If I could locate her and reassure them without ruining whatever new life she planned to create for herself, I would feel I'd performed the job I'd been hired to do. But right now I was weary, chilled to the bone, and out of leads. I decided to go back to All Souls and consider my next moves in warmth and comfort.

All Souls Legal Cooperative is housed in a ramshackle Victorian on one of the steeply sloping side-streets of Bernal Heights, a working-class district in the southern part of the city. The co-op caters mainly to clients who live in the area: people with low to middle incomes who don't have much extra money for expensive lawyers. The sliding fee scale allows them to obtain quality legal assistance at reasonable prices—a concept that is probably outdated in the self-centered 1980s, but is kept alive by the people who staff All Souls. It's a place where the lawyers care about their clients, and a good place to work.

I left my MG at the curb and hurried up the front steps through the blowing fog. The warmth inside was almost a shock after the chilliness at Fort Point; I unbuttoned my jacket and went down the long deserted hallway to the big country kitchen at the rear. There I found my boss, Hank Zahn, stirring up a mug of the Navy grog he often concocts on cold November nights like this one.

He looked at me, pointed to the rum bottle, and said, "Shall I make you one?" When I nodded, he reached for another mug.

I went to the round oak table under the windows, moved a pile of newspapers from one of the chairs, and sat down. Hank added lemon juice, hot water, and sugar syrup to the rum; dusted it artistically with nutmeg; and set it in front of me with a flourish. I sampled it as he sat down across from me, then nodded my approval.

He said, "How's it going with the DiCesare investigation?"

Hank had a personal interest in the case; Vanessa's fiancé, Gary Stornetta, was a long-time friend of his, which was why I, rather than one of the large investigative firms her father normally favored, had been asked to look into it. I said, "Everything I've come up with points to it being a disappearance, not a suicide."

"Just as Gary and her parents suspected."

"Yes. I've covered the entire area around the bridge. There are absolutely no witnesses, except for the tour bus driver who saw her park her car at four and got suspicious when it was still there at seven and reported it. But even he didn't see her walk off toward the bridge." I drank some more grog, felt its warmth, and began to relax.

Behind his thick horn-rimmed glasses, Hank's eyes became concerned.

"Did the DiCesares or Gary give you any idea why she would have done such a thing?"

"When I talked with Ernest and Sylvia this morning, they said Vanessa had changed her mind about marrying Gary. He's not admitting to that, but he doesn't speak of Vanessa the way a happy husband-to-be would. And it seems an unlikely match to me—he's close to twenty years older than she."

"More like fifteen," Hank said. "Gary's father was Ernest's best friend, and after Ron Stornetta died, Ernest more or less took him on as a protégé. Ernest was delighted that their families were finally going to be joined."

"Oh, he was delighted all right. He admitted to me that he'd practically arranged the marriage. 'Girl didn't know what was good for her,' he said. 'Needed a strong older man to guide her.' " I snorted.

Hank smiled faintly. He's a feminist, but over the years his sense of outrage has mellowed; mine still has a hair trigger.

"Anyway," I said, "when Vanessa first announced she was backing out of the engagement, Ernest told her he would cut off her funds for law school if she didn't go through with the wedding."

"Jesus, I had no idea he was capable of such . . . Neanderthal tactics."

"Well, he is. After that Vanessa went ahead and set the wedding date. But Sylvia said she suspected she wouldn't go through with it. Vanessa talked of quitting law school and moving out of their home. And she'd been seeing other men; she and her father had a bad quarrel about it just last week. Anyway, all of that, plus the fact that one of her suitcases and some clothing are missing, made them highly suspicious of the suicide."

Hank reached for my mug and went to get us more grog. I began thumbing through the copy of the morning paper that I'd moved off the chair, looking for the story on Vanessa. I found it on page three.

> The daughter of Supervisor Ernest DiCesare apparently committed suicide by jumping from the Golden Gate Bridge late yesterday afternoon.
>
> Vanessa DiCesare, 22, abandoned her 1985 Honda Civic at Vista Point at approximately four p.m., police said. There were no witnesses to her jump, and the body has not been recovered. The contents of a suicide note found in her car have not been disclosed.
>
> Ms. DiCesare, a first-year student at Hastings College of Law, is the only child of the supervisor and his wife, Sylvia. She planned to be married next month to San Francisco attorney Gary R. Stornetta, a political associate of her father. . . .

Strange how routine it all sounded when reduced to journalistic language. And yet how mysterious—the "undisclosed contents" of the suicide note, for instance.

"You know," I said as Hank came back to the table and set down the fresh mugs of grog, "that note is another factor that makes me believe she staged this whole thing. It was so formal and controlled. If they had samples of suicide notes in etiquette books, I'd say she looked one up and copied it."

He ran his fingers through his wiry brown hair. "What I don't understand is why she didn't just break off the engagement and move out of the house. So what if her father cut off her money? There are lots worse things than working your way through law school."

"Oh, but this way she gets back at everyone, and has the advantage of actually being alive to gloat over it. Imagine her parents' and Gary's grief and guilt—it's the ultimate way of getting even."

"She must be a very angry young woman."

"Yes. After I talked with Ernest and Sylvia and Gary, I spoke briefly with Vanessa's best friend, a law student named Kathy Graves. Kathy told me that Vanessa was furious with her father for making her go through with the marriage. And she'd come to hate Gary because she'd decided he was only marrying her for her family's money and political power."

"Oh, come on. Gary's ambitious, sure. But you can't tell me he doesn't genuinely care for Vanessa."

"I'm only giving you her side of the story."

"So now what do you plan to do?"

"Talk with Gary and the DiCesares again. See if I can't come up with some bit of information that will help me find her."

"And then?"

"Then it's up to them to work it out."

The DiCesare home was mock-Tudor, brick and half-timber, set on a corner knoll in the exclusive area of St. Francis Wood. When I'd first come there that morning, I'd been slightly awed; now the house had lost its power to impress me. After delving into the lives of the family who lived there, I knew that it was merely a pile of brick and mortar and wood that contained more than the usual amount of misery.

The DiCesares and Gary Stornetta were waiting for me in the living room, a strangely formal place with several groupings of furniture and expensive-looking knickknacks laid out in precise patterns on the tables. Vanessa's parents and fiancé—like the house—seemed diminished since my previous visit: Sylvia huddled in an armchair by the fireplace, her gray-blonde hair straggling from its elegant coiffure; Ernest stood behind her, haggard-faced, one hand protectively on her shoulder. Gary paced, smoking and clawing at his hair with his other hand. Occasionally he dropped ashes on the thick wall-to-wall carpeting, but no one called it to his attention.

They listened to what I had to report without interruption. When I finished, there was a long silence. Then Sylvia put a hand over her eyes and said, "How she must hate us to do a thing like this!"

Ernest tightened his grip on his wife's shoulder. His face was a conflict of anger, bewilderment, and sorrow.

There was no question of which emotion had hold of Gary; he

smashed out his cigarette in an ashtray, lit another, and resumed pacing. But while his movements before had merely been nervous, now his tall, lean body was rigid with thinly controlled fury. "Damn her!" he said. "Damn her anyway!"

"Gary." There was a warning note in Ernest's voice.

Gary glanced at him, then at Sylvia. "Sorry."

I said, "The question now is, do you want me to continue looking for her?"

In shocked tones, Sylvia said, "Of course we do!" Then she tipped her head back and looked at her husband.

Ernest was silent, his fingers pressing hard against the black wool of her dress.

"Ernest?" Now Sylvia's voice held a note of panic.

"Of course we do," he said. But the words somehow lacked conviction.

I took out my notebook and pencil, glancing at Gary. He had stopped pacing and was watching the DiCesares. His craggy face was still mottled with anger, and I sensed he shared Ernest's uncertainty.

Opening the notebook, I said, "I need more details about Vanessa, what her life was like the past month or so. Perhaps something will occur to one of you that didn't this morning."

"Ms. McCone," Ernest said, "I don't think Sylvia's up to this right now. Why don't you and Gary talk, and then if there's anything else, I'll be glad to help you."

"Fine." Gary was the one I was primarily interested in questioning, anyway. I waited until Ernest and Sylvia had left the room, then turned to him.

When the door shut behind them, he hurled his cigarette into the empty fireplace. "Goddamn little bitch!" he said.

I said, "Why don't you sit down."

He looked at me for a few seconds, obviously wanting to keep on pacing, but then he flopped into the chair Sylvia had vacated. When I'd first met with Gary this morning, he'd been controlled and immaculately groomed, and he had seemed more solicitous of the DiCesares than concerned with his own feelings. Now his clothing was disheveled, his graying hair tousled, and he looked to be on the brink of a rage that would flatten anyone in its path.

Unfortunately, what I had to ask him would probably fan that rage. I braced myself and said, "Now tell me about Vanessa. And not all the stuff about her being a lovely young woman and a brilliant student. I heard all that this morning—but now we both know it isn't the whole truth, don't we?"

Surprisingly he reached for a cigarette and lit it slowly, using the time to calm himself. When he spoke, his voice was as level as my own. "All right, it's not the whole truth. Vanessa *is* lovely and brilliant. She'll make a top-notch lawyer. There's a hardness in her; she gets it from Ernest. It took guts to fake this suicide . . ."

"What do you think she hopes to gain from it?"

"Freedom. From me. From Ernest's domination. She's probably taken off somewhere for a good time. When she's ready she'll come back and make her demands."

"And what will they be?"

"Enough money to move into a place of her own and finish law school. And she'll get it, too. She's all her parents have."

"You don't think she's set out to make a new life for herself?"

"Hell, no. That would mean giving up all this." The sweep of his arm encompassed the house and all of the DiCesares's privileged world.

But there was one factor that made me doubt his assessment. I said, "What about the other men in her life?"

He tried to look surprised, but an angry muscle twitched in his jaw.

"Come on, Gary," I said, "you know there were other men. Even Ernest and Sylvia were aware of that."

"Ah, Christ!" He popped out of the chair and began pacing again. "All right, there were other men. It started a few months ago. I didn't understand it; things had been good with us; they still *were* good physically. But I thought, okay, she's young; this is only natural. So I decided to give her some rope, let her get it out of her system. She didn't throw it in my face, didn't embarrass me in front of my friends. Why shouldn't she have a last fling?"

"And then?"

"She began making noises about breaking off the engagement. And Ernest started that shit about not footing the bill for law school. Like a fool I went along with it, and she seemed to cave in from the pressure. But a few weeks later, it all started up again—only this time it was purposeful, cruel."

"In what way?"

"She'd know I was meeting political associates for lunch or dinner, and she'd show up at the restaurant with a date. Later she'd claim he was just a friend, but you couldn't prove it from the way they acted. We'd go to a party and she'd flirt with every man there. She got sly and secretive about where she'd been, what she'd been doing."

I had pictured Vanessa as a very angry young woman; now I realized she was not a particularly nice one, either.

Gary was saying, ". . . the last straw was on Halloween. We went to a costume party given by one of her friends from Hastings. I didn't want to go—costumes, a young crowd, not my kind of thing—and so she was angry with me to begin with. Anyway, she walked out with another man, some jerk in a soldier outfit. They were dancing . . ."

I sat up straighter. "Describe the costume."

"An old-fashioned soldier outfit. Wide-brimmed hat with a plume, frock coat, sword,"

"What did the man look like?"

"Youngish. He had a full beard and wore granny glasses."

Lee Gottschalk.

The address I got from the phone directory for Lee Gottschalk was on California Street not far from Twenty-fifth Avenue and only a couple of miles from where I'd first met the ranger at Fort Point. When I arrived there and parked at the opposite curb, I didn't need to check the mailboxes to see which apartment was his; the corner windows on the second floor were ablaze with light, and inside I could see Gottschalk, sitting in an armchair in what appeared to be his living room. He seemed to be alone but expecting company, because frequently he looked up from the book he was reading and checked his watch.

In case the company was Vanessa DiCesare, I didn't want to go barging in there. Gottschalk might find a way to warn her off, or simply not answer the door when she arrived. Besides, I didn't yet have a definite connection between the two of them; the "jerk in a soldier outfit" *could* have been someone else, someone in a rented costume that just happened to resemble the working uniform at the fort. But my suspicions were strong enough to keep me watching Gottschalk for well over an hour. The ranger *had* lied to me that afternoon.

The lies had been casual and convincing, except for two mistakes—such small mistakes that I hadn't caught them even when I'd read the newspaper account of Vanessa's purported suicide later. But now I recognized them for what they were: The paper had called Gary Stornetta a "political associate" of Vanessa's father, rather than his former campaign manager, as Lee had termed him. And while the paper mentioned the suicide note, it had not said it was *taped* inside the car. While Gottschalk conceivably could know about Gary managing Ernest's campaign for the Board of Supes from other newspaper accounts, there was no way he could have known how the note was secured—except from Vanessa herself.

Because of those mistakes, I continued watching Gottschalk, straining my eyes as the mist grew heavier, hoping Vanessa would show up or that he'd eventually lead me to her. The ranger appeared to be nervous: He got up a couple of times and turned on a TV, flipped through the channels, and turned it off again. For about ten minutes, he paced back and forth. Finally, around twelve-thirty, he checked his watch again, then got up and drew the draperies shut. The lights went out behind them.

I tensed, staring through the blowing mist at the door of the apartment building. Somehow Gottschalk hadn't looked like a man who was going to bed. And my impression was correct: In a few minutes he came through the door onto the sidewalk carrying a suitcase—pale leather like the one of Vanessa's Sylvia had described to me—and got into a dark-colored Mustang parked on his side of the street. The car started up and he made a U-turn, then went right on Twenty-fifth Avenue. I followed. After a few minutes, it became apparent that he was heading for Fort Point.

When Gottschalk turned into the road to the fort, I kept going until I could pull over on the shoulder. The brake lights of the Mustang flared, and then Gottschalk got out and unlocked the low iron bar that blocked the road from sunset to sunrise; after he'd driven through he closed it again, and the car's lights disappeared down the road.

Had Vanessa been hiding at drafty, cold Fort Point? It seemed a strange choice of place, since she could have used a motel or Gottschalk's apartment. But perhaps she'd been afraid someone would recognize her in a public place, or connect her with Gottschalk and come looking, as I had. And while the fort would be a miserable place to hide during the hours it was open to the public—she'd have had to keep to one of the off-limits areas, such as the west side—at night she could probably avail herself of the heated employees' lounge.

Now I could reconstruct most of the scenario of what had gone on: Vanessa meets Lee; they talk about his work; she decides he is the person to help her fake her suicide. Maybe there's a romantic entanglement, maybe not; but for whatever reason, he agrees to go along with the plan. She leaves her car at Vista Point, walks across the bridge, and later he drives over there and picks up the suitcase. . . .

But then why hadn't he delivered it to her at the fort? And to go after the suitcase after she'd abandoned the car was too much of a risk; he might have been seen, or the people at the fort might have noticed him leaving for too long a break. Also, if she'd walked across the bridge, surely at least one of the people I'd talked with would have seen her—the maintenance crew near the north tower, for instance.

There was no point in speculating on it now, I decided. The thing to do was to follow Gottschalk down there and confront Vanessa before she disappeared again. For a moment I debated taking my gun out of the glovebox, but then decided against it. I don't like to carry it unless I'm going into a dangerous situation, and neither Gottschalk nor Vanessa posed any particular threat to me. I was merely here to deliver a message from Vanessa's parents asking her to come home. If she didn't care to respond to it, that was not my business—or my problem.

I got out of my car and locked it, then hurried across the road and down the narrow lane to the gate, ducking under it and continuing along toward the ranger station. On either side of me were tall, thick groves of eucalyptus; I could smell their acrid fragrance and hear the fog-laden wind rustle their brittle leaves. Their shadows turned the lane into a black winding alley, and the only sound besides distant traffic noises was my tennis shoes slapping on the broken pavement. The ranger station was dark, but ahead I could see Gottschalk's car parked next to the fort. The area was illuminated only by small security lights set at intervals on the walls of the structure. Above it the bridge arched, washed in fog-muted yellowish light; as I drew closer I became aware of the grumble and clank of traffic up there.

I ran across the parking area and checked Gottschalk's car. It was empty, but the suitcase rested on the passenger seat. I turned and started toward the sally port, noticing that its heavily studded door stood open a few inches. The low tunnel was completely dark. I felt my way along it toward the courtyard, one hand on its icy stone wall.

The doors to the courtyard also stood open. I peered through them into the gloom beyond. What light there was came from the bridge and more security beacons high up on the wooden watchtowers; I could barely make out the shapes of the construction equipment that stood near the west side. The clanking from the bridge was oppressive and eerie in the still night.

As I was about to step into the courtyard, there was a movement to my right. I drew back into the sally port as Lee Gottschalk came out of one of the ground-floor doorways. My first impulse was to confront him, but then I decided against it. He might shout, warn Vanessa, and she might escape before I could deliver her parents' message.

After a few seconds I looked out again, meaning to follow Gottschalk, but he was nowhere in sight. A faint shaft of light fell through the door from which he had emerged and rippled over the cobblestone floor. I went that way, through the door and along a narrow corridor to where an archway was illuminated. Then, realizing the archway led to the unrestored cell of the jail I'd seen earlier, I paused. Surely Vanessa wasn't hiding in there. . . .

I crept forward and looked through the arch. The light came from a heavy-duty flashlight that sat on the floor. It threw macabre shadows on the water-stained walls, showing their streaked paint and graffiti. My gaze followed its beams upward and then down, to where the grating of the cistern lay out of place on the floor beside the hole. Then I moved over to the railing, leaned across it, and trained the flashlight down into the well.

I saw, with a rush of shock and horror, the dark hair and once-handsome features of Vanessa DiCesare.

She had been hacked to death. Stabbed and slashed, as if in a frenzy. Her clothing was ripped; there were gashes on her face and hands; she was covered with dark smears of blood. Her eyes were open, staring with that horrible flatness of death.

I came back on my heels, clutching the railing for support. A wave of dizziness swept over me, followed by an icy coldness. I thought: He killed her. And then I pictured Gottschalk in his Union Army uniform, the saber hanging from his belt, and I knew what the weapon had been.

"God!" I said aloud.

Why had he murdered her? I had no way of knowing yet. But the answer to why he'd thrown her into the cistern, instead of just putting her into the bay, was clear: She was supposed to have committed suicide; and while bodies that fall from the Golden Gate Bridge sustain a great many injuries, slash and stab wounds aren't among them. Gottschalk could not count on the body being swept out to sea on the current; if she washed up somewhere along the coast, it would be obvious she had been murdered—and eventually an investigation might have led back to him. To him and his soldier's saber.

It also seemed clear that he'd come to the fort tonight to move the body. But why not last night, why leave her in the cistern all day? Probably he'd needed to plan, to secure keys to the gate and fort, to check the schedule of the night patrols for the best time to remove her. Whatever his reason, I realized now that I'd walked into a very dangerous situation. Walked right in without bringing my gun. I turned quickly to get out of there. . . .

And came face-to-face with Lee Gottschalk.

His eyes were wide, his mouth drawn back in a snarl of surprise. In one hand he held a bundle of heavy canvas. "You!" he said. "What the hell are you doing here?"

I jerked back from him, bumped into the railing, and dropped the flashlight. It clattered on the floor and began rolling toward the mouth of the cistern. Gottschalk lunged toward me, and as I dodged, the light fell into the hole and the cell went dark. I managed to push past him and ran down the hallway to the courtyard.

Stumbling on the cobblestones, I ran blindly for the sally port. Its doors were shut now—he'd probably taken that precaution when he'd returned from getting the tarp to wrap her body in. I grabbed the iron hasp and tugged, but couldn't get it open. Gottschalk's footsteps were coming through the courtyard after me now. I let go of the hasp and ran again.

When I came to the enclosed staircase at the other end of the court, I started up. The steps were wide at the outside wall, narrow at the inside. My toes banged into the risers of the steps; a couple of times I teetered and almost fell backwards. At the first tier I paused, then kept going. Gottschalk had said something about unrestored rooms on the second tier; they'd be a better place to hide than in the museum.

Down below I could hear him climbing after me. The sound of his feet—clattering and stumbling—echoed in the close space. I could hear him grunt and mumble: low, ugly sounds that I knew were curses.

I had absolutely no doubt that if he caught me, he would kill me. Maybe do to me what he had done to Vanessa. . . .

I rounded the spiral once again and came out on the top floor gallery, my heart beating wildly, my breath coming in pants. To my left were archways, black outlines filled with dark-gray sky. To my right was blackness. I went that way, hands out, feeling my way.

My hands touched the rough wood of a door. I pushed, and it opened. As I passed through it, my shoulder bag caught on something; I yanked it loose and kept going. Beyond the door I heard Gottschalk curse loudly, the sound filled with surprise and pain; he must have fallen on the stairway. And that gave me a little more time.

The tug at my shoulder bag had reminded me of the small flashlight I keep there. Flattening myself against the wall next to the door, I rummaged through the bag and brought out the flash. Its beam showed high walls and arching ceilings, plaster and lath pulled away to expose dark brick. I saw cubicles and cubbyholes opening into dead ends, but to my right was an arch. I made a small involuntary sound of relief, then thought *Quiet!* Gottschalk's footsteps started up the stairway again as I moved through the archway.

The crumbling plaster walls beyond the archway were set at odd angles—an interlocking funhouse maze connected by small doors. I slipped through one and found an irregularly shaped room heaped with debris. There didn't seem to be an exit, so I ducked back into the first room and moved toward the outside wall, where gray outlines indicated small high-placed windows. I couldn't hear Gottschalk any more—couldn't hear anything but the roar and clank from the bridge directly overhead.

The front wall was brick and stone, and the windows had wide waist-high sills. I leaned across one, looked through the salt-caked glass, and saw the open sea. I was at the front of the fort, the part that faced beyond the Golden Gate; to my immediate right would be the unrestored portion. If I could slip over into that area, I might be able to hide until the other rangers came to work in the morning.

But Gottschalk could be anywhere. I couldn't hear his footsteps above the infernal noise from the bridge. He could be right here in the room with me, pinpointing me by the beam of my flashlight. . . .

Fighting down panic, I switched the light off and continued along the wall, my hands recoiling from its clammy stone surface. It was icy cold in the vast, echoing space, but my own flesh felt colder still. The air had a salt tang, underlaid by odors of rot and mildew. For a couple of minutes the darkness was unalleviated, but then I saw a lighter rectangular shape ahead of me.

When I reached it I found it was some sort of embrasure, about four feet tall, but only a little over a foot wide. Beyond it I could see the edge of the gallery where it curved and stopped at the chain link fence that barred entrance to the other side of the fort. The fence wasn't very high—only five feet or so. If I could get through this narrow opening, I could climb it and find refuge . . .

The sudden noise behind me was like a firecracker popping. I whirled, and saw a tall figure silhouetted against one of the seaward windows. He lurched forward, tripping over whatever he'd stepped on. Forcing back a cry, I hoisted myself up and began squeezing through the embrasure.

Its sides were rough brick. They scraped my flesh clear through my clothing. Behind me I heard the slap of Gottschalk's shoes on the wooden floor.

My hips wouldn't fit through the opening. I gasped, grunted, pulling with my arms on the outside wall. Then I turned on my side, sucking in my stomach. My bag caught again, and I let go of the wall long enough to rip its strap off my elbow. As my hips squeezed through the embrasure, I felt Gottschalk grab at my feet. I kicked out frantically, breaking his hold, and fell off the sill to the floor of the gallery.

Fighting for breath, I pushed off the floor, threw myself at the fence, and began climbing. The metal bit into my fingers, rattled and clashed with my weight. At the top, the leg of my jeans got hung up on the spiky wires. I tore it loose and jumped down the other side.

The door to the gallery burst open and Gottschalk came through it. I got up from a crouch and ran into the darkness ahead of me. The fence began to rattle as he started up it. I raced, half-stumbling, along the gallery, the open archways to my right. To my left was probably a warren of rooms similar to those on the east side. I could lose him in there. . . .

Only I couldn't. The door I tried was locked. I ran to the next one and hurled my body against its wooden panels. It didn't give. I heard myself sob in fear and frustration.

Gottschalk was over the fence now, coming toward me, limping. His breath came in erratic gasps, loud enough to hear over the noise from the bridge. I twisted around, looking for shelter, and saw a pile of lumber lying across one of the open archways.

I dashed toward it and slipped behind, wedged between it and the pillar of the arch. The courtyard lay two dizzying stories below me. I grasped the end of the top two-by-four. It moved easily, as if on a fulcrum.

Gottschalk had seen me. He came on steadily, his right leg dragging behind him. When he reached the pile of lumber and started over it toward me, I yanked on the two-by-four. The other end moved and struck him on the knee.

He screamed and stumbled back. Then he came forward again, hands outstretched toward me. I pulled back further against the pillar. His clutching hands missed me, and when they did he lost his balance and toppled onto the pile of lumber. And then the boards began to slide toward the open archway.

He grabbed at the boards, yelling and flailing his arms. I tried to reach for him, but the lumber was moving like an avalanche now, pitching over the side and crashing down into the courtyard two stories below. It carried Gottschalk's thrashing body with it, and his screams echoed in its wake. For an awful few seconds the boards continued to crash down on him, and then everything was terribly still. Even the thrumming of the bridge traffic seemed muted.

I straightened slowly and looked down into the courtyard. Gottschalk lay unmoving among the scattered pieces of lumber. For a moment I breathed deeply to control my vertigo; then I ran back to the chain link fence, climbed it, and rushed down the spiral staircase to the courtyard.

When I got to the ranger's body, I could hear him moaning. I said, "Lie still. I'll call an ambulance."

He moaned louder as I ran across the courtyard and found a phone in the gift shop, but by the time I returned, he was silent. His breathing was so shallow that I thought he'd passed out, but then I heard mumbled words coming from his lips. I bent closer to listen.

"Vanessa," he said. "Wouldn't take me with her. . . ."

I said, "Take you where?"

"Going away together. Left my car . . . over there so she could drive across the bridge. But when she . . . brought it here she said she was going alone. . . ."

So you argued, I thought. And you lost your head and slashed her to death.

"Vanessa," he said again. "Never planned to take me . . . tricked me. . . ."

I started to put a hand on his arm, but found I couldn't touch him. "Don't talk any more. The ambulance'll be here soon."

"Vanessa," he said. "Oh God, what did you do to me?"

I looked up at the bridge, rust red through the darkness and the mist. In the distance, I could hear the wail of a siren.

Deceptions, I thought.

Deceptions. . . .

ROBERT J. RANDISI

Robert J. Randisi (1951–) cofounded *Mystery Scene* magazine, single-handedly created The Private Eye Writers of America, and has edited a number of cutting-edge anthologies showcasing contemporary hard-boiled fiction at its best.

And somehow, despite all these time-consuming accomplishments, he's managed to grow into a major writer in the field he so clearly loves.

While Randisi's early crime novels were swift, sure, singular looks at working-class Brooklyn (two of which were deservedly nominated for Shamus awards), his more recent books demonstrate the true depth of his skills, in particular his novels about detective Joe Keough. The Keough books work both as excellent thrillers and serious novels.

Randisi is also an excellent Western writer, with a number of novels to his credit in that genre, most notably perhaps *The Ham Reporter*, about Bat Masterton's days in New York City as a sports reporter.

The Nickel Derby

(Henry Po)

Kentucky Derby time is a special time of year for anyone involved in thoroughbred horse racing. The air crackles with excitement and tension as the big day approaches. My involvement with the Derby is usually as a non-betting spectator, but this year it had suddenly become a more substantial part of my life.

My boss, J. Howard Biel, president of the New York State Racing

Club, had phoned me at home that morning, something which has customarily come to mean bad—or "serious"—news.

Invariably, every year there is a "Big Horse" from the east coast, and a "Big Horse" from the west coast. The Kentucky Derby is usually the first meeting between these two special thoroughbreds. This year, the west coast horse was a big, strapping colt named Dreamland, and the east coast entry was a sleek, rather smallish bundle of energy called Runamuck. So imposing were the credentials of these two horses that, to date, only five other horses had been named to run against them in the Derby. Of those, however, one had been felled by injury and another by illness, cutting the total field to five. This had caused this year's Run For The Roses to be dubbed by the media as "The Nickel Derby."

Arriving at Howard's office after his phone summons and accepting his offer of some of that mud he calls coffee, I took a seat while he started to tell me about it.

"I've had a meeting with officials from both California and Kentucky."

"About what?"

"There have been some threats against Dreamland and his camp."

"What sort of threats?"

"They've ranged from kidnapping to actually killing the horse."

"And the people on his camp?"

"They've been threatened with bodily harm, but no death threats as of yet."

"Well, that's all a real shame, Howard. But why would that cause you to have a meeting with the racing officials of two other states and then call me?"

He hesitated a moment, then said, "Because they don't have a team of special investigators, and I do."

He did have a team of investigators, for which he had fought long and hard with the Board of Directors of the NYSRC. They had finally agreed to give him a grant to hire *not* the twenty people he'd requested, but four. Take it or leave it, they told him, and he had taken it.

He took it and promptly contacted me because I had done some work for him before. I accepted the job, and helped find the other three people.

"Such as we are," I replied now.

"A poor lot, but mine own," he said, spreading his hands.

"So they want to borrow a man, is that it?"

"That's about the size of it. You'd be in charge of security for the animal while he's in California as well as when he's taken to Kentucky." He leaned forward and added, "Henry, if this horse were stolen or harmed, it would be a serious blow to all of thoroughbred racing. That's why I've decided it's important for us to work with these people."

"You mean you've decided that *I* should work with them."

He smiled grimly and said, "Yes, that's exactly what I mean."

"What about Runamuck?"

"No threats, no calls. Thank God."

"All right, Howard." I stood up. "I'll get going."

"I appreciate this, Henry," he said, opening his top drawer. He withdrew a brown envelope and held it out. "Here's your ticket, and some expense money."

"Think you know me pretty well, huh?" I asked, taking the envelope. "I'll need some background info on the people I'll be dealing with."

He reached down and brought an attache case out from behind his desk. "It's been prepared."

"Boy," I said, taking that, too, "I really like being unpredictable."

"Good luck, Henry."

"I'll keep in touch."

On the plane, I went through the material in the attache case. It told me a little about the people in the Dreamland camp: Donald McCoy, his rider, who had ridden him in all of his previous races; his owner, Mrs. Emily Nixon, who had taken the stable over from her father when he died ten years ago and had not had a Derby winner since; and his trainer, Lew Hale, who had been hired by Mrs. Nixon at the time she took over the stable.

It sounded like there could be some pressure on Hale to come through with a Derby winner, so I decided he'd be a good place to start.

When I landed at LAX, I took a cab to a hotel, changed into some California duds, and then took another cab to the racetrack, where I sought and found Lew Hale.

It was early, and workouts were just concluding. I approached Hale as he was looking over a two-year-old filly that was being galloped around the track, and introduced myself.

"Oh, you're the investigator from New York," he said, holding out his hand. "Glad to have you aboard, Mr. Po."

Deeply lined, be it from constant exposure to the weather, or otherwise, his face had character. His eyes were grey and his nose prominent. His mouth was what made him look ugly, though. His lips were heavy, and twisted, so that he always looked as if he had just sucked a lemon. He was taller than me by some four inches, which put him at least at six-two. He was in good shape for a man in his late fifties—hell, he was in good shape for a man my own age.

"I don't mind telling you, I've been plenty worried since those threats started."

"How long has that been?"

He thought a moment, then said, "A couple of weeks, I guess. First there was a note saying that Dreamland would never make it to the Derby."

"That sounds more like an opinion than a threat," I pointed out.

"Which was why we didn't react to it."

"Did you keep it?"

"I'm sorry, no. I threw it out. I never realized it was a threat until I got the phone call."

"Where did you receive the phone call?"

"Here, at the track."

"What time of day?"

"Early, before the day's racing began."

"Was the caller a man or a woman?"

"Uh, now that's hard to say. It could have been a woman with a deep voice . . . It sounded sort of muffled, as if the person had their hand over the phone."

"What did they say?"

"That Dreamland was going to take a ride, but that it wouldn't be to Kentucky."

"How many other calls did you get after after that?"

"Two. The last one said that Dreamland would be dead before he could reach the finish line."

"What about the threats against you and his jock?"

"I don't scare, Mr. Po, but he sure did."

"What?"

"No, you wouldn't know about that yet," he said. "He quit yesterday. He got a call and wouldn't even tell me what was said. He just wanted out, and I let him go. I don't need a gutless jock."

"In what way were you threatened?"

"They told me I'd be dead if Dreamland won the Derby. Bullshit!"

"I wonder if I could see where you keep the colt now?"

"Of course. Just let me finish watching Miss Emily work."

"The filly?" I asked.

"Yeah."

"She looks like a beauty. Is she named for Mrs. Nixon?"

He nodded. "She bid on the filly herself, and went for more bucks than I would have. But then, it's her money and I guess she knows what she's doing."

We watched the filly work until, apparently satisfied, Hale said, "Come on, let's go and see Dreamy. He's impressive as all hell just standing in his stall."

We walked out to a parking lot and got into a '73 Chevy that was covered with dust. We drove into the stable area on a dirt road, which explained the thick layers on the car. Most tracks have either dirt or gravel roads running through their stable areas.

Hale stopped the car in front of one of the larger stables and we got out. I could see a uniformed guard standing outside one of the stalls, so it wasn't hard to figure out where Dreamland was.

"I've had a guard on him day and night for three days now, since the last call," Hale explained.

When we reached the stall, the guard nodded at Hale but made no attempt to stop me or have me identify myself.

"This is Mr. Po," Hale told him. "He's from New York, and he will be in charge of security from now on."

"Yes, sir," the guard replied, and he nodded at me now that we'd been introduced.

"Are you private, or track security?" I asked the guard.

"Private, sir."

Hale said, "He's actually from the same company the track uses, but he's not assigned to the track permanently. Mrs. Nixon hired his company and they send us our own guards."

"Do you want to see my ID?" I asked the uniformed man.

"Uh, that won't be necessary, sir," he answered.

"Yes, it will," I said, taking out my ID and showing it to him. "I don't care whose company a stranger is in," I added, "I want his ID checked. Understand?"

The guard compressed his lips at the scolding and said, "Yes, sir, I understand."

I stepped past him, leaned on the stall door and peered in. Hale had been right; Dreamland was impressive. He picked up his head and looked me straight in the eye, wondering who the interloper was.

"Well, hello, your majesty," I greeted him.

"You get that feeling too, huh?" Hale asked. "He's regal-looking as all hell, eh?"

"That he is," I agreed.

"And he runs like all hell, too."

"How many shifts do you have the guards working on?"

"Three."

"When are you flying to Kentucky?"

"Day after tomorrow."

"Okay, until that time I want two guards on every shift. One here, and one moving about."

"I'll arrange it."

"It'll cost more."

"Lady Emily doesn't care about the cost," he assured me.

"Is that a nickname?"

"One of the milder ones," he answered, "and they're usually used behind her back."

"Has McCoy been around today?" I asked.

"Not today," he said. He turned his attention to the horse and said, "See you later, Dreamy." Dreamland gave him a sideways glance and then raised his head up high, as if ignoring us.

"Not very friendly," I commented.

"And that may be his only idiosyncrasy. But the way he runs, who cares? Come on, let's go to my office. If you can't locate McCoy around here, you might find him there, lickering his wounds."

"Why wouldn't I find him around here?" I asked. "He didn't quit riding altogether, did he?"

"When he quit me, he might as well have."

Hale gave me McCoy's address and phone number, and then I spent the better part of an hour trying to locate him on the track. When the day's racing began and I still hadn't found him, I gave up. None of the trainers I spoke to would admit that McCoy had been blackballed, but none of them were using him as a rider.

When I left the track, I grabbed a cab and gave the driver McCoy's home address, which turned to be an apartment building in a middle class neighborhood. Asking the driver to wait, I went into the lobby and rang McCoy's bell, but received no answer. I returned to the cab and had him take me back to my hotel, where I'd plan out my next move.

I checked in at the desk to see if there were any messages, not really expecting any, but when you're staying at a hotel you tend to do that. To my surprise, there was a message in my box. I controlled my curiosity until I got to my room. Once inside, I opened the envelope and took out a neatly typewritten note.

I read: "Mrs. Emily Nixon requests that you dine with her tonight. A car will come by your hotel to pick you up at seven sharp."

No signature.

It was some hell of a "request," but since I wanted to talk to the lady anyway, I wouldn't argue.

I read the note again, then put it down on a writing desk. Before showering, I dialed McCoy's number but got no answer. I showered, then tried again, still getting no response. I wanted very much to talk to McCoy and find out from him why he withdrew from a mount that very likely would have made him a lot of money. Hale had told me his version, but Hale—and Emily Nixon—were management; and management always had their own ideas about how things should be.

I got dressed and was ready when "Miss Emily's" driver knocked on the door.

I didn't expect to find anyone else in the car, since I thought that the vehicle was being sent specifically to take me somewhere, but there she was. When I stuck my head in, the first thing I saw were a pair of shapely legs. The second thing I saw was the face of an extremely handsome woman, which at the moment was wearing an amused smile.

"Good evening, Mr. Po," she greeted.

"Mrs. Nixon."

"Please, step all the way in and take a seat."

When I stepped in, the driver slammed the door behind me, got behind the wheel, and got under way.

"Let me say how grateful I am that you agreed to come to California and help us with our problem."

"I'm happy to be of help, Mrs. Nixon."

She had violet eyes that were very bright and intelligent. She appeared to be in her early forties, but was exceptionally attractive and radiated a youthful vitality.

"I hope you like expensive food, Mr. Po," she said then. "It's the only kind I ever eat."

"I only indulge when someone else is paying, Mrs. Nixon."

"Then you're in luck, aren't you?"

We spoke idly of racing until we reached our destination, an extremely expensive-looking Italian restaurant on Wilshire. When we entered we received the preferential treatment a woman of her station deserved—and craved—and were shown to "her" table.

After we had ordered dinner and had drinks in our hands, she said, "Well, what will your first step be in finding the man who has been making all these ghastly threats against us?"

"I think I should explain," I replied, "that my primary concern is not in finding the person making the threats, but to make sure that no harm comes to Dreamland or any of the people around him."

"I see," she said. "I'm afraid I misunderstood then. I was under the impression you were a special 'investigator' for the New York State Racing Club."

"I am," I assured her.

"Oh? Then what is it that a special investigator does?" she asked. "Investigate, no?"

"Under normal circumstances, yes," I said, trying not to lose my temper with her. "But not in this instance, I'm afraid."

"What have you done, then, to assure Dreamland's safety?" she asked. Her tone was considerably colder than what it had been to that point.

I explained that I had been to the track and had increased the security around Dreamland's stall. I also told her that I had spoken to Lew Hale, and was looking for McCoy.

"I don't want to talk about McCoy," she said vehemently. "How dare he do that to me!"

"You're talking about withdrawing from the mount?"

"Of course! What else?" she shot back. "I cannot believe—" She stopped herself in midsentence, closed her eyes, and said, "I do not want to talk about that little man."

"What about Hale?"

"Hale is fired if Dreamy doesn't win the Derby," she said. "I've given him long enough."

"Ten years, isn't it?"

"Yes, ever since my father died. My father, George Gregg, had two Derby winners and three other horses who finished in the money. I have not had a horse accomplish any of that."

"Lew Hale seems fairly confident," I observed.

"We are all confident," she agreed, "but confidence does not win horse races."

Dinner came and I asked if she minded talking while we ate.

"Well, well, a gentleman," she said. "How nice. No, of course I don't mind. Thank you for asking."

As we cut into our food, I asked, "Will you be going to Kentucky with, uh, Dreamy?"

"No, but I'll be there later in the week, the day before the race," she answered. "I don't want to miss the Derby Eve festivities."

"Mrs. Nixon, about the threats. The notes, the calls—"

"One call," she said. "I received only one call."

"I understood there were more. And at least one note."

"The other calls, and the note, were received by Lew Hale."

"Did you see the note?"

"No, I did not. He told me about it, but said he threw it away."

"What about the call you did get?"

"A voice—"

"Male or female?"

That stopped her, as it had Hale, and she had to think about it.

"That voice was rather deep. I did not get the impression that I was speaking to a woman."

I put a lot of stock into her "impression"—or lack of one. I reasoned that a woman would know instinctively if she were speaking to another woman.

"Go on," I said.

"The voice said that if I made the trip to Kentucky, I'd be lucky as all hell to make it back."

This time I was the one who was stopped for a moment. Then I said, "Was that verbatim?"

"What?" she asked, hesitating over a forkful of linguini.

"The message you got on the phone, the way you gave it to me just now—was that word for word?"

She thought a moment, then said, "Yes. That's the way I remember it. Why?"

"Nothing," I said, not wanting to voice my thoughts at that moment. It would take more than what I was thinking to build a case. I went on, "How much contact have you had with Lew Hale over your ten-year association?"

"Actually, not all that much. Outside of the winner's circle—when we get there—I don't think I see him more than two or three times a year."

"Isn't that unusual?"

"Perhaps. But, unlike my father, I do *not* like the way horses smell. I don't spend that much time around the stables, and if I'm at the track it's either in the clubhouse or my private box."

"I see."

She put her fork down and said, "Why are you asking all these questions about the threats if you don't intend to investigate them?"

I was caught.

"Curiosity," I pleaded, "an investigator's curiosity. A few questions can't hurt, and if I *can* find something out, I naturally will. But security is still my prime concern. I'll be satisfied just to see Dreamland run in the Derby."

"And win?" she asked.

I put my right hand out, palm down, and wiggled it back and forth a few times. "I'm like that about who wins, although I *am* an Easterner at heart," I confessed.

There was less tension between us after that, and at times I thought she might even be coming on to me. But I feigned ignorance.

When her driver arrived, we got up to leave and I asked if she minded if I made a phone call. She said she'd wait for me in the car.

I found a pay phone and dialed Don McCoy's number again and this time got a busy signal. I hung up, dialed again, got the same thing. On a hunch, I called the operator and had her check the line. She informed me there was no ongoing conversation and said the phone was either out of order or off the hook.

When I got back to Mrs. Nixon's car, I said, "Would you take me by Don McCoy's apartment?"

She compressed her lips and I thought she was going to refuse, but instead she said, "I'll have Arthur take me home, and then drive you over there."

"Thank you."

We dropped her at "one of" her residences, a ritzy apartment house near Beverly Hills, and then her driver took me to McCoy's less ostentatious residence.

"Mrs. Nixon instructed me to wait if you wanted," Arthur told me.

"I appreciate that," I said, "but I'll find my way back. Thanks."

He touched the tip of his cap, then drove off.

I went into the lobby of McCoy's building and rang his bell. There was no answer. I tried the oldest trick in the official Private Eye Handbook. I pushed a few of the other buttons and was buzzed in. With access to the elevators now, I rode up to McCoy's floor—the fifth—and found his apartment. I knocked and rang his buzzer and when I still didn't get an answer, I used my lock picks to get in.

The apartment was lit by a small lamp in the living room. On the desk next to the lamp was the phone, its receiver hanging by the cord, dangling just above the floor.

I went from room to room—there were only three—and finally found what I wasn't looking for in the bathroom.

Don McCoy was in the tub, but he wasn't taking a bath.

He was dead.

"How did you get in?" Lt. Taylor of the L.A.P.D. Homicide Squad asked me.

"The door was open," I lied.

"Is that so? If I searched you right now, Mr. Po, I wouldn't just happen to come up with a dandy little set of lock picks, would I?"

"You might," I admitted. "But that still wouldn't mean that I didn't find the door open."

He had to concede me that point, and he did so, grudgingly.

After getting over the shock of finding McCoy in the tub, with his blood running down the drain, I put the phone back on the hook and called for the police. A squad car had responded first, taken one look at the tub, and put in a call for Homicide, Forensics, and the M.E.

Homicide was Lt. Bryce Taylor, who reminded me a little of my sometime friend, sometime adversary on the N.Y.P.D., Detective James Diver. Taylor had a ruddy complexion and salt-and-pepper hair, and he also had a spare tire around his middle-aged middle. It didn't look so bad on him, though, because he was tall enough to carry it. Actually, at six-six or so, he was tall enough to carry almost anything.

The M.E., a Doctor Zetnor, came out of the bathroom and Taylor asked, "What can you tell me, Doc?"

Zetnor, a small, neat, precise-looking man of indeterminable ancestry—and his name didn't help—said, "He was shot twice, at close range. Either bullet looks like it could've done the trick, but I'll know more after I go inside."

"Report on my desk in the morning?" Taylor asked.

"As soon as I can," Zetnor promised. He supervised the removal of the body, and followed it out.

"You toss the place?" Taylor asked, turning to me. Before I could speak, he added, "Don't dummy up on me, Po. I won't come down on you if you level with me, but you're out of town talent. If you hold out on me I could cause you a lot of heartache."

He was tough, but didn't come on as tough as he could have, so I decided to level.

"I did look around," I said. "Just for something to do while I waited."

"What did you come up with that we'll eventually come up with anyway?"

"A note," I said.

"What kind of note?"

I explained to him my reason for being in town, and told him that McCoy had received a note that had caused him to withdraw from the mount of Dreamland.

"Horses," he said, shaking his head. "You know, even my wife makes a bet at Kentucky Derby time. Waste of money. Where's the note?"

"Top drawer of his dresser."

"Not in your pocket?"

"Lieutenant," I scolded.

"Sorry," he said, touching his forehead, "I don't know what came over me. Come on."

I followed him into the bedroom.

"You dust this dresser yet?" he asked one of the Forensics men.

"Yes, sir."

He opened the drawer, looked around, and came up with an envelope.

"This it?" he asked me.

"That's it."

"Looks like a letter," he said. It was addressed to McCoy, with a stamp and a postmark, the date of which was earlier that week. He opened it, scanned it, and said, "Reads like a note."

"Read it out loud," I told him.

"What?"

"Humor me. I think I may be able to help you wrap this one up quick."

"I'm all for that," he said, and proceeded to read out loud.

When he'd finished, I said, "Let's check that note for prints, and I think I can tell you whose to check it against."

"If there *are* any prints," he said. "People who make death threats aren't usually that helpful."

"Why don't you give me a ride to my hotel," I suggested, "and I'll tell you a story about a man and a slip of the tongue."

"All right, but you better have something worth the cab fare."

He drove me to my hotel, listened to what I had to say, and agreed to pick me up the next day. He admitted that I might have something, however slim a hook I was hanging it on.

"What did you get?" I asked as I got in his car the next morning.

"Enough to keep me going along," he said. "The man owes a bundle, his job is in danger, and we already had his prints on file from an old gambling bust. They matched the ones taken from the note."

"All right," I said. "Let me go in to talk to him first. Maybe I can get him to say something that will make your case easier."

"Okay," he said. "Here's the note."

"We going alone?"

"I'm shorthanded on my squad. That's the only reason I responded myself last night." He started the car, then added, "I'll have a unit meet us at the track."

"Quietly," I suggested.

"Natch."

I found Lew Hale watching the workouts and persuaded him to accompany me to his office. I told him I had some news about McCoy, and about the man making the threats.

"Man?" he asked me on the way. "So you've determined that it *was* a man?"

"Oh, yes," I said. "I'm dead sure it was a man."

When we got to his office, he sat down behind his desk and said, "Well, what about McCoy and the guy making the threats? You don't mean it was him, do you?"

I shook my head. "No, it wasn't him. McCoy's dead. According to the M.E.'s report, he was killed night before last."

"That's too bad," Hale said. "He was gutless, but that's not a reason for a man to have to die."

"My thoughts exactly, Mr. Hale," I said. "And yet, you *did* kill him."

"Me!?" he replied in surprise. "Are you crazy?"

"And there must have been more of a reason than the fact he was gutless."

"Have you got any proof of what you're saying?" he demanded.

"I think I do," I replied.

"Well, you'd better be sure as all hell that you do!"

"That's what first put me onto you, Hale," I told him. "That phrase you keep using. Most people say 'sure as hell' or 'fast as hell,' but you always add the word 'all.' You said Dreamland was 'impressive as all hell,' remember?"

"And that makes me guilty of murder?"

"Not necessarily, but that's what made me start to think you might be guilty of fabricating and making threats."

"Fabricating? Didn't Miss Emily tell you she got a call—"

"She did. She told me that the caller said she'd be 'lucky as all hell' to make it back from Kentucky."

"So?" he demanded, looking uncomfortable.

"And then there's this," I said, taking the envelope and note from my pocket.

"Now what's that?"

"A note Don McCoy received earlier this week, which probably caused him to withdraw from his mount on Dreamland. The note says he would be 'deader than all hell' if he rode Dreamland in the Derby."

"I don't say—"

"Yes, you do, Hale. You don't notice it because it's become habit with you. But I noticed it right away. It didn't dawn on Mrs. Nixon because she didn't spend enough time around you that she would notice."

"This is ridiculous," he sputtered. "You have to have more proof than—"

"You owe a lot of money," I said, cutting him off. "Gambling debts. You stood to make plenty if Dreamland lost, but if he lost you also stood to lose your job."

"You're saying that I wanted him to run and lose, and that I didn't want him to run at all. You should make up your—"

"And then there are your prints on this piece of paper," I said.

"Prints?"

"Fingerprints. You probably had no way of knowing that McCoy would keep the note, and—not being a true criminal—it probably never occurred to you to wear gloves when you wrote it. Your prints are on file with the police because of an old gambling arrest, aren't they?"

He made a quick move, opening his top drawer and pulling out a .38.

"All right," he said, "all right." He was nervous, flexing his fingers around the gun, making me nervous. "I didn't mean to kill McCoy."

"Tell me about it," I said, sensing that he needed little prodding to do so.

"You were right, there were two ways I could go. I could allow Dreamland to run, hoping that he'd win and save my job, but that wouldn't pay my debts. Of course if he ran and lost, without my job I wouldn't be able to make any payments at all."

"Let me guess. First you scared McCoy, then you offered him a deal."

Hale nodded. "To pull the horse, throw the race. I'd make a bundle and the people I owe money to would make a bundle, too."

"What happened?"

"McCoy got irate, the little fool," he hissed. "He said he'd rather be scared off than bought off. When I showed him the gun, he jumped me. We struggled and it went off."

"Why were there no calls or threats for the past four days?" I asked.

"The people I owe found out what I was trying to do," he explained. "They said that keeping the horse from running so he wouldn't lose and cost me my job was small thinking. They said I'd lose my job anyway, sooner or later. They made me see that the only way to get square with them—and even make some money for myself—was to make sure Dreamland ran and lost. So I changed my plans." He flexed his fingers around the gun some more. "Now I've got to change my plans again."

"Did you find a jockey that could be bought?"

"There are enough of them," he said. "I'll give one of them the mount . . . but first I've got to take care of you."

"You're not going to kill me, Hale," I said. "Look at how nervous you are. You killed McCoy by accident. I don't think you can kill me in cold blood."

A drop of persperation rolled down his cheek to the corner of his mouth, where he licked it off.

"Besides," I went on, "the police are right outside listening to everything. Kill me, and you'll be a lot of worse off than you already are." I raised my voice and said, "Lieutenant?"

The door opened and Taylor walked in, followed by two uniform cops.

I took a step towards Hale, holding out my hand. "Let me have the gun, Hale. It's all over."

He hesitated long enough to scare me a little, but finally handed over the weapon.

"Okay," Taylor told his men, "take him out and read him his rights."

As they led the trainer from the office, Taylor walked over and relieved me of the .38.

"I guess he could look on the bright side," I said.

"What's that?"

"Maybe in prison he'll be safe from the people he owes money to."

"Maybe," the tall cop said, shaking his head, as if something were still eating at him.

"What's on your mind, Lieutenant?"

"Hm? Oh, nothing much," he said. "This is just the first time I've ever built a case around a slip of the tongue, that's all."

ED GORMAN

Ed Gorman (1941–) has been called "one of the most original crime writers around" by *Kirkus Reviews* and "a powerful storyteller" by Charles Champlin of the *Los Angeles Times*. He works in horror and Westerns as well as crime and writes many excellent short stories. To date there have been six Gorman collections, three of which are straight crime, the most recent being *Such a Good Girl and Other Crime Stories*. He is probably best known for his Sam McCain series, set in small-town Iowa of the 1950s ("good and evil clash with the same heartbreaking results as Lawrence Block or Elmore Leonard"). He has also written a number of thrillers, including *The Marilyn Tapes* and *Black River Falls,* the latest being *The Poker Club*.

He is among the best writers of short crime fiction today—or ever.

The Reason Why

"I'm scared."

"This was your idea, Karen."

"You scared?"

"No."

"You bastard."

"Because I'm not scared I'm a bastard?"

"You not being scared means you don't believe me."

"Well."

"See. I knew it."

"What?"

"Just the way you said 'Well.' You bastard."

I sighed and looked out at the big red brick building that sprawled over a quarter mile of spring grass turned silver by a fat June moon.

Twenty-five years ago a 1950 Ford fastback had sat in the adjacent parking lot. Mine for two summers of grocery store work.

We were sitting in her car, a Volvo she'd cadged from her last marriage settlement, number four if you're interested, and sharing a pint of bourbon the way we used to in high school when we'd been more than friends but never quite lovers.

The occasion tonight was our twenty-fifth class reunion. But there was another occasion, too. In our senior year a boy named Michael Brandon had jumped off a steep clay cliff called Pierce Point to his death on the winding river road below. Suicide. That, anyway, had been the official version.

A month ago Karen Lane (she had gone back to her maiden name these days, the Karen Lane-Cummings-Todd-Browne-LeMay getting a tad too long) had called to see if I wanted to go to dinner and I said yes, if I could bring Donna along, but then Donna surprised me by saying she didn't care to go along, that by now we should be at the point in our relationship where we trusted each other ("God, Dwyer, I don't even look at other men, not for very long anyway, you know?"), and Karen and I had had dinner and she'd had many drinks, enough that I saw she had a problem, and then she'd told me about something that had troubled her for a long time . . .

In senior year she'd gone to a party and gotten sick on wine and stumbled out to somebody's backyard to throw up and it was there she'd overheard the three boys talking. They were earnestly discussing what had happened to Michael Brandon the previous week and they were even more earnestly discussing what would happen to them if "anybody ever really found out the truth."

"It's bothered me all these years," she'd said over dinner a month earlier. "They murdered him and they got away with it."

"Why didn't you tell the police?"

"I didn't think they'd believe me."

"Why not?"

She shrugged and put her lovely little face down, dark hair covering her features. Whenever she put her face down that way it meant that she didn't want to tell you a lie so she'd just as soon talk about something else.

"Why not, Karen?"

"Because of where we came from. The Highlands."

The Highlands is an area that used to ring the iron foundries and factories of this city. Way before pollution became a fashionable concern, you could stand on your front porch and see a peculiarly beautiful orange haze on the sky every dusk. The Highlands had bars where men lost ears, eyes, and fingers in just garden-variety fights, and streets where nobody sane ever walked after dark, not even cops unless they were in pairs. But it wasn't the physical violence you remembered so much as the emotional violence of poverty. You get tired of hearing your mother scream because there isn't enough money for food and hearing your father scream back because there's nothing he can do about it. Nothing.

Karen Lane and I had come from the Highlands, but we were smarter and, in her case, better looking than most of the people from the area, so when we went to Wilson High School—one of those nightmare conglomerates that shoves the poorest kids in a city in with the richest—we didn't do badly for ourselves. By senior year we found ourselves hanging out with the sons and daughters of bankers and doctors and city officials and lawyers and riding around in new Impala convertibles and attending an occasional party where you saw an actual maid. But wherever we went, we'd manage for at least a few minutes to get away from our dates and talk to each other. What we were doing, of course, was trying to comfort ourselves. We shared terrible and confusing feelings—pride that we were acceptable to those we saw as glamorous, shame that we felt disgrace for being from the Highlands and having fathers who worked in factories and mothers who went to Mass as often as nuns and brothers and sisters who were doomed to punching the clock and yelling at ragged kids in the cold factory dusk. (You never realize what a toll such shame takes till you see your father's waxen face there in the years-later casket.)

That was the big secret we shared, of course, Karen and I, that we were going to get out, leave the place once and for all. And her brown eyes never sparkled more Christmas-morning bright than at those moments when it all was ahead of us, money, sex, endless thrills, immortality. She had the kind of clean good looks brought out best by a blue cardigan with a line of white button-down shirt at the top and a brown suede car coat over her slender shoulders and moderately tight jeans displaying her quietly artful ass. Nothing splashy about her. She had the sort of face that snuck up on you. You had the impression you were talking to a pretty but in no way spectacular girl, and then all of a sudden you saw how the eyes burned with sad humor and how wry the mouth got at certain times and how absolutely perfect that straight little nose was and how the freckles enhanced rather than detracted from her beauty and by then of course you were hopelessly entangled. Hopelessly.

This wasn't just my opinion, either. I mentioned four divorce settlements. True facts. Karen was one of those prizes that powerful and rich men like to collect with the understanding that it's only something you hold in trust, like a yachting cup. So, in her time, she'd been an ornament for a professional football player (her college beau), an orthodontist ("I think he used to have sexual fantasies about Barry Goldwater"), the owner of a large commuter airline ("I slept with half his pilots; it was kind of a company benefit"), and a sixty-nine-year-old millionaire who was dying of heart disease ("He used to have me sit next to his bedside and just hold his hand—the weird thing was that of all of them, I loved him, I really did—and his eyes would be closed and then every once in a while tears would start streaming down his cheeks as if he was remembering something that really filled him with remorse; he was really a sweetie, but then cancer got him before the heart disease and I never did find out what he regretted so much, I mean if it was about his son or his wife or what"), and now she was comfortably fixed for the rest of her life and if the crow's feet were a little more pronounced around eyes and mouth and if the slenderness was just a trifle too slender (she weighed, at five-three, maybe ninety pounds and kept a variety of diet books in her big sunny kitchen), she was a damn good-looking woman nonetheless, the world's absurdity catalogued and evaluated in a gaze that managed to be both weary and impish, with a laugh that was knowing without being cynical.

So now she wanted to play detective.

I had some more bourbon from the pint—it burned beautifully—and said, "If I had your money, you know what I'd do?"

"Buy yourself a new shirt?"

"You don't like my shirt?"

"I didn't know you had this thing about Hawaii."

"If I had your money, I'd just forget about all this."

"I thought cops were sworn to uphold the right and the true."

"I'm an ex-cop."

"You wear a uniform."

"That's for the American Security Agency."

She sighed. "So I shouldn't have sent the letters?"

"No."

"Well, if they're guilty, they'll show up at Pierce Point tonight."

"Not necessarily."

"Why?"

"Maybe they'll know it's a trap. And not do anything."

She nodded to the school. "You hear that?"

"What?"

"The song."

It was Bobby Vinton's "Roses Are Red."

"I remember one party when we both hated our dates and we ended up dancing to that over and over again. Somebody's basement. You remember?"

"Sort of, I guess," I said.

"Good. Let's go in the gym and then we can dance to it again."

Donna, my lady friend, was out of town attending an advertising convention. I hoped she wasn't going to dance with anybody else because it would sure make me mad.

I started to open the door and she said, "I want to ask you a question."

"What?" I sensed what it was going to be so I kept my eyes on the parking lot.

"Turn around and look at me."

I turned around and looked at her. "Okay."

"Since the time we had dinner a month or so ago I've started receiving brochures from Alcoholics Anonymous in the mail. If you were having them sent to me, would you be honest enough to tell me?"

"Yes, I would."

"Are you having them sent to me?"

"Yes, I am."

"You think I'm a lush?"

"Don't you?"

"I asked you first."

So we went into the gym and danced.

Crepe of red and white, the school colors, draped the ceiling; the stage was a cave of white light on which stood four balding fat guys with spit curls and shimmery gold lamé dinner jackets (could these be the illegitimate sons of Bill Haley?) playing guitars, drum, and saxophone; on the dance floor couples who'd lost hair, teeth, jaw lines, courage, and energy (everything, it seemed, but weight) danced to lame cover versions of "Breaking Up Is Hard To Do" and "Sheila," "Runaround Sue" and "Running Scared" (tonight's lead singer sensibly not even trying Roy Orbison's beautiful falsetto) and then, while I got Karen and myself some no-alcohol punch, they broke into a medley of dance tunes—everything from "Locomotion" to "The Peppermint Twist"—and the place went a little crazy, and I went right along with it.

"Come on," I said.

"Great."

We went out there and we burned ass. We'd both agreed not to dress up for the occasion so we were ready for this. I wore the Hawaiian shirt she found so despicable plus a blue blazer, white socks and cordovan penny-loafers. She wore a salmon-colored Merikani shirt belted at the waist and tan cotton fatigue pants and, sweet Christ, she was so adorable half the guys in the place did the kind of double-takes usually reserved for somebody outrageous or famous.

Over the blasting music, I shouted, "Everybody's watching *you*!"

She shouted right back, "I know! Isn't it wonderful?"

The medley went twenty minutes and could easily have been confused with an aerobics session. By the end I was sopping and wishing I was carrying ten or fifteen pounds less and sometimes feeling guilty because I was having too much fun (I just hoped Donna, probably having too much fun, too, was feeling equally guilty), and then finally it ended and mate fell into the arms of mate, hanging on to stave off sheer collapse.

Then the head Bill Haley clone said, "Okay, now we're going to do a ballad medley," so then we got everybody from Johnny Mathis to Connie Francis and we couldn't resist that, so I moved her around the floor with clumsy pleasure and she moved me right back with equally clumsy pleasure. "You know something?" I said.

"We're both shitty dancers?"

"Right."

But we kept on, of course, laughing and whirling a few times, and then coming tighter together and just holding each other silently for a time, two human beings getting older and scared about getting older, remembering some things and trying to forget others and trying to make sense of an existence that ultimately made sense to nobody, and then she said, "There's one of them."

I didn't have to ask her what "them" referred to. Until now she'd refused to identify any of the three people she'd sent the letters to.

At first I didn't recognize him. He had almost white hair and a tan so dark it looked fake. He wore a black dinner jacket with a lacy shirt and a black bow tie. He didn't seem to have put on a pound in the quarter century since I'd last seen him.

"Ted Forester?"

"Forester," she said. "He's president of the same savings and loan his father was president of."

"Who are the other two?"

"Why don't we get some punch?"

"The kiddie kind?"

"You could really make me mad with all this lecturing about alcoholism."

"If you're not really a lush then you won't mind getting the kiddie kind."

"My friend, Sigmund Fraud."

We had a couple of pink punches and caught our respective breaths and squinted in the gloom at name tags to see who we were saying hello to and realized all the terrible things you realize at high school reunions, namely that people who thought they were better than you still think that way, and that all the sad little people you feared for—the ones with blackheads and low IQs and lame left legs and walleyes and lisps and every other sort of unfair infirmity people get stuck with—generally turned out to be deserving of your fear, for there was a sadness in their eyes tonight that spoke of failures of every sort, and you wanted to go up and say something to them (I wanted to go up to nervous Karl Carberry, who used to twitch—his whole body twitched—and throw my arm around him and tell him what a neat guy he was, tell him there was no reason whatsoever for his twitching, grant him peace and self-esteem and at least a modicum of hope; if he needed a woman, get him a woman, too), but of course you didn't do that, you didn't go up, you just made edgy jokes and nodded a lot and drifted on to the next piece of human carnage.

"There's number two," Karen whispered.

This one I remembered. And despised. The six-three blond movie-star looks had grown only slightly older. His blue dinner jacket just seemed to enhance his air of malicious superiority. Larry Price. His wife Sally was still perfect, too, though you could see in the lacquered blond hair and maybe a hint of face lift that she'd had to work at it a little harder. A year out of high school, at a bar that took teenage IDs checked by a guy who must have been legally blind, I'd gotten drunk and told Larry that he was essentially an asshole for beating up a friend of mine who hadn't had a chance against him. I had the street boy's secret belief that I could take anybody whose father was a surgeon and whose house included a swimming pool. I had hatred, bitterness, and rage going, right? Well, Larry and I went out into the parking lot, ringed by a lot of drunken spectators, and before I got off a single punch, Larry hit me with a shot that stood me straight up, giving him a great opportunity to hit me again. He hit me three times before I found his face and sent him a shot hard enough to push him back for a time. Before we could go at it again, the guy who checked IDs got himself between us. He was madder than either Larry or me. He ended the fight by taking us both by the ears (he must have trained with nuns) and dragging us out to the curb and telling neither of us to come back.

"You remember the night you fought him?"

"Yeah."

"You could have taken him, Dwyer. Those three punches he got in were just lucky."

"Yeah, that was my impression, too. Lucky."

She laughed. "I was afraid he was going to kill you."

I was going to say something smart, but then a new group of people came up and we gushed through a little social dance of nostalgia and lies and self-justifications. We talked success (at high school reunions, everybody sounds like Amway representatives at a pep rally) and the old days (nobody seems to remember all the kids who got treated like shit for reasons they had no control over) and didn't so-and-so look great (usually this meant they'd managed to keep their toupees on straight) and introducing new spouses (we all had to explain what happened to our original mates; I said mine had been eaten by alligators in the Amazon, but nobody seemed to find that especially believeable) and in the midst of all this, Karen tugged my sleeve and said, "There's the third one."

Him I recognized, too. David Haskins. He didn't look any happier than he ever had. Parent trouble was always the explanation you got for his grief back in high school. His parents had been rich, truly so, his father an importer of some kind, and their arguments so violent that they were as eagerly discussed as who was or who was not pregnant. Apparently David's parents weren't getting along any better today because although the features of his face were open and friendly enough, there was still the sense of some terrible secret stooping his shoulders and keeping his smiles to furtive wretched imitations. He was a paunchy balding little man who might have been a church usher with a sour stomach.

"The Duke of Earl" started up then and there was no way we were going to let that pass so we got out on the floor; but by now, of course, we both watched the three people she'd sent letters to. Her instructions had been to meet the anonymous letter writer at nine-thirty at Pierce Point. If they were going to be there on time, they'd be leaving soon.

"You think they're going to go?"

"I doubt it, Karen."

"You still don't believe that's what I heard them say that night?"

"It was a long time ago and you were drunk."

"It's a good thing I like you because otherwise you'd be a distinct pain in the ass."

Which is when I saw all three of them go stand under one of the glowing red EXIT signs and open a fire door that led to the parking lot.

"They're going!" she said.

"Maybe they're just having a cigarette."

"You know better, Dwyer. You know better."

Her car was in the lot on the opposite side of the gym.

"Well, it's worth a drive even if they don't show up. Pierce Point should be nice tonight."

She squeezed against me and said, "Thanks, Dwyer. Really."

So we went and got her Volvo and went out to Pierce Point where twenty-five years ago a shy kid named Michael Brandon had fallen or been pushed to his death.

Apparently we were about to find out which.

The river road wound along a high wall of clay cliffs on the left and a wide expanse of water on the right. The spring night was impossibly beautiful, one of those moments so rich with sweet odor and even sweeter sight you wanted to take your clothes off and run around in some kind of crazed animal circles out of sheer joy.

"You still like jazz," she said, nodding to the radio.

"I hope you didn't mind my turning the station."

"I'm kind of into Country."

"I didn't get the impression you were listening."

She looked over at me. "Actually, I wasn't. I was thinking about you sending me all those AA pamphlets."

"It was arrogant and presumptous and I apologize."

"No, it wasn't. It was sweet and I appreciate it."

The rest of the ride, I leaned my head back and smelled flowers and grass and river water and watched moonglow through the elms and oaks and birches of this new spring. There was a Dakota Staton song, "Street of Dreams," and I wondered as always where she was and what she was doing, she'd been so fine, maybe the most underappreciated jazz singer of the entire fifties.

Then we were going up a long, twisting gravel road. We pulled up next to a big park pavillion and got out and stood in the wet grass, and she came over and slid her arm around my waist and sort of hugged me in a half-serious way. "This is all probably crazy, isn't it?"

I sort of hugged her back in a half-serious way. "Yeah, but it's a nice night for a walk so what the hell."

"You ready?"

"Yep."

"Let's go then."

So we went up the hill to the Point itself, and first we looked out at the far side of the river where white birches glowed in the gloom and where beyond you could see the horseshoe shape of the city lights. Then we looked down, straight down the drop of two hundred feet, to the road where Michael Brandon had died.

When I heard the car starting up the road to the east, I said, "Let's get in those bushes over there."

A thick line of shrubs and second-growth timber would give us a place to hide, to watch them.

By the time we were in place, ducked down behind a wide elm and a mulberry bush, a new yellow Mercedes sedan swung into sight and stopped several yards from the edge of the Point.

A car radio played loud in the night. A Top 40 song. Three men got out. Dignified Forester, matinee-idol Price, anxiety-tight Haskins.

Forester leaned back into the car and snapped the radio off. But he left the headlights on. Forester and Price each had cans of beer. Haskins bit his nails.

They looked around in the gloom. The headlights made the darkness beyond seem much darker and the grass in its illumination much greener. Price said harshly, "I told you this was just some goddamn prank. Nobody knows squat."

"He's right, he's probably right," Haskins said to Forester. Obviously he was hoping that was the case.

Forester said, "If somebody didn't know something, we would never have gotten those letters."

She moved then and I hadn't expected her to move at all. I'd been under the impression we would just sit there and listen and let them ramble and maybe in so doing reveal something useful.

But she had other ideas.

She pushed through the undergrowth and stumbled a little and got to her feet again and then walked right up to them.

"Karen!" Haskins said.

"So you did kill Michael," she said.

Price moved toward her abruptly, his hand raised. He was drunk and apparently hitting women was something he did without much trouble.

Then I stepped out from our hiding place and said, "Put your hand down, Price."

Forester said, "Dwyer."

"So," Price said, lowering his hand, "I was right, wasn't I?" He was speaking to Forester.

Forester shook his silver head. He seemed genuinely saddened. "Yes, Price, for once your cynicism is justified."

Price said, “Well, you two aren’t getting a goddamned penny, do you know that?”

He lunged toward me, still a bully. But I was ready for him, wanted it. I also had the advantage of being sober. When he was two steps away, I hit him just once and very hard in his solar plexus. He backed away, eyes startled, and then he turned abruptly away.

We all stood looking at one another, pretending not to hear the sounds of violent vomiting on the other side of the splendid new Mercedes.

Forester said, “When I saw you there, Karen, I wondered if you could do it alone.”

“Do what?”

“What?” Forester said. “What? Let’s at least stop the games. You two want money.”

“Christ,” I said to Karen, who looked perplexed, “they think we’re trying to shake them down.”

“Shake them down?”

“Blackmail them.”

“Exactly,” Forester said.

Price had come back around. He was wiping his mouth with the back of his hand. In his other hand he carried a silver-plated .45, the sort of weapon professional gamblers favor.

Haskins said, “Larry, Jesus, what is that?”

“What does it look like?”

“Larry, that’s how people get killed.” Haskins sounded like Price’s mother.

Price’s eyes were on me. “Yeah, it would be terrible if Dwyer here got killed, wouldn’t it?” He waved the gun at me. I didn’t really think he’d shoot, but I sure was afraid he’d trip and the damn thing would go off accidentally. “You’ve been waiting since senior year to do that to me, haven’t you, Dwyer?”

I shrugged. “I guess so, yeah.”

“Well, why don’t I give Forester here the gun and then you and I can try it again.”

“Fine with me.”

He handed Forester the .45. Forester took it all right, but what he did was toss it somewhere into the gloom surrounding the car. “Larry, if you don’t straighten up here, I’ll fight you myself. Do you understand me?” Forester had a certain dignity and when he spoke, his voice carried an easy authority. “There will be no more fighting, do you both understand that?”

“I agree with Ted,” Karen said.

Forester, like a teacher tired of naughty children, decided to get on with the real business. “You wrote those letters, Dwyer?”

“No.”

“No?”

"No. Karen wrote them."

A curious glance was exchanged by Forester and Karen. "I guess I should have known that," Forester said.

"Jesus, Ted," Karen said, "I'm not trying to blackmail you, no matter what you think."

"Then just what exactly are you trying to do?"

She shook her lovely little head. I sensed she regretted ever writing the letters, stirring it all up again. "I just want the truth to come out about what really happened to Michael Brandon that night."

"The truth," Price said. "Isn't that goddamn touching?"

"Shut up, Larry," Haskins said.

Forester said, "You know what happened to Michael Brandon?"

"I've got a good idea," Karen said. "I overheard you three talking at a party one night."

"What did we say?"

"What?"

"What did you overhear us say?"

Karen said, "You said that you hoped nobody looked into what really happened to Michael that night."

A smile touched Forester's lips. "So on that basis you concluded that we murdered him?"

"There wasn't much else to conclude."

Price said, weaving still, leaning on the fender for support, "I don't goddamn believe this."

Forester nodded to me. "Dwyer, I'd like to have a talk with Price and Haskins here, if you don't mind. Just a few minutes." He pointed to the darkness beyond the car. "We'll walk over there. You know we won't try to get away because you'll have our car. All right?"

I looked at Karen.

She shrugged.

They left, back into the gloom, voices receding and fading into the sounds of crickets and a barn owl and a distant roaring train.

"You think they're up to something?"

"I don't know," I said.

We stood with our shoes getting soaked and looked at the green green grass in the headlights.

"What do you think they're doing?" Karen asked.

"Deciding what they want to tell us."

"You're used to this kind of thing, aren't you?"

"I guess."

"It's sort of sad, isn't it?"

"Yeah. It is."

"Except for you getting the chance to punch out Larry Price after all these years."

"Christ, you really think I'm that petty?"

"I know you are. I know you are."

Then we both turned to look back to where they were. There'd been a cry and Forester shouted, "You hit him again, Larry, and I'll break your goddamn jaw." They were arguing about something and it had turned vicious.

I leaned back against the car. She leaned back against me. "You think we'll ever go to bed?"

"I'd sure like to, Karen, but I can't."

"Donna?"

"Yeah. I'm really trying to learn how to be faithful."

"That been a problem?"

"It cost me a marriage."

"Maybe I'll learn how someday, too."

Then they were back. Somebody, presumably Forester, had torn Price's nice lacy shirt into shreds. Haskins looked miserable.

Forester said, "I'm going to tell you what happened that night."

I nodded.

"I've got some beer in the back seat. Would either of you like one?"

Karen said, "Yes, we would."

So he went and got a six pack of Michelob and we all had a beer and just before he started talking he and Karen shared another one of those peculiar glances and then he said, "The four of us—myself, Price, Haskins, and Michael Brandon—had done something we were very ashamed of."

"Afraid of," Haskins said.

"Afraid that, if it came out, our lives would be ruined. Forever," Forester said.

Price said, "Just say it, Forester." He glared at me. "We raped a girl, the four of us."

"Brandon spent two months afterward seeing the girl, bringing her flowers, apologizing to her over and over again, telling her how sorry we were, that we'd been drunk and it wasn't like us to do that and—" Forester sighed, put his eyes to the ground. "In fact we had been drunk; in fact it wasn't like us to do such a thing—"

Haskins said, "It really wasn't. It really wasn't."

For a time there was just the barn owl and the crickets again, no talk, and then gently I said, "What happened to Brandon that night?"

"We were out as we usually were, drinking beer, talking about it, afraid the girl would finally turn us into the police, still trying to figure out why we'd ever done such a thing—"

The hatred was gone from Price's eyes. For the first time the matinee idol looked as melancholy as his friends. "No matter what you think of me, Dwyer, I don't rape women. But that night—" He shrugged, looked away.

"Brandon," I said. "You were going to tell me about Brandon."

"We came up here, had a case of beer or something, and talked about it some more, and that night," Forester said, "that night Brandon just snapped. He couldn't handle how ashamed he was or how afraid he was of being turned in. Right in the middle of talking—"

Haskins took over. "Right in the middle, he just got up and ran out to the Point." He indicated the cliff behind us. "And before we could stop him, he jumped."

"Jesus," Price said, "I can't forget his screaming on the way down. I can't ever forget it."

I looked at Karen. "So what she heard you three talking about outside the party that night was not that you'd killed Brandon but that you were afraid a serious investigation into his suicide might turn up the rape?"

Forester said, "Exactly." He stared at Karen. "We didn't kill Michael, Karen. We loved him. He was our friend."

But by then, completely without warning, she had started to cry and then she began literally sobbing, her entire body shaking with some grief I could neither understand nor assuage.

I nodded to Forester to get back in his car and leave. They stood and watched us a moment and then they got into the Mercedes and went away, taking the burden of years and guilt with them.

This time I drove. I went far out the river road, miles out, where you pick up the piney hills and the deer standing by the side of the road.

From the glove compartment she took a pint of J&B, and I knew better than to try and stop her.

I said, "You were the girl they raped, weren't you?"

"Yes."

"Why didn't you tell the police?"

She smiled at me. "The police weren't exactly going to believe a girl from the Highlands about the sons of rich men."

I sighed. She was right.

"Then Michael started coming around to see me. I can't say I ever forgave him, but I started to feel sorry for him. His fear—" She shook her head, looked out the window. She said, almost to herself, "But I had to write those letters, get them there tonight, know for sure if they killed him." She paused. "You believe them?"

"That they didn't kill him?"

"Right."

"Yes, I believe them."

"So do I."

Then she went back to staring out the window, her small face childlike there in silhouette against the moonsilver river. "Can I ask you a question, Dwyer?"

"Sure."

"You think we're ever going to get out of the Highlands?"

"No," I said, and drove on faster in her fine new expensive car. "No, I don't."

JOHN JAKES

Say John Jakes (1932–) and you instantly think bestselling writer. But think John Jakes before his reign on all the bestseller lists, and you find a writer adept at virtually every kind of genre fiction, from spy to Western to hard-boiled crime.

He was one of the last writers to use the pulps as a training ground. You find his name in the pulp-edged magazines dating from approximately 1950 to 1957, at which point most of these magazines were gone.

He was good from the git-go, particularly with crime fiction, and especially in the private eye novels about the diminutive Johnny Havoc, books that hold up well for two very good reasons. They're fun to read and they do a good job of telling you what America was like in the early 1960s. Recently his mystery short fiction was collected in the anthology *Crime Time*.

No Comment

The gruesome Slub Canal murders had a long history.

The start of it could be dated 1953. A developer from nearby Buffalo bought some land within sight of the main plant of Metrochemical, Inc., and the waterway for which the tract was eventually named. Young couples, most with husbands employed at Metrochem, snapped up all the houses before they were built; those were the days when a Philco TV, a carport, and a chain link fence consummated the American Dream, and you knew your company would take care of you till you retired or died.

Soon children from the tract houses were playing along the canal bank. Under a slaggy winter sky at twilight, mothers who came to call them in began to notice the slow, sludgelike quality of the canal that had flowed briskly and noisily only a couple of years before, when the lots were being sold. Looking along the canal to the huge tangle of pipes and smokestacks of Metrochem, the mothers could see two large conduits in the bank spilling more sludge. Flames from the stacks snapped like flags, and even on sunny days a deep lavender haze filled the air. No one thought much of it, though.

One night in 1963, Mrs. Sheila Johnson of 22 Crystal Court went into the bedroom belonging to her twins and screamed. Kimmy, the girl, the frail one, slept to the left of the door. Near her bed a small night-light glowed. In the bed, Kimmy's forearm bones glowed. They glowed a faint but unmistakable green through her pale translucent skin. Seven months later—two days after her sixth birthday—Kimmy breathed her last. For the final two months she had screamed almost constantly as the cancer ate her bones away.

By this time the nation was beginning to wake up to the dangers of chemical pollution. Metrochemical, meanwhile, was expanding, increasing production and changing its name to Metrochem World-Wide. A young man named Hollister (Buddy) Wood was promoted from accountant to sales assistant, to broaden his background. He was considered a comer.

Not everyone in the tract worked for MWW. Stan Krasno did not. Stan lived at 36 Sparkling Avenue with his wife and three tiny daughters. Stan's house backed up to Slub Canal. Sometimes on a summer night, getting a beer from the Frigidaire, he could hear turgid bubbles popping on the canal's surface. If he glanced out the window at the right time, he could see the same popping bubbles briefly emit a yellow-green glow. It worried him in an unfocused way.

Stan's wife Helen took a job in the sales literature department at MWW when the last of her three girls entered school. Stan worked in the meat department of the Sav-All Supermart in one of the new Buffalo suburbs creeping out toward Slub Canal. The meat department occupied the right wall as you entered. From behind the work area's one-way glass Stan could see the MWW executives driving to and from work in their company Cadillacs. At this point they did not yet have chauffeurs.

By the late sixties, when MWW was making chemicals for Vietnam, four children and two adults from the tract had died of forms of cancer. Several women held a meeting which Helen Krasno attended. They prepared a sincere if crudely written petition and presented it to the company, requesting an inquiry into possible links between the deaths and the plant's waste-dumping practices. Assistant to the President Buddy Wood returned the petition through the mail, having written on the front page THE COMPANY HAS NO COMMENT.

In the early seventies three more deaths occurred. By now cause and effect were no longer in doubt, at least to the residents of Slub Canal. This caused some agonizing moments in the Krasno household.

The Krasnos were devout Catholics. Stan never missed a Sunday mass and went regularly, compulsively, to confession. "*Bless me, Father . . .*" His list of sins, some real, some fanciful, was always long. Helen had the deep misfortune of believing that the basic teachings of her religion should be practiced universally. She lived by standards of honesty, decency, fairness, personal responsibility, and took it on faith that everyone else did, too. She assumed everyone's word was good, without exception.

Helen also believed in loyalty to her employer. But her ideals, her family, and her neighbors won out. She began to write Congressmen and organize Saturday coffees. She invited a young and hairy environmentalist to sleep on the couch after he addressed a group in the living room. She took a night school course in better letter writing, and bought a book on improving telephone skills. Finally the government sent investigators to Slub Canal. At this point Helen lost her job. It was claimed that she misdirected a huge shipment of sales literature to the Bangkok branch when it was urgently needed in Frankfurt.

Stan Krasno expressed his outrage to his bowling buddies. One of the best of them, Chief of Police Milt Dubofsky, a pal since high school, warned him, "Don't do anything rash. I'd have to haul you in and knock a confession out of you and then you'd be on your way to jail." He was only half-joking.

There were six more harrowing cancer deaths in the next three years. Buddy Wood, now president of MWW, turned aside questions from teams of TV and newspaper reporters who swarmed into Slub Canal, photographing the green-brown "water" which now hardly moved at all. While Buddy Wood certainly didn't own the company, he was a large stockholder thanks to his option programs, and he had become the target of the anger of Slub Canal householders, including Stan Krasno. Chopping or packaging meat, Stan would stare out through the one-way glass, watch Buddy Wood's silver stretch whisk by and angrily recall that Helen couldn't even get work as a domestic, cleaning the homes of the executives of MWW; as soon as someone learned her name, the door closed in her face.

The news media practically camped in Slub Canal. Buddy Wood, now plump and middle-aged, was occasionally photographed coming out the gate in his silver limo; he wore rimless bifocals at this point in life, and dyed his hair dark brown to promote a youthful image, as so many businessmen did. He never smiled for cameras.

The day the government announced its twenty-million-dollar suit against MWW for violations of environmental laws, Buddy Wood issued a statement from his office before dashing off to Scottsdale on the company jet with his wife Chrissy. Buddy was scheduled to address a conference of high-level corporate executives on the subject of the dangers of executive stress. Chrissy carried their tennis rackets and her ankle-length mink coat. The departing statement consisted of two words. "No comment."

That was all you ever heard from the company, Stan Krasno thought as he sat in front of his flickering TV that evening, a beer can in one hand and the lights turned off to hide the increasing shabbiness of the deteriorating house. That was all you heard, "no comment," or "the company declines comment," or "spokesmen for the company declined comment," or "the New York attorneys representing the company declined comment at this time. . . ." Stan belched and stood and listened because he thought he'd heard a sound. Yes, there it was again. A bubble went *pop* in Slub Canal. The smell made him gag.

Stan slouched to the door of the bedroom where his teenage daughter, Cherylanne, slept; the other girls were grown and gone, Babette married, Lynne Marie in cosmetology school. Stan opened the door, looked in, and practically tore the phone off the wall before he got Helen on the line; she was night manager at the local Señor Speedy Taco Hacienda.

"She's green, her bones are green, I can see 'em," Stan screamed into the phone.

Ten and a half months later, lying mewling in a pool of her own green diarrhea, Cherylanne died at three-ten A.M. In the adjoining bedroom Helen was likewise dying; she expired a week after her daughter's burial. Stan was hysterical most of that night.

Next day he summoned reporters from the Buffalo media and accused MWW of murdering his wife and child. This provoked a surprising personal appearance by Buddy Wood on evening news shows. Looking grave and correct in his seven hundred dollar custom-tailored suit, the lights reflecting off his rimless glasses, he said:

"At this point in time we have no comment other than to extend the sympathy of the entire Metrochem family to Mr. Krasno in his hour of loss. We will of course launch a thorough and objective investigation. Beyond that, I must say again that we cannot comment at this time. Now if you'll excuse me, I have to make a flight out of JFK to Zurich this evening for a conference on the merger announced last week. I have no further comment." Off camera, his wife Chrissy waited with their skis. The camera caught a glimpse of her and, at home, Stan went wild.

"No comment, no comment," he screamed. "Fucking coward. Fucking CRIMINAL. Always hiding, hiding behind your fucking lawyers and your fucking hired help to save your fucking profits and your fucking greedy ass." Stan no longer believed in the carport-and-chain-link dream, or that MWW, or any other company, would take care of an ordinary Joe unless it served some cold-blooded purpose.

Ten days later the Woods returned to their suburban Buffalo home, severely jet-lagged and exhausted. At five-fourteen in the morning, alarms went off in the central office of the security service which looked after their property. The service automatically dialed the local police, who rushed to the site of the alarm. They found the huge house broken into on the first floor. Upstairs, in the enormous master bedroom suite (two complete baths and his-and-hers walk-in closets in which you could hold a small dinner party) they found carnage.

Buddy and Chrissy Wood had been stabbed to death through their night clothes. Many cuts were visible on both bodies, but his had been mutilated. The bedding was blood-soaked; the walls resembled huge wet abstract paintings done in red. In the warm ashes in the bedroom hearth, a detective discovered something black and meaty. It turned out to be most of Buddy Wood's tongue.

When Chief Milt Dubofsky got the call, he was only mildly surprised. He'd watched his bowling buddy Stan slowly come apart following his wife's firing and then her death a week after their daughter's. "The poor son of a bitch," the chief said, strapping on his hip holster with considerable reluctance. He drove to the shoebox house on Sparkling Avenue with two deputies. Guns drawn, they knocked at the front door.

"Stan? This is Milt. Got to talk to you."

From inside came a weird gargling noise.

"Stan, if you come out peaceably, you won't get hurt. But you've got to come out. We've got to talk about what you did."

The noise again, a kind of moist glottal choking sound. Chief Milt Dubofsky cautiously tested the door.

Not locked. Unhappily, he gestured his deputies forward with his gun.

They found Stan seated in an old armchair in his living room. The arms of the chair were soaked with blood. Pools of it glistened under his shoes. Stan was still alive—barely—with a delirious smile on his blood-stained mouth. He made another of those weird gagging sounds as if to demonstrate that he couldn't speak. One of the deputies turned away to be sick.

"Stan, you got to tell me—" But Stan was shaking his head. Grinning, very pleased, he pointed to his bloody mouth with the butcher knife in his right hand. Then the Chief saw the bloody object lying in Stan's lap. What he had done to Wood, he had done to himself.

LAWRENCE BLOCK

Is it all right to prefer Bernie Rhodenbarr to Matt Scudder? That question was asked, in all seriousness, in a recent on-line exchange.

Because the Bernies are hilarious and the Scudders dark and brooding, the e-mail inquirer apparently wanted to know if her preference revealed a certain, shall we say, shallowness in her reading tastes. Not at all. Lawrence Block (1938–) is one of the best crime fiction writers in the world, whatever his literary mood of the moment happens to be.

Block's career is one of those up-from-the-trenches, decades-in-the-making sagas that makes you cheer him on. He's written just about every kind of fiction—high, low, and unmentionable—and he's done virtually all of it with style, wit, and enormous acumen.

Recently he has turned to editing books, with five stellar anthologies published, *Master's Choice*, volumes 1 and 2; *Opening Shots*, volumes 1 and 2; and *Speaking of Lust*. His latest novel is *Everybody Dies*.

While everybody talks about his newer Bernies and Scudders, and how wonderful they are (and they damned well are), do yourself a favor and read some of his earlier books, such as *After the First Death*, *The Specialists*, and *Such Men Are Dangerous*.

He is also one of the best short story writers the crime field has ever produced. Of the dozens of marvelous stories to pick from, this one shows his talents in full swing.

How Would You Like It?

I suppose it really started for me when I saw the man whipping his horse. He was a hansom cab driver, dressed up like the chimney sweep in *Mary Poppins* with a top hat and a cutaway tailcoat, and I saw him on

Central Park South, where the horse-drawn rigs queue up waiting for tourists who want a ride in the park. His horse was a swaybacked old gelding with a noble face, and it did something to me to see the way that driver used the whip. He didn't have to hit the horse like that.

I found a policeman and started to tell him about it, but it was clear he didn't want to hear it. He explained to me that I would have to go to the stationhouse and file a complaint, and he said it in such a way as to discourage me from bothering. I don't really blame the cop. With crack dealers on every block and crimes against people and property at an all-time high and climbing, I suppose crimes against animals have to receive low priority.

But I couldn't forget about it.

I had already had my consciousness raised on the subject of animal rights. There was a campaign a few years ago to stop one of the cosmetic companies from testing their products on rabbits. They were blinding thousands of innocent rabbits every year, not with the goal of curing cancer but just because it was the cheapest way to safety-test their mascara and eye liner.

I would have liked to sit down with the head of that company. "How would you like it?" I would have asked him. "How would you like having chemicals painted on your eyes to make you blind?"

All I did was sign a petition, like millions of other Americans, and I understand that it worked, that the company has gone out of the business of blinding bunnies. Sometimes, when we all get together, we can make a difference.

Sometimes we can make a difference all by ourselves.

Which brings me back to the subject of the horse and his driver. I found myself returning to Central Park South over the next several days and keeping tabs on that fellow. I thought perhaps I had just caught him on a bad day, but it became clear that it was standard procedure for him to use the whip that way. I went up to him and said something finally, and he turned positively red with anger. I thought for a moment he was going to use the whip on me, and I frankly would have liked to see him try it, but he only turned his anger on the poor horse, whipping him more brutally than ever and looking at me as if daring me to do something about it.

I just walked away.

That afternoon I went to a shop in Greenwich Village where they sell extremely odd paraphernalia to what I can only suppose are extremely odd people. They have handcuffs and studded wrist bands and all sorts of curious leather goods. Sadie Mae's Leather Goods, they call themselves. You get the picture.

I bought a ten-foot whip of plaited bullhide, and I took it back to Central Park South with me. I waited in the shadows until that driver finished for the day, and I followed him home.

You can kill a man with a whip. Take my word for it.

* * *

Well, I have to tell you that I never expected to do anything like that again. I can't say I felt bad about what I'd done. The brute only got what he deserved. But I didn't think of myself as the champion of all the abused animals of New York. I was just someone who had seen his duty and had done it. It wasn't pleasant, flogging a man to death with a bullwhip, but I have to admit there was something almost shamefully exhilarating about it.

A week later, and just around the corner from my own apartment, I saw a man kicking his dog.

It was a sweet dog, too, a little beagle as cute as Snoopy. You couldn't imagine he might have done anything to justify such abuse. Some dogs have a mean streak, but there's never any real meanness in a hound. And this awful man was hauling off and savaging the animal with vicious kicks.

Why do something like that? Why have a dog in the first place if you don't feel kindly toward it? I said something to that effect, and the man told me to mind my own business.

Well, I tried to put it out of my mind, but it seemed as though I couldn't go for a walk without running into the fellow, and he always seemed to be walking the little beagle. He didn't kick him all the time—you'd kill a dog in short order if you did that regularly. But he was always cruel to the animal, yanking hard on the chain, cursing with genuine malice, and making it very clear that he hated it.

And then I saw him kick it again. Actually it wasn't the kick that did it for me, it was the way the poor dog cringed when the man drew back his foot. It made it so clear that he was used to this sort of treatment, that he knew what to expect.

So I went to a shoe store on Broadway in the teens where they have a good line of work shoes, and I bought a pair of steel-toed boots of the kind construction workers wear. I was wearing them the next time I saw my neighbor walking his dog, and I followed him home and rang his bell.

It would have been quicker and easier, I'm sure, if I'd had some training in karate. But even an untrained kick has a lot of authority to it when you're wearing steel-toed footwear. A couple of kicks in his legs and he fell down and couldn't get up, and a couple of kicks in the ribs took the fight out of him, and a couple of kicks in the head made it absolutely certain he would never harm another of God's helpless creatures.

It's cruelty that bothers me, cruelty and wanton indifference to another creature's pain. Some people are thoughtless, but when the inhumanity of their actions is pointed out to them they're able to understand and are willing to change.

For example, a young woman in my building had a mixed-breed dog that barked all day in her absence. She didn't know this because the dog never started barking until she'd left for work. When I explained that the poor fellow couldn't bear to be alone, that it made him horribly anxious, she went to the animal shelter and adopted the cutest little part-Sheltie to keep him company. You never hear a peep out of either of those dogs now, and it does me good to see them on the street when she walks them, both of them obviously happy and well cared for.

And another time I met a man carrying a litter of newborn kittens in a sack. He was on his way to the river and intended to drown them, not out of cruelty but because he thought it was the most humane way to dispose of kittens he could not provide a home for. I explained to him that it was cruel to the mother cat to take her kittens away before she'd weaned them, and that when the time came he could simply take the unwanted kittens to the animal shelter; if they failed to find homes for them, at least their deaths would be easy and painless. More to the point, I told him where he could get his mother cat spayed inexpensively, so that he would not have to deal with this sad business again.

He was grateful. You see, he wasn't a cruel man, not by any means. He just didn't know any better.

Other people just don't want to learn.

Just yesterday, for example, I was in the hardware store over on Second Avenue. A well-dressed young woman was selecting rolls of flypaper and those awful Roach Motel devices.

"Excuse me," I said, "but are you certain you want to purchase those items? They aren't even very efficient, and you wind up spending a lot of money to kill very few insects."

She was looking at me oddly, the way you look at a crank, and I should have known I was just wasting my breath. But something made me go on.

"With the Roach Motels," I said, "they don't really kill the creatures at all, you know. They just immobilize them. Their feet are stuck, and they stand in place wiggling their antennae until I suppose they starve to death. I mean, how would you like it?"

"You're kidding," she said. "Right?"

"I'm just pointing out that the product you've selected is neither efficient nor humane," I said.

"So?" she said. "I mean, they're cockroaches. If they don't like it let them stay the hell out of my apartment." She shook her head, impatient. "I can't believe I'm having this conversation. My place is swarming with roaches and I run into a nut who's worried about hurting their feelings."

I wasn't worried about any such thing. And I didn't care if she killed roaches. I understand the necessity of that sort of thing. I just don't see the need for cruelty. But I knew better than to say anything more to her. It's useful to talk to some people. With others, it's like trying to blow out a lightbulb.

So I picked up a half-dozen tubes of Super Glue and followed her home.

SARA PARETSKY

Sara Paretsky (1947–) is regularly reviewed in places where other mystery writers are never mentioned. Her novels, dealing as they do with the lives of contemporary women, have found an audience outside genre. She appeals to people who rarely if ever read mystery stories. And she appeals to that generation known as boomers, who has learned the hard way that despite some major advances for women, there is still a substantial way to go before we reach anything like parity between the sexes. But where they're climbing and clawing their way to the top, detective V. I. Warshawski will be there right beside them.

Here is Paretsky at the top of her game, much as she is in her latest novel, *Total Recall.*

Grace Notes

I

GABRIELLA SESTIERI OF PITIGLIANO.
Anyone with knowledge of her whereabouts
should contact the office of Malcolm Ranier.

I was reading the *Herald-Star* at breakfast when the notice jumped out at me from the personal section. I put my coffee down with extreme care, as if I were in a dream and all my actions moved with the slowness of dream time. I shut the paper with the same slow motion, then opened it again. The notice was still there. I spelled out the headline letter by letter, in case my unconscious mind had substituted one name for another, but the text remained the same. There could not be more than one Gabriella

Sestieri from Pitigliano. My mother, who died of cancer in 1968 at the age of forty-six.

"Who could want her all these years later?" I said aloud.

Peppy, the golden retriever I share with my downstairs neighbor, raised a sympathetic eyebrow. We had just come back from a run on a dreary November morning and she was waiting hopefully for toast.

"It can't be her father." His mind had cracked after six months in a German concentration camp, and he refused to acknowledge Gabriella's death when my father wrote to inform him of it. I'd had to translate the letter, in which he said he was too old to travel but wished Gabriella well on her concert tour. Anyway, if he was alive still he'd be almost a hundred.

Maybe Gabriella's brother Italo was searching for her: he had disappeared in the maelstrom of the war, but Gabriella always hoped he survived. Or her first voice teacher, Francesca Salvini, whom Gabriella longed to see again, to explain why she had never fulfilled Salvini's hopes for her professional career. As Gabriella lay in her final bed in Jackson Park Hospital with tubes ringing her wasted body, her last messages had been for me and for Salvini. This morning it dawned on me for the first time how hurtful my father must have found that. He adored my mother, but for him she had only the quiet fondness of an old friend.

I realized my hands around the newspaper were wet with sweat, that paper and print were clinging to my palms. With an embarrassed laugh I put the paper down and washed off the ink under the kitchen tap. It was ludicrous to spin my mind with conjectures when all I had to do was phone Malcolm Ranier. I went to the living room and pawed through the papers on the piano for the phone book. Ranier seemed to be a lawyer with offices on La Salle Street, at the north end where the pricey new buildings stand.

His was apparently a solo practice. The woman who answered the phone assured me she was Mr. Ranier's assistant and conversant with all his files. Mr. Ranier couldn't speak with me himself now, because he was in conference. Or court. Or the john.

"I'm calling about the notice in this morning's paper, wanting to know the whereabouts of Gabriella Sestieri."

"What is your name, please, and your relationship with Mrs. Sestieri?" The assistant left out the second syllable so that the name came out as "Sistery."

"I'll be glad to tell you that if you tell me why you're trying to find her."

"I'm afraid I can't give out confidential client business over the phone. But if you tell me your name and what you know about Mrs. Sestieri we'll get back to you when we've discussed the matter with our client."

I thought we could keep this conversation going all day. "The person you're looking for may not be the same one I know, and I don't want to violate a family's privacy. But I'll be in a meeting on La Salle Street this morning; I can stop by to discuss the matter with Mr. Ranier."

The woman finally decided that Mr. Ranier had ten minutes free at twelve-thirty. I gave her my name and hung up. Sitting at the piano, I crashed out chords, as if the sound could bury the wildness of my feelings. I never could remember whether I knew how ill my mother was the last six months of her life. Had she told me and I couldn't—or didn't wish to—comprehend it? Or had she decided to shelter me from the knowledge? Gabriella usually made me face bad news, but perhaps not the worst of all possible news, our final separation.

Why did I never work on my singing? It was one thing I could have done for her. I didn't have a Voice, as Gabriella put it, but I had a serviceable contralto, and of course she insisted I acquire some musicianship. I stood up and began working on a few vocal stretches, then suddenly became wild with the desire to find my mother's music, the old exercise books she had me learn from.

I burrowed through the hall closet for the trunk that held her books. I finally found it in the farthest corner, under a carton holding my old case files, a baseball bat, a box of clothes I no longer wore but couldn't bring myself to give away. . . . I sat on the closet floor in misery, with a sense of having buried her so deep I couldn't find her.

Peppy's whimpering pulled me back to the present. She had followed me into the closet and was pushing her nose into my arm. I fondled her ears.

At length it occurred to me that if someone was trying to find my mother I'd need documents to prove the relationship. I got up from the floor and pulled the trunk into the hall. On top lay her black silk concert gown: I'd forgotten wrapping that in tissue and storing it. In the end I found my parents' marriage license and Gabriella's death certificate tucked into the score of *Don Giovanni*.

When I returned the score to the trunk another old envelope floated out. I picked it up and recognized Mr. Fortieri's spiky writing. Carlo Fortieri repaired musical instruments and sold, or at least used to sell music. He was the person Gabriella went to for Italian conversation, musical conversation, advice. He still sometimes tuned my own piano out of affection for her.

When Gabriella met him, he'd been a widower for years, also with one child, also a girl. Gabriella thought I ought to play with her while she sang or discussed music with Mr. Fortieri, but Barbara was ten years or so my senior and we'd never had much to say to each other.

I pulled out the yellowed paper. It was written in Italian, and hard for me to decipher, but apparently dated from 1965.

Addressing her as *"Cara signora Warshawski,"* Mr. Fortieri sent his regrets that she was forced to cancel her May 14 concert. "I shall, of course, respect your wishes and not reveal the nature of your indisposition to anyone else. And, *cara signora*, you should know by now that I regard any confidence of yours as a sacred trust: you need not fear an indiscretion." It was signed with his full name.

I wondered now if he'd been my mother's lover. My stomach tightened, as it does when you think of your parents stepping outside their prescribed roles, and I folded the paper back into the envelope. Fifteen years ago the same notion must have prompted me to put his letter inside *Don Giovanni*. For want of a better idea I stuck it back in the score and returned everything to the trunk. I needed to rummage through a different carton to find my own birth certificate, and it was getting too late in the morning for me to indulge in nostalgia.

II

Malcolm Ranier's office overlooked the Chicago River and all the new glass and marble flanking it. It was a spectacular view—if you squinted to shut out the burnt-out waste of Chicago's west side that lay beyond. I arrived just at twelve-thirty, dressed in my one good suit, black, with a white crepe-de-chine blouse. I looked feminine, but austere—or at least that was my intention.

Ranier's assistant-cum-receptionist was buried in Danielle Steel. When I handed her my card, she marked her page without haste and took the card into an inner office. After a ten-minute wait to let me understand his importance, Ranier came out to greet me in person. He was a soft round man of about sixty, with gray eyes that lay like pebbles above an apparently jovial smile.

"Ms. Warshawski. Good of you to stop by. I understand you can help us with our inquiry into Mrs. Sestieri." He gave my mother's name a genuine Italian lilt, but his voice was as hard as his eyes.

"Hold my calls, Cindy." He put a hand on the nape of my neck to steer me into his office.

Before we'd shut the door Cindy was reabsorbed into Danielle. I moved away from the hand—I didn't want grease on my five-hundred-dollar jacket—and went to admire a bronze nymph on a shelf at the window.

"Beautiful, isn't it." Ranier might have been commenting on the weather. "One of my clients brought it from France."

"It looks as though it should be in a museum."

A call to the bar association before I left my apartment told me he was an import-export lawyer. Various imports seemed to have attached themselves to him on their way into the country. The room was dominated by a slab of rose marble, presumably a work table, but several antique chairs were also worth a second glance. A marquetry credenza stood against the far wall. The Modigliani above it was probably an original.

"Coffee, Ms."—he glanced at my card again—"Warshawski?"

"No, thank you. I understand you're very busy, and so am I. So let's talk about Gabriella Sestieri."

"D'accordo." He motioned me to one of the spindly antiques near the marble slab. "You know where she is?"

The chair didn't look as though it could support my hundred and forty pounds, but when Ranier perched on a similar one I sat, with a wariness that made me think he had them to keep people deliberately off balance. I leaned back and crossed my legs. The woman at ease.

"I'd like to make sure we're talking about the same person. And that I know why you want to find her."

A smile crossed his full lips, again not touching the slate chips of his eyes. "We could fence all day, Ms. Warshawski, but as you say, time is valuable to us both. The Gabriella Sestieri I seek was born in Pitigliano on October thirtieth, 1921. She left Italy sometime early in 1941, no one knows exactly when, but she was last heard of in Siena that February. And there's some belief she came to Chicago. As to why I want to find her, a relative of hers, now in Florence, but from the Pitigliano family, is interested in locating her. My specialty is import-export law, particularly with Italy: I'm no expert in finding missing persons, but I agreed to assist as a favor to a client. The relative—Mrs. Sestieri's relative—has a professional connection to my client. And now it is your turn, Ms. Warshawski."

"Ms. Sestieri died in March 1968." My blood was racing; I was pleased to hear my voice come out without a tremor. "She married a Chicago police officer in April 1942. They had one child. Me."

"And your father? Officer Warshawski?"

"Died in 1979. Now may I have the name of my mother's relative? I've known only one member of her family, my grandmother's sister who lives here in Chicago, and am eager to find others." Actually, if they bore any resemblance to my embittered Aunt Rosa I'd just as soon not meet the remaining Verazi clan.

"You were cautious, Ms. Warshawski, so you will forgive my caution: do you have proof of your identity?"

"You make it sound as though treasure awaits the missing heir, Mr. Ranier." I pulled out the copies of my legal documents and handed them over. "Who or what is looking for my mother?"

Ranier ignored my question. He studied the documents briefly, then put them on the marble slab while condoling me on losing my parents. His voice had the same soft flat cadence as when he'd discussed the nymph.

"You've no doubt remained close to your grandmother's sister? If she's the person who brought your mother to Chicago it might be helpful for me to have her name and address."

"My aunt is a difficult woman to be close to, but I can check with her, to see if she doesn't mind my giving you her name and address."

"And the rest of your mother's family?"

I held out my hands, empty. "I don't know any of them. I don't even know how many there are. Who is my mystery relative? What does he—she—want?"

He paused, looking at the file in his hands. "I actually don't know. I ran the ad merely as a favor to my client. But I'll pass your name and address along, Ms. Warshawski, and when he's been in touch with the person I'm sure you'll hear."

This runaround was starting to irritate me. "You're a heck of a poker player, Mr. Ranier. But you know as well as I that you're lying like a rug."

I spoke lightly, smiling as I got to my feet and crossed to the door, snatching my documents from the marble slab as I passed. For once his feelings reached his eyes, turning the slate to molten rock. As I waited for the elevator I wondered if answering that ad meant I was going to be sucker-punched.

Over dinner that night with Dr. Lotty Herschel I went through my conversation with Ranier, trying to sort out my confused feelings. Trying, too, to figure out who in Gabriella's family might want to find her, if the inquiry was genuine.

"They surely know she's dead," Lotty said.

"That's what I thought at first, but it's not that simple. See, my grandmother converted to Judaism when she married Nonno Mattia—sorry, that's Gabriella's father—Grandpa Matthias—Gabriella usually spoke Italian to me. Anyway, my grandmother died in Auschwitz when the Italian Jews were rounded up in 1944. Then, my grandfather didn't go back to Pitigliano, the little town they were from, after he was liberated—the Jewish community there had been decimated and he didn't have any family left. So he was sent to a Jewish-run sanatorium in Turin, but Gabriella only found that out after years of writing letters to relief agencies."

I stared into my wineglass, as though the claret could reveal the secrets of my family. "There was one cousin she was really close to, from the Christian side of her family, named Frederica. Frederica had a baby out of wedlock the year before Gabriella came to Chicago, and got sent away in disgrace. After the war Gabriella kept trying to find her, but Frederica's family wouldn't forward the letters—they really didn't want to be in touch with her. Gabriella might have saved enough money to go back to Italy to look for herself, but then she started to be ill. She had a miscarriage the summer of sixty-five and bled and bled. Tony and I thought she was dying then."

My voice trailed away as I thought of that hot unhappy summer, the summer the city burst into riot-spawned flames and my mother lay in the stifling front bedroom oozing blood. She and Tony had one of their infrequent fights. I'd been on my paper route and they didn't hear me come in. He wanted her to sell something which she said wasn't hers to dispose of.

"And your life," my father shouted. "You can give that away as a gift? Even if she was still alive—" He broke off then, seeing me, and neither of them talked about the matter again, at least when I was around to hear.

Lotty squeezed my hand. "What about your aunt, great-aunt in Melrose Park? She might have told her siblings, don't you think? Was she close to any of them?"

I grimaced. "I can't imagine Rosa being close to anyone. See, she was the last child, and Gabriella's grandmother died giving birth to her. So some cousins adopted her, and when they emigrated in the twenties Rosa came to Chicago with them. She didn't really feel like she was part of the Verazi family. I know it seems strange, but with all the uprootings the war caused, and all the disconnections, it's possible that the main part of Gabriella's mother's family didn't know what became of her."

Lotty nodded, her face twisted in sympathy; much of her family had been destroyed in those death camps also. "There wasn't a schism when your grandmother converted?"

I shrugged. "I don't know. It's frustrating to think how little I know about those people. Gabriella says—said—the Verazis weren't crazy about it, and they didn't get together much except for weddings or funerals—except for the one cousin. But Pitigliano was a Jewish cultural center before the war and Nonno was considered a real catch. I guess he was rich until the Fascists confiscated his property." Fantasies of reparations danced through my head.

"Not too likely," Lotty said. "You're imagining someone overcome with guilt sixty years after the fact coming to make you a present of some land?"

I blushed. "Factory, actually: the Sestieris were harness makers who switched to automobile interiors in the twenties. I suppose if the place is even still standing, it's part of Fiat or Mercedes. You know, all day long I've been swinging between wild fantasies—about Nonno's factory, or Gabriella's brother surfacing—and then I start getting terrified, wondering if it's all some kind of terrible trap. Although who'd want to trap me, or why, is beyond me. I know this Malcolm Ranier knows. It would be so easy—"

"No! Not to set your mind at rest, not to prove you can bypass the security of a modern high rise—for no reason whatsoever are you to break into that man's office."

"Oh, very well." I tried not to sound like a sulky child denied a treat.

"You promise, Victoria?" Lotty sounded ferocious.

I held up my right hand. "On my honor, I promise not to break into his office."

III

It was six days later that the phone call came to my office. A young man, with an Italian accent so thick that his English was almost incomprehensible, called up and gaily asked if I was his "Cousin Vittoria."

"Parliamo italiano," I suggested, and the gaiety in his voice increased as he switched thankfully to his own language.

He was my cousin Ludovico, the great-great-grandson of our mutual Verazi ancestors, he had arrived in Chicago from Milan only last night, terribly excited at finding someone from his mother's family, thrilled that I knew Italian, my accent was quite good, really, only a tinge of America in it, could we get together, any place, he would find me—just name the time as long as it was soon.

I couldn't help laughing as the words tumbled out, although I had to ask him to slow down and repeat. It had been a long time since I'd spoken Italian, and it took time for my mind to adjust. Ludovico was staying at the Garibaldi, a small hotel on the fringe of the Gold Coast, and would be thrilled if I met him there for a drink at six. Oh, yes, his last name—that was Verazi, the same as our great-grandfather.

I bustled through my business with greater efficiency than usual so that I had time to run the dogs and change before meeting him. I laughed at myself for dressing with care, in a pantsuit of crushed lavender velvet which could take me dancing if the evening ended that way, but no self-mockery could suppress my excitement. I'd been an only child with one cousin from each of my parents' families as my only relations. My cousin Boom-Boom, whom I adored, had been dead these ten years and more, while Rosa's son Albert was such a mass of twisted fears that I preferred not to be around him. Now I was meeting a whole new family.

I tap-danced around the dog in my excitement. Peppy gave me a long-suffering look and demanded that I return her to my downstairs neighbor. Mitch, her son, had stopped there on our way home from running.

"You look slick, doll," Mr. Contreras told me, torn between approval and jealousy. "New date?"

"New cousin." I continued to tap-dance in the hall outside his door. "Yep. The mystery relative finally surfaced. Ludovico Verazi."

"You be careful, doll," the old man said severely. "Plenty of con artists out there to pretend they're your cousins, you know, and next thing—phht."

"What'll he con me out of? my dirty laundry?" I planted a kiss on his nose and danced down the sidewalk to my car.

Three men were waiting in the Garibaldi's small lobby, but I knew my cousin at once. His hair was amber, instead of black, but his face was my mother's, from the high rounded forehead to his wide sensuous mouth. He leapt up at my approach, seized my hands, and kissed me in the European style—sort of touching the air beside each ear.

"Bellissima!" Still holding my hands he stepped back to scrutinize me. My astonishment must have been written large on my face, because he laughed a little guiltily.

"I know it, I know it, I should have told you of the resemblance, but I didn't realize it was so strong: the only picture I've seen of Cousin Gabriella is a stage photo from 1940 when she starred in Jommelli's *Iphigenia*."

"Jommelli!" I interrupted. "I thought it was Gluck!"

"No, no, *cugina*, Jommelli. Surely Gabriella knew what she sang?" Laughing happily he moved to the armchair where he'd been sitting and took up a brown leather case. He pulled out a handful of papers and thumbed through them, then extracted a yellowing photograph for me to examine.

It was my mother, dressed as Iphigenia for her one stage role, the one that gave me my middle name. She was made up, her dark hair in an elaborate coil, but she looked absurdly young, like a little girl playing dress-up. At the bottom of the picture was the name of the studio, in Siena where she had sung, and on the back someone had lettered, *"Gabriella Sestieri fa la parte d'Iphigenia nella produzione d'Iphigenia da Jommelli."* The resemblance to Ludovico was clear, despite the blurring of time and cosmetics to the lines of her face. I felt a stab of jealousy: I inherited her olive skin, but my face is my father's.

"You know this photograph?" Ludovico asked.

I shook my head. "She left Italy in such a hurry: all she brought with her were some Venetian wineglasses that had been a wedding present to Nonna Laura. I never saw her onstage."

"I've made you sad, cousin Vittoria, by no means my intention. Perhaps you would like to keep this photograph?"

"I would, very much. Now—a drink? Or dinner?"

He laughed again. "I have been in America only twenty-four hours, not long enough to be accustomed to dinner in the middle of the afternoon. So—a drink, by all means. Take me to a typical American bar."

I collected my Trans Am from the doorman and drove down to the Golden Glow, the bar at the south end of the Loop owned by my friend Sal Barthele. My appearance with a good-looking stranger caused a stir among the regulars—as I'd hoped. Murray Ryerson, an investigative reporter whose relationship with me is compounded of friendship, competition, and a disastrous romantic episode, put down his beer with a snap and came over to our table. Sal Barthele emerged from her famous mahogany horseshoe bar. Under cover of Murray's greetings and Ludovico's accented English she muttered, "Girl, you are strutting. You look indecent! Anyway, isn't this cradle snatching? Boy looks *young*!"

I was glad the glow from the Tiffany table lamps was too dim for her to see me blushing. In the car coming over I had been calculating degrees of consanguinity and decided that as second cousins we were eugenically safe; I was embarrassed to show it so obviously. Anyway, he was only seven years younger than me.

"My newfound cousin," I said, too abruptly. "Ludovico Verazi—Sal Barthele, owner of the Glow."

Ludovico shook her hand. "So, you are an old friend of this cousin of mine. You know her more than I do—give me ideas about her character."

"Dangerous," Murray said. "She breaks men in her soup like crackers."

"Only if they're crackers to begin with," I snapped, annoyed to be presented to my cousin in such a light.

"Crackers to begin with?" Ludovico asked.

"Slang—*gergo*—for *'pazzo,'* " I explained. "Also a cracker is an oaf—a *cretino*."

Murray put an arm around me. "Ah, Vic—the sparkle in your eyes lights a fire in my heart."

"It's just the third beer, Murray—that's heartburn," Sal put in. "Ludovico, what do you drink—whiskey, like your cousin? Or something nice and Italian like Campari?"

"Whiskey before dinner, Cousin Vittoria? No, no, by the time you eat you have no—no tasting sensation. For me, Signora, a glass of wine please."

Later over dinner at Filigree we became "Vic" and "Vico"—"Please, Veek, no one is calling me 'Ludovico' since the time I am a little boy in trouble—" And later still, after two bottles of Barolo, he asked me how much I knew about the Verazi family.

"Niente," I said. "I don't even know how many brothers and sisters Gabriella's mother had. Or where you come into the picture. Or where I do, for that matter."

His eyebrows shot up in surprise. "So your mother was never in touch with her own family after she moved here?"

I told him what I'd told Lotty, about the war, my grandmother's estrangement from her family, and Gabriella's depression on learning of her cousin Frederica's death.

"But I am the grandson of that naughty Frederica, that girl who would have a baby with no father." Vico shouted in such excitement that the wait staff rushed over to make sure he wasn't choking to death. "This is remarkable, Vic, this is amazing, that the one person in our family *your* mother is close to turns out to be *my* grandmother.

"Ah, it was sad, very sad, what happened to her. The family is moved to Florence during the war, my grandmother has a baby, maybe the father is a partisan, my grandmother was the one person in the family to be supporting the partisans. My great-grandparents, they are very prudish, they say, this is a disgrace, never mind there is a war on and much bigger disgraces are happening all the time, so—poof!—off goes this naughty Frederica with her baby to Milano. And the baby becomes my mother, but she and my grandmother both die when I am ten, so these most respectable Verazi cousins, finally they decide the war is over, the grandson is after all far enough removed from the taint of original sin, they come fetch me and raise me with all due respectability in Florence."

He broke off to order a cognac. I took another espresso: somehow after forty I no longer can manage the amount of alcohol I used to. I'd only drunk half of one of the bottles of wine.

"So how did you learn about Gabriella? And why did you want to try to find her?"

"Well, *cara cugina*, it is wonderful to meet you, but I have a confession I must make: it was in the hopes of finding—something—that I am coming to Chicago looking for my cousin Gabriella."

"What kind of something?"

"You say you know nothing about our great-grandmother, Claudia

Fortezza? So you are not knowing even that she is in a small way a composer?"

I couldn't believe Gabriella never mentioned such a thing. If she didn't know about it, the rift with the Verazis must have been more severe than she led me to believe. "But maybe that explains why she was given early musical training," I added aloud. "You know my mother was a quite gifted singer. Although, alas, she never had the professional career she should have."

"Yes, yes, she trained with Francesca Salvini. I know all about that! Salvini was an important teacher, even in a little town like Pitigliano people came from Siena and Florence to train with her, and she had a connection to the Siena Opera. But anyway, Vic, I am wanting to collect Claudia Fortezza's music. The work of women composers is coming into vogue. I can find an ensemble to perform it, maybe to record it, so I am hoping Gabriella, too, has some of this music."

I shook my head. "I don't think so. I kept all her music in a trunk, and I don't think there's anything from that period."

"But you don't know definitely, do you, so maybe we can look together." He was leaning across the table, his voice vibrating with urgency.

I moved backward, the strength of his feelings making me uneasy. "I suppose so."

"Then let us pay the bill and go."

"Now? But, Vico, it's almost midnight. If it's been there all this while it will still be there in the morning."

"Ah: I am being the cracker, I see." We had been speaking in Italian all evening, but for this mangled idiom Vico switched to English. "*Mi scusi, cara cugina*: I have been so engaged in my hunt, through the papers of old aunts, through attics in Pitigliano, in used bookstores in Florence, that I forget not everyone shares my enthusiasm. And then last month, I find a diary of my grandmother's, and she writes of the special love her cousin Gabriella has for music, her special gift, and I think—ah-ha, if this music lies anywhere, it is with this Gabriella."

He picked up my right hand and started playing with my fingers. "Besides, confess to me, Vic: in your mind's eye you are at your home feverishly searching through your mother's music, whether I am present or not."

I laughed, a little shakily: the intensity in his face made him look so like Gabriella when she was swept up in music that my heart turned over with yearning.

"So I am right? We can pay the bill and leave?"

The wait staff, hoping to close the restaurant, had left the bill on our table some time earlier. I tried to pay it, but Vico snatched it from me. He took a thick stack of bills from his billfold. Counting under his breath he peeled off two hundreds and a fifty and laid them on the check. Like many

Europeans he'd assumed the tip was included in the total: I added four tens and went to retrieve the Trans Am.

IV

As we got out of the car I warned Vico not to talk in the stairwell. "We don't want the dogs to hear me and wake Mr. Contreras."

"He is a malevolent neighbor? You need me perhaps to guard you?"

"He's the best-natured neighbor in the world. Unfortunately, he sees his role in my life as Cerberus, with a whiff of Othello thrown in. It's late enough without spending an hour on why I'm bringing you home with me."

We managed to tiptoe up the stairs without rousing anyone. Inside my apartment we collapsed with the giggles of teenagers who've walked past a cop after curfew. Somehow it seemed natural to fall from laughter into each other's arms. I was the first to break away. Vico gave me a look I couldn't interpret—mockery seemed to dominate.

My cheeks stinging, I went to the hall closet and pulled out Gabriella's trunk once more. I lifted out her evening gown again, fingering the lace panels in the bodice. They were silver, carefully edged in black. Shortly before her final illness Gabriella managed to organize a series of concerts that she hoped would launch her career again, at least in a small way, and it was for these that she had the dress made. Tony and I sat in the front row of Mandel Hall, almost swooning with our passion for her. The gown cost her two years of free lessons for the couturier's daughter, the last few given when she had gone bald from chemotherapy.

As I stared at the dress, wrapped in melancholy, I realized Vico was pulling books and scores from the trunk and going through them with quick careful fingers. I'd saved dozens of Gabriella's books of operas and lieder, but nothing like her whole collection. I wasn't going to tell Vico that, though: he'd probably demand that we break into old Mr. Fortieri's shop to see if any of the scores were still lying about.

At one point Vico thought he had found something, a handwritten score tucked into the pages of *Idomeneo*. I came to look. Someone, not my mother, had meticulously copied out a concerto. As I bent to look more closely, Vico pulled a small magnifying glass from his wallet and began to scrutinize the paper.

I eyed him thoughtfully. "Does the music or the notation look anything like our great-grandmother's?"

He didn't answer me, but held the score up to the light to inspect the margins. I finally took the pages from him and scanned the clarinet line.

"I'm no musicologist, but this sounds baroque to me." I flipped to the end, where the initials "CF" were inscribed with a flourish: Carlo Fortieri might have copied this for my mother—a true labor of love: copying music is a slow, painful business.

"Baroque?" Vico grabbed the score back from me and looked at it more intensely. "But this paper is not that old, I think."

"I think not, also. I have a feeling it's something one of my mother's friends copied out for a chamber group they played in: she sometimes took the piano part."

He put the score to one side and continued burrowing in the trunk. Near the bottom he came on a polished wooden box, big enough to fit snugly against the short side of the trunk. He grunted as he prised it free, then gave a little crow of delight as he saw it was filled with old papers.

"Take it easy, cowboy," I said as he started tossing them to the floor. "This isn't the city dump."

He gave me a look of startling rage at my reproof, then covered it so quickly with a laugh that I couldn't be sure I'd seen it. "This old wood is beautiful. You should keep this out where you can look at it."

"It was Gabriella's, from Pitigliano." In it, carefully wrapped in her winter underwear, she'd laid the eight Venetian glasses that were her sole legacy of home. Fleeing in haste in the night, she had chosen to transport a fragile load, as if that gained her control of her own fragile destiny.

Vico ran his long fingers over the velvet lining the case. The green had turned yellow and black along the creases. I took the box away from him, and began replacing my school essays and report cards—my mother used to put my best school reports in the case.

At two Vico had to admit defeat. "You have no idea where it is? You didn't sell it, perhaps to meet some emergency bill or pay for that beautiful sports car?"

"Vico! What on earth are you talking about? Putting aside the insult, what do you think a score by an unknown nineteenth-century woman is worth?"

"Ah, *mi scusi*, Vic—I forget that everyone doesn't value these Verazi pieces as I do."

"Yes, my dear cousin, and I didn't just fall off a turnip truck, either." I switched to English in my annoyance. "Not even the most enthusiastic grandson would fly around the world with this much mystery. What's the story—are the Verazis making you their heir if you produce her music? Or are you looking for something else altogether?"

"Turnip truck? What is this turnip truck?"

"Forget the linguistic excursion and come clean, Vico. Meaning, confession is good for the soul, so speak up. What are you really looking for?"

He studied his fingers, grimy from paging through the music, then looked up at me with a quick frank smile. "The truth is, Fortunato Magi may have seen some of her music. He was Puccini's uncle, you know, and very influential among the Italian composers of the end of the century. My great-grandmother used to talk about Magi reading Claudia Fortezza's music. She was only a daughter-in-law, and anyway, Claudia Fortezza was dead years before she married into the family, so I never paid any attention to it. But then when I found my grandmother's diaries, it seemed possible that there was some truth to it. It's even possible that Puccini used some of Claudia Fortezza's music, so if we can find it, it might be valuable."

I thought the whole idea was ludicrous—it wasn't even as though the Puccini estate were collecting royalties that one might try to sue for. And even if they were—you could believe almost any highly melodic vocal music sounded like Puccini. I didn't want to get into a fight with Vico about it, though: I had to be at work early in the morning.

"There wasn't any time you can remember Gabriella talking about something very valuable in the house?" he persisted.

I was about to shut him off completely when I suddenly remembered my parents' argument that I'd interrupted. Reluctantly, because he saw I'd thought of something, I told Vico about it.

"She was saying it wasn't hers to dispose of. I suppose that might include her grandmother's music. But there wasn't anything like that in the house when my father died. And believe me, I went through all the papers." Hoping for some kind of living memento of my mother, something more than her Venetian wineglasses.

Vico seized my arms in his excitement. "You see! She did have it, she must have sold it anyway. Or your father did, after she died. Who would they have gone to?"

I refused to give him Mr. Fortieri as a gift. If Gabriella had been worried about the ethics of disposing of someone else's belongings she probably would have consulted him. Maybe even asked him to sell it, if she came to that in the end, but Vico didn't need to know that.

"You know someone, I can tell," he cried.

"No. I was a child. She didn't confide in me. If my father sold it he would have been embarrassed to let me know. It's going on for three in the morning, Vico, and I have to work in a few hours. I'm going to call you a cab and get you back to the Garibaldi."

"You work? Your long lost cousin Vico comes to Chicago for the first time and you cannot kiss off your boss?" He blew across his fingers expressively.

"I work for myself." I could hear the brusqueness creep into my voice—his exigency was taking away some of his charm. "And I have one job that won't wait past tomorrow morning."

"What kind of work is it you do that cannot be deferred?"

"Detective. Private investigator. And I have to be on a—a—"—I couldn't think of the Italian, so I used English—"shipping dock in four hours."

"Ah, a detective." He pursed his lips. "I see now why this Murray was warning me about you. You and he are lovers? Or is that a shocking question to ask an American woman?"

"Murray's a reporter. His path crosses mine from time to time." I went to the phone and summoned a cab.

"And, Cousin, I may take this handwritten score with me? To study more leisurely?"

"If you return it."

"I will be here with it tomorrow afternoon—when you return from your detecting."

I went to the kitchen for some newspaper to wrap it in, wondering about Vico. He didn't seem to have much musical knowledge. Perhaps he was ashamed to tell me he couldn't read music and was going to take it to some third party who could give him a stylistic comparison between this score and something of our grandmother's.

The cab honked under the window a few minutes later. I sent him off on his own with a chaste cousinly kiss. He took my retreat from passion with the same mockery that had made me squirm earlier.

V

All during the next day, as I huddled behind a truck taking pictures of a handoff between the vice president of an electronics firm and a driver, as I tailed the driver south to Kankakee and photographed another handoff to a man in a sports car, traced the car to its owner in Libertyville and reported back to the electronics firm in Naperville, I wondered about Vico and the score. What was he really looking for?

Last night I hadn't questioned his story too closely—the late night and pleasure in my new cousin had both muted my suspicions. Today the bleak air chilled my euphoria. A quest for a great-grandmother's music might bring one pleasure, but surely not inspire such avidity as Vico displayed. He'd grown up in poverty in Milan without knowing who his father, or even his grandfather were. Maybe it was a quest for roots that was driving my cousin so passionately.

I wondered, too, what item of value my mother had refused to sell thirty summers ago. What wasn't *hers* to sell, that she would stubbornly sacrifice better medical care for it? I realized I felt hurt: I thought I was so dear to her she told me everything. The idea that she'd kept a secret from me made it hard for me to think clearly.

When my dad died, I'd gone through everything in the little house on Houston before selling it. I'd never found anything that seemed worth that much agony, so either she did sell it in the end—or my dad had done so—or she had given it to someone else. Of course, she might have buried it deep in the house. The only place I could imagine her hiding something was in her piano, and if that was the case I was out of luck: the piano had been lost in the fire that destroyed my apartment ten years ago.

But if it—whatever it was—was the same thing Vico was looking for, some old piece of music—Gabriella would have consulted Mr. Fortieri. If she hadn't gone to him, he might know who else she would have turned to. While I waited in a Naperville mall for my prints to be developed I tried phoning him. He was eighty now, but still actively working, so I wasn't surprised when he didn't answer the phone.

I snoozed in the president's antechamber until he could finally snatch ten minutes for my report. When I finished, a little after five, I stopped in his secretary's office to try Mr. Fortieri again. Still no answer.

With only three hours sleep, my skin was twitching as though I'd put it on inside out. Since seven this morning I'd logged a hundred and ninety miles. I wanted nothing now more than my bed. Instead I rode the packed expressway all the way northwest to the O'Hare cutoff.

Mr. Fortieri lived in the Italian enclave along north Harlem Avenue. It used to be a day's excursion to go there with Gabriella: we would ride the Number Six bus to the Loop, transfer to the Douglas line of the el, and at its end take yet another bus west to Harlem. After lunch in one of the storefront restaurants, my mother stopped at Mr. Fortieri's to sing or talk while I was given an old clarinet to take apart to keep me amused. On our way back to the bus we bought polenta and olive oil in Frescobaldi's Deli. Old Mrs. Frescobaldi would let me run my hands through the bags of cardamom, the voluptuous scent making me stomp around the store in an exaggerated imitation of the drunks along Commercial Avenue. Gabriella would hiss embarrassed invectives at me, and threaten to withhold my gelato if I didn't behave.

The street today has lost much of its charm. Some of the old stores remain, but the chains have set out tendrils here as elsewhere. Mrs. Frescobaldi couldn't stand up to Jewel, and Vespucci's, where Gabriella bought all her shoes, was swallowed by the nearby mall.

Mr. Fortieri's shop, on the ground floor of his dark-shuttered house, looked forlorn now, as though it missed the lively commerce of the street. I rang the bell without much hope: no lights shone from either story.

"I don't think he's home," a woman called from the neighboring walk.

She was just setting out with a laundry-laden shopping cart. I asked her if she'd seen Mr. Fortieri at all today. She'd noticed his bedroom light when she was getting ready for work—he was an early riser, just like her, and this time of year she always noticed his bedroom light. In fact, she'd just been thinking it was strange she didn't see his kitchen light on—he was usually preparing his supper about now, but maybe he'd gone off to see his married daughter in Wilmette.

I remembered Barbara Fortieri's wedding. Gabriella had been too sick to attend, and had sent me by myself. The music had been sensational, but I had been angry and uncomfortable and hadn't paid much attention to anything—including the groom. I asked the woman if she knew Barbara's married name—I might try to call her father there.

"Oh, you know her?"

"My mother was a friend of Mr. Fortieri's—Gabriella Sestieri—Warshawski, I mean." Talking to my cousin had sunk me too deep in my mother's past.

"Sorry, honey, never met her. She married a boy she met at college, I can't think of his name, just about the time my husband and I moved in here, and they went off to those lakefront suburbs together."

She made it sound like as daring a trip as any her ancestors had undertaken braving the Atlantic. Fatigue made it sound funny to me and I found myself doubling over to keep the woman from seeing me shake with wild laughter. The thought of Gabriella telling me "No gelato if you do not behave this minute" only made it seem funnier and I had to bend over, clutching my side.

"You okay there, honey?" The woman hesitated, not wanting to be involved with a stranger.

"Long day," I gasped. "Sudden—cramp—in my side."

I waved her on, unable to speak further. Losing my balance, I reeled against the door. It swung open behind me and I fell hard into the open shop, banging my elbow against a chair.

The fall sobered me. I rubbed my elbow, crooning slightly from pain. Bracing against the chair I hoisted myself to my feet. It was only then that it dawned on me that the chair was overturned—alarming in any shop, but especially that of someone as fastidious as Mr. Fortieri.

Without stopping to reason I backed out the door, closing it by wrapping my hand in my jacket before touching the knob. The woman with the laundry cart had gone on down the street. I hunted in my glove compartment for my flashlight, then ran back up the walk and into the shop.

I found the old man in the back, in the middle of his workshop. He lay amid his tools, the stem of an oboe still in his left hand. I fumbled for his pulse. Maybe it was the nervous beating of my own heart, but I thought I felt a faint trace of life. I found the phone on the far side of room, buried under a heap of books that had been taken from the shelves and left where they landed.

VI

"Damn it, Warshawski, what were you doing here anyway?" Sergeant John McGonnigal and I were talking in the back room of Mr. Fortieri's shop while evidence technicians ravaged the front.

I was as surprised to see him as he was me: I'd worked with him, or around him, anyway, for years downtown at the Central District. No one down there had told me he'd transferred—kind of surprising, because he'd been the right-hand man of my dad's oldest friend on the force, Bobby Mallory. Bobby was nearing retirement now; I was guessing McGonnigal had moved out to Montclare to establish a power base independent of his protector. Bobby doesn't like me messing with murder, and McGonnigal sometimes apes his boss, or used to.

Even at his most irritable, when he's inhaling Bobby's frustration, McGonnigal realizes he can trust me, if not to tell the whole truth, at least not to lead him astray or blow a police operation. Tonight he was exasperated simply by the coincidence of mine being the voice that summoned him to a crime scene—the nature of their work makes most cops a little superstitious. He wasn't willing to believe I'd come out to the Montclare neighborhood just to ask about music. As a sop, I threw in my long-lost cousin who was trying to track down a really obscure score.

"And what is that?"

"Sonatas by Claudia Fortezza Verazi." Okay, maybe I sometimes led him a little bit astray.

"Someone tore this place up pretty good for a while before the old guy showed up. It looks as though he surprised the intruder and thought he could defend himself with—what did you say he was holding? an oboe? You think your cousin did that? Because the old guy didn't have any Claudia whoever whoever sonatas?"

I tried not to jump at the question. "I don't think so." My voice came from far away, in a small thread, but at least it didn't quaver.

I was worrying about Vico myself. I hadn't told him about Mr. Fortieri, I was sure of that. But maybe he'd found the letter Fortieri wrote Gabriella, the one I'd tucked into the score of *Don Giovanni*. And then came out here, looking for—whatever he was really hunting—and found it, so he stabbed Mr. Fortieri to hide his—Had he come to Chicago to make a fool of me in his search for something valuable? And how had McGonnigal leaped on that so neatly? I must be tired beyond measure to have revealed my fears.

"Let's get this cousin's name . . . Damn it, Vic, you can't sit on that. I move to this district three months ago. The first serious assault I bag, who should be here but little Miss Muppet right under my tuffet. You'd have to be on drugs to put a knife into the guy, but you know something or you wouldn't be here minutes after it happened."

"Is that the timing? Minutes before my arrival?"

McGonnigal hunched his shoulders impatiently. "The medics didn't stop to figure out that kind of stuff—his blood pressure was too low. Take it as read that the old man'd be dead if you hadn't shown so pat—you'll get your citizen's citation the next time the mayor's handing out medals. Maybe Fortieri'd been bleeding half an hour, but no more. So, I want to talk to your cousin. And then I'll talk to someone else, and someone else and someone after that. You know how a police investigation runs."

"Yes, I know how they run." I felt unbearably tired as I gave him Vico's name, letter by slow letter, to relay to a patrolman. "Did your guys track down Mr. Fortieri's daughter?"

"She's with him at the hospital. And what does *she* know that you're not sharing with me?"

"She knew my mother. I should go see her. It's hard to wait in a hospital while people you don't know cut on your folks."

He studied me narrowly, then said roughly that he'd seen a lot of that himself, lately, his sister had just lost a kidney to lupus, and I should get some sleep instead of hanging around a hospital waiting room all night.

I longed to follow his advice, but beneath the rolling waves of fatigue that crashed against my brain was a sense of urgency. If Vico had been here, had found what he was looking for, he might be on his way to Italy right now.

The phone rang. McGonnigal stuck an arm around the corner and took it from the patrolman who answered it. After a few grunts he hung up.

"Your cousin hasn't checked out of the Garibaldi, but he's not in his room. As far as the hall staff know he hasn't been there since breakfast this morning, but of course guests don't sign in and out as they go. You got a picture of him?"

"I met him yesterday for the first time. We didn't exchange high school yearbooks. He's in his mid-thirties, maybe an inch or two taller than me, slim, reddish-brown hair that's a little long on the sides and combed forward in front, and eyes almost the same color."

I swayed and almost fell as I walked to the door. In the outer room the chaos was greater than when I'd arrived. On top of the tumbled books and instruments lay gray print powder and yellow crime-scene tape. I skirted the mess as best I could, but when I climbed into the Trans Am I left a streak of gray powder on the floor mats.

VII

Although her thick hair now held more gray than black, I knew Barbara Fortieri as soon as I stepped into the surgical waiting room (now Barbara Carmichael, now fifty-two, summoned away from flute lessons to her father's bedside). She didn't recognize me at first: I'd been a teenager when she last saw me, and twenty-seven years had passed.

After the usual exclamations of surprise, of worry, she told me her father had briefly opened his eyes at the hospital, just before they began running the anesthetic, and had uttered Gabriella's name.

"Why was he thinking about your mother? Had you been to see him recently? He talks about you sometimes. And about her."

I shook my head. "I wanted to see him, to find out if Gabriella had consulted him about selling something valuable the summer she got sick, the summer of 1965."

Of course Barbara didn't know a thing about the matter. She'd been in her twenties then, engaged to be married, doing her masters in performance at Northwestern in flute and piano, with no attention to spare for the women who were in and out of her father's shop.

I recoiled from her tone as much as her words, the sense of Gabriella as one of an adoring harem. I uttered a stiff sentence of regret over her father's attack and turned to leave.

She put a hand on my arm. "Forgive me, Victoria: I liked your mother. All the same, it used to bug me, all the time he spent with her. I thought he was being disloyal to the memory of my own mother . . . anyway, my husband is out of town. The thought of staying here alone, waiting on news. . . ."

So I stayed with her. We talked emptily, to fill the time, of her classes, the recitals she and her husband gave together, the fact that I wasn't married, and, no, I didn't keep up with my music. Around nine one of the surgeons came in to say that Mr. Fortieri had made it through surgery. The knife had pierced his lung and he had lost a lot of blood. To make sure he didn't suffer heart damage they were putting him on a ventilator, in a drug-induced coma, for a few days. If we were his daughters we could go see him, but it would be a shock and he wanted us to be prepared.

We both grimaced at the assumption that we were sisters. I left Barbara at the door of the intensive care waiting room and dragged myself to the Trans Am. A fine mist was falling, outlining street lamps with a gauzy halo. I tilted the rearview mirror so that I could see my face in the silver light. Those angular cheekbones were surely Slavic, and my eyes Tony's clear deep gray. Surely. I was surely Tony Warshawski's daughter.

The streets were slippery. I drove with extreme care, frightened of my own fatigue. Safe at home the desire for sleep consumed me like a ravening appetite. My fingers trembled on the keys with my longing for my bed.

Mr. Contreras surged into the hall when he heard me open the stairwell door. "Oh, there you are, doll. I found your cousin hanging around the entrance waiting for you, least, I didn't know he was your cousin, but he explained it all, and I thought you wouldn't want him standing out there, not knowing how long it was gonna be before you came home."

"Ah, *cara cugina*!" Vico appeared behind my neighbor, but before he could launch into his recitative the chorus of dogs drowned him, barking and squeaking as they barreled past him to greet me.

I stared at him, speechless.

"How are you? Your working it was good?"

"My working was difficult. I'm tired."

"So, maybe I take you to dinner, to the dancing, you are lively." He was speaking English in deference to Mr. Contreras, whose only word of Italian is "grappa."

"Dinner and dancing and I'll feel like a corpse. Why don't you go back to your hotel and let me get some sleep."

"Naturally, naturally. You are working hard all the day and I am playing. I have your—your *partitura*—"

"Score."

"*Buono*. Score. I have her. I will take her upstairs and put her away very neat for you and leave you to your resting."

"I'll take it with me." I held out my hand.

"No, no. We are leaving one big mess last night, I know that, and I am greedy last night, making you stay up when today you work. So I come with you, clean—*il disordine*—disorderliness?, then you rest without worry. You smell flowers while *I* work."

Before I could protest further he ducked back into Mr. Contreras's living room and popped out with a large portmanteau. With a flourish he extracted a bouquet of spring flowers, and the score, wrapped this time in a cream envelope, and put his arm around me to shepherd me up the stairs. The dogs and the old man followed him, all four making so much racket that the medical resident who'd moved in across the hall from Mr. Contreras came out.

"Please! I just got off a thirty-six-hour shift and I'm trying to sleep. If you can't control those damned dogs I'm going to issue a complaint to the city."

Vico butted in just as Mr. Contreras, drawing a deep breath, prepared to unleash a major aria in defense of his beloved animals. "*Mi scusa, Signora, mi scusa*. It is all my doing. I am here from Italy to meet my cousin for the first time. I am so excited I am not thinking, I am making noise, I am disturbing the rest your beautiful eyes require. . . ."

I stomped up the stairs without waiting for the rest of the flow. Vico caught up with me as I was closing the door. "This building attracts hard-working ladies who need to sleep. Your poor neighbor. She is at a hospital where they work her night and day. What is it about America, that ladies must work so hard? I gave her some of your flowers; I knew you wouldn't mind, and they made her so happy, she will give you no more complaints about the ferocious beasts."

He had switched to Italian, much easier to understand on his lips than English. Flinging himself on the couch he launched happily into a discussion of his day with the "partitura." He had found, through our mutual acquaintance Mr. Ranier, someone who could interpret the music for him. I was right: it was from the Baroque, and not only that, most likely by Pergolesi.

"So not at all possibly by our great-grandmother. Why would your mother have a handwritten score by a composer she could find in any music store?"

I was too tired for finesse. "Vico, where were you at five this afternoon?"

He flung up his hands. "Why are you like a policeman all of a sudden, eh, *cugina*?"

"It's a question the police may ask you. I'd like to know, myself."

A wary look came into his eyes—not anger, which would have been natural, or even bewilderment—although he used the language of a puzzled man: I couldn't be jealous of him, although it was a compliment when we had only just met, so what on earth was I talking about? And why the police? But if I really wanted to know, he was downstairs, with my neighbor.

"And for that matter, Vic, where were you at five o'clock?"

"On the Kennedy Expressway. Heading toward north Harlem Avenue."

He paused a second too long before opening his hands wide again. "I don't know your city, Cousin, so that tells me nothing."

"*Bene*. Thank you for going to so much trouble over the score. Now you must let me rest."

I put a hand out for it, but he ignored me and rushed over to the mound of papers we'd left in the hall last night with a cry that I was to rest, he was to work now.

He took the Pergolesi from its envelope. "The music is signed at the end, with the initials 'CF.' Who would that be?"

"Probably whoever copied it for her. I don't know."

He laid it on the bottom of the trunk and placed a stack of operas on top of it. My lips tight with anger I lifted the libretti out in order to get at the Pergolesi. Vico rushed to assist me but only succeeded in dropping everything, so that music and old papers both fluttered to the floor. I was too tired to feel anything except a tightening of the screws in my forehead. Without speaking I took the score from him and retreated to the couch.

Was this the same concerto Vico had taken with him the night before? I'd been naive to let him walk off with a document without some kind of proper safeguard. I held it up to the light, but saw nothing remarkable in the six pages, no signs that a secret code had been erased, or brought to light, nothing beyond a few carefully corrected notes in measure 168. I turned to the end where the initials "CF" were written in the same careful black ink as the notes.

Vico must have found Fortieri's letter to my mother stuffed inside *Don Giovanni* and tracked him down. No, he'd been here at five. So the lawyer, Ranier, was involved. Vico had spent the day with him: together they'd traced Mr. Fortieri. Vico came here for an alibi while the lawyer searched the shop. I remembered Ranier's eyes, granite chips in his soft face. He could stab an old man without a second's compunction.

Vico, a satisfied smile on his face, came to the couch for Gabriella's evening gown. "This goes on top, right, this beautiful concert dress. And now, *cugina*, all is tidy. I will leave you to your dreams. May they be happy ones."

He scooped up his portmanteau and danced into the night, blowing me a kiss as he went.

VIII

I fell heavily into sleep, and then into dreams about my mother. At first I was watching her with Mr. Fortieri as they laughed over their coffee in the little room behind the shop where McGonnigal and I had spoken. Impatient with my mother for her absorption in someone else's company I started smearing strawberry gelato over the oboe Mr. Fortieri was repairing. Bobby Mallory and John McGonnigal appeared, wearing their uniforms, and carried me away. I was screaming with rage or fear as Bobby told me my naughtiness was killing my mother.

And then suddenly I was with her in the hospital as she was dying, her dark eyes huge behind a network of tubes and bottles. She was whispering my name through her parched lips, mine and Francesca Salvini's. "*Maestra Salvini . . . nella cassa . . . Vittoria, mia carissima, dale . . .*" she croaked. My father, holding her hands, demanded of me what she was saying.

I woke as I always did at this point in the dream, my hair matted with sweat. "Maestra Salvini is in the box," I had told Tony helplessly at the time. "She wants me to give her something."

I always thought my mother was struggling with the idea that her voice teacher might be dead, that that was why her letters were returned unopened. Francesca Salvini on the Voice had filled my ears from my earliest childhood. As Gabriella staged her aborted comeback, she longed to hear some affirmation from her teacher. She wrote her at her old address in Pitigliano, and in care of the Siena Opera, as well as through her cousin Frederica—not knowing that Frederica herself had died two years earlier.

"*Cassa*"—"box"—isn't the usual Italian word for coffin, but it could be used as a crude figure just as it is in English. It had always jarred on me to hear it from my mother—her speech was precise, refined, and she tolerated no obscenities. And as part of her last words—she lapsed into a coma later that afternoon from which she never awoke—it always made me shudder to think that was on her mind, Salvini in a box, buried, as Gabriella was about to be.

But my mother's urgency was for the pulse of life. As though she had given me explicit instructions in my sleep I rose from the bed, walked to the hall without stopping to dress, and pulled open the trunk once more. I took out everything and sifted through it over and over, but nowhere could I see the olivewood box that had held Gabriella's glasses on the voyage to America. I hunted all through the living room, and then, in desperation, went through every surface in the apartment.

I remembered the smug smile Vico had given me on his way out the door last night. He'd stuffed the box into his portmanteau and disappeared with it.

IX

Vico hadn't left Chicago, or at least he hadn't settled his hotel bill. I got into his room at the Garibaldi by calling room service from the hall phone and ordering champagne. When the service trolley appeared from the bar I followed the waiter into the elevator, saw which room he knocked on as I sauntered past him down the hall, then let myself in with my picklocks when he'd taken off again in frustration. I knew my cousin wasn't in, or at least wasn't answering his phone—I'd already called from across the street.

I didn't try to be subtle in my search. I tossed everything from the drawers onto the floor, pulled the mattress from the bed, and pried the furniture away from the wall. Fury was making me wanton: by the time I'd made sure the box wasn't in the room the place looked like the remains of a shipwreck.

If Vico didn't have the box he must have handed it off to Ranier. The import-export lawyer, who specialized in remarkable *objets*, doubtless knew the value of an old musical score and how to dispose of it.

The bedside clock was buried somewhere under the linens. I looked at my watch—it was past four now. I let myself out of the room, trying to decide whether Ranier would store the box at his office or his home. There wasn't any way of telling, but it would be easier to break into his office, especially at this time of day.

I took a cab to the west Loop rather than trying to drive and park in the rush-hour maelstrom. The November daylight was almost gone. Last night's mist had turned into a biting sleet. People fled for their home-bound transportation, heads bent into the wind. I paid off the cab and ran out of the ice into the Caleb Building's coffee shop to use the phone. When Ranier answered I gave myself a high nasal voice and asked for Cindy.

"She's left for the day. Who is this?"

"Amanda Parton. I'm in her book group and I wanted to know if she remembered—"

"You'll have to call her at home. I don't want this kind of personal drivel discussed in my office." He hung up.

Good, good. No personal drivel on company time. Only theft. I mixed with the swarm of people in the Caleb's lobby and rode up to the thirty-seventh floor. A metal door without any letters or numbers on it might lead to a supply closet. Working quickly, while the hall was briefly empty, I unpicked the lock. Behind lay a mass of wires, the phone and signal lines for the floor, and a space just wide enough for me to stand in. I pulled the door almost shut and stared through the crack.

A laughing group of men floated past on their way to a Blackhawks game. A solitary woman, hunched over a briefcase, scowled at me. I thought for a nervous moment that she was going to test the door, but she was apparently lost in unpleasant thoughts all her own. Finally, around six, Ranier emerged, talking in Italian with Vico. My cousin looked as debonair as ever, with a marigold tucked in his lapel. Where he'd found one in mid-November I don't know but it looked quite jaunty against his brown worsted. The fragment of conversation I caught seemed to be about a favorite restaurant in Florence, not about my mother and music.

I waited another ten minutes, to make sure they weren't standing at the elevator, or returning for a forgotten umbrella, then slipped out of the closet and down to Ranier's import-export law office. Someone leaving an adjacent firm looked at me curiously as I slid the catch back. I flashed a smile, said I hated working nights. He grunted in commiseration and went on to the elevator.

Cindy's chair was tucked against her desk, a white cardigan draped primly about the arms. I didn't bother with her area but went to work on the inner door. Here Ranier had been more careful. It took me ten minutes to undo it. I was angry and impatient and my fingers kept slipping on the hafts.

Lights in these modern buildings are set on master timers for quadrants of a story, so that they all turn on or off at the same time. Outside full night had arrived; the high harsh lamps reflected my wavering outline in the black windows. I might have another hour of fluorescence flooding my search before the building masters decided most of the denizens had gone home for the day.

When I reached the inner office my anger mounted to murderous levels: my mother's olivewood box lay in pieces in the garbage. I pulled it out. They had pried it apart, and torn out the velvet lining. One shred of pale green lay on the floor. I scrabbled through the garbage for the rest of the velvet and saw a crumpled page in my mother's writing.

Gasping for air I stuck my hand in to get it. The whole wastebasket rose to greet me. I clutched at the edge of the desk but it seemed to whirl past me and the roar of a giant wind deafened me.

I managed to get my head between my knees and hold it there until the dizziness subsided. Weak from my emotional storm, I moved slowly to Ranier's couch to read Gabriella's words. The page was dated the 30th of October 1967, her last birthday, and the writing wasn't in her usual bold, upright script. Pain medication had made all her movements shaky at that point.

The letter began *"Carissima,"* without any other address, but it was clearly meant for me. My cheeks burned with embarrassment that her farewell note would be to her daughter, not her husband. "At least not to a lover, either," I muttered, thinking with more embarrassment of Mr. Fortieri, and my explicit dream.

My dearest,

I have tried to put this where you may someday find it. As you travel through life you will discard that which has no meaning for you, but I believe—hope—this box and my glasses will always stay with you on your journey. You must return this valuable score to Francesca Salvini if she is still alive. If she is dead, you must do with it as the circumstances of the time dictate to you. You must under no circumstances sell it for your own gain. If it has the value that Maestra Salvini attached to it it should perhaps be in a museum.

It hung always in a frame next to the piano in Maestra Salvini's music room, on the ground floor of her house. I went to her in the middle of the night, just before I left Italy, to bid her farewell. She feared she, too, might be arrested—she had been an uncompromising opponent of the Fascists. She gave it to me to safeguard in America, lest it fall into lesser hands, and I cannot agree to sell it only to buy medicine. So I am hiding this from your papa, who would violate my trust to feed more money to the doctors. And there is no need. Already, after all, these drugs they give me make me ill and destroy my voice. Should I use her treasure to add six months to my life, with only the addition of much more pain? You, my beloved child, will understand that that is not living, that mere survival of the organism.

Oh, my darling one, my greatest pain is that I must leave you alone in a world full of dangers and temptations. Always strive for justice, never accept the second-rate in yourself, my darling, even though you must accept it from the world around you. I grieve that I shall not live to see you grown, in your own life, but remember: *Il mio amore per te è l'amor che muove il sole e l'altre stelle.*

My love for you is the love that moves the sun and all the other stars. She used to croon that to me as a child. It was only in college I learned that Dante said it first.

I could see her cloudy with pain, obsessed with her commitment to save Salvini's music, scoring open the velvet of the box and sealing it in the belief I would find it. Only the pain and the drugs could have led her to something so improbable. For I would never have searched unless Vico had come looking for it. No matter how many times I recalled the pain of those last words, "*nella cassa*," I wouldn't have made the connection to this box. This lining. This letter.

I smoothed the letter and put it in a flat side compartment of my case. With the sense that my mother was with me in the room some of my anger calmed. I was able to begin the search for Francesca Salvini's treasure with a degree of rationality.

Fortunately Ranier relied for security on the building's limited access: I'd been afraid he might have a safe. Instead he housed his papers in the antique credenza. Inside the original decorative lock he'd installed a small modern one, but it didn't take long to undo it. My anger at the destruction of Gabriella's box made me pleased when the picklocks ran a deep scratch across the marquetry front of the cabinet.

I found the score in a file labeled "Sestieri-Verazi." The paper was old, parchment that had frayed and discolored at the edges, and the writing on it—clearly done by hand—had faded in places to a pale brown. Scored for oboe, two horns, a violin, and a viola, the piece was eight pages long. The notes were drawn with exquisite care. On the second, third, and sixth pages someone had scribbled another set of bar lines above the horn part and written in notes in a fast careless hand, much different from the painstaking care of the rest of the score. In two places he'd scrawled "da capo" in such haste that the letters were barely distinguishable. The same impatient writer had scrawled some notes in the margin, and at the end. I couldn't read the script, although I thought it might be German. Nowhere could I find a signature on the document to tell me who the author was.

I placed the manuscript on the top of the credenza and continued to inspect the file. A letter from a Signor Arnoldo Piave in Florence introduced Vico to Ranier as someone on the trail of a valuable musical document in Chicago. Signor Ranier's help in locating the parties involved would be greatly appreciated. Ranier had written in turn to a man in Germany "well-known to be interested in 18th-century musical manuscripts," to let him know Ranier might soon have something "unusual" to show him.

I had read that far when I heard a key in the outer door. The cleaning crew I could face down, but if Ranier had returned . . . I swept the score from the credenza and tucked it in the first place that met my eye—behind the Modigliani that hung above it. A second later Ranier and Vico stormed into the room. Ranier was holding a pistol, which he trained on me.

"I knew it!" Vico cried in Italian. "As soon as I saw the state of my hotel room I knew you had come to steal the score."

"Steal the score? My dear Vico!" I was pleased to hear a tone of light contempt in my voice.

Vico started toward me but backed off at a sharp word from Ranier. The lawyer told me to put my hands on top of my head and sit on the couch. The impersonal chill in his eyes was more frightening than anger. I obeyed.

"Now what?" Vico demanded of Ranier.

"Now we had better take her out to—well, the place name won't mean anything to you. A forest west of town. One of the sheriff's deputies will take care of her."

There are sheriff's deputies who will do murder for hire in unincorporated parts of Cook County. My body would be found by dogs or children under a heap of rotted leaves in the spring.

"So you have Mob connections," I said in English. "Do you pay them, or they you?"

"I don't think it matters." Ranier was still indifferent. "Let's get going. . . . Oh, Verazi," he added in Italian, "before we leave, just check for the score, will you?"

"What is this precious score?" I asked.

"It's not important for you to know."

"You steal it from my apartment, but I don't need to know about it? I think the state will take a different view."

Before Ranier finished another cold response Vico cried out that the manuscript was missing.

"Then search her bag," Ranier ordered.

Vico crossed behind him to snatch my case from the couch. He dumped the contents on the floor. A Shawn Colvin tape, a tampon that had come partially free of its container, loose receipts, and a handful of dog biscuits joined my work notebook, miniature camera, and binoculars in an unprofessional heap. Vico opened the case wide and shook it. The letter from my mother remained in the inner compartment.

"Where is it?" Ranier demanded.

"Don't ask, don't tell," I said, using English again.

"Verazi, get behind her and tie her hands. You'll find some rope in the bottom of my desk."

Ranier wasn't going to shoot me in his office: too much to explain to the building management. I fought hard. When Ranier kicked me in the stomach I lost my breath, though, and Vico caught my arms roughly behind me. His marigold was crushed, and he would have a black eye before tomorrow morning. He was panting with fury, and smacked me again across the face when he finished tying me. Blood dripped from my nose onto my shirt. I wanted to blot it and momentarily gave way to rage at my helplessness. I thought of Gabriella, of the love that moves the sun and all the other stars, and tried to avoid the emptiness of Ranier's eyes.

"Now tell me where the manuscript is," Ranier said in the same impersonal voice.

I leaned back in the couch and shut my eyes. Vico hit me again.

"Okay, okay," I muttered. "I'll tell you where the damned thing is. But I have one question first."

"You're in no position to bargain," Ranier intoned.

I ignored him. "Are you really my cousin?"

Vico bared his teeth in a canine grin. "Oh, yes, *cara cugina*, be assured, we are relatives. That naughty Frederica whom everyone in the family despised was truly my grandmother. Yes, she slunk off to Milan to have a baby in the slums without a father. And my mother was so impressed by her example that she did the same. Then when those two worthy women died, the one of tuberculosis, the other of excess heroin, the noble Verazis rescued the poor gutter child and brought him up in splendor in Florence. They packed all my grandmother's letters into a box and swept them up with me and my one toy, a horse that someone else had thrown in the garbage, and that my mother brought home from one of her nights out. My aunt discarded the horse and replaced it with some very hygienic toys, but the papers she stored in her attic.

"Then when my so-worthy uncle, who could never thank himself enough for rescuing this worthless brat, died, I found all my grandmother's papers. Including letters from your mother, and her plea for help in finding Francesca Salvini so that she could return this most precious musical score. And I thought, what have these Verazis ever done for me, but rubbed my nose in dirt? And you, that same beautiful blood flows in you as in them. And as in me!"

"And Claudia Fortezza, our great-grandmother? Did she write music, or was that all a fiction?"

"Oh, no doubt she dabbled in music as all the ladies in our family like to, even you, looking at that score the other night and asking me about the notation! Oh, yes, like all those stuck-up Verazi cousins, laughing at me because I'd never seen a piano before! I thought you would fall for such a tale, and it amused me to have you hunting for her music when it never existed."

His eyes glittered amber and flecks of spit covered his mouth by the time he finished. The idea that he looked like Gabriella seemed obscene. Ranier slapped him hard and ordered him to calm down.

"She wants us excited. It's her only hope for disarming me." He tapped the handle of the gun lightly on my left kneecap. "Now tell me where the score is, or I'll smash your kneecap and make you walk on it."

My hands turned clammy. "I hid it down the hall. There's a wiring closet. . . . The metal door near the elevators. . . ."

"Go see," Ranier ordered Verazi.

My cousin returned a few minutes later with the news that the door was locked.

"Are you lying?" Ranier growled at me. "How did you get into it?"

"Same as into here," I muttered. "Picklocks. In my hip pocket."

Ranier had Vico take them from me, then seemed disgusted that my cousin didn't know how to use them. He decided to take me down to unlock the closet myself.

"No one's working late on this side of the floor tonight, and the cleaning staff don't arrive until nine. We should be clear."

They frog-marched me down the hall to the closet before untying my hands. I knelt to work the lock. As it clicked free Vico grabbed the door and yanked it open. I fell forward into the wires. Grabbing a large armful I pulled with all my strength. The hall turned black and an alarm began to blare.

Vico grabbed my left leg. I kicked him in the head with my right. He let go. I turned and grabbed him by the throat and pounded his head against the floor. He got hold of my left arm and pulled it free. Before he could hit me I rolled clear and kicked again at his head. I hit only air. My eyes adjusted to the dark: I could make out his shape as a darker shape against the floor, squirming out of reach.

"Roll clear and call out!" Ranier shouted at him. "On the count of five I'm going to shoot."

I dove for Ranier's legs and knocked him flat. The gun went off as he hit the floor. I slammed my fist into the bridge of his nose and he lost consciousness. Vico reached for the gun. Suddenly the hall lights came on. I blinked in the brightness and rolled toward Vico, hoping to kick the gun free before he could focus and fire.

"Enough! Hands behind your heads, all of you." It was a city cop. Behind him stood one of the Caleb's security force.

X

It didn't take me as long to sort out my legal problems as I'd feared. Ranier's claim, that I'd broken into his office and he was protecting himself, didn't impress the cops: if Ranier was defending his office why was he shooting at me out in the hall? Besides, the city cops had long had an eye on him: they had a pretty good idea he was connected to the Mob, but no real evidence. I had to do some fancy tap dancing on why I'd been in his office to begin with, but I was helped by Bobby Mallory's arrival on the scene. Assaults in the Loop went across his desk, and one with his oldest friend's daughter on the rap sheet brought him into the holding cells on the double.

For once I told him everything I knew. And for once he was not only empathetic, but helpful: he retrieved the score for me—himself—from behind the Modigliani, along with the fragments of the olivewood box. Without talking to the state's attorney, or even suggesting that it should be impounded to make part of the state's case. It was when he started blowing his nose as someone translated Gabriella's letter for him—he didn't trust me to do it myself—that I figured he'd come through for me.

"But what is it?" he asked, when he'd handed me the score.

I hunched a shoulder. "I don't know. It's old music that belonged to my mother's voice teacher. I figure Max Loewenthal can sort it out."

Max is the executive director of Beth Israel, the hospital where Lotty Herschel is chief of perinatology, but he collects antiques and knows a lot about music. I told him the story later that day and gave the score to him. Max is usually imperturbably urbane, but when he inspected the music his face flushed and his eyes glittered unnaturally.

"What is it?" I cried.

"If it's what I think—no, I'd better not say. I have a friend who can tell us. Let me give it to her."

Vico's blows to my stomach made it hard for me to move, otherwise I might have started pounding on Max. The glitter in his eye made me demand a receipt for the document before I parted with it.

At that his native humor returned. "You're right, Victoria: I'm not immune from cupidity. I won't abscond with this, I promise, but maybe I'd better give you a receipt just the same."

XI

It was two weeks later that Max's music expert was ready to give us a verdict. I figured Bobby Mallory and Barbara Carmichael deserved to hear the news firsthand, so I invited them all to dinner, along with Lotty. Of course, that meant I had to include Mr. Contreras and the dogs. My neighbor decided the occasion was important enough to justify digging his one suit out of mothballs.

Bobby arrived early, with his wife Eileen, just as Barbara showed up. She told me her father had recovered sufficiently from his attack to be revived from his drug-induced coma, but he was still too weak to answer questions. Bobby added that they'd found a witness to the forced entry of Fortieri's house. A boy hiding in the alley had seen two men going in through the back. Since he was smoking a reefer behind a garage he hadn't come forward earlier, but when John McGonnigal assured him they didn't care about his dope—this one time—he picked Ranier's face out of a collection of photos.

"And the big guy promptly donated his muscle to us—a part-time deputy, who's singing like a bird, on account of he's p-o'd about being fingered." He hesitated, then added, "If you won't press charges they're going to send Verazi home, you know."

I smiled unhappily. "I know."

Eileen patted his arm. "That's enough shop for now. Victoria, who is it who's coming tonight?"

Max rang the bell just then, arriving with both Lotty and his music expert. A short skinny brunette, she looked like a street urchin in her jeans and outsize sweater. Max introduced her as Isabel Thompson, an authority on rare music from the Newberry Library.

"I hope we haven't kept dinner waiting—Lotty was late getting out of surgery," Max added.

"Let's eat later," I said. "Enough suspense. What have I been lugging unknowing around Chicago all this time?"

"She wouldn't tell us anything until you were here to listen," Max said. "So we are as impatient as you."

Ms. Thompson grinned. "Of course, this is only a preliminary opinion, but it looks like a concerto by Marianne Martines."

"But the insertions, the writing at the end," Max began, when Bobby demanded to known who Marianne Martines was.

"She was an eighteenth-century Viennese composer. She was known to have written over four hundred compositions, but only about sixty have survived, so it's exciting to find a new one." She folded her hands in her lap, a look of mischief in her eyes.

"And the writing, Isabel?" Max demanded.

She grinned. "You were right, Max: it is Mozart's. A suggestion for changes in the horn line. He started to describe them, then decided just to write them in above her original notation. He added a reminder that the two were going to play together the following Monday—they often played piano duets, sometimes privately, sometimes for an audience."

"Hah! I knew it! I was sure!" Max was almost dancing in ecstasy. "So I put some Krugs down to chill. Liquid gold to toast the moment I held in my hand a manuscript that Mozart held."

He pulled a couple of bottles of champagne from his briefcase. I fetched my mother's Venetian glasses from the dining room. Only five remained whole of the eight she had transported so carefully. One had shattered in the fire that destroyed my old apartment, and another when some thugs broke into it one night. A third had been repaired and could still be used. How could I have been so careless with my little legacy.

"But whose is it now?" Lotty asked, when we'd all drunk and exclaimed enough to calm down.

"That's a good question," I said. "I've been making some inquiries through the Italian government. Francesca Salvini died in 1943 and she didn't leave any heirs. She wanted Gabriella to dispose of it in the event of her death. In the absence of a formal will the Italian government might make a claim, but her intention as expressed in Gabriella's letter might give me the right to it, as long as I didn't keep it or sell it just for my own gain."

"We'd be glad to house it," Ms. Thompson offered.

"Seems to me your ma would have wanted someone in trouble to benefit." Bobby was speaking gruffly to hide his embarrassment. "What's something like this worth?"

Ms. Thompson pursed her lips. "A private collector might pay a quarter of a million. We couldn't match that, but we'd probably go to a hundred or hundred and fifty thousand."

"So what mattered most to your ma, Vicki, besides you? Music. Music and victims of injustice. You probably can't do much about the second, but you ought to be able to help some kids learn some music."

Barbara Carmichael nodded in approval. "A scholarship fund to provide Chicago kids with music lessons. It's a great idea, Vic."

We launched the Gabriella-Salvini program some months later with a concert at the Newberry. Mr. Fortieri attended, fully recovered from his wounds. He told me that Gabriella had come to consult him the summer before she died, but she hadn't brought the score with her. Since she'd never mentioned it to him before he thought her illness and medications had made her delusional.

"I'm sorry, Victoria: it was the last time she was well enough to travel to the northwest side, and I'm sorry that I disappointed her. It's been troubling me ever since Barbara told me the news."

I longed to ask him whether he'd been my mother's lover. But did I want to know? What if he, too, had moved the sun and all the other stars for her—I'd hate to know that. I sent him to a front-row chair and went to sit next to Lotty.

In Gabriella's honor the Cellini Wind Ensemble had come from London to play the benefit. They played the Martines score first as the composer had written it, and then as Mozart revised it. I have to confess I liked the original better, but as Gabriella often told me, I'm no musician.

BILL PRONZINI

The Nameless books by Bill Pronzini (1943–) will someday be regarded as the major body of noir work they are. And they will be taken seriously as novels, too, because they form nothing less than the autobiography of a man of our times, sometimes likeable, sometimes not, but always interesting.

In recent years, Pronzini has also turned to mainstream suspense novels. In books such as *Blue Lonesome*, he has brought serious concerns to the clichéd standard-issue suspense books that crowd the bookstands. Of our time and about our time, he is.

And he is a powerful short story writer, as well. One senses in his shorter work a restless literary sensibility that finds its ultimate freedom in these stories, no longer confined by the severe limitations put on most writers by bottom-line-oriented publishers today.

One Night at Dolores Park

A "Nameless Detective" Story

Dolores Park used to be the hub of one of the better residential neighborhoods in San Francisco: acres of tall palms and steeply rolling lawns in the Western Mission, a gentrifying area up until a few years ago. Well-off Yuppies, lured by scenic views and an easy commute to downtown, bought and renovated many of the old Victorians that rim the park. Singles and couples, straights and gays, moved into duplexes that sold for $300,000 and apartments that rented for upwards of a grand a month. WASPs, Latinos, Asian Americans . . . an eclectic mix that lived pretty much in harmony and were dedicated to preserving as much of the urban good life as was left these days.

Then the drug dealers moved in.

Marijuana sellers at first, aiming their wares at students at nearby Mission High School. The vanguard's success brought in a scruffier variety and their equally scruffy customers. As many as forty dealers allegedly had been doing business in Dolores Park on recent weekends, according to published reports. The cops couldn't do much; marijuana selling and buying is a low-priority crime in the city. But the lack of control, the wide-open open-air market, brought in fresh troops: heroin and crack dealers. And where you've got hard drugs, you also have high stakes and violence. Eight shootings and two homicides in and around Dolores Park so far this year. The firebombing of the home of a young couple who tried to form an activist group to fight the dealers. Muggings, burglaries, intimidation of residents. The result was bitterly predictable: frightened people moving out, real estate values dropping, and as the dealers widened their territory to include Mission Playground down on 19th Street, the entire neighborhood beginning to decline. The police had stepped up patrols, were making arrests, but it was too little too late: they didn't have the manpower or the funds, and there was so damned much of the same thing happening elsewhere in the city. . . .

"It's like Armageddon," one veteran cop was quoted as saying. "And the forces of evil are winning."

They were winning tonight, no question of that. It was a warm October night and I had been staked out on the west side of the park, nosed downhill near the intersection of Church and 19th, since a few minutes before six o'clock. Until it got dark I had counted seven drug transactions within the limited range of my vision—and no police presence other than a couple of cruising patrol cars. Once darkness closed down, the park had emptied fast. Now, at nine-ten, the lawns and paths appeared deserted. But I wouldn't have wanted to walk around over there, as early as it was. If there were men lurking in the shadows—and there probably were—they were dealers armed to the teeth and/or desperate junkies hunting prey. Only damned fools wandered through Dolores Park after nightfall.

Drugs, drug dealers, and the rape of a fine old neighborhood had nothing to do with why I was here; all of those things were a depressing by-product. I was here to serve a subpoena on a man named Thurmond, as a favor to a lawyer I knew. Thurmond was being sought for testimony in a huge stock fraud case. He didn't want to testify because he was afraid of being indicted himself, and he had been hiding out as a result. It had taken me three days to find out he was holed up with an old college buddy. The college buddy owned the blue-and-white Stick Victorian two doors down Church Street from where I was sitting. He was home—I'd seen him arrive, and there were lights on now behind the curtained bay windows—but there was still no sign of Thurmond. I was bored as well as depressed, and irritated, and frustrated. If Thurmond gave me any trouble when he finally put in an appearance, he was going to be sorry for it.

That was what I was thinking when I saw the woman.

She came down 19th, alone, walking fast and hard. The stride and the drawn-back set of her body said she was angry about something. There was a streetlight on the corner, and when she passed under it I could see that she was thirtyish, dark-haired, slender. Wearing a light sweater over a blouse and slacks. She waited for a car to roll by—it didn't slow—and then crossed the street toward the park.

Not smart, lady, I thought. Even if she was a junkie looking to make a connection, it wasn't smart. I had been slouched down on my spine; I sat up straighter, to get a better squint at where she was headed. Not into the park, at least. Away from me on the sidewalk, downhill toward Cumberland. Moving at the same hard, angry pace.

I had a fleeting impulse to chase after her, tell her to get her tail off the street. Latent paternal instinct. Hell, if she wanted to risk her life, that was her prerogative; the world is full of what the newspeakers call "cerebrally challenged individuals." It was none of my business what happened to her—

Yes, it was.

Right then it became my business.

A line of trees and shrubs flanked the sidewalk where she was, with a separating strip of lawn about twenty yards wide. The tall figure of a man came jerkily out of the tree-shadow as she passed. There was enough starlight and other light for me to make out something extended in one hand and that his face was covered except for the eyes and mouth. Gun and ski mask. Mugger.

I hit the door handle with my left hand, jammed my right up under the dash and yanked loose the .38 I keep clipped there. He was ten yards from her and closing as I came out of the car; she'd heard him and was turning toward him. He lunged forward, clawing for her purse.

There were no cars on the street. I charged across at an angle, yelling at the top of my voice, the only words that can have an effect in a situation like this: "Hold it, police officer!" Not this time. His head swiveled in my direction, swiveled back to the woman as she pulled away from him. She made a keening noise and turned to run.

He shot her.

No compunction: Just threw the gun up and fired point blank.

She went down, skidding on her side, as I cut between two parked cars onto the sidewalk. Rage made me pull up and I would have fired at him except that he pumped a round at me first. I saw the muzzle flash, heard the whine of the bullet and the low, flat crack of the gun, and in reflex I dodged sideways onto the lawn. Mistake, because the grass was slippery and my feet went out from under me. I stayed down, squirming around on my belly so I could bring the .38 into firing position. But he wasn't going to stick around for a shootout; he was already running splayfooted toward the trees. He disappeared into them before I could get lined up for a shot.

I'd banged my knee in the fall; it sent out twinges as I hauled myself erect, ran toward the woman. She was still down but not hurt as badly as I'd feared: sitting up on one hip now, holding her left arm cradled in against her breast. She heard me, looked up with fright shining on the pale oval of her face. I said quickly, "It's all right, I'm a detective, he's gone now," and shoved the .38 into my jacket pocket. There was no sign of the mugger. The park was empty as far as I could see, no movement anywhere in the warm dark.

She said, "He shot me," in a dazed voice.

"Where? Where are you hurt?"

"My arm . . ."

"Shoulder area?"

"No, above the elbow."

"Can you move the arm?"

"I don't . . . yes, I can move it."

Not too bad then. "Can you stand up, walk?"

"If you help me . . ."

I put an arm around her waist, lifted her. The blood was visible then, gleaming wetly on the sleeve of her sweater.

"My purse," she said.

It was lying on the sidewalk nearby. I let go of her long enough to pick it up. When I gave it to her she clutched it tightly: something solid and familiar to hang onto.

The street was still empty; so were the sidewalks on both sides. Somebody was standing behind a lighted window in one of the buildings across Church, peering through a set of drapes. No one else seemed to have heard the shots, or to want to know what had happened if they did. Just the woman and me out here at the edge of the light. And the predators—one predator, anyway—hiding somewhere in the dark.

Her name was Andrea Hull, she said, and she lived a few doors up 19th Street. I took her home, walking with my arm around her and her body braced against mine as if we were a pair of lovers. Get her off the street as quickly as possible, to where she would feel safe. I could report the shooting from there. You have to go through the motions even when there's not much chance of results.

Her building was a one-story, stucco-faced duplex. As we started up the front stoop, she drew a shuddering breath and said, "God, he could have killed me," as if the realization had just struck her. "I could be dead right now."

I had nothing to say to that.

"Peter was right, damn him," she said.

"Peter?"

"My husband. He keeps telling me not to go out walking alone at night and I keep not listening. I'm so smart, I am. Nothing ever happened, I thought nothing ever would . . ."

"You learned a lesson," I said. "Don't hurt yourself anymore than you already are."

"I hate it when he's right." We were in the vestibule now. She said, "It's the door on the left," and fumbled in her purse. "Where the hell did I put the damn keys?"

"Your husband's not home?"

"No. He's the reason I went out."

I found the keys for her, unlocked the door. Narrow hallway, a huge lighted room opening off of it. The room had been enlarged by knocking out a wall or two. There was furniture in it but it wasn't a living room; most of it, with the aid of tall windows and a couple of skylights, had been turned into an artist's studio. A cluttered one full of paintings and sculptures and the tools to create them. An unclean one populated by a tribe of dust mice.

I took a better look at its owner as we entered the studio. Older than I'd first thought, at least thirty-five, maybe forty. A sharp featured brunette with bright, wise eyes and pale lips. The wound in her arm was still bleeding, the red splotch grown to the size of a small pancake.

"Are you in much pain?" I asked her.

"No. It's mostly numb."

"You'd better get out of that sweater. Put some peroxide on the wound if you have it, then wrap a wet towel around it. That should do until the paramedics get here. Where's your phone?"

"Over by the windows."

"You go ahead. I'll call the police."

". . . I thought *you* were a policeman."

"Not quite. Private investigator."

"What were you doing down by the park?"

"Waiting to serve a subpoena."

"Lord," she said. Then she asked, "Do you have to report what happened? They'll never catch the man, you know they won't."

"Maybe not, but yes, I have to report it. You want attention for that arm, don't you?"

"All right," she said. "Actually, I suppose the publicity will do me some good." She went away through a doorway at the rear.

I made the call. The cop I spoke to asked half a dozen pertinent questions, then told me to stay put, paramedics and a team of inspectors would be out shortly. Half hour, maybe less, for the paramedics, I thought as I hung up. Longer for the inspectors. This wasn't an A-priority shooting. Perp long gone, victim not seriously wounded, situation under control. We'd just have to wait our turn.

I took a turn around the studio. The paintings were everywhere, finished and unfinished: covering the walls, propped in corners and on a pair of easels, stacked on the floor. They were all abstracts: bold lines and interlocking and overlapping squares, wedges, triangles in primary colors. Not to my taste, but they appeared to have been done by a talented artist. You couldn't say the same for the forty or so bronze, clay, and metal sculptures. All of those struck me as amateurish, lopsided things that had no identity or meaning, like the stuff kids make free-form in grade school.

"Do you like them? My paintings?"

I turned. Andrea Hull had come back into the room, wearing a sleeveless blouse now, a thick towel wrapped around her arm.

"Still bleeding?" I asked her.

"Not so badly now. *Do* you like my paintings?"

"I don't know much about art but they seem very good."

"They are. Geometric abstraction. Not as good as Mondrian or Glarner or Burgoyne Diller, perhaps. Or Hofmann, of course. But not derivative, either. I have my own unique vision."

She might have been speaking a foreign language. I said, "Uh-huh," and let it go at that.

"I've had several showings, been praised by some of the most eminent critics in the art world. I'm starting to make a serious name for myself—finally, after years of struggle. Just last month one of my best works, 'Tension and Emotion,' sold for fifteen thousand dollars."

"That's a lot of money."

"Yes, but my work will bring much more someday."

No false modesty in her. Hell, no modesty of any kind. "Are the sculptures yours too?"

She made a snorting noise. "Good God, no. My husband's. Peter thinks he's a brilliant sculptor but he's not—he's not even mediocre. Self-delusion is just one of his faults."

"Sounds like you don't get along very well."

"Sometimes we do. And sometimes he makes me so damn mad I could scream. Tonight, for instance. Calling me from some bar downtown, drunk, bragging about a woman he'd picked up. He *knows* that drives me crazy."

"Uh-huh."

"Oh, not the business with the woman. Another one of his lies, probably. It's the drinking and the taunting that gets to me—his jealousy. He's so damned jealous I swear his skin is developing a green tint."

"Of your success, you mean?"

"That's right."

"Why do you stay married to him, if he has that effect on you?"

"Habit," she said. "There's not much love left, but I do still care for him. God knows why. And of course he stays because now there's money, with plenty more in the offing . . . *oh*! Damn!" She'd made the mistake of trying to gesture with her wounded arm. "Where're those paramedics?"

"They'll be here pretty quick."

"I need a drink. Or don't you think I should have one?"

"I wouldn't. They'll give you something for the pain."

"Well, they'd better hurry up. How about you? Do you want a drink?"

"No thanks."

"Suit yourself. Go ahead and sit down if you want. I'm too restless."

"I've been doing nothing but sitting most of the evening."

"I'm going to pace," she said. "I have to walk, keep moving, when I'm upset. I used to go into the park, walk for an hour or more, but with all the drug problems . . . and now a person isn't even safe on the sidewalk—"

There was a rattling at the front door. Andrea Hull turned, scowling, in that direction. I heard the door open, bang closed; a male voice called, "Andrea?"

"In here, Peter."

The man who came duck-waddling in from the hall was a couple of inches over six feet, fair-haired and pale except for red-blotched cheeks and forehead. Weak-chinned and nervous-eyed. He blinked at her, blinked at me, blinked at her again with his mouth falling open.

"My God, Andrea, what happened to you? That towel . . . there's blood on it . . ."

"I was mugged a few minutes ago. He shot me."

"*Shot* you? Who . . . ?"

"I told you, a mugger. I'm lucky to be alive."

"The wound . . . it's not serious . . ."

"No." She winced. "What's *keeping* those paramedics?"

He went to her, tried to wrap an arm around her shoulders. She pushed him away. "The man who did it," he said, "did you get a good look at him?"

"No. He was masked. This man chased him off."

Hull remembered me, turned and waddled over to where I was.

"Thank God you were nearby," he said. He breathed on me, reaching for my hand. I let him have it but not for long. "But I don't think I've seen you before. Do you live in the neighborhood?"

"He's a private investigator," Andrea Hull said. "He was serving a subpoena on somebody. His name is Orenzi."

"No it isn't," I said. I told them what it was, not that either of them cared.

"I can never get Italian names right," she said.

Her husband shifted his attention her way again. "Where did it happen? Down by the park, I'll bet. You went out walking by the park again."

"Don't start in, Peter, I'm in no mood for it."

"Didn't I warn you something like this might happen? A hundred times I've warned you but you just won't listen."

"I said don't start in. If you hadn't called drunk from that bar, got me upset, I wouldn't have gone out. It's as much your fault as it is mine."

"*My* fault? Oh sure, blame me. Twist everything around so you don't have to take responsibility."

Her arm was hurting her and the pain made her vicious. She bared her teeth at him. "What are you doing home, anyway? Where's the bimbo you claimed you picked up?"

"I brushed her off. I kept thinking about what I said on the phone, what a jerk I was being. I wanted to apologize—"

"Sure, right. You were drunk, now you're sober; if there was any brushing off, she's the one who did it."

"Andrea . . ."

"What's the matter with your face? She give you some kind of rash?"

"My face? There's nothing wrong with my face. . . ."

"It looks like a rash. I hope it isn't contagious."

"Damn you, Andrea—"

I'd had enough of this. The bickering, the hatred, the deception—everything about the two of them and their not-so-private little war. I said sharply, "All right, both of you shut up. I'm tired of listening to you."

They gawked at me, the woman in disbelief. "How dare you. You can't talk to me like that in my own home—"

"I can and I will. Keep your mouth closed and your ears open for five minutes and you'll learn something. Your husband and I will do the talking."

Hull said, "I don't have anything to say to you."

"Sure you do, Peter. You can start by telling me what you did with the gun."

"Gun? I don't—what gun?"

"The one you shot your wife with."

Him: hissing intake of breath.

Her: strangled bleating noise.

"That's right. No mugger, just you trying to take advantage of what's happened to the park and the neighborhood, make it look like a street killing."

Him: "That's a lie, a damn lie!"

Her, to me in a ground-glass voice: "Peter? How can you know it was Peter? It was dark, the man wore a mask. . . ."

"For openers, you told me he was drunk when he called you earlier. He wasn't, he was faking it. Nobody can sober up completely in an hour, not when he's standing here now without the faintest smell of alcohol on his breath. He wasn't downtown, either; he was somewhere close by. The call was designed to upset you so you'd do what you usually do when you're upset—go out for a walk by the park.

"It may have been dark, but I still got a pretty good look at the shooter coming and going. Tall—and Peter's tall. Walked and ran splayfooted, like a duck—and that's how Peter walks. Then there are those blotches on his face. It's not a rash; look at the marks closely, Mrs. Hull. He's got the kind of skin that takes and retains imprints from fabric, right? Wakes up in the morning with pillow and blanket marks on his face? The ones he's got now are exactly the kind the ribbing on a ski mask would leave."

"You son of a bitch," she said to him. "You dirty rotten son of a—!"

She went for him with nails flashing. I got in her way, grabbed hold of her; her injured arm stopped her from struggling with me. Then he tried to make a run for it. I let go of her and chased him and caught him at the front door. When he tried to kick me I knocked him on his skinny tail.

And with perfect timing, the doorbell rang. It wasn't just the paramedics, either; the law had also arrived.

Peter Hull was an idiot. He had the gun, a .32 revolver, *and* the ski mask in the trunk of his car.

She pressed charges, of course. She would have cut his throat with a dull knife if they'd let her have one. She told him so, complete with expletives.

The Hulls and their private war were finished.

Down in Dolores Park—and in the other neighborhoods in the city, and in cities throughout the country—the other war, the big one, goes on. Armageddon? Maybe. And maybe the forces of evil are winning. Not in the long run, though. In the long run the forces of good will triumph. Always have, always will.

If I didn't believe that, I couldn't work at my job. Neither could anybody else in law enforcement.

No matter how bad things seem, we can't ever stop believing it.

LIA MATERA

Laura Di Palma is the creation of Lia Matera (1952–), who has written several novels about the no-nonsense lawyer. Matera's other Edgar- and Anthony-nominated series character is Willa Jansson, a California attorney whose approach to life is a little more laid back, as seen in the recent novel *Last Chants*. In whichever series Matera's writing, there is always a refreshing sensibility about her characters, a sense that, even though everything may be crumbling around them, they will always persevere and find a way through the urban jungle. A former teaching fellow at Stanford University Law School, Matera lives in Santa Cruz, California.

Dead Drunk

My secretary, Jan, asked if I'd seen the newspaper: another homeless man had frozen to death. I frowned up at her from my desk. Her tone said, *And you think you've got problems?*

My secretary is a paragon. I would not have a law practice without her. I would have something resembling my apartment, which looks like a college crash pad. But I have to cut Jan a lot of slack. She's got a big personality.

Not that she actually says anything. She doesn't have to, any more than earthquakes bother saying "shake shake."

"Froze?" I murmured. I shoved documents around the desk, knowing she wouldn't take the hint.

"Froze to death. This is the fourth one. They find them in the parks, frozen."

"It has been cold," I agreed.

"You really haven't been reading the papers!" Her eyes went on highbeam. "They're wet, that's why they freeze."

She sounded mad at me. Line forms on the right, behind my creditors.

"Must be the tule fog?" I guessed. I've never been sure what tule fog is. I didn't know if actual tules were required.

"You have been in your own little world lately. They've all been passed out drunk. Someone pours water on them while they lie there. It's been so cold they end up frozen to death."

I wondered if I could get away with, *How terrible*. Not that I didn't think it was terrible. But Jan picks at what I say, looking for hidden sarcasm.

She leaned closer, as titillated as I'd ever seen her. "And here's the kicker. They went and analyzed the water on the clothes. It's got no chlorine in it—it's not tap water. It's bottled water! Imagine that, Perrier or Evian or something. Can you imagine? Somebody going out with expensive bottled water on purpose to pour it over passed-out homeless men." Her long hair fell over her shoulders. With her big glasses and serious expression, she looked like the bread-baking natural foods mom that she was. "You know, it probably takes three or four bottles."

"What a murder weapon."

"It is murder." She sounded defensive. "Being wet drops the body temperature so low it kills them. In this cold, within hours."

"That's what I said."

"But you were . . . anyway, it is murder."

"I wonder if it has to do with the ordinance."

Our town had passed a no-camping ordinance that was supposed to chase the homeless out of town. If they couldn't sleep here, the theory went, they couldn't live here. But the city had too many parks to enforce the ban. What were cops supposed to do? Wake up everyone they encountered? Take them to jail and give them a warmer place to sleep?

"Of course it has to do with the ordinance! This is someone's way of saying, if you sleep here, you die here."

"Maybe it's a temperance thing. You know, don't drink."

"I know what temperance means." Jan could be touchy.

She could be a lot of things, including a fast typist willing to work cheap. "I just don't believe the heartlessness of it, do you?"

I had to be careful; I did believe the heartlessness of it. "It's uncondonable," I agreed.

Still she stooped over my desk. There was something else.

"The guy last night," Jan said bitterly, "was laid off by Hinder. Years ago, but even so."

Hinder was the corporation Jan had been fired from before I hired her.

She straightened. "I'm going to go give money to the guys outside."

"Who's outside?" Not my creditors?

"You are so oblivious, Linda! Homeless people, right downstairs. Regulars."

She was looking at me like I should know their names. I tried to look apologetic.

Ten minutes later, she buzzed me to say there was someone in the reception area. "He wants to know if you can fit him in."

That was our code for, *He looks legit*. We were not in the best neighborhood. We got our share of walk-ins with generalized grievances and a desire to vent at length and for free. For them, our code was, "I've told him you're busy."

"Okay."

A moment later, a kid—well, maybe young man, maybe even twenty-five or so—walked in. He was good-looking, well dressed, but too trendy, which is why he'd looked so young. He had the latest hairstyle, razored in places and long in others. He had shoes that looked like inflatable pools.

He said, "I think I need a good lawyer."

My glance strayed to my walls, where my diploma announced I'd gone to a night school. I had two years' experience, some of it with no caseload. I resisted the urge to say, *Let me refer you to one*.

Instead, I asked, "What's the nature of your problem?"

He sat on my client chair, checking it first. I guess it was clean enough.

"I think I'm going to be arrested." He glanced at me a little sheepishly, a little boastfully. "I said something kind of stupid last night."

If that were grounds, they'd arrest me, too.

"I was at the Club," a fancy bar downtown. "I got a little tanked. A little loose." He waggled his shoulders.

I waited. He sat forward. "Okay, I've got issues." His face said, *Who wouldn't?* "I work my butt off."

I waited some more.

"Well, it burns me. I have to work for my money. I don't get welfare, I don't get free meals and free medicine and a free place to live." He shifted on the chair. "I'm not saying kill them. But it's unfair I have to pay for them."

"For who?"

"The trolls, the bums."

I was beginning to get it. "What did you say in the bar?"

"That I bought out Costco's Perrier." He flushed to the roots of his chichi hair. "That I wish I'd thought of using it."

"On the four men?"

"I was high, okay?" He continued in a rush. "But then this morning, the cops come over." Tears sprang to his eyes. "They scared my mom. She took them out to see the water in the garage."

"You really did buy a lot of Perrier?"

"Just to drink! The police said they got a tip on their hot line. Someone at the bar told them about me. That's got to be it."

I nodded like I knew about the hot line.

"Now"—his voice quavered—"they've started talking to people where I work. Watch me get fired!"

Gee, buddy, then you'll qualify for free medical. "What would you like me to do for you, Mr. . . ."

"Kyle Kelly." He didn't stick out his hand. "Are they going to arrest me or what? I think I need a lawyer."

My private investigator was pissed off at me. My last two clients hadn't paid me enough to cover his fees. It was my fault; I hadn't asked for enough in advance. Afterward, they'd stiffed me.

Now the PI was taking a hard line: he wouldn't work on this case until he got paid for the last two.

So I made a deal. I'd get his retainer from Kelly up front. I'd pay him for the investigation, but I'd do most of it myself. For every hour I investigated and he got paid, he'd knock an hour off what I owed him.

I wouldn't want the state bar to hear about the arrangement. But the parts that were on paper would look okay.

It meant I had a lot of work to do.

I started by driving to a park where two of the dead men were found. It was a chilly afternoon with the wind whipping off the plains, blowing dead leaves over footpaths and lawns.

I wandered, looking for the spots described in police reports. The trouble was, every half-bare bush near lawn and benches looked the same. And many were decorated with detritus: paper bags, liquor bottles, discarded clothing.

As I was leaving the park, I spotted two paramedics squatting beside an addled-looking man. His clothes were stiff with dirt, his face covered in thick gray stubble. He didn't look wet. If anything, I was shivering more than him.

I watched the younger of the two paramedics shake his head, scowling, while the older talked at some length to the man. The man nodded, kept on nodding. The older medic showed him a piece of paper. The man nodded some more. The younger one strode to an ambulance parked on a nearby fire trail. It was red on white with "4–12" stenciled on the side.

I knew from police reports that paramedics had been called to pick up the frozen homeless men. Were they conducting an investigation of their own?

A minute later, the older medic joined his partner in the ambulance. It drove off.

The homeless man lay down, curling into a fetal position on the lawn, collar turned up against the wind.

I approached him cautiously. "Hi," I said. "Are you sick?"

"No!" He sat up again. "What's every damn body want to know if I'm sick for? 'Man down.' So what? What's a man got to be up about?"

He looked bleary-eyed. He reeked of alcohol and urine and musk. He was so potent, I almost lost my breakfast.

"I saw medics here talking to you. I thought you might be sick."

"Hassle, hassle." He waved me away. When I didn't leave, he rose. "Wake us up, make us sign papers."

"What kind of papers?"

"Don't want to go to the hospital." His teeth were in terrible condition. I tried not to smell his breath. "Like I want yelling from the nurses, too."

"What do they yell at you about?"

"Cost them money, I'm costing everybody money. Yeah, well, maybe they should have thought of that before they put my-Johnny-self in the helicopter. Maybe they should have left me with the rest of the platoon."

He lurched away from me. I could see that one leg was shorter than the other.

I went back to my car. I was driving past a nearby sandwich shop when I saw ambulance 4–12 parked there. I pulled into the space behind it.

I went into the shop. The medics were sitting at a small table, looking bored. They were hard to miss in their cop-blue uniforms and utility belts hung with flashlights, scissors, tape, stethoscopes.

I walked up to them. "Hi," I said. "Do you mind if I talk to you for a minute?"

The younger one looked through me; no one's ever accused me of being pretty.

The older one said, "What about?"

"I'm representing a suspect in the . . ." I hated to call it what the papers were now calling it, but it was the best shorthand. "The Perrier murders. Of homeless men."

That got the younger man's attention. "We knew those guys," he said.

"My client didn't do it. But he could get arrested. Do you mind helping me out? Telling me a little about them?"

They glanced at each other. The younger man shrugged.

"We saw them all the time. Every time someone spotted them passed out and phone in a 'man down' call, we'd code-three it out to the park or the tracks or wherever."

The older paramedic gestured for me to sit. "Hard times out there. We've got a lot more regulars than we used to."

I sat down. The men, I noticed, were lingering over coffee. "I just saw you in the park."

"Lucky for everybody, my-Johnny-self was sober enough to AMA." The younger man looked irritated. " 'Against medical advice.' We get these calls all the time. Here we are a city's got gang wars going on, knifings, drive-bys, especially late at night; and we're diddling around with passed-out drunks who want to be left alone anyway."

The older man observed, "Ben's new, still a hot dog, wants every call to be the real deal."

"Yeah, well, what a waste of effort, Dirk," the younger man, Ben, shot back. "We get what? Two, three, four man-down calls a day. We have to respond to every one. It could be some poor diabetic, right, or a guy's had a heart attack. But you get out there, and it's some alcoholic. If he's too out of it to tell us he's just drunk, we have to transport and work him up. Which he doesn't want—he wakes up pissed off at having to hoof it back to the park. Or worse, with the new ordinance, he gets arrested."

"Ridiculous ordinance," the older medic interjected.

"And it's what, maybe five or six hundred dollars the company's out of pocket?" his partner continued. "Not to mention that everybody's time gets totally wasted and maybe somebody with a real emergency's out there waiting for us. Your grandmother could be dying of a heart attack while we play taxi. It's bullshit."

"It's all in a night's work, Ben," Dirk looked at me. "You start this job, you want every call to be for real. But you do it a few years, you get to know your regulars. Clusters of them near the liquor stores—you could draw concentric circles around each store and chart the man-down calls, truly. But what are you going to do? Somebody sees a man lying in the street or in the park, they've got to call, right? And if the poor bastard's too drunk to tell us he's fine, we can't just leave him. It's our license if we're wrong."

"They should change the protocols," Ben insisted. "If we know who they are, if we've run them in three, four, even ten times, we should be able to leave them to sleep it off."

Dirk said, "You'd get lawsuits."

"So these guys either stiff the company or welfare picks up the tab, meaning you and me pay the five hundred bucks. It offends logic."

"So you knew the men who froze." I tried to get back on track. "Did you pick them up when they died?"

"I went on one of the calls," Ben said defensively. "Worked him up."

"Sometimes with hypothermia," Dirk added, "body functions slow down so you can't really tell if they're dead till they warm up. So we'll spend, oh God, an hour or more doing CPR. Till they're warm and dead."

"While people wait for an ambulance somewhere else," Ben repeated.

"You'll mellow out," Dirk promised. "For one thing, you see them year in, year out, you stop being such a hard-ass. Another thing, you get older, you feel more sympathy for how hard the streets got to be on the poor bones."

Ben's beeper went off. He immediately lifted it out of his utility belt, pressing a button and filling the air with static. A voice cut through: "Unit four-twelve, we have a possible shooting at Kins and Booten streets."

The paramedics jumped up, saying " 'Bye" and "Gotta go," as they strode past me and out the door. Ben, I noticed, was smiling.

My next stop was just a few blocks away. It was a rundown stucco building that had recently been a garage, a factory, a cult church, a rehab center, a magic shop. Now it was one of the few homeless shelters in town. I thought the workers there might have known some of the dead men.

I was ushered in to see the director, a big woman with a bad complexion. When I handed her my card and told her my business, she looked annoyed.

"Pardon me, but your client sounds like a real shit."

"I don't know him well enough to judge," I admitted. "But he denies doing it, and I believe him. And if he didn't do it, he shouldn't get blamed. You'd agree with that?"

"Some days," she conceded. She motioned me to sit in a scarred chair opposite a folding-table desk. "Other days, tell the truth, I'd round up all the holier-than-thou jerks bitching about the cost of a place like this, and I'd shoot 'em. Christ, they act like we're running a luxury hotel here. Did you get a look around?"

I'd seen women and children and a few old men on folding chairs or duck-cloth cots. I hadn't seen any food.

"It's enough to get your goat," the director continued. "The smugness, the condemnation. And ironically, how many paychecks away from the street do you think most people are? One? Two?"

"Is that mostly who you see here? People who got laid off?"

She shrugged. "Maybe half. We get a lot of people who are frankly just too tweaked-out to work. What can you do? You can't take a screwdriver and fix them. No use blaming them for it."

"Did you know any of the men who got killed?"

She shook her head. "No, no. We don't take drinkers, we don't take anybody under the influence. We can't. Nobody would get any sleep, nobody would feel safe. Alcohol's a nasty drug, lowers inhibitions—you get too much attitude, too much noise. We can't deal with it here. We don't let in anybody we think's had a drink, and if we find alcohol, we kick the person out. It's that simple."

"What recourse do they have? Drinkers, I mean."

"Sleep outside. They want to sleep inside, they have to stay sober; no ifs, ands, or buts."

"The camping ban makes that illegal."

"Well," she said tartly, "it's not illegal to stay sober."

"You don't view it as an addiction?"

"There's AA meetings five times a night at three locations." She ran a hand through her already disheveled hair. "I'm sorry, but it's a struggle scraping together money to take care of displaced families in this town. Then you've got to contend with people thinking you're running some kind of flophouse for drunks. Nobody's going to donate money for that."

I felt a twinge of pity. No room at the inn for alcoholics, and not much sympathy from paramedics. Now, someone—please God, not my client—was dousing them so they'd freeze to death.

With the director's permission, I wandered through the shelter. A young woman lay on a cot with a blanket over her legs. She was reading a paperback.

"Hi," I said. "I'm a lawyer. I'm working on the case of the homeless men who died in the parks recently. Do you know about it?"

She sat up. She looked like she could use a shower and a makeover, but she looked more together than most of the folks in there. She wasn't mumbling to herself, and she didn't look upset or afraid.

"Yup—big news here. And major topic on the street."

"Did you know any of the men?"

"I'll tell you what I've heard." She leaned forward. "It's a turf war."

"A turf war?"

"Who gets to sleep where, that kind of thing. A lot of crazies on the street, they get paranoid. They gang up on each other. Alumni from the closed-down mental hospitals. You'd be surprised." She pushed up her sleeve and showed me a scar. "One of them cut me."

"Do you know who's fighting whom?"

"Yes." Her eyes glittered. "Us women are killing off the men. They say we're out on the street for their pleasure, and we say, death to you, bozo."

I took a backward step, alarmed by the look on her face.

She showed me her scar again. "I carve a line for every one I kill." She pulled a tin St. Christopher medal out from under her shirt. "I used to be a Catholic. But Clint Eastwood is my god now."

I pulled into a parking lot with four ambulances parked in a row. A sign on a two-story brick building read "Central Ambulance." I hoped they'd give me their records regarding the four men.

I smiled warmly at the front-office secretary. When I explained what I wanted, she handed me a records-request form. "We'll contact you within five business days regarding the status of your request."

If my client got booked, I could subpoena the records. So I might, unfortunately, have them before anyone even read this form.

As I sat there filling it out, a thin boy in a paramedic uniform strolled in. He wore his medic's bill cap backward. His utility belt was hung with twice the gadgets of the two men I'd talked to earlier. Something resembling a big rubber band dangled from his back pocket. I supposed it was a tourniquet, but on him it gave the impression of a slingshot.

He glanced at me curiously. He said, "Howdy, Mary," to the secretary.

She didn't look glad to see him. "What now?"

"Is Karl in?"

"No. What's so important?"

"I was thinking instead of just using the HEPA filters, if we—"

"Save it. I'm busy."

I shot a sympathetic look. I know how it feels to be bullied by a secretary.

I handed her my request and walked out behind the spurned paramedic.

I was surprised to see him climb into a cheap Geo car. He was in uniform. I'd assumed he was working.

All four men had been discovered in the morning. It had probably taken them most of the night to freeze to death; they'd been picked up by ambulance in the wee hours. Maybe this kid could tell me who'd worked those shifts.

I tapped at his passenger window. He didn't hesitate to lean across and open the door. He looked alert and happy, like a curious puppy.

"Hi," I said, "I was wondering if you could tell me about your shifts? I was going to ask the secretary, but she's not very . . . friendly."

He nodded as if her unfriendliness were a fact of life, nothing to take personally. "Come on in. What do you want to know?" Then, more suspiciously, "You're not a lawyer?"

I climbed in quickly. "Well, yes, but—"

"Oh, man. You know, we do the very best we can." He whipped off his cap, rubbing his crewcut in apparent annoyance. "We give a hundred and ten percent."

I suddenly placed his concern. "No, no, it's not about medical malpractice, I swear."

He continued scowling at me.

"I represent a young man who's been falsely accused of—"

"You're not here about malpractice?"

"No, I'm not."

"Because that's such a crock." He flushed. "We work our butts off. Twelve hour shifts, noon to midnight, and a lot of times we get force-manned onto a second shift. If someone calls in sick or has to go out of service because they got bled all over or punched out, someone's got to hold over. When hell's a-poppin' with the gangs, we've got guys working forty-eights or even seventy-twos." He shook his head. "It's just plain unfair to blame us for everything that goes wrong. Field medicine's like combat conditions. We don't have everything all clean and handy like they do at the hospital."

"I can imagine. So you work—"

"And it's not like we're doing it for the money! Starting pay's eight-fifty an hour; it takes years to work up to twelve. Your garbage collector earns more than we do."

I was a little off balance. "Your shifts—"

"Because half our calls, nobody pays the bill—Central Ambulance's probably the biggest pro bono business in town. So we get stuck at eight-fifty an hour. For risking AIDS, hepatitis, TB."

I didn't want to get pulled into his grievances. "You work twelve-hour shifts? Set shifts?"

"Rotating. Sometimes you work the day half, sometimes the night half."

Rotating—I'd need schedules and rosters. "The guys who work midnight to noon, do they get most of the drunks?"

He shrugged. "Not necessarily. We've got 'em passing out all day long. It's never too early for an alcoholic to drink." He looked bitter. "I had one in the family," he complained. "I should know."

"Do you know who picked up the four men who froze to death?"

His eyes grew steely. "I'm not going to talk about the other guys. You'll have to ask the company." He started the car.

I contemplated trying another question, but he was already shifting into gear. I thanked him and got out. As I closed the door, I noticed a bag in back with a Garry's Liquors logo. Maybe the medic had something in common with the four dead men.

But it wasn't just drinking that got those men into trouble. It was not having a home to pass out in.

I stood at the spot where police had found the fourth body. It was a small neighborhood park.

Just after sunrise, an early jogger had phoned 911 from his cell phone. A man had been lying under a hedge. He'd looked dead. He'd looked wet.

The police had arrived first, then firemen, who'd taken a stab at resuscitating him. Then paramedics had arrived to work him up and transport him to the hospital where he was pronounced dead. I knew that much from today's newspaper.

I found a squashed area of grass where I supposed the dead man had lain yesterday. I could see pocks and scuffs where workboots had tramped. I snooped around. Hanging from a bush was a rubber tourniquet. A paramedic must have squatted with his back against the shrubbery.

Flung deeper into the brush was a bottle of whiskey. Had the police missed it? Not considered it evidence? Or had it been discarded since?

I stared at it, wondering. If victim number four hadn't already been pass-out drunk, maybe someone helped him along.

I stopped by Parsifal MiniMart, the liquor store nearest the park. If anyone knew the dead man, it would be the proprietor.

He nodded. "Yup. I knew every one of those four. What kills me is the papers act like they were nobodies, like that's what 'alcoholic' means." He was a tall, red-faced man, given to karate-chop gestures. "Well, they were pretty good guys. Not mean, not full of shit, just regular guys. Buddy was a little"—he wiggled his hand—"not right in the head, heard voices and all that, but not violent that I ever saw. Mitch was a good guy. One of those jocks who's a hero as a kid but then gets hooked on the booze. I'll tell ya, I wish I could have made every kid comes in here for beer spend the day with Mitch. Donnie and Bill were . . . how can I put this without sounding like a racist? You know, a lot of older black guys are hooked on something . . . Check out the neighborhood. You'll see groups of them talking jive and keeping the curbs warm."

Something had been troubling me. Perhaps this was the person to ask. "Why didn't they wake up when the cold water hit them?"

The proprietor laughed. "Those guys? If I had to guess, I'd say their blood alcohol was one-point-oh even when they weren't drinking, just naturally from living the life. Get enough Thunderbird in them, and you're talking practically a coma." He shook his head. "They were just drunks; I know we're not talking about killing Mozart here. But the attitude behind what happened—man, it's cold. Perrier, too. That really tells you something."

"I heard there was no chlorine in the water. I don't think they've confirmed a particular brand of water."

"I just saw on the news they arrested some kid looks like a fruit, one of those hairstyles." The proprietor shrugged. "He had a bunch of Perrier. Cases of it from a discount place—I guess he didn't want to pay full price. Guess it wasn't even worth a buck a bottle to him to freeze a drunk."

Damn, they'd arrested Kyle Kelly. Already.

"You don't know anything about a turf war, do you?" It was worth a shot. "Among the homeless?"

"Sure." He grinned. "The drunk sharks and the rummy jets." He whistled the opening notes of *West Side Story*.

I got tied up in traffic. It was an hour later by the time I walked into the police station. My client was in an interrogation room by himself. When I walked in, he was crying.

"I told them I didn't do it." He wiped tears as if they were an embarrassing surprise. "But I was getting so tongue-tied. I told them I wanted to wait for you."

"I didn't think they'd arrest you, especially not so fast," I said. "You did exactly right, asking for me. I just wish I'd gotten here sooner. I wish I'd been in my office when you called."

He looked like he wished I had, too.

"All this over a bunch of bums," he marveled. "All the crime in this town, and they get hard-ons over winos!"

I didn't remind him that his own drunken bragging had landed him here. But I hope it occurred to him later.

I was surrounded by reporters when I left the police station. They looked at me like my client had taken bites out of their children.

"Mr. Kelly is a very young person who regrets what alcohol made him say one evening. He bears no one any ill will, least of all the dead men, whom he never even met." I repeated some variation of this over and over as I battled my way to my car.

Meanwhile, their questions shed harsh light on my client's bragfest at the Club.

"Is it true he boasted about kicking homeless men and women?" "Is it true he said if homeless women didn't smell so bad, at least they'd be usable?" "Did he say three bottles of Perrier is enough, but four's more certain?" "Does he admit saying he was going to keep doing it till he ran out of Perrier?" "Is it true he once set a homeless man on fire?"

Some of the questions were just questions: "Why Perrier?" "Is it a statement?" "Why did he buy it in bulk?" "Is this his first arrest?," "Does he have a sealed juvenile record?"

I could understand why police had jumped at the chance to make an arrest. Reporters must have been driving them crazy.

After flustering me and making me feel like a laryngitic parrot, they finally let me through. I locked myself into my car and drove gratefully away. Traffic was good. It only took me half an hour to get back to the office.

I found the paramedic with the Geo parked in front. He jumped out of his car. "I just saw you on TV."

"What brings you here?"

"Well, I semi-volunteered, for the company newsletter. I mean, we picked up those guys a few times. It'd be good to put something into an article." He looked like one of those black-and-white sitcom kids. Opie or Timmy or someone. "I didn't quite believe you, before, about the malpractice. I'm sorry I was rude."

"You weren't rude."

"I just wasn't sure you weren't after us. Everybody's always checking up on everything we do. The nurses, the docs, our supervisors, other medics. Every patient care report gets looked at by four people. Our radio calls get monitored. Everybody jumps in our shit for every little thing."

I didn't have time to be Studs Terkel. "I'm sorry, I can't discuss my case with you."

"But I heard you say on TV your guy's innocent. You're going to get him off, right?" He gazed at me with a confidence I couldn't understand.

"Is that what you came here to ask?"

"It's just we knew those guys. I thought for the newsletter, if I wrote something . . ." He flushed. "Do you need information? You know, general stuff from a medical point of view?"

I couldn't figure him out. Why this need to keep talking to me about it? It was his day off; didn't he have a life?

But I *had* been wondering: "Why exactly do you carry those tourniquets? What do you do with them?"

He looked surprised. "We tie them around the arm to make a vein pop up. So we can start an intravenous line."

I glanced up at my office window, checking whether Jan had left. It was late, there were no more workers spilling out of buildings. A few derelicts lounged in doorways. I wondered if they felt safer tonight because someone had been arrested. With so many dangers on the street, I doubted it.

"Why would a tourniquet be in the bushes where the last man was picked up?" I hugged my briefcase. "I assumed a medic dropped it, but you wouldn't start an intravenous line on a dead person, would you?"

"We don't do field pronouncements—pronounce them dead, I mean—in hypothermia cases. We leave that to the doc." He looked proud of himself, like he'd passed the pop quiz. "They're not dead till they're warm and dead."

"But why start an IV in this situation?"

"Get meds into them. If the protocols say to, we'll run a line even if we think they're deader than Elvis." He shrugged. "They warm up faster, too."

"What warms them up? What do you drip into them?"

"Epinephrine, atropine, normal saline. We put the saline bag on the dash to heat it as we drive—if we know we have a hypothermic patient."

"You have water in the units?"

"Of course."

"Special water?"

"Saline and distilled."

"Do you know a medic named Ben?"

He hesitated before nodding.

"Do you think he has a bad attitude about the homeless?"

"No more than you would," he protested. "We're the ones who have to smell them, have to handle them when they've been marinating in feces and urine and vomit. Plus they get combative at a certain stage. You do this disgusting waltz with them where they're trying to beat on you. And the smell is like, whoa. Plus if they scratch you, you can't help but be paranoid what they might infect you with."

"Ben said they cost your company money."

"They cost you and me money."

The look on his face scared me. Money's a big deal when you don't make enough of it.

I started past him.

He grabbed my arm. "Everything's breaking down." His tone was plaintive. "You realize that? Our whole society's breaking down. Everybody sees it—the homeless, the gangs, the diseases—but they don't have to deal with the physical results. They don't have to put their hands right on it, get all bloody and dirty with it, get infected by it."

"Let go!" I imagined being helpless and disoriented, a drunk at the mercy of a fed-up medic.

"And we don't get any credit"—he sounded angry now—"we just get checked up on." He gripped my arm tighter. Again I searched my office window, hoping Jan was still working, that I wasn't alone. But the office was dark.

A voice behind me said. "What you doin' to the lady, man?"

I turned to see a stubble-chinned black man in layers of rancid clothes. He'd stepped out of a recessed doorway. Even from here, I could smell alcohol.

"You let that lady go. You hear me?" He moved closer.

The medic's grip loosened.

The man might be drunk, but he was big. And he didn't look like he was kidding.

I jerked my arm free, backing toward him.

He said. "You're Jan's boss, aren't ya?"

"Yes." For the thousandth time, I thanked God for Jan. This must be one of the men she'd mother-henned this morning. "Thank you."

To the medic, I said. "The police won't be able to hold my client long. They've got to show motive and opportunity and no alibi on four different nights. I don't think they'll be able to do it. They were just feeling pressured to arrest someone. Just placating the media."

The paramedic stared behind me. I could smell the other man. I never thought I'd find the reek of liquor reassuring. "Isn't that what your buddies sent you to find out? Whether they could rest easy, or if they'd screwed over an innocent person?"

The medic pulled his bill cap off, buffing his head with his wrist.

"Or maybe you decided on your own to come here. Your coworkers probably have sense enough to keep quiet and keep out of it. But you don't." He was young and enthusiastic, too much so, perhaps. "Well, you can tell Ben and the others not to worry about Kyle Kelly. His reputation's ruined for as long as people remember the name—which probably isn't long enough to teach him a lesson. But there's not enough evidence against him. He won't end up in jail because of you."

"Are you accusing *us* . . . ?" He looked more thrilled than shocked.

"Of dousing the men so you didn't have to keep picking them up? So you could respond to more important calls? Yes, I am."

"But who are you going to—? What are you going to do?"

"I don't have a shred of proof to offer the police," I realized. "And I'm sure you guys will close ranks, won't give each other away. I'm sure the others will make you stop 'helping,' make you keep your mouth shut."

I thought about the dead men; "pretty good guys," according to the MiniMart proprietor. I thought about my-Johnny-self, the war veteran I'd spoken to this morning.

I wanted to slap this kid. Just to do *something*. "You know what? You need to be confronted with your arrogance, just like Kyle Kelly was. You need to see what other people think of you. You need to see some of your older, wiser coworkers look at you with disgust on their faces. You need your boss to rake you over the coals. You need to read what the papers have to say about you."

I could imagine headlines that sounded like movie billboards: "Dr. Death." "Central Hearse."

He winced. He'd done the profession no favor.

"So you can bet I'll tell the police what I think," I promised. "You can bet I'll try to get you fired, you and Ben and whoever else was involved. Even if there isn't enough evidence to arrest you."

He took a cautious step toward his car. “I didn’t admit anything.” He pointed to the other man. “Did you hear me admit anything?”

“And I’m sure your lawyer will tell you not to.” If he could find a halfway decent one on his salary. “Now, if you’ll excuse me, I have a lot of work to do.”

I turned to the man behind me. “Would you mind walking me in to my office?” I had some cash inside. He needed it more than I did.

“Lead the way, little lady.” His eyes were jaundiced yellow, but they were bright. I was glad he didn’t look sick.

I prayed he wouldn’t need an ambulance anytime soon.

MAX ALLAN COLLINS

Max Allan Collins's (1948–) Nathan Heller series about a private eye who meets and works with celebrities from Al Capone to Amelia Earhart during the course of his decades-long career . . . is the best hard-boiled historical series ever written. And don't let anybody tell you differently.

The Shamus Award–winning series has been so often imitated (i.e., ripped off in the way Ed McBain's 87th Precinct books have been ripped off) that their original impact has been forgotten. Collins gave us something brand-new. His latest Nathan Heller novel is *Angel in Black*.

In addition, Collins has written an excellent series about a contract killer (Quarry) and an equally good series about a thief named Nolan. Oh, yes, and he's become King of the Movie Novelization, one of the most in-demand writers walking that particular path, perhaps because he's an accomplished filmmaker in his own right. He never just does the script. He fleshes it out so that it has the inner tension and depth of a real novel. Which explains why he's so much in demand. His most recent novelization, *Road to Perdition*, is based on his own graphic novel, now a feature film starring Tom Hanks and Paul Newman.

Kaddish for the Kid

The first operative I ever took on in the A-1 Detective Agency was Stanley Gross. I hadn't been in business for even a year—it was summer of '33—and was in no shape to be adding help. But the thing was—Stanley had a car.

Stanley had a '28 Ford coupe, to be exact, and a yen to be a detective. I had a paying assignment, requiring wheels, and a yen to make a living.

So it was that at three o'clock in the morning, on that unseasonably cool summer evening, I was sitting in the front seat of Stanley's Ford, in front of Goldblatt's department store on West Chicago Avenue, sipping coffee out of a paper cup, waiting to see if anybody came along with a brick or a gun.

I'd been hired two weeks before by the manager of the downtown Goldblatt's on State, just two blocks from my office at Van Buren and Plymouth. Goldblatt's was sort of a working-class Marshall Field's, with six department stores scattered around the Chicago area in various white ethnic neighborhoods.

The stores were good-size—two floors taking up as much as half a block—and the display windows were impressive enough; but once you got inside, it was like the push-carts of Maxwell Street had been emptied and organized.

I bought my socks and underwear at the downtown Goldblatt's, but that wasn't how Nathan Heller—me—got hired. I knew Katie Mulhaney, the manager's secretary; I'd bumped into her on one of my socks and underwear buying expeditions, and it blossomed into a friendship. A warm friendship.

Anyway, the manager—Herman Cohen—had summoned me to his office, where he filled me in. His desk was cluttered, but he was neat—moon-faced, moustached, bow- (and fit-to-be-) tied.

"Maybe you've seen the stories in the papers," he said, in a machine-gun burst of words, "about this reign of terror we've been suffering."

"Sure," I said.

Goldblatt's wasn't alone; every leading department store was getting hit—stench bombs set off, acid sprayed over merchandise, bricks tossed from cars to shatter plate-glass windows.

He thumbed his moustache; frowned. "Have you heard of 'Boss' Rooney? John Rooney?"

"No."

"Well, he's secretary of the Circular Distributors Union. Over the past two years, Mr. Goldblatt has provided Rooney's union with over three thousand dollars of business—primarily to discourage trouble at our stores."

"This union—these are guys that hand out ad fliers?"

"Yes. Yes, and now Rooney has demanded that Mr. Goldblatt order three hundred of our own sales and ad people to join his union—at a rate of twenty-five cents a day."

My late father had been a die-hard union guy, so I knew a little bit about this sort of thing. "Mr. Cohen, none of the unions in town collect daily dues."

"This one does. They've even been outlawed by the AFL, Mr. Heller. Mr. Goldblatt feels Rooney is nothing short of a racketeer."

"It's an extortion scam, all right. What do you want me to do?"

"Our own security staff is stretched to the limit. We're getting *some* support from State's Attorney Courtney and his people. But they can only do so much. So we've taken on a small army of night watchmen, and are fleshing out the team with private detectives. Miss Mulhaney recommended you."

Katie knew a good dick when she saw one.

"Swell. When do I start?"

"Immediately. Of course, you do have a car?"

Of course, I lied and said I did. I also said I'd like to put one of my "top" operatives on the assignment with me, and that was fine with Cohen, who was in a more-the-merrier mood where beefing up security was concerned.

Stanley Gross was from Douglas Park, my old neighborhood. His parents were bakers two doors down from my father's bookstore on South Homan. Stanley was a good eight years younger than me, so I remembered him mostly as a pestering kid.

But he'd grown into a tall, good-looking young man—a brown-haired, brown-eyed six-footer who'd been a star football and basketball player in high school. Like me, he went to Crane Junior College; unlike me, he finished.

I guess I'd always been sort of a hero to him. About six months before, he'd started dropping by my office to chew the fat. Business was so lousy, a little company—even from a fresh-faced college boy—was welcome.

We'd sit in the deli restaurant below my office and sip coffee and gnaw on bagels and he'd tell me this embarrassing stuff about my being somebody he'd always looked up to.

"Gosh, Nate, when you made the police force, I thought that was just about the keenest thing."

He really did talk that way—gosh, keen. I told you I was desperate for company.

He brushed a thick comma of brown hair away and grinned in a goofy boyish way; it was endearing, and nauseating. "When I was a kid, coming into your pop's bookstore, you pointed me toward those Nick Carters, and Sherlock Holmes books. Gave me the bug. I *had* to be a detective!"

But the kid was too young to get on the force, and his family didn't have the kind of money or connections it took to get a slot on the PD.

"When you quit," he said, "I admired you so. Standing up to corruption—and in *this* town! Imagine."

Imagine. My leaving the force had little to do with my "standing up to corruption"—after all, graft was high on my list of reasons for joining in the first place—but I said nothing, not wanting to shatter the child's dreams.

"If you ever need an op, I'm your man!"

He said this thousands of times in those six months or so. And he actually did get some security work, through a couple of other, larger agencies. But his dream was to be my partner.

Owning that Ford made his dream come temporarily true.

For two weeks, we'd been living the exciting life of the private eye: sitting in the coupe in front of the Goldblatt's store at Ashland and Chicago, waiting for window smashers to show. Or not.

The massive gray-stone department store was like the courthouse of commerce on this endless street of storefronts; the other businesses were smaller—resale shops, hardware stores, pawn shops, your occasional Polish deli. During the day, things were popping here. Now, there was just us—me draped across the front seat, Stanley draped across the back—and the glow of neons and a few pools of light on the sidewalks from streetlamps.

"You know," Stanley said, "this isn't as exciting as I pictured."

"Just a week ago you were all excited about 'packing a rod.' "

"You're making fun of me."

"That's right." I finished my coffee, crumpled the cup, tossed it on the floor.

"I guess a gun is nothing to feel good about."

"Right again."

I was stretched out with my shoulders against the rider's door; in back, he was stretched out just the opposite. This enabled us to maintain eye contact. Not that I wanted to, particularly.

"Nate . . . if you hear me snoring, wake me up."

"You tired, kid?"

"Yeah. Ate too much. Today . . . well, today was my birthday."

"No kidding! Well, Happy Birthday, kid."

"My pa made the keenest cake. Say, I . . . I'm sorry I didn't invite you or anything."

"That's okay."

"It was a surprise party. Just my family—a few friends I went to high school and college with."

"It's okay."

"But there's cake left. You want to stop by Pa's store tomorrow and have a slice with me?"

"We'll see, kid."

"You remember my pa's pastries. Can't beat 'em."

I grinned. "Best on the West Side. You talked me into it. Go ahead and catch a few winks. Nothing's happening."

And nothing was. The street was an empty ribbon of concrete. But about five minutes later, a car came barreling down that concrete ribbon, right down the middle; I sat up.

"What is it, Nate?"

"A drunk, I think. He's weaving a little . . ."

It was a maroon Plymouth coupe; and it was headed right our way.

"Christ!" I said, and dug under my arm for the nine millimeter.

The driver was leaning out the window of the coupe, but whether man or woman I couldn't tell—the headlights of the car, still a good thirty feet away, were blinding.

The night exploded and so did our windshield.

Glass rained on me as I hit the floor; I could hear the roar of the Plymouth's engine and came back up, gun in hand, saw the maroon coupe bearing down on us, saw a silver swan on the radiator cap, and cream-colored wheels, but people in the car going by were a blur, and as I tried to get a better look, orange fire burst from a gun and I ducked down, hitting the glass-littered floor. Another four shots riddled the car and the night, the side windows cracking, and behind us the plate glass of display windows was fragmenting, falling to the pavement like sheets of ice.

Then the Plymouth was gone.

So was Stanley.

The first bullet must have got him. He must have sat up to get a look at the oncoming car and took the slug head-on; it threw him back, and now he still seemed to be lounging there, against the now-spiderwebbed window, precious "rod" tucked under his arm; his brown eyes were open, his mouth too, and his expression was almost—not quite—surprised.

I don't think he had time to be truly surprised before he died.

There'd been only time enough for him to take the bullet in the head, the dime-sized entry wound parting the comma of brown hair, streaking the birthday boy's boyish face with blood.

Within an hour I was being questioned by Sergeant Charles Pribyl, who was attached to the state's attorney's office. Pribyl was a decent enough guy, even if he did work under Captain Daniel "Tubbo" Gilbert, who was probably the crookedest cop in town. Which in this town was saying something.

Pribyl had a good reputation, however; and I'd encountered him, from time to time, back when I was working the pickpocket detail. He had soft, gentle features and dark alert eyes.

Normally, he was an almost dapper dresser, but his tie seemed hastily knotted, his suit and hat looked as if he'd thrown them on—which he probably had; he was responding to a call at four in the morning, after all.

He was looking in at Stanley, who hadn't been moved; we were waiting for a coroner's physician to show. Several other plainclothes officers and half a dozen uniformed cops were milling around, footsteps crunching on the glass-strewn sidewalk.

"Just a kid," Pribyl said, stepping away from the Ford. "Just a damn kid." He shook his head. He nodded to me and I followed him over by a shattered display window.

He cocked his head. "How'd you happen to have such a young operative working with you?"

I explained about the car being Stanley's.

He had an expression you only see on cops: sad and yet detached. His eyes tightened.

"How—and why—did stink bombs and window smashing escalate into bloody murder?"

"You expect me to answer that, Sergeant?"

"No. I expect you to tell me what happened. And, Heller—I don't go into this with any preconceived notions about you. Some people on the force—even some good ones, like John Stege—hold it against you, the Lang and Miller business."

They were two crooked cops I'd recently testified against.

"Not me," he said firmly. "Apples don't come rottener than those two bastards. I just want you to know what kind of footing we're on."

"I appreciate that."

I filled him in, including a description of the murder vehicle, but couldn't describe the people within at all. I wasn't even sure how many of them there were.

"You get the license number?"

"No, damnit."

"Why not? You saw the car well enough."

"Them shooting at me interfered."

He nodded. "Fair enough. Shit. Too bad you didn't get a look at 'em."

"Too bad. But you know who to go calling on."

"How's that?"

I thrust a finger toward the car. "That's Boss Rooney's work—maybe not personally, but he had it done. You know about the Circular Union and the hassles they been giving Goldblatt's, right?"

Pribyl nodded, somewhat reluctantly; he liked me well enough, but I was a private detective. He didn't like having me in the middle of police business.

"Heller, we've been keeping the union headquarters under surveillance for six weeks now. I saw Rooney there today, myself, from the apartment across the way we rented."

"So did anyone leave the union hall tonight? Before the shooting, say around three?"

He shook his head glumly. "We've only been maintaining our watch during department-store business hours. The problem of night attacks is where hired hands like you come in."

"Okay." I sighed. "I won't blame you if you don't blame me."

"Deal."

"So what's next?"

"You can go on home." He glanced toward the Ford. "We'll take care of this."

"You want me to tell the family?"

"Were you close to them?"

"Not really. They're from my old neighborhood, is all."

"I'll handle it."

"You sure?"

"I'm sure." He patted my shoulder. "Go home."

I started to go, then turned back. "When are you going to pick up Rooney?"

"I'll have to talk to the state's attorney first. But my guess? Tomorrow. We'll raid the union hall tomorrow."

"Mind if I come along?"

"Wouldn't be appropriate, Heller."

"The kid worked for me. He got killed working for me."

"No. We'll handle it. Go home! Get some sleep."

"I'll go home," I said.

A chill breeze was whispering.

"But the sleep part," I said, "that I can't promise you."

The next afternoon I was having a beer in a booth in the bar next to the deli below my office. Formerly a blind pig—a speakeasy that looked shuttered from the street (even now, you entered through the deli)—it was a business investment of fighter Barney Ross, as was reflected by the framed boxing photos decorating the dark, smoky little joint.

I grew up with Barney on the West Side. Since my family hadn't practiced Judaism in several generations, I was shabbas goy for Barney's very Orthodox folks, a kid doing chores and errands for them from Friday sundown through Saturday.

But we didn't become really good friends, Barney and me, till we worked Maxwell Street as pullers—teenage street barkers who literally pulled customers into stores for bargains they had no interest in.

Barney, a roughneck made good, was a real Chicago success story. He owned this entire building, and my office—which, with its Murphy bed, was also my residence—was space he traded me for keeping an eye on the place. I was his night watchman, unless a paying job like Goldblatt's came along to take precedence.

The lightweight champion of the world was having a beer, too, in that back booth; he wore a cheerful blue and white sportshirt and a dour expression.

"I'm sorry about your young pal," Barney said.

"He wasn't a 'pal,' really. Just an acquaintance."

"I don't know that Douglas Park crowd myself. But to think of a kid, on his twenty-first birthday . . ." His mildly battered bulldog countenance looked woeful. "He have a girl?"

"Yeah."

"What's her name?"

"I don't remember."

"Poor little bastard. When's the funeral?"

"I don't know."

"You're going, aren't you?"

"No. I don't really know the family that well. I'm sending flowers."

He looked at me with as long a face as a round-faced guy could muster. "You oughta go. He was working for you when he got it."

"I'd be intruding. I'd be out of place."

"You should do kaddish for the kid, Nate."

A mourner's prayer.

"Jesus Christ, Barney, I'm no Jew. I haven't been in a synagogue more than half a dozen times in my life, and then it was social occasions."

"Maybe you don't consider yourself a Jew, with that Irish mug of yours your ma bequeathed you . . . but you're gonna have a rude awakening one of these days, boyo."

"What do you mean?"

"There's plenty of people you're just another 'kike' to, believe you me."

I sipped the beer. "Nudge me when you get to the point."

"You owe this kid kaddish, Nate."

"Hell, doesn't that go on for months? I don't know the lingo. And if you think I'm putting on some stupid beanie and . . ."

There was a tap on my shoulder. Buddy Gold, the bartender, an ex-pug, leaned in to say, "You got a call."

I went behind the bar to use the phone. It was Sergeant Lou Sapperstein at Central Headquarters in the Loop; Lou had been my boss on the pickpocket detail. I'd called him this morning with a request.

"Tubbo's coppers made their raid this morning, around nine," Lou said. Sapperstein was a hard-nosed, balding cop of about forty-five and one of the few friends I had left on the PD.

"And?"

"And the union hall was empty, 'cept for a bartender. Pribyl and his partner Bert Gray took a whole squad up there, but Rooney and his boys had flew the coop."

"Shit. Somebody tipped them."

"Are you surprised?"

"Yeah. Surprised I expected the cops to play it straight for a change. You wouldn't have the address of that union, by any chance?"

"No, but I can get it. Hold a second."

A sweet union scam like the Circular Distributors had "Outfit" written all over it—and Captain Tubbo Gilbert, head of the State Prosecutor's Police, was known as the richest cop in Chicago. Tubbo was a bagman and police fixer so deep in Frank Nitti's pocket he had Nitti's lint up his nose.

Lou was back: "It's at seven North Racine. That's Madison and Racine."

"Well, hell—that's spitting distance from Skid Row."

"Yeah. So?"

"So that explains the scam—that 'union' takes hobos and makes day laborers out of them. No wonder they charge daily dues. It's just bums handing out ad circulars. . . ."

"I'd say that's a good guess, Nate."

I thanked Lou and went back to the booth, where Barney was brooding about what a louse his friend Heller was.

"I got something to do," I told him.

"What?"

"My kind of kaddish."

Less than two miles from the prominent department stores of the Loop they'd been fleecing, the Circular Distributors Union had their headquarters on the doorstep of Skid Row and various Hoovervilles. This Madison Street area, just north of Greek town, was a seedy mix of flop-houses, marginal apartment buildings, and storefront businesses, mostly bars. Union headquarters was on the second floor of a two-story brick building whose bottom floor was a plumbing supply outlet.

I went up the squeaking stairs and into the union hall, a big high-ceilinged open room with a few glassed-in offices toward the front, to the left and right. Ceiling fans whirred lazily, stirring stale smoky air; folding chairs and card tables were scattered everywhere on the scuffed wooden floor, and seated at some were unshaven, tattered "members" of the union. Across the far end stretched a bar, behind which a burly blond guy in rolled-up white shirt-sleeves was polishing a glass. More hobos leaned against the bar, having beers.

I ordered a mug from the bartender, who had a massive skull and tiny dark eyes and a sullen kiss of a mouth.

I salted the brew as I tossed him a nickel. "Hear you had a raid here this morning."

He ignored the question. "This hall's for union members only."

"Jeez, it looks like a saloon."

"Well, it's a union hall. Drink up and move along."

"There's a fin in it for you, if you answer a few questions."

He thought that over; leaned in. "Are you a cop?"

"No. Private."

"Who hired you?"

"Goldblatt's."

He thought some more. The tiny eyes narrowed. "Let's hear the questions."

"What do you know about the Gross kid's murder?"

"Not a damn thing."

"Was Rooney here last night?"

"Far as I know, he was home in bed asleep."

"Know where he lives?"

"No."

"You don't know where your boss lives."

"No. All I know is he's a swell guy. He don't have nothin' to do with these department-store shakedowns the cops are tryin' to pin on him. It's union-busting, is what it is."

"Union-busting." I had a look around at the bleary-eyed clientele in their patched clothes. "You have to be a union, first, 'fore you can get busted up."

"What's *that* supposed to mean?"

"It means this is a scam. Rooney pulls in winos, gets 'em day-labor jobs for $3.25 a day, then they come up here to pay their daily dues of a quarter, and blow the rest on beer or booze. In other words, first the bums pass out ad fliers, then they come here and just plain pass out."

"I think you better scram. Otherwise I'm gonna have to throw you down the stairs."

I finished the beer. "I'm leaving. But you know what? I'm not gonna give you that fin. I'm afraid you'd just drink it up."

I could feel his eyes on my back as I left, but I'd have heard him if he came out from around the bar. I was starting down the stairs when the door below opened and Sergeant Pribyl, looking irritated, came up to meet me on the landing, halfway. He looked more his usual dapper self, but his eyes were black-bagged.

"What's the idea, Heller?"

"I just wanted to come bask in the reflected glory of your triumphant raid this morning."

"What's that supposed to mean?"

"It means when Tubbo's boys are on the case, the Outfit gets advance notice."

He winced. "That's not the way it was. I don't know why Rooney and Berry and the others blew. But nobody in our office warned 'em off."

"Are you sure?"

He clearly wasn't. "Look, I can't have you messing in this. We're on the damn case, okay? We're maintaining surveillance from across the way . . . that's how we spotted you."

"Peachy. Twenty-four-hour surveillance, now?"

"No." He seemed embarrassed. "Just day shift."

"You want some help?"

"What do you mean?"

"Loan me the key to your stakeout crib. I'll keep night watch. Got a phone in there?"

"Yeah."

"I'll call you if Rooney shows. You got pictures of him and the others you can give me?"

"Well . . ."

"What's the harm? Or would Tubbo lower the boom on you if you really did your job?"

He sighed. Scratched his head and came to a decision. "This is unofficial, okay? But there's a possibility the door to that apartment's gonna be left unlocked tonight."

"Do tell."

"Third floor—three-oh-one." He raised a cautionary finger. "We'll try this for one night . . . no showboating, okay? Call me if one of 'em shows."

"Sure. You tried their homes?"

He nodded. "Nothing. Rooney lives on North Ridgeland in Oak Park. Four kids. Wife's a pleasant, matronly type."

"Fat, you mean."

"She hasn't seen Rooney for several weeks. She says he's away from home a lot."

"Keeping a guard posted there?"

"Yeah. And that *is* twenty-four hour." He sighed, shook his head. "Heller, there's a lot about this case that doesn't make sense."

"Such as?"

"That maroon Plymouth. We never saw a car like that in the entire six weeks we had the union hall under surveillance. Rooney drives a blue LaSalle coupe."

"Any maroon Plymouths reported stolen?"

He shook his head. "And it hasn't turned up abandoned, either. They must still have the car."

"Is Rooney *that* stupid?"

"We can always hope," Pribyl said.

I sat in an easy chair with sprung springs by the window in Room 301 of the residential hotel across from the union hall. It wasn't a flophouse cage, but it wasn't a suite at the Drake, either. Anyway, in the dark it looked fine. I had a flask of rum to keep me company, and the breeze fluttering the sheer, frayed curtains remained unseasonably cool.

Thanks to some photos Pribyl left me, I now knew what Rooney looked like: a good-looking, oval-faced smoothie, in his mid forties, just starting to lose his dark, slicked-back hair; his eyes were hooded, his mouth soft, sensual, sullen. There were also photos of the union's so-called business agent Henry Berry, a mousy little guy with glasses, and pockmarked, cold-eyed Herbert Arnold, V.P. of the union.

But none of them stopped by the union hall—only a steady stream of winos and bums went in and out.

Then, around seven, I spotted somebody who didn't fit the profile.

It was a guy I knew—a fellow private op, Eddie McGowan, a Pinkerton man, in uniform, meaning he was on night-watchman duty. A number of the merchants along Madison must have pitched in for his services.

I left the stakeout and waited down on the street, in front of the plumbing-supply store, for Eddie to come back out. It didn't take long—maybe ten minutes.

"Heller!" he said. He was a skinny, tow-haired guy in his late twenties with a bad complexion and a good outlook. "What no good are you up to?"

"The Goldblatt's shooting. That kid they killed was working with me."

"Oh! I didn't know! Heard about the shooting, of course, but didn't read the papers or anything. So you were involved in that? No kidding."

"No kidding. You on watchman duty?"

"Yeah. Up and down the street here, all night."

"Including the union hall?"

"Sure." He grinned. "I usually stop up for a free drink 'bout this time of night."

"Can you knock off for a couple of minutes? For another free drink?"

"Sure!"

Soon we were in a smoky booth in back of a bar and Eddie was having a boilermaker on me.

"See anything unusual last night," I asked, "around the union hall?"

"Well . . . I had a drink there, around two o'clock in the morning. *That* was a first."

"A drink? Don't they close earlier than that?"

"Yeah. Around eleven. That's all the longer it takes for their 'members' to lap up their daily dough."

"So what were you doing up there at two?"

He shrugged. "Well, I noticed the lights was on upstairs, so I unlocked the street-level door and went up. Figured Alex . . . that's the bartender, Alex Davidson . . . might have forgot to turn out the lights 'fore he left. The door up there was locked, but then Mr. Rooney opened it up and told me to come on in."

"Why would he do that?"

"He was feelin' pretty good. Looked like he was workin' on a bender. Anyway, he insists I have a drink with him. I says, sure. Turns out Davidson is still there."

"No kidding?"

"No kidding. So Alex serves me a beer. Berry—the union's business agent—he was there, too. He was in his cups also. So was Rooney's wife—she was there, and also feeling giddy."

I thought about Pribyl's description of Mrs. Rooney as a matronly woman with four kids. "His *wife* was there?"

"Yeah, the lucky stiff."

"Lucky?"

"You should see the dame! Good-lookin' tomato with big dark eyes and a nice shape on her."

"About how old?"

"Young. Twenties. It'd take the sting out of a ball and chain, I can tell you that."

"Eddie . . . here's a fin."

"Heller, the beer's enough!"

"The fin is for telling this same story to Sergeant Pribyl of the state's attorney's coppers."

"Oh. Okay."

"But do it tomorrow."

He smirked. "Okay. I got rounds to make, anyway."

So did I.

At around eleven-fifteen, bartender Alex Davidson was leaving the union hall; his back was turned, as he was locking the street-level door, and I put my nine-millimeter in it.

"Hi, Alex," I said. "Don't turn around, unless you prefer being gut-shot."

"If it's a stickup, all I got's a couple bucks. Take 'em and bug off!"

"No such luck. Leave that door unlocked. We're gonna step back inside."

He grunted and opened the door and we stepped inside.

"Now we're going up the stairs," I said, and we did, in the dark, the wooden steps whining under our weight. He was a big man; I'd have had my work cut out for me—if I hadn't had the gun.

We stopped at the landing where earlier I had spoken to Sergeant Pribyl. "Here's fine," I said.

I allowed him to face me in the near-dark.

He sneered. "You're that private dick."

"I'm sure you mean that in the nicest way. Let me tell you a little more about me. See, we're going to get to know each other, Alex."

"Like hell."

I slapped him with the nine-millimeter.

He wiped blood off his mouth and looked at me with hate, but also with fear. And he made no more smart-ass remarks.

"I'm the private dick whose twenty-one-year-old partner got shot in the head last night."

Now the fear was edging out the hate; he knew he might die in this dark stairwell.

"I know you were here with Rooney and Berry and the broad last night, serving up drinks as late as two in the morning," I said. "Now you're going to tell me the whole story—or you're the one who's getting tossed down the fucking stairs."

He was trembling now; a big hulk of a man trembling with fear. "I didn't have anything to do with the murder. Not a damn thing!"

"Then why cover for Rooney and the rest?"

"You saw what they're capable of!"

"Take it easy, Alex. Just tell the story."

Rooney had come into the office about noon the day of the shooting; he had started drinking and never stopped. Berry and several other union "officers" arrived and angry discussions about being under surveillance by the state's attorney's cops were accompanied by a lot more drinking.

"The other guys left around five, but Rooney and Berry, they just hung around drinking all evening. Around midnight Rooney jotted a phone number on a matchbook and gave it to me to call for him. It was a Berwyn number. A woman answered. I handed him the phone and he said to her, 'Bring one.' "

"One what?" I asked.

"I'm gettin' to that. She showed up around one o'clock—good-looking dame with black hair and eyes so dark they coulda been black, too."

"Who was she?"

"I don't know. Never saw her before. She took a gun out of her purse and gave it to Rooney."

"That was what he asked her to bring."

"I guess. It was a thirty-eight revolver, a Colt, I think. Anyway, Rooney and Berry were both pretty drunk; I don't know what *her* excuse was. So Rooney takes the gun and says, 'We got a job to pull at Goldblatt's. We're gonna throw some slugs at the windows and watchmen.' "

"How did the girl react?"

He swallowed. "She laughed. She said, 'I'll go along and watch the fun.' Then they all went out."

Jesus.

Finally I said, "What did you do?"

"They told me to wait for 'em. Keep the bar open. They came back in, laughing like hyenas. Rooney says to me, 'You want to see the way he keeled over?' And I says, 'Who?' And he says, 'The guard at Goldblatt's.' Berry laughs and says, 'We really let him have it.' "

"That kid was twenty-one, Alex. It was his goddamn birthday."

The bartender was looking down. "They laughed and joked about it till Berry passed out. About six in the morning, Rooney has me pile Berry in a cab. Rooney and the twist slept in his office for maybe an hour. Then they came out, looking sober and kind of . . . scared. He warned me not to tell anybody what I seen, unless I wanted to trade my job for a morgue slab."

"Colorful. Tell me, Alex. You got that girl's phone number in Berwyn?"

"I think it's upstairs. You can put that gun away. I'll help you."

It was dark, but I could see his face well enough; the big man's eyes looked damp. The fear was gone. Something else was in its place. Shame? Something.

We went upstairs, he unlocked the union hall and, under the bar, found the matchbook with the number written inside: Berwyn 2981.

"You want a drink before you go?" he asked.

"You know," I said, "I think I'll pass."

I went back to my office to use the reverse-listing phone book that told me Berwyn 2981 was Rosalie Rizzo's number; and that Rosalie Rizzo lived at 6348 West 13th Street in Berwyn.

First thing the next morning, I borrowed Barney's Hupmobile and drove out to Berwyn, the clean, tidy hunky suburb populated in part by the late Mayor Cermak's patronage people. But finding a Rosalie Rizzo in this largely Czech and Bohemian area came as no surprise: Capone's Cicero was a stone's throw away.

The woman's address was a three-story brick apartment building, but none of the mailboxes in the vestibule bore her name. I found the janitor and gave him Rosalie Rizzo's description. It sounded like Mrs. Riggs to him.

"She's a doll," the janitor said. He was heavy-set and needed a shave; he licked his thick lips as he thought about her. "Ain't seen her since yesterday noon."

That was about nine hours after Stanley was killed.

He continued: "Her and her husband was going to the country, she said. Didn't expect to be back for a couple of weeks."

Her husband.

"What'll a look around their apartment cost me?"

He licked his lips again. "Two bucks?"

Two bucks it was; the janitor used his passkey and left me to it. The well-appointed little apartment included a canary that sang in its gilded cage, a framed photo of slick Boss Rooney on an end table, and a closet containing two sawed-off shotguns and a repeating rifle.

I had barely started to poke around when I had company: a slender, gray-haired woman in a flowered print dress.

"Oh!" she said, coming in the door she'd unlocked.

"Can I help you?" I asked.

"Who are you?" Her voice had the lilt of an Italian accent.

Under the circumstances, the truth seemed prudent. "A private detective."

"My daughter is not here! She and her-a husband, they go to vacation. Up north some-a-where. I just-a come to feed the canary!"

"Please don't be frightened. Do you know where she's gone, exactly?"

"No. But . . . maybe my husband do. He is-a downstairs. . . ."

She went to a window, threw it open, and yelled something frantically down in Italian.

I eased her aside in time to see a heavy-set man jump into a maroon Plymouth with a sliver swan on the radiator cap, and cream-colored wheels, and squeal away.

And when I turned, the slight gray-haired woman was just as gone. Only she hadn't squealed.

The difference, this time, was a license number for the maroon coupe; I'd seen it: 519-836. In a diner I made a call to Lou Sapperstein, who made a call to the motor vehicle bureau, and phoned back with the scoop: The Plymouth was licensed to Rosalie Rizzo, but the address was different—2848 South Cuyler Avenue, in Berwyn.

The bungalow was typical for Berwyn—a tidy little frame house on a small, perfect lawn. My guess was this was her folks' place. In back was a small matching, but unattached, garage, on the alley. Peeking in the garage windows, I saw the maroon coupe and smiled.

"Is Rosalie in trouble again?"

The voice was female, sweet, young.

I turned and saw a slender, almost beautiful teenage girl with dark eyes and bouncy, dark, shoulder-length hair. She wore a navy-blue sailor-ish playsuit. Her pretty white legs were bare.

"Are you Rosalie's sister?"

"Yes. Is she in trouble?"

"What makes you say that?"

"I just know Rosalie, that's all. That man isn't really her husband, is he? That Mr. Riggs."

"No."

"Are you here about her accident?"

"No. Where is she?"

"Are you a police officer?"

"I'm a detective. Where did she go?"

"Papa's inside. He's afraid he's going to be in trouble."

"Why's that?"

"Rosalie put her car in our garage yesterday. She said she was in an accident and it was damaged and not to use it. She's going to have it repaired when she gets back from vacation."

"What does that have to do with your papa being scared?"

"Rosalie's going to be mad as h at him, that he used her car." She shrugged. "He said he looked at it and it didn't look damaged to him, and if Mama was going to have to look after Rosalie's g.d. canary, well, he'd sure as h use *her* gas not his."

"I can see his point. Where did your sister go on vacation?"

"She didn't say. Up north someplace. Someplace she and Mr. Riggs like to go to, to . . . you know. To get away?"

I called Sergeant Pribyl from a gas station where I was getting Barney's Hupmobile tank refilled: I suggested he have another talk with bartender Alex Davidson, gave him the address of "Mr. and Mrs. Riggs," and told him where he could find the maroon Plymouth.

He was grateful but a little miffed about all I had done on my own.

"So much for not showboating," he said, almost huffily. "You've found everything but the damn suspects."

"They've gone up north somewhere," I said.

"Where up north?"

"They don't seem to've told anybody. Look, I have a piece of evidence you may need."

"What?"

"When you talk to Davidson, he'll tell you about a matchbook Rooney wrote the girl's number on. I got the matchbook."

It was still in my pocket. I took it out, idly, and shut the girl's number away, revealing the picture on the matchbook cover: a blue moon hovered surrealistically over a white lake on which two blue lovers paddled in a blue canoe—Eagle River Lodge, Wisconsin.

"I suppose we'll need that," Pribyl's voice over the phone said, "when the time comes."

"I suppose," I said, and hung up.

Eagle River was a town of 1,386 (so said the sign) just inside the Vilas County line at the junction of US 45 and Wisconsin State Highway 70. The country was beyond beautiful, green pines towering higher than Chicago skyscrapers, glittering blue lakes nestling in woodland pockets.

The lodge I was looking for was on Silver Lake, a gas station attendant told me. A beautiful dusk was settling on the woods as I drew into the parking of the large resort sporting a red city-style neon sign saying: DINING AND DANCE. Log-cabin cottages were flung here and there around the periphery like Paul Bunyan's Tinkertoys. Each one was just secluded enough—ideal for couples, married or un-.

Even if Rooney and his dark-haired honey weren't staying here, it was time to find a room: I'd been driving all day. When Barney loaned me his Hupmobile, he'd had no idea the kind of miles I'd put on it. Dead tired, I went to the desk and paid for a cabin.

The guy behind the counter had a plaid shirt on, but he was small and squinty and Hitler-moustached, smoking a stogie, and looked more like a bookie than a lumberjack.

I told him some friends of mine were supposed to be staying here.

"We don't have anybody named Riggs registered."

"How 'bout Mr. and Mrs. Rooney?"

"Them either. How many friends you got, anyway?"

"Why, did I already catch the limit?"

Before I headed to my cabin, I grabbed some supper in the rustic restaurant. I placed my order with a friendly brunette girl of about nineteen with plenty of personality, and makeup. A road-company Paul Whiteman outfit was playing "Sophisticated Lady" in the adjacent dance hall, and I went over and peeked in, to look for familiar faces. A number of couples were cutting a rug, but not Rooney and Rosalie. Or Henry Berry or Herbert Arnold, either. I went back and had my green salad and fried trout and well-buttered baked potato; I was full and sleepy when I stumbled toward my guest cottage under the light of a moon that bathed the woods ivory.

Walking along the path, I spotted something: snuggled next to one of the secluded cabins was a blue LaSalle coupe with Cook County plates.

Suddenly I wasn't sleepy. I walked briskly back to the lodge check-in desk and batted the bell to summon the stogie-chewing clerk.

"Cabin seven," I said. "I think that blue LaSalle is my friends' car."

His smirk turned his Hitler moustache Chaplinesque. "You want I should break out the champagne?"

"I just want to make sure it's them. Dark-haired doll and an older guy, good-looking, kinda sleepy-eyed, just starting to go bald?"

"That's them." He checked his register. "That's the Ridges." He frowned. "Are they usin' a phony name?"

"Does a bear shit in the woods?"

He squinted. "You sure they're friends of yours?"

"Positive. Don't call their room and tell 'em I'm here, though—I want to surprise them. . . ."

I knocked with my left hand; my right was filled with the nine-millimeter. Nothing. I knocked again.

"Who is it?" a male voice said gruffly. "*What* is it?"

"Complimentary fruit basket from the management."

"Go away!"

I kicked the door open.

The lights were off in the little cabin, but enough moonlight came in with me through the doorway to reveal the pair in bed, naked. She was sitting up, her mouth and eyes open in a silent scream, gathering the sheets up protectively over white skin, her dark hair blending with the darkness of the room, making a cameo of her face. He was diving off the bed for the sawed-off shotgun, but I was there to kick it away, wishing I hadn't, wishing I'd let him grab it so I could have had an excuse to put one in his forehead, right where he'd put one in Stanley's.

Boss Rooney wasn't boss of anything now: He was just a naked, balding, forty-four-year-old scam artist, sprawled on the floor. Kicking him would have been easy.

So I did; in the stomach.

He clutched himself and puked. Apparently he'd had the trout, too.

I went over and slammed the door shut, or as shut as it could be, half off its hinges. Pointing the gun at her retching, naked boyfriend, I said to the girl, "Turn on the light and put on your clothes."

She nodded and did as she was told. In the glow of a nightstand lamp, I caught glimpses of her white, well-formed body as she stepped into her step-ins; but you know what? She didn't do a thing for me.

"Is Berry here?" I asked Rooney. "Or Arnold?"

"N . . . no," he managed.

"If you're lying," I said, "I'll kill you."

The girl said shrilly, "They aren't here!"

"You can put your clothes on, too," I told Rooney. "If you have another gun hidden somewhere, do me a favor. Make a play for it."

His hooded eyes flared. "Who the hell are you?"

"The private cop you *didn't* kill the other night."

He lowered his gaze. "Oh."

The girl was sitting on the bed, weeping; body heaving.

"Take it easy on her, will you?" he said, zipping his fly. "She's just a kid."

I was opening a window to ease the stench of his vomit.

"Sure," I said. "I'll say kaddish for her."

I handcuffed the lovebirds to the bed and called the local law; they in turn called the state prosecutor's office in Chicago, and Sergeants Pribyl and Gray made the long drive up the next day to pick up the pair.

It seemed the two cops had already caught Henry Berry—a tipster gave them the West Chicago Avenue address of a second-floor room he was holed up in.

I admitted to Pribyl that I'd been wrong about Tubbo tipping off Rooney and the rest about the raid.

"I figure Rooney lammed out of sheer panic," I said, "the morning after the murder."

Pribyl saw it the same way.

The following March, Pribyl arrested Herbert Arnold running a Northside handbill-distributing agency.

Rooney, Berry, and Rosalie Rizzo were all convicted of murder; the two men got life, and the girl twenty years. Arnold hadn't been part of the kill-happy joyride that took Stanley Gross's young life, and got only one to five for conspiracy and extortion.

None of it brought Stanley Gross back, nor did my putting on a beanie and sitting with the Gross family, suffering through a couple of stints at a storefront synagogue on Roosevelt Road.

But it did get Barney off my ass.

AUTHOR'S NOTE: While Nathan Heller is a fictional character, this story is based on a real case—names have not been changed, and the events are fundamentally true; source material included an article by John J. McPhaul and information provided by my research associate, George Hagenauer, whom I thank for his insights and suggestions.

BENJAMIN M. SCHUTZ

"Mary, Mary, Shut The Door" is one of the most stunning short stories ever written in the private eye genre. Benjamin M. Schutz (1949–) won both the Edgar and the Shamus for it. In larger perspective, it is but one part of his fine Leo Haggerty saga, one of the truly underappreciated bodies of work in today's private eye field.

Schutz hasn't published much of late, busy, one assumes, with his work as a clinical psychologist specializing in child custody and child sexual abuse cases. One hopes to see another novel from him soon.

Lost and Found

Acknowledgments:

I'd like to thank the following people for the gracious donation of their expertise. Any errors are entirely my responsibility. Chanda Kinsey, defense attorney; Johnny Ringo of Carefree Jeep Tours; Paula Edgin, JoAnne Reiss and Arllys Filmer-Ennett, concierges at The Boulders; Sherry Mehalic of Travel Partners; and Rhoda K. Schutz.

"So, how would you like another shot at Derek Marshall?"

Inside, you learned to speak once and listen twice. I listened.

"Not interested?"

"Not saying. What does a 'second shot' mean?"

"He's come out of hiding. He left San Francisco, drove to San Diego and jumped on a cruise ship to Mexico. He has a woman with him."

"You think he plans to kill her?"

"I don't know. That's one of the things I want you to find out."

I looked at the old man. I hadn't seen Enzo Scolari in six, maybe seven years. Time had leached a lot of life out of him. He was frail and bony. Waiting for my reply, he massaged the swollen arthritic knuckles of his hands. His wispy, white eyebrows were now as unruly as smoke.

Six years ago he had hired me to prevent his niece's marriage to Derek Marshall. I wasn't able to do that. She married Marshall, and in short order he murdered her and became a millionaire. For two years after that I kept tabs on him, hoping that he'd step wrong and I'd be there to drop a net over him. It didn't happen.

"Why me?"

"I can't think of anyone better qualified, Mr. Haggerty. You know Marshall. You know how he works. You have a personal stake in this, or at least you did. And you're available. You can follow him wherever he goes."

"Marshall knows me, too. I can't get near him. He'll make me and that's the end of that."

"I don't think so, Mr. Haggerty. I knew you then and I would never recognize you now. You've changed quite a bit. How much weight have you put on?"

I shrugged. "Thirty-six pounds."

"It looks good on you. All muscle. How did you do that? I hear the food is not fit for animals."

"I lifted weights four hours a day, seven days a week. That and good genes. I can turn shit into muscle."

"That seems to be the case. With your shaved head and goatee, sunglasses and a hat, he'll never recognize you."

I let it pass. "I lost my license. I can't carry a gun. I have no contacts anymore. I don't know how I could be of any use to you."

Scolari waved my words away with a swat of his bony hand. "You didn't get stupid, did you? You were a bright man. I'm betting you still are. You don't need a license or a gun, just your wits. As for contacts, I know all you'll ever need to about Derek Marshall. I maintained my own surveillance on Mr. Marshall after he left Virginia."

Scolari touched the switch on his wheelchair, spun towards the desk and poured himself a glass of water. His hand shook so badly that he had to stop two inches from his mouth and let his head close the distance. He drained the glass and put it on the desk.

Scolari turned back to me.

"What was prison like, Mr. Haggerty?"

"Just like any gated community, Mr. Scolari. Too many rules."

"How does it feel to be back in the world?"

"I wouldn't know. I'm just out. I'm not back."

"Yes, well let me tell you about Derek Marshall. After he settled in San Francisco, I had our local office keep track of all the women he dated.

After the first date, we sent them a press kit, so to speak. All the clippings about Gina's death, the inquest, the unanswered questions. Most of them never went out with him again. There were a few that we could not dissuade. However, Derek Marshall spent many, many nights alone. I also tried to recover the money he got when Gina died. I was not quite as successful there. I have many business contacts all over the country. Those that I could influence in San Francisco made it hard for him to get loans, or closed mutual funds to him. I ruined a couple of his investments; cost him and some other people quite a bit of money. All of this forced Mr. Marshall into a very low profile lifestyle. He wasn't enjoying the spoils of his crime.

"I'm worried about this trip to Mexico. It's his first attempt to shake my surveillance. I want to know what he's up to. Is he planning to disappear? Who is the woman with him? Is she an accomplice to his plans? Is she in danger from him? That's where you come in, Mr. Haggerty. As I said, you know Derek, how he thinks. You have no ties to this area anymore, am I correct?"

I just listened.

"I kept track of you, too. You have no license, no job, and no career. No family. Your friends in the police department can't help you because you're a felon. Same with your friends at other agencies. No one can use you. You have no home, no money. Your lawyer got all that.

"I, however, have a plane ticket for you, a car waiting at the airport in Tucson, and a cabin on the ship where he's staying. Right now they are wet-docked at Puerto Penasco for repairs. They'll be there for three days. I also have a company credit card for you. While you're on the job, all your living expenses will be covered."

"What do you want from me?"

"Find out what he's up to. I don't want to lose him. That's the first thing. Find out who the girl is. If she's in danger, warn her off. I don't want anyone else to go through what I've gone through."

"That's it?"

"That's it. Report to me as soon as you find out anything. I don't care what time it is. I sleep badly when I sleep at all. That's your 'second shot.' Are you interested?"

Scolari's offer beat everything else I had going. I was too old to be starting over from scratch.

"When's the next plane out?"

In the air over Tucson, I thought about my talk with old man Scolari. He was awfully eager to get me out here with Marshall. Why? Maybe he blamed me for Gina's death. Maybe he'd decided to have us both killed? No. I went to prison two years after Derek left. He never tried it then and he had plenty of time. Maybe he wants to set me up for Derek's death, do it that way. Why now? He can maneuver me into position a lot easier than before. Five years ago a lot more people would have cared about what happened to me, not now. Maybe he was tired of waiting and decided to make something happen. How sick was he?

Maybe what I should do is milk this for all it's worth. File dummy reports, stay away from Marshall in case it's a frame and see how long I can ride this until he catches on. They say living well is the best revenge. Besides, what's the worst that he could do, fire me? Why am I not scared?

We began to descend over Tucson. I looked out the window at the ground rushing up at us. Most crashes occur on takeoffs and landings. I watched all the way down. We bounced once on the runway, then settled down and began to slow.

Scolari had asked me how it felt to be back. I really didn't know. I remember thinking about Humpty Dumpty when I was sentenced. How some men shattered when they hit bottom, while others armored themselves all the way down and they didn't feel a thing. Not then, not ever.

My rental car was in a lot across the street from the airport. I threw my bag in the passenger seat, got in and turned on the air conditioner. The airport information board said it was 110 degrees today. The rental agent had given me a courtesy map of the area. I unfolded it and decided on a route. I pulled out of the lot and entered the freeway traffic that ran by the airport.

I drove south out of America into Mexico. My last case had started in Mexico. It ended in the Maryland State Penitentiary Maximum Security Facility at Jessup. There was only one thing I knew for certain. I was not going into a Mexican prison.

I crossed the border at Nogales and headed towards Hermosillo. Halfway there I turned west towards Mexicali, then south again to the Gulf of California.

God must have had only a few crayons left in his box when he got to the desert. Everything was one shade of brown or another. Scraggly plants sprouted up on the hills that flanked the road. Each group had its own shepherd; a tall cactus watching over it. Some were as straight and narrow as Giacometti's men. Others had arms: some up; some down; some both, signalling each other like giant green semaphores.

An hour or so later I saw the sign for the docks, pulled off the road and stopped at the guard's station. Razor wire ringed the area.

"Name, sir?"

"Haggerty, Leo Haggerty."

"Yes sir. You are registered on the *Calypso Moonbeam*. Drive straight ahead to the parking lot. Check in with security at the gangway."

I surrendered my passport, got my security pass, room key, and directions to my cabin. It was clean. It was bigger than I was used to, it was all mine, and I had the key to the door.

I dropped my bag on the floor and lay down on the bed. I took off my sunglasses and stared at the ceiling fan. Its blades seemed to move as slowly as the hands of a prison clock. It wasn't long before I was asleep.

I awoke lying on my back and looked at my watch. It was after four o'clock. I checked the ship's map and found the lounge. I left the room and went there.

I sat in a soft chair and ordered a gin and tonic from the waitress. My seat allowed me to watch the entrance to the bar and the dining room. At the very least, I ought to see what Derek looked like these days. No use letting him surprise me. I sipped my drink and watched the people come and go. It was almost eight when Marshall showed up. The last seven years had not hurt him any. He'd put on a few pounds and erased his jawline along the way. His hair was still fine and brown, but he parted it on the left now. The glasses were gone, so I guessed he wore contacts.

He had his arm around a tall blonde, whose pale blue eyes and bright smile stood out against her tan face like turquoise and ivory in the sandy desert. Derek laughed at something the maitre d' said, squeezed his friend to him and kissed her ear. I took a long slow pull on my drink and thought of Gina Dalesandro. I could still see her wiping tears off her cheek on her wedding day and asking me, "What's so wrong with me? Can you tell me that?"

I whispered what I hadn't said then. "Nothing, Gina, not one single thing. I'm sorry I've darkened your day. I'm sorry I didn't do better." I hadn't been able to save her back then and I'd tried my best. This grinning bastard had murdered her and gotten rich doing it. I raised that drink to Gina's memory and asked her to "wish me better luck this time." I raised the rest to forget.

I nursed a port until Marshall and the girl were done eating and then followed them out of the dining room. They walked back to the cabins and entered room 116, a deck below me.

Still haunted by Gina Dalesandro, I went back to my room and called Scolari. It was 1:30 a.m. back east, and, good as his word, he picked up on the second ring.

"Yes."

"Mr. Scolari, this is Leo Haggerty. I've located Derek Marshall. I saw him at dinner this evening. He has a woman with him. A blonde, tall and very tanned. Do you know anything about her?"

"No, we're still working on it. What else have you found out?"

"Not much. I'll follow him tomorrow, see if I can get a line on what he's doing here. If I have to, I'll try to get closer to the woman, see if she's in any danger and warn her off."

"Careful, Mr. Haggerty. I don't want Marshall spooked. He hasn't recognized you, I presume?"

"No."

"We'll try to find out who she is and if she's in any danger."

"Call me here anytime with any information you get. Especially on the girl."

"Of course, Mr. Haggerty. You'll be the first to know. Goodnight."

I hadn't lifted or run today, so I did seven hundred sit-ups as penance, showered and lay naked on the cool, clean sheets of the bed. I listened hard into the darkness. No one was crying, or cursing. No one was praying or screaming. No one was begging for the mercy that never came. In the middle of the night, I got up and left my room, just because I could.

I awoke around seven, slipped into a T-shirt, shorts and running shoes, and trotted down the gangway. I showed the security guy my pass and headed for the guard's station. I passed him and turned right down the road and ran off into the desert. I came back an hour later.

I trudged back up the gangway. At the top, a woman was putting up a notice on the bulletin board. I stopped to read it.

She looked at me. "How far did you go?"

I shrugged. "Six miles."

"You take any water with you?"

"Nah, it wasn't that far."

"Provided you don't turn an ankle, step on a rattler, and you stay on the road. But if things go wrong, you'll need that water because you're sweating quite a bit. Heatstroke and dehydration can drop anyone. You ever been out in the desert before?"

"No, I haven't. Maybe my ignorance has led to disrespect."

"Why don't you come on my hike this morning." She tapped the notice. "You'll learn more about the desert than you ever wanted to know."

Her chestnut hair was pulled back under a beige baseball cap and flowed out the back, thick and smooth as a thoroughbred's well-curried tail. Silvered sunglasses shielded her eyes like a beetle's shiny shell. I found that strangely reassuring.

"When is it?"

"Nine."

"Okay," I said, and walked away. I went into my room, stripped down and took a shower, ending it with the icy needle spray I knew so well was only one mistake away.

I had a light breakfast, then went outside to find my guide. She was standing out by the notice board alternately staring at her clipboard and looking all around to see who was missing. I'd once heard a camp counselor call it "urchin searchin."

I pulled up in front of her.

"Looks like you're it."

"Hike still on?"

"Sure. Here, take this." She gave me a water bottle on a belt. I saw she had one on her hip, so I strapped mine on.

"We may as well start with the rules of the desert. They're real simple. This is God's country, not man's. We're not welcome here. It's not user friendly. If you don't respect that, it will kill you. There are three absolutes: Never travel without water; never go out in the desert alone; always tell someone where you are going. Got that?"

"Got it."

"You ought to wear a hat. That shiny scalp of yours is a solar collector."

"I'll get one after the hike."

"Here, put this on your head, like a do-rag." She handed me a bandanna from her back pocket. "You look like you're in pretty good shape.

Why don't we go out to those mountains over there." She pointed into the distance. "It's probably a couple of hours out. We can see a number of things on the way."

"Sounds good."

She held out her hand. "My name's Kiki. Kiki Davenport."

"Leo Haggerty." I shook it, and then tied the bandanna around my head.

"Where are you from?" she asked and turned to lead the way. She had on a small fanny pack.

"Back east."

We left the road and walked out into the desert. After about twenty minutes she stopped by a twisted tree decorated with a fuzzy necklace.

"This is a chain fruit cholla. It's a kind of cactus. I like to start with them to show people the enormous variety of the cactus family."

"The big ones with the arms. They look like they're guarding the others. What are they?"

"Those are Saguaro. The largest of all the cacti. It's funny you should describe them like that. Saguaro means *sentinel* in Spanish.

"I find cacti fascinating. This is a very harsh environment. Great heat and light, very little water. The parameters for survival are very narrow, not only do they survive, they thrive. And they do so in many, many ways. They remind me of how creative the will to live can be."

She looked out across the desert. "Here, let's look at this one." She walked off the path into the bush. I followed.

She looked like the land itself. All variations of brown, from her beige hiking boots, white socks and tanned skin, to her khaki shorts and cream shirt. She'd be hard to see at a distance. I made a note of that.

"This is a jumping cholla. Very, very nasty."

The cactus was covered with very fine spines so thick that they looked like a soft yellow fur. "Why?"

"This plant reproduces asexually. These last segments of the stalks get carried off by animals that brush up against them. The spines are hooked and so fine that they're almost impossible to get out. When the animal finally gets it off them it falls to the ground, roots and starts to grow."

"Why jumping cholla?"

"When it breaks off, it looks like it jumped onto you. The slightest contact leaves you covered in these spines. Bend down and take a closer look."

She squatted down and I got down next to her and looked at the tiny barbs on the spines. Six inches away, they were invisible.

I avoided looking at her but I could smell her; sweet and clean, flowers and spice.

"You go out into the desert, you should always carry a comb. That way you can get the cholla off if you have to. You slide the teeth down into the spines and flip it off. You can't use your other hand. They'll both wind up full of spines."

"I'll bet falling into one of these is a real mess."

"Oh yeah," she said, nodding in sincere agreement.

"Let's head for those rocks over there. It's a mile or so. We'll climb them, check out the valley beyond, and then head back." I followed her extended arm. She wore a large ring on her right hand, an oval, rose-colored stone in a heavy silver and gold setting.

I followed her back to the path and we set off in silence. For twenty minutes I walked in her footsteps up a gradual incline on a narrow, winding path. Eyes down, I watched her legs move, each step a precise placement on a flat rock surface. The steeper the incline, the closer the attention I paid. We stopped on a plateau.

"Look there," she said. I saw a paddle-shaped cactus with several of its paddle half chewed off.

"Javelinas."

"What's that?"

"Javelinas, peccaries, wild pigs. They eat prickly pears—spines and all. They travel in packs. Nasty customers if you're hunting them."

"Are they interested in hunting us?" I asked.

"No. I suppose if you got between a mother and her young they'd charge and drive you off.

"They've got very sharp tusks, and they'd give you a bad bite. I had an old boyfriend who used to hunt them with a bow and arrow. When they were cornered, they'd charge. Then they were real dangerous. They were really fast and they'd be on you before you could get a shot off."

"You go hunting with him?"

"Yeah."

"Ever get one?"

"No. Too fast. One of them opened my leg up, though."

She pointed down to her thigh. I saw a long white scar on the inside. "Up near the artery. I left the javelinas alone after that. You ever hunt?"

I waited too long to answer. It was a simple question. "No."

"Funny, I'd have thought you did. You have that look."

"And what look is that?"

"Patient, watchful. A stalker. You don't say much. Most people talk my ear off on these hikes. They tell me all about themselves, ask me all about myself. You take information in but you don't offer any. That's hunter behavior. Plus, you don't look like a businessman."

"Really? Now why is that?"

"Your muscles. Getting those is a full time job. You wouldn't have time for an office."

"Maybe muscles are my business, like Arnold Schwarzenegger."

"Sorry. I've never seen you in any muscle magazines."

"You read that many of them?"

She nodded her head. "For years. The boyfriend with the bow and arrows, he was a body builder. Mister Southwest 1990."

"I like the way your mind works, but I'm not a hunter. I'm just out here to relax and enjoy the scenery. So tell me, are there any animals to be worried about out here?"

She smiled, chuckled softly and shook her head. "Okay. Let's see. Everyone will tell you about the rattlesnakes, the Gila Monsters, the scorpions, and the tarantulas. They're all here, they're all dangerous, but you need to be stupid and unlucky to get bit. Simple rules for the biters: Look where you put your hands and feet; shake out your shoes before you put them on; don't reach into dark places, and watch where you step. That's about it, for them.

"Then there's cougars and bears. Bears aren't a big problem in the desert. Much more so up in the mountains. We do get cougars down here. They like javelina. They're pretty shy of humans, and attacks are rare but not unheard of. If you meet one, stop, then back away slowly. Don't turn your back to them. Don't run. If they attack, protect your neck. Cats kill by asphyxiation. They'll try to bite your throat and cut off your air. Keep your hands up, protect your eyes and throat, and try to stay on your feet. If you can find something to hit them with, a thick stick or a heavy rock, so much the better. Keep backing away. We're not on their regular diet, so unless they're starving to death or protecting their young they're not likely to keep up the attack in the face of resistance."

She turned and headed up the path. As the grade steepened, we slowed as the footing got worse. I gave her more of a lead. No reason if she fell to take us both down the hill. We went into a cave made of fallen boulders and climbed up through an opening between the stones to the top of a giant boulder. Two rocks were on top of it in the center like the crown of a hat.

She walked over near the edge, squatted down, took the water bottle off her belt, and squeezed out a long drink. I walked over next to her and did the same.

"Beautiful out here," I said.

"Sure is. I just love it. I don't ever want to leave."

"What brought you out here?"

She turned and looked at me. I saw my sunglasses in hers.

"An '85 Chevy with a black interior, a busted tape player and no A/C."

I laughed. She smiled. She sipped her water, then leaned back onto her butt and crossed her legs Indian-style. I stayed squatting. One time the warden wanted to talk to me about an accident in the laundry. He wanted to talk to me so badly that I was listed as escaped for two days. Turned out to be a mistake of course. I had fallen into a box in the power plant. It was only thirty inches deep but I couldn't get out. Not until the warden and I had that talk. Every day after that, I practiced being folded up like a shirt in case I ever escaped again. I can squat a good long while.

"What do you like about it?" I said.

"It's empty out here. I like empty. You don't have to work to keep your distance. It's big and it's old out here. Not human time or human efforts. It helps me keep a good perspective on things, not take them too seriously. How about you? Do you like it out here?"

"Yeah, I like it out here. Like you said, it's empty. Empty is good. I don't ever want to be crowded again."

I looked around. You could see for miles in any direction. Dark clouds were forming to the south, and the wind said they were headed this way.

I closed my eyes and tilted my face against the breeze.

"There's a storm coming. Summer storms are filled with lightning. We don't want to be up on the heights. Let's start down."

"I think I'll tempt fate a little longer. I haven't felt rain in a long time."

"Not smart. The storm isn't that far away. You'll get all the rain you want if we don't start back now. Monsoons can fill up these arroyos in a minute."

When I didn't move right away, she stood up and headed back down.

I sat on the hill and waited for the rain to come. The breeze picked up and caressed my face. A bolt of lightning flashed a jagged path to the ground. A thunderclap boomed almost immediately afterward. Time to go.

I caught up with her at the base of the rocks. "Uh, Mister Southwest 1990 . . . you still with him?"

She shook her head. "No, he left me for Mister Southwest 1993."

I hadn't said this much to a woman in years. I decided to press my luck. Prison, like the desert, helps you with perspective. "Could I buy you dinner tonight?"

She thought about that for a minute. "Okay."

"What time should I come by?"

"Oh," she tilted her head, "you wanted to eat it with me, too."

I must have made a face.

"I'm kidding. I'm kidding," she said.

"Staff isn't supposed to fraternize with the guests. Why don't we meet off the ship. There's a little place in town called the Aztec Café. How about I meet you there, say, eight o'clock?"

"Great."

She checked the sky. The clouds were rolling on while we stood still. "We really ought to head back."

"Sure." I followed her back into the desert. All the way back I wondered what color her eyes were.

At the ship's store I purchased a water bottle, some sunscreen and a soft, wide-brimmed hat.

I found Derek by the pool, reading a book about moneyless investing. He had a drink on the table next to him. His soft white body was starting to get a little pink: medium-rare. His legs were crossed at the ankles, and the upper foot tapped the lower one incessantly.

I walked around the pool and into the spa area. The weight room was beyond a pair of doors in the far wall. The blonde stood in line behind an enormously fat man. I brought up the rear.

The whale wanted a massage. He looked like he'd have to be stirred. I checked the blonde out head to toe, looking for any distinguishing marks. She had on a pair of clogs. They looked like hooves back in the '70s and they still did today. She adjusted her cover-up, and I saw a nice bruise on her right thigh. I glanced down into her bag, but it was fastened. She had a tennis bracelet on. It could have been diamonds, could have been rock candy for all I knew. No rings, but long hot pink nails.

"The couples massage, how long does that last?"

"It's about an hour," the attendant said.

"Okay. We'd like to schedule one this afternoon. Cabin 116. How late do you do them?"

"We schedule the last ones of the day at five p.m."

"Okay, let's do it then. We'd also like room service at seven thirty."

"Do you want to order now?"

"No. We'll call it in later."

"Very good. Your masseurs will be Carl and Rita."

"Where is the Jacuzzi?"

"Through the doors and into the ladies' locker room."

She picked up a towel from a woven basket next to the counter and glided off towards the locker room.

I took a quick glance at the schedule book to see what was entered. Just cabin numbers, no names. That made sense. Everything was automatically billed to the cabin to be settled up at departure.

"May I help you, sir?" asked a stocky girl with short dark hair wearing a green and beige uniform that made her look like a park ranger.

"Weights?"

"Through those doors."

"Anybody inside to spot?"

"No sir, we don't have free weights, just machines."

I nodded. I picked up a towel and walked into the weight room. It was empty and silent. I walked around the circuit of machines, looking at their maximum settings. No work here. I sat on a bench, pulled out my gloves and belt, and tossed my bag into the corner.

I saw Marshall through the glass. He was having a nice vacation. I was having a nice vacation. He didn't have the jumpy, worried look of a man on the run. No furtive glances of the frightened schemer trying to lose a shadow. Maybe he's up here having a nice time with some bimbo. They go back to San Francisco, I go to San Francisco. This is a good gig. I'm paid to live the good life watching someone else live the good life. Don't fuck this up, Derek, I thought to myself. I could get used to this. A life sentence of pointless luxury. Guilty, your honor. Show me no mercy.

I did the circuit slowly, drawing out the negatives on each rep, squeezing the most work out of the machines. The weights slid smoothly, silently, up and down their spines like a steel bellows I inflated with each effort.

In the yard, you set your load by hand, hoisting each plate onto the bar, slamming it against the others, metal on metal, clanging like a cell door. When I finished my workout, I rubbed my face and scalp with my towel and draped it around my neck.

I looked around the empty room. Here the weight meant nothing. There, you were watched by everyone. Sheer physical strength was important.

Early on I met all the animals. The spiders who run the joint; the great apes who did their bidding; the zombies; and the bunk bunnies. The great apes don't do the same time as everyone else, so I became a great ape and things got better.

The fact that I was in for killing a cop didn't hurt my status any. I didn't correct anyone who thought it was murder, but I also didn't claim it. Inside, you don't say anything you can't back up.

One thousand eight hundred and twenty-five days later they opened a door and returned me to the world. Bigger. Stronger. Harder.

You go to the property room before you leave in your shiny black state suit. They hand you a bus ticket and then give you your belongings in a brown manila envelope. They open it up and dump it out; your wallet, watch, some coins, a ring, keys, and a pen. Then they slide a form over for you to sign. I remember reading:"CHECK YOUR BELONGINGS. YOUR SIGNATURE CONFIRMS THAT EVERYTHING TAKEN FROM YOU HAS BEEN RETURNED IN ITS ORIGINAL CONDITION."

I looked into the bag. I turned it over and shook it. I tapped it with my hand. The guard asked me what I was looking for.

"Somehow, I don't think this is quite everything you took when I came in here."

"We didn't take anything you didn't deserve to lose," was his reply.

I stopped in front of the mirror and looked at myself. A bullet head, a mask for a face, empty eyes, and a miser's mouth. My shirt was soaked in sweat and hugged my wedge-shaped torso, armor-plated in muscle. Kiki was right. Everything that survives adapts to its environment. Well, I've changed environments again. Can I change myself again?

The blonde must have come out of the sauna by another door because I never saw her pass me but there she was sitting next to Derek. Derek's hand stroked lazy figure eights on her thigh with the tip of his index finger like a tiny figure skater.

I went back to my room, showered and lay down for a nap. At six, I got up and dressed for dinner. I knew where Derek and his friend would be for the evening.

I sat by the pool and ordered a Salty Dog. I sat sipping it in the fading daylight and stared at the jagged peaks of the distant mountains. It looked like someone had torn off the edge of the sky.

I finished my drink and waved the waitress over for a second. She was dark skinned with thick, black hair, held in place by a bright multicolored ribbon. Her hair was stiff and wiry like a cord of very fine kindling. Her eyes were as dark as her hair, without discernible pupils. I imagined her hair ablaze with gold and crimson flames.

"Another one, please."

She nodded, took the glass and left.

I drank steadily until the sun flattened itself on the horizon like the yolk of a dropped egg. My day now had a wavy, shimmery edge to it, like the air on a hot, still day.

I got directions to the cafe from the excursion desk and arrived a little before eight. Inside, the big room was divided into three separate areas. To the left was a small dance floor. Something Spanish with pedal steel was playing on the sound system—Country-Mexican, I guess. A long bar ran across the back wall of the middle area. A couple of the men at the bar spotted me in the mirror and watched me walk across the room. I stared into their broad, flat Indian faces. They didn't like what they saw and returned to their conversation. A waitress in a white shirt with a string tie showed me to one of the tables in the dining section and handed me a menu. I glanced at it. Mostly Mexican, with some steaks, chili, and barbeque.

Kiki showed up a little after eight. She wore tooled mid-calf boots, the leather a brown and white patchwork and a short, clingy white sleeveless dress, cut low in the back. Her white Stetson had a turquoise ornament on the crown.

I stood up and pulled out a chair for her. She scooped her dress underneath herself and sat down.

"May I get you something to drink?" the waitress asked.

"I'm fine," I said. "I got an early start."

"Iced tea will be fine," she said.

"You look great." I nodded in agreement with myself.

Easy boy, you're just passing through. What would a good-looking young woman want with a beat-up old man like you? Nothing. Don't go thinking about it or wishing for it. Just do what you said you would. Enjoy some pleasant company, for a change. If you wanted to get laid, you should have lined up a pro.

"Thank you," she said and smiled. Her eyes were green.

"So what's good here?" I asked.

"Everything. I usually get the Carne Asada."

I sipped my water and just looked at her. Her face was a narrow oval with a thin straight nose and mouth. With her thick red hair, I thought of a fox. I could do this for hours, I thought. Not say a word. Just look. Prisons are the tower of Babel. Everyone scrambling over each other to be heard, to make their point, to tell it like it ain't. Silence reminds you what a sloth time is.

"Did you hear what I said?"

"I'm sorry. I wasn't paying attention."

"I could tell."

"I was, but not to what you were saying, just how you look."

"There was a time that would have pleased me, but I know I'm not that good looking. You looked at me like you'd never seen a woman before."

She drank her iced tea. "Let's see. How bad is this? You haven't felt rain in years, you hardly say a word about yourself, and you look at me like I'm a Martian." She paused then clapped her hands. "Hospital. You've been in a hospital. In a coma and now you have amnesia."

She shook her head. "No, not a coma. Where'd you get the muscles? I've got it. A monastery. Lot's of time on your hands. You pump iron for Jesus. You're some kind of ninja monk."

"Why is this so important to you? I don't like to talk about myself. That's all. You're like a starfish on a clam. The harder you pull the harder I'm gonna pull."

"No. You aren't a monk. Not now, not ever. I got it wrong again. When will I learn?" She took another drink, picked up her purse and pulled out her wallet. "I'll pay for the tea, thank you very much, don't bother to get up."

"What are you doing?"

"I'm leaving is what I'm doing."

"Why? What did I do?"

She put her elbows on the table and leaned forward to speak. "Just do me this, answer one question, okay?"

She didn't say tell the truth. "Okay, what is it?"

"You're a con, aren't you? You're just out of prison. That would explain things. Am I right?"

I weighed the effort in constructing and carrying off a good lie against her green eyes, the wisp of hair that had eluded her French braid, and her fragrance riding across the table at me.

"That's it, I'm outta here." She started to get up.

I reached out and grabbed her wrist. She stared down at my hand. She was shackled to me, unable to move.

"Don't go," I said, and released her. "Please. I'm sorry I touched you, that was wrong. Yes, I'm an ex-con, and yes, I'm just out of prison."

She sat down, rubbing her wrist.

"Did I hurt you?"

"No. You just scared me."

I shook my head, amazed at my stupidity. Maybe I did want to go back inside. "I'll pay for the tea. I'm sorry I scared you. You're the first woman I've spent any time with in five years. Just looking at you is enough for me. I can imagine that's not as much fun for you."

She stared at me, considering what I had just said. "What did you do?"

"Does it matter?"

"Yes. It does."

"What makes you think I'd tell you the truth?"

"I think you will. Let's leave it at that."

I exhaled long and slow, and closed my eyes to gather my thoughts.

"I was charged with felony murder of a police officer, a capital offense. I was found guilty of involuntary manslaughter, and sentenced to and served the maximum, five years. Any questions?"

"Did you do it?"

I nodded yes. "Sure did. He was trying to kill me and a witness I was protecting. There was a gunfight in the street. I was chasing him. He got hit by a car."

"You say you were protecting a witness. Were you a police officer?"

"No. I was a private investigator. She was a witness who could expose the involvement of the police and the district attorney in a pornography ring. He was sent out to kill her. He bought it instead."

"If that's true, why were you found guilty?"

"I couldn't prove the conspiracy part. By the time it went to trial, all the other witnesses had had fatal accidents. All that was left to see was that he was a police officer pursuing a legitimate warrant on a fugitive. I was assisting her in escaping. That's a felony. Chanda—that's my lawyer—she did a good job in getting it knocked down from murder to man two. For felony murder I'd have gotten the chair. Considering what could have happened, five years was a bargain. But then again, I don't often look at it that way."

She sat staring at me, her mouth pursed in thought.

"So," I said. "It's been nice having this talk. I'm glad we got that all cleared up. I won't try to stop you if you want to leave." I hoisted up a dead smile.

"I'll stay," she said.

"I'm glad. Why don't we order something."

She ordered the Carne Asada and I followed her lead.

"You said you got it wrong again? What did you mean?"

"I can't say 'nothing' can I?"

"Not a chance."

"Thought so. My track record with guys isn't so great. There's a line out there between exciting and dangerous that always confuses me. My compass goes haywire and I always wind up on the wrong side of that line. That's what I meant. That's why I was being such a pain. I had all these questions about you. I figured let's just go straight to the bottom, avoid the whole disappointment part. That's really gotten old."

"If you had all those questions, why did you say 'yes' to dinner?"

"How else was I going to get them answered? Besides, you look like no two days with you would be the same. That's exciting."

Her food arrived, and she ordered a beer to go with it. I stayed with water.

"You know an awful lot about cactus. Are you a botanist?"

"No. I mean, I read a lot about them, but I don't have a degree or anything."

"You could have fooled me."

"Good. You see, I invented my job. So, if I sound like I know what I'm talking about they won't replace me with a trained botanist."

"What do you mean 'invented' it?"

"Well, I was living up in the desert with Ricky. Ricky Mendoza—Mr. Switch-hitter 1990. We both worked in gyms in Tucson. Anyway, after we split I didn't want to be part of that crowd anymore so I got a job as a trainer for the cruises. It was okay but I hated being indoors all the time and around all those pampered bitches, waiting on them hand and foot. I started going for hikes on my own whenever we pulled into port. People started going with me, and they liked them. It got back to the cruise director, and I made a pitch to make it my full-time job. And now it is. I'm always afraid I'll screw up and they'll replace me, so I read all the time: botany, zoology, geology.

"What about you? What are you really doing out here?" she asked.

"I'm working—following a guy who's on board. He murdered his first wife and got away with it. He even inherited her estate. I'm here to see that he doesn't do it again."

"What do you feel when you see a guy like that? Someone who got away with murder."

"What do I feel? I feel like picking up a steak knife and burying it up to the hilt in his chest and then breaking off the blade. That's what I feel. Then I try not to feel anything. That's the way back inside. I don't want to go back inside."

"Are you working as a private investigator?"

"No. I can't do that anymore. I can't ever do that again. This is just something I'm doing until I can find a permanent job."

"Do you have any offers?"

"Oh yeah, I've got a permanent job waiting for me in Fresno."

"That's good."

"No, it's not. How shall I put this? Chief of Security for a west coast pharmaceutical distributor. How's that? The head of a biker gang liked my work in prison so much that they want me to handle security for all of their west coast runs. In return, I get the pick of the litter for my woman, a company chopper and all the product my body can process. What's not to like?"

"You aren't going to do that are you?"

"I don't know. Most of the time I think 'no.' Then there are some days I get up and think 'why not?' I was one of the good guys once. What did it get me? Maybe it's my way of getting to the bottom in a hurry, avoid all that pointless wishing and hoping that things will be different.

"The only thing I know for sure is that I'm not the man I once was. The man I am now is not an improvement. I'd like to get back the good things I lost, but it hasn't happened yet."

We finished eating and lingered over our coffee. I paid the check and escorted Kiki out of the café.

"How'd you get here?"

"Over there," she pointed to a white jeep in a corner of the lot.

"I'll walk you over."

"That's okay. I had a nice time. I hope you find those pieces that you're looking for."

"Thanks. Maybe your compass is starting to work a little better. You're still on the right side of things."

"Maybe," she said, smiling.

"Goodnight." I turned and walked away. Three steps later, I felt a hand on my arm. I turned. She was already backing away.

"Don't go to Fresno, Leo. That's not you. Keep looking. You'll find something better."

I started to speak, but she was already too far away, so I told myself, "I'll try. I really will."

The next day I saw Kiki after my run. She was taking two couples horseback riding. We exchanged smiles but nothing else. I was following Derek and his lady on a guided tour to some local ruins.

Throughout the tour, I kept my distance. I asked no questions and did nothing to draw attention to myself.

After lunch we went back to the ship. I was able to eavesdrop on Derek's plans to go soaring in the afternoon and got my own directions to the airfield. I spent the afternoon in the weight room and then just sitting in the lounge.

At four, I got into my car and headed for the airfield. Five miles from the dock there were no signs of human life, except the dirt road running towards the distant mountains. Up ahead, I saw the dust of Derek's cab and kept my distance. I knew where he was going, and a car in the desert gives itself away.

I turned into the lot off the road and parked on the far side of the office, away from their car. A bi-plane idled on the runway by the office. A white glider was descending out of the still, blue sky. It bounced twice on its tiny wheels and then rolled to a halt when one wing tilted over to touch the ground. A young man, tanned and muscular with silvered sunglasses, jumped out of the cockpit and began to talk excitedly with an older couple sitting on a bench under some trees. He shook the hand of the man who exited the cockpit, walked over to the couple, and all three went to their car.

I watched Derek and the blonde talk to the glider pilot and then to the pilot in the tow plane. The woman shook her head 'no,' and Derek pointed to the bench under the trees. He helped the pilot roll the glider over to the cable and attach it to the tow plane. Derek and the pilot got inside, and the blonde helped keep the wing level until the tow plane began to taxi down the runway. Then she walked over to the bench.

How long would Derek be up, I wondered? How far could one of these gliders go? They couldn't go too far. Not with Blondie on the ground. She wouldn't want to spend her afternoon sitting out here in the middle of nowhere. But suppose Derek wasn't coming back? No way to follow him. Can't ride with him. There's only one tow plane. By the time it gets back he could be anywhere. I began to manufacture possibilities in my mind. You take a parachute with you. You don't need a big landing strip. You can bail out in the desert. With a four-wheel-drive vehicle you don't need to be near a road. These planes don't file flight plans. Nobody would know where you were going until you're up in the air.

I got out of the car and walked over to the office. The man behind the counter squinted up at me.

"Can I help you?"

"Yes. These flights—how long do they last?"

"Thirty minutes to an hour, depending on whether you want to do any fancy maneuvers."

"Is that the maximum?"

"Oh, hell no. Depends on how high up you want to go. I've ridden the thermals here for almost four hours."

"How far would a trip like that take you?"

"Two hundred, two hundred and fifty miles. Why? Would you like a trip like that?"

"I don't know. How much is it?"

"A hundred dollars an hour."

"You got any scheduled like that now? Before I put out that kind of money, I think I'd like to talk to someone who's done it, see how they liked it."

"Nah. Nothing on the books right now."

"Okay, thanks."

I turned to walk away but saw the blonde at the other end of the porch by the soda machine. She bent over to pick up her drink, looked at me for an instant without recognition, and walked back to her seat.

I got into my car, left the parking lot and drove back toward the ship. A half-mile away I found a flat, open space, turned off and drove into the desert. I turned around so that I could see the road and waited for a dust plume leaving the airfield. A half-hour later one appeared. I pulled back onto the road, followed it to the paved road and then back to the ship.

I sat in the bar and watched for them in its mirror. A half-hour later they walked in. I watched the blonde pull him close to her and whisper in his ear. I bowed my head and reached for some nuts. They walked past me towards the pool. Time to go before my cover gets blown. Once is nothing; twice a coincidence; three times is a pattern. I'd give them a day or so without me in their space. I waved to the bartender for the check.

"You've been following me all day. What is this? I told them I'd make . . ." Derek, in full umbrage, had pulled up next to me.

I watched him in the mirror and spoke to his image, giving him only my profile to stare at.

"I have no idea what you're talking about." I picked up my drink and hid my face behind it.

He stared at the mirror. "No . . . Wait a minute. It's you. You can't fool me. Haggerty, Leo Haggarty. You son of a bitch. Old man Scolari sent you after me." He pointed a finger at me.

I looked past him to see if heads were turning. They were. The blonde was standing at the far wall near the door. Her arms across her chest, she was worrying a nail.

"I won't be hounded like this. You have no right to harass me. This is stalking."

I focused on his soft, pale face, the color of outrage in his cheeks, his quivering lips, and his thin brown hair.

"I'm not stalking you, Derek. I'm not doing anything to you. I'm just out here on vacation, relaxing. It's nice to see a familiar face in a strange place." I smiled at him and began to raise my voice. "Old man Scolari didn't send me, Derek, Gina did. She can't rest, Derek. She wants to know why you killed her? Was it the money?" He stumbled, backing away from me, as my voice grew louder.

"What am I supposed to tell her? She loved you. Why did you kill her?" I smiled at everyone in the lounge.

Marshall disappeared into the hall. I returned to my drink. No sense in going anywhere. They'd just come to my cabin. I gobbled a few more nuts and held up my drink for a refill. No need to be parched when they arrived.

Ten minutes later, a gentleman in a suit came up next to me. I turned towards him and made my face a wall. I kept my hands in plain sight.

"My name is Munson. I'm chief of security here. We have a little problem. I'd like you to follow me to the captain's office."

"And if I don't?"

Munson stepped back so he'd have room to swing or draw. He had a high, square forehead and a flat nose dividing his broad, flat face. He looked like a mallet to me. A mallet that needed swinging, that cried out for John Henry to slam it against a steel spike. I grimaced as I suppressed that impulse.

"Then I'd have to call for backup and have you thrown into the brig."

"Really? You think so?" I started rocking, then stopped. "Let's do it the easy way," I said, and followed Munson to the captain's office.

He opened the door and motioned me inside. I sat in the chair facing the desk. The captain, a Nils Lennartson, had a phone to his ear nodding at what he heard. He put the phone down and spoke to Munson.

"No need for you to be here, Tom. I can handle this."

Lennartson's hair was cut short and waxed stiff like a blonde bristle brush. Ruddy-cheeked and fair, he had the penetrating gaze of a man who had no doubts.

"Mr. Marshall says you are here to harass him. That you are an agent for his ex-wife's family and that there's a long history of that sort of thing."

I laughed. "*Ex*-wife? Oh she's *ex* all right; ex as in dead. Derek Marshall murdered her. I know because he confessed to me." I held up my hands. "Don't ask why he's not in jail. He was very clever. He killed her in a way that left no evidence. I'm out here at the insistence of his 'ex' wife's guardian. Whenever Mr. Marshall shows an interest in a young woman, Mr. Scolari gets very concerned. He doesn't want another family to know the misery he's gone through."

Lennartson put his elbows on the desk and leaned forward.

"Let me make myself perfectly clear, Mr. Haggerty. I have no idea what went on before. Frankly, I don't care. There's nothing I can do about that. What I do care about is the ship's reputation and the comfort of its guests. I've informed Mr. Marshall that you are forbidden from coming within one hundred yards of him. If you disobey me, Mr. Haggerty, I'll either clap you in irons or turn you over to the local authorities. Gringos fare very poorly in Mexican jails. As for your concern for the young lady who is with him, I think your tantrum created so much attention that she's probably the safest person here. I know security will keep an eye on her from now on. You should be able to go about the rest of your stay without that on your mind. So there's no reason for you to be near Derek Marshall. Are we clear?"

"Yes sir, warden, we are clear." I stood up and left.

I went back to my room, showered, ordered room service, and put in a call to Enzo Scolari. It was after eight when he returned my call.

"Mr. Haggerty?"

"Mr. Scolari. We've got some problems here."

"Oh?"

"Marshall made me this afternoon, and now the captain has made it clear I'm not to be anywhere near Marshall or he'll arrest me. I can't even be an open shadow. I also think you're right about why he came up here. He's found a beautiful way to lose a tail. Soaring. You go up alone, and aren't subject to the same rules as engined aircraft, so you can't be followed. You parachute out in the middle of the desert to a waiting car, and you've got at least a half-day lead on anyone following you."

"Mr. Haggerty, it seems your usefulness has ended. You're to leave the ship tomorrow morning and return the car to the airport. If you don't want to return to this area, feel free to convert your ticket to any other destination you'd like."

"Are you going to be able to get someone else out here that soon?"

"Don't worry, Mr. Haggerty, that's all been taken care of."

"Okay, when are they going to get here? I'll brief them on everything I've learned."

"That won't be necessary, Mr. Haggerty."

"What about the girl? Have you found out anything about her? What is she? Accomplice? Victim?"

"Mr. Haggerty, that is no longer your business."

"Wait a minute, that is my business. You don't want me out here because my cover's been blown, fine. You don't care if Derek Marshall disappears, lives the good life without ever paying for what he did, fine. I thought that was why you sent me out here, but I must have been mistaken. But don't tell me it's none of my business that *that* woman could still be a target. That's why I came out here."

"You're right, Mr. Haggerty, I'm sorry. You can rest assured that we've determined she's in no danger."

"That's nice, Mr. Scolari. Tell you what, though; I'm not convinced. How about a name and address? How is it she's here with Marshall? Give me that and then I'll rest assured."

"Mr. Haggerty, I don't have those details here with me. I'm at home. I'll call you with them tomorrow morning. How is that? Then you can leave without any concerns."

"Fine. I'll be waiting."

I hung up the phone, sat there and stared at it. Fuck him. Fuck Derek Marshall. Why was I getting all churned up? Because my easy ride was over? Sure. This was sweet. All expenses paid. Did I really think this would last forever? If old man Scolari didn't care what happened to Derek Marshall, why should I? It wasn't my niece he murdered. I wasn't the law. He'd gotten away with that one. Once upon a time I'd hoped to catch him at something, anything, and to help put him away, for him to pay even a little bit for what he'd done, but I'd lost my chance at that when I went to prison. Just an empty threat I made a long time ago in another life. Who cares? Not me.

I took a long look around the cabin. So long good life. So long warm showers. So long heated towels, so long maid service, clean sheets every day. I pulled down my suitcase, threw it on the bed, opened the dresser and tossed everything inside. Zipping up that side, I flipped the bag over, went into the bathroom and scooped up my toilet articles and dumped them into the bag and closed it up. Packed. I had the impulse to just walk out, get in the car and leave, let Scolari clean up after me. But another night on clean sheets and a hot breakfast wouldn't hurt any. I opened up my plane ticket and fished out a piece of paper. Sitting up on the bed, I dialed a long-distance number.

"Yeah," was followed by a belch.

"Is 'The Kurgen' there?"

"Who wants to know?"

"Tell him it's Leo Haggerty. Slag told me to call." Slag was at the top of the prison food chain. He had no natural predators but time.

"Hold on."

I heard feet shuffle in the background, then someone picked up the phone.

"Yo, so you're out. Where are you?"

"Mexico."

"That's too bad. You coming up this way?"

"Looks like it. That job still open?"

"Yeah. There's a couple guys out here think it should be theirs, but if you're everything Slag says you are you'll have no trouble convincing them otherwise."

"I got some business to clean up here first. You should see me in a couple of days."

"Alright. We'll party first, then we'll talk."

"Sounds good."

I went to the mini-bar, poured myself a gin and tonic, and turned on the TV. I muted the sound and just stared at the screen. I stared and I sipped, then closed my eyes and got very still. Five years ago I could play a spider's web like a harp without anybody knowing I was there. At least I thought that, right up to "we the jury."

I was on another web now and I could feel it vibrate under my feet. Somebody was moving out there and it wasn't me. I played back everything that had happened since Scolari first called me, rethinking every slip, every stumble as a feint.

I went back to the bedroom and dialed the switchboard.

"I'd like the phone number for Kiki Davenport."

"I'm sorry. We can't give out crew member's numbers."

"Can I leave a message?"

"I'll connect you with her voice mail."

"Hi, this is Kiki. I'm not available to take your call. At the tone, please leave your name and number and a brief message. I'll get back to you."

"Kiki, this is Leo Haggerty. I need your help. It's kind of an emergency. Call when you get in no matter what the time."

I hung up and waited.

Around 1:30 I put down my drink and then my head. At 8:30 I heard a pounding on the door.

"Leo, are you okay?"

I stumbled across the room and opened the door. She didn't come in. "I didn't check my messages until this morning. Are you okay?"

"Yeah, yeah. I'm okay. Come on in. I need to talk to you."

She slipped inside.

"Does this have anything to do with Derek Marshall?"

"Yeah. How'd you know?"

"Everybody got briefed on it by Tom Munson. If you're anywhere near Marshall, he's to be called."

"That's why I need your help because I can't go near him. I think he's being set up for a hit."

"If what you said is true, why do you care?"

"I'm not sure I do. What I do care about is being hustled out of the way so somebody can get a clean shot at him. I wanted him to pay for

Gina Dalesandro. I don't think this has anything to do with her. I don't like the idea that somebody thinks I'll just bow out so murder can be done or that I'm too stupid to know what's going on. Besides, I'm still not convinced that the woman that's with him isn't in danger, also."

"Why don't you tell the captain? Let him take care of it?"

"Because I have nothing but hunches, and my hunches have nothing but questions dangling from them."

Kiki sat down on the sofa. "What do you want me to do?"

"Hear me out. I used to be pretty smart. These days I don't trust myself. But if this sounds plausible to you there may be something to it.

"When Derek Marshall blew my cover, he didn't recognize me at first. He said, 'I told them I'd make the . . . ' He didn't finish his sentence. Then he recognized me. He was surprised that someone was there. He thought some 'they' had sent me and it was because he hadn't *made* something for them. Made what? Made it good? Made payments?

"He was reading some book on moneyless investing. Scolari said he'd ruined some of his investments, cost him and some other people a lot of money. Maybe more than he told me.

"If Marshall needs money, she could be a potential victim. If Marshall's a target, they may not care who goes with him. Especially if Scolari's not behind this."

"Why do you think Scolari is not behind this?"

"Let's look at what Scolari did. He hears I'm blown so he fires me. Okay so far. He shows no interest in how Marshall might disappear. *That's* why I'm suppose to be out here, so he can't escape Scolari's scrutiny. I tell him I'll brief my replacement; he says don't bother. He shows no concern for this girl until I raise it. Why? Because the 'them' Marshall thought sent me out here are going to whack him. So Scolari doesn't have to worry about him getting away, or the girl being harmed by him. He just pulls me out of here so there's nobody watching, nobody in the way. That gives them the go ahead. Hell, I have no idea if Marshall's even in the wrong with these people."

"That's it?"

"Yeah."

"I can see why you didn't go to the captain. I can think of half a dozen other explanations that this guy Scolari didn't want to share with you."

"So can I, but this is the one that worries me."

"Okay, what do you want me to do?"

"Find out what you can about the girl. If you can get into the cabin while they're out, look in her purse, get a name, address, whatever. I need to know where she fits in. The other thing is to try to get to Marshall. See if he'll agree to meet me somewhere public. Away from the ship. I ought to warn him that he's a target and it isn't me who's after him. After that, he's on his own."

"All right. I'll go over to his cabin and try to talk to him or the girl, whoever's there. Where will you be?"

"I've got to check out. I'll go down the road towards town, sit in the first gas station I come to and wait for him there. If he comes. If he doesn't, I'll take the car back to Tucson. Then I've got a plane ticket to wherever."

"You going to Fresno?"

"I don't know. The job's still there."

"You called?"

"Yeah."

Kiki shook her head.

"When should I tell him to meet you?"

"I have to be off the ship by eleven. Say ten after."

"I'll call you here as soon as I get in touch with him."

"Okay."

She got up off the sofa and walked to the door. I went to open it for her. She turned in the space between me and the door, reached up to pat my chest and straighten out my collar. I looked down into her green eyes, at the little tug at the corner of her mouth where a smile was struggling to be, and felt an enormous ache in my chest as a huge bubble of longing moved in my blood like a case of the bends.

Kiki kissed my cheek, spun under my arm and out the door.

At nine thirty she called back. "I talked to the woman. Marshall was in the spa getting a fitness evaluation from Joey. He's the personal trainer. She said she'd give him the message. I also got a quick peek into her purse. She was putting on her makeup when I got there. Her name is Leslie Bowen. She lives at 931 Euclid Avenue in San Francisco."

"Great. Thanks."

At ten my phone rang again. It was Scolari.

"Mr. Haggerty. I've got that information you wanted. The woman with him is named Leila Kurland, she's from San Diego. Two priors for prostitution. Not a likely target for a man like him, wouldn't you say?"

"No, not the Derek Marshall we all know and love. I feel a lot better knowing she's okay. I'll be checking out at eleven, then I'll take the car back to Tucson. I have to stop and gas it up before I turn it in."

"Then what?"

"I don't know. See how far this ticket will take me I guess."

"Well, good luck Mr. Haggerty."

"Yeah, thanks."

I grabbed my bag, checked out, went to the car, threw it in the back seat and drove out of the lot. A couple of hundred yards up the road was a driveway that meandered up into the hills to a house that sat up above the Saguaro. I pulled into it and waited.

At 10:45 a white Camry nosed out of the dock's entrance. Leslie/Leila was behind the wheel. A moment of truth. The car turned east towards the mountains and flashed past me. I sat and watched it pull away.

She told Kiki she'd give Marshall the message. She's driving the other way. She didn't give him the message. She's in it with them. Or she did give him the message and he blew her off. Fuck them. It's their problem, not mine. They've been warned.

I pulled out and headed north towards America. I'd be in Fresno tonight. I turned on the radio, looking for something fast, loud and stupid. Look out bottom, here I come. You never bounce back as far as you fall. That's a law of nature. Doesn't matter if it's a basketball, a rock or a man. So why bother?

That worked for about five miles, but a cowlick of doubt kept popping up no matter how hard I tried to slick it down with bitterness or cynicism or self-pity. It just wouldn't go away. Once it came up with Kiki's face. That was easy to dismiss. No future there. Do it for yourself. Then it came back with a question. What would you have done five years ago? Would you drive away and let murder be done? What's different now?

"I am," I said to no one.

"Only if you let yourself be," was the reply.

If you never bounce back as far as you fall, then maybe you shouldn't fall any farther than you have to.

All important journeys begin with a U-turn, so I made one. I pushed the needle past ninety and held it there until I caught sight of Derek's car. I confirmed the tag number and then fell behind.

She was doing a steady seventy going rapidly into the desert, but not so fast that anyone would notice. I looked ahead at oncoming traffic for an opportunity to pull along side and force them over. Dust devils swirled off to either side of the road.

Almost immediately she turned south at an unmarked crossroads. I followed. We were still on paved road, but now there was no traffic at all. Then we had company. I kept flicking my eyes from the road to the mirror. The Camry hadn't changed speed, but the jeep kept expanding in my mirror. I saw its turn signal flash as it moved to pass me. Smoked glass hid the occupants. I looked for the tag number. There was none. I went to slam on the brakes and let them shoot past me when the jeep hit me broadside and I flew off the road. The car slammed up and down as it bounced across the desert like a brahma bull. I gritted my teeth and strangled the wheel trying to keep control. A giant Saguaro stood in front of me, his lone arm up and extended towards me like a traffic cop. I threw myself sideways on the seat as I slammed into it. The giant green cop came crashing down on the roof, and everything went black.

I came to with a throbbing headache. The rest of me checked in as a battered presence. I was on my back and immediately tried to move my toes and hands. That was good. I flexed my limbs and felt their entirety. I opened my eyes and saw that the roof was gone. A bright light made me squint.

"Where am I?" I asked.

Surprisingly, a deep voice said, "You're in the hospital, Mr. Haggerty."

I turned toward the voice. I saw a badge on his chest, the word *policia*, the black string tie, and the long black hair swept back over his ears, like a cutaway jacket behind a holster. His mouth was hidden behind a cookie duster.

"You're a lucky man. That Saguaro you hit must have weighed five tons. Crushed your car flat. You're damn lucky we found you. We weren't even looking for you."

I swallowed. My throat felt creased and raw.

"Water."

He handed me a glass with a straw. I sucked long and hard.

"Thanks. Who were you looking for?"

"Guy named Derek Marshall, a guest on the ship. He missed the boat when it departed. Captain called me because of some trouble with you. We got a call about a vulture dance in the desert so I figured we ought to go check it out. Might be a cow, might be Marshall. We found you on the way there. Which brings me to my next question. What were you doing out there?"

You never tell the law the truth. Because there is no truth. Only your lies and somebody else's.

"I got lost. I wanted to go out into the desert, see it up close for myself, so I left the main road to do a little exploring."

"And what happened?"

"Some kind of pig ran across the road. I swerved to avoid hitting it. Next thing I know, I'm aimed at the Saguaro."

I asked for more water. "You find Marshall?"

"Yeah, we found him, or what was left of him. Between the sun and the vultures, he looked like a half-eaten piece of beef jerky when we got to him."

"How'd he die?"

"Stupidity, I'd say. We have no idea what he was doing out there. He was alone. No one knew where he'd gone. He had no water with him, although he did have a bottle of wine. We found that on the way to his body. Alcohol's the worst thing to drink in the desert. It just accelerates the dehydration. His car was just stopped. It had run out of gas. We guess he thought he could walk out, got disoriented, wandered deeper into the desert, got thirsty, drank the wine he had with him, got dehydrated, then sunstroke. Somewhere along the way he fell into a jumping cholla. His face and hands were covered in spines. Eventually he sat down and died. That's how we found him. Sitting up against a rock with his hands in his lap. They were covered in spines. He had spines in his eyelids, his lips. He was a mess.

"You're lucky we found you. You'd never have gotten out of that car by yourself. We needed a winch to get the Saguaro off you, then we had to use metal cutters to pry you out. Another day and you'd have been as dead as Marshall."

The cop got up to leave, then he turned back towards me.

"You see, that's the only reason I'm not arresting you. You couldn't have killed Marshall, and you wouldn't have staged that as an accident because nobody called us about you. You'd have died for sure. So I'm ignoring all the captain's stuff about you harassing Marshall, or the amazing coincidence of two accidents on that road at the same time. No evidence of foul play, but lots of stupidity, so we're gonna close it up as death by misadventure, unless you've got something you want to tell me?"

"No, I know justice when I see it."

The cop nodded goodbye and left. The door was swinging closed when Kiki pushed through.

She sat down in the chair, threw one leg over the other and clasped her hands around her knees. Her sandaled foot tapped away to silent music. "How are you doing?"

"I guess I'm okay. I've got this drip in me, but nothing seems to be broken."

"That's what the doctor said. You were pinned but not crushed. He thinks you can leave tomorrow."

"That's good. I don't know how I'll pay this bill, so the sooner I get out of here the better."

Her sunglasses were pushed up into her hair and she was nodding though I hadn't said a word.

"Oh, I've got your suitcase and your plane ticket. They gave me your belongings when they cut your clothes off."

"Thanks."

"Yeah, they weren't going to at first, but I told them you had been staying with me. Otherwise, they were going to hold onto everything, and I figured you wouldn't want a policeman holding your ticket out of here, so I told him that and they gave it to me. I hope that was okay."

Her brow wrinkled like a raised blind.

"Yeah, that was good thinking."

"Well, I'll go get your stuff."

"Kiki, thanks for coming. How will you get back to the ship?"

"I've got the company's jeep. I told the cruise director we were old friends, so he let me stay behind to make sure you were okay. I promised him I'd catch up at the next port of call."

"Where is that?"

"We're headed around Baja back to Ensenada. I'll probably get there before the ship does."

"So you wouldn't have to leave right away?"

"No, I wouldn't have to."

"You know, if you were here tomorrow, you could have company for that trip back."

"Really? What would I want with company?"

"I don't know. I hear your compass doesn't work so well. A girl could get lost like that."

"Oh? And you don't get lost?"

"Oh, I get lost, too. That's why you should have me along. That's how I learned what it takes to get found."

A Century of Noir copyright notices:

right renewed © 1983 by the Estate of Gil Brewer. Reprinted by permission of the agency for the author's Estate, the Scott Meredith Literary Agency.

"The Plunge" by David Goodis. Copyright © 1958 by David Goodis. First published in *Mike Shayne's Mystery Magazine*, October 1958. Reprinted by permission of the agent for the author's Estate, the Scott Meredith Literary Agency.

"Tomorrow I Die" by Mickey Spillane. Copyright © 1960, renewed 1984 by Mickey Spillane. First published in *Cavalier*, March 1960. Reprinted by permission of the author.

"Never Shake a Family Tree" by Donald E. Westlake. Copyright © 1961; renewed Copyright © 1989 by Donald E. Westlake. First published in *Alfred Hitchcock's Mystery Magazine*, March 1961. Reprinted by permission of the author.

"Somebody Cares" by Talmage Powell. Copyright © 1962 by Davis Publications, Inc. First published in *Ellery Queen's Mystery Magazine*, December 1962. Reprinted by permission of Paul Talmage Powell.

"The Granny Woman" by Dorothy B. Hughes. Copyright © 1963 by Dorothy B. Hughes. First published in *Gamma #2,* 1963. Reprinted by permission of the Executrix for the Dorothy B. Hughes Trust, Suzy Sarna.

"Wanted—Dead and Alive" by Stephen Marlowe. Copyright © 1963 by Flying Eagle Publications, Inc. First published in *Manhunt*, October 1963. Reprinted by permission of the author.

"The Double Take" by Richard S. Prather. Copyright © 1963 by Fawcett Publications, Inc.; Copyright renewed © 1991 by Richard Scott Prather. First published in *Shell Scott's Seven Slaughters*. Reprinted by permission of the author.

"The Real Shape of the Coast" by John Lutz. Copyright © 1971 by John Lutz. First published in *Ellery Queen's Mystery Magazine*, June 1971. Reprinted by permission of the author.

"Dead Men Don't Dream" by Evan Hunter. Copyright © 1982 by Evan Hunter. Reprinted by permission of the author and his agents, Gelfman Schneider Literary Agents.

"The Used" by Loren D. Estleman. Copyright © 1982 by Loren D. Estleman. First published in *Alfred Hitchcock's Mystery Magazine*, June 1982. Reprinted by permission of the author.

"Busted Blossoms" by Stuart M. Kaminsky. Copyright © 1986 by Double Tiger Productions, Inc. First published in *Mean Streets*. Reprinted by permission of the author.

"The Kerman Kill" by William Campbell Gault. Copyright © 1987 by William Campbell Gault. First published in *Murder in Los Angeles*, 1987. Reprinted by permission of Shelley Gault.